The Turning Place

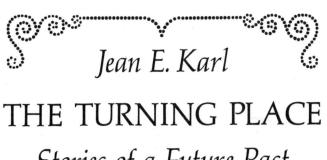

Jean E. Karl

THE TURNING PLACE

Stories of a Future Past

E. P. DUTTON & CO., INC. · NEW YORK

SC
KAR

Library of Congress Cataloging in Publication Data

Karl, Jean E.   The turning place

SUMMARY: Nine short stories reveal various aspects
of future life on Earth and other planets.

1. Science fiction. [1. Science fiction] I. Title.
PZ7.K139Tu [Fic]   75–33669   ISBN 0–525–41573–4

Published simultaneously in Canada by Clarke,
Irwin & Company Limited, Toronto and Vancouver

Designed by Riki Levinson
Printed in the U.S.A.   First Edition
10 9 8 7 6 5 4 3 2 1

Most of all, for R. and W.

Contents

The Turning Place

I don't know what to write. How much of what's happened should I put down? Where will I put this when I finish? Will anyone else ever see it? I can't be sure. I can't be sure of anything. That's one of the awful things. It's too hard to think about. There is nothing left to think about. No pattern. No matrix. Only the future. And the future is as blank as the desert below us.

It began four days ago. A morning like any other. At breakfast my father was reading his paper. He always did that. And my mother said, "Anything new in the paper? Anything cheerful for a change?" She almost always said that.

My father looked up and shook his head. "If anything it's worse."

"It can't be!"

"They can attack," said my father.

"But why?" my mother demanded. "Why?"

"I've explained," my father said. "Earth is too crowded. We need more room. A little more technical skill, and we can begin to plant some colonies in some nearby systems. But the Clordians don't want that to happen. They have this part of the galaxy sewn up. Or they thought they did until they discovered us."

"But surely there's enough space out there for all of us."

"Not enough within the technical limitations of either of us. It's a rotten shame that Clord is so close." He always said that. As if he were explaining again and again to himself. Trying to make sense of the whole senseless problem. "And worse still, they're so little ahead of us, just enough to be out there settling in while we've been feeling around here in the solar system. If only we'd moved a little faster. But, of course, we didn't know."

"Why didn't we? And why can't we do something? Work out an agreement of some sort? I don't understand why there can't be some reasonable way of settling this thing."

It was an old conversation in our house.

"I have nothing to do with that end of it. I don't know. I—well—some of our stuff may be useful in an attack; but we don't really have enough of anything to defend ourselves completely. And of course the Clordians know that."

My father is, or was, a particle physicist. We lived in a town on the desert, with mountains all around. It was nice. There were houses and green grass and stores and schools and the laboratory. The laboratory was where most of the fathers and mothers worked. It was a big place, run by the government mostly, although some private industries contributed. Everyone in the lab was working on atoms, not atoms really, but mesons and quarks and all that. Basic energy, my father called it. "Nothing," I used to tell him, "you're dealing with nothing." Because that's what it seemed like to me.

But that was four days ago. And that morning I didn't worry too much about the Clordians. We discovered them (or they discovered us, however you want to look at it) fifteen years ago, and I was only born thirteen years ago, so the problem's always been there for me. As my father said, it was tough that they were so near us in the galaxy and so little ahead of us technically. Far enough ahead, and we wouldn't have been in their way. Behind us, and we would have been their problem. As it was, it's been one threat after another. We hardly even dared go to the moon. We could have just given up, I guess, but nobody wanted to. Not that they wanted to conquer us. They don't need this planet. They just didn't want us out there competing with them while they moved colonies into the planets they did want. They saw that we too were crowded, even with all our population-control laws. And they didn't trust us.

Yet, four days ago the Clordians didn't seem any bigger a problem than usual, and I ignored them. As soon as I could, I dealt with something more important.

"Can I go out on the desert with Krishna today?" He lived next door. His father was part of the international team at the lab. Krishna and I both liked the desert. Every once in a while we hiked out there together. No one else we knew liked to go.

"Well, I don't know, Georgia . . ." My mother didn't like the desert much. She was a people lover, the town pediatrician. There were times when I felt as if all the kids I knew were related to me. She was proxy mother to all of them.

3

"Oh, why not," said my father, who didn't understand about the desert either, but who kept feeling I was being overprotected. "It's December. It won't be too hot. Christmas vacation is the ideal time to go to the desert, if you have to go."

My mother gave in. She always did. So Krishna and I set out about half an hour later. We each had a compass, a knapsack with plenty of water, some food, the usual first-aid stuff, and a communicator.

When we walked in the desert, we almost always went the same way. In fact, our parents had laid down rules about desert-walking. They weren't too rigid, so we really tried to keep them. We stayed on established trails. We never walked more than three or four hours out. We wore hats and all the usual desert gear. And we took along a small communicator in case we got lost or in trouble, although neither of us would have wanted to use it. We both felt we'd have to be pretty stupid to get into the kind of fix where we'd need it. After all, we were never very far from civilization, and we almost always ran into at least one person, out walking or riding.

There was only one trail up into the desert. It started at the north edge of town, led up a smallish hill, then down and up into the mountains. After a while it branched off. There were at least ten branches that we knew of. Krishna and I had explored most of them. Some led to abandoned mines, others to tumbledown shacks, and some went on over the mountains to places beyond our four-hour range.

There was one branch, though, that we hadn't followed. It turned off about two kilometers down the main trail. And, though we couldn't understand why, we had noticed it for the first time just a couple of weeks ago. We'd

4

been that far at least a dozen times before, but we hadn't seen the path. And we felt we ought to check it out. At least I felt that way. Krishna didn't care as long as he was in the desert.

So four days ago, we started down this new trail. It surprised us. It curved around, out of sight of the main path, and almost immediately it took us into really strange country. There were more rocks, loose rocks, along the way than usual. And the path, narrow at the start, got even narrower. We had to walk single file, and sometimes we were pressed close against the sharp rocks of a canyon wall.

The path led at first up a fairly wide canyon, where the walls beside us were not too steep. After about a half hour, however, we turned into a much narrower canyon, almost a gorge.

We moved steadily up a path on our side of the canyon. On the other side, another path moved up also. Both lay some distance above the canyon floor, but I felt from the look of things that the two paths, and perhaps the canyon floor also, would meet at the head of the canyon. I couldn't tell for sure because there were slight twists to the canyon itself that made it impossible to see that far ahead.

As we moved forward the canyon sides above us gradually became more sloping. We rounded a curve, and then suddenly I stopped. The end of the canyon was about five hundred meters ahead. But I couldn't go on. I had come to something that blocked me. It was a wall that didn't look like a wall. In fact, it was a wall I couldn't see at all. There was a bit of haziness, no more. Yet I couldn't move through it.

"See if you can feel this, too," I said to Krishna, who

5

had stopped to look at a rock, and now came strolling up. Without saying anything, he came up next to me. We squeezed together on the path, and he put his hands ahead.

"What do you make of it?" I asked.

He didn't answer. Instead he felt along the wall. It curved out over the drop across to the other side of the canyon. At least it went as far as we could reach. It also went up the slope beside us. We could see through it, and yet it blocked our way.

Without words, acting almost instinctively, we pulled ourselves up and climbed above the path. We followed the wall far enough to see that it curved on and on—probably right around the mountain at the canyon head. Then we hurried back to the path. I think we both wanted to be on something that felt familiar.

As far as we could see, the head of the canyon was perfectly ordinary. It had a shallow cave, or the entrance to an old mine, at the end, just above the path. The path did curve around just above the slanting floor of the canyon, as I had thought it would.

"Maybe the men from the lab are doing something here," I said. "That could explain why we didn't see the path before. It could be new. This wall could be some kind of force field."

"No," said Krishna, "no. It isn't that. There'd be NO TRESPASSING signs. And besides, there's no machinery."

"It could be projected from something below. Even from town," I said.

"No," said another voice, a strange voice from behind me, a man. Krishna and I hadn't heard anyone coming, and the voice frightened us. "You could be right, but you're not," it went on.

I turned nervously to look at the man. We both did, both more upset than we normally would have been because we were still puzzled by the wall. The stranger didn't seem to be a monster or a man from some planet of Alpha Centauri. He was a plain man, in everyday hiking clothes, with a pack and a walking stick.

"Don't worry," he said. "I'm not dangerous. And I'm not sure this is a danger. But it's something to check out. They've been aware of it for several days at the Central Energy Bank. And I'm the one who's supposed to decide what it is. More to the point, I'm the only one who was willing to climb out here."

"What do you think it is?" I asked, louder than I meant to.

"I'm not sure," he said again. "It's not a normal force field. I know that. And it's not from the lab in your town. It's different from anything they could make there."

"Then where's it from?" I asked.

"I haven't seen enough to know," he said. "I'm an electrical engineer, and I've done a lot of work with the new uses of nuclear binding forces. But I've never seen anything quite like this—not so big and strong, and yet so neutral. It made a lot of static over at the lab. Even so, I didn't expect something so solid."

"Which lab?" I said. "If not ours."

"The one over at Clistra. The unified field project."

He grinned and rubbed his chin. "I was down at your place seeing some people to get their ideas. And then came up here. I'm mostly Indian. American Indian," he added, looking at Krishna. "My ancestors roamed these mountains, so they always seem like home, even though I've never lived in them. I was glad for a chance to get up here. But now I'm not so sure this is where I want to be."

"You didn't make the path?" I asked. It seemed a foolish question, but the path was puzzling me too. Why hadn't we seen it before? Did it have something to do with the wall?

He shrugged. "No. But you're right, it could be quite new; the edges are sharp." I hadn't had sense enough to realize that.

He turned and felt the wall again, then reached into his pack and took out some small instruments. We watched him as he poked and prodded. After a bit, he took out some other gear and did more quick tests. When he turned to us again, his face was tense.

"This is not created by anything on Earth," he said positively.

"From where, then?" I whispered.

"From Clord?" Krishna murmured.

The man rubbed his chin and nodded. "Maybe."

"We'd better go," I said, getting my voice back. "We'd better tell somebody."

"Look," he said, "stay a while. I may need you. I've got to do some more checking. I want to be sure before I report anything. And I may need some help."

He ran through his tests again, very intensely. When he finished, he turned to us, obviously baffled. "It's a field, of some sort. But what kind, and what for?"

"Do you want me to use my communicator?" I asked.

He shook his head. "Too dangerous so close," he said.

8

"The wrong ones might hear. In fact, I think walking down to your place would be the best way to report. The safest."

That really threw me.

"He's right," Krishna said slowly. "We've got to be careful. My father has been worried. . . ." He drifted off. "For now we should stay here—learn all we can. Then we should go down."

I was outvoted. Well, not really. I had nothing to cast my vote for except going home. And suddenly I didn't want that either. There seemed to be more to do where we were. Maybe it was wrong, but we stayed.

For a few minutes we just stood there, thinking. Then without a word we all put our hands on the wall and pushed. Nothing happened.

"Maybe it takes a fourth, like bridge." This time there were three of us to be startled by a strange voice. It belonged to a woman in riding clothes.

"Why, there is a wall here," she said, reaching out, as if she thought we'd all been pushing on air. "Whatever is it?"

We told her what we knew.

"Is there a break in it anywhere?" she asked.

"Not that we've found," the man answered.

"We went way up," I said. "And we couldn't find a break."

"We might know more about it if we could get inside," the man said. "Let's see what we can do."

So all four of us trooped up the way Krishna and I had gone, but this time we went farther up along the wall. Krishna was first, and all at once he gave a little cry.

"It's here," he said. "The entrance."

Sure enough, there was a break of about a meter, as if two huge plates of steel hung for a wall didn't quite meet at the joining. The woman pushed on through, and hardly thinking, we all walked in behind.

Inside was much like outside, the same rock, the same contours. There was a little more vegetation, but that was normal since we had reached the more shaded areas at the head of the canyon. I felt along the curve. The wall was as firm on one side as on the other. We explored around, then climbed down to the path inside the wall and marched to the head of the canyon. There was no sign of anyone or anything. We stood there, looking from side to side, surrounded by a strange translucent haze.

"Nothing more here," said the man reluctantly.

"Not even my runaway horse," said the woman, ruefully. "I thought he might be up here. Got spooked by a snake when I got off to look at a new rockfall. I thought he came this way."

None of us had seen a horse.

"Well, let's go back," said the man. "No more to find here. We might as well report what we can."

We went back to the break in the wall. We had marked the way with cairns, and left a special pile of rocks just at the hole. But the hole wasn't there. We felt around the wall, slowly at first, then with a frantic desperation. There was no hole. The opening was gone.

I got mad then. I had been curious, like the rest. But not curious enough to get caught in a trap. "Get us out," I shouted at the woman. "We have to go home. Our parents will worry. You led us in here. Now get us out."

The woman looked upset with herself. "I just didn't

think," she said. "I was so intent on finding my horse. I'm Leslie Frame. I have a ranch about ten miles away—down near Corba. I ride up this way often, especially at this time of year, and I suppose I've been in this canyon a dozen times. It never occurred to me to be afraid. I just wasn't thinking."

"It was my fault," said the man, looking at me. "I should have known better. I didn't want to admit the truth. And now we're trapped."

"But what is it?" Leslie asked. "What is the wall?"

"A field of some sort," the man said. "Clordian, I suspect. Not dangerous now, but it could be. Though how they intend to use it, I don't know."

"Where from?" Krishna asked.

"A spaceship of some sort, I would judge—maybe even a space platform. If it's high enough, we wouldn't catch it. Not with the kind of diffusion screen they're likely to use. By the way, I'm Victor Tallhill."

"I'm Georgia West, and this is Krishna Raspinti."

"Can we get out?" Krishna asked.

"We can try," Victor said. "There may be another break. But I rather doubt it. If this one is closed, any others are probably closed too."

We moved along the wall, staying together. But there was no break, not even a place where the wall didn't quite touch the ground. We were well out of sight of the path when Victor stopped us.

"If we haven't found a break by now," he said, "we won't find one. After all, this wall is not here by accident. What is sealed, is sealed. Let's stop and see what we do know. The wall is a field, neutral now, probably projected

11

by equipment shielded from our protective warning systems. If I read the field right, it can be used to transmit a lot of things. It may also be able to move, to enlarge. If the transmitter is strong enough, and the thing can move, it may be able to sweep a large area. If it's Clordian, it must be a new thing. They haven't had this before. We'd have known. They've been working very quietly." His face was very drawn now. And all of us sensed why. This was a threat, a danger bigger than we had thought before.

I felt as if I couldn't breathe. We were all quiet—too long. I had to say something.

"Can't we warn somebody? The communicator. . . ."

"Will never penetrate the wall," said Victor.

"You can't be sure," I said.

"Of that much I can be sure," he answered. "But the strange thing is—the really terrible part for us—is that we may be safe."

"Safe?" murmured Leslie.

"If it moves out, we may not be touched by what it carries. It all depends, of course, on what they plan."

I had to think a minute about that. And then I realized why that was so terrible. I beat against the wall then, and Krishna kicked at it. But it did no good. We were inside to stay.

"Can't we warn anyone?" Krishna asked at last.

"What good would it do?" Victor asked. "We couldn't get even all the people in your town inside this circle. And, of course, we don't know for sure that we'll be safe here. We don't even know what's going to happen. Maybe it's nothing. Or maybe it's better for people not to know. I think that whatever happens will come soon. A field of this size can be detected and checked. It won't stand idle long."

"What about our parents?" I said. "Will they die?"

"Depends on what the plans for this are," he said.

"Will it be only here—or everywhere?" Krishna asked.

I looked at him, startled. "What difference does it make?" I asked. "If our parents are gone, what will we do?"

"Don't panic. It won't help," Krishna said, as if he hadn't been close to panic too, a moment before. "There are many ways of living. In spite of entropy, my father says, nothing is ever really lost."

Krishna is my age. But sometimes he seems too old. How could he be so abstract when everyone we knew was in danger?

"But our parents!" I shouted at him. "Our parents may die!"

His face crumpled, and I was immediately sorry. He was only trying to help.

"We don't know for sure," Victor said softly. "We are here by chance, maybe, and we have to do the best we can, until we see what happens."

Leslie Frame looked thoughtful. "If that's true, then we'd better start working. The nights are cold up here in December."

"There was a cave or an old mine or something at the head of the canyon," I said dully. I had to pull myself together. I couldn't keep making things worse for us. After all, as Victor said, we didn't really know anything.

We made our way back to the path, then moved to the head of the canyon again. It was an old mine. Most of it had fallen in, but there was enough that seemed safe at the front to shelter us. There were even some old timbers around, evidently intended for the mine and never used. They would make fine firewood.

We had begun to check our resources when we heard voices coming up the path. We were startled, then hopeful. Was the wall gone? Had someone found a way through?

We raced out of the mine and saw a group of people coming toward us, not from our path, but the path on the other side of the canyon. There were four kids and two adults, who seemed to be together. Behind them were two men who seemed separate. The family looked frightened; the men looked puzzled.

In a few minutes we met. One of the men spoke first.

"What in blazes is this? Do you know? I never saw anything like it!"

Victor and Leslie explained as best they could. It took a long time for the new people to understand. It helped me, in a way, to hear it all said once again. It made it more real, and at the same time, more unreal, if that makes sense.

When the talking was finished, the men sat on the ground, and so did the kids. The other adults were leaning against the entrance to the mine. We knew what they were thinking. The men probably had wives and kids outside. A couple of the kids maybe had other parents. Four was too many for one family. We felt sorry for them—and us.

"I'm Georgia West," I said finally, to break the awful silence. I introduced the other three in our group. Then the others gave their names. The men were John Biggs and Gray Skopotkin, mining engineers. They'd flown in by helicopter at dawn to look for an old mine, supposed to be in the area somewhere, that they thought would yield up some Rare Earths. They'd come through a haze, but not a wall, searched the other side of the mountain, then found that the haze had hardened and they couldn't get through. The wall ringed the whole upper part of the mountain as far as they could tell.

"And this may be your mine," I said.

They nodded grimly.

The family was Peter and Susan De Fleshe, and Betsy (10), Tony (7), Jill (11), and Tom (8). Only Jill and Tom were De Fleshes. Betsy and Tony were cousins, on their way to visit their grandparents for a couple of weeks. The six of them had seen a strange haze from their air car and stopped to check it out, just for a lark. Like us, they had come through a crack and been trapped. They hadn't even planned to come this way. Just taken a new route for a change.

Now here we all were. We looked at each other, then went into the mine to finish what the four of us had begun, only now there were twelve of us. We went to work in silence, getting a fire ready, checking on the space available, and wondering how long we would have to wait, what would happen before we could leave. No one spoke, except the little kids, and even they were quiet, as if they sensed the dreadful chasm that lay before the rest of us.

"What about food?" asked Susan.

"We four had started a pool," said Leslie. "I didn't have much with me. I was chasing a runaway horse. But I always carry a few things when I go into the desert. Victor and Georgia and Krishna had quite a bit."

"We've got some," said John Biggs, quietly. "We'd

planned to camp. We left our gear over the ridge a way. I think maybe we'd better get it."

The two men left, plodding along heavily, yet moving swiftly. Like the rest of us, they seemed to be moving in a purposeful dream, a dream we would wake up from and know had been a nightmare.

"Let's go over to the wall again," I said to Krishna. I wanted to be sure, really sure, that we were trapped before I finally gave in.

Nothing had changed. The wall was there. If anything, it was a bit more obvious, and a bit thicker. You could see through, but not as much.

"It's heavier," I said to Krishna.

He nodded, and we walked back to the mine.

Victor was outside, and the mining engineers came soon after, with their gear. They dumped it, and we all stood watching, looking at the wall. It was growing visibly thicker, even from a distance.

"Back into the mine entrance," Victor said finally. "We might as well be as safe as we can."

We moved, but not all the way in. Something was happening, and we had to watch.

Five minutes passed—maybe—or five hours. We stared as if our eyes were tied to the distance ahead. Eventually the wall grew green. Then flashes of yellow sparked through it. And slowly it began to move out. At first it was almost as if one man was trying to push a heavy truck over the top of the hill. The wall didn't want to go. But then its pace quickened as if the top of the hill had been reached and the weight was being pushed along a plane.

By the time it really started to move, everyone was

watching, even the little kids, who didn't know at all what was happening. Of course, none of us did either, not for sure.

"There she goes," called Tony. But his tone was subdued.

The huge flickering green and yellow cylinder, or what we could see of it, began spreading faster. It moved quietly for a bit, drawing away, then suddenly *whooshed* out with a roar that deafened us and left us weak with fright and wonder. It was gone before we knew.

"Can it go all around the Earth?" Krishna asked.

Victor and the miners nodded. "This one, or maybe a bunch of them," one said.

I hadn't thought of that. More than one. Were there others trapped as we were, then, in the middle of a circle?

Finally we all went into the mine entrance. We had watched, and now we couldn't stand to watch anymore. It was better not to see. Not to think.

"Now that it's gone, can we go?" Jill asked.

She still didn't understand. So Victor explained what we were afraid had happened. Jill's mouth dropped. The two boys began to cry. I felt like it. And so did all the others, I guess. We all just sat still, unable to move, unable to lift the terrible burden of what we believed.

"We have to plan," said Victor, finally, trying once again to get us into motion—to save us from our thoughts. "For now, we must stay here. Tomorrow, maybe the day after, we'll move down a bit. But not before. Maybe someone will miss us and come looking. Then we'll know it's safe."

"Can we check the food?" said Susan De Fleshe,

weakly, looking up from Tony, who now sat on her lap. It turned out that when it was all pooled, there was quite a bit of food. The two miners had planned to stay several days. While I was checking to make sure all of mine was in the pool, I came upon my communicator. I held it out wordlessly.

Leslie shook her head, but Victor took it. "Might work now," he said. Somehow, he had become a sort of leader, although what little we were doing was largely by common consent. We were doing the best we could. But we were all slow, drugged by terror and horror. We didn't know what was happening, what to think.

Victor turned on my communicator. "The band?" he asked. I told him. He tried, and there was nothing. But that was the closest place. He tried some others that he knew. Nothing there either. "A hundred-mile range at most. And the field may still be in the way," he said.

It was no comfort.

We made our arrangements then. The mine wasn't very big, not room enough in the safe part for twelve. And only the mining engineers had sleeping bags. It would be cold at night, but even so, I decided I would prefer the outside. Finally it was decided that the two women and the two young boys would stay inside. The rest of us would find places on the mountain. There were flat places, and we could gather some brush for mattresses and blankets.

"Just stay away from snake holes," said Victor. Somehow snakes didn't seem such a menace just then. We even made some arrangements for sanitation facilities. Victor was very thorough. He kept us busy, and at the same time kept himself busy too. It was the only way to keep your mind from groping at the future.

Water was going to be our next problem. We had enough for the night. But after that we'd need more. Tomorrow would be time enough to search, Victor decided. For water and whatever else we might try to find.

That night out in the open was strange. The sky wasn't right, but none of us knew what was wrong. Something was still happening in the atmosphere. But what it was we did not know, and did not even want to imagine. None of us slept much. John Biggs and Gray Skopotkin paced a small piece of mountain most of the night, never speaking, just pacing, until, almost at the same moment, they both dropped into their sleeping bags, worn out. I envied them in a way and wished I had done the same—exercise until I dropped. Krishna had stayed near the mine, and he said later that the women talked quietly most of the night. Only the two little boys really slept.

Morning was clear. It almost always is in this part of the country. But the horizon was too near, and dusty. It was hard to tell why. We knew about the moving field, of course. But it was gone. What was the dust?

After breakfast, tired as we all were, we felt that we had to do something. Do anything. So we divided up and set out in different directions. We were to stay pretty much inside the area the field had once enclosed. Krishna and Victor and I were to climb to the top of the mountain, the rise above the mine. The others, in three groups, were going to follow the path both ways and also explore the canyon floor below the mine. Water was our main need, the spoken object of our search. But all of us knew that everyone would be looking for some sign of what might lie in the world beyond.

We all three picked our way up the hill. Five hundred

meters is a long way up, stumbling back and forth across a mountain, even when it is not too steep. We didn't say much. At the top we slumped down and took a small sip of water from the canteen we shared. Then we looked out to see what was there. It had never been a place where you could see people. That was clear. But we didn't like the haze that still muddied the distance. Something had been stirred up that wasn't yet ready to settle. And there were fewer green spots than we might have expected. But we'd never, any of us, seen the view from up there before. We couldn't say it looked different.

"Better stay in the canyon until it's clear," Victor said.

We just nodded. It sounded good. We weren't eager to go down. Unless someone came up for us.

We picked our way back to the mine, looking for water and maybe something edible. Not much luck. The others had been a little more successful, especially the ones who went down the canyon floor—Leslie Frame, Jill, and Tom. Leslie had found water. There had been some edible greens down there too. Jill and Tom each had a handful. John Biggs, who had wandered off the path onto the hill with Peter De Fleshe, had shot a rabbit with the small rifle he carried. The others, like us, had found nothing. We sat just looking into the distance then, not seeing anything. Most of the rest of the day we were still, except for a water-carrying, green-gathering expedition in the middle of the afternoon. The frantic activity of yesterday no longer seemed an answer to our worry. Some of us slept finally. But none of us slept all through the night when it came. I kept seeing my parents, wondering. . . .

The next day the haze began to settle. And surprisingly

there was rain. Not the torrential rain of the desert, but a gentle rain that came and stayed a while. I wondered if the whole world was raining. We caught what we could, and Victor and Gray tested it with their equipment. It seemed safe, and we drank it.

The rain stopped before night, and the ground was not too wet for sleeping. Rain disappears quickly in the desert.

"We'll go down tomorrow," Victor said. "Slowly. Testing our way. Not taking chances. We could live here a while longer but we need to move out, I think. We need to know more. We can't just sit. We have to keep going."

"Why not take chances," said John Biggs, almost laughing. "What have we got to lose?"

"It's not what *we* have to lose," said Victor. "It's what the world has to lose."

No one said anything more. We all understood. But no one could say it. What if everyone were dead? Could we stand it? How would we act? We drew together, needing each other and all the bravery each of us had to give. A group. That's what we had to be. Not individuals, but all one. Yet inside we were still separate from each other. We each had our own hopes and our own griefs. We were afraid alone. We could not share our fears because we each hoped privately that we would not have to face them. As a group we knew better, and we needed each other in order to do what we had to do, in order to go on.

Finally Victor told us an old Indian tale—one about the world being destroyed three times, and each time new life emerging better than before. The story made too much sense, and no sense at all. Betsy was the only one who cried. The rest of us were too old or too young.

We went to bed under clear skies and the stars we have always known. There was nothing strange left up there. Yet none of us was sure, I think, if the sky was a good place or just a place of death.

It is morning now. I started this yesterday because the others said I must. I did it while we waited out the rain in the mine, and later, by the campfire. Leslie Frame had a pad of paper in her knapsack. I've written before. For the school paper. But I didn't want to do this. I had to, they said.

We are going down. At least we are going to start down. We will go the way Krishna and I came up, down to our town. If we find what we expect, Krishna and I will meet our sorrow first. But in what form, we do not know.

"If the worst is what we find," said John Biggs this morning, "then we've got to stick together. We aren't a family. There's no love between us. Yet apart we can't survive. And we must survive." He seemed grim but determined. Better than yesterday. We are all learning to consider only the moment as individuals. To plan for the future as a whole. Then he added, "We will not be all alone, surely. There have to be others, somewhere. We may find them, and we may not. We may have no way of finding them. Either way, those left are Victor's new emergence. For whatever it means."

We stood silent a moment. And Victor threw up his hand and looked at the sky.

No one cried this morning. It is too late for that here. But below, who knows?

We may be stronger than I think. It may be chance

that brought us together, and it may not be. Yet I believe we must try to live; we must try to flourish together, alone in the world, if need be.

This story is for us; for anyone we may find; and for those who must come after us. It goes down the mountain with us.

Over the Hill

Carpa paused to catch her breath. Tired, and it was barely past dawn. She wished she had slept better these nights in the open. It would make the long, trudging days easier. Yet she would not stop. She would not give in. She would find a place. Wearily she lifted her feet. Better to get as far as she could before the sun got too high and the heat made motion more difficult. It was warm already. Good growing weather. She made a face to herself. What difference did it make? Yet it did matter—it mattered for the place she would find. But where was it? How far? If she could find a resting place only for a day, it would help. The chance of finding a home or even a spot where she would be welcomed for more than a few hours seemed unlikely now. It had been five days—or was it six? Yet—surely soon —there would at least be people somewhere.

Why had her mother, her father, even, seemed to think it would not be hard? Because she was strong and determined? Maybe. But maybe too, because that's what they had wanted to think. She had had to leave. They knew it and so had put the best face on it. They would never know what happened. Could always think the best. Only she would know for sure. And she had to make it! She was going to make it!

She sighed again. Curse the land! The endless, barren, hard land, with its only occasional lush valleys. Growing space for so little. Each valley a place for so few. Her parents, her grandparents too, were all alive, and there was her brother. Their land had been enough for six. But when the woman came over the hill and her brother wanted her to stay, to become his wife, someone had had to go. There would be children, maybe more than the two she and her brother had been. Their land was not enough.

Sometimes, she had heard her grandmother say, it was a man who left when a growing place grew too crowded. But more often it was a woman. She wandered until she found a place where she was wanted, or until her food gave out. Whichever came first.

Her food supply was low, but not too low. She had been careful. And in one or two places she had found plants. That had surprised her. You didn't expect to see plants growing just anywhere. These had been near a stream. Washed down, maybe. But still, growing in the dead earth. And good to eat.

With a tug she pulled herself to the top of the rise. Up another obstacle. Another climb behind her. Down would be easier. Not looking up—after all, one dead valley was like another—she put one foot in front of the other, easing herself down the casual grade.

Water. She could use water. Glancing up then, she hoped to see water ahead. The last valley had been dry.

26

She looked and then focused her gaze sharply. It was hard to believe. She was seeing things because she'd been alone so long! But no, there was water, and more. Stopping, she stared in wonder. This was a growing valley! Crops high and lush. A house and small planted fields. Oats, corn, vegetables. All the things she knew. Even some trees! Her brother's wife had told of them. But there were none in Carpa's home valley. Was it possible? After all this time!

She moved cautiously down. There was no way of knowing who lived here. How many people. They might be welcoming. They might not. No one was to be seen. Yet she had to be careful. They'd have no cause to hurt her. Still, it was best to be cautious.

She moved into the corn. It rose high on either side, but not high enough to hide her. She half bent down, covering herself; wanting time to observe, to see who was here, to decide what to do.

It was too late. She had been seen. A boy, her own age she guessed, was coming. He strode toward her, then bent to pick up a stick. Why that? What was he afraid of? What was the matter?

She stood up quickly, wanting the advantage of her full height. She stepped out, moving to meet him, head held high. He should see she came honestly, not to steal. The stick rose menacingly in his hand, then dropped. Had he decided she wasn't dangerous?

He spoke. The words were clear. They almost made sense, and yet they didn't. Her brother's wife had been the same—yet her words had been more like theirs, Carpa felt.

She replied, speaking the words of morning greeting

27

carefully. But she could see he didn't understand. She smiled, pointed to her knapsack, then to the hill from which she had come. He nodded gravely, but looked upset again. Was it possible no wanderer had ever come to this valley in his lifetime?

Motioning to her to follow, he led the way toward the house. She wondered if she should go. With the boy so unsettled, would there be trouble at the house? Yet she needed water. And maybe there would be food and a chance to rest. Even a little food would make what she carried last longer. And a day of rest would give the strength she had to have.

They came to the house, and he pointed to a bench outside. She was to sit there. She did so gratefully. It was a nice place. A good house—fine stones. A good garden too, but in need of some weeding and picking. That was easily done. And the trees! Two stood behind the bench, reaching up, with leaves, and roundish green fruit of some sort. Almost yellow, those at the top.

She glanced back at the boy and smiled again. He looked puzzled. Then he smiled, just a little, himself. Why didn't he get the others, she wondered. She pointed at the house and nodded. Best to get it over with.

He didn't understand. He glanced at the house, then at her. Motioning her to be still, he disappeared inside. In a few moments he was out with some meat. Rabbit. And some raw carrots. She ate hungrily. She hadn't realized how dull her diet had become. The boy just stood and stared at her. Then when she had finished all he had given her, he came and stood on the bench and reached high up, up to the yellow fruit at the top. She held her breath. Was she to taste it? It was more than she had hoped for. If only no one came to stop him. Maybe that's what worried him.

He handed her the fruit. She smiled, grinned really, at him. It was all she could do in thanks. Then she bit into the fruit. It was soft and sweet and juicy. The juice ran down her chin and she reached down as far as she could with her tongue. Swept the rest up with her finger and into her mouth. It was too good to lose any. Again the boy just stood and stared.

She glanced around once more as she swallowed the last of the fruit. Where were the others? She looked at the vegetables. Surely someone should be weeding. She got up and stepped over to the beans, pulled a weed. Maybe he would let her weed a little in payment for food. The boy looked at her in alarm again. Picked up the stick he had dropped.

That was no good. What next? He looked desperate now. As if he didn't know which way to turn. Maybe she should leave. She reached for her bag. But he stopped her. Put out his hand. Then he made a sweeping, reaping motion. He pointed to the oats. Maybe that's where the others were. But she saw no one. The oats did need harvesting. It was almost past time. With another gesture that seemed to indicate she should stay, he disappeared toward the oats. In a few minutes she saw him cutting away at it, alone.

What did it mean? What was she to do? Stay as long as she was welcome, obviously. And show that she could be useful. Maybe that would at least earn a night's rest. And a bit more of that fruit.

With a practiced hand she moved down a row of beans.

29

First she drew out the weeds. They robbed the soil, her father had said. Then she picked the beans that were ready. From one row she went to the next. And from beans to peas and squash. It was a good garden, in spite of the weeds. But under her care, it could be even better. She thought with satisfaction of the garden she had left behind. It had been hers alone for the past two summers. It wasn't fair to have to leave! She sighed. It couldn't be helped.

The quiet oppressed her again. There was something wrong here. Why was she picking someone else's beans and peas and squash, weeding them, when she had seen only the boy? Better to leave before something happened.

She rose suddenly, her back tired. She had been weary before she began. Would there really be a place for her, somewhere? Or would her food give out first? Better not to think of that! She looked ruefully at the beans she had gathered, the peas. All in a safe little pile. Better leave them. No sense in calling down trouble. At least she'd paid for what she'd eaten.

The boy was coming, whistling. A lot more cheerful than he had been. What now? He waved. Too late to leave before he came.

The boy looked in surprise at the vegetables she had picked, put on the bench, and at the weeded rows. Did he think she was ignorant? He smiled then, more than before, and beckoned toward the house. Should she go in? What kind of trap could it be? She hesitated. Then decided to take a chance. She had so little to lose.

Hesitantly she followed the boy in. It was pleasant, well furnished. Spare but comfortable. She looked around

30

with pleasure. Would there be some other such house to receive her somewhere?

The boy went to the fire, still burning from the morning, took up some pots, and went to a cupboard. Dried meat, vegetables, all in the pot. And some water. But was there no one else?

For the first time it struck her that the boy might be alone. But how could that be? He should have parents, grandparents, maybe even a brother or a sister. She looked around again. But there was no one.

The boy stood up and looked at her. She saw that he knew what she was thinking, and a flash of fear crossed his face. Of course. That was the answer. He was alone. Everyone dead or gone for some reason. No wonder he acted so oddly. She was a stranger, and he was alone. She remembered how her father had warned of the dangers a stranger might bring. Yet there had been only three or four who had come in all the years she could remember, and none of them had ever been dangerous. There weren't many people to come, she knew that now. This boy was the first person she had seen since she left her own valley. Yet her family had been afraid. Was it because they didn't know? Her mother had come over the hill, though she said little of it. Maybe not from so far. This boy, she knew, had never been away. He couldn't know. Maybe, too, no one had ever told him how girls sometimes came over the hills. Could she tell him? Was there any way to say it that wouldn't frighten him? There was certainly room here if he would let her stay.

She smiled at the boy, to reassure him. And she made herself as useful as she could without being too forward.

Before long they were eating together. Then the boy tried again at conversation. She could see that the words were not unlike. Some she almost recognized. And with signs she made him understand that she had come from far, that she was seeking a new home. She conveyed her approval of his house, his fields. And she saw pride mingle with unease and fear, still. Fear was greater when you felt alone and vulnerable. She was alone too, and knew. Yet to try to say this would only frighten him more.

The meal ended in an unsettled haze. Should she stay or should she go? It would mean so much to stay in a comfortable place, if only for one night. If she could just sleep before she went on, that would be something. For a moment she had the stark notion of overcoming the boy, driving him off. Stupid. She couldn't, and she really didn't want to. Then she would always have to be afraid of the same thing herself: if she knew for sure people did that, because she had done it herself, she could not rest easy.

They left the house together after the meal-cleaning was done. He motioned to the bench and said a few words. Was she to stay? It seemed so. But she saw that he was agitated. She knew how the pattern of life went on a farm, the pressures he was under, alone at this season. No wonder the weeding wasn't done. There was too much work for one. And if he were newly alone, he might wonder, as she did, if he could cope with the future.

Did she want to stay here with this boy? For more than a day? The question made her stop. He was such a stolid sort. A child almost, though surely of her age. At ease with her himself, he might be different. Yet it was nothing for her to ponder now. It was his land and his decision. If he wanted her to stay, then it would be her turn to decide. She could stay or she could go. She was no beggar to remain in a sorry place, just to live.

She turned again to the garden to keep from thinking. Warring against her sensible thoughts, her pride, was a feeling of desperation. She had to find a place, and soon. This was the first in five—or was it six—days. Could she manage to get to another? And would she be welcomed there if she found it? These were not the thoughts she wanted. She tried to put them away, but they kept coming back.

The afternoon wore on. The boy, when she looked, was not in the oats. Where had he gone? She gathered up what she had picked and put them with the ones from the morning, on the bench. Enough here to dry, she thought absently.

The futility of it struck her. What chance did she have? How could she survive another six days, let alone winter, if she didn't find a place? And this boy! It was clear he was too confused, too unsettled, to let her stay long. She dropped her head, willing herself not to cry. And as she did, he came up. She looked at him and knew. She had been right. She was to go.

What had happened? Agitated, he motioned for her to be gone, to pick up her bag and go. Fear had won over his obvious need for companionship. Well, so be it. She couldn't say what she thought because he wouldn't understand. She seized what was hers and set off. Head high again, she almost ran. She wouldn't even look back. What was there here for her? Her future lay beyond.

Halfway to the hill ahead, she felt an urgent tap on

her arm. The boy. Had he changed his mind? Was he calling her back? No, some vegetables. For her bag. He motioned for her to open it. That was thoughtful, at least. She opened the bag, and he put them in; but she didn't look at him. Couldn't bear to let him see her disappointment. And her anger. Suddenly she blazed with fury. He had everything, and she had nothing. And he shared a few vegetables! What did he think she was? Well, she didn't need him. She'd find her own place, her own way. And so much for the likes of him.

"All right," she said, still not looking at him. "You choose to live alone. I cannot help you then. Even in a few days I could have done a lot for that neglected garden. But the choice is yours, and you made it. I wish you well of it."

She looked at him, determined and grim, and he seemed bewildered. She had no intention of smiling, yet she did; because, she saw, his need was almost as great as hers, though he didn't know it. Then she hurried off. Let him think what he would.

She moved quickly toward the hill and up. Anger and determination alike surged through her, made her strong. But as she climbed, the old weariness overcame her and she moved more slowly, less positively. Still, she did not look back. And she kept moving.

It was late afternoon when she reached the hilltop. A lovely time of day. She yearned to stop, to rest there. And maybe she would. Yet she needed water; she'd forgotten to get it; or rather, she had hardly been given time or opportunity. Water would more likely lie below than on the hilltop.

She sank to the ground for a rest and became aware for

the first time that she had not been traveling over dry, hard dirt. There were bits of lichen and mosses, and in many places, where the dirt was loosened, scatterings of other plants as well. Some of them she recognized as edible. Up here! Not close along a stream! What did it mean? Always the land had been dry and hard, except in the scattered places, in the protected valleys, where all things grew. Did this mean that all land might now grow things, if it were dug up and planted? If that was true, she need never have left home. She could go back.

The idea was curiously unappealing. Her leave-taking had been too final. And her journey had changed her. She could not go home and be the person she had been. She didn't want to be the child in the family anymore. She could only go on.

Rising, she moved to the edge of the hill and looked down. What she saw took her breath away. Made her momentarily afraid. A city of the old ones! She had heard of such. One who had come through their valley had said that there were places where many had once lived. Though how, no one understood. And here was such a place. She had never been sure she could believe in them before. But it was true.

She seized her sack and hurried on. Was this the answer? If there was growth here too, could she not live here alone? These dwellings must surely still provide some shelter. She could harvest the things she knew, range far and wide if need be, kill rabbits. They must like such old warrens as these houses were. The idea gave her feet wings. She all but ran down the hill to arrive before the twilight was upon her.

Once at the bottom of the hill, she moved more slowly.

Best to be sure no one was there. Though the place looked deserted.

She moved cautiously into the ruins, amazed. There must have been a hundred houses here once. Some seemed to have been of wood, but almost none of the wood was left. Only a hint here and there, on hard stone-like foundations. Others were of hard oblong stones. Not natural, she felt sure. Made by someone. These had fared better.

Peering in, she saw few other remains—scraps of metal in odd shapes, much of it weathered and rusted. What these things had once been, she could not say.

Moving on down what had been a path—a hard path, she realized, because the ground was covered with something—she came to a building unlike the others. It was one small room, not many as the others were, and part of a roof remained, a clay-like substance, yet different from the oblong house-blocks. In front were some bent and rusted metal objects—large. Inside a scattering of metal objects, mostly small, made the place messy, but not impossible. If she could find something to sweep with. . . . She stepped to the door and then went around and looked behind. A small stream ran about fifty steps away, and some plants grew there—quite large. A few branches might act as a broom. More important, she realized, was the fact that she had been right: the land could be farmed. There was a place for her here, her own place.

She broke off some branches, swept the floor of the small house clean, and settled in. Only as she sat down to eat a bit of the food she carried did she realize how hard the floor was, however. Like the path, it was covered with something to make it flat and very solid.

36

Well, tomorrow she would work something out for sleeping inside on this hardness. For one more night she could sleep in the open. But this would be her house. She surveyed it with pride in the dwindling light. It was better than any house she had ever seen.

Full of hope and joy, she moved to a pleasant place near the stream, sheltered by a bit of the new growth. She drank her fill, ate some of the boy's vegetables raw, and fell asleep happy. Tomorrow a new life would begin.

She struggled awake soon after dawn, trying to remember where she was. It was morning. She had slept the whole night through. And where was she? She struggled to recollect. Then a glance showed her, and her delight returned. She was in a ruined city. In a place that was to be her very own. She sighed with pleasure, sure now that everything would be all right. If there were more problems, she could cope. The nagging thought that there might not be enough food for winter she poked inside. She would find a way. She would live. She had come this far, and she would survive.

Through the haze of her thoughts, she heard a noise. Was that what had awakened her? She listened carefully. There was something! A call! But there was no one here. She was sure there was no one here. She couldn't be disappointed, driven away again. And the ground was becoming fertile. Many could live here now. Maybe it wouldn't matter if there were others.

Slowly, cautiously, she lifted herself, seeking in every direction with her eyes.

The call came again. From far away. She lifted her eyes to the hill she had run down. Was the caller over that way?

Yes, yes, on top. The boy. It had to be the boy. He had left his precious valley, his house, his farm. He had come seeking her. There was no one else he could be calling.

Her first instinct was to call back, to tell him she was here. Then she remembered: the fine house, the promise of food here. And it would be hers.

She fought within herself. Which was it to be? If she didn't call, the boy would never know she was here—would never come. She could make something that was hers alone.

Alone, that was it too. She would be as alone as the boy she had pitied, had scolded. Was it right to be so alone? Sometimes yes. But all the time? Never to see anyone, to speak to anyone, to hear a voice?

Looking up again, she saw him still standing, alone and dejected. She understood him. It was hard to make a decision thrust on you by someone else. She knew what he had been told, that no one must ever be allowed to stay. To cast aside a lifetime of teaching in one day was not easy. Perhaps, she thought again, no one had ever told him that girls sometimes came, and sometimes were allowed to stay.

With a sudden inner joy, she called, "Boy, boy, here I am."

She saw his body turn, his feet spring down the hill as hers had last sunset. And she too, ran, ran to the foot of the hill. She'd show him the place she'd found, the house, and the good new growth. He'd know then that she came not out of mere hunger, not out of need for shelter, but out of wanting. He'd know she came as an equal. As one who wanted not simply a place, but a person. A sharing.

She smiled as he came up to her, threw his arms around her, startling her with the strength of his wanting. She knew then that he too, had suddenly seen the future alone and had rejected it.

She led him toward the house and the bush where her things were. Everything had worked out fine.

Enough

The following is a transcript of a broadcast made by Velta Akhbar on her eighty-fifth birthday. It was part of the Central Communications series for young people, "Ideas into Action."

First, I want to tell you that when they asked me to do this broadcast, I laughed. Me, Velta Akhbar, to talk about my life and about that old hack slogan, "Put Ideas to Work"? Absurd! They used that slogan when I was a child. And they didn't really believe it then. I can't imagine that they believe it now. It stirs up too much trouble.

When I said this, the Central Com people looked at me as if my mind were gone. And that made me laugh too. They were so earnest, those people from Central Com. Deliver me from the earnest! They never see beyond their noses. "Any child I've ever known who put ideas to work had trouble," I said. "It's time you stopped telling children things you don't mean. But if you want me to tell them the truth, then I'll do your broadcast." So here I am. And as you can see, I've at least started with the truth.

When I was a child, I was always putting ideas to work. It was a mistake every time. Everybody hated it. Most of my ideas were for new ways of doing things. And even when they worked, they got me in trouble. Once, on the same day, I got an idea for a way to fold a leaf so it would sail through the air, using the breeze to bolster it up, and carry some small items on top. I folded and folded until I got it just right, then launched it, right into the path of old Mrs. Wokker, who was so frightened by this thing that sailed past, she nearly had a fit. She did fall and skin her knee. To get away from her, and my mother, I went off to finish an idea I had had for a new kind of pulley. The only decent place to try it was from the schoolhouse roof. It was nearly dark by the time I was ready, and no one could see me, so I climbed up, fastened the pulley, and started to pull my pet rabbit to the roof in a sling I had rigged up. Halfway up, the rabbit got scared and jumped through a window into the schoolhouse, where the town council was having a meeting. It didn't interrupt the meeting for long, but you would have thought I had caused an earthquake, the way everyone carried on. There was no encouragement there to "put ideas to work." And that was the way my life went as a child.

Was I never given any encouragement, people always ask when I tell them about my childhood? If not, how did you ever come to do so much? Well, I did get encouragement, in a negative sort of way. The more people encouraged me not to put ideas to work, the more I did it. I was just perverse, I guess. Or maybe I really liked the image I had created for myself. I was the town bad girl. And goodness knows what might have happened to me. My future was fairly uncertain at the time I came to school-leaving age.

That was just at the time the first sequesterings were being held. The Pre-Clordian Sweep Scientific Recovery Group had decided it needed young recruits. Our schoolmaster, along with four or five others, had been asked to bring one or two of his best—or most apt—students to a sort of camp where it could be seen if any of them showed the proper potential. This was done in several places where there were enough villages near a suitable location to make it practical. In those days people had to walk to any place they couldn't reach by boat.

The choice for the camp from our village was obvious—a young dolt named Dolbin. He was everybody's favorite. He always did the right thing. I hated him. And I wanted to go. This seemed my one chance to get help on some of my bigger projects, the ones I hadn't been able to carry out on my own. There was no one in the village who could, or would, help me. My small projects made trouble enough. But I was sure the Sweep people would be different.

I was persistent in those days, and I was determined. I had also discovered how the Central Com worked. Each village then had only one outlet. Generally some one person listened all day and spread the news to the rest of the village, though everyone came to listen to special programs. If there was a message to send from the village to some other place, the person in charge knew how to do that too. I had watched at the window of the house where all this was lodged in my village, until I knew not only what the operator did, but also something of how messages came in.

So at one point when the Central Com people were quiet, I was able to put my own message through to the machine. It said, "Velta Akhbar is to go to the Recovery Group sequestering next week." The operator, in fact the whole town, was so stunned by my message that no one stopped to ask how anyone outside the village had ever heard of me. I was notorious, they thought, known Earthwide.

As a result, it was just assumed that I was going. I think everyone was a little relieved. It meant a week without me. The only one really upset was Dolbin. He had been strutting around, airing his self-importance, because he had been chosen. Now I, who was always in trouble, was going too. It was a fine joke on him. Not the least of my triumph.

We set out on a fine morning, the three of us—the schoolmaster, Dolbin, and I—for a broad open meadow that lay almost a day's walk away in the middle of the Northeast Woods.

"I hope this trip will give you enough, Velta," my mother said as we left. "Enough what?" I asked. "Just enough," she said. And I was left to wonder what she meant. It irritated me that she had said something like that just as I was leaving. It was something I had to puzzle over, instead of using all my time on the way to think about the questions I wanted to ask and the projects on which I wanted help. For I was sure the people from the

Recovery Group could do anything I wanted. After all, they had made the Central Com. I had confidence in them.

We walked through the woods, I saying nothing, dividing my thoughts between my projects and my mother's comment. The others kept to themselves too. Maybe they were thinking of projects. Or maybe they were just content to walk and enjoy the day. That had never been my style.

When we arrived at the meadow, the two men from the Recovery Group who were to lead the camp were there, but none of the other schoolmasters or children had come yet. We were shown where to put our tents, and when they were up, were asked to help the men and the others, who had begun to arrive. I went to help the men. They were setting up a large tent, some cooking equipment, and some other gear they had pulled in on a cart, from a closer village than ours. A couple of times I saw easier ways to handle things and said so, but these men were no more eager to hear my ideas than anyone in the village. I couldn't believe it.

Enough! I said to myself. I've already had enough of this at home. I thought things would be different here.

But already I had discovered that these two men were not doers, not makers of things. They were local people whose job it was to take care of Recovery Group details in the area. And they did the best they could. I know that now. But that day I was mad clear through.

We had dinner finally. I met all the others. The sort of lot I should have expected. Mostly Dolbins, although a few seemed to have a spark of fun, at least. I did feel more at home in the group than I generally felt in my village. Most of these people at least understood what I was talk-

45

ing about when I asked some questions about the Central
Com. Some of them had obviously studied it too. But I
didn't think any of them had ever used it. Certainly none
of them were at the camp under false pretenses because
they had.

After dinner we had the first session. It was a time of
quiet. Quiet, it seemed, was to be an important part of
what we did at that camp, or sequestering, as they preferred to call it. We were supposed to think about what we
wanted to get out of the experience. To plan for what we
would bring home with us. To decide what things interested us most, what we wanted to do with our lives. I had
answered some of those questions long before. My problem was that no one had ever agreed with me. No one really
wanted me to put new ideas to work. Instead, they simply
wanted me to work at ideas that had already been over-
worked, as far as I could see.

I went to bed disappointed. I think even I hadn't realized how much I had wanted this week to do for me. I
couldn't sleep at first. I was desperate. *Enough*, my mother
had said, and I wasn't going to get even a little. Yet, as I
thought it over, I decided I could make something happen. I had done that before. And I'd do it again.

The next morning we had breakfast, and then the program began in earnest. First we had an introductory talk
by one of the men, named Gwester. He explained the work
of the Recovery Group, and I found myself interested. He
said that, as we all knew, people had once lived on Earth
who knew far more than we. They had developed all sorts
of machines, most of which would be of little use to us.
But some of their ideas and some of their inventions could

be very helpful. The Recovery Group tried to find places where the records of these old people had been preserved. From some of these records the idea for the Central Com had come. Now people were working on other ideas they had found, even some medical ones. We were, it seemed, not quite like those people. This fact fascinated me, and I would have begun to think about it if Gwester had not gone on to say that the one thing we really needed most was some kind of practical, reliable transportation on land. The Old Ones had had more kinds than they needed. But we had none, not even large animals, which had once served them well. Not enough had been discovered yet about how the Old Ones' mechanical transportation had worked to enable us to make something of our own.

"But why don't we just work something out for ourselves?" I asked. "Why wait to see what the Old Ones did?"

Gwester frowned at me. "Because we don't know enough theory. And we don't have enough people and resources to spend a lot of time learning," he said. That made sense. I decided Gwester was smarter than I had thought.

"But the Old Ones didn't have just exactly what we need," I went on. "And some things they had, we don't want. Don't we have to be ourselves?"

That was too much for Gwester. He would have none of that. All the answers lay with the Old Ones, he was sure. And I knew I couldn't disagree entirely. It did seem silly to try to invent something that had already been invented. Yet, if you couldn't find what you needed. . . .

I forgot what was going on around me, then. A transportation system! That was really a big idea. Could one really be developed? The idea was staggering. Not to have to walk everywhere over land. Not to have to carry on your back what you needed, or push or pull it in a wheeled cart. The Central Com had put us in touch with many places in the world. What if we could not only hear about all those far places, but see them as well? My mind reeled, and then went to work. They had to shout at me to tell me we were each supposed to find a quiet place and think about ourselves and what we wanted to do.

I was glad to have a little quiet. I had already begun to think. I drifted to the edge of the great clearing and sat down under a tree. Transportation. What was the answer? In those days I was convinced I could do anything. But the transportation problem was too big even for one morning, so gradually my mind drifted onto other things. I cursed the fact that I had been cheated again, and wondered how I could make the best of the week. Not by following the camp program, that was clear. At the same time, I didn't want to be sent home. If there was to be a lot of quiet, I could at least think in peace. Maybe I could get enough of that, though not enough of what I really wanted.

I looked around at the place where we were, then, more carefully than I had before. It was an odd place, a huge rectangle of grass—an open meadow, in the midst of a dense forest. An ideal place for a quiet retreat. It was as if someone had planned it, had cut away the trees in that vast shape. Yet I know no one had. Why would this happen?

Once again I was seeking an answer I couldn't quite grasp. What kept the trees from moving into the meadow?

The ground was good. Would the dense grass keep the seeds of the trees from rooting? Some of them maybe, but not all. Surely a tree or two would make its way in. Yet not one had. A few low bushes. And yes, there was one lone tree. But it was small, scrawny, pale. It looked as if it wasn't going to live long. Was the soil below the grass roots, where the tree roots would go, no good? Maybe. But why in so regular a pattern?

When we were called for lunch, I asked Gwester if he knew why this meadow was here, what made it so regular in shape. Of course, he didn't. He hadn't even thought about it. I should have expected that. But I was disgusted just the same.

In the afternoon we were to wander around, get acquainted with the area, find plants and things that interested us, and ask questions about them. Gwester and the other Recovery man, Syntron, would be waiting to explain what we had found. I laughed to myself, wondering what kinds of questions they could answer. Not mine, surely. Yet it was a fine day, a good place. And with a little effort on my part, I would have a maximum of freedom for a week. It had been worth the effort of coming.

I spent the afternoon walking the edge of the forest. There wasn't a break in the even pattern, except in one place. There, the clearing moved a few paces into the forest. That had to have some meaning. I measured that small space. Twenty steps up and down. Six long steps across. All grassy, except for a few bushes and an odd stone with plants on top. This was the only place in the rim of the meadow where the long straight sides were broken.

I brought no plants back to Gwester and Syntron. And

49

I didn't even mention the questions I had. Instead, I had decided to look for some answers myself. What would happen if I dug down below the sod? Would I find out what made the place so peculiar? It was an idea. And to put it to work, I told about the stone I had seen, the one with plants almost covering it; I proposed to dig out that stone and bring it in. And I did intend to do that; I just didn't say I also planned to dig a little deeper and see what lay below. Could I have a spade to use for my project? I asked.

The schoolmaster looked a little askance at my request. He knew me well enough to know that things were not always as they seemed with me. Yet, there wasn't much I could do with a spade. So he let it pass. And the next morning, I set off for my stone with the one spade available.

Most people had gone in another direction that day, looking for small stones to bring in. Each one was to go alone. By being alone, we were to face ourselves. We were all being taught to think for ourselves, choose for ourselves. My project fit in perfectly. What could be better than a stone with plants on top?

I began to dig around the stone to free it, and soon discovered it was bigger than it had seemed. It had been too well covered with growth for me to see it clearly. I dug deeper and deeper, and it soon became apparent that I might not be able to deliver it. I couldn't find the bottom of the stone, nor the edges. Below the soil it moved out in all directions.

At noon I went back and described my problem; but no one offered to help, and no one came to see. The others had become interested in their own projects. Some had begun plant collections to take home. Others were trying to see how many small stones they could find on the forest floor. Still others were examining the trees to see how many varieties there were. No one else seemed concerned by the overall strangeness of the place, the uniqueness of where we were.

I went back alone, resolved to dig as deep as I needed to, to find the bottom of that stone. Something about it excited me. I felt that it had something to offer, even though I knew I could never carry it to the camp, to say nothing of home. Maybe I alone would have no memento of my week.

I dug until I thought I could dig no more. And then I did dig some more. Finally, I was in the hole, throwing the dirt out. By that time, I knew the stone was not a stone. It was some of the stone-like material the Old Ones had used. I had read about it. They made buildings, roads, everything with it. It was hard as stone, whatever they made it of. This was the first time I had seen it.

By dinnertime, I had discovered that my stone was connected to more of the stone-like material at a distance of almost my height below the soil. That had to be the reason no trees grew in all that huge rectangle. There was hard stone beneath it all. I was sure of it. But was there just a flat expanse of it—a playing field of some sort? Had it been the bottom of something? Or, was it maybe the top? I don't know where the later idea came from, it wasn't an idea that would have seemed logical to anyone else. We did not build underground. But I was overcome with it. I began to visualize a huge underground retreat. It was the most romantic idea I had ever had. I was in love with it at once.

I should have known better, but I raced back to the

camp full of my thoughts. I had not yet learned to stop and think before I exploded with an idea that excited me. I told everyone what I had found, and what I had decided. And then realized that once more I had done it. I had put the wrong ideas to work. Everyone laughed. No one had ever heard such a strange tale. Dolbin began telling some of the things I had done at home. He didn't have to do it. He did it for free. And I was not grateful. I stormed at him, at everyone, trying to make them see. Until no one would even look at me. The schoolmaster took me aside and said he would send me home if he could. No good would come of my being there. He had always known that. He had no way of knowing why I had been asked, but he was sure it was a mistake. He was right, of course. But I had no intention of telling him so.

Gwester and Syntron, to their credit, were not so scornful as the others. They didn't offer to help, but they questioned me. I think they were afraid of committing themselves to what might be a scatterbrained idea. Yet they knew enough of the ways of the Old Ones to know that what I had suggested was not impossible.

So the next day I was allowed to pursue my project. The others went on with their collections. Insects had been added now. And some of the children had begun to think deeply about their futures. This was supposed to be the climax of the week. Each one of us was to have discovered her or himself by the time we left. And, supposedly, some one or two would have discovered a future with the Recovery Group. I was more interested in discovering the Old Ones. I still think it strange no one was even curious about what I had found. Yet maybe Dolbin's stories turned away those who might have come to look. I never knew.

I had decided how I would proceed. I would dig all around the stone that had started my work. I would discern its dimensions. If anything held the key to what lay below, I thought, that did.

First I cleared the top of the outcropping, my stone. When I looked at its hugeness I wondered what had ever made me think that I could carry it to camp. However, only a tiny bit of it, higher than the rest, had shown in the beginning.

Next, I worked my way down the sides, clearing evenly as I went, until on one side I saw a piece of metal, fastened to the stone. It had been put there at some time by some person. I was sure of it. My excitement was almost more than I could bear. There were words on the metal, words I did not understand, and an arrow. Below, as I hastily uncovered more, I found a big piece of metal, a kind of door.

Was that what it was? And if so, how did it open? More arrows—these painted in colors on the rock—so faint they were hardly visible any longer, pointed to a small additional piece of metal set in the stone. It was just a round place, with no writing. I touched it, to see what it felt like, and suddenly there was a noise. I jumped back.

A rattle, then some sounds as if a great monster was awakening inside. And slowly, almost as if it wasn't going to happen, the little door slid open. Would it stay open? I put my head through. Steps lay ahead, down into the dark. Again there was a button and arrows, these far more visible, as if they had been waiting for me to see them. I pushed the button, and the stairs below were lighted.

Did I dare go down? What would happen to me if the

door closed, or the light went off when I could no longer see the door, even if it stayed open? Yet how could I not take a chance? I stepped in, then gingerly crept down the stairs. It was foolish of me. I can say that now. I think I knew it even then. But I had never been a careful child.

At the foot of the stairs a long corridor opened. Many doors lay along that corridor. I opened the first I came to and saw a bed, a chair, a comfortable room. Yet everything was old. If I touched something, it would surely fall apart, I thought. Yet when I did touch something, it felt firm. Being shut up in a dry place had preserved everything, but I didn't know that then. I crept to the next door and found the same. People had lived here!

I grew bolder. Stole on until I came to a door that opened into a very large room. I had never seen an inside place so enormous. Our whole village could have fit in just that one vast hall! And it was all lighted somehow. With what I did not know. I stood on a high balcony, and below me were machines. Some like birds. Others tall—rockets, I can say now. The sight frightened me, awed me, fascinated me. I could have stood and looked all day. It was long past lunchtime, but I gave that no thought. I moved on. Beyond the huge room—far, far down the corridor—was a room lined with books. This is where it is, I thought. This is where I can find out. And for once I agreed with someone else. Why work something out for myself, if someone had already done it for me? Could I learn to read those books, learn those languages? Oh, yes, if someone would only let me, I could. I knew I could. To do that would be enough.

I spent the whole afternoon with those books. I

couldn't read what they said, but I could look at the pictures and marvel. Suddenly, I realized how late it must be, and I hurried back down the corridor, past the big room, past the sleeping rooms, and up the stairs. At the top of the stairs, I pushed the button and the lights went out. Outside I saw that it was indeed late in the day. On the chance that if I pushed the outside button again it would close the door, I touched it, and the door slid down, with the same heavy rumble.

Now I had a new problem. Should I tell what I had found? It was so big a question that for once I took some time to plot a sensible answer. I had found myself in those hours underground. I had found my life, if anyone would let me have it. And I didn't want to spoil my chances. What was I to do?

I couldn't tell everyone. They had had their chance and missed it. But I must tell someone. I couldn't not. This was too important. It wasn't just for me. The knowledge a lot of people might need could be in those books. So after dinner I told Gwester. He was the one who had talked about the knowledge of the Old Ones. He was the one who might understand, I thought.

At first he didn't believe me. We sat apart from the others, where he had reluctantly come at my insistence. But as I went on, I think he couldn't believe that anyone could make up such a story. He agreed to come with me the next morning. He said nothing to anyone else, nor did I.

In the morning he casually set out with me, saying he wanted to see where I had been digging. We entered the underground chambers in the same way I had entered the day before. And all was as I had said. I told him then how

I felt. What I longed to do. And once more he listened. He even said he thought something could be done for me.

We spent the day in that underground place, exploring. The light was electric, he said. But he didn't know how it could possibly still work, after so many years with no one there. It was something to find out, I decided.

Some of the machines were transportation. They were meant to fly in the air, we decided. People on Earth now would never agree to that. Even to me it seems a bit obscene. But those machines started me thinking. If I could find out what made them go. . . .

It was many years before I finally invented what did become the Mechanized Transport. But my ideas for it began that day. I have put ideas to work. I have done it all my life. But as you can see, it wasn't popular when I was young. And I suspect it's still not popular for some of you.

We told no one at the camp of the discovery. It seemed better that no one know until the area could be protected in some way. A few days later we were all back in our villages, and Gwester and Syntron were in a place where they could send a message to the Recovery Group headquarters. Eventually those who really knew about the Old Ones came to explore, and they came to me too. My sequestering was supposed to have been a failure. I had brought nothing back as Dolbin had. A waste, people had said. But when my mother asked if it had been enough, I had said, "Yes, enough. At least I hope it will be."

And when the new people came from the Recovery Group and took me back to the meadow, back to that library, and taught me to discover what was in those books, she understood, I knew.

It was enough. And yet, never enough. For there is always something ahead. I don't want to make things anymore, not as I did when I was young. Things are not so important to me now. Not even the Mechanized Transport. Now I feel that ideas, themselves, are more important than the work they lead to or the things they create. Things put to work are important only when they free us for ideas. It may be that all those others there during that sequestering week knew this, knew then what I have come to know only in these last years. Yet I do not regret my life.

Put ideas to work. That phrase still makes me laugh. Yet it has been my life. And I have loved it. It's enough for me, whether others like it or not.

Accord

Casselia Sorchum had never wanted to travel. At least not to another planet. No one on Earth had ever wanted to travel that far. She kicked at the plastic floor of the terrace and a little dust blew into her face, from her motion and from the wind that was always on the move on Clord. The few specks of dust were very like the dust of home. They reminded her of how absurd it was to be in a place where the only thing that seemed like home was dust. Yet Earth was more light-years away than she cared to think. And she had no idea of when she might return. She kicked at the plastic again. This time there was no dust.

Clordians were like the wind that blew around their planet, she thought. Always on the move. Busy. And yet she couldn't see that it got them anywhere. To places, yes. But they never got down into things. They were always racing off without having really seen the place they had been. And with all that racing around, their children never went on a sequestering. At least she didn't think they did. She'd never actually had a chance to talk to any of them.

If they didn't go sequestering, it was no wonder they were so restless; they had never had to face themselves, these people, never had to find out what they were. Never learned to focus. That had to be what made all the Clordians she knew so thrusting and jumpy. She didn't like them.

"Casselia!"

Casselia sighed. It was her mother, with more instructions, she was sure, for the stupid banquet they were going to tonight. Another one! The third in a week. It used to be that she hadn't had to go. Which was much better. She hated banquets. Staying at home in this too-confined apartment might be lonely, but at least she didn't have to flutter and smile at all those Clordians. She had never had to say much to them; her parents had always said she should be as quiet as possible. But just being with them was unpleasant. They seemed to shove at you so.

"Remember, Casselia, we are envoys. We represent our entire planet here on Clord. We must not take our responsibility lightly." She had heard that too often. And she had seen too often what it meant. A strange, quiet retreat. Her parents behaved differently, were not themselves, when they were with the Clordians. She hated to watch them. It didn't seem necessary. They weren't owned by Clord, not yet, anyway.

Casselia made a face to herself as she walked from the terrace into the impossibly rigid and ridiculously orderly apartment she and her mother and father had been given for their "brief visit." Apartment! It was just a fancy name for a prison. The three of them always being watched. She was glad her parents didn't even try to pretend that the Clordians weren't most interested in know-

60

ing if Earth was safe, or if the people of Earth were likely to make new problems for Clord. Everyone on Earth had known the Clordians would want to investigate thoroughly after a spaceship from Clord had gotten in trouble and landed on Earth.

The only question Earth people had had was what the Clordians would do. A Clordian research team—ambassadors of friendship—had arrived soon after, which was expected. But they had stayed only a few days, which was unexpected. There had been no attempt at a takeover, though surely they had seen that the people of Earth had no weapons. The Clordians had simply come, asked for an ambassador to accompany them home, and then gone. It was they, the Sorchums, who had been chosen to go. So here they were, ambassadors. And Casselia hated it. Had hated every day of the four absurd fifty-day Clordian months they had been there.

"Casselia! Hurry!"

"I'm here," she answered, strolling through the door to the gathering room, where her mother was standing. "Why do I have to go? You never let me say anything. I just smile. And all those heavy-handed clods pat me on the head. I never see anyone my own age. And nobody ever pays any attention to me."

The atmosphere as she made her usual complaint was not the usual patient-but-tense "do as we say." As she walked up to her mother, there was more of a smile in the air, not the half-formed sense of dread she so often caught from her parents. Her mother was thumbing absently through the clothes in a huge wall wardrobe—some Clordian-style clothes, some Earth clothes.

"Sit down," she said.

Casselia slid into one of the slippery Clordian chairs and waited, perplexed. Something had changed. There was a sureness in her mother. It hung all over the glossy surface of the room like an alien skin. Not that the three of them had ever been really unsure of themselves inside. They were what they were, most of the time; yet there was something new today.

"I think you should wear this dress of mine, this Earth dress, to the dinner with the Commander of All the Clords tonight."

"Oh, Mother, not him," Casselia began, before she took in all her mother had said. A grown-up dress! And an Earth dress! She hated the Clordian clothes she usually wore to dinners. Clordians were built differently, and no matter how their clothing styles were altered, their clothes simply didn't fit Earth people. The dress her mother held out was the one thing in her mother's wardrobe she had always wanted to try on.

"You're about my size now, you know," her mother went on, as if she hadn't seen Casselia's surprise. "You've grown a lot in the year and a half since we left Earth."

She's giving me a chance to recover, Casselia thought. There was something going on.

"Let's try it," her mother said. "Of course, if you'd rather wear one of your own dresses, you can." The look on her face said she knew better.

The dress fit just as Casselia had known it would. She'd often wondered why her mother had brought it. It wasn't like the things she usually wore. In fact she'd never had it on. Never had it on! Had it been brought for her?

"It was for me. You brought this for me!" She turned to

62

her mother almost accusingly. "Did you bring it for to-night? How could you know?"

"I brought it for you to wear when the right time came," her mother said. "And that time has come, I think." The sureness Casselia had sensed before still filled her mother's voice.

"Does this mean I don't have to be a child anymore? That I can talk?" she asked hopefully. She had, after all, had her sequestering before she left Earth. And she could focus better than anyone she knew. She was not a child, although they had persisted in treating her like one on this trip. She wasn't full grown, of course, but she had a right to more consideration than she had had.

She sighed, thinking as she often had before that she'd had more sequestering than most, but had never had a chance to try out its benefits. Even her curiosity was hedged about by rules. On the long trip here, they'd made her stay in her small room, except for exercise and times with her parents. Her mother had taught her the same things she would have learned at school. But she'd been alone so much. No friends, no one her own age to talk to. No one to explore with. She'd actually looked forward to arriving in Clord, in the hope that she might see more people. She'd even had the notion that she might go to a school here. But life on Clord had been much like life on the spaceship. There'd been lots of time to think, lots of time to become herself. Lots of time to develop her inner unity. Too much time. You needed people too, in the end, to find out what you were and to learn what was really true.

"Can I talk tonight?" she asked. "Really talk? I can

speak Clordian. I won't make any stupid mistakes."

Her mother nodded. "Say what you will, when you will. But," she added softly, "remember why we are here. The Earth depends on us. And yet not on us so much, I think, as on the slender thread of what we all are as individuals and as a people. And you, Casselia, are Earth, the Earth the Clordians want to know, as much as any. More than many, perhaps, for away from Earth we see its delights, its wonders most clearly, enjoy them most thoroughly. Be what you are, and let the winds of Earth run through you."

"Earth is fifty light-years away," Casselia murmured. "Ten months of travel."

"But not far in your thoughts."

"No, always there."

"Then be of Earth, and be it fully. You are not yet a woman, Casselia, not yet fully grown; but tonight you must be the best of us. That's all I can tell you, and by the Guardians, I hope it's enough." A flit of worry crossed her face. Then she smiled again, and turned to select a dress for herself.

The best of us. The thought was frightening. Why her? And so all-at-once when she had hardly opened her mouth before. She had been the unheard child forever, there on demand but quiet. Now all of a sudden she was to be the "best of us." And with the worst of them, as far as she was concerned. Well, maybe not the very worst. The Clordians were all so heavy. That was the only word—*heavy*. They didn't seem to have any sense of discovery. When they came into a room, they just came. They blunted in. And they said things without knowing what they said. She had envied them once. It had seemed so easy. She had thought they didn't care. But now she knew they did; they just didn't see what lay below the surface of things. And it made her feel sorry. They did awful things to each other.

"They're so heavy to handle," she said, voicing a part of her thoughts to her mother.

Her mother smiled, in the same warm carefree way she had shown earlier.

"Just be yourself," she said again. "But be all you are. Remember all you know. That will be enough, I think."

It was so confusing. Casselia pushed her thoughts aside and looked at the dress again. Why couldn't her mother be more specific? Be all she was . . . what, by the Guardians, did that mean?

When the time came to go, she was nervous. It was strange to feel that way. She never had. Her parents smiled and talked in the air car, and she felt better after a bit. Her father was as light and confident as her mother, and that gave her further support. It was almost as if they were at home on Earth. The guardedness she had seen in them here was gone. Her father hadn't joked like this since they'd climbed on the spaceship. She tried to share their mood, but didn't quite make it; she couldn't look forward to the evening as they seemed to be doing. Dinner parties on Clord were so somber, so stiff and proper. What she really wanted was fun. And she didn't think this was going to be.

As usual, the dinner was to be out-of-doors. Even though the air held no sparkle, the ground was fake, and most plants everywhere had been trimmed into shapes beyond all recognition as living things, the Clordians seemed to like getting out of their all-the-same rooms into their almost all-the-same gardens. The garden at the palace of the Commander of All the Clords, she saw to her surprise, had some real ground, well plasticized to prevent dust, but real ground nevertheless. The trees had been trimmed into the shapes of long extinct Clordian animals. The bushes too. All carefully placed in very geometric patterns. The last garden she had been in had had only bushes—cut and trimmed into little buildings. This was a bit better. The tables were set down one long aisle between huge lizard-like creatures of trees, and small rodent-like bushes, alternating on either side. Stiff, stiff, stiff!

Casselia looked at the sky and wished it would rain. That would be really different. It never rained on Clord. She wasn't sure, but she thought it had never happened there. The water was all under the ground. Or maybe she'd heard that some clouds sometimes did hold water, but they were drained and the water stored. Certainly nothing was ever left to chance on Clord. It was a pity. Casselia sighed. A little rain would do a lot for one of these state occasions.

There were evidently not to be as many guests tonight as usual. Only a dozen tables for ten, instead of the customary thirty or forty tables. There were always representatives from conquered and dependent planets who had to be included. Whether the smaller size boded good or ill, she decided, might depend on who was invited to a smaller dinner. Were all Clordians old? Surely not. Then why did she have to come if no young Clordians ever did?

Walking between her mother and father, she was conscious of many eyes upon her, a staring look even from those who had seen her many times before. What was happening? She looked down at her dress, not really sure now that she was ready to be grown-up. At home it would be fine. But here? What did it mean? Her mother had never been so secretive before. And telling her only to be herself, instead of going into one of those long lectures she always gave before a dinner. When was she to be herself? And how could she really be herself here? Suddenly she felt nervous again. Something was obviously expected of her tonight, and she didn't know what. She felt very much alone.

Her mother smiled at her, as if she knew, and the fear and the aloneness retreated a little. But not the question. What was she expected to do?

The Commander of All the Clords was coming. A dreary bore. Almost the worst of the Clordians, she thought again. Yet in many ways she felt sorry for him too. He tried so hard to be nice—to express what seemed to be real regret about what had happened so long ago. He seemed to be obsessed with the past. Too much so, she thought. No matter what he said, he would do the same thing again if it seemed necessary to him. He was afraid of Earth. Odd, wasn't it? The Clordians had so much power—and yet so little knowledge. They couldn't see beyond themselves and their own ways; couldn't really cope with the unexpected. People on Earth had been almost too much of a shock.

"Ah, my great good friends, the honorable envoys, Sorchum. And you, my dear—Casselia, is it not? How elegant you are tonight. You are becoming a fine young woman among us. We are honored."

The Commander held up his hands to touch those of her parents, and then turned to her. She moved her hands up slowly and with reluctance. She had never had to do this before. No one had really noticed her, except to pat her on the head. The big hands came forward toward hers and stopped. Realizing she would have to observe the silly custom, she poked her hands on and touched his.

Looking at his face for a moment, she caught an expression of surprise, instead of the customary stony smile. What had surprised him? Maybe something behind her that she couldn't see. But what could possibly surprise the Commander of All the Clords at one of these machine-made dinners? She turned to look, and to her amazement a young man was coming down the avenue—a boy, really, not much older than she, by Clordian standards. Glancing back, she saw that the Commander was smiling again. It must be all right then. And what a relief to know that Clordians were sometimes young.

"You see him," said the Commander of All the Clords, smiling as real a smile as she had ever seen him give. "Then come meet him. It is time you knew our Vester."

Casselia looked up at her parents, who nodded, pleased, and let her follow the Commander alone. She was to meet a young Clordian at last. She regretted that he was in uniform. It seemed to limit his possibilities. But never mind. He was young. And that was enough for now.

"Casselia Sorchum, Vester Wrang. Vester is the son of my son, one you may have heard of." His face held a proud look. "The one who alone convinced the Southeast Quadrant that it should be a part of us, accept our protection."

Casselia shuddered. She'd heard. The Southeast Quadrant was a new territory for Clord. They were about to give it the "advantages" of Clordian ownership and protection. She barely managed to smile at Vester. The thought struck her that he might be worse than nothing. How could she be herself with the son of the conqueror of the Southeast Quadrant? Yet he was young. And something new had to happen to her or she'd explode.

"Why don't you two young people find a place to get acquainted?" A smile covered the Commander's face, but his words were really a command. The smile on Vester's face was too wide.

"Be yourself," her mother had said. And suddenly, unaccountably, the lightness that had held her parents seized her. She was tired of the whole dreary business, but she'd show them that she could be all she knew. She focused her thoughts on Vester and grinned, which gave her the satisfaction of seeing both the Commander and his grandson look startled.

"Marvelous," she said. "I'm delighted to meet you, Vester. What about that bench over there?"

He looked a bit dazed as she moved confidently to the bench. But he came. His face, however, seemed a bit blue.

"Have you ever been to Earth?" she asked sweetly, knowing he hadn't. There had been only two ships of Clordians on Earth, as far as she knew, and only one of any consequence. Sequestered as she had been on the return journey of that second ship, she had still seen everyone aboard and knew that Vester had not been among them. None of them had been young.

Numbly he shook his head. He seemed to be a little

dizzy. Maybe he hadn't been prepared for this meeting either. Did young Clordians not go to fancy dinners at all? If they didn't, he might be even more dazed than she, though she had never noticed any Clordians before who seemed weak and ineffectual in any situation. Blunt, yes. And driving. But never weak. Or were young Clordians different? Were they kept apart from others—at least from adults—until they had that hard outside? Of course, she had never really spoken to adult Clordians either, just observed them. Yet it was strange that he didn't say anything. The only thing to do seemed to be to go on.

"I'm very fond of Earth, though Clord is nice too," she added quickly. She concentrated on him, trying to bring him out of his quiet, to make him a part of the place and the event, as she'd been taught to do. "We're comfortable here. Your people have provided well for us," she added hastily at his look of lost amazement. "Though I sometimes miss our out-of-doors. I went on my sequestering almost two years ago now. That's when you go off alone to discover yourself. I spent three days in a canyon by a little stream. I found some old bottles that my mother said might have been made before the Clordian Sweep."

That was a mistake, especially when his grandfather felt so embarrassed about it. "We're not sure but what it didn't help us in the end, the Clordian Sweep," she said, trying to recoup her error. "We're different now, the scientists say. And maybe better." She stopped short as a pale green color swept over Vester's face. What was wrong. Was it the Clordian Sweep still? That had been a mistake. Should she talk about something he knew more about?

"I wish I could see more of Clord. There hasn't been

much chance for me to get out. And I haven't met anyone young before. You can't imagine how glad I am to get to know you. I haven't talked to anyone my own age in a whole Earth year and a half. And everyone needs someone to talk to, not just parents."

Vester remained silent. Would nothing bring him out? Could he talk at all? His color was now pale mauve. She wondered briefly if he had ever seen a rainbow. No, of course not, unless he had traveled away from Clord, and that didn't seem likely if he was as much of a lump as he seemed. Yet she was supposed to be the best of Earth for him! This must have been what her mother meant. This whole thing was so obviously planned. Did that mean she was supposed to get Vester to talk? Was it some kind of test? She felt a moment's panic, then decided to throw caution to the winds. Earth was what she really wanted to talk about, so that was what she would talk about.

"Do you go on sequestering? I think about mine all the time. It was really beautiful there. There was a gorgeous rainbow while I was in the canyon. You've never seen one, I guess. It's an arch in the sky, and it's all colors. From the rain and the sun. The sun, that's our star. I had never seen such a perfect rainbow. But it wasn't just that it was so perfect, it was that it happened while I was there."

She remembered it very clearly. It had been a sort of promise, of what she did not know. Lost in thought, she stopped talking a moment. The rainbow had been the answer then. She had been seeking deep inside, as she'd been taught, for a strong inner unity, for a sense of direction, and suddenly she'd known that for her it would al-

71

ways come from seeing and holding steady one thing out-side herself. Her director had said later that that was a bit of oversimplification, but it would do until she moved on.

Thinking back still to that moment, she held Vester in her gaze and decided to put her discovery to work at last. She'd concentrate on Vester as if he were a double rain-bow, even though he seemed to have no voice at all. How could the Clordians have done so much, when their young people couldn't even hold up one end of a conversation?

"What is your school like? Do you have to find a focus, a unity, as we do? Do you have to explore and discover? Or do you just learn facts and things, as we do some-times? My mother's taught me a lot on the spaceship and here, but the exploring has been a bit limited. What I'd really like is to go to school with others again. It's more fun. Do you go to school?" She smiled the brightest smile she had and gave Vester the full force of it.

He fainted. At least he slumped over and fell to the ground.

Startled, she gave a short scream. What had she done? Surely her conversation wasn't so dull it put people into a dead faint. She'd never had that trouble at home. And if what she was saying was so bad, why hadn't he changed the subject? Why hadn't her parents warned her, told her what to talk about? She reached down to lift his head, but other hands reached him first, motioned to her to move, and stretched him out on the bench. There had been peo-ple closer than she had realized. The Commander and her parents and several others.

"I don't know what happened," Casselia said, puzzled more than ever. "He just fainted."

The Commander looked at her sternly, accusingly. But it didn't matter to her. She was too upset. The first young Clordian she'd seen, and it had gone so badly. Was she going to be alone forever?

"He never said anything," she murmured, trying to understand. "He turned all sorts of colors and then he fainted."

The Commander looked at her for a second, turned white, and took a step toward Vester, where he lay on the bench.

Casselia took a few quick steps toward her parents, needing them. It was a relief to find that they were not worried or even angry. The Clordians around them were so upset. The air was all stirred up. But her parents were an island of peace and, yes, gaiety—the same laughing gaiety she had sensed earlier, though on the outside both seemed concerned and sober. She had never seen them this way with Clordians before.

"This is most unusual. And most unexpected," said the Commander of All the Clords ominously. "You must understand, my dear Sorchums, that Vester is in perfect health. He has never had the least problem. We were all watching. We saw nothing. But he is my heir. You know, of course, that we must examine the girl."

Casselia looked at her parents. Were they going to let that happen? She'd only talked at the boy. Silly thing! What weaklings the Clordians were if they couldn't even take a little conversation.

"We understand," her father said, speaking directly at the Commander, in a way she had not seen her father speak on Clord before. The withdrawal, the hesitation were gone. It was, in fact, the Commander who was withdrawing. "It will be simply a superficial physical examination, I assume, to make sure she has no concealed weapon. And we will be allowed to be present."

The Commander of All the Clords rubbed his hand over his eyes. "Yes, of course," he said, almost softly.

What a strange turn of events. Walking slowly between her parents, who in turn walked between the precisely trimmed trees and bushes, she gave up for the third time that day. Once more she didn't know what was going on.

Before the curious stares of the other guests, a little parade wound its way toward the sheath building at the head of the garden. Vester and his bearers were first, then Casselia and her parents, then two guards, then the Commander of All the Clords, and then two more guards.

We need a little music, Casselia thought, and almost giggled. She glanced at her parents and somehow had the idea they were thinking the same. All three shared a smile. Good, then they weren't worried. But why? She didn't have a weapon, of course, and they knew it. But the Clordians could do anything in that building and no one would ever know, no one on Earth, at least. The building didn't even have any windows. She drew herself up very straight. She would not be afraid.

The march continued slowly, moving deliberately toward the door. Nearer, Casselia felt a sudden moment of panic, but her mother, probably feeling her tense up, squeezed her hand and said softly, "Remember the Earth. Focus on those who come to you here. Be concerned for them and not for yourself. Yet be yourself. Relax and be easy." Another smile. From her father too. She relaxed.

She could do that all right. Her focus was fine. And the Earth was always hard to forget. It was winter at home now; hard to imagine in the everlasting sameness of Clordian weather. The bite of cold came to mind and she held it there, willing away the present. Then she dropped the thought. It was the present that needed her concentration.

They were inside the door. Soft lights were everywhere and nowhere. The eternal hard chairs of Clord gave way here to a few with some upholstery, but only a few. It was nevertheless, she realized, a fine home. The home of the Commander of All the Clords. Of course, it would be fine. But why was she here, and in such a predicament?

A woman came in then, glanced at Casselia where she and her parents had stopped, and moved to Vester. She looked down at him, shook her head, and led the bearers down the hall beyond.

"You understand that further association may now be impossible—certainly it is unlikely that we can look for a marriage—but of course any action depends on what we find."

Casselia looked up, startled. She had not seen the Commander come over, busy watching Vester disappear.

"Marriage?" she murmured, almost without thinking.

"She doesn't know?" he asked quickly.

Her parents shook their heads.

"We had not agreed to it, nor, of course, had she. It was better to see how the meeting went. Such things cannot be forced, especially under such abnormal circumstances. Obviously it could never be a true marriage, only a marriage of state."

"Cannot be forced," the Commander puffed. "But such

things, even under these circumstances, are expected. No force is needed. I myself have many wives from other planets."

"Which is just the point," murmured her mother. "On Earth, marriage when it occurs is never expected. It simply is. But once a true marriage comes about, both parties have a right to expect something of each other. Formal agreements are not enough for us. We cannot live in patterns."

The Commander did not reply.

Casselia looked at the floor, then up at her parents. Had they expected her to like him? To marry Vester? Had they wanted it? Would that protect Earth from Clord? Be yourself, they had said. And she had been. That Vester was a limp old toadstool! He'd never said a word. And then he'd fainted. How could she marry that? Besides, she was too young. And more than that, she wanted to go home. Vester would never fit in on Earth. They'd as much as said that a marriage between an Earth person and a Clord person wouldn't really work. So why did they want her to have that kind of marriage?

"If you want my thoughts, it was a silly plan," she said, looking up at the Commander of All the Clords defiantly. "I never would have come tonight if I had known. I don't intend to marry for at least ten Earth years and maybe never. Nobody has to. And that Vester is a. . . ." She stopped. It might be best not to voice her opinion of him to his grandfather. She'd probably said enough already.

She looked up to see if she had offended him too much and discovered that his face was almost as colorful as Vester's had been. He seemed about to explode. What right had he to feel that way, no matter who he was?

Focusing on him, angry now beyond caring, she exploded first. "Who do you think you are, pushing people around? We all have a right to be just what we are, and you can't make us anything else."

The Commander was suddenly white.

"Casselia," her mother cautioned lightly, "better calm down. Save yourself for the two ladies here."

The Commander dropped to a padded chair as two women, large and burly, approached.

"Are you the girl to be searched?" one asked, not unkindly.

Casselia nodded. But as the woman put out a hand to take her, she felt a sudden return of her earlier fears and anger; she gazed at the woman stonily, wishing her away. The woman's hand did not touch her.

"Well, come on," said the other, shoving the first aside.

That woman's hand reached out, and as Casselia turned her attention there, it dropped also.

"Perhaps," said her father quietly, "if you'd lead us to the room you wish, we could follow. That might be easier for you." He took Casselia's hand, and they both looked at the women.

"I'm not going to touch her," said the second woman, backing away. She turned and all but ran from the room, the first woman following.

"Perhaps you should get some other women," Casselia's father murmured to one of the guards who stood near the Commander. "Those seem to behave strangely."

The guard did not move.

"No one will come now," another guard said. "Something peculiar here. It's better not to find out. We know what we know. And that's good enough."

"Yes, it is good enough," Casselia's father said. "Clord is a great empire. It is the greatest we know. You have much to be proud of. And we are pleased to have been among you and to have had this chance to learn your ways. They are not our ways, but we all have a right to accept what we will and to let others enjoy what they will."

He meant it, Casselia saw. He was trying to smooth over a hard moment for the Clordians. And yet the meaning of it all still wasn't quite clear. What had she done? She was sorry she had shown fear and anger, and would apologize if the women came back. Yet why had they gone away? Surely in their job they had had people afraid before. She'd heard that fear was a defense. But you had to do something with it beside focus on the person, didn't you? Or didn't you? Something had happened to everyone she had focused on today. Was there something in her?

"I'm sorry," she said, looking at her father. "I didn't mean to be afraid. I didn't mean to drive her away, if I did. Did my focusing do it?"

"Casselia, don't be sorry," said her mother. "You did only what any of us might have done in your place."

Her mother still wasn't angry and neither was her father. The light feeling remained. The joy and warmth of Earth.

The Commander of All the Clords lifted his head now, although it seemed an effort for him. "We have no records to indicate that any of the people of Earth were . . . well, were as this child seems to be."

"Your records are from a time long past," said Casselia's father. "And the child is not alone. We are all the same, it is just that we who know our strength have learned to mask it. It is an inheritance, perhaps, from your ancestors."

"You were changed—by what we did?" whispered the Commander.

"Perhaps. Or perhaps this power is something we always had and only developed after your coming," said Mr. Sorchum. "We have found old medical records, and there is much in them that does not agree with what we find in ourselves today. We are seldom ill, seldom even injured. We do not multiply rapidly. And we seem to have an affinity for and a power over the other living things on Earth. Yet we have small effect on each other, perhaps because we do not care to have, perhaps because we neutralize each other. We have done no research on the matter, because we know so little of it ourselves. We simply know we have a force, an energy, within ourselves that may have many uses. Only recently have some of us begun to learn its control. A few adults have been experimenting. But we all have the power and can use it in crude ways. And we are sure that what one can do alone, many can do together."

"How did we land?"

"We wanted you to land. We were as curious as you. Partly because we did not really know the extent of our strength. We were not sure until you came, until we could test ourselves quietly against you. Only a few of us knew enough of what we might possibly be able to do to be a part of the test. So you saw only those who could control their powers, test them in unfelt ways."

"But why should the girl damage the boy? What had he done?"

"She did not mean to do anything but speak. She didn't know what we know about the power of focusing. At home it is a polite thing to do. You focus on those to whom you speak. And because she sensed the importance of the meeting, she focused her full attention on him. He simply was unprepared for the energy that she was beaming toward him."

"Why did you let it happen if you knew?" the Commander barked, almost himself again.

"I didn't know what would happen myself. We none of us know just how we measure in this thing. Casselia has been kept apart because we did not dare expose her to others too soon. My wife and I needed to test you first. We had to have time before we revealed what we knew, time to find out the extent of our powers. We needed the chance to do this as much as you needed two or three envoys from Earth to study."

"What have you learned? How strong is it?" the Commander pressed on.

"We are not wholly sure yet. To know the whole of the matter, we would have to test openly, and that would be too dangerous, for you more than us, I suspect."

Casselia looked at her parents in amazement. Was all this really true? And why hadn't she known it? But was it true? No. Only some of it was. And some of it might be. They were bluffing. There was a power there. And they had known, had hoped, at least, that it would help. They had given her all the strength they could, and then hoped it would be enough. And it had been. Her mother gave a small smile that said she was right. She knew her mother well enough for that. What would happen next? It didn't matter, she guessed, as long as the Clordians knew for sure that some power existed. It was marvelous! She wanted to laugh.

"You should be wiped out," the Commander was saying.

"We cannot be wiped out. We three perhaps, but not, we are sure, a whole, focusing Earth. It is possible that no spaceship will ever land again, or even come close, without the consent of Earth. In our absence, no one will be allowed to land. No spaceship will touch Earth until we have returned.

"All Earth now knows something of what has been discovered. Every child on Earth has been taught to focus for years. It's been a way of learning things quickly and of complimenting your friends. Now it may be a defense as well."

The Commander dropped his hands to his side. "Will the boy recover?" he asked.

"I think he will," murmured Mrs. Sorchum. "I hope so."

"And what is to be done?" The Commander seemed confused.

"Nothing," said Casselia's father. "We exist, we of Earth, and we have a right to be. There are five hundred planets in all the Clords, and we want none of them. We have our own problems. And they are not problems of going beyond ourselves. Not yet, and probably not ever. We are no threat to you. Except that we exist apart from you. And you surely know that we are not alone in that."

"You know that too," the Commander whispered, as if

a great secret had been spoken. This time Casselia felt he was truly afraid, more afraid than he had been of them. And she understood his fear. They, the people of Earth, were the first minded beings he had actually encountered who could not be talked or fought into becoming a part of Clord. One such planet might be tolerated. But if there were others, and he had to admit it, then Clord would never seem as powerful again.

"We have seen ships in the sky that were not Clordian," said her father. "None have landed. It may be that we have driven them away, unknowing. Or perhaps they have not needed to land to see what we are. Yet they have been there, and we have seen them."

"I knew . . . I felt sure . . . Reports have said . . . Soon it will all end for us, I know." The Commander was dejected beyond reason, Casselia thought. Who needed an empire? Earth didn't have one, and it was better by far than Clord.

"No, no," she said, focusing her thoughts on him, "don't feel that way. There's room for all of us. You can't just disappear. We might even come to like you." Surprised at herself, she drew back. She'd forgotten that you couldn't focus on a Clordian. But she had meant what she said.

"In my school they tell a joke," she said hesitantly, looking away. "They say, 'And who is Earth's greatest enemy?' 'Clord,' everyone says. And then they say, 'And who is Earth's greatest friend?' 'Clord,' everyone says. 'Why?' they ask. 'Because they're the only ones we have to talk to beside ourselves, and who on Earth can live without talking?' It's a kind of silly joke. Not all of us talk a lot." She ended rather lamely. On Clord it didn't make as much sense, somehow, as it did on Earth. Clordians didn't have the same feeling of all being one as people on Earth did.

The Commander, however, gave her a weak smile. "How hungry are you?" he asked unexpectedly.

Casselia gave a start. She hadn't thought of that. But now that the question had come up, she knew that she was starved.

"I could eat," she said truthfully.

"Then let's to dinner, if you'll just concentrate on the food."

The Commander bowed, and she stepped beside him. Together they moved out the door and down the rows of trees and bushes to the tables. Her parents followed; and the other guests, who had been waiting outside the door, fell in. The dinner was somewhat overdone, but Casselia didn't care. She had the feeling that life on Clord was about to pick up. And Earth didn't seem quite so distant anymore.

Catabilid Conquest

You would never believe it, but our greatest adventure actually began one day a couple of months ago as Vana, my twin, and I sat under a tree, wallowing in absolute misery.

"Vana," I said, "what are we going to do? We'd counted on their coming now." Neither one of us could understand why our parents had decided not to come home. They'd been gone for months. It just wasn't fair.

Vana looked at me, at a loss for words for the first time I could ever remember. "I don't know," he said finally. "There doesn't seem to be any way out for us. We ought to go on our sequestering in the next three or four weeks, if we're going to have any choice at all in what we do at school next year. I don't think I can stand another year of that standard course."

"Almost everyone else is gone," I added.

Vana nodded and didn't reply. We both knew the fix we were in. We live with our grandparents because our parents own and fly a small spaceship, one that delivers supplies to archaeological digs on other planets. As a result, they are seldom home.

We had always liked the freedom this gave us. Our grandparents both teach at the Master Level School and are deep into subjects that have to do with hidden areas of the mind: Earth Power and what it can do. So unless we did something that really called attention to ourselves, we could pretty much do as we pleased.

This had all worked very well until it came time for us to go on a sequestering. Everyone has to go on one in order to move from the standard course in school to one that meets one's own interests and talents. On a sequestering you pull yourself together and find out who you are and what you want of the future. But adults, and especially parents, have to be a part of it.

Our grandparents couldn't understand our need for a sequestering. "It's an old-fashioned concept," they said. "You children are secure enough. And in the end all education must come from within you."

At school, everyone said it had to be parents who were involved anyway. "Wait until your parents come home," we were told again and again.

The real trouble, we had decided, was that we simply didn't fit into any pattern that anyone else considered normal, and no one knew what to do with us. Even our grandparents sometimes seemed a little embarrassed by us. Earth people don't have many children. Twins are something no one knows anything about. And to make it worse, most people don't think it's wise to leave Earth unless they really have to. Archaeologists leave, and government people, to work in other places for a while. But to choose to be gone almost all the time—well, that's just not normal. So by being twins and by having parents who are always away, by choice, we had become outsiders. We had hoped that a sequestering would prove that we really were like other people and deserved a place to belong.

We sat under the tree in silence, going over and over our problem. Only the really stupid kids, the ones who had no choice about their futures, would be left in the standard school next year. And we had been bored this year. We had counted on the promised three-week visit from our parents. Surely they would listen, we felt, would understand, would care, would arrange things. But now they weren't coming. Instead they were taking emergency equipment off to some weird place called Frod, where a small dig was taking place. A number of different planets were participating, but this particular gear only Earth could supply. Earth is big on archaeology because of its history. Its archaeologists are called in on special projects in lots of places, even by planets that are more developed.

"We've got to do something," I said at last. "Think of something, Vana."

"Think of something yourself," he muttered.

I did have an idea in the back of my mind, but I hadn't wanted to say anything for fear he would laugh. We had to find some answer, though. So I blurted it out.

"Well, why don't we plan our own sequestering? If we went away, and kept careful notes to show people, maybe that would be enough. There wouldn't be the rituals at the start and end, but we could show we have some ability anyway. Getting away would prove that."

Vana looked at me with amazement. He always thinks

87

boys should be the ones with ideas. "That might just work," he said. "It just might." His whole face brightened.

"Look," he went on, "no one would miss us, at least not at first, if we planned right. We could go far enough away so no one would think to look for us where we were, then come back after three or four days. It would be great. If nothing else, it would be something different to do, and we sure need that."

There's no place we can walk to where no one would look for us," I said, a little annoyed that he had taken over my idea so completely. "In fact, I can't think of any place we could get to that someone wouldn't look, except maybe Frod." Frod was simply the farthest away place I could think of at the moment. But then suddenly. . . .

An electric spark jumped between us, and we both grinned. We knew we both had the same idea. It was so obvious. Why had it taken us so long to think of? We could go to Frod. Our sequestering would be a stolen trip to Frod! It was the greatest idea we had ever had.

"It would work," Vana said, almost breathless. "We could do it. I know we could." And thinking it over, I agreed. Together we could make it happen.

According to the report we had received, our parents were expected at the space port they used in just a week. They would arrive late one evening and leave early the next morning. They were bringing in only a few things that would have to be unloaded, and only a few new things would have to be loaded for the trip to Frod. We would have one night in which to get aboard the spaceship and find places to hide.

We had visited the space port and the spaceship several times in the past. We knew of places at the space port where we could wait unseen, and we could think of several places in the ship that would probably be empty on the trip to Frod.

Almost before we knew it, our plans were roaring along and were almost completed. We tried to nail down every detail of our going. And the more we planned, the more confident we became.

We told our grandparents that a message had come from the space port saying that our parents had asked us to come for a short visit while they were in. It sounded logical because they had been gone so long. Our grandparents believed us. They had no reason not to.

Our next chore was to gather condensed food and the kinds of liquids that you only need a little of to keep from being thirsty. That was harder, but we managed. We both had some money, and we found ways to buy quietly and in small bits.

The hardest part was to keep the excitement out of our voices and faces. That was the thing that would give us away, if anything did. We didn't wholly succeed, but luckily no one noticed.

When the time came for us to leave, we were all ready. We set off with more gear than anyone should have thought necessary for a brief trip to a space port. But no one asked any awkward questions. We took the Mechanized Transport, which was very safe. People mind their own business on the Transport.

The base was just as we remembered it. We found a place to hide, and saw our parents' ship come down just after sundown. We watched them get off, obviously tired and ready to sleep. Good, there was no danger of their taking time to call us or our grandparents.

A gang of workers took a few things from the ship and put a few more things on. The steps to the cabin were left in place, and the door was left open because the ship was leaving so early in the morning. Other workers, on the far side of the ship, would be refueling it all night, so obviously no one thought there was any danger in leaving things open.

Under cover of dark, and the scant vegetation of the desert area where the space port was, we crept to the ship, slipped up the stairs, and were in. It was almost too easy.

We had remembered two special closets, generally used for fragile artifacts, that we were sure would be available to us. It was dark in the ship, with only a few landing lights on, but we found the closets after a short search and crept in. We felt very safe in our hideaways. Only in emergencies were they used for supplies. And like most of the ship, they had oxygen outlets.

The next day the ship took off. We were a bit shaken up by the blast-off, but our closets were padded, so we weren't hurt. We had made it into space! I felt like cheering as soon as I came out of my blackout. Now, even when our grandparents discovered we were gone, which wasn't likely for another day or two, no one could do a thing. No one was likely to guess where we were. And we would have our sequestering.

We had been in our closets for almost twenty-four earth hours when Vana called me.

"What are we going to do now?" I asked, coming out.

"Stretch," Vana said.

"And then what?"

"Plot our course," he muttered.

"It's plotted for us," I said. "We're going to Frod."

"Don't be stupid. The question is, what do we do when we get there? And how do we get back if these closets are filled for the return?"

I looked at him in amazement. I hadn't thought of that. But I was sure he had. He's generally so thorough.

"I was busy planning how to get away, of course," he said, to my unspoken question. "Coming back wasn't important until we left."

"What are the options?" I asked.

"Do we want to be found?" he said.

At first it seemed a silly question, then it didn't. If we were found it would solve some of our problems, problems that now seemed all too obvious, although we had both evidently overlooked them before. Yet being found would create other problems that could be much worse. We wouldn't have to worry about food and getting home. But we would have to worry about a scolding or more—the Guardians only know what—and about being watched too closely, maybe forever. Certainly if we were found before we got to Frod, we wouldn't see much of that planet.

"I say no," I answered at last.

"Me too," said Vana. "If we can make it. It all depends on Frod. And on what they pick up there."

We had done some research on Frod, but hadn't been able to find out much about it. It wasn't a large planet, but it was quite heavy, so gravity was close to Earth's. It had once had intelligent life, but that life now seemed gone. Archaeologists were trying to find out what had happened. Why, we didn't know, because as far as we had been able to discover there had never been the kind of life that would make such research worthwhile. Yet it must have been important if Earth archaeologists were there. They only go out when they're really needed. People on other planets still feel a little strange about being with Earth people.

"We won't have enough food if we can't get some there," I said.

"Or water," Vana said. "Of course, in an emergency we can get it from the ship's tanks, but we can hardly do that often without someone's noticing."

"I'll fix that," I said.

"How?" Vana asked.

"Put in a few pebbles each time, to keep the level up."

"You don't have any pebbles."

"I can get some on Frod." I couldn't imagine a planet without stones of some kind.

He let that pass, not having a better suggestion.

"Can we stand a week in these closets? Maybe a week each way?" I asked, stretching my stiff muscles again.

"We have to. We chose it," Vana said.

I grinned wryly. He was right, we had.

So we both stretched some more and didn't talk. There was nothing more to say. We had made all the plans we could. The rest depended on Frod.

It seems a miracle that we were not discovered on that trip out. The spaceship was compact. There was little room that wasn't filled with something. And we did move around a bit in our compartments. We must have made some noise in our sleep, when our parents were awake. But I guess the idea of stowaways had never occurred to them, so they just didn't hear the noises.

It was a sequestering, all right. Sleeping was hard. We

were so tired sometimes, we could have slept standing up in broad daylight. But after only a little sleep huddled in those closets, we woke up feeling cramped again. There wasn't much time, we found, when we could be out of our nests. One or the other of our parents was generally awake. A short trip takes more navigation than a longer one. You pass through time bumps more often.

I got a bit of thinking done, and Vana did too. Part of it was about our problem. What we would do on Frod. Food. Water. We rationed what we had brought carefully to last the trip out, so these things became more and more important. You always think about what you can't have, I guess. At least you do if you want it.

I discovered a few things about myself. I like people and I like new things and new ideas. And suddenly I didn't blame our parents for the life they led. I decided that given a chance I'd do the same myself. Vana, I discovered later, came to the same decision on that outward trip. Maybe it was mental telepathy. Don't laugh. Some places have it. And our Earth Power is not so different. Since one is supposed to develop one's powers on a sequestering, maybe ours were moving in new directions because we were going on a new kind of sequestering. Actually, we both knew how to focus, which is why our grandparents hadn't worried and said we were secure.

The time went by slowly. It was hard to keep track of days. But eventually we felt the ship enter a new phase. There was a change of power, and a sense of direction to what we were doing. We were nearing Frod.

Vana and I held fast in our closets, afraid the landing would jar us out of our senses. But, although we were tossed around a bit, it wasn't as bad as blast-off. Worst of all was a gradual clamping at us, a feeling of heaviness that we could hardly bear. There was a sharp smack, a swaying, and we were down. It was strange to be still, and stranger still to feel the gravity of Frod.

We heard all sorts of things going on almost at once. Obviously someone had been waiting for the ship. We were really quiet then, listening to the sounds of unloading. Someone nearly opened my door, but I held it shut, and whoever it was thought it was locked. A strange voice said something I didn't understand, and the person at the door went away.

Eventually it was quiet, but I waited until Vana called before I crept out. He was on the door side and could hear what was going on there better than I. It was dark in the ship, but I could tell that all the stuff had been unloaded.

"Let's go," Vana whispered. "Take all your gear."

We crept down the passageway, alert, waiting for any breath of sound. None came. So far so good. No one around inside. The door to the outside was at the left. Closed? Locked? I tried it softly, quietly. No! Not locked.

"Not all the way," Vana murmured at me.

I shook my head and shoved the door open a crack. There was no sound. Another crack. Still no sound. And now I could see that stairs outside led to the ground. Fortunately it was night on Frod. No one would see us, I hoped. I slid through the crack and went down the steps. Vana followed, carefully closing the door behind him. Again, everything seemed almost too easy. We were on Frod. We had done what we had planned to do.

We lay flat on the soil of Frod, hidden by the stairs and the spaceship from any eyes that might be near. In the distance we saw someone, a watchman, perhaps. But there was no sign that he had seen us.

Sliding on our stomachs, we moved slowly over the dark ground, our packs on our backs. It seemed most important that we not be discovered. We had come to see Frod, and now we were going to see it. By ourselves. We moved away from the watchman and the one building in the distance. Which meant we were also moving away from any signs of habitation and gliding toward a forest where the plants looked something like tropical plants on Earth. Broad heavy leaves. Some small. Some large. The whole was so dense we wondered if we could force ourselves into the protection of it.

Because we had to, we managed. By the time the moon of Frod came up, huge and brilliant, we were sitting under and surrounded by the oddest plants we had ever seen. They were strong and thick and seemed to grow while we watched.

"Whew!" said Vana. "Here we are, and now what?"

"I thought you were working that out," I said.

"Couldn't till we got here to see what it was like."

"How long have we got?"

"That I do know. They're due back at sunset on the twenty-fifth of Westerg. We left on the fourth. This is the eleventh, I think. If it takes as long to get back as it did to come, we've got seven days, or six days, if we want to play it safe."

I did. "Six days then," I said. "Six days to find food and water and a place on the ship to hide."

"I thought we came for a sequestering," Vana said, laughing.

"I've had it," I said. "Seven days on the way out. And if we're lucky, seven days on the way back. That's enough. Besides, to find food and water, we have to explore. And I'd rather do that. If we can get through all this greenery, that is." As I spoke, I felt doubtful and must have sounded it. It was such an odd place.

"Frod is different," Vana admitted. "I didn't think it would be like this."

We both looked around carefully. The field where we had landed seemed to be cut out of a solid bed of growth. It was like an oasis in the middle of a terrarium gone wild. At least as far as we could see. Which wasn't all that far.

"We've got a little food," Vana said. "So we don't have to worry right away about how much of this is edible. Why don't we sleep until it's light. Things may look better then."

The Frodian night was not as dark as ours. In addition to the moon, something in the atmosphere seemed to glow. But no light would have been enough to keep us awake. It felt too good to stretch out on the ground.

We woke to a Frodian day that turned out to be not quite so bright as ours on Earth. It seemed strange after that bright night sky. Whatever made the sky glow at night seemed to hold out some of the rays of Frod's star in the day. It still was bright enough, considering we had seen very little light in almost eight days. We both blinked as we woke.

"Forgot my dark glasses," Vana said.

I laughed. It seemed such a normal thing to forget. "What else do you need?" I asked.

"Food first," he said.

So it was food first. Our careful ration. And a little water. Then we looked around. There wasn't much to see that we hadn't already seen. Plants everywhere. Light green. Medium green. Dark green. Yellow green, blue green, all shades of green. And all succulents of a sort. Yet not desert plants. Lush, the products of a rain forest, and dense. The soil had to be very rich to support such growth, I thought. But even given that, the growth seemed over-much.

"If we go far into this, how will we know where we are?" I said. "We may never find the field again. Do you have a compass?"

"Silly!" Vana thought he was being smart. "We have no idea of where the magnetic poles are here, or even if there are any."

"Well, if there is one, does it matter where it is, as long as we know what direction we're moving in?" I asked.

Vana looked at me in surprise. "You're right," he said. "And I think I do have a compass. Left from that last hiking trip." He searched in his bag and pulled out a tiny compass. The needle swung to a fixed position, so the place did have a magnetic pole of some sort.

We set out in the direction the compass pointed, which happened to be parallel to the field. It was hard going. Some of the plants had sharp edges. The ones near the ground obviously needed little light because they flourished under a canopy of heavy leaves made by the tree-like plants. And in between there was a bush level. It was almost dark on the ground.

We moved on for an hour or an hour and a half.

"How long is a day here?" I asked.

"About twenty of our hours," Vana answered.

"Will the ship be here six or seven of our days or theirs?"

Vana just shrugged his shoulders. He had no way of knowing. So we had less time on Frod than I had thought. We'd have to be back in six Frodian days. Or maybe be left behind. And the job of finding what we needed looked bigger every minute. We saw no water and didn't know what was edible among these plants.

We plodded on, or rather pushed and pressed our way —silently. We had no idea where we were going or what we hoped to find. We were alone on a strange planet, and no one knew we were there. Yet not for a minute did we want to be found. It was still an adventure.

"Where do you suppose the archaeological team is working?" Vana asked as we slowed to rest.

"How can they find anything at all in this?" I asked. "What ever made them think there was intelligent life here once?"

"I think they must be on the other side of the clearing," he said. "That's where the building was. The dig or whatever it is must be near the clearing. You couldn't carry supplies very far in this. Of course," he added, "it may not all be like this."

"Do we try to find the dig?" I asked.

"I don't know. We don't want to be found. But food and water may be easier to find there." It was the first time I had ever heard Vana be really uncertain. And suddenly the six Frodian days seemed long, longer than six Earth days. Especially if we had to spend them near some stupid dig with an uncertain future at the end.

"We've been walking inside the forest but parallel to

the field," Vana said at last. "If we make a sharp right, we should go over the top of the field—somewhat beyond it, I expect. Let's walk a hundred or a hundred and fifty paces to the right and see what we come to."

We moved slowly to the right, but the scenery remained the same. The field was not there. The compass said we were doing what we had planned. We had been going due north by the compass. And now we were headed due east, or as near to it as we could manage with all the stuff growing in our way.

"Shall we go back south a way?" I asked.

We did and still saw no open space. Yet we had moved so slowly through the heavy growth we couldn't have come too far beyond it.

"Is there really a magnetic pole here?" I asked timidly.

"You and your fancy ideas!" Vana sank to the ground. And I settled heavily beside him. The compass needle seemed true. But was it? Where were we? And where was the spaceship? I began to be afraid for the first time.

"We could follow our trail back," I said.

We both looked in the direction we thought we had come. Nothing. All around. Nothing. We had pushed through and left no trail. But how was that possible, especially when we had sometimes broken off the stiff leaves as we came along? Why were there no signs of our passage anywhere?

"Where are we?" I whispered.

"You are on his majesty's planet Cheriba," a voice answered.

It was a pleasant voice. But that didn't keep it from being electrifying, even terrifying.

Vana and I looked at each other. Frod was uninhabited,

except for plants. And no archaeologist would have said a thing like that. Had our spaceship made an unscheduled landing? I had never heard of Cheriba.

Vana looked shaken. We moved closer together and glanced around. There was no one anywhere. We looked up at the high plants. They covered the sky. We couldn't have seen the ship if it had left. But it was scheduled only for Frod. And the supplies had been taken off. This must be Frod!

"Here, under the bush," the voice said.

We hardly dared to look. But there under the bush was a little brown lump. A cross between a stone and a turtle shell. Nothing that looked alive. Certainly nothing that could talk. Yet as I watched, the whole thing rose, hovered in the air a moment, and then slowly moved toward us. It was an amazing sight. I drew back, ready to stand and run if necessary. Vana, I could feel, was as tense as I.

"You don't look like the others. Earth, aren't you? But smaller," said the voice from the turtle-rock, as it settled before us.

Neither of us replied.

"No matter. The question is, what's to be done with you? None of the others were foolish enough, or venturesome enough, to wander off. You really aren't lost, you know. You just came too far. As others of you have discovered, directions aren't easy here for those who don't know the place. Your noisy airfield is over there." The creature hopped a little back and to the right. We nodded and remained still.

"I'm not sure I can let you go there, though. You may not be like the rest. But this may have been planned. Can't be sure. Can't take a chance. Yet you seemed less certain than the others. More friendly, and really lost. I felt sorry. . . ." Its voice trailed off into nothing, as if it were thinking deeply.

"But we don't want to go back. At least not right away. If this really is Frod," I ventured. The thing sounded so friendly I felt I had to take a chance.

The creature said nothing for a moment.

"This is what they call Frod," it said finally. "But it really is Cheriba."

"But Frod is uninhabited," I said, "except for plants. At least that's what the archaeologists think."

"There are some who think this planet is uninhabited," said the creature with dignity. "We who live here think otherwise. However, we are not eager that those who have come should discover our presence."

"I guess not," said Vana. "Not if they're here to dig up a dead civilization. You might complicate things. And besides, you can't tell what they might do with you. Can you protect yourselves?"

"We have our ways," our turtle-rock said slyly. "And as for dead civilizations, that's absurd." The creature seemed to chuckle. "I shouldn't be telling you this, though. There are those of us who will never trust outlings. And that is what you are."

"We are, and we aren't," Vana muttered.

"Why do you talk like us, if you're from here?" I asked, before the creature could say any more.

"Learned from those digging fools." Our companion chuckled again. "They're digging up our garbage pile, and they don't even know we're here." With that, our friend rolled over and over in the underbrush, howling with laughter. We were so amazed we simply sat and watched until there was another question.

"You're with the Earth bunch?"

I looked at Vana, and he looked at me.

"Not really," I began slowly. "We're more like you. Unseen." And then, hardly realizing what I was doing, I told our whole story, all of it.

When I finished, our turtle-rock gave a quick snort.

"Serves them right," it muttered. "No sense. None at all. Looking into other people's garbage."

"Are you all like you?" Vana asked.

"Of course. Always have been. No reason to change. Very comfortable shape. And especially good these days. They think we're stones. Now, how long did you say you have?"

I told it what we had figured. Six Frodian days—Cheriban days.

"Good," it said. "Plenty of time. Come with me." And it set off with its queer flying jumps that seemed to have no means of propulsion behind them whatsoever.

I looked at Vana and he looked at me, and we followed. It was the airfield or our new friend. And our new friend seemed to offer the best chance for adventure. Though what else we might be getting into, we didn't even dare guess.

"Why don't they realize about you?" I asked finally.

"Because they've got no sense," our friend said quickly. Then it added, "Though, of course, we don't give them much chance." It chuckled again, but didn't go on.

Vana and I found the going hard. The undergrowth,

which had seemed dense before, grew denser. Our friend flew over the lower plants in high hops. But we couldn't. Still we went on, and after a bit I began to feel good about it all, even though I was getting very tired.

"Whew!" Vana said finally. "We can't move as fast as you. By the way, do you have a name? My name is Vana, and this is my sister, Chory."

Our friend stopped, and if an almost-rock can bow, it did. "Honored," it said. "Not every creature gives its name so easily. I'm Quelot. And I forgot that you Earthlings have never learned to bounce. Do you want to learn? It'll be easier for you to get around here, even at your size."

Quelot spoke as if we might take our choice. But who wouldn't want to! Although I didn't for a minute believe I could. Vana nodded his head, yet I could tell he was dubious, too.

"We'd love to, Mister Quelot," he said.

"Not 'Mister,' just Quelot. No fanciness here. All alike."

We nodded. Then Quelot seemed to ponder a moment.

"You creatures from Earth, you have a great power. Not like most who come. You should find this easy. I wouldn't try otherwise. Can you do the Earth-Power thing?"

We nodded. We could focus. It was a useful thing, focusing, though not so all-powerful as some minded planets might think.

"It's not so different from that, I guess. Same sort of concentration. Just use the pressure in another way. Instead of holding things still, just push the ground away."

It sounded easy, but it wasn't as simple as it sounded. I pushed and pushed and nothing happened. Vana looked finally as if he were about to explode. And still he didn't move. I suppose I looked just as silly.

Quelot looked on patiently, seemingly convinced we would master it before long. We were not so sure.

We tried some more.

Still nothing.

"Not with part of you," Quelot said finally. "All of you, and don't force it. Relax and pressure down. I forgot that you sometimes use tension to trigger your power. That doesn't work with this."

I stopped a moment, worn out with trying. Vana, I could see, was working to relax and still getting nowhere.

Finally I pulled myself together and gave it another go. Maybe it was because I had almost given up. Maybe it was because I had really relaxed for a moment. Or maybe it was because I accidentally found the key to how to place the pressure. But suddenly I rose about a decimeter into the air. It was the strangest thing that had ever happened to me. And I must have looked as surprised as I felt because Quelot was once more off into that wild, happy hysteria we had seen before. I let go and settled to the ground, but before I said anything, I did it again, this time propelling myself just a bit higher and a little forward.

"How . . . ?" Vana began, looking at me in amazement. And at that moment he too rose into the air. We had both done it. And the most astonishing thing was that it was easy, once you felt how.

"Will this work at home?" Vana asked.

"Of course," said Quelot. "If you need it there. You have all kinds of machines."

"Not so many on Earth," I said. "We're not big machine people."

Quelot bobbled in surprise. "I thought you outlings were all alike underneath."

"Oh, no," Vana cried. "You might even like Earth. You wouldn't like Clord or Campion or Gammer. At least not from what I've heard. I've never been there. But Earth has a lot of peace on it."

"I'm content with Cheriba," Quelot said.

"You sound like most Earth people," Vana said.

Quelot made no reply, just went hopping off, and we followed. It was obvious at once that it was a lot easier to bounce than to walk over and through the vegetation.

We went on for what seemed hours, with no idea of where we were going. I began to worry, and I saw a questioning look on Vana's face too. We were hungry and tired, and we didn't know where we were. Neither of us said anything. But Quelot must have sensed our mood.

"Nearly there," our guide said, stopping a moment. "Are you hungry? I've noticed that outlings eat a lot."

We nodded. "It's time to eat," I ventured.

"Can you wait a bit?"

We nodded again. And once more we bounced off.

"Are we going to see the king?" Vana asked tentatively.

That set Quelot off once more. Our new friend was the jolliest creature I had ever encountered. Earth people laugh sometimes. But not like that. Quelot seemed to find laughter in everything.

"Oh, my," our turtle-rock mumbled at last. "I'd almost forgotten. His majesty's planet Cheriba! Of course you believed it. But I was just being like an outling. I didn't know you then. There's no king. We all just live. Well, it's not quite that simple, but you'll see. Just don't expect a king."

So we didn't expect a king, or an emperor, or a Commander of All the Cheribas. Or even a Core Council. But what were we to expect?

We bounced along in silence. If we hadn't left any trail pushing and shoving our way through the lush growth, we were leaving less of one now, bouncing from spot to spot. We were totally dependent on Quelot and others of Cheriba, if we ever got to them. If they were all as friendly and helpful as Quelot seemed, we were fine. But if not and we were left alone in the jungle, we were going to be very lost.

I was so busy trying to digest our situation that at first I didn't notice that the scene was changing. The undergrowth was as heavy as ever, but the taller plants were thinning. I first realized it when I felt a bit of sun on my face. It was the first time I had felt the sun of Frod—or Cheriba as I had now begun to think of it—since we had left our sleeping place at the edge of the clearing.

"Well, here we are," said Quelot unexpectedly. "Why don't you just sit down? The others will be along."

Vana and I looked at each other, surprised again. The trees, if you could call them that, were thinner. But this did not look like a place where even someone like Quelot might live. So we just sat down and waited. It was all too peculiar to do anything different.

"Be back in a minute," Quelot mumbled, preoccupied. "Eat if you have something."

Again, because there seemed to be nothing else to do,

we did what we were told. We ate. And we looked around. Once again we were struck by the strangeness of the vegetation. A deep, deep green, most of it here. The leaves were thick, almost leathery, and in every kind of shape. Even in the more open surroundings in which we sat, they seemed to press down and in. Yet it wasn't hot and sticky, as such a place might have been on Earth. It was warm and moist, but pleasant. Only when we had had to walk, pushing through the dense growth, had the climate felt uncomfortable.

"I like it," Vana said. "I could stay here forever. If there were things to eat and drink, of course."

"Glad you do," said a voice. "And, of course, there's food you can eat. What's all this stuff around for, if not to eat?"

"Is that you, Quelot?" I asked tentatively, not seeing anyone.

"No, Turstive here. And you? Not the usual fool diggers, I gather, or you wouldn't be sitting there so still."

A small rock at the base of a large tree-like plant seemed to be the source of the sound. I nodded to it. "I'm Chory, and this is my brother, Vana."

"Pleased! Quelot bring you?"

"Yes."

"Gone for the others?"

"I think so," Vana said.

"Good. I guess Quelot thought you could help."

"Help with what?" Vana asked.

"Plans," Turstive replied simply. And with that we had to be satisfied, because the rock gave a quick bounce and was gone.

We sat there in the quiet, and slowly I found myself feeling more a part of the scene than I had ever felt a part of Earth. I felt blended in. I belonged. Which was strange because, of course, I didn't. And even more peculiar, the blending gave me an open bubbly feeling inside. I wanted to laugh and to roll on the ground in delight.

Which is just what Vana commenced to do. In a moment we were both roaring around the clearing, rolling over plants and whatever else lay in our way, skittering around trees, somersaulting over stones (real stones, we decided), and in general celebrating just being alive and having succeeded in getting ourselves into what, all at once, seemed the most marvelous place in the galaxy.

I was so full of glee that at first I didn't even realize anyone else was there. But when I bumped into a rolling rock, I knew that Vana and I weren't the only ones howling with laughter and spinning in delight. The clearing was alive with friends of Quelot and Turstive. It was almost like a ceremony, a convention, a demonstration, or maybe a dance, with everyone taking an active part.

I didn't want it to stop, but quite suddenly it did. And I stopped with everyone else. Vana did too.

"Oh, my!" said one of our friends. "That was the best ever. Quelot, where did you find them?"

"Lost," another rock-like creature said, Quelot obviously, though we hadn't yet learned to tell one from another. Our friend summarized the whole story.

"Allies?" another rock asked.

"Oh, yes," Quelot said.

Then before we knew what was happening, we were surrounded by dense circles of rocks, all of them the living creatures of Cheriba. We were surrounded, but not frightened.

"Who and what are you?" Vana asked.

"We are Catabilids, or so we call ourselves," said one, stepping out of the inner circle and up to us. "We live in these forests of Cheriba, and the Daphamaris live in the more open places. You could not tell the difference between us, the Catabilids and the Daphamaris, but we know ourselves. Yet we are friends. And together we cultivate and enjoy our place in the galaxy."

"How do you talk? Have you hands or feet?" I asked.

"Mostly mind we are, covered with a hard outer protection. We bounce, as you have seen. And we have several small openings through which we absorb certain chemicals that are our foods, and through which we can project sounds made by certain of our organs within. We also have a couple of things you might call hands." He put out a stringy sort of appendage at an odd angle, with two fingers and a thumb at the end. "We have a language of our own. But we have been able to learn yours and those of the others quite quickly."

"And where do you live?" I asked. "I mean, do you have houses?"

"Most certainly," said the spokesman. "We have holes in some of our larger plants. Very comfortable. Not your size, of course. But good for us, and full of the sorts of things that make us happy. Now, how much time do you have?"

"Five days after this, we think," Vana said.

"Five days, then," said the speaker. "And by the way, my name is Ganid. I am the current leader of the Catabilids in this area. Quelot and Turstive are two of my assistants. Although we really don't have governments as you do. No need, really. Ours is a simple life."

"Let's get on," said a voice I recognized as Turstive's. "Five days. Time enough."

For what, I wondered.

A snicker, that was all I could call it, passed through the ranks of Catabilids.

"What do you want of us?" Vana asked, suddenly alarmed.

"To help us convince the outlings they should leave," said Ganid.

"But we can't do that!" Vana said. "They would never listen to us."

"Didn't say they would," Quelot spoke up. "We have our ways, but we could use some help."

"You're not going to hurt them?" I asked hesitantly.

"No need," said Quelot.

"Let me explain," said Ganid. "We Catabilids farm the forest. The plants are our friends, so to speak. They provide us with the chemicals we need, and we in turn provide them with what they need. The growth in this area is a bit heavier than we really like it, except right here; but it's all planned. As I'm sure you realize, growth is a protection for us. Those fool diggers have tried everything, chemicals from every planet, to stop the growth, and nothing works. Because we neutralize what they bring, and put down the things that will make our plants grow. That airfield, for example, is a real problem to them. Ten of them spend all day every day keeping it cut. And it grows faster than they can work. The dig site—where they're finding our old stools and other things we make to have around, all worn out, of course—is overgrown every morning. They spend half of every day cutting plants. A little more growth, and they'll all go home. But the chemicals we use we make ourselves, mostly, inside us, and we're using all we can make. The next complex of Catabilids would give us some of theirs. Any complex anywhere would, for that matter. It's to everyone's good that we get rid of these outlings. But each group is needed where it is. Can't leave for long. And as you can see, we can't carry much. So we have trouble bringing in the extra supplies we need. But you can do it. You're big, and you have big hands."

The idea was clear at once. And I loved it. Those diggers had no right to be here, really. Even our parents were interlopers. The Catabilids had first rights. People could dig up their own past. But why explore someone else's garbage heap? The outlings were just being nosy. More to the point, someone from some overcrowded planet probably wanted to settle here and wanted to be sure it was safe before a ship and colonists were sent in. The idea made me shudder.

"I'm with you," Vana said.

"When do we start?" I asked.

"It's nearly dark now." It was Quelot again. "Morning is time enough. We'll bring food then. Do you need water?"

We said yes.

"Fine. Why don't you sleep now? Right here will be fine. It should be warm enough for you."

In an amazing surge, the Catabilids all bounded off. I

111

wanted to talk to Vana, but I was too sleepy. I didn't even eat. I just fell asleep.

The morning light slid obliquely through the tall plants as I awoke, only vaguely aware of someone beside me. It was a Catabilid. Another was waking Vana.

"Time to be up." My Catabilid was Quelot. The other was Turstive. "But here, eat." Quelot pointed to specific leaves. I took one and found it wasn't tough, but rather solid and quite sweet. Another had a rather melony texture and a spicy taste.

"Good," I said.

"Cheriba has everything," Quelot said.

Vana, meanwhile, was getting the same treatment from Turstive.

"There's water on the way," Quelot told me. "Better get started, to be there and back before night."

We bounced off through the forest at a faster pace than the day before. But we seemed to have no trouble, Vana and I. We didn't even get tired. No one said much. Yet I knew Vana was pleased with our project, and so was I.

We moved through the forest for several hours, stopping now and then at small pools for water and a carefully pointed-out leaf or bud. Our guides seemed to know just what plants we should have. I wondered if some were poisonous, but didn't ask. It didn't matter, so long as we had friends.

Finally we came to a rather new kind of vegetation, less dark, less dense.

"New territory," Quelot said.

Vana and I nodded, not really understanding.

"Here they come," said Turstive.

And there they did come. A whole flying army of Catabilids. I wondered why they didn't just fly at the diggers. That should scare them away, certainly. But then I realized that once the Catabilids had let themselves be discovered, they would be hunted down and carried all over our part of the galaxy, as a curiosity. Which would be a shame. They loved their planet so, and they were happy here.

There was a conference in their own language. Obviously only the Catabilids in the invaded area had become linguists. Then we all went over to what seemed to be a log hollowed out from one end and filled with a sweet-smelling liquid. That was what we were to carry. But how could we do it and not spill anything, bouncing along as we must.

Quelot sensed our question and said, "We'll put a heavy leaf on top. That should do it."

And in a few minutes it was ready. A tough leathery leaf had been fastened to the stump with sticky stuff from another plant. The plants of Cheriba did seem to provide everything. On request? Maybe so, since they were considered friends.

The leaf cover was strong enough that we could turn the log end for end and carry it between us. It took a while for Vana and I to coordinate our bounces, but after a few tries, we did pretty well. The return trip took longer, though. It was nearly dark when we arrived back at our clearing.

"Good, just what we need for tonight," Ganid greeted us. "But you are tired. We have water here for you in small containers and some leaves." We looked gratefully at small cups made of thick stems, full of water, and a pile of leaves. It had not been easy for our friends to gather so much and bring it all to the clearing. The Catabilids had very small "hands." They were obviously a thoughtful people.

"Thank you," Vana said.

"You are really kind," I added.

"No, it is you who are kind. Or perhaps we are helping each other, as we and our plants do," Ganid said.

We ate and fell asleep at once.

Morning came in the same way it had the day before. But it was not quite so light.

"Early," said Quelot, confirming my observation. "We thought you'd like to see what we've done. Lots of plants at the dig."

Vana and I were up in a moment, bouncing after Quelot and Turstive. We had not seen the dig before; and we soon discovered that we weren't really going to see it then. Bush-size plants were growing all over it. From a place well hidden, we saw people of several outling varieties looking dazed. And then we realized that not only had the bushes grown more than usual overnight, but the tree trunks that ringed the dig site had become so much thicker that the three small tractors the diggers had used could not get out. They sat there trapped.

I giggled.

"Sh!" Quelot warned. "See the field."

We nodded.

The field beyond was more of the same. The spaceship was surrounded by bushes. There were tractors there, too, but even with them that field wasn't going to get cleared in one day.

114

"One night, maybe two more," said Turstive with a chuckle.

"What if our parents leave before they planned?" I asked.

"We will know. You won't be left. You'll have food and water too," Quelot said.

How it would all be managed, we didn't know. But we trusted the Catabilids. They seemed amazingly competent.

That day and the next were repetitions of the first, except that we went to different places, each about the same distance as the first.

The morning after the third night of extra feeding, the whole outling camp was in a state of alarm. The tractors were totally useless, all hemmed in. In fact, some of the heavier members of the digging party had to pass sideways between the taller, thicker plants when they went to the dig site. They might just as well not have gone. The dig was obliterated. The diggers could only stand and stare. Yet all of them were there. Our parents too, as confused as the rest. I wondered what they would think if they knew. It seemed best, somehow, that they not find out. I wondered if the Catabilids thought that too.

"What if our parents go home early?" I asked again.

"Won't happen," Quelot murmured. "Strange winds in those buildings. All loose things held down with Catabilids."

For a minute I could hardly hold in my laughter. A perfect spy system. Quelot shook with inner laughter too. We backed away quietly. And Vana followed.

"What's wrong with you two?" he asked.

I explained. He howled aloud before he remembered where we were. Quelot hastily beckoned for us to move more quickly, and we did. Then back in the clearing we laughed until we thought we'd shake apart. Only when we were so weak we couldn't laugh anymore did we really begin to cope with the problem of getting home.

"Do you think," Turstive asked, "that you could make one more trip, a short one this time? Only half a day. Just in case. And we'll keep watch and have everything ready. We won't let them go without you. And you needn't worry about food and water or even quarters for your trip. We'll take care of that."

We could only agree. We couldn't solve our problems for ourselves. And so far the Catabilids had done well for us, and, of course, we had helped them a lot in return. So we went to a nearer group of Catabilids where we got another log full of growing juice. I wondered what would happen if I tasted some, but decided it was better not to know.

We got back in the middle of the Cheriban afternoon, and Ganid was there to greet us.

"Glad to see you!" the leader exclaimed loudly. "The results of your work have certainly been better than even we anticipated." Only remarkable self-restraint seemed to keep Ganid from rolling into a great spasm of laughter. "Spaceships have been called for everyone. Dangerous planet, they say. Too small to bother with. Wild growth of no use, even for animal food. Your parents are leaving in the morning with the most important Earth diggers."

"And what about us?" I asked, afraid once again. Now the ship would really be full. I was sure we'd be found. And that would ruin everything.

"No problem," said Ganid. "There are a number of

116

crates being loaded now, in the pressurized cargo area. Two of them hold samples of Cheriban plant life, of obvious interest to scientists everywhere. These are not solidly packed. And they are not air-tight. One of you in each, with several containers of water, will work quite well. We have seen to it that all the plants in each box are edible and useful to you."

"But won't they wonder about its all being gone if we eat it?"

"Who knows what happens to Cheriban plant stuffs when they come into an alien atmosphere? They may just go *poof!* Certainly we Catabilids could not exist elsewhere." Ganid did begin to laugh then.

It would be the final joke. Vana and I looked at each other and roared until we remembered it meant leaving. Then the joke almost seemed to be on us.

That night the Catabilids helped us into the proper boxes. They had even seen to it that the boxes were placed on top of the other cargo so we could get in and out easily. We had no trouble getting to the ship without being seen because by that time the new growth was so high even a giant would have been hidden. A narrow trail was kept open from the camp building, but otherwise the field was completely overgrown. There were no guards. None of the outlings would stay apart from the others. They were afraid they'd be lost forever. So we moved in easily, settled down, and waited for morning.

The parting with the Catabilids went quickly. None of us could say what we felt. I really wished I could stay, and Vana did too. But we couldn't. We belonged on Cheriba no more than the diggers did. The Catabilids had a right to

117

keep their planet for themselves, and to live as they chose to live.

The next morning the Earthlings came out—our parents and two men and a woman. They carried small bags. The rest of their gear had obviously been stowed earlier.

"Do you think you can lift off?" one of the men said in a worried tone.

"Positive," said my father. "Strangest things I've ever seen, these plants. But we've taken off from worse places."

The man grunted. No one else spoke. And in a few minutes we felt the now almost familiar swift rise. We were facing seven days in our crates, Vana and I. Although we might find moments when we could crawl out, obviously they would be few. Still, we had a lot to think about. And surely there would be some moments to move and stretch.

We needed to move about less than we had thought we would. The plants seemed to keep us in a state where a lot of movement was unnecessary. All of our bodily functions were slowed down. Yet, except when I slept, my mind was clear.

In those hours we had our real sequestering. But we did not find what others usually found. I discovered that the nicest thing I had ever known was the laughter I had heard and experienced on Cheriba. It was gentle, even kind, and it came from true delight. That was what I wanted more than anything. That kind of laughter. And the life that went with it.

Vana said that he decided he wanted to explore in a spaceship, not to dig, but to find more unlikely places where he felt at home. I liked that idea too.

It was a strange goal for an Earthling. But I believed it was something to be jolly about. In fact in the few times we met out of our boxes, we were both very jolly. We recalled the things that had happened to us on Cheriba and felt again the delight we had known in being there.

"And just wait until we bounce on Earth!" Vana said.

We had agreed to get out of our boxes as soon as possible on Earth, but not to be discovered near the space port, if possible. We hoped the ship would not be unloaded right away. Then we would have a chance to disappear before our empty boxes were found. Once out, we would move as far away as we could, then let ourselves be picked up. Somehow, it didn't matter what happened after that. We knew we'd be all right. We would say we'd gone on a sequestering ourselves, since no one would take us, and we'd gotten lost. That was, after all, sort of the truth of the matter.

We landed late in the day, as we had hoped we might. Whether or not the Catabilids had arranged that too, we didn't know, but they certainly had taken care of everything else. Just before coming down, we heard a loud exclamation and a rumble of voices that told us our parents had been informed of our absence. That was both good and bad, but mostly good. They'd be off in a hurry, looking for us. Even though we'd said we were coming to the base, no one would believe that, since no one had seen us.

In the excitement of landing and getting people out and away, we found plenty of chance to slip off. We wanted to stay and see what happened when those cases of greens turned out to be empty (we had the remaining leaves in our knapsacks), but even our new carefree state

119

would not allow that. We hurried off into the night.

Two days later we were "found." We had spent the days wandering away from the field, following the Mechanized Transport lines as much as possible so as not to get completely lost. We had eaten up the plants we had with us and used up our water. On our wanderings, we had spent a good deal of our time bouncing. It worked very well on Earth.

The second day we noticed a town in the distance, and after getting our story straight between us, we wandered in as if we had been lost a long time. In a way we had been and still were; we had no idea of what place we had come to.

At first the people in the town would not believe us. But they sent our pictures to Central Com and discovered that we were the twins we said we were. Our parents and a variety of officials arrived soon after.

They were all remarkably glad to see us. Vana and I were both surprised. It was apparent that our parents did care, after all. We told our story: we hadn't been allowed to go on a sequestering, so we had had to go on our own and had gotten lost. We had lived on plants. And we had discovered and learned all we were supposed to learn and more. None of what we said was false. We didn't even give any false impressions. We just didn't tell everything.

They questioned us, of course. And when the questioning got a little tight, we brought up bouncing. That finished the questions. We had to bounce over and over. And everyone seemed as amazed at our not being worn out by it as by our doing it at all.

Then we began to teach them. It was funny to see

adults try. Our father and mother got it very quickly, and some others soon after. They looked so funny, we had to laugh. We rolled on the ground with laughter, but only we knew that we had learned bouncing and laughing at the same time, from a Catabilid.

The next day they brought in a woman from the sequestering unit in the Central Core group; she also learned to bounce quickly. We liked her.

"Will you come and teach my leaders to bounce?" she asked.

"Sure, if we can," we said.

And we did.

People all over Earth, young and old, have learned to bounce now. But not many of them have learned to laugh as we do. Vana and I still roll with laughter, to the amazement of most people we know. Those plants we ate must have made us part Catabilid. I hope so.

The diggers are all gone from Cheriba, we've heard. The plants are a mystery still, both the ones on the planet and the missing ones we ate. We still hold to our dreams, though there is more of a place for us here on Earth than we had ever hoped there would be. We like it here, but we also hope to find new places where we will feel at home. Until then, Earth can be a good place. It is a good place, even if your parents fly a spaceship. Providing, of course, you find a way to go sequestering.

Quiet and a White Bush

She woke slowly, almost as if she were pulling herself together, physically drawing herself in, letting herself become one again after she had been exploded into the diverse parts of her oneness. Where was she? That was the question to be settled first. She almost thought she knew. But then she knew she didn't. What she saw was like nothing she had seen before. The misty forms, the white rocks that were not real rocks, and the deep gray of the sky were not her world. But what world were they? And why?

She pushed a finger of thought into her mind and probed. Home? Yes, there was such a place. Earth. A comfortable bed? Yes, not just mushroom-like rocks that made hard pillows and knee rests and, if she wanted, places for sitting. Family? After a fashion. A mother and father and a brother. None of whom wholly understood her need for wildness, for distance. Aloneness was a part of them, but not apartness.

Where were they now? A hole. There had been a hole. In the place she had gone for quiet. An old stone quarry, left maybe from the pre-Clordian Sweep days. No one had ever checked. But the stones in the hole had been dark and in deep shadow. Not these queer white ones. And the sky there had been high and blue, not near and misty white.

Yet here she was. She rose on her side, propping herself on one elbow, and looked with deep concern at her surroundings. No one. A few growing things, also white. And the quiet. It was haunted, and yet it had a loveliness about it that she could not explain, even to herself. It was lonely too, and a bit frightening. What did one do here? Where did one go? Was the ground hard, like the rocks? No, it felt soft beneath her.

She rose unsteadily to her feet, drew herself up. She could stand. Her feet did not find the soil unyielding, but neither did they find it unsupporting. She took one step and then another. It was a tree, she suddenly realized, that stood above her. Strange, she hadn't noticed it. Or had it not been there before? Had it come because she suddenly perceived it? The thought made her mind reel. This was no time for guesses. It was a time to think wisely. The tree was there, and so was she. But what else? She sank to the rocks again.

She was reluctant to move from under the tree. The outer world seemed bare. Misty. Uncertain. If she left the tree, she might not find her way back. And the spot under the tree was the most familiar place she could be in, her one shelter. It seemed a slim and tenuous link with her past. It was the place she had come to. Somehow.

Yet she had never believed that the past alone made the future. She had always wanted to venture, to push just a little farther, to go beyond the edge. She had always wanted to go on a spaceship. She would be willing to go and never come back, she had sometimes thought. Though that was not Earth-like. She would go not for adventure or for newness, but for the wonder of it, for the pushing back of walls. Physical walls, quite unlike the idea walls most people worked at.

She had not gone on a spaceship. Her parents were too content on Earth, and she was too young to go alone. The people who did go on spaceships for long distances were mostly older and married, because of the long times of going and coming. So she knew she had not been on a spaceship. She had been in her own world. In a quarry in a green forest, in a place of retreat. A place with an unexpected hole.

The scene around her did not change. The gray-white mistiness was the same. There was no movement. The tree was surely alive. But in all its whiteness, there was no sign of vital flow. Where was she?

She could not stay. If the whole of the place was so misty, so uncertain, so bland and yet so oppressive, she could not stay. She was afraid, and restless. She must move. Picking herself up again carefully, she looked about more searchingly. But with no discernible result. A bump here, a rock there, a small gray-white shrub somewhere else broke the formless pattern, but nothing else, nothing of note. Here was the only tree. The sky too was uniform. More uniform than the ground. There was light, but no difference in light, no deepening colors, no clouds in the uniform depths above. She thought of Earth on a lowering, gray, misty day. Was it this uniform? She thought not. Was this place always thus? Or were there other kinds of days too?

She put one foot in front of the other, moved out from under the tree. The view was the same, in all directions. She had no compass, if a compass would have worked. Nor did she have any other means of direction-finding. She had herself and nothing more. She sighted a bush, as far away as she could see, which was not terribly far, and began to walk. If she could reach that bush, she might see something more appealing to move to. And if not, she could come back to the tree.

The walking was hard. Harder than she had expected. The ground was more solid than she would have imagined. Only under the tree had it been soft. What made walking difficult then? It took several moments to realize that it was the place itself. She was heavy. Too heavy to move easily. She was on a large planet, or a very dense one. Yet she did not think it could be the latter—not when some ground was soft. A large planet then. That was something to know. Larger than Earth. That offered many possibilities. The day, too, might be bigger, longer. But that was harder to be sure of.

The bush was closer, and the horizon had moved beyond it. But there was no change in the landscape. A few more rocks. A few more bumps. And maybe the start of another bush at the edge. She reached her bush and collapsed. She was worn thin. And she had come only a hundred meters or so.

The bush was much like the tree, grayish-white, and the ground beneath it a bit soft. She stayed out on the harder ground.

She was not on her own planet. Unless she was dreaming. Unless the hole had taken her out of her normal consciousness. But would even a fall make such a strange world enter her mind? She felt the ground beside her, pinched herself, wrestled to wake up. And in the end she knew for certain that she was awake, and that somehow, in her flesh, she was elsewhere. It was no time to panic. It was a time for clear thought.

Something inside of her said, "Well, get on with it, girl." Or was it inside? That thought wasn't like her. And what was she to get on with? Pondering? That must be it.

She had been in her lovely world, green and cool and quiet. But not this quiet. Her mind had been busy. There had been that strange thing she had done. The day before. In school. The school head had sent for her, to scold her for gently lifting herself out the window during a class. Everyone could do it, of course. But she had always found it easier than others. Too easy. Just thinking about it sometimes was enough. It happened every once in a while when she was bored. The head had really been angry this time. But the class had been so dull. Pre-Clordian Sweep archaeology didn't interest her very much. She had thought it would, but it didn't. And seeing the outside and wanting it, she had simply gone, because she had willed it. Then while the head had lectured on staying put, she had thought of her hidden corner in the garden near home. She had yearned to be there, physically yearned for it with all her being. It had been a new sort of yearning. She had wanted before, but not like that. And then she had been there. In her flesh, she had been there. It had been too frightening. Lifting up gently and moving out a window

127

was one thing. But being someplace else with no preparation was another. In horror she had yearned with a deep intentness to be back where she had been with the head. And she had been. The head hadn't even missed her. Yet she had been gone. She knew it. For afterward Fraisy had laughed and asked how she'd done it. She'd been outside the window and seen.

She had pondered on that, sitting near the quarry, and then had gone on to think about her cousin Borin. He was something like her, but he was not in school anymore. He was on a spaceship, and she was the only one in the family who really understood why. He needed a physical unknown too. Generally he traveled on a small, short-trip cargo vessel. But lately he had gone on a much longer voyage, with some Core Council people. They had been to a number of planets, making agreements with those who lived there. Back on Earth he had come to tell about it; to tell her mostly, because he knew she cared. And she had listened eagerly. When he left, she had gone to the woods to think about what he had said, about that and about her own strange trip. Yes, that was it. That was what she had done.

She reared up in her thoughts. She was close, close.

"Now you're coming on there." Was it she who had spoken?

No, she was sure it was not. There was someone, something else nearby—but where? It couldn't be just a voice. That was silly. Was it something in another dimension, one she couldn't see? That sounded absurd too. But not so ridiculous as just a voice. Whatever it was, it knew her thoughts and could speak in her language. That in itself was a miracle.

"Not so strange," said the voice. "We sense rather than hear. We transmit ideas, rather than words. You simply make words of ideas to suit your own needs. And we welcome visitors. There is little that is new when you can't move."

"Can't move!" She turned quickly and looked at the bush.

"Of course," it said. "Moving is too hard on this planet. You discovered that yourself. So we are what you call plants, I guess. If by a plant you mean an unmoving living creature with higher sensitivities."

"No, not exactly," she murmured. "Our plants don't talk. Or at least they don't transmit thought."

There was silence for a moment, as if the idea was hard for the bush to understand.

"I grasp, I grasp," came the reply at last. "Then on your world there are moving creatures who think and unmoving creatures who seem not to think. An amazing innovation. A place I'd like to touch. I've heard of things—there are rumors, others of us have encountered things. But I didn't really believe."

"How do you know what others think," she asked, "when none of you can move?"

"Why, we sense each other thinking, of course," the bush replied. "Don't you on your planet sense each other thinking? No, of course you don't. You were surprised at me."

"We speak aloud," she said. "But we don't expect bushes to speak."

"Then maybe that's why they do not speak. No, no, you may be right." The bush sounded apologetic, as if it were at fault in questioning her. Then it was silent. But the silence was filled with thought. It seemed to beg for conversation.

"What planet is this? How do I get home? Where are you in the galaxy?" They were the first ideas that came to mind. If only she could get some clue, she might find a way to project herself home, she decided. If that was how she had gotten here in the first place.

"Why, how should I know?" asked the bush. "We are where we are. Where I have always been. Why don't you stay? It's nice to have someone so close. I never thought of it before. The winds come and bring pollen from my neighbors, take away the seeds that I have made. I hear the thoughts of my neighbors, and sometimes of the young that I myself have helped create. But we must not grow too close together. We cannot. We need much space beneath the soil. Strange, I think none of us have ever thought how good it might be to have another near. Yet what is, must be. We must grow apart. Still, stay a while, and let us feel together the goodness of the rain that comes quite soon."

She looked across the plain then—to the tree that she had left—the nearest bit of life, and to other bushes, most of them farther than she cared to walk on that heavy world.

"Do you speak often with your neighbors?" she asked.

"There is often something in the air. But not often thoughts as strange as yours. I sense much in you I do not entirely understand. It excites me. It makes me restless. Stay, and ease the strangeness you have brought."

"Bush," she said. "Is it always like this—the gray, the white, the mist, the stillness?"

130

"Until—until you asked, I would have said what else can there be? But you are here. And in your mind are things that seem strange and frightening. Yet oddly exciting. I have never lacked for thought. I contemplate a stone. There are many that my roots can touch. I think of things I pick from others' thoughts; often there are odd quirks that must be studied. The mists are here, sometimes heavier than now, sometimes lighter when the winds come. There are long thoughts in the mists. Yet not much new as you would sense it. I grasp that now."

"Have you no longings, bush? Do you not wish to know your world at least beyond that tree? Or do you know your world at all?"

"I do not know what your knowing is. I am aware of much, if that is what you mean. The land beyond that tree is like my land here. The stones may differ—new shapes, new sizes. But I do not know all my own stones well, not yet, though my roots reach a long way out. They bring word of new things as they grow a bit now and then —new directions, new earth, new contours, new rock."

The weight of the land was more than the weight of its mass. She saw that now. It was a heavy land, one of stolid immobility. She panicked against it. Yet she did not move. She was too tired with merely the exertion of thought.

She looked down at her lap, then up again at the bush, knowing she must not stay. She must make herself move. The bush might be content, but she needed things she did not find here. It was quiet and alone. She could daydream in peace. Yet she could not stay. She dare not stay. She must eat, for one thing. Though she felt no real hunger as yet.

131

"I understand. Each of us needs his own kind. Let me enjoy you while I may. Think and I will hear."

"Bush, bush!" she cried. "If only you could see my world. Could know its beauties."

"I cannot. But I have known you."

"Oh bush, bush, have you seen me? Can you see?"

"In my own fashion. Though not yours, I suspect."

"Then maybe you can grasp my world. If I can get home, I can come again sometime. And maybe I can bring things, let you understand what you can never come to grasp yourself."

"Perhaps." The thought was resigned. The bush did not believe. "Go home. You must, but you will not come again. I will be content. Once, once in my time, a wonder has been near me. That is enough."

She had a feeling the bush was wrong. Having invaded the bush's world, she might have brought discontent forever. She resolved to return even if all the Earth tried to stop her. But first she had to get back to Earth. Her thoughts went back to her cousin Borin and his spaceship. What did that have to do with the place where she was? And how had she come? Was it like floating out of a classroom window? No, it was more like yesterday—the trip to the garden. But how, and why?

Once more she pondered on the green, thick woods of home. The place of noisy quiet. She had started after school, running from Fraisy and Chara. She had gone to think about her own strange adventure and about the places Borin had been. He had seen many solar systems and many planets, minded creatures of many kinds. He had seen other worlds where no one lived.

"There was a white planet," he had said. "With a heavy, breathable atmosphere—a huge planet that held in great clouds of gas and water. We dipped beneath some of those clouds and saw a white surface, bare except for a few almost-white plants. A strange, quiet place. A still, wild world."

She had longed for that planet. It revolved around a star—something in the constellation Crespid. She had thought of her own night sky. She had envisioned the large W in the north and imagined where that star might be in that group. A tree toad had hopped by. Then a chipmunk. And a butterfly had wobbled along. The place she had been was light, too light, too distracting for real thought. There had been a hole nearby, a place of deeper quiet. She had retreated there. And in her mind, in the dark and the stillness, she had conjured up the night sky.

The True Relation of that distant planet in Crespid, that was what she had wanted. Slowly it came back. Yes, a True Relation of 500–20–15–50060321–603212. Borin had written it down. That was it. She could never have re-membered it. She had conjured up that world. She had held its True Relation in her mind. What more? Nothing more, except that odd, heightened sense of wanting, of more than wanting, of bending the whole sense of her presence toward something. It was the same as the day be-fore. And then she had pulled herself into oneness in this new world. Was she then at a True Relation of 500–20–15–50060321–603212? On a white planet? And what was the True Relation of Earth? That at least she ought to know. She struggled to remember. And she felt the bush helping her. How, she did not know.

133

She was sure she would never remember. She decided she would never see Earth again. For it was clear that you had to know—really know—where you were going if you wanted to get there. She had to do more than remember the beauty of Earth, the face of her brother, the look of her home, the marvel of food. She tore her mind apart looking. And the answer eluded her.

"My, you are a busy one, aren't you?" said the bush calmly. "It's a wonder you ever pull yourself together at all."

She quieted then. And in a deep inner peace she let ideas come. Not questing so much as inviting. And eventually the numbers came.

"That's better," said the bush. "Now go home, and don't feel you must keep your promise to return. It may not even be wise."

She did not dispute the voice. She could not. All her thoughts were bent toward reaching that instant of total desire. How did one do it? She worked and nothing happened. Was the planet too heavy to leave? She looked at the bush, at the landscape. Were these to be her life? The bush looked sad, sad in its own way. And she knew in her inner self that it was sad both for her and for itself. It might never again meet the unusual, the unexpected. She looked again at the landscape. Flat and quiet. Too much room for thought here, and maybe too little thought to fill it. Was that her destiny?

They were sad together, the bush and she, until suddenly the wanting in her grew greater than she had ever known. It was a wanting of two together, a wanting mixed with parting and sadness. Could such wanting go on forever?

It was dark around her then. Did it grow dark so quickly on that strange planet? For the first time she reached to touch the bush and felt instead a wall, a dirt wall. Was she where she had been—on Earth—the hole she had left? She had given the True Relation; she had held the latitude and longitude of her place as close as she knew it; she had conjured up the roads and the paths from town. Was that enough?

On all fours, she crawled ahead in the dark until at last she saw a light, very dim. She moved out into that light, the last of daylight. It was not the same woods. But yes it was! The woods were a great belt along the low hills that ringed the town. This was another part of them. She knew it. It was a part she loved, but one that was too far from home for an afternoon's jaunt. Even the hole she remembered now. Another remnant of the days of mining. She even knew where the road was, the old road, almost overgrown, that people took to come here now and then. Kids from old-fashioned families that still insisted on sequestering often came out here.

She stood up, took a step, and moved more quickly than she had planned. She fell and skinned her knee. It hurt, and she wondered if she could walk as far as she must to get home. Yet she couldn't stay in the woods all night. It would get cold, and she didn't have even a coat. Besides, the woods were too alone, too quiet and yet not quiet enough, especially after the place she had been. She needed to go home.

She stood up once more and, holding herself steady and slow, moved toward the road. She felt jumpy and tired and not quite herself. In a panic she tried to run, and fell again, hurting the same knee and the other as well. Misery lurked all around, and she sought frantically for a way out of it.

"My, you are a busy one." The words were as clear in her mind as when the bush had thought them at her. Yet it had to be memory. Once more she grew quiet.

And then the solution was obvious. If she could think herself to a planet in the constellation Crespid, she could think herself home. Of course she could. But once having thought of it, she found she was almost too tired to do it. She panicked again. Then let herself grow calm. Pulled all of herself in. And then she was ready. She thought of home, of the relation of home to the place where she was, the roads and the distances. And she wanted it. Oh, how she wanted it. And all at once, it worked. She was outside her own door.

She was late for dinner, of course.

"Menta, where in the world have you been?" her mother cried, more in relief than in anger. Generally she would have replied with silence, or said some noncommittal thing. She liked her privacy. And her mother knew it. The whole family knew it too well. But now she could not just let it pass.

"To the woods," she said. "I fell," she added, "and had trouble getting home."

"Menta," her mother said, half in fear for her and half in a real attempt to understand, "you simply cannot go off like that. Something really bad could happen to you. Those woods are full of old holes. You know that. And you know you never look where you're going. You could fall into something and never get out. And we wouldn't know where to find you. Why do you do it?"

"You needn't worry about me, not now," Menta said, looking at her mother, understanding her as never before and loving her with a kind of giving love that was new and exciting.

"Whatever do you mean by that?" her mother asked in a sharper tone. Then she looked at Menta, really looked, and an odd expression came over her face. "Menta, has something happened to you? Something, something. . . ." She did not finish, but she seemed disturbed. "Hurry and clean up. I'll have your dinner ready when you come down."

Menta grinned. "I'm starved," she said.

Later, after she ate, she tried to explain, just to her mother, what had happened. She was too tired to even think of demonstrating. And her mother was too amazed to think it was anything but a fairy tale, a dream, a result of falling, maybe.

And so it remained. Menta did not speak of it again. Her mother watched her closely, she knew. And she knew that her mother was perplexed. For she had been right, there was a change. And even she didn't know why or what. She was more whole, more herself. She was quiet, and yet she no longer needed a place apart, a wild freedom in the woods and hills. She had it inside herself, where she had strange memories to ponder.

She reached out to others more. Like her friend the bush, she tried to know and understand the stones around her. And with her roots and her mind, she sought the meanings that lay in her own tight world. They produced riches she had never dreamed existed. Her father, her mother, her brother were people with a dimension she had never anticipated. Even school became different. She saw it as the bush would have seen it, savored it as that bush would have done.

She used the power sparingly, but she did use it. She did not want to forget how. Yet she took only small jumps to places she knew. She yearned to visit the bush again. But something inside her was afraid. What would happen if she went to the wrong place? Sometimes in her mind-moving, as she came to think of it, she did wind up in a place she had not chosen. Why, she could not be sure. What would happen if she found herself on a dangerous planet, or even a star? Yet she yearned to speak once more to a bush, to share that sort of wisdom.

Eventually her cousin Borin came to visit again. He had been on a short shuttle trip to Clord. He came with more restlessness in him than ever before. As if that one long trip into far space had left him unable to be content with less.

The first night he was there, after the evening meal, Menta had to speak. "Borin, I've thought a lot about that strange planet you saw, the white one. Can you show me where in Crespid it is?"

Her mother looked at her strangely, as if she thought the odd dream-adventure had long been forgotten. It had never been mentioned after that first night, though it had been clear that she herself had not forgotten it. The strange careful looks she had given Menta had been enough to display that. Now there was nothing she could say. She had to let them go to see the constellation. Menta was glad that no questions could be asked.

Menta and Borin walked down to an open field at the

edge of the town and sat looking toward the north. There, looking toward her planet, for she had begun to feel that way about it, she told Borin the tale of her adventure. And he didn't believe her.

"Menta," he said, "you fell. You were dazed, and you dreamed."

"But I came back in another place," she said. "And I've done short trips around here since."

"No, you're having some sort of delusions."

She was desperate. Someone had to believe her, and he had been her one hope. She had waited for him, believing that he would understand. Hardly knowing what she did, she concentrated on the school yard and instantly found herself there; it was deserted and quiet as it never was in the day. She waited a minute or two, then brought herself back to Borin. When she returned, he was standing, looking around. But her agony was only increased because he was sure she had tricked him.

"Menta, you've learned some clever tricks, and somehow you've gotten a good impression of a planet that fascinated me, but you can't convince me of anything more." He laughed.

Once more she disappeared. This time, although she hated to do it, she put herself at home in the room where the family was gathered. Her father saw her and her mother and her brother. They were wondering aloud what had happened to the two of them, and there she was. But only long enough for her to nod at them and return to the edge of town. Her powers of concentration had improved for her to be able to do that, she realized. What a shame no one believed her.

Again Borin laughed when she was back beside him. "You must teach me that trick sometime," he said.

"I'd like to," she cried. And then she changed the subject. They walked home talking of things in a casual way, and he, at least, was unprepared for the stir the two of them created when they walked into the house.

"Menta," said her father, "if you go for a walk with Borin to see the stars, you ought at least to stay with him. There was no call for you to come home alone. And why didn't you answer when I spoke to you? Where did you go so quickly?"

Her mother was silent. Borin looked at her in awe. But even so his mind was quick. "She ran in to get me a range finder," he said. "I'd forgotten it."

Her parents turned away then, as if the explanation had been given. But she could sense that they were puzzled. Borin said nothing more. She went off to do some schoolwork, and he to his ever-present calculations. You'd think, she had often said, that he'd never heard of a computer. But he always replied that it took a sharp mind to keep a computer alert on a short journey. And besides, he liked calculations. They kept him awake. The men watched two weeks on and two weeks off on short trips. And it could be dull, Menta supposed. She decided she liked her way of travel better, even if it might not always be so dependable. She wondered how soon it would be before he appeared to ask questions.

Eventually he came to the door of her room and opened it a crack, whispering through as if he didn't want others to hear what he said. "Menta, I've got to talk to you. You know that, don't you? And you know I'm sorry."

She nodded. "Tomorrow," she said.

The next day Borin met her after school. They walked off to the woods, the place she'd first gone to, and she told him, all over again, the whole story. This time in more detail because he wanted to know every bit of it.

"Tell me again how your mind sets," he said at the end.

She explained it once more, and then again.

"It's as if you were breaking into another compartment of your mind," she said finally. "Or maybe breaking into a new kind of being." The last she whispered. She had hardly said it before, even to herself. Yet she had been different, ever since that day.

He tried and tried and nothing happened.

"Do it for me again," he said.

She quieted, drew into herself. Then she thought of home, and there she was. She still had her school films in her hand, so she dropped them on the table inside the door. Then she took herself back to Borin. It was hard to place herself exactly in the midst of a forest, so she arrived about forty meters from him. He watched her walk toward him.

"What is the secret?" he asked, puzzled.

"It's the quiet, I think," she said. "And the wanting, the really wanting. It's wanting to be there that matters. Not wanting to do it."

He looked even more puzzled. Then he relaxed and sat back. He motioned for her to sit beside him, and she did. They talked of many things. Until all at once he was still. And then he wasn't there. He didn't return for at least ten minutes, and she began to be afraid that he had gone way off and couldn't get back. But finally he was beside her, chuckling.

"Got caught with your mother," he said. "She's worried

141

about you. You're in and out so fast these days. And you seem different."

Menta laughed with him. It was a warm, rich, understanding laugh. For they now shared a dimension known, as far as they could tell, to no one but themselves. They were unique. It was frightening, but it also gave them a warm sense of comradeship. She felt secure, knowing that Borin would learn more, would perhaps tell a few others. And there would be trips with others someday. Safer trips than she could make alone. Maybe even a trip to a certain white planet, to see a very important bush.

The Talkaround

Not many people these days remember Jalish Dozent. Except that he did something strange when he was young—and that he wandered around a whole lot in the galaxy. Not many remember what he found, and their forgetting is not entirely an accident.

It's true that Jalish Dozent was young, purely and simply young, when he took off that first time for someplace else. Most that go, even now, are twenty, maybe twenty-five, before they make even little jumps away. And then they don't stay for long. They don't make a vacation of it; it's just a short adventure or a brief research expedition. It isn't that they can't go younger, of course—that they don't have the roots of it. It's just that no one lets them do it. There are all those controls still. Just as there were in Jalish's time.

Then too, the inner searchings, the unity of Earth life, have always made travel by the young seem unwise. And other planets have always had their own reasons for keeping the young at home. For example, there's always been

143

the thought that the young might not be able to cope if they came into a really rough spot. It's a handy idea, so although it's never been proved, it stays around. There are other reasons, some sensible and some not, why the young cannot leave their own planets. And so, things being as they are and were, it wasn't really so amazing that Jalish managed to go where he went as it was surprising that he got to do it at all. He was sixteen at the time.

By the year it happened, all the space-oriented planets, even the ones where the minded species hadn't yet gotten the knack of self-space-placement, had the usual psychic screens around them so one couldn't just project from planet to planet whenever one wanted. They were cruder screens then than the ones now in use, more like the ones people have to shelter their homes; still, they were effective. People could come and go, but they had to get a permit, and they had to schedule the opening of any screen they wanted to go through. Much like now.

Screens have always created some nuisances, but people have always thought the safety was worth the trouble. In fact, as far as some of the people then were concerned, the screens saved a lot of difficulty. There were still those who remembered the days before screens had become universal, and they could still conjure up the horrors of it. People had gone jumping around and no one had ever been sure of who or what might turn up within a hundred meters or so. It was almost impossible to try to find somebody, because everybody was always off someplace else. It was a craze even Earth people fell for. The screens and the permits and the records cleaned all that up.

So even if the screens did put a damper on people's

free travel, in the end only a few Universal Movement Association members stayed upset about the new situation. And kids complained too. They had the hardest time getting permits. Like now, they were taught from the time they started school, at three, how to get around. By the time they were nine or ten, they were as good as adults— they could pinpoint themselves almost anywhere they wanted on the home planet. By sixteen the galaxy, or the near parts, the local sectors, could have been open. But they weren't. And lots of kids didn't like it. Even Earth kids, who realized more than most that the far and the near can have a unity that nullifies distance.

Some people thought after Jalish made his trip that the Universal Movement Control Agency had simply tried to make an example of him to keep the kids quiet. But anyone who knew Jalish didn't really think that. They knew he'd just done his usual job of getting what he wanted when he wanted it. Jalish could talk himself into or out of almost anything.

It really started the day Jalish was late to cosmology class. Not that that mattered. Teachers seldom cared if Jalish was late. It gave them a few minutes alone with the class. Anyway, that day the class was up at one of Earth's astronomy satellites, checking out some far parts of the galaxy. It was a double period class—10 to 12 Earth time. Jalish had stopped off before taking himself up to the satellite to ask the movement teacher (that's where he'd been the class before—in movement) a whole spill of questions. The kind that made teachers hate to see him come, though most did take him with good grace. He was a nice enough kid, after all. And he really meant those questions.

He actually wanted to know. The trouble was that most of the time no one had the answers. This teacher hemmed and hawed around until Jalish was late to cosmology class.

As it turned out, he hadn't missed a thing. He'd gotten acquainted with the parts of the galaxy they were looking at that day when he was eight. But he listened to the teacher, once he'd settled in, with half a mind anyway, just in case he might have a question. The rest of his mind was taking in everything he could see through the huge ceiling lens. It was maybe an hour down the line, halfway through the class time, when it happened.

The lens was sweeping from one part of the Milky Way to another, and as it went, Jalish got a fleeting impression of a pink and green star. When he thought about it later, he wasn't even sure he had seen it. Just felt it was there. It seemed a bit odd, to say the least, and it didn't take Jalish long to figure out just where it had to be, if it actually existed, the True Relation. He was a genius at True Relations, even at sixteen. The star was outside the core of the galaxy, where even he had sense enough not to want to go, but not far out. Maybe because it was so close to the core, it was in an area that was almost always marked "mostly unexplored" on galactic survey maps. There were a lot of places like that in those days, of course, but this was an unusually large one.

No one had been able to explain to Jalish why this huge unexplored patch existed, or why any existed at all. It had always surprised him that anything outside the core had not been visited by someone. The young don't always grasp the size of things or the complexities of going to out-of-the-way places. But Jalish, more than most, wondered

146

why when people went someplace they went to a place they knew. That just didn't make sense to him. When he left Earth, it would be for some decent purpose, like investigating an unexplored solar system.

Anyway, by the time Jalish left that class, he had his mind made up. He was going to find out if that pink and green star existed, and he also intended to go there, if what he discovered made it appear to be even one-tenth as strange as it seemed to him then. The more he thought about it, the more peculiar the whole thing got. Though the star had looked odd enough, that wasn't the end. It had seemed almost to make a sound. Nonsense, of course, but he couldn't shake the idea, and it raised all kinds of questions in his mind that, as usual, had no answers.

Sitting in the eating room back on Earth, he pondered; after eating he went to the library. There he checked tapes and holographic photographs made by research expeditions. A star was there, where he had placed the True Relation. No question of that. The sky maps showed it, though he could find nothing much written about it. And—this became the major issue for him then—it was not shown as being pink and green. It was a plain yellow sun. Yet he knew it was pink and green. He was convinced of it.

There was a time discrepancy between the research material and his own look at the star. Did that matter? Of course it did. The research material was newer, taken closer. It made a difference. The star might once have been pink and green and now be yellow. But even that didn't make sense. It didn't fit any pattern of star development he had ever heard of.

Before he crawled into bed that night, he had checked

again to make sure of his True Relation. Everything was in order. He'd been looking up the right star. And he'd found everything known about it. It was such a deep void star, it didn't even have a number, much less a name. And no one was sure it had a planet, although it was the right magnitude for planets, and its motion seemed to indicate that some were likely. For no reason he could determine, Jalish was sure it did have them. Yet all that he had discovered had only added to the questions that he needed to have answered; and it was obvious that no one was going to be able to help him. For once he was not going to be satisfied with evasions. He was going to go to one of the planets of the pink and green star. Having made his decision, Jalish went to sleep.

There was no one at school the next day who could give him permission to go. He had known that even before he asked. But he had to begin there. His space action teacher said maybe he ought to go to the Remote Regions Guidance Council. As far as the teacher was concerned, it was a place to send him, a way of achieving a morning's rest. Jalish went at once. He was at the council office immediately. And there they finally sent him on to Remote Space Missions, where they said he didn't qualify for their programs and he ought to go to Youth in Space. It was the man there who pushed him off onto the Universal Movement Control Agency. The feeling was that the UMCA permitters were tough enough to send him home. No one else had quite managed that.

But the UMCA had had too many young ones coming in with arguments for going off to someplace else. It seemed as if the under-twenty crowd was the only group that hadn't settled into the typical Earth pattern of deep focus on inner matters, and of staying at home except when there was good reason for leaving. Life would have been dull at the agency if it hadn't been for the kids, but they were the ones who couldn't go anywhere. It seemed a shame sometimes, the permitters thought. Most of the still-in-schools would have been scared to go much beyond Uranus or Pluto—a harmless jaunt. But even that couldn't be done, so the whole thing was a perpetual nuisance.

Jalish, though he was something of a novelty, proved more a trial than a nuisance. To begin with, he was more persistent than most. And he was persuasive. The extent of his knowledge was alarming, and he used it like no one at the agency had heard before. His mother wore ear plugs or turned up the white noise full blast when Jalish really wanted something. But the UMCA people didn't know about that. And finally, they didn't know how—short of easing him out of his mind for a while, which wasn't allowed either—they were ever going to get rid of him.

At last they called his school for advice. That was, after all, where he belonged. It was also a mistake. The school recommended the trip. It had been such a pleasant day there with Jalish gone. Everyone had relaxed.

Next the UMCA called his mother. She sometimes worked at home, and that's where she was that day. But she'd forgotten to turn down the white noise, and she didn't really hear the request. She understood that it was something about Jalish. A permission for something. And since, as far as she knew, he was at school and the school must know what it was doing, she said yes.

There was no further recourse. The UMCA permitters

put the usual space gear on Jalish, the equipment they had on hand for trips to blank spots—oxygen and a cosmic ray shield and all the rest. Enough to get him through a couple of minutes at a planet near his pink and green star and back again, even if it was as dangerous as they thought it might be. Then they let him go, with the usual warning to come back soon and not to be swallowed by monsters.

One minute he was there with them laughing. And the next minute he was on the fifth planet of the pink and green star. Why the fifth planet? Well, he didn't know for sure just how many planets there were. Why should he? No one else even knew if there were planets at all. It had just seemed a good place to aim for, and he had worked out a reasonable True Relation. He had no real basis for what he did, and yet he had felt sure of himself. Why, he did not know. Even Jalish sometimes knew when questions were useless.

The UMCA people were sure Jalish would be back in five minutes or so, disappointed and quiet. But they were wrong. After an hour they began to worry. He had seemed so intelligent, and so persistent, they had never dreamed he would get lost—forget the way home. They began to wonder if they should send someone after him. But when they stopped to think, they realized they didn't know where he had gone. A pink and green planet. Whoever heard of such a thing? And where in the galaxy? What was the True Relation? They called up the school in a real panic when two hours had passed, but no one there could help them, not even the cosmology teacher. Who could pick out a single star in the sweep of a lens? Only Jalish.

They called his mother, but she still had the white noise on and was no help at all. His father didn't even

know Jalish had wanted to go anywhere, let alone that he
had already gone. He yelped when he heard, and the next
minute he was right there at UMCA. He didn't blame anyone. He knew Jalish too well. He just wanted to add his
brain to the tangle. A whole crew began to work on the
problem.

At that moment, for a change, Jalish wasn't thinking
nearly so hard as they were. In fact, there wasn't a question
in his mind. He'd outdone himself at last. He'd found a
place that left him speechless and empty.

When he had first come, there had been the colors. Not
just pink and green, but all colors. The star seemed to
emit light of every color in the spectrum, though Jalish
knew that wasn't how things worked. But he didn't start
trying to figure it out. He just looked. At the star, and at
the fifth planet where his feet were. The whole planet was
jumping with color. Not just in the sky. There were tall
waves of color sweeping back and forth over the ground.
Some were big—sixty, eighty meters high—he estimated.
Others were smaller. And the space between was white.
A white you felt without its being anything you could
touch. What vegetation there was, was sparse and a shiny
gray. These gray things caught the color and reflected it.
Electromagnetic waves of some sort—a giant aurora—was
the thought that flashed into his mind a few moments after
he landed. And then he stopped thinking.

He simply had no thoughts of his own. The waves
filled his mind, and not only color waves, but music
waves as well. Because there was music too. It all came
into his mind, and there was no room left for anything else.
The music moved with the waves of light, keeping time
with them. Each wave had a beat of its own, and yet all

the waves worked together. And together they really rocked him. They took over and left him standing there with nothing at all going on inside. And that's how it still was two hours after he came.

Eventually he sat down and leaned back against one of the big flat-bladed gray plants, a little like a cactus he'd seen once. But he hardly knew what he was doing. He was only a little part of a big color and a big sound. He didn't know anything else existed, not even himself.

Later, a lot later, his mind began to creep back underneath and around the sides of the waves that were still in the middle. It took a little pressure, a little force to do it, but there was something in Jalish that never could leave well enough alone; he had to push against things. So he made a wedge for himself, and his thoughts began to take shape; it occurred to him then that all that sound wasn't just sound. It was music, but it wasn't just music. The light was color, but not just color.

He pushed a bit farther and it hit him that all that sight and sound might be what passed for people on that planet. It was about the second real thought he'd had on that fifth planet, and at first he was afraid he'd lost his mind entirely. Usually a new thought like that picked Jalish up and left him feeling pretty good, but this one just left him sitting, lower and lower, if possible. The problem was that if he was right, he had no way of knowing what was going to happen to him. When the waves sort of bounced up and down a little harder and the sound took on a pleasant murmur, he could feel he was right. But that still didn't give him a clue to his future, if he had one, or to when he might have his whole mind back again.

That was only the beginning. It took a while longer

before Jalish really got a sense of what was going on. And when he did, he felt almost worse than before. He knew then that he had put himself in a real mess. Because it was clear that those waves were pumping his mind. All his questions and all his answers were being siphoned out. Everything he'd ever known. Or rather, it was all being absorbed. The waves had come in and were just soaking it up. There was no real need for language. The waves didn't use it. His mind waves simply blended with their mind waves. Were these people, if you could call them that, all mind? Were the waves themselves mind? He couldn't think that far. There wasn't room enough for his thoughts to work that out. So he just sat and let it all happen. It wasn't usual with Jalish to let things go like that, but this wasn't a usual situation.

And soon things became even more unusual. Because Jalish almost relaxed. And with that, he actually felt the waves prodding around in his mind. And because he sensed them there, for the first time he really understood something of what they were. That was when he nearly blew apart. Energy, nothing but energy. Not even atoms, really. Waves of particles. Something so basic that the whole universe seemed contained in just one. What they knew seemed to go all the way back to the big bang his cosmology teacher liked to explain, maybe even to something before. Though that was hard to think about. He sensed it all, breathed it in through his mind, absorbed it, and then he nearly collapsed. For the first time in his life he was not in charge.

Once they all knew each other better, that is once the waves had taken in everything Jalish had on his mind, including the fact that he dimly perceived what they were, more of the waves came closer. They crowded around him and all but ran up against him. He felt them, and yet he didn't. Of course he had the suit on; but there was a gentle pressure here and there on the outside. They were really giving him the once over, he decided. And sometimes he dimly sensed that they didn't wholly believe what they had found, anymore than he believed what he had found. It was hard for them to admit that he was as solid as he was, though of course they could move right through him; and it was even harder for them to accept his thoughts, especially the idea that there were lots more like him, back where he came from. This seemed to scare them. The lights and the music began to clash and to move a bit faster. But eventually the uproar settled, and it seemed as if they had decided to live with what they had learned, after all.

After a while the waves made it clear that they wanted Jalish to stand up and go along on a little trip. They flicked all around him, and he could see that he didn't have much choice. They might be transparent, but he had an idea they had a lot of power within them; this was an idea he thought it was better not to check out.

The planet had a glossy, solid surface, which the waves slid over rather smoothly as they squired him along. There was water, or something of the sort, here and there, and the strange gray plants were scattered around. Once in a while they passed a huge chunk of raw metal, big as a house, barren and a bit rusty looking. And other times there were odd-looking stones. Jalish tried to store away pictures of everything he saw.

It began to get dark as they moved, and Jalish was unreasonably glad that the planet was like other planets at least in that way. But even in the dark the waves went on, a little darker maybe, but still there. They now cast strange shadows on the ground.

Moving forward, Jalish felt more and more of his mind coming back. The waves were through searching it at last, he guessed. But he was still too stunned, and too tired now, to think very much. He did decide he wasn't really afraid any longer, and he wasn't in much danger. In fact, it was all rather nice by that time—the music and the lights. He was used to it, and he liked it. The only thing he needed was a bit of supper.

That was what actually made him decide it was time to go home. With his mind back, he could think of things like that if he wanted to. So with a real jerk on himself, he pulled in and set things up for going. He hated to, in a way. But he couldn't just stay. He tried to think out an explanation to the waves around him, a sort of apology for running off, and then he put himself in mind to leave. But nothing happened. The usual system didn't work. He didn't move a meter toward home. And that's when he really discovered what it means to be afraid. He could see that he'd soon know what hunger really was, too. And more than that, he decided he was homesick. It was all very fine to go away, but home had its advantages if you hadn't planned for a long stay, which he hadn't.

The waves, he saw, understood what was happening. They crowded around, as if to keep him cool and happy. Still he might have given way to a real case of the shakes if the biggest wave he had seen all day hadn't suddenly come bolting in. It hit down right there in front of him, gently. And then he understood. They'd sent for the head wave—if that's what this was.

It was the same round all over. His mind was borrowed again, and he could only guess what questions and what answers they were waving out of it. All perfectly friendly, but at the same time more than a little wearing, especially when you were hungry. That was a thing the waves didn't seem to understand. It slipped into him finally that if they ate anything at all it would be natural field forces or cosmic rays or something of that type. Not especially appetizing. Probably didn't even come in different flavors. He almost laughed. Even pills would be better.

The search was over all at once. The head wave backed off and left. The waves all drew back in a circle, the ones that were left. They bowed, that was all he could call it, and waited around him, as if something was about to happen. And at that instant Jalish realized that for the first time since he had landed, he truly had all of his mind back, including the part that could take him home. He was so pleased, he bowed in return. And at the same moment questions flooded in, not their questions, but his. It was his turn now, he decided. No sense in going back so soon, even if he was hungry. He hadn't come all that way and gone through all that for nothing. But when he began to try to ask the things he felt he had to know, the waves were gone. In despair he realized that there was nothing he could do now but go home. He'd never felt so frustrated, so utterly defeated, in his life. Obviously these waves had never heard of fair play. They had called him. That was the only way he had seen the star as pink and green from Earth. Though how they had done it, he couldn't say. And now, without doing anything for him, they had left him. He set himself up for home, and the next thing he knew he was in the UMCA office.

It looked the same, yet not the same. What was wrong?

To begin with, everyone there was just a little too solid. Once he got over that shock, Jalish decided that no one looked as if he or she had eaten for at least twelve hours or slept for twenty-four. Which was more or less the truth of it. Some word of Jalish's trip had leaked out, and what worry hadn't done, questions from the outside had. The Core Council was in steady contact, and the local Sector Group had been warned in case Jalish got stuck in someone else's screen. With all that, everyone there looked half dead, and was. Each agency officer in the room was so wrapped up in one little corner of the problem that no one saw Jalish for at least three minutes. And then no one had strength enough to say anything. For Jalish it was like being back on the fifth planet again, only harder. This time he had to talk.

When things finally settled down, and everyone had had a late supper, Jalish showed them where he'd been. The showing wasn't hard. It was the telling that took time. There wasn't an easy thing to believe in the whole strange story. But Jalish stuck to the truth, and since no one could prove it wasn't the truth, UMCA and everyone else finally had to believe.

Of course, when word really got out, the experts came tumbling in, and then Jalish had his hands full. What helped him most at that point were all the things he knew. There were things in his mind that had never been in any-one's mind before, at least not in any mind on Earth or in

157

the immediate sector. The more he probed around, the more he found. He had so many ideas and so many questions that were so new that nobody could doubt he'd been some place strange. Slowly it dawned on him that while those waves had been in there probing, he'd picked up a whole lot from them in return. It hadn't been a one-sided venture after all. He had learned things about the whole system that nobody on any planet anyone had visited had ever learned before. The experts looked at him in awe.

They made him a Universal Spokesman and a Man of Honor in cosmology, planetology, radiology, and various branches of primary matter study and energy concerns, all at the same time. Then to both Jalish's and the school's relief, it was decided that he didn't have to finish even quarter school. He knew more than almost anyone—about some things, anyway—and he was still only sixteen.

When they finally left him alone, there was no doubt about his being able to do anything he wanted to do. His whole life was ahead of him, and he was on his own to shape it.

What he did was to start watching the pink and green star—the planet, of course, couldn't be seen from any place reasonable for observation. Others went with him to the nearest possible observation post, and everyone agreed that the star was pink and green. But it seemed dimmer to him than it had before. And as time went by, this proved to be the case. The pink and green dimmed until it was finally gone, and a plain old yellow star was left. Other scientists were puzzled, but not Jalish. He'd seen those waves whipping back and forth up there. And he'd sensed how upset they'd been over what they'd learned from him.

So he knew they'd decided they didn't want to be visited again, not for a while, anyway. It was why he hadn't gone back. He had sensed that they were afraid of solid creatures. All that was clear. The only real question was: Were the planets and the star empty? Yes, he decided, the waves had gone. They had simply picked up and moved. But where?

The whole problem made Jalish uneasy. He really wanted to think that his friends (he'd come to think of them as friends; after all, they'd gotten him out of school and into something much better) were all still someplace. But he didn't know how to find them. For the second or third time in his life, he was really baffled. He felt he had to find some waves again. Others, perhaps, that weren't afraid. He had to know more about them. They alone had the answers to the questions that still filled his mind. Questions about the galaxy and about the universe, but most of all questions about the waves themselves. How old were they? Were they all different, or were they all basically alike? Did they have more than one sex? Were there children? And if he found some again, would they answer his questions? Would they let him come near them? Obviously the ones he had met already knew all he knew, and they hadn't liked some of what they saw. Would they or any others be willing to take him in again?

As time passed, his attention gradually moved to other unexplored places in the galaxy. He mapped huge uncharted regions, exploring tirelessly, always by himself. He was free to go whenever he chose, and he was always snapping out to really wild places, and coming home with strange stories, all of which made him pretty much an

159

outer galactic hero. But he was never really satisfied. Those who knew him best said he'd never have a quiet day until he found another pink and green solar system. Not that another would be the same, maybe. But he wanted another chance at some of those waves, whatever the color. He didn't know for sure what would happen if he found some. But he was willing to take a chance.

They still don't let sixteen-year-olds off their home planets much. And it still makes some of them mad. But then there aren't too many people anymore who remember Jalish Dozent's first trip. Everyone in the fifty sectors of the galactic arms lives by some of his ideas and discoveries. But few remember that so much came out of one trip made by one sixteen-year-old. To the few who do remember, it seems wiser that the others do not.

A Central Question

Ganser Wekot looked up at the sky—close, encircling, and too enticing. It was too much like home. Strange that the sky on Cora C should remind him so of Earth. Though maybe not. Cora C was about the same distance from its sun as Earth was from its. And the suns were near in size. The atmospheres were remarkably similar; physically he'd adapted easily. So it was understandable, the similarity in the sky. Still, he hated it, hated to be reminded of Earth.

Most of those who'd come to the Outer Galactic Council's new school for service trainees were content. They didn't seem to have the affection for their home planets that he did. Yet there was Bilee from Groad and Flu-on from Xenos D. They weren't really happy on Cora C either. He'd mentioned the sky to them; but they saw other things. For Bilee it was the rocks: same colors, same cut as Groad. For Flu-on it was the wind: always sharp the way it was on Xenos D. The three of them had tried to like the school, tried to like the place where they found themselves, to adjust as the others had, but somehow they simply could not.

They had been on Cora C for two years, but it seemed a lot longer. Ganser hadn't wanted to come; he had had no choice. His mother was Council Leader for Sector 5, and so he had had to set an example when he was chosen. He had wondered why, and still did. It was his mother's job to lead, not his.

Each one of the fifty sectors of the outer galaxy had been asked to send two or three of their young—only two or three, so it was very selective—to the school. It was experimental, as was almost everything the council undertook. After all, the council itself was new. It was just exploring means to unify the outer galactic sectors into doing some things together. The students at the school, when they finished their training, would carry out special galaxy-wide projects. They were being taught to look at the outer galaxy as a whole, something few representatives from any minded species were equipped to do. Ganser wasn't sure that he and his schoolmates were going to be much better equipped, but he guessed someone had to at least try.

On Earth everyone beyond a certain level in school had had to take the exams the council had sent around, for choosing those who would come to the school. He had had the feeling that they especially wanted someone from Earth, though why he wasn't sure. At any rate, he had been chosen. Why that had happened, he wasn't sure either. Maybe since he knew so much about sector government, because of his mother. Most people on Earth didn't pay too much attention to governments of any kind. And now Earth was half a galaxy away. And it was likely to remain that way even during their short school vacations, with travel controls so tight.

162

Lately the whole outer galaxy had gotten so precise about travel; it didn't make sense. He knew there were dangers. You could accidentally land in the wrong place and be in trouble. And some minds got upset on long trips —bodies even. So there had to be protection, he supposed. But not to let anyone go anywhere at all. That didn't seem reasonable.

"Ganser, you haven't made a sound in ten minutes."

Ganser grinned at Bilee. "It's the sky today. It's—well, it makes me think too much. I'm not really here."

Bilee grinned back. She looked around at the broad flat gravel plain, the steep brown cliffs in the distance, and the deep blue vegetation that made small circles here and there. "Fillets on your sky. Give me good brown stone any-time."

They both laughed out loud.

"What's the meeting for tonight?" Ganser asked, changing the subject. It wasn't often the whole school was called together. But word had been passed down at the midday meal that there was to be a big meeting tonight. And nothing had been the same the rest of the day. Flu-on hadn't even been able to come walking. He was stuck setting up the amphitheater.

Bilee shrugged. "Some visiting wonder, I suppose," she said. "Some Outer Galactic Council member. Or maybe a Sector Council Leader."

Ganser toyed with the idea. His mother, maybe? The idea flooded him with anticipation. He hadn't seen anyone in his family in two years. But then he shrugged it off. The meeting might not be because of visitors at all. And even if it were, the chance of his mother being there was remote.

"Your mother hasn't said she was coming, has she?" Bilee asked, all but reading his thoughts.

"She wouldn't tell me if she were coming," he said. "It wouldn't be right, with others not knowing."

Ganser's thoughts bounded away again. Why did Earth people need each other so much, when others didn't seem to have the same need? Why did Earth people seem so drawn toward home? It wasn't that they didn't like to travel. Most went off on business or pleasure now and then and enjoyed it. And a few found space absolutely fascinating. Yet Earth always called them back.

His mind turned to some of the jaunts he had made with his Uncle Britter before he had come to Cora C, before travel restrictions had become so tight. He'd spent a lot of time with his Aunt Kirry and Uncle Britter, because both of his parents were gone a good deal. He and Uncle Britter had often traveled to strange places for a day or two. It had been fun, even if his mother hadn't always approved when she found out. Uncle Britter could make any trip an adventure, but some of the ones they had shared together had given him experiences he would never forget. Uncle Britter liked odd planets. Yet, no matter how exciting a trip had been, the coming home had always been a joy. There was a warmth, a welcoming feeling, about Earth that no other planet shared.

"I hope it's not a lecture," Bilee said suddenly. "I'm so tired of sitting. It's too settled here. All those classes on problems of the galaxy where we just talk. Yet it's not peaceful here either, really. All those minds are always pushing at you, for no reason."

Ganser looked over sympathetically. He hadn't really

164

known that she felt it so strongly, the weariness of sitting and learning and never doing. Coming from Groad, she was square and firm, built for action. And of course her four arms made it obvious that her race did things.

"I don't mind learning," Ganser said slowly. "I like to know things. It's being stuffed with it until you could explode and never being given a chance to make something happen. Some of the others here seem like blotters; they soak up everything that's given them and never stop, but it all stays just where it's put. They never get beyond their endless dead-end games. We're not like that home, and it's hard for me to understand."

Bilee shrugged. "Better start back. If we're too late, they'll keep us in tomorrow."

That was true, although the school had shown the three of them unusual consideration when their restlessness had become apparent. Sometimes some of the teachers had almost seemed to approve.

They turned and ran toward the low flat building—mostly roofs, since the largest part of the school was underground—in the distance. Unable to talk, not wanting to think, Ganser ran toward the sky—the sky over the buildings.

Flu-on met them at the door, at the bottom of the steps.

"Where have you been? You're almost late for dinner."

Ganser shrugged. Food here didn't interest him. Mostly concentrates with a few tasteless bulk items to make those who needed them feel full.

The three moved to the room that served as a mess hall and generally as an assembly room as well, though tonight they were to meet in the more formal amphitheater. The meal was eaten quickly and almost in silence, though there was an electric quality to the air. Only twice before had there been a formal general assembly, and neither of them had been called suddenly.

Ganser looked around, studying the others. Most of them were busy all the time with their minds, looking for ways to test themselves against other minds or soaking up information that would help them when they did find an opponent. They did not need to move much physically, yet each seemed to be struggling for space, mental space. They seemed to define themselves by pushing against others, yet it didn't seem to matter who the others were. Earth people, on the other hand, found themselves inside, and worked with others who shared their interests to discover new things. Was that why he felt himself so different here?

Yet tonight the rest did not seem so different. He sensed around him a reflection of his own curiosity and more than a vague apprehension about the meeting to be held. He didn't know why he felt as he did. Did they? What were they afraid of? Maybe they knew something he didn't. They soaked up knowledge, and in spite of their combativeness, they did sometimes use their knowledge in interesting ways, creating patterns and puzzles and hypothetical situations that were really fascinating. And they were not all alike, even though sometimes they did seem almost like building blocks, each occupying a given space and filling a given function. Maybe underneath they were more like him and Bilee and Flu-on than he had thought. The idea interested him.

At a signal from the Head, everyone began to move

toward the amphitheater, each in his or her own way. Some rolled, some were propelled by jets of air, some walked as he did. Those who could only move by thought projection, naturally arrived first.

Ganser, Flu-on, and Bilee took their time. Ganser was still thoughtful.

"I was wrong, Bilee," he muttered, letting his mind run on. "They're not blotters. They were once like us, or at least their ancestors were. But their worlds are so crowded, they've had to make their lives a mental contest just to continue to exist as individuals, or at least as intelligent individuals. I wonder if they can ever be different."

Bilee and Flu-on looked at him curiously. He was a little amazed at himself. Why hadn't he realized that before!

"Why?" asked Flu-on. "Why is it that way? It wouldn't have to be. And I think even the ones who move out to new planets stay the same. Maybe they're what happens to minded species—and we on our planets just haven't evolved that far."

"Then I don't want to evolve," said Bilee. "There has to be something more."

"Yes," said Ganser. "There does have to be something more. Because that's a dead end. But what else can happen?"

A teacher appeared at the door ahead.

"No place for chatter," the teacher murmured at them.

The three had to separate. There were no places together. Ganser made his way to the first spot he saw, quietly, his head down, his mind still wrestling with the questions he had raised. He hardly noticed the Head come

167

in with a lot of others following. They had all mounted to the low stage at the front before he saw them. His mother was there! She was on the Central Committee of the Outer Galactic Council this year, but what did her presence mean? He counted the people on the stage. The whole Central Committee and the Central Convener must be there. The feeling of anxiety around him was stronger than ever, and strangely it seemed to be shared by those on the platform.

The Head stepped forward and began to speak.

"I will be brief. You see before you the entire Central Committee of the Outer Galactic Council and its Convener. They bring a perplexing problem that faces them; they come to enlist your help. I will not explain further, but will leave it to the Council Convener, who will speak to you now."

The Convener gave a long speech. Ganser felt it could all have been said more directly and in one quarter the time. But reflecting again on his newfound evaluation of the others at the school, he decided maybe the Convener knew what he was doing. Abstract ideas came quickly to his classmates, but not concepts of real physical change.

What it all came down to was that, as everyone knew, the outer galaxy was divided into fifty sectors. In each sector the majority of the stars and planets were known, although many had not really been explored. The fifty sectors, however, covered only the great spiral arms of the galaxy. The core, beyond a hypothetical perimeter, was still largely unknown. It was a place of gas clouds, of masses of dust, and of many strange stars. Exploration had tended to take place in safer, more ordinary areas. Besides, no one had believed that life of any recognizable sort could exist at the galactic center. But in recent years scientists and the Outer Galactic Council had not been so sure earlier conclusions were correct. There were signs of strange, unnatural movements in the core. Odd things had happened in the fringe areas of sectors surrounding the core. It was possible that danger could come from the core, and come fairly soon, to all the settled planets of the outer galaxy. Travel in most parts of the galaxy had been limited even more than usual while the situation was being studied.

"Because your training and inclinations fit you for such service, and because, quite frankly, we have no comparable group to call upon, we are transferring each of you to a separate command and observation post, on a planet near the edge of the unknown. Most of these will be on uninhabited planets, because as you well know, few planets near the core have been settled or currently have minded life that naturally evolved there. Unfortunately, it will be necessary, in order to cover a maximum area, for each of you to be stationed alone. You will be well provided for, of course, and will be expected to report any and all occurrences you see in the core area within your range of surveillance."

He went on with details, but Ganser's mind wandered. They had been well prepared for the Convener's deputation by his earlier remarks, but even so there was shock all around him. Shock and outright fear. Regardless of what their ancestors might have been, Ganser's classmates had never been alone, had never had an individual responsibility. He went back to his earlier thoughts. They needed

169

others around for their own identification. They'd die of being alone, he realized. Even here they were afraid of it. Most of them had never had to realize that a challenge could be real, not a hypothetical game, and could come to the whole person, not just the mind. They were afraid of the real, and afraid of those who could deal with it. But the Convener should know that! Well, of course he did, Ganser saw. He simply had no other choice. There were too few he could call on for service of this kind. Most people were too busy on their own planets and in their own sectors to leave, even to fend off what could be real danger. Few would be willing to isolate themselves for the good of the galaxy, or would even be able to appreciate what danger was, the kind of danger the Convener saw.

The amphitheater was silent. No one spoke. The Central Committee on the platform gazed anxiously, eagerly, at the students. The students sat frozen. And then, almost without thinking, Ganser moved. He stood and began speaking. His thoughts were not formed. The idea he began to pour out was not consciously put together, yet he knew with a deep inner excitement that it was a good idea and that he believed in it.

"Why can't someone go to the core and see what's there?" he asked. "Has someone gone? Why just observe from the outside?"

The Convener seemed impatient. "Of course, we've thought of that. Tried it, even. But no one who has gone has returned. The forces are too strong for ships. And it is too hard for an individual to place himself. You know the dangers of transportation to wholly unknown planets, surely?"

"Yes," Ganser went on, his excitement growing. "Not

ships, of course. But why must people land? Why not someone, or maybe even two or three, with proper suits, after some experimenting and working together, going to the space between? Looking around. There's no need to stay long. Ten or twelve places, even a hundred, could be approached in a few days' time. And then maybe you'd know. With a proper set of True Relations, and whatever other information you do have, I think it could be done. Surely some information is available."

"My dear boy, don't be preposterous. In the first place, who would volunteer for such a mission? And we certainly can't force anyone to go. It would be murder. But even beyond that, you must surely know, if you are bright enough to be here, that even those most capable of self-transportation require a specific destination and a positive landing site. A True Relation is hardly enough. No, our plan is the only solution for the present."

Ganser saw his mother frown and nod her head. But he had no intention of letting go.

"I would volunteer," he said, and saw his mother look both shocked and horrified. "And I'm fairly certain Flu-on and Bilee would too."

They both stood up and nodded yes.

"And," Ganser went on, quickly before the Convener could object again, "if you'll give us permission and gear, I think we might find a way to pinpoint ourselves in space." He began then to put as much authority as he could into technical details, drawing on all he'd learned at the school, but more on what he'd learned from Uncle Britter. Until now, he hadn't realized how much his uncle had taught him.

The Convener began to look less gruff. He listened more

171

and more intently. "Yes, yes, go on," he said at one point. When Ganser finished, there was another moment of silence.

"You speak well, boy," the Convener said. "It's not that we haven't thought of many of these things. It's just that you seem to have had some travel experiences no one else has had. I'm inclined to think your ideas may be worth further consideration, if they are indeed based in knowledge and experience. What is your name, and where are you from?"

Before he could reply, his mother spoke. "Will you let a boy change the course the entire Central Committee has set?"

"When a boy seems to speak wisdom, yes," said the Convener. "What is your name? And where are you from?" he asked again.

"Ganser Wekot," he said firmly. "From Sector 5, Earth."

The Convener started, then looked at his mother.

"Council Leader Wekot," he said, "you have a son worthy of you."

His mother nodded weakly.

"This assembly is dismissed. Will the three volunteers come with us? We may decide to follow the plan previously set. But I feel we must at least discuss Ganser's plan, since he speaks with such confidence. You will be kept informed."

There was a small meeting room behind the stage. The Central Committee members, Ganser, Bilee, and Flu-on filed in and settled around a raised platform. It was very like a classroom, a place made for discussion.

The Convener rapped for silence and began at once.

"You seem to have a wide knowledge of transportation, Ganser, more than I would have thought possible for one your age," he said.

"I grew up on Earth, sir. Sometimes with my mother and father, and sometimes with my uncle and aunt. My uncle teaches theory of transportation and has done some experimenting. He sometimes took me." He glanced at his mother quickly, remembering that she had seldom approved of those trips. Her face was now impassive. "He could get permission. And we never went for long. But we went to some really odd places, and we often tried new ways of getting there. Even though people on Earth like it at home, some of us like wildness and uncertainty too. And you sure get that when you travel with Uncle Britter." He grinned in spite of himself. "Anyway, I've always been interested in transportation, and I've read all I can—even here, especially here. You have to do something that takes you away sometimes, if only in your mind."

"You find this place stifling, then, and think staying alone in an outpost somewhere might be even worse," the Convener finished, giving him a sympathetic look. "Ganser, we are all different. Each of us from every place is a little different from all others, and each planet with minded beings has made a life that is in some way different from life anywhere else. Earth has an odd history and perhaps because of that has given more than its share of the new to us all. Don't be ashamed of your feelings, or be afraid to say what you know. We respect you for what you are."

"But he's so young," his mother burst out, the first time Ganser had ever seen her lose her objectivity. "And he's

173

my only child. We on Earth have so few children. If we've given so much, why must we give more?"

"You sent me here," Ganser said. "And it seems as if from here you never get back home, even on vacation. If I can't go to Earth, why shouldn't I do something worth doing?"

"Every good thing is worth doing, Ganser," said the Convener. "And at the end of your training here, had there been no emergency, you would surely have had a chance to go home, perhaps even to stay a while as a representative of the Outer Galactic Council. That may still happen. Is that why you volunteered? And you too, Bilee and Fluon? To get away from here? To perhaps go home?"

Ganser went through his mind. Was that the reason? No, no it wasn't. Not all of it, at least.

"I want to go home," he said truthfully. "But that wasn't it. It was more. We'd been talking, Bilee and I, about the others—all mind and no body, they seem, a lot of them. They seem satisfied here mostly because they have others to push against, just as they do at home. They need others around all the time to give them a sense of existing at all. When you told us about the outposts, they froze up. On their planets, only minds have adventures. They'd die at an outpost alone. I'd hate it, being trapped there, unable to get around, having to spend all my time on one thing. But they couldn't function at all."

"You're at least partly right, Ganser," said another committee member. "I come from a crowded planet, as indeed most of us do. Survival would be hard at an outpost for one of us. Yet, in the Central Committee, we seemed to find no alternative. What you propose is a more venturesome plan than any of us could conceive. We called on the school because no other institution represents all of the outer galaxy, and because you are all being trained for service to the galaxy. The watchers obviously had to be made up of people who had a concern for all fifty sectors. We hoped that most of you might still be young enough and open enough to adapt to the new."

Ganser was quiet, and the Convener looked at Flu-on and Bilee.

"I thought it was something to do," Flu-on said. "I need to move; and Ganser's right about the others."

"And I'm not going to be left behind if Ganser and Flu-on go," said Bilee. "I couldn't stand it here alone. There's really nobody else. That is, no one who seems to be thinking and growing the same way we are."

The Convener was thoughtful. "I wasn't going to bring this up," he said. "But when the school was founded, those of us who dreamed of what it might be, believed that by bringing together young representatives of all the kinds of minded life we know in the outer galaxy we might develop not only a sense of galactic unity in all of them, but a new direction, a new way that minded life in a united galaxy might move. We felt this might happen in some, if not in all who came, because the school would provide a totally new situation and a new look at patterns of life everywhere. For some races, it may be too late for this to happen. I cannot say. But I have a stirring of hope that in you three there is evidence that it could happen. You have not lost the essence of what you are as individuals and as representatives of your planets, and yet there is more in you—an understanding and a daring that goes beyond.

"Ganser, your plan holds promise, if it can be made to work. You say your uncle was experimenting?"

"Yes, sir. He has some really interesting ideas. But it's hard for him to get time for testing. I've been away two years, though. And he had done some marvelous things before I left."

"My brother-in-law is slightly mad on the subject of transportation," Council Leader Wekot put in dryly. "And I suspect Ganser is right about what Britter knows. You will also find him more than eager to cooperate. But you may not always be pleased with what you get. Britter is not like anyone else."

"We all have our madnesses," the Convener observed mildly. "Gormist," he nodded to his aide, "can you tack in on Earth and bring Britter Wekot here? And until he comes, why don't we all plan to stay. I'm sure the school can accommodate us."

The Head, who was in the room, nodded and led the way to the door. "For as long as you need," he said. The others began to follow.

Ganser hesitated. He felt he couldn't face the school just yet, nor his mother. And he needed to talk to Bilee and Flu-on. They were not moving either, as unsure as he.

"Oh, you three stay with me a bit," said the Convener. "I'm sure you're tired and ready to sleep, but I need a few more words with you."

His mother frowned, hesitated near the door, then followed the others down the hall. For a moment he had an urge to follow her, to try to explain. He was torn between his need to see her and a fear that she might talk him out of the whole thing when he did, though why she should want to, he couldn't quite see.

"Stay here, Ganser," said the Convener. "There'll be plenty of time to talk to your mother. It'll be a day or two before your uncle comes."

Ganser felt relieved. The final decision had been taken from him. He turned to join the Convener and Bilee and Flu-on.

The next two days were hectic. That was the only way Ganser could describe them. He and Bilee and Flu-on did not go to classes. And when they went out walking, the Convener went with them. In fact the four of them spent a great deal of time out-of-doors. It was quieter, for one thing. Bilee's and Flu-on's parents, and their planet and sector heads, had been reached. They had all arrived and were no happier than Ganser's mother. So there was little peace inside.

For Ganser—and for Flu-on and Bilee, he was sure—the project became more and more concrete, more and more frightening—and yet more and more attractive. Nothing had ever seemed more important. And everything beyond it—if there was to be a time beyond—lost any sense of reality.

Ganser's uncle arrived on the second day, even more pleased with the project than Ganser had thought he would be. There was another conference of the Central Committee, with Ganser, Flu-on, Bilee, Britter, and a few added specialists who had been called in. Ganser had been right, his uncle did have some new techniques—some tried and some not—all of which might help.

"But if Britter is the proponent and originator of these untried ideas," said Council Leader Wekot, in a last attempt to change the direction of things, "why shouldn't he be the one to go and perhaps some other adults with him?"

"Because these young people, with their new approach to the galaxy, an approach you yourself hoped would develop, are without a doubt the best observers in this thing," said the Convener, wearily. He'd said almost the same thing to too many people too many times, Ganser thought. Why didn't they leave him alone and get on with it?

Several committee members nodded in agreement with the Convener, and there was no more debate. The issue was settled.

There was a sense of relief in knowing it was really going to happen, Ganser found. That the training for the actual travel could begin. And when the committee and the Convener left to go back to their more usual concerns, the work did begin.

"Your uncle is a slave driver!" Flu-on complained one day.

"Wouldn't you think three or four hours a day would be enough?" Bilee asked. "I'm so tired, I can't think."

"Which is just what we want to help you with," Uncle Britter said, coming up. "The probability is that you'll be gone at least a day and maybe two. Or you may decide to come and go over a longer period of time instead, making many short trips. But either way, you have to be prepared to keep going, if necessary, for long periods of time. You don't know what may happen to you. You need to be able to think for several days, not just three or four hours, no matter how tired you become. And you've got to have your technique so firmly established that you can use it even asleep."

No one of the three could argue with that.

The days were spent not only in studying theory and experimenting with travel, including trips over quite long distances, but also in studying available core charts. They also had to learn from various specialists where the key spots for observation were—those nearest seeming centers of core activity—develop the needed skills to operate the miniature observation equipment they would carry along, discover what to look for, and be fitted with special space suits that would maintain life for a minimum of two days, it was hoped, in core space.

The project became more and more the only reality. The rest of the galaxy, even life at the school—which went on all around—was generally a haze at the periphery of existence for all three of them. Ganser thought of the other students sometimes, wishing he had tried harder to understand them, to get to know them. Maybe when he came back. . . . But that was even farther beyond the haze. That was unreal.

The date and site for the first exploration were set. They were all to go to Worrly D, an uninhabited planet near the core boundary. Not a bad planet, they were told. Some stationary, unminded life, but that was all. A planet that might have been colonized if it were not so near the core. There had always been a hesitancy about getting too close, based on an unfounded but persistent fear of powerful, deadly rays from the core.

From Worrly D they would make a short jump over the hypothetical boundary to a relatively known area that had been under surveillance from a distance for a long time. If that went well, they would make farther jumps on other days to lesser known places. It had been decided that many short jumps would be better than an extended trip. It sounded reasonable.

"And when you're too tired, we'll simply hold up a while," said the specialist who was making the general arrangements as the time grew close.

"Oh, we've been trained not to get tired," said Bilee blithely. "We can go on thinking for two days, at least."

Everyone laughed and looked at Uncle Britter.

"Just don't get too big for your space suits," he said, smiling. "Or, I'll have to come and get you. And I'm too old for space rescue." It had been determined that he would go along to Worrly D to continue to coach them. Ganser's mother and father and Bilee's and Flu-on's parents were to be there also. The planet site was being readied by a team and supplies from the nearest inhabited system. The three were to start from near the core not because they needed to be near for transporting themselves, but for what limited tracking of their journeys could be done.

Finally, when it was only the completion of the camp and the tracking station on Worrly D that held them back, the three began to get impatient. You could only look forward to danger and prepare for it for so long, Ganser decided. Then something had to happen.

Finally the Convener, himself, returned and announced, "We're ready. We're going tomorrow."

The three were glad, and yet Cora C had seldom looked so good.

"How long will we be there?" asked Ganser the next day, as the group gathered for departure.

"No one knows. In part it depends on you three. And in part it depends on what you find."

Ganser nodded. That made sense. It was so obvious, in fact, he felt he should never have asked the question. Yet he went on, "And after?"

"That will be decided later on," the Convener said quietly. "First we have to begin."

There was no putting it off anymore. And a large black hole of fear opened in Ganser's mind. He wondered if the others felt the same. He supposed they did. How could they not? He looked around at Cora C. At the pleasant sky. The two years here had been all right.

"You all know the landscape and the True Relation and the exact coordinates for Worrly D?" the Convener asked. Everyone nodded. "Then let's go before we change our minds." The Convener almost grinned at them.

He knows, Ganser thought, pleased. He knows how we feel. But he can't help us. It's too late now. He bent his mind on Worrly D. One thing at a time. That was the way to keep going.

"It's always so quick," Bilee said. "Even after all we've done, I never quite get used to it. Sometimes you wish it took longer so you could be ready. . . ." she trailed off lamely. "This is nice," she added, looking around at the low building that had been thrown up for them, the rather lush vegetation that crowded around the flat area, and high rocky cliffs in the distance. "Not at all what I thought a planet so near the core would be like. I guess I expected something wild and stormy." She giggled.

"It's a quiet place," said Flu-on. "Not even a breeze. Strange no one's ever settled here, even though it is so close to the core."

"This is one of the better parts of it," said Uncle Britter, unexpectedly. "There are places as barren as you might imagine, and almost as wild, Bilee. Windier than even you might like, Flu-on."

The Convener looked surprised. "You've been here? This has been pretty much off limits for a long time."

"I did some experimental work in this area once. Some core perimeter research."

"A group?"

"Alone. It was a final school project."

"Did you make a report?"

Uncle Britter nodded.

"What happened to it?"

"School-holding, I guess. Probably no one's encountered it in years. They had to accept it, but no one really believed what I found."

"Did you go into the core?"

"No, just here on the perimeter. I found some of the things your stationary observers, had you sent them, might have gotten, though things may have changed. I was only one, of course, but a lot more mobile than your students might have been. There's life out there, all right, if that's what you want to know. People have laughed for a long time at Jalish Dozent's pink and green waves; but legends die hard. And I, for one, haven't laughed at that one for a long time." He seemed distant—dreaming—as if he longed for another time, another place. Ganser had never seen him like this. Had never heard about his search.

"Have you ever wanted to penetrate the core?" They all just stood there outside the buildings, no one making a move, as the Convener reached into Uncle Britter's knowing.

"Of course. But not anymore. You have to go young. You have to be prepared for change by the kinds of training these three have had, and you have to have a young body able to take new experiences. Yet, going there is the only way, I think, that communication can be initiated. It will cost. Exactly what I don't know. We simply have to be ready to pay." He gave the three an odd look, and Ganser felt a chill inside him, deeper than the fear he had already felt.

"Why didn't you say all this before?" the Convener asked, obviously irritated. "It might have made us think differently."

"No sense in it. You would have put too much stock, and too little, in what I said. Your plans are good. And these three can do the job, if anyone can. I'm just glad to be here to see it. I wish it were me." He was still in his abstracted mood, and Ganser wondered what more he did know.

Was knowing something more what made Uncle Britter different? The thought struck Ganser sharply. Uncle Britter was not like other people. He never had been. Had his research made him different? He had only been here on the edge. Could that have changed him? And if so, what changes would actually going into the core make? Ganser had been afraid he might die or be lost in some unknown place. But the idea that he might change, might come out a different person, had never occurred to him. Of course, as the Convener had pointed out, the school had changed him. But this seemed different, more threatening. Could he lose himself in the core and still come out a whole person? Would they all three not be themselves at all?

The idea tore him apart, opened a raw fear he wished

he could have left covered. And yet with the idea there came an unexplainable excitement, bigger than any he had ever felt before. Had Uncle Britter known this feeling long ago; did he feel it now? Looking at Uncle Britter, Ganser wasn't sure. The abstraction was still there; was he held by something no one else could yet grasp?

"Well," said the Convener abruptly, obviously deciding he would get little more from Uncle Britter, "shall we go in? And will the first trip be today or tomorrow?" He smiled at them.

Ganser looked at the others.

"Today, please," said Flu-on. "That is, if the others want that too. I don't want to wait until tomorrow."

Bilee looked at him with obvious relief, and Ganser nodded. Today for him too.

Two hours later they stood in their special core suits in the departure room, where equipment stood that was supposed to keep track of them. Although their trip could not really be completely monitored, as most trips in the galactic arms could be, there were devices of many kinds around for communication and emergency action. It was the suit, though, that was the real marvel. Ganser looked down at his—pockets for viewing equipment, a sturdy lightness all over that spoke of strength and of wave-and-force repulsion without being cumbersome. They could see and move with ease.

"You know the True Relation and the coordinates here." The Convener was making the last routine check.

The three nodded. They had memorized all that to the point of knowing it in a state beyond the deepest sleep.

"And you each know your coordinate point." They had

each been given a destination a little apart from the other two. There were sometimes difficulties when more than one person aimed at exactly the same place at the same time. Even in core space it was assumed that three bodies could not occupy the same location at the same time. Ganser muttered his number and tried to fix his mind on it.

"Then when I count four, go, all of you, and don't stay too long, if you can avoid it. Remember, we'll be waiting. Don't kill us with anxiety." The Convener was serious.

Here it comes, Ganser thought.

"One . . . two . . . three . . . four."

It worked, just as it had in practice. The three were within easy seeing distance of each other, and a few puffs of propulsion brought them together. They communicated by the finger signs they'd learned. It looked strange done by gloved hands, but it worked. Bilee, Ganser had always thought, had an unfair advantage in this. But it wasn't her fault.

They hung back to back in a circle, each surveying with a scanner in a different direction, each noting on an outside pad anything seen.

The main thing was the brightness of the sky. And the colors, Ganser decided, hastily mapping as best he could the area before him. They were in the heart of a planetary system, and one of the planets seemed especially beautiful, bathed in a soft blue-green light. He jerked himself up—a planet bathed in light? Some large planets did make their own heat. And some atmospheres had color. But not like this. He tapped Bilee and Flu-on and pointed. They turned and looked. Then Bilee pointed out a more distant planet, barely visible to the naked eye, but quite clear in the scanner. That planet was pink, and Flu-on had spotted one that seemed violet.

They had done the best they could, and it was enough for a first day. In fact, it took almost more energy than they had to get back to Worrly D.

"I never knew you were such a sleepyhead, Ganser," said his uncle. "And just to drop off like that without telling us a thing!"

Britter was joking, but his mother and father looked upset.

"Ganser, this can be called off," said his father.

"Flu-on and Bilee?" he asked.

"Still asleep, or maybe just waking," said his uncle. "Your maps and notes were just what we hoped to get."

"Ganser, are you sure you want to go on with this?" his mother asked.

"Of course," said Ganser, surprised at his own strength of feeling. "Nothing in the galaxy could keep me from going back."

It was true. He had never been so sure of anything in his life. The core didn't have the answers to all the questions he'd ever asked. No place did, not in this galaxy, anyway. But there were a lot of things he could find out in the core. He felt sure of that. His mother, he could see, knew it too. And his father. But they were not as happy about it as he. Had he changed already? He looked down and decided he looked like himself. Why were they worried? He didn't dare ask.

There were reports to make. The three made them in more detail than they had expected. They remembered every sight, every single moment of the trip. Though they had seen no real sign of life, the Convener was pleased. And even the six parents were impressed.

"Now can we go again," Flu-on pleaded. "There's more to know. We've got to get back there."

"Yes, of course," said the Convener, thoughtfully. "To-morrow. Get some more sleep. You look as if you need it, all three of you. In the meantime, I'll call for more supplies and a larger crew. We may be here a while. It may take longer than we had planned. You were right, Britter, about our not really knowing," he said.

"Then tomorrow again," said Bilee eagerly.

"Tomorrow," said the Convener.

"And who knows what then," Ganser murmured. The excitement inside him was almost more than he could contain. Yet somehow he knew he shouldn't show too much of it. Though why, he couldn't be sure.

Two more trips were made, without incident—except for unexpected bits of information they brought back. No life had been seen, but that seemed logical. All was according to plan, except for what was going on inside of them. Ganser knew something was happening there. But he found no way to speak of it, not even to Flu-on and Bilee, although he saw that they also felt it. There were no words for it. The second and third trips had taken them progressively deeper into the core. With each trip they had returned more tired, slept longer, reported as fully. They had little time to talk alone together, yet Ganser knew that for the others as well as for himself, something was drawing them in, something was fighting to hold them in core space, maybe even take them to a core planet. It was the struggle to leave that tired them so.

Still, he would die, he felt, if he could never return to the core. He was frightened when he thought about it all; yet he didn't know what to do. Even the hope of Earth had left him. All that mattered was going in and then coming out. The going-in grew larger and larger; would the demand to come out always stay as strong? Would it always be strong enough? They didn't have to go. They could explain the problem of the coming-out. But that would be worse. They had to go. There was something there in the core that was so important, so attractive, the idea of not going was unendurable. It was all so strange, so different, Ganser finally gave up thinking about it.

"Are you sure you want to make this trip so soon?" the Convener asked, the parents looking on, as the three dressed for the fourth trip.

Ganser's mind had been concentrating on the physical details of getting ready.

"I have to go," he answered automatically, knowing he did.

The adults looked upset. They obviously knew more about the problem than he had realized. They could see the change. Maybe he was beginning to look different. He didn't know.

"You know your destination?" Uncle Britter said in his usual firm, quiet voice.

The three nodded.

"Come back, come back," Ganser's mother whispered. And Ganser was flooded with love for her. She looked tense and worried. His father looked upset and drawn. So did Bilee's and Flu-on's parents.

For a moment Ganser almost spoke, almost said, "Maybe we should wait." But he didn't. He couldn't.

Bilee's fists were clenched, all four of them. Flu-on's mouth was tight.

"One . . . . . . two . . . . three . . . . four. . . ." The familiar counting, and they were off.

They were in an area much like the others they had been to, but closer to the center of the core; brighter, more dust, more gas. And much nearer to a planet than they'd been, closer than they'd planned to be, Ganser thought fleetingly. He glanced around at the other planets in the system. They were smaller than those in the arms of the galaxy, he realized, and closer to the stars they circled. Probably heavy. A strong gravity. That might be what held the three of them and had brought them in so close, a physical force, not anything more powerful than that. Yet it seemed more.

Among the planets in the system around them, the one before them was the only odd-colored one, predominantly green. Unsignaled, together, and against all plans and instructions, they moved to the planet. It happened so quickly, Ganser wondered if he had willed it. Surely he had. Yet when and why?

It was bare. Lots of rocks. He grinned through his face glass at Bilee, and she grinned back. But at the same time she looked as perplexed as he felt. What were they doing here? Why had they come?

The three stood facing each other. It was a planet of dense gravity. They could feel it pulling at them, like lift-off in one of the supply rockets still used occasionally to take large quantities of materials from one planet to another. All three wondered the same thing, Ganser saw, without needing to speak. Would they be able to lift themselves off this planet? Was it a trap of some kind? Their apprehension became almost tangible.

And then there was nothing. Ganser was aware of his existence, and no more. The emptiness came on all at once and left him helpless, mindless. It was a trap then, was his last real thought, as he felt the change come. Standing, sitting, lying down, he didn't know. He was, he existed, and no more. For how long, he didn't know.

He moved a toe, a thought came into his mind, he brought his hands to his face glass, opened his eyes and saw his gloved hands, his space scope still held tight in one of them. Moving his hands, he gave a quick glance at his surroundings. He was in the departure room, Bilee on one side of him and Flu-on on the other. They were motionless yet, or almost. Flu-on seemed to be staring at his fingers. Ganser glanced up and saw a ring of adults above them. None of them were speaking aloud, but anxiety spoke on every face.

Ganser raised his hand to his helmet, pushed at it, and Uncle Britter bent down to loosen the grippers. Of course, he couldn't hear them with the helmet on. But they hadn't been talking. Their lips hadn't moved. Yet, you didn't always have to make sounds to speak. Did you? Silly! Still a memory came into his mind. A hint of something. What was it?

"You've been gone two days," Uncle Britter was saying. "We were frantic. I even did a quick spec on your location myself, and you weren't there. Had a hard time getting back. Almost didn't make it. Then here you were like this!" He babbled on, totally unlike himself.

Relieved, Ganser thought. He's relieved, and he needs to talk. But Ganser couldn't. Not yet. He wasn't sure of the answers. He'd have to talk to Flu-on and Bilee. Together maybe they'd know what had happened.

"Not yet," he managed to murmur. "Too tired. Need to talk to Flu-on, Bilee. Got to straighten it out!" Things were flooding into his mind now, and he sat up, caught up in a new restlessness. Flu-on and Bilee were stirring too, trying to sit up, looking at him and at each other. They had to talk.

It was impossible to sleep. And they didn't even need to be alone, as long as the others were quiet. Had there been a kind of hypnotism practiced on them by some minded creature—a hypnotism with a strong post-recovery suggestion? None of the three knew. All they knew for certain was that once the remembering began, it went on and on and they had little control over it.

There were the green waves on the rocky planet. Uncle Britter nodded at that. He had learned not to laugh at Jalish Dozent's waves, Ganser remembered. And then all the information. Some minded creatures with bodies in the core. Mostly small. But most life was waves. Easier to get around. Less confining. Easier to think, though harder to do things.

Most important seemed to be the need the core felt, or at least the core as represented by the planet they had reached, for some contact with the arms of the galaxy. Not possible before. Too much conflict, too much fear, too many differences. But now, maybe, in spite of some planets

191

in both places still in earlier stages. Maybe ready now to help each other. Make a unit to discover and work with other units, other galaxies.

The ideas tumbled out one after the other. They were all there, though how or why no one of the three was sure.

"Do they represent the core government? Is there one? A council or something of the sort?" the Convener asked faintly.

Ganser sat blank, plumbing his mind.

"I think so," said Flu-on beside him, hesitantly. "But I'm not sure."

"The core center is at 84–283–60/251, and it's on a pink planet," said Bilee, unexpectedly.

"Yes," said Ganser, "it is."

"Can you go there?" asked the Convener.

"Yes." There was no question about it. Flooded with a heartening warmth and joy, he knew they could. Now. Right away.

"No, not now," said Uncle Britter. "After you calm down and get some sleep. And when you go, I'm going too."

The Convener started to shake his head, then changed his mind.

"I'd go too, if I could," he said. "Maybe someday I shall go. I hope so." He sounded wistful, longing.

They all felt it, Ganser realized, the drawing power of it. Perhaps because they all cared so much. And they were so close to the perimeter of the core. Was it good? That didn't seem to matter. What was important was that the core and its strangeness, its mysteries were there. No one would stop them now. No one could.

"If I get into trouble, don't stop for me," Uncle Britter cautioned.

"We won't know it," Flu-on murmured. "Not if it's like the last time. I hope it is," he added. "Or maybe better. Awake."

They were all three eager. Only Uncle Britter seemed apprehensive. Yet they all knew he would never decide not to go.

The Convener began to count. "One . . . two . . . three. . . ."

Ganser could not hold himself. At three he was gone, Bilee and Flu-on with him. They were at True Relation 84–283–60/251 at almost the same instant. Uncle Britter did not appear. They waited, expecting him. Then, they knew, just knew, he would not come. Too late for him, something seemed to say. But whether it was too late because he was no longer young, or too late because he had not come on the other trips, or too late because he had waited for "four," no one said.

Without a word, impelled by an idea, the three walked slowly forward. It was a heavy, pink-wave planet, as promised. Ahead were rocks, a huge circular formation of them. It looked natural. And yet it didn't. It was a ring of stone with an entrance at each of the four sides, all perfectly aligned. Yet the stone seemed to have erupted from the flat ground—to have grown there, if stones in the core could grow. Its roughness and its sheer size spoke of cliffs and canyons on any wind- or water-swept planet. Yet there was no wind or water that the three could see.

They walked boldly forward, as if they belonged, as if they knew what lay ahead. A fear caught at them, but curiosity and the sense of needing to move on were far stronger.

The walls of the stone ring rose on either side of the entranceway above them. They walked through, dwarfed, like insects coming into a human abode. The circular space within was perfect—even—and yet the rock still seemed hewn only by whatever unthinking forces might tend the planet.

The inside was not like a trap, though the entrances were small and the sides high and tight. Ganser thought of traps and dismissed the idea. It was an open place, for all of its roundness and its walls.

They stood and waited. They looked and waited. Time had no meaning. The waiting was neither long nor short. They had no desire to leave. They stood and did not tire. It was a lovely place. A place to be alive.

"Yes, to be alive."

The three looked startled, glanced at each other. The sound came again.

"To be alive. And so you are. And so you will be. Alive in a world where your time does not exist. No, not that, perhaps. You bring your time with you. As some of us did, long ago. Yet, this is where you are to be. For longer than your own time would allow. Longer than you can account for. And Earth and Groad and Xenos D will all be here, for you. For all things can be—here, and in the deeper places."

There were no words to answer. But none were needed. Ganser believed what he had heard, and that was enough. Earth was a feeling. And that feeling was here. The wildness of the sky was here—as it was on only the best days of Earth. That wildness and wonder was inside him as never before. And perhaps the rocks and the winds were here too, for the others.

"Yes," Bilee said aloud. And he and Flu-on heard in spite of their suits. Was there atmosphere here then? But that would not explain the other voice. Was there another way of speaking—maybe another way of hearing?

"This is not our central place, an entrance rather," the voice went on. "But all will come in time." A pink wave formed out of the nothingness before them, grew deeper, grew smaller, almost their size. "First, however, we must plan. You are our first. The first of the new order. And it will always be so. There was another, once long ago, when some of us ventured out foolishly. That was too soon. And a few others on the periphery. And of course there are those here whose sources lay in the outside. But theirs was a different coming. Now, if time is important, and that is questionable, the moment is now for what is to be. And you are chosen."

Ganser felt confused. His mind was his own, and he remembered that this had been his idea. How then had he been chosen? He was bothered only a minute. Better not to wonder. Just listen.

The pink wave led, and they followed—through the rock ring—through the ring! And then they were in another place. And the ring was nowhere. It was a dream. Ganser was sure it was a dream.

Yet, much later he knew it was not. Hours had gone by —or among those who had no time, or no time that could be explained—was it hours? There were minded creatures in the core. Some with bodies, some only waves, as they had learned before. Not all were advanced; this they had known too. But as in the galaxy's arms, many were striving

195

for—they didn't know what—a goal ahead. And unity within the galaxy seemed the next thing to accomplish. Yet life within the core was different. More different even than life from planet to planet in the arms. Some advanced races from the outer galaxy had come here long before. Yet not all could bridge the gap over the periphery. Not all on either side. But some could. They, the three of them, could.

"We would not have imagined three," one of the waves said."One of three perhaps, but all . . . you are amazing."

"No, only lucky," said Flu-on.

"It is more—much more," said another wave. "It is training, learning, and a nature that accepts the new. It is we who are lucky. You are among those few who can go beyond the immediate. For that we are more than grateful."

"And together we will unite the galaxy," said a new wave that swept into the center of the open—yet clearly defined—space where they all stood.

"But we are children." Ganser was overwhelmed at the prospect laid out for them.

"You are no longer children. And will not be again. You are with us, a part of us. And though we multiply, slowly, we have no children, not as you know them. You will be listened to. You will go back. And you will be heard. Then you will come to us. And together, arms and core will be one. Come with me. There is much to be done."

Once again Ganser woke on the floor of the departure room. Flu-on on one side, Bilee on the other. All three sat up. No one was there. Strange! They stood, shook them-

196

selves, and looked. They were the same. Yet not the same. With clumsy space-glove-covered hands they helped each other unsuit. In their underclothes they were, again, the same and not the same.

"You kind of glow," said Flu-on.

"You too," said Bilee.

"To us, or to others as well?" Ganser asked.

They stepped to the door, found it open, and walked into a night. But what night?

"Three days, I think," said Flu-on.

"Yes," said Bilee. "Three days."

"Whose days? Oh, Worrly D. Yes, three here," said Ganser.

"It's different, isn't it?" said Bilee. "I didn't know a place could seem so different, without really changing. Or that we could be so different."

"We have a job," said Flu-on. "Then we've got to go. Do you think we need those suits next time?"

"No," said Ganser, sure. "It will be better without." He yearned for the moment of return. They would do their job and then go back.

The others were asleep, worn out with watching and waiting. But they woke up when the three approached. Uncle Britter had come home, spent and upset. There was no 84–283–60/251, not where he had gone. After that they had watched and waited, then slept.

None of the adults needed convincing, strangely enough, when the three said what had to be said. It was because they were different, more different by far than they had been before, they realized. The changes were greater, more obvious to others, than to themselves.

"There may be others someday," said Ganser, comforting all those who would stay behind on Worrly D when the three of them left again. He felt they sensed a deep loss—the thought that none of them might ever know what the three had learned. "We are only the first. The work has only begun. Listen."

The plans were laid, the discussions held, the communications planned, so those who could not cross the border would not need to. There could be a sharing of minds and ideas and wonders across the barriers—across the gap. The three made it all as clear as they could. But some ideas were never meant for words. It was hard. Words were so puny. Why had they never known that before? Or at least not known it so thoroughly.

"We will fill the gap," said the Convener. "There will be no gap eventually."

"No, that may not be," said Ganser. "There is a gap. We can't ignore it. It may always be there—at least a little. We have crossed the gap, we three, and we have not wholly returned, nor can we ever. It would be no good if everyone went. We must be side by side, not together, for we all have something to give, something we must not lose. They must absorb something of what we are. And we of what they are. But we must not all become wholly alike. Some of them may cross this way. The gap will slowly be bridged. But a bridge is enough. Uncle Britter, they send regrets. They said you'd understand, when you thought it through."

Uncle Britter smiled wryly and nodded. "I came too early—and too late."

The talks went on for five days. Others were called to

join. The three seemed to have no need for sleep, and those that did worked with the three in relays. At the end of the five days, the three were impatient. Yet they went on to the last of what they had to do. And finally it was over. They were free to go. And by going, the chain would be drawn tight—a beginning would truly be made.

They left from the departure room, and everyone in the room smiled. It was the right thing. The chances were that the three would never return, could never return. They would never see Earth or Groad or Xenos D again; yet all three planets and much more would exist for them. They would be in the core, where there was work to do, and things to know, and joys to be experienced.

Where there might come the beginning of a great understanding, of a great galactic unity.

Out for the Flicker Path

Why am I writing this? Maybe so some sneaky archaeologist of the future can know the truth about today. Or maybe, just maybe, so I can find a sensible explanation for what we saw. After all it couldn't have happened, could it?

And why am I plunked down in this ridiculous isolation chamber? Its technical name, the one they like us to use, is dry carrel, but it really is an isolation chamber. Well, I didn't choose it. And I've got to sit in this dirt-down hole reading this crawly book for another twenty minutes. And Chip isn't even looking at me—maybe not even speaking to me! *Your Stars Tonight!* Dut!

Don't get me wrong. I'm not really excited. Just hysterical, that's all. And I don't believe any of it. But Chip was there too. At least I think he was. And I think he thinks he saw what I think I saw. It's all very confusing.

You see, we were on our own again last night. His folks were out, and mine were busy with some drools from the Chamber Society. There was another one of those stupid brown-outs, just as we left my house. So the movies were out, even in that new all laser-beam place.

"Let's lift off to the park," Chip said.

"The park," I said. "In all this dark!"

"Sure," he said, and he grinned. "We'll really be able to see the Flicker Path tonight."

"The Flicker Path," I said. "Are you blued out? Since when have you taken up with the stars?"

He looked kind of sheepish and grinned again, and then I decided maybe he really had. And I thought I knew all about Chip. Sometimes you get surprised.

"Oh, come on," he said. "What else is there to do?"

So we went to the park. And he was right. The Flicker Path looked good. Like a solid thing, hanging there. All those stars. You don't see them much in the city. You forget how big the Flicker Path is. I liked it. They say someday there may be things that go out into space, right off beyond gravity, and from there the stars will be even clearer. I don't believe all that, though. At least I didn't last night.

We hunkered down on the ground and sort of stretched out and looked up. I could even see the Jar. It was as clear as anything, curving around the Great West Star.

"Creag," I said finally. "I never saw it like this before."

Chip was quiet. But I felt a tap on my shoulder. "Hey," I said, "we didn't come here for that. To see the Flicker Path, you said."

"I beg your pardon," said a voice. Well, sort of a voice. High and soft. I jumped. That wasn't Chip. It wasn't Chip by a whistle. "I beg your pardon," the sound said, like some soft loudspeaker.

"Chip," I said. "Chip?" I was scared.

"Yah," he said, and his voice was there too, but kind of brittle and hollow. The park isn't all that safe at night. We weren't supposed to be there.

"Please, you two," said the high voice again.

Chip and I were on our feet like a bolt, ready to run. And then we saw it. Or I guess we saw him. Actually there were two sorts of hims—or hers. But they weren't really. I don't know what they were. Big heads and not much more.

It was enough to make you shrivel.

"I think I need to go home and read a book for tomorrow," I squeaked.

Chip muttered, "What you kids think you're doing? You think it's Waste Weather Night or something?"

"Listen, you two," said another voice, a deeper one this time. Kind of heavy and *ruh! ruh! ruh!* We both stopped. It was the kind of voice you stop for. And we listened.

"We're visitors," the deep voice said. "We have no desire to be known here or to meet any other of your people. But we wanted to talk to someone at your stage of development in your galactic system."

Chip was feeling a little more tied together by then. They weren't very big, those two. Mostly head. "Don't put us on," he croaked. "Our galactic system! Huh!"

The first one, the higher voice, said, "Just tell us a few things. That's all we want. There are a few things we need to know. Your language we have absorbed through observation. But there are some things we can't discover that way. For example, what do you on this planet call this system?"

"What do you mean, this system?" I said, even dumber than I usually am.

"This galaxy?"

"The Flicker Path?" I said, sure now that these whispos had escaped from some wild place.

"The Flicker Path. That sounds right. Roughly comparable to the Milky Way, an old local term for our galaxy." He turned to the other and nodded. "Tell me," he went on, turning back to me again, "a little more about yourself. Your school. What is it like? Grammar, history, math, science? Or do you also have a little mind direction and space equation?"

I looked at those two again. If there hadn't been something in those voices, I would have called the gops for sure. I'm not all that much for gops, but sometimes they give you a feeling of confidence. Instead I found myself answering.

"Look," I said, "I don't know what you're after. And I sure don't know anything about mind direction and space equation. But if you're taking a public opinion poll on public education, I can tell you plenty." And then I really gave it to them. Dumb teachers. Stupid textbooks. Ridiculous parents. Useless subjects. And all for what? To stay on the same old treadmill, as far as I could see. Most of the other kids thought so too.

That opened Chip up, of course. He's hung up on world problems and how we ought to save people. He's fed up with the mess we've got here. That, and bullet-ball cars are his crates. Sometimes I think he's two people—the bullet-ball half and the world-problems half, with not much left over for anything else, including me.

Those two whispos listened, and sometimes they said a word or two to each other. But I got the feeling they didn't always have to say everything out loud to each other. Isn't that a funny idea? I don't really believe it. I couldn't see their ears, though.

Chip went on and on until he'd run down his whole clutch. Then, without really meaning to, we began to ask them questions, Chip and I. Sometimes the answers didn't make much sense. You can't tell me a star can have nine planets. Four is enough. And once when Chip asked them how they got to the park, they looked down and we looked down, and we felt as if we were all ten feet off the ground. Chip and I just looked at each other and then we began to sort of squirm, and suddenly we were on the ground again. I could have sworn I heard a giggle out of those two. You can't trust grown-ups, if that's what they were, even though they were so small and so sort of all head.

Well, we talked a little more. We were kind of having fun, Chip and I. It was so ridiculous, it was a crash, except for that up-in-the-air business. But then Chip said, "Now stop pulling us out. Where are you guys from? And what are you doing here?"

"Look," said deep voice, "look up there. It's very dark tonight, thanks to your brown-out. Your usual smog even seems to have settled down. Now look. Right there, down from your Great West Star and to the left of the Jar, do you see that fuzzy speck?"

I looked hard, and all at once I saw it. Chip did too, but he wouldn't admit it.

"That's our galaxy, the one I said was once called the Milky Way. It's about two million light-years away. You can't see our planet, of course, or even our star. But there's no need to. They're much like yours. Or once were."

"Now tell us another," said Chip. "Two million light-years. You'd have to spend that much time getting here, and you can't be anywhere near that age. Not even one million." Chip thought he had them there.

"No, we left home two years ago, and we've been exploring around here ever since," said high voice. "We . . . well . . . it's longer than that on Earth, where we come from. But not all that long. There are ways. . . ." The words stopped as if high voice thought we were too dumb to understand what he was trying to tell us.

"Never mind!" I said, using my best sarcastic tone. "We wouldn't understand, I'm sure."

"No, you wouldn't, you're right. But what I can't understand," deep voice said, "is how you can be so like us—like us as we were in time before our time really began. As we were in some of our oldest records. You're almost the same, in all kinds of ways. We have a few planets left in the system that retain some of these old ways. But very few. Some newly evolving ones, of course, that may produce something." He spoke almost to himself.

"Now that's enough!" Chip said. "If you're so far beyond us—then what should we do with all our problems? I told you what they are. Then how should we solve them? You ought to know."

"Don't be in too much of a hurry," said deep voice. "There are always problems. They change. Patterns change. And sometimes things get worse, sometimes better. But no matter what happens, problems remain."

"Yah! You just don't know the answer," said Chip. "You think you know a lot, and you don't."

"We think nothing of the sort," said high voice. "We

see some patterns you don't see, that's all. But patterns are surprising. They don't follow as you might expect. Learn everything and then jump to the unexpected, that's about all we can tell you."

"Yah, yah," I said, suddenly tired of the whole thing. "Listen, I have to go home. And if you guys have a place to go, maybe you'd better go there too."

"I guess you're right," said high voice, with a sigh.

And all of a sudden they weren't there. They just weren't there!

Well, Chip and I started to run then. We didn't say anything, we just ran. We ran until we fell up the steps at my place. Then we caught our breaths. And Chip left, almost right away, without saying anything. I went in and all at once it hit me. What had we done? What had happened to us? And who would ever believe us?

Today I headed, first chance I got, for the library. I wanted a book on galaxies. But I was a minute too late. Chip was there first, reaching for the only decent book in the place. We both grabbed the thing. And he yelled at me. And I yelled at him. We nearly pulled the ramming book apart. And that's when the librarian came.

"What's your problem?" she said, sweet and sour at the same time.

We both began at once. And then we both shut up. Who would believe us? We couldn't explain at all. Not to a grown-up. Maybe not even to a kid. Most kids aren't much for space.

"This is quite a technical book," the librarian said, taking it away. We both knew it. It was the only one that held any chance of helping us. "Here are some that may be of more interest to you. Why don't you each take one and come with me?"

So here I am in this dumb isolation booth, reading *Your Stars Tonight.* And there's Chip reading *Briley Sees Stars.* And what we both want to know is: Is there a galaxy called the Milky Way—or once long ago called the Milky Way? (But how would anyone know that?) Or, is there a galaxy about two million light-years away where they know a lot we don't? But then, no one here knows that either, but us. Or do other people know, and we just don't know it? It's all so confusing. And *Your Stars Tonight* is no help. At this rate I may never have any answers. And maybe I really don't want any.

It's kind of scary, either way. If they were from here . . . or somewhere else. It's not really about that Milky Way I want to know. (And by the way, isn't that a silly name for a whole galaxy? The Flicker Path is much better. Maybe we're smarter than they were.) What I want, I guess, is a book about the jumping. Learn everything and jump to the unexpected. I wish books were different like that. Sort of leaping out in whammy directions. I wonder if we really were ten feet up in the air last night, Chip and I? Do you think we could learn to do that for ourselves? Do you think those whispos will ever come back? Chip and I may go to see. We may go to the park tonight. I think maybe we have to go, even if no one ever comes again.

Some Notes on Sources

The Turning Place

Very little is known of exactly what did happen on the day of the Clordian Sweep. Clordian records do not reveal what the deadly rays projected from several spaceships, carefully concealed, consisted of. The result, however, was a rapid disintegration of all carbon compounds, which destroyed all life, since all living things on Earth have a carbon base. Clusters of people in places untouched by the rays did live—some of them in underground complexes, others in areas where natural configurations of land blocked the rays, and still others, perhaps, in the centers of the initial fields, where they were not touched. There are no known written records of the event as seen from Earth, but there is an oral tradition that carries some survivor stories.

Over the Hill

Just as some people were preserved after the Clordian Sweep, the fertility of some land remained. Actually the rays did not poison the ground. They simply killed the life in it, sterilized it, so that it became hard and unproductive. Only when bacteria, earthworms, and other organic matter had once more invaded the barren places, could they become productive. People lived on the small plots of productive land. They did not reproduce quickly, both because food was limited and because, scientists now know, certain physical changes in body chemistry limited their reproductive ability. Again, our knowledge of this period is based largely on oral tradition.

Enough

When land became more plentiful, the population did increase more quickly, mostly because people were able to live in larger communities and mating was easier. However, communities did not grow too large. A fear, perhaps left from the time of the Clordian Sweep, prevented this. In the new communities there was greater leisure, and eventually some of the more venturesome people began to investigate what were clearly remains of large towns and cities. A small group of people grew quite excited about what might be learned from these areas and banded together as the Pre-Clordian Sweep Scientific Recovery Group. They were able to produce an amazing number of technological improvements over a very short time. Velta Akhbar of this story was a real person, and she did invent the first land transportation system—a kind of hovercraft railroad. No tracks were needed, but long trains of cars were floated over varying terrains. Little is known of her life, but records do reveal the general tenor of existence at the time.

Accord

This story is based on fact. The Sorchum family were the first ambassadors from Earth to Clord and did in fact reveal the new nature of Earth people to the Clordian government, in much the way this story is told. Casselia Sorchum is a heroine still, though to most young people she is more myth than reality.

Catabilid Conquest

At the time this story represents, the people of Earth had entered one of their rare, stagnant, self-satisfied epochs. Though the underlying unity of Earth people was by this time clearly established, largely through the development of the sequestering system, which by this time had passed its period of greatest usefulness, the sense of gathering in all, and cherishing all for the breadth of understanding to be garnered, had not yet been completely understood. Therefore, those who were different stood outside. Since Earth was an inward-, rather than an outward-directed planet, those who went to other planets, and even their children, were often outside the mainstream of Earth life. The twins of this story are fiction, but they represent a small group who brought needed changes to Earth. The early movements toward self-space-placement did come from other planets. There is a planet named Cheriba, which was once called Frod. And there was some research done on that planet at about the time this story is set. The Catabilids do exist, although few of the other inhabitants of the galaxy have ever seen them. Catabilids do not leave Cheriba, and Cheriba is now off limits to travelers of any sort, except in great emergencies.

Quiet and a White Bush

The true mechanics of a self-space-placement are, as far as the outer galaxy is concerned, a contribution of Earth. It developed in several areas of the planet almost simultaneously. This story is fiction, but it comes close to some of the true stories that are told of this time. Records for this period are, of course, very complete, so research into these developments is not difficult. Planets like the white planet are known, although they are not common. Few intelligent species have no capacity to move.

The Talkaround

Jalish Dozent still receives less honor than he should. His discoveries changed life throughout the galaxy. His life is well documented and there have been several significant biographical studies. But few people credit him for as much as he did.

A Central Question

The events of this story are too recent not to be known to most of the readers of this book. The story is, of course, based on what did occur. The three young people who moved into the core of the galaxy were not seen again, but they did communicate with relatives and with officials in the outer galaxy on a regular basis. With their help, the galactic government was instituted.

Out for the Flicker Path

As we reach out to our neighboring galaxies, we of course do a great deal of research that does not involve contact with individuals on specific planets. Sometimes, however, it seems necessary to check certain hypotheses by actually visiting a planet. When this is done, planets at every state of development are reached. Earth people on these missions sometimes find themselves confronting people and situations that only a course in pre-Clordian Sweep archaeology can help them understand. This story is not based on an actual occurrence, but might certainly be true, given the information contained in some research reports.

86 89 90 91 92 <del>93</del> <del>82</del> 81 +7710

88 SC   Karl, Jean E
    Kar
         The turning place

MY 1

                              7710

    SC   Karl, Jean E
    Kar   7.95
            The turning place

93

ADVANCES IN
LEARNING AND
BEHAVIORAL DISABILITIES

Supplement 2 • 1987

MEMORY AND LEARNING DISABILITIES

ADVANCES IN
LEARNING AND
BEHAVIORAL DISABILITIES

A Research Annual

MEMORY AND LEARNING DISABILITIES

Editor: H. LEE SWANSON
Educational Psychology
University of Northern Colorado

SUPPLEMENT 2 • 1987

 JAI PRESS INC.

Greenwich, Connecticut   *London, England*

ISBN: 0-89232-836-3

Manufactured in the United States of America

CONTENTS

LIST OF CONTRIBUTORS

Jacqueline G. Baker

Department of Human Development
    and Family Studies
Cornell University

Richard H. Bauer

Department of Psychology
Middle Tenessee State University

Sara M. Bowen

Department of Educational
    Psychology
University of Georgia

Stephen J. Ceci

Department of Human Development
    and Family Studies
Cornell University

Laird S. Cermak

Research Career Scientist
Veterans Administration Medical
    Center
Boston

John B. Cooney

Department of Educational
    Psychology
University of Northern Colorado

Lynn M. Gelzheiser

Department of Educational
    Psychology and Statistics
State University of New York
Albany

Jonathan Greenstein

Department of Psychology
Florida State University

John W. Hagen

Center for Human Growth and
     Development
University of Michigan

Doug Herrmann

Department of Psychology
University of Manchester
England

James W. Hall

Department of Psychology
Northwestern University

Michael S. Humprheys

Department of Psychology
University of Queensland

Griffith Houck

Department of Psychology
Florida State University

George W. Hynd

Department of Educational
     Psychology
University of Georgia

Eric D. Laywell

Center for Human Growth and
     Development
University of Michigan

Joel R. Levin

Department of Educational
     Psychology
University of Wisconsin

Isabelle Y. Liberman

Haskins Laboratories
New Haven, Connecticut

Margo A. Mastropieri

Department of Education
Purdue University

Patti R. Miliotis

Research Speech Pathologist
Veterans Administration Medical
     Center
Boston

John E. Obzrut

Department of Educational
     Psychology
University of Arizona

Carol A. Rashotte   Department of Psychology
                             Florida State University

David A. Saarnio   Center for Human Growth and
                                 Development
                             University of Michigan

Margaret Jo Shepherd   Department of Special Education
                             Teachers College
                             Columbia University

Thomas E. Scruggs   Department of Education
                             Purdue University

Donald Shankweiler   Haskins Laboratories
                             New Haven, Connecticut

H. Lee Swanson   Department of Educational
                                 Psychology
                             University of Northern Colorado

Margaret B. Tinzmann   National College of Education

Joseph K. Torgesen   Department of Psychology
                             Florida State University

Bernice Y. L. Wong   Faculty of Education
                             Simon Fraser University

PREFACE

The primary objective of this Supplement to *Advances in Learning and Behavioral Disability* is to stimulate research towards a more comprehensive understanding of learning disabled (LD) children's memory development and to provide direction for the application of research findings in the assessment and treatment of memory difficulties experienced by such children. This is the first book of its kind, and Dr. Swanson has done an excellent job of bringing together experimental psychologists currently active in research on memory to formulate a truly instructive and thought provoking text. The contributors discuss some of the most promising areas for advancing our understanding of memory processes and structures as they relate to learning disabilities.

The orientation of this Supplement relies somewhat on the basic assumptions of the information process model, which is in many respects the *sine qua non* of the field (see Swanson, 1982, 1987). The central assumption of this model is that a number of elementary operations or processing stages occur between a stimulus and a response. Stimulus presentation initiates a sequence of processing stages, and each stage operates on information available to it. The response (output) of each processing stage provides "transformed" information, which is the input to the succeeding stage. Typically, two theoretical components are postulated in information processing analysis: dynamic components that perform specific operations (e.g., strategies) and structural components that define or describe the nature of information at a particular processing stage.

One criticism of the field of learning disabilities is that relatively few principles have emerged from the myriad of published distinctions made between LD and nonLD children. A possible solution to this problem is the construction of complex models that capture a wide range of deficient abilities in LD children. Such an approach, however, provides very little in terms of what information is relevant or irrelevant to children's functioning. An alternative perspective (one explored in this Supplement) is that LD children's performance is related to fundamental information processing operations and that the identification of such operations could provide a basis for the study of (a) individual differences between and within ability groups, and (b) changes as a result of learning and instruction and, most importantly, (c) the division of LD deficiencies into reasonable sets of mental operations. In addition, an analysis of information processing components may be useful in discovering the neurophysiological bases of learning disabilities that are implicit in many of its definitions.

This Supplement will be of special interest to researchers in the field of learning disabilities, particularly those seeking to identify new and fruitful areas of research, or to examine the parallels between their own efforts and contemporary thinking. Professionals who are challenged by the task of applying current research findings and "thoughts" to the diagnosis and treatment of LD children will also find this volume to be a storehouse of exciting possibilities.

The introductory paper in the series is by Cooney and Swanson, and they present an overview of research on memory and learning disabilities. Each of the contributions is discussed with regard to the major theories and empirical issues in this area, and they make an excellent case for the potential benefits of continued investigation of the cognitive aspects of learning disability. The reader is cautioned, however, that each contribution represents a particular bias in research and orientation, and that we are a long way from reaching a consensus of opinion on the role of memory in the etiology of learning disabilities. There are, nevertheless, at least a few common underlying themes, which does suggest that some progress is being made toward an understanding of this socially important group of disorders.

REFERENCES

Swanson, H. L. (1982). In the beginning was a strategy: Or was it a constraint? *Topics in Learning and Learning Disabilities, 2,* 10–14.
Swanson, H. L. (1987). Information processing theory and learning disabilities: An overview. *Journal of Learning Disabilities, 20,* 3–7.

K.D. Gadow
Series Editor

MEMORY AND LEARNING DISABILITIES:

AN OVERVIEW

John B. Cooney and H. Lee Swanson

ABSTRACT

In this chapter, an overview and critical evaluation of memory research with learning disabled (LD) populations is presented. The historical antecedents of memory research with the learning disabled are traced to the work of Kussmaul in 1877, and contemporary research related to attention; encoding, storage, and retrieval processes; and memory development are reviewed. The three central themes of this chapter focus on the contributions of LD-based research to the understanding of memory, sources of ability differences, and future directions for the field. It was concluded that over the past decade LD-based research has contributed to the mainstream of memory research and our understanding of the sources of ability differences.

Memory and Learning Disabilities
Advances in Learning and Behavioral Disabilities, Suppl. 2, pages 1–40.
Copyright © 1987 by JAI Press Inc.
All rights of reproduction in any form reserved.
ISBN: 0-89232-836-3

These advances can be attributed to researchers' tacit adherence to the theoretical infrastructure of human information processing models of memory. However, research in the field remains characteristic of a discipline in the very earliest stage of scientific development. Continued progress in the field is viewed as being dependent on the development of and adherence to a scientific paradigm.

Recommendations for the development of a paradigm, described in the final section of the chapter, include: greater percision in the description of subject characteristics, greater detail in the analysis of behavior and more precise measurements, longitudinal studies of memory development and cognitive skill acquisition, greater theoretical precision, the study of memory in context, and research designed to evaluate the utility competing theoretical models of memory.

During the past few years, the study of learning disabled (LD) children's memory has become a cornerstone of research in the field. The increase in the volume of memory research with LD students has been fueled by advances in cognitive science, implications of memory research for educational intervention, and the search for a theoretical framework that would "tie" the fragmented field together. This fragmentation will be discussed later in this chapter, but suffice to say that the field of learning disabilities is still contending with such basic questions as: "What is the nature of learning disabilities?" and "What should research in learning disabilities entail?" (e.g., Farnham-Diggry, 1978; Kavale & Forness, 1985b; Keogh, 1982). Unfortunately, for the psychologist interested in memory and individual differences, research in the field of learning disabilities has not provided much insight into memory processes. In part, the reason for the poor interaction between the two fields of learning disabilities research and memory research is that, as suggested by Humphreys, Lynch, Revelle and Hall (1983), "enormous conceptual and methodological problems characterize the body of research in learning disabilities and it has yielded little (if any) reliable information for psychology" (p. 56). In a similar vein, Pressley, Heisel, McCormick and Nakamura (1982) stated:

> an inspection of the learning disabilities literature on memory gives the impression that much of the research has been generated out of a *shotgun* approach rather than a carefully planned body of research guided by either practical or theoretical concerns. This state of affairs is understandable given the immensity of the task of evolving a reasonable set of hypotheses for such a diverse population. Nonetheless, it is still disturbing that there is little research on anything except rehearsal in list learning." (p. 139)

Thus to date, active communication between the two fields has been minimal, and when such communication has occurred, it usually has taken the form of clinical facts about learning abilities or that such children's performance may be viewed as an extension of mentally retarded children's memory performance (e.g., see Campione, Brown, & Ferrara, 1983).

There are, however, some indications that researchers are beginning to address some of the more general issues in the field of memory through the study of memory processes in LD children. One indication is the appearance of articles in developmental, experimental and neuropsychological journals that address the timely issues related to learning and memory. These articles suggest that insights into memory can be obtained by studying LD children. For example, studies appearing in *Child Development, Developmental Psychology,* and the *Journal of Educational Psychology* have identified links between memory development and learning disabilities (e.g., Gelzheiser, 1984; Howe, Brainerd, & Kingma, 1985; Obrzut, Hynd, Obrzut, & Pirozzola, 1981; Swanson, 1977a; Torgesen & Goldman, 1977; Vellutino, Smith, Steger, & Kamin, 1975b). Research published in the *Journal of Experimental Child Psychology* and the *Journal of Experimental Psychology: Learning, Memory, and Cognition* link learning disabilities to verbal coding theory (e.g., Bauer, 1977a, 1979a; Ceci, Lea, & Ringstrom, 1980; Shankweiler, Liberman, Mark, Fowler, & Fischer, 1979; Vellutino & Scanlon, 1985), while articles published in *Brain and Language* and *Neuropsychologia* have established links between learning disabilities and hemispheric time-sharing (e.g., Obrzut, Hynd, Obrzut, & Leitgeb, 1980; also see Denckla & Rudel, 1976). Furthermore, the appearance of theoretical and methodological frameworks, such as ones by Barclay and Hagen (1982), Jorm (1983), Cermak (1983), Shankweiler et al. (1979), and Hall, Tinzmann, and Humphreys (this volume) have provided the basis for integrating the insights of experimental and/ or developmental psychology with the memory functioning of the learning disabled.

Another indication of increased communication is that memory research in learning disabilities has become embedded in contemporary models of child development (e.g., Bauer, 1977a,b; Hagen, Saarnio, & Laywell, this volume; Liberman & Shankweiler, this volume; Jorm, 1979; Siegel & Linder, 1984; Torgesen, 1977; Wong, this volume). It should be noted, however, that LD researchers are not necessarily in agreement about which developmental model best captures memory performance. Researchers, especially contributors to this volume, are however in agreement that what we know about LD children's memory is somewhat paralleled by what we know about the differences between older and younger children's memory (e.g., Ceci, 1984; Torgesen, 1977; Wong, this volume). That is, LD children's memory performance, in most cases, has been likened to younger children's memory performance. Thus, it is important to review some parallels between LD children's memory performance and research on the development of nondisabled (NLD) children's memory.

PARALLELS TO MEMORY DEVELOPMENT

The parallels between LD memory research and age-related research is apparent in, (a) the distinctions made between automatic and effortful processing, (b) the focus on effortful processing or cognitive strategies (such as rehearsal and organization), (c) the development of a knowledge-base, and (d) children's awareness of their own memory processes (meta-cognition). We briefly review each of these parallels. A large body of research suggests that remembering becomes easier with age because mental operations become more automatic through repeated use (e.g., Case, Kurland, & Goldberg, 1982; Chase & Ericsson, 1981; Craik, 1977; Craik & Simon, 1980; Dempster, 1985; Hasher & Zacks, 1979). Research in memory suggests, however, that a distinction can be made between the development of memory processes that are dependent upon overt conscious "effort" and those that are not (e.g., Hasher & Zacks, 1979). Memory that results only after some conscious intent to remember is said to be effortful; that which occurs *without* intent or effort is considered to be automatic (e.g., Hasher & Zacks, 1979; Shiffrin & Schneider, 1977). Effortful memory is assumed to be dependent upon the development of an available store of "cognitive resources." Thus, differences in memory performance between ability groups (LD vs. NLD) and children of various ages are presumed to be dependent upon effortful memory since individual differences exist in the amount of cognitive resources available (e.g., Dempster, 1981; Friedrich, 1974; Geiselman, Woodward, & Beatty, 1982; Guttentag, 1984; Swanson, 1984a). In contrast, automatic memory is considered to be independent of these types of processing limitations, and thus some theorists (e.g., Ceci, 1983, 1984) suggest that there should minimal ability group differences across age in the efficiency of automatic memory processes. The empirical evidence for this effortful-automatic distinction is emerging with respect to the presence or absence of individual differences across ages in measures of memory functioning (e.g., Dempster, 1985; see Samuels, in press; Spear & Sternberg, 1986; Worden, 1986).

To date, the research on LD children's memory directly parallels memory development in the area of effortful processing. For example, it has been shown that NLD children below the age of 9 years and LD children perform quite poorly relative to older children or age-related counterparts, respectively, on tasks such as free recall. Older children and NLD age-related counterparts have been found to utilize deliberate mnemonic strategies to remember information (e.g., see Cohen, 1978, 1981; Dawson, Hallahan, Reeves, & Ball, 1980; Hallahan & Reeves, 1980; Koorlan & Wolking, 1982; Tarver, Hallahan, Kauffman, & Ball, 1976; Torgesen, 1977; Wong, 1978, for a review). An excellent example of research on mnemonic strategies is provided in a series of studies conducted by Bauer (1979a) involving the primacy effect in free recall. LD and NLD children were asked to perform a free-recall task in which children were required to recall as many words as possible from lists of monosyllabic nouns. Recall for each serial position showed that LD children were deficient in the recall of items early in the list (primacy). Primacy performance has traditionally been associated with rehearsal (Ornstein & Naus, 1978, 1983), as well as elaborative encoding (e.g., Bauer & Emhert, 1984). In contrast to research on primacy performance, studies which examined the recency effect note that LD are not unlike NLD youngsters, and that younger and older children are comparable in performance (e.g., Bauer, 1977a; Swanson, 1977a; Tarver et al., 1976; however see Cohen, Netley, & Clarke, 1984). It is assumed that recall of the most recent items presented represents the encoding of information in an automatic fashion (i.e., without the benefit of using deliberate mnemonic strategies). Thus, the trend found with free recall tasks suggested that ability group and age-related differences tend to be limited to items that occur at the beginning and middle serial position and thus reflect control processing deficits, such as rehearsal.

In addition to the ability group and age-related differences in the use of rehearsal, differences in the use of organizational strategies have been investigated. Ability group and age-related differences (e.g., see Ornstein & Corsale, 1979; Shepard & Gelzheiser, this volume; Torgesen, 1978, for a review) have suggested that LD and younger children are less likely to organize or take advantage of the organizational structure of items. Intervention strategies (i.e., directing children to sort or cluster items prior to recall) have in many cases lessened or eliminated ability group differences (e.g., Dallego & Moely, 1980; Torgesen, Murphy, & Ivey, 1979; Wong, Wong, & Foth, 1977). Although LD and younger children tend to make less use of semantic relationships inherent in the free recall material, when organizational instructions are provided, both LD and younger children are capable of using a semantic organizational strategy with some degree of effectiveness (e.g., Dallego & Moely, 1980; Worden, 1983).

Another important parallel between LD research and NLD memory development is the focus on children's knowledge about the world (e.g., Baker, Ceci, & Herrmann, this volume; Bjorklund, 1985; Chi, 1978, 1981; Chi & Koeske, 1983; Naus & Ornstein, 1983; Ornstein & Corsale, 1979). For example, familiarity with words, objects, and events permits subjects to integrate new information into established cognitive structures (e.g., see Bjorklund, 1985, for a review). One of the ways in which a knowledge base may affect memory performance is through its influence on the efficiency of mental operations performed upon the to-be-memorized items. Several authors (Chi, 1981; Ornstein & Naus, 1983; Swanson, in press) have suggested that an individual's knowledge base may mediate, in some situations, strategy use. That is, organizational and rehearsal strategies may be executed more spontaneously and efficiently contingent on an individual's knowledge base. Indirect support for this view was provided by Torgesen and Houck (1980). LD students with severe short-term memory (STM) problems, LD youngsters with normal STM, and normal children were compared for their recall of material scaled for familiarity. Their results indicate that children who learn normally and LD children who do not have STM problems gained an advantage in recall as their familiarity with the items increased. That is, recall differences were reduced with less familiar material. This finding suggests that an individual's knowledge base (i.e., an individual's familiarity with material) influences the development or utilization of memory processes.

Another important link between LD memory research and age-related research is the focus on children's *thinking* about cognitive strategies and executive functions. Ann Brown (1975) summarized this development as "knowing how to know" and "knowing about knowing." Developmental improvement in remembering and the advantage accrued by nondisabled children is associated with the use of strategies in rehearsal, organization and elaboration to facilitate encoding and retrieval (e.g., Hagen, Jongeward, & Kail, 1975). Recent research (e.g., see Forrest, Pressley, & Gillies, 1983; Pressley, Borkowski, & O'Sullivan, 1984; Pressley & Levin, 1986; Wong, 1979) has focused on how and to what degree is the effective use of effortful processes (such as cognitive strategies) relates to metacognition. Metacognition refers to knowledge of general cognitive strategies (e.g., rehearsal); awareness of one's own cognitive processes along with monitoring, evaluating and regulating those processes; and beliefs about factors that affect cognitive activities (e.g., Brown, 1978; Brown & Campione, 1981; Brown & Palinscar, 1982; Flavell, 1976, 1979). Differences in metacognition have been proposed as one source of individual differences in intelligence (e.g., Borkowski & Cavanaugh, 1981). Comparisons of various groups of children (e.g., normal, mentally retarded, disabled) have revealed substantial differences in metacognitive knowledge, at least about memory and the memorial processes (see Campione, Brown, & Ferrara, 1982, for a review). At present, what we know from the literature is that children between 4 and 12 years of age become progressively more aware of the person, task, and strategy variables that influence remembering (e.g., Borkowski & Cavanaugh, 1981; Cavanaugh & Perlmuter, 1982; Pressley et al., 1984; Rabinowitz, Ackerman, Craik, & Hinchley, 1982). For example, Wong (1982) compared learning disabled, normal achieving, and gifted children in their recall of prose under cue retrieval conditions. Her results indicated that when compared to the NLD and gifted children, LD children lacked self-checking skills, and they were less exhaustive in their selective search of retrieval cues. These results suggest that LD children were less aware of efficient strategies related to prose recall. Children's awareness of strategies as well as knowledge about "when" and "how" strategies are efficiently applied is discussed by Wong in this volume.

Because several chapters in the volume describe in more detail the similarities between LD memory performance and NDL memory development, our review has been cursory. To better understand the mainstream of memory research with LD children, we turn next to a description of the extant research.

CATEGORIZING LD RESEARCH

LD research on memory may be categorized in terms of the orientation of existing research programs. Three categorizations are apparent. First, many of the studies of LD children's memory processes are descriptive in that they report *how* LD children of various ages compare with NLD children in their ability to remember a stimulus array. The ages vary from elementary school age children to adults (e.g., Gelzheiser, 1984; Golden, McCutcheon, Delay, & Issac, 1982; Worden, Malmgren, & Gabourie, 1982; Worden & Nakamura, 1983) and utilize tasks that require recognition, recall, or reconstruction (i.e., story recall) of information, and the stimuli might include words, digits, visual patterns or prose. A simple study of ability group comparison is provided by Swanson (1977b). Ten-year-old LD and mentally retarded children were compared on a probe-memory task for their recall of pictorial or three-dimensional representations (concrete objects). The results of the study indicated that both LD and MR children were better able to recall concrete rather than pictorial material although ability group differences in favor of the LD children were found only on the concrete representations. Similar recall strategies occurred for both ability groups (e.g., primacy effects) in both conditions suggesting that similar information processing algorithms were used.

A second group of studies in the LD field focuses on memory instruction. The emphasis in these studies is on teaching LD children under various conditions or with different types of memory devices how to remember presented material (e.g., Batey & Sonnerschein, 1981; Gelzheiser, 1984; Haines & Torgesen, 1979). These studies have generally shown that LD children can be taught through instructions (e.g., Gelzheiser, 1984), modeling (e.g., Dawson et al., 1980), and reinforcement (e.g., Torgesen & Houck, 1980) to use some simple strategies that they do not produce spontaneously (e.g., Dallego & Moely, 1980). In a sample study, Mastropieri, Scruggs, Levin, Gaffney, and McLoone (1985) conducted two experiments in which LD adolescents recalled the definitions of 14 vocabulary words either according to a pictorial mnemonic strategy (the "keyword method") or via a traditional instructional approach. The keyword method involved constructing an interactive visual image of the to-be-associated items. For example, to remember that the English word *carlin* means old *woman* via the keyword method, the learner is directed to the fact that the first part of carlin sounds like the familiar word *car*. Then, the learner constructs an interactive image that relates a car and an old women such as an elderly woman driving an old car (see chapter by Scruggs, Mastropieri, and Levin, for further discussion). The results of the first experiment (experimenter generated mnemonic illustrations) and the second experiment (student generated mnemonic images) indicated that the former strategy was substantially more effective in learning vocabulary.

A third group of studies could be regarded as theoretical pieces in which a focus is placed upon individual differences and methodological issues in the study of memory (e.g., Ceci, Ringstrom, & Lea, 1980; Shankweiler et al., 1979). The purpose of this work is to relate various dimensions of memory to specific-performance deficits. These studies have been relatively rare compared with the preponderance of descriptive and instructional studies. As a consequence, much of what we know about learning disabilities is derived from description at a clinical or instructional level rather than a comprehensive theoretical framework.

COMMENTS ON CURRENT RESEARCH PRACTICE

The aforementioned categorization does not exhaust important memory dimensions. Nevertheless, the distinctions allow one to make some comments in reference to research on learning disabilities. First, these various types of studies, if they are distinct, require somewhat different investigative procedures and, therefore, are more likely to raise different methodological concerns (see Hall, et al., this volume for a review). For example, different procedures are required to measure metamemory, strategy variables, and automatic memory. Second, regardless of the validity of these distinctions when applied to learning disabilities, some types of memory have been subject to a lot more investigation than others. Until recently, the majority of studies have focused on effortful (i.e., strategies) and episodic forms of memory. This disproportionate emphasis has important implications for the overall evaluation of LD children's memory , particularly if it is eventually discovered that LD memory functioning is composed of operations over and above the processes that are a natural consequence of carrying out the task (e.g., see Pressley, Forrest-Pressley, Elliot-Faust, & Miller, 1985, for a related discussion).

A number of excellent reviews relating memory and LD research have appeared (e.g., Hall & Humphreys, 1982; Jorm, 1983; Torgesen, 1985; Torgesen & Greenstein, 1982). In addition, two chapters within this edition address important methodological issues, and therefore little comment is made here about them. The majority of the problems related to current research practice in the area of memory and learning disabilities have been (a) an over estimation of discrepancies between a child's potential and measures of achievement, (b) insensitivity to statistical regression, (c) interpreting the causal relations from the existing data, (d) sample identification that is not under experimental control (e.g., school district definitions), and (e) sample process definitions (e.g., reading) of learning disabilities that are insensitive to fine-grained measurement. Perhaps the most serious problem with previous research that attempts to link memory processes to learning disabilities is related to the narrowness of conceptualization. This may be illustrated by the fact, as suggested earlier, that the majority of LD children's memory functioning is described in terms of younger normal children's functioning. The problem is that whether the researcher is concerned with the development of memory organization, selective attention, or whatever, his or her conceptualization rarely matches the complexities of the processes used by the sample to perform the particular task(s). For example, clustering or item organization during retrieval operations is an extremely complex process consisting of several component behaviors (see Mandler, 1979). Yet, a number of investigators (ourselves included) treat memory organization as a unitary concept. (This point is discussed by Torgesen, Rashotte, Greenstein, Houck, and Portes and Hall et. al. in this volume and is, therefore, not elaborated upon here.) There are two obvious problems, however, related to memory research and learning disabilities that need to be discussed further: sample selection and ability matching.

Sample Selection

A fundamental problem underlying research in the field of learning disabilities is the lack of a commonly accepted definition and of a lack of consensus about which terms (e.g., learning disabled, reading disabled, retarded, poor readers, or dsylexics) should be used. As a result, the incidence of learning disabilities has not been established, nor are the demographic characteristics of this population precisely known (e.g., Farnham-Diggory, 1978; Owen, Adams, Forrest, Stolz & Fischer, 1971). The struggle to formulate a definition has continued since the inception of the field. The most widely accepted definition is that which is part of Public Law 94–142, the Education of All Handicapped Children Act (USOE, August 23, 1977). This definition has become the basis for federal and state law as well as many research programs. There are two parts to the federal definition. One part adopts an earlier report from the National Advisory Committee on Handicapped Children (1968), which defines learning disabilities as

> a disorder in one or more of the basic psychological processes involved in the understanding or in using the language spoken or written, which may manifest itself in an imperfect ability to listen, think, speak, read, write, spell, or to do mathematical calculation. The term includes such conditions as perceptual handicaps, brain injury, minimal brain dysfunction, dyslexia, and developmental aphasia. The term does not include children who have learning problems which are primarily the result of visual, hearing, or motor handicaps, of mental retardation, of emotional disturbance, or of environment, cultural, or economic disadvantage.

The second part of the definition appeared as a second set of regulations (USOE, December 29, 1977) applying to PL 94–142. This definition focuses on the child's ability to achieve commensurate with his/her age and ability levels in one or more of the specific academic areas. The focus on a *discrepancy* between achievement and intellectual ability is to accrue in one or more of the following areas: oral expression, listening comprehension, written expression, basic reading skill, reading comprehension, mathematic calculation and mathematical reasoning. Thus, the definition of learning disabilities emphasizes below average academic achievement, IQ of normal range, and exclusion of the conditions noted in the federal definition.

Although the federal definition has had a substantial impact on the procedures used to identify learning disabilities, there remains considerable variability in the definitions and criteria used by State Department of Education to define learning disabilities (Mercer, Hughes, & Mercer, 1985). Equally disturbing is the heterogeneity of definitions in the professional research literature (Kavale and Nye, 1981; Torgesen & Dice, 1980). Of the 307 studies reviewed by Kavale and Nye (1981), 24% relied on psychometric definitions (discrepancy or formula driven) for subject selection; approximately 20% used federal or state guidelines as selection criteria; and over half of the studies selected subjects who were receiving services from established programs for the learning disabled. In view of the generally acknowledged heterogeneity of the population labeled *learning disabled,* it is interesting to note that Torgesen and Dice (1980) did not find one study that attempted to reduce subject heterogeneity as part of the sample selection procedure.

Given that more than half of the published research is based on students receiving services from established programs for the learning disabled, it is reasonable to ask what characterizes this population? In at least one state, it was estimated that over 50% of the students receiving services did not match conventional definitions of learning disabilities (Shepard, Smith, & Vojir, 1983). In a companion study, Shepard and Smith (1983) analyzed the records of 1,000 pupils receiving services from programs designed for the learning disabled and reported that only 28% of the students were found to meet the strict definitions of learning disabilities. More than 50% of the students were better described by other indicators (e.g., non-English dominant, minor behavior disorders, slow learners).

The problems associated with sample selection criteria severely limit the generalizations that one might be able to make from the research on the memory processes of LD children. Recent efforts to remedy this state of affairs have resulted in attempts to develop minimum standards for describing the subjects in research reports on learning disabilities (Deutsch-Smith et al., 1984; Keogh, Major-Kinsley, Omori-Gordon, & Reid, 1982). Such descriptions would, at least, permit more objective methods for comparing research reports and would be a major improvement in view of the fact that approximately 40% of the studies reviewed by Harber (1981a) did not adequately report classification criteria.

Another recent approach to the solution of problems associated with subject selection is the identification of subgroups or subtypes of learning disabilities. Some of the recent subgrouping schemes have included behavioral characteristics (Speece, McKinney, & Applebaum, 1985), memory performance (Torgesen & Houck, 1980), language ability (Ceci, Ringstrom, & Lea (1981), and neuropsychological profiles (Boder, 1973; Lyon & Watson, 1981; Satz & Morris, 1981). (The search for distinct subtypes is thoroughly addressed by Torgesen et al. and Hynd et al. in this volume.) Although subtyping is an important enterprise, there are two stumbling blocks. First, any taxonomy of subtypes will not be readily accepted by fellow researchers until the issues associated with the definition of learning disabilities are resolved.

Second, the establishment of subtypes is based on the assumption that any specific disability can be assigned to a category having a unitary cause and a well defined effect. That is, a long held observation is that LD students have high inter-subject, as well as intra-subject, variability on most cognitive measures. One strategy to handle this variability has been to identify subgroups of LD children. If successful, variability would be less within subgroups and greater from one subgroup to another. These attempts have often led to subgroupings that look like only graduations in severity. When this happens, it suggests one common underlying disorder: learning disabilities. Some view these assumptions as tenuous (e.g., see Torgesen et al., this volume) and suggest that more theoretically provocative findings occur when one defined subgroup of LD children differs significantly in one direction and another subgroup differs in the opposite direction from the NLD group. Such has been demonstrated in measures of auditory (Torgesen & Houck, 1980) and visual recall (see Swanson chapter, final experiment reviewed).

In criticizing the subtyping approach, Jorm (1983) implies a possible solution to the problem of subject selection. That is, to study the rela-

tionship between memory processes and human abilities in the population
as a whole. The study of subgroups of students at the extremes of the
ability distribution provides an incomplete account of the sources of individual differences (Hall et al., this volume, alludes to this). The focus
on overlapping disabilities has certainly paid off in terms of a general theory
of reading ability. According to Perfetti (1985), reading ability can be
viewed on a continuum with reading disabled children occupying the extreme or low end of the continuum. Most importantly, specific reading
disability can be understood in terms of the verbal processing factors that
account for reading ability in the general population (e.g., lexical processes,
working memory processes, comprehension processes).

Ability Matching

Many of the problems related to learning disabilities are related to
matching experimental and control subjects on measures of specific ability
(see also Hall, Tinzman, and Humphreys, in this volume). These problems
include: (a) the way learning disabilities are defined, (b) the degree of
discrepancy between intellectual potential and achievement, and (c) the
matching of groups on general ability. For example, a common approach
used in LD research is to match subjects for age and IQ. The groups are
then given some experimental task that taps memory ability. Thus, average
intelligence in the LD and NLD samples is viewed as a critical criterion
in ability matching. However, as noted by several reviewers (e.g., Hallahan
& Cruichshank, 1973), intelligence test scores are quite variable for LD
children. This variability is influenced by motivation, nature of test demands, and other internal and external factors. Thus, many LD children
(and NLD youngsters for that matter) can be expected to show regression
effects in IQ performances. The insensitivity to regression effect creates
an over or underestimation in IQ (this argument also applies to achievement measures). In short, there is an inherent limitation on what information can be generalized from LD studies on memory. In support of this
observation, Hall and Humphreys (1982) have noted that the majority of
research on learning disabilities reports only IQ and reading scores. However, since reading is correlated with many other academic areas, it is
possible that such reading samples may be at odds with classic notions
of reading disabilities (i.e., reading disabilities is assumed to reflect a normal achievement in other academic areas).

HISTORICAL PERSPECTIVES

As a formal area of inquiry, learning disabilities have only recently been
subjected to experimental investigation. The number of experimental

studies investigating LD childrens' memory processes prior to 1976 is meager, however a survey of LD journals between 1976 and 1979 revealed that 18% of the reports were concerned with memory processes (Torgesen & Dice, 1980).

A majority of the research published prior to 1970 was concerned with perceptual-motor behavior of brain injured and/or reading disabled children, and little if any experimental research dealt directly with memory difficulties (Hallahan & Cruickshank, 1973). Of the studies that were available prior to 1970, most merely stated that LD children perform poorly on certain tasks (e.g., digit span, see Mishra, Ferguson, & Priscilla, 1984, for a recent review). Few if any attempts were made to isolate the nature of children's memory deficits. Most studies focused on children with reading difficulties. For example, one early experimental study (Rizzo, 1939) compared retarded and nonretarded readers on three different STM tasks. For one task, children were presented letter strings simultaneously; in another, letters were presented visually but in succession; and in the third, letters were presented auditorily but in a sequential fashion. For all three tasks retarded readers were inferior to normal readers. Unfortunately, the author did not adequately discuss the mental processing mechanisms that might account for retarded readers' poor memory performance.

A second characteristic of the early research concerned with the memory processes in LD children was that constructs such as perception, attention, memory, and cognition were conceptualized as independent of one another. Several founders of the field argued, for example, that word perception must be adequately developed and/or remediated before subsequent learning or memory can take place (e.g., Strauss & Kephart, 1955). Thus, the reciprocal interaction between various processes was not taken into consideration.

The historical link between learning disabilities and memory was clearly established in the early literature on reading disabilities. In 1877 Kussmaul called attention to a disorder he called *word blindness,* which was characterized as an inability to read, although vision, intellect, and speech were normal. Following Kussmaul's contribution, several cases of reading difficulties acquired by adults due to cerebral lesions, mostly involving the angular gyri of the left hemisphere, were reported in the literature (see Hinshelwood, 1917, for a review). One important case study was published by Morgan (1896) in which a 14-year-old boy of normal intelligence had difficulty recalling letters of the alphabet. Written words were also difficult to recall and seemed to convey "no impression to this mind." Interestingly, Morgan stated that the child appeared to have good memory for oral information. This case study was important since word blindness did not appear to occur as a result of a cerebral lesion. Since Morgan's description of this condition, designated as a specific reading disability, research was expanded to include children of normal intelligence who exhibited difficulties in reading but not with achievement in other subjects. Hinshelwood's (1917) classic monograph presents a number of case studies describing reading disabilities in children of normal intelligence. On the basis of these observations, Hinshelwood inferred that reading problems of these children were related to "a pathological condition of the visual memory center" (p. 21).

At the same time Hinshelwood's monograph was published, a little known text by Bronner (1917) reviewed case studies linking mental processing difficulties to children of normal intelligence. For example, consider case number 21.

> Henry J., 16 years old, was seen after he had been in court on several occasions. The mental examination showed that the boy was quite intelligent and in general capable, but had a very specialized defect. The striking feature of all the test work with this boy was the finding that he was far below for his age in the matter of rote memory. When a series of numerals was presented to him auditorily he could remember no more than four. His memory span for numerals presented visually was not much better . . . he succeeded here with five. Memory span for syllables was likewise poor . . . on the other hand when ideas were to be recalled, that is, where memory dealt with logical material, the results were good. (p. 120)

A majority of case studies reviewed in the Bronner's text suggested that disabled children's immediate memory (STM) was deficient and that remote (long-term) memory was somewhat intact (a conclusion not unlike Wordens, 1983, recent review of the literature). Bronner also noted that memory and its application to complex learning activities was not known (this point is also made in current reviews, e.g., see Torgesen & Greenstein, 1982). For example, the author stated:

> very many practically important laws of memory have not yet been determined; those most firmly established concern themselves mainly with nonsense or other type of material quite unlike the activities of everyday life. In a common sense way we are aware that both immediate and remote memory are essential, that we need to remember what we see and hear . . . that to remember an idea is probably more useful in general, than to have a good memory for rote material, but a defect for the latter may be of great significance in some kinds of school work. (p. 110)

Researchers during the time between 1900s to 1940s generally viewed reading difficulties as being associated with structural damage to portions of the brain that support visual memory (e.g., see Geschwind, 1962, for review; also see Monroe, 1932). A contrasting position was provided by Orton (1925, 1937) in which he suggested that reading disorders were reflective of a neurological-maturational lag resulting from a delayed lateral cerebral dominance for language. An excellent critique of Orton's work and the history of the neuropsychological basis of learning disabilities is provided in the chapter by Hynd, Obrzut and Bowen in this volume. Orton described the phenomena of a selective loss or diminished capacity to remember words as *strephosymbolia* (twisted symbols). Orton (1937) noted that while:

> these children show many more errors of a wide variety of kinds it is clear that their difficulty is not in hearing and not in speech mechanism . . . but in recalling words previously heard again or used in speech, and that one of the outstanding obstacles to such recall is remembering all of the sounds in their proper order. (P. 147)

In cases of visual memory, Orton stated that such children with reading disabilities have major difficulties in "recalling the printed word in terms of its spatial sequence or proper order in space" (p. 148). Thus, for Orton, reading disabled children's memory difficulties were seen as reflecting spatial sequences in visual memory or temporal sequences in auditory memory. While the conceptual foundation of much of Orton's research has been challenged (see Vellutino, 1977, 1979; Hynd et al., this issue), much of the evidence for linking learning disabilities and memory processes has been established from the earlier clinical studies of Morgan, Hinshelwood, and Orton. To date, reading difficulties are primarily viewed as related to language skills (Liberman, Shankweiler, Orlando, Harris, & Berti, 1971; Vellutino, Harding, Phillips, & Steger, 1975a; however see Mason, 1980), and memory difficulties are popularly conceptualized in terms of language processes (see Baddeley, 1974; Stanovich, 1982, for a review).

Unfortunately for the field of learning disabilities, theories accounting for reading difficulties were not as influential in shaping our historical understanding of cognitive processes in LD children as was the work of Strauss and Werner and their colleagues (Strauss & Kephart, 1955; Strauss & Lehtinen, 1947; Werner, 1948). Many recent commentaries have questioned the earlier paradigms and conclusions of Strauss and Werner (see Kavale & Forness, 1985a, 1985b, for a review). Their work with exogenous brain-injured mentally retarded children has been a foundation for many of the concepts in the field to date (see Hallahan & Cruickshank, 1973). Strauss and Werner viewed learning disabilities as a process disturbance that occurred most notably in the areas of perceptual-motor functioning. Such processing disturbances were assumed to be caused by neurological dysfunctions, which in turn produced discrepancies in academic performance (high and low achievement scatters).

Unfortunately, the relationship between memory and learning disabilities was somewhat obscured by the work of Strauss and Werner. In their classical text on the *Psychopathology and Education of the Brain Injured Child* Strauss and Lehtinen suggested that memory skills of brain-injured children were intact or at least normal. For example, in a case report of a brain injured female child they noted that "her most outstanding capacity is her excellent auditory memory. This is consistently good with respect to digits, sentences, and meaningful material, scoring on every level and accounting for the only success above chronological age. Vocabulary development is adequate for abstract words. Word naming is fluent" (p. 4). Based on several case studies, the authors further stated that "the characteristic excellent verbal memory and tendency to automatization has a profound significance for the teaching methods of brain injured children" (p. 142). The authors suggested that educational remediation should not focus on automatization (i.e., repeated practice) but rather on "insight and analysis." No doubt, such conclusions reflected the authors' theoretical orientation (Gestalt psychology).

In a revision of Strauss and Lehtinen's earlier text (Strauss & Kephart, 1955), little empirical research (although emerging clinical support) related memory processes to LD children's functioning was provided. Some case histories began to report an adequate memory for remote information (long-term memory) but not of immediate information (STM, e.g., see case histories on p. 229). In addition, a chapter by Goldberg (pp. 144–164) in Strauss and Kephart's text suggested that brain injured children of normal intelligence have poor retention for visual designs. Current research has not supported the notion that LD children have difficulties remembering designs (e.g., see Vellutino & Scanlon, 1985, for a review) or that recall deficiencies are related to problems in perceptual processes (e.g., Vellutino, 1977).

It was not until the late 1960s and early 1970s that systematic studies appeared comparing LD and NLD children's performance on memory tasks. These studies focused on modality specific memory processes (i.e., auditory or visual memory) and cross-modality instructional conditions, but they provided conflicting evidence. For example, two studies on *auditory memory* were found focusing on children labeled learning disabled. (Several other studies were available on brain-damaged, mentally retarded, or aphasic children.) Conners, Kramer, and Guerra (1969) compared LD and normal achieving children on their ability to remember numbers presented to them on a dichotic listening task. The results of their study were that LD children *did not differ* from their counterparts in their STM recall. In contrast, Bryan (1972) compared LD and normal achieving children on a task that required subjects to recall a list of words presented by a tape recorder and words presented by slide projector. LD and comparison samples performed better with the visual than the auditory stimulus, but LD children performed more poorly than the NLD group under both conditions.

Conflicting results were also found among studies investigating visual memory information processing abilities of reading disabled children. Goyan and Lyle (1971, 1973) investigated young reading disabled children's (children under 8.5 years) recall of critical details of visual stimuli presented tachistoscopically for various exposure duration intervals. Their results showed that the reading disabled students were less accurate in the recall of critical details than older disabled readers as well as younger and older normal readers. In another study, Guthrie and Goldberg (1972) compared disabled and skilled readers on several tests designed to measure visual STM. In contrast to Goyan and Lyle, it was found that childrens' scores on memory subtests from the Illinois Test of Psycholinguistic Abilities did not clearly differentiate the ability groups. In view of the conflicting results, it was not possible to develop any definitive conclusions regarding the visual memory processes of LD children.

Cross-modality research with LD students also began to appear during this time period. For example, Senf and Feshback (1970) found differences between good and poor readers' memory on cross-modality presentation conditions. Samples included elementary and junior high school age, culturally deprived, LD and normal control readers. Subjects were compared on their recall of auditory and visual digits and combinations of both presentations (e.g., auditory-visual). The LD sample exhibited poor recall of stimuli organized into audiovisual pairs, which was attributed to problems of cross-modality matching. Older culturally deprived and normal children recalled the digits in paired order more accurately than their younger counterparts, while older LD children were no better than the young learning disabled. The LD sample also exhibited a higher prevalence of visual *encoding* errors. The implication of this research was that some prerequisite skills of pairing stimuli had not developed in the LD child, and the possession of these skills was essential for reading. In contrast to this study, Denckla and Rudel (1974) found that LD children's poor recall was not related to encoding errors, but rather to temporal sequencing. Their results suggested that subjects who had difficulties in temporal sequencing would have difficulty recalling information from spatial tasks or tasks that required matching of serial and spatial stimuli (as in the Senf & Feshback, 1970 study). To date, research on cross-modality matching is equivocal (e.g., see Koppitz, 1971; then see Torgesen, Bowen, & Ivey, 1978).

To summarize, the studies in the late 1960s and early 1970s, while contradictory, did establish a foundation for the study of learning disabilities in the context of memory. We now turn to a discussion of the more recent conceptualizations related to LD childrens' memory.

CURRENT RESEARCH

Since the mid 1970s, research has consistently revealed that LD children exhibit poorer performance than NLD youngsters on a variety of memory tasks including free recall (e.g., Bauer, 1977a, 1977b; Torgesen, 1977), serial recall (Torgesen, 1978b), and story recall (see Worden, 1983, 1986). Somewhat less clear are the sources of these differences in memory performance.

After conducting our survey of the contemporary research literature, we elected to organize the findings according to the basic memory processes of encoding, storage, and retrieval. Research on attention was also included because of its relationship to encoding (e.g., Hallahan, 1975; Tarver et al., 1976; Torgesen, 1981) and retrieval (e.g., Bauer, 1977a, 1977b). We were motivated to use this organizational scheme for two reasons. First, the necessity for postulating the processes of trace formation, retention of a memory trace over time, and utilization of memory traces have been well documented (Murdock, 1972; Postman, 1976). Unfortunately, it has been extremely difficult to separate these processes experimentally (Postman, 1976). By acknowledging this problem, we hope to encourage further work by LD researchers to develop procedures that more clearly separate encoding, storage, and retrieval processes (see Brainerd, 1985, for a review). Second, the basic processes of attention, encoding, storage, and retrieval are not linked to any one model of memory but rather to a general class of memory models.

Attention

Several lines of evidence suggest that LD children exhibit attentional deficits that may interfere with encoding processes (e.g., Hallahan, Gajar, Cohen, & Tarver, 1978; Tarver et al., 1976). Studies that have examined attentional resources and strategies directly report a variety of differences between LD and NLD children (Atkinson & Seunath, 1973; Cherry & Kruger, 1983; Dykman, Walls, Suzuki, Akerman, & Peters, 1970; Mazer, McIntyre, Murray, Till, & Blackwell, 1983; McGrady & Olson, 1970; McIntyre, Murray, Coronin & Blackwell, 1978; Sykes, Douglas, Weiss, & Minde, 1971). Using a psychophysical technique free of memory confounds, McIntyre et al. (1978) reported a lower than normal span of apprehension in children identified as learning disabled (also see Hynd et al., this volume, for a review). Subsequently, Mazer et al. (1983) attributed the lower span of apprehension to a slower rate of information pick-up from the iconic sensory store.

Ability differences in selective auditory attention have also been reported. Cherry and Kruger (1983) studied children's performance on a dichotic listening task under three different distractor conditions: nonlinguistic, linguistic-nonsemantic, and linguistic-semantic. Their results indicated that all three distractors had a more deleterious effect on the performance of the LD children. They exhibited the most difficulty focusing attention on the primary task when the distractor was semantic. Thus, LD children were found to differ in their ability to attend to relevant information in the auditory sensory store.

Despite these differences between LD and NLD children in attention to visual and auditory stimuli, Bauer (1982) has argued that the attentional resources of the LD children are *adequate* for performance on a variety of *memory* tasks. In other words, the residual differences are not great enough to account for the differences in memory performance. For example, LD and NLD children were comparable in their ability to recall aurally presented sets of three letters or three words within 4 seconds after presentation (Bauer, 1977a, 1977b). Similarly LD and NLD students were comparable in their ability to recognize letters and geometric shapes after a brief visual presentation when recognition was less than 300 msec after stimulus offset (Morrison, Giordani, & Nagy, 1977). In view of these findings, it would appear that the retrieval of information from sensory storage is an important, although not a major factor, in the memory deficits exhibited in LD children.

Likewise, Bauer has argued that reports of a diminished recency effect in LD populations have often been misinterpreted, and it is difficult to replicate. There is a considerable amount of evidence suggesting that for the majority of memory tasks, LD and NLD children are comparable in their ability to store and retrieve sensory information (Bauer, 1977a, 1977b, 1979a; Morrison, Giordani, & Nagy, 1977). Thus, the LD child's ability to attend to and recognize the items of most memory tasks is adequate (see Bauer, 1982, for further discussion).

Swanson (1981c, 1983a) has also suggested, via a signal detection analysis, that LD children are able to sustain attentional resources (vigilance) in a fashion comparable to NLD children. On the Continuous Performance Task, LD children did not exhibit a decline in attention as time on task increased. They did, however, make fewer correct detections and more false responses than their NLD counterparts. LD children also appeared to exhibit the application of different attention strategies when compared to NLD peers across age (Swanson, 1983a). The role of strategies in allocation of attention is underscored by the findings of Copeland and Reiner (1984). Studying the performance of LD and NLD children on a sorting task, the former were found to be slower at sorting items based on their attributes than the latter. More importantly, only the NLD children exhibit improvement in the accuracy of the sorting task with practice (Copeland & Reiner, 1984).

Strong developmental trends in the awareness of attentional processes have been found in NLD (Miller & Bigi, 1979) and LD children (Loper, Hallahan, & Ianna, 1982). Younger children focus on external reasons for attending (e.g., rewards), while older children tend to focus on internal reasons (e.g., interest). Although there were no differences between the ability groups, performance on the meta-attentional task was correlated with achievement of the NLD sample, but not for the LD group (see Kneedler & Hallahan, 1984; Loper et al., 1982). In a second experiment, Loper et al. found that attentional performance was correlated with academic achievement after the LD students received academic intervention. Loper et al. interpreted these results as suggesting that LD children may have difficulty with the application of their knowledge about attentional processes.

Taken as a whole, research on attention suggests that the attentional resources of LD children are adequate for performance on most learning and memory tasks (also see Copeland & Wisniewski, 1981; Samuels & Miller, 1985).

Encoding

On the assumption that attentional deficits may not directly underlie ability group differences in memory performance, current studies have focused on the processes of encoding information. For our purposes, encoding processes refer to the construction or activation of mental representations of concepts or events.

Findings from the research on the encoding of semantic information is mixed. There is some evidence which suggests that LD students do exhibit some difficulty in the activation of word features (Ceci, 1984; Lorsbach, 1982; Maisto & Sipe, 1980; Shankweiler et al., 1979; Swanson & Obrzut, 1985; Vellutino & Scanlon, 1985). In contrast, other investigators find no encoding differences (see Gerber, 1981, for a review). For example, Elbert (1984) has provided evidence that LD and NLD students are comparable at the encoding stage of word recognition, but that LD children require more time to conduct a memory search (also see Manis, 1985). Additional evidence that LD and NLD children are comparable at the encoding stage of information processing was provided by Lehman and Brady (1982). Using a release from proactive inhibition procedure (see Dempster & Cooney, 1981), Lehman and Brady found that reading disabled and normal readers were comparable in their ability to encode word information (e.g., indicating whether a word was heard or seen and information concerning a word's category). However, reading disabled children relied on smaller subword components in the decoding process than normal readers.

One means of unifying these conflicting findings is to suggest that LD children exhibit encoding deficiencies on some types of tasks, but not others (Ceci et al., 1980, 1981). For example, Ceci (1982) has suggested that LD children exhibit encoding deficiencies on tasks that require effortful or purposive semantic processing but are not deficient on tasks that measure automatic processing (e.g., spreading activation). Lorsbach and Gray (1982) also provided data to support the idea that LD children do not spontaneously engage in effortful semantic processing.

Swanson (1984a) has suggested that cognitive effort (mental input a limited-capacity attentional system expends to encode information) may also play a critical role in the encoding of words. Tasks that require high levels of cognitive effort result in better recall by NLD than LD students. In contrast, low effort tasks result in better recall by LD than NLD students. This finding was found to be invariant with age. Skilled readers under the high effort condition also produced memory traces that contained more distinctive semantic information than the less skilled readers. Thus, it is possible that one source of ability group differences in encoding performance is the cognitive effort that can be effectively allocated to generate a distinctive memory trace.

Storage vs Retrieval

In comparison to the volume of research on attention and encoding processes, research on the storage and retrieval of information in long-term memory is meager. The available research, however, provides considerable support for the assertion that storage and retrieval problems are primary sources of individual diffferences in long-term memory performance (e.g., Ackerman, 1985; Howe, Brainerd, & Kingma, 1985; Vellutino & Scanlon, 1982, 1985).

Numerous studies have also shown that LD children are less skilled than NLD peers in the use of rehearsal strategies used to store information in long-term memory (Bauer, 1977a, 1977b, 1979a; Tarver et al., 1976; Torgesen, 1978a; Torgesen & Goldman, 1977). The primary source of support for the assertion of rehearsal deficits in LD children is the diminished primacy effect of the serial position curve (Bauer, 1979a). Primacy performance reflects the accessing of items placed in long-term storage (e.g., Watkins, 1974). In addition, the primacy effect (i.e., better recall of items at the beginning of a list over the middle items of the list) is thought to reflect greater rehearsal of those items at the beginning of the list. Additional support for the rehearsal deficiency hypothesis was provided by Torgesen and Goldman (1977) who studied the lip movements of children during memorization task. LD children were found to exhibit fewer lip movements than the NLD students. To the extent that these lip movements reflect the quantity of rehearsal, these data lend support to rehearsal deficiency hypothesis. Haines and Torgesen (1979) and others (e.g., Dawson et al., 1980; Koorland & Wolking, 1982) also reported that incentives could be used to increase the amount of rehearsal, and thus, recall by LD students.

More recently, Bauer and Emhert (1984) have suggested that the difference between LD and NLD students is in the quality of the rehearsal rather than the quantity of rehearsal per se. In other words, LD children use less effective rehearsal strategies. For example, Wong and Sawatsky (1984) found that good readers used more precise elaboration of sentences to aid their recall than average or poor readers. Teaching students a self-questioning procedure was found to improve sentence elaborations and recall by average and poor readers.

In terms of retrieval, LD children are able to use organized strategies for selecting retrieval cues (Wong, 1982) and are capable of using different word attributes (e.g., graphophonic, syntactic, semantic) to guide retrieval (Blumenthal, 1985). They appear, however, to select less efficient strategies, conduct a less exhaustive search for retrieval cues, and lack self checking skills in the selection of retrieval cues (Wong, 1982). Several investigators have also provided evidence consistent with the idea that long-term memory deficits may arise from the failure to integrate visual and verbal memory traces of visually presented stimuli at the time of storage or retrieval (Ceci et al., 1980; Perfetti & Hogaboom, 1975; Swanson, 1983, 1984a; Vellutino, Steger, Harding, & Phillips, 1975c). For example, Swanson (1984) has suggested that the LD child's failure to integrate verbal and visual codes is due to semantic memory limitations. In contrast, Ceci et al. (1980) present data that suggest that there are separate pathways for auditory and visual inputs to the semantic memory system and that LD children may have an impairment in one or both of these pathways. For children with visual and auditory impairments, the recall deficit arises at the time of storage and retrieval. When only one modality is impaired, the long-term memory deficit is hypothesized to arise at the time of storage. Furthermore, semantic orienting tasks were found to ameliorate the recall deficits of the children with single modality impairments but not those with impairments in both visual and verbal modalities (Ceci et al., 1980, Experiment 2).

Unfortunately, a persistent problem that has plagued research on long-term memory deficits in LD children is the lack of quantitative methods for separating storage and retrieval processes. Extant research has relied primarily on qualitative methodology (Howe et al., 1985). Howe et al. (1985), using a stages-of-learning model based on a two-stage Markov process, have conducted perhaps the most precise investigation of storage and retrieval processes in LD children to date. The stages-of-learning model contains 11 parameters that provide quantitative estimates of storage processes, processes related to the acquisition of a retrieval algorithm, and heuristic retrieval processes (see Brainerd, 1985, for detailed discussion of this approach). Comparisons involving the parameter values of NLD and LD children found that the latter were deficient in their ability to store both pictures and words; however, there were no differences between the ability groups in retaining a memory trace once it was stored. LD children also exhibited a deficiency in the acquisition of algorithmic retrieval process. Interestingly, there were no differences in heuristic retrieval processes used between the time a trace was stored and errorless recall occurred (i.e., algorithmic retrieval). Finally, the ability-age group comparisons revealed that the storage deficit was invariant with age. In contrast, ability group differences in the acquisition of a retrieval algorithm increased with age.

Taken as a whole, the results reviewed here suggest that the processes involved in entering a memory trace into the long-term store and acquiring an algorithim for retrieval of that information are primary sources of ability group differences in LD children's long-term recall. Additional research to discover methods for remediating these deficits is certainly warranted. One promising avenue is the mnemonic keyword method (see Scruggs, Mastropieri, & Levin, this volume). Ostensibly, the success of the keyboard method is a function of the strategy it provides for recoding novel items into a familiar form (encoding), relating novel items to familiar items in long-term memory (storage), and retrieving items from long-term memory. Application of the stages-of-learning model to the data from keyword experiments could be fruitful in pinpointing the effects of the keyword method on storage and retrieval processes.

FUTURE DIRECTIONS

If research on the role of memory in learning disabilities is to fulfill the promise of resolving "acute" issues in the field, it will be necessary for researchers to converge on a paradigm for the study of memory phenomena. In the absence of a paradigm, researchers confronted with a similar range of phenomena describe and interpret them in many different ways (Kuhn, 1979). As a result, fact-gathering appears to be random, and their is much confusion. This is indeed the case for research on the role of memory in learning disabilities. According to Kuhn's (1979) scheme, the LD field can be characterized at the very earliest stages of scientific development. In view of this state of affairs, adoption of a paradigm is the necessary first step toward putting memory research with LD children on the "route to normal science". The paradigm selected will identify the theoretical infrastructure, critical questions to be researched, and acceptable methods for conducting research.

Although the field is far from a consensus on the most appropriate theoretical model, there is an implicit adherence to a theoretical infrastructure, i.e., the language and methods of information processing models of human memory and cognition (Cermak, 1983; Jorm, 1983). Within this infrastructure, however, there are many different viewpoints, and confusion about the distinctions between each of the viewpoints continues to plague the field (see the special issues of *Topics in Learning and Learning Disabilities*, 1982a, 1982b). In many cases the instructional implications for the different cognitive models vary widely (Reid & Hresko, 1981). We do not presume to know what model might best characterize human memory and cognition. An answer to this question must be sought in the laboratory and the classroom. Rather, we propose a strategy for reducing the number of alternative models and map a route toward "normal" science: the development of a paradigm. What form would the paradigm take? We believe that the guidelines for the development of a paradigm can be sketched as follows:

Subject Selection

Much more precise descriptions of the subjects used in research are essential if we are to arrange our facts into a coherent body of knowledge with any generalizability. The findings presented by Herber (1981), Kavale and Nye (1981), Torgesen and Dice (1980), Shepard and Smith (1983), and Shepard, Smith and Vojir (1983) clearly document the need for more precision in the description of subject characteristics. The recommendations offered by Deutsch-Smith et al. (1984), Hall et al. (this volume), and Keogh et al. (1982) are a step in the right direction. The detailed descriptions of subjects called for in these reports would also permit investigators to conduct secondary analysis of the research (i.e., meta-analyses) with greater precision by linking effect size to quantitative subject characteristics.

Analysis of Behavior

More detailed descriptions of all behaviors occurring in relation to the tasks would indeed provide a more complete picture of the cognitive processes involved in children's intellectual performances (Swanson, 1985). Our data must go beyond the number of items recalled. Detailed analyses intended to discover patterns of errors are likely to be much more revealing (Brown & Burton, 1978). Children's thinking aloud protocols collected during the performance of tasks are also likely to be profitable for both theory testing and theory construction. Here, the analysis of verbal reports as data presented by Erickson of Simon (1980) is relevant. For example, a study of mathematical strategy transformations was conducted by Swanson and Cooney (1985). Although the primary data used to infer strategy development was time needed to perform mathematical operations, detailed descriptions of cognitive strategies emerged as a result of verbal protocol analysis (see Kail & Bisanz, 1982; also see Swanson, 1985). As a result, a more complete picture of children's mathematical performance emerged than if only reaction time data were included in the analysis.

Longitudinal Studies

Much of the data on children exhibiting learning disabilities are snapshots of performance on tasks of short duration. We do not yet have a clear picture of how cognitive skills are acquired or how memory develops in children with learning disabilities in the classroom (see Shephard & Gelzheiser, this volume). The methodology of comparing LD students with younger NLD students is wholly inadequate for making developmental inferences. Only longitudinal studies can provide answers to the questions of skill acquisition and memory development in the learning disabled.

Theoretical Precision

There is currently much confusion in the field about the exact nature of the cognitive structures and processes that compose an information processing system. From our purview, the confusion stems from the lack of precise characterization of the cognitive processes and structures. Kosslyn (1985) aptly points out that cognitive theories are not always theories of mental representations:

> Mental representations are entities that are taken to actually exist in the head, which not only must be labeled but must be characterized. Often cognitive psychologists supply the label but do not go on to present a theory of the entities themselves. (p. 93)

There are numerous examples of this state of affairs in the LD literature. For example, consider the constructs of working memory and STM. In many cases the terms have been used synonomously (see Jorm, 1983, for a review), however there are major differences in these entities that preclude the interpretation of previous findings involving traditional STM tasks (e.g., digit span) as working memory deficits (e.g., Brainerd, 1981).

The work of Baddeley and his colleagues (Baddeley & Hitch, 1974, 1977; Baddeley & Liberman, 1980) provide a theory of the entity of working memory that includes three components: a central executive, an articulatory loop, and a buffer for holding a small amount of visuo-spatial code. Thus, at best, the majority of research on STM deficits could be described as research on the articulatory loop of working memory.

A second example involves the constructs of semantic and episodic memory. Often researchers speak of these two structures but do not describe the structure of information in these memory systems or the processes whereby information in these structures are activated. There are numerous theories of spreading activation (Anderson, 1976, 1983; Collins & Loftus, 1975; Collins & Quillian, 1972; McClelland & Rumelhart, 1981), yet we could find few studies in the LD literature conducted at this level of analysis (Ceci, 1982; Lorsbach, 1982). The study of LD children in the context of long-term memory representations and activation processes would most certainly advance our knowledge about normal memory development and the structure of memory.

Other examples of theoretical constructs or entities that lack theoretical precision could be cited (e.g., executive monitor), but our point about the need for greater theoretical precision, we hope, has become obvious in the two examples provided. It is *not* our intention to advocate the adoption of any one model or theory of long-term memory or working memory, however, we are suggesting that researchers in the field exercise more precision in the description of mental representations that permit evaluation of their utility.

MEMORY IN CONTEXT

Memory research involving LD children has been sharply criticized for its narrow focus on "list learning" (Pressley et al., 1982). We concur with this assessment and recommend a shift toward tasks that more closely resemble activities that children are expected to master in school and at home. It is possible that measures of memory derived from learning lists are poor facsimiles of the way that memory is used when performing tasks embedded in the child's daily routine (Bronner, 1917). The way that a child uses the articulatory loop of working memory to memorize a list of words is very likely to be different from the way s/he uses working memory to comprehend spoken or written discourse, and there may be differences among the various measures of working memory. Data collected by one of our colleagues (Cochran, 1986) revealed only moderate correlations between tasks modeled after Baddeley and Hitch (1974) and Daneman and Carpenter (1980).

An excellent example of the approach we have in mind is the assessment of working memory capacity using the continuous reading task (Goldman, Hogaboom, Bell, & Perfetti, 1980; Perfetti & Lesgold, 1977). In this task, the subject is asked to read a short passage of prose, and at various points the experimenter asks the reader to recall the most recent words read. In the context of reading, working memory is presumed to be the processing mechanism responsible for maintaining words in an active state, assembling the words into propositions, and linking (integrating) the propositions of one sentence with the next sentence. In this type of task there are at least four factors that may affect measures of working memory capacity and control processes (Perfetti, 1985): knowledge base, lexical processes, the number of propositions, and phonological processes.

An individual's knowledge base may affect the demands placed on working memory. Students who differ in their knowledge of a subject, but equated on general reading ability, show substantial differences in their ability to recall the details of an episode (Chiesi, Spilich, & Voss, 1979; Spilich, Vesonder, Chiesi, & Voss, 1979). A more elaborate knowledge base (or schema) would be likely to reduce the processing demands placed on working memory for integrating the text into long-term memory. An interesting comparison would involve reading disabled students who differ only in terms of their knowledge of the subject they are reading about.

Lexical variables are another potential source of variability in measures of working memory capacity. Working memory resources that must be devoted to the activation of symbols in memory decrease resources that can be devoted to maintaining words in an active state and assembling them into propositions. The speed of activating symbols in memory largely determines the speed at which an individual can read (Jackson & McClelland, 1979). Thus, when readers are presented with a timed task, those experiencing difficulties at the level of lexical access may appear to have less working memory capacity.

Another variable that could affect the assessment of working memory are the structural properties of the text (see Taylor & Williams, 1983). The more complex the text, in terms of the number of propositions, the greater the demands placed on working memory (Kintsch & Van Dijk, 1978). Successful comprehension and memory for text depends on the reader's ability to link the propositions from one sentence to the next. This requirement does not appear to be present in the methods used by Baddeley and Hitch (1974) or the reading task suggested by Daneman and Carpenter (1980), where students are asked to remember the last word of a series of unrelated sentences.

Phonologically based processes may also affect the way that working memory is used (see Liberman & Shankweiler, this volume). Perfetti and

McCutchen (1984), for example, proposed that speech sounds are automatically activated as a by-product of lexical access, which in turn facilitates the comprehension processes being carried out in working memory. Resources that must be devoted to activating phonological codes reduce the processing that could be allocated to integrating propositions in working memory.

It should be apparent that there are many task-specific requirements placed on working memory when the goal is comprehension and memory for discourse that are not present in the typical laboratory tasks (cf. Baddeley & Hitch, 1974; Daneman & Carpenter, 1980). This is also likely to be true of other activities such as mathematics, spelling, and problem solving.

Another example of a strategy for the study of memory in context is the teaching experiment. A notable application of this approach involves the use of the mnemonic keyword method with LD students to enhance vocabulary acquisition and scientific classification schemes (see Scruggs, Mastropieri, Levin, & Gaffney, 1985, for a review). Results from this research show that LD students instructed with the keyword method exhibited superior memory performance when compared with similar students receiving direct instruction. From our point of view, learning and remembering the meaning of novel words is altogether different from remembering which words have recently been presented and is more similar to learning required of students in school (see Shephard & Gelzheiser, this volume, for a contrary position).

The significance of an individual's vocabulary becomes apparent when one considers that measures of vocabulary are often considered to be one of the best single indicies of general intellectual ability (e.g., Hunt, 1985). More specifically, word knowledge has been found to be a source of individual differences in the ability to comprehend complex and ambiguous texts (e.g., Small, 1980). It would be of considerable theoretical importance to find that vocabulary were alterable to the extent that it could influence measures of general verbal ability. This appears to be the case. Beck, Perfetti, and McKeown (1983), for example, exposed normal fourth grade students to a 5-month vocabulary training program wherein the students learned 100 new vocabulary words. Students receiving the training, which emphasized speed of activating word knowledge and the elaboration of word knowledge, performed better than the control group on tasks requiring semantic decisions, sentence verification tasks, memory for discourse, and standardized reading comprehension measures. Furthermore, Beck et al. reported a practice effect: words receiving more practice were processed more quickly during the test tasks.

Research involving LD students and instructional strategies derived from different theoretical models are likely to provide information about the role of memory in learning disabilities, the adequacy of the theoretical models of memory, and intellectual functioning in general.

EVALUATION OF THEORETICAL MODELS

If research with LD children is to make contributions to knowledge about memory in general, it will be necessary to design experiments that permit evaluation of competing theoretical models. Often researchers implicitly assume that a particular theoretical model is correct and then proceed to compare normal and LD students in terms of the entities postulated by the model. A notable exception to this rule is the work of Ceci and his colleagues (Ceci, Lea, & Ringstrom, 1980; Ceci et al., 1980, 1981). In the Ceci et al. (1980) study, students were first screened for the presence of specific types of memory deficits: visual, auditory, or both visual and auditory. In Experiment 1, the students were presented with pictures of objects or the spoken names of objects. The pictures were generated from four semantic categories, and each picture was one of four colors (perceptual). The spoken names of objects varied in terms of three attributes: semantic (e.g., animals, fruit), phonetic (homophones), and acoustic (gender/age of voice). Subsequently, students attempted free recall of the objects followed by cued recall. Results from the first experiment show that the effectiveness of semantic cues presented in the impaired modality was diminished. In contrast, perceptual cues were found to be effective regardless of modality impairment. A second experiment was then designed to identify the locus of the memory deficit (encoding vs storage). The procedure for Experiment 2 was similar to the first except that students were presented with either a semantic or perceptual orienting task. The results show that requiring students to process information semantically, when presented in their impaired modality, eliminated the memory deficits observed in Experiment 1. The semantic orienting task did not improve the memory performance of the students identified as having both visual and auditory memory deficits. Thus, the memory deficits are believed to arise at the time of encoding and retrieval.

Results from the two experiments supported the diagnosis of specific memory impairment, however, the findings also have implications for the functional properties (cf., Kosslyn, 1985) of memory. The functional implications of these findings include support for (a) the distinction between a semantic and episodic memory system, (b) independent pathways linking visual and verbal stimuli with the semantic memory system, (c) the duplication of associative networks in the semantic memory system, (d) a unitary pathway that links stimuli with an episodic memory system, and (e) the hypothesis that semantic information is automatically encoded even at the sensory level of processing. Continued research in this vein is likely to yield rich ore. In view of our comments regarding theoretical precision, the structure of the associative networks and the process of spreading activation could be more fully described and investigated. Analyses of memory functions at this level have a close correspondence with neural constructs (Hinton & Anderson, 1981) and would be particularly revealing when studied in the context of learning disabilities.

In retrospect, we believe that considerable advances have occurred in the last decade regarding our understanding of the memory processes that underlie learning disabilities and that the evolution of a paradigm is now taking place within the field. The contents of the present volume represent the continued efforts of researchers to converge on a paradigm for the study of learning disabilities.

ACKNOWLEDGMENTS

This work was supported by the Office of Special Education and Rehabilitative Services awarded to the second author. Authorship was equal and determined by a flip of a coin.

REFERENCES

Ackerman, B. P. (1985). Children's retrieval deficit. In C. J. Brainerd (Ed.), *Basic processes in memory development* (pp. 1–46). New York: Springer-Verlag.

Anderson, J. R. (1976). *Language, memory, and thought*. Hillsdale, NJ: Erlbaum.

Anderson, J. R. (1983). *The architecture of cognition*. Cambridge, MA: Harvard University Press.

Atkinson, B. R., & Seunath, D. H. M. (1973). The effect of stimulus change on attending behavior in normal children and children with learning disorders. *Journal of Learning Disabilities, 6*, 518–523.

Baddeley, A. (1984). Reading and working memory, *Visible Language, 18*, 311–322.

Baddeley, A. D., & Hitch, G. T. (1974). Working memory. In G. A. Bower (Ed.), *The psychology of learning and motivation* (Vol. 8, pp. 47–89). Orlando, FL: Academic Press.

Baddeley, A. D., & Lieberman, K. (1980). Spatial working memory. In R. S. Nickerson (Ed.), *Attention and performance (VIII)*. Hillsdale, NJ: Erlbaum.

Barclay, C. R., & Hagen, J. W. (1982). The development of mediated behavior in children: An alternative view of learning disabilities. In J. P. Das, R. Mulachy, & A. E. Wall (Eds.), *Theory and research in learning disabilities* (pp. 61–84). New York: Plenum.

Batey, O. B., & Sonnerschein, S. (1981). Reading deficits in learning disabled children. *Journal of Applied Developmental Psychology, 2*, 237–246.

Bauer, R. H. (1977a). Memory processes in children with learning disabilities: Evidence for deficient rehearsal. *Journal of Experimental Child Psychology, 24*, 415–430.

Bauer, R. H. (1977b). Short-term memory in learning disabled and nondisabled children. *Bulletin of the Psychonomic Society, 10,* 128–130.

Bauer, R. H. (1979a). Memory, acquisition, and category clustering in learning-disabled children. *Journal of Experimental Child Psychology, 27,* 365–383.

Bauer, R. H. (1979b). Recall after a short delay and acquisition in learning disabled and nondisabled children. *Journal of Learning Disabilities, 12,* 596–608.

Bauer, R. H. (1982). Information processing as a way of understanding and diagnosing learning disabilities. *Topics in Learning and Learning Disabilities, 2,* 33–45.

Bauer, R. H., & Emhert, J. (1984). Information processing in reading-disabled and nondisabled children. *Journal of Experimental Child Psychology, 37,* 271–281.

Beck, I. L., Perfetti, C. A., & McKeown, M. G. (1982). The effects of long-term vocabulary instruction on lexical access and reading comprehension. *Journal of Educational Psychology, 74,* 506–521.

Bjorklund, D. F. (1985). The role of conceptual knowledge in the development of organization in children's memory. In C. J. Brainerd (Ed.), *Basic processes in memory development* (pp. 103–134). New York: Springer-Verlag.

Brown, J. S., & Burton, R. R. (1978). Diagnostic models for procedural bugs in basic mathematical skills. *Cognitive Science, 2,* 155–192.

Bryan, T. (1972). The effect of forced mediation upon short-term memory of children with learning disabilities. *Journal of Learning Disabilities, 5,* 605–609.

Campione, J., Brown, A., & Ferrara, R. (1982). Mental retardation and intelligence. In R. J. Sternberg (Ed.), *Handbook of human intelligence* (pp. 392–473). New York: Cambridge.

Case, R., Kurland, M., & Goldberg, J. (1982). Operational efficiency and the growth of short-term memory span. *Journal of Experimental Child Psychology, 33,* 386–404.

Cavanagh, J. C., & Perlmuter, M. (1982). Metamemory: A critical examination. *Child Development, 53,* 11–28.

Ceci, S. J. (1982). Extracting meaning from stimuli: Automatic and purposive processing of the language-based learning disabled. *Topics in Learning and Learning Disabilities, 2,* 46–53.

Ceci, S. J. (1983). Automatic and purposive semantic processing characteristics of normal and language/learning-disabled children. *Developmental Psychology, 19,* 427–439.

Ceci, S. J. (1984). Developmental study of learning disabilities and memory. *Journal of Experimental Child Psychology, 38,* 352–371.

Ceci, S. J., Ringstrom, M. D., & Lea, S. E. G. (1981). Do language/learning disabled children (L/LDs) have impaired memories? In search of underlying processes. *Journal of Learning Disabilities, 14,* 159–163.

Blumenthal, S. H. (1980). A study of the relationship between speed of retrieval of verbal information and patterns of oral reading errors. *Journal of Learning Disabilities, 3,* 568–570.

Boder, E. (1973). Developmental dyslexia: A diagnostic approach based on three atypical reading patterns. *Developmental Medicine and Child Neurology, 15,* 663–687.

Borkowski, J. G., & Cavanaugh, J. C. (1981). Metacognition and intelligence theory. In M. Friedman, J. P. Das, & N. O'Connor (Eds.), *Intelligence and learning* (pp. 253–258). New York: Plenum.

Brainerd, C. J. (1981). Working memory and the developmental analysis of probability judgement. *Psychological Review, 88,* 463–502.

Brainerd, C. J. (1985). Model-based approaches to storage and retrieval development. In C. J. Brainerd (Ed.), *Basic processes in memory development* (pp. 143–208). New York: Springer-Verlag.

Brown, A. L. (1975). The development of memory: Knowing, knowing about knowing, and knowing how to know. In H. W. Reese (Ed.), *Advances in child development and behavior* (Vol. 10). Orlando, FL: Academic Press.

Brown, A. (1978). Knowing when, where, and how to remember: A problem of medatation. In R. Glaser (Ed.), *Advances in instructional psychology* (Vol. 2, pp. 104–152). Hillsdale, NJ: Erlbaum.

Brown, A. L., & Campione, J. C. (1981). Inducing flexible thinking: The problem of access. In M. Friedman, J. P. Das, & N. O'Connor (Eds.), *Intelligence and learning* (pp. 515–530). New York: Plenum.

Brown, A., & Palincsar, A. (1982). Inducing strategic learning from texts by means of informed self-control training. *Topics in Learning and Learning Disabilities, 2,* 1–8.

Ceci, S. J., Lea, S. E. G., & Ringstrom, M. D. (1980). Coding characteristics of normal and learning-disabled 10-year-olds: Evidence for dual pathways to the cognitive system. *Journal of Experimental Psychology: Human Learning and Memory, 6,* 785–797.

Cermak, L. (1983). Information processing deficits in children with learning disabilities. *Journal of Learning Disabilities, 16,* 599–605.

Cermak, L. S., Goldberg, J., Cermak, S. A., & Drake, C. (1980). The short-term memory ability of children with learning disabilities. *Journal of Learning Disabilities, 13,* 20–24.

Chase, W. G., & Ericsson, J. A. (1981). Skilled memory. In J. R. Anderson (Ed.), *Children's thinking: What develops?* (pp. 73–96). Hillsdale, NJ: Erlbaum.

Cherry, R., & Kruger, B. (1983). Selective auditory attention abilities of learning disabled and normal achieving children. *Journal of Learning Disabilities, 16,* 221–225.

Chi, M. T. H. (1978). Knowledge structure and memory development. In R. Siegler (Ed.), *Children's thinking: What develops?* Hillsdale, NJ: Erlbaum.

Chi, M. T. H. (1981). Knowledge development and memory performance. In M. P. Friedman, J. P. Das, & N. O'Connor (Eds.), *Intelligence and learning* (pp. 221–230). New York: Plenum.

Chiesi, H. L., Spilich, G. J., & Vass, J. F. (1979). Acquisition of domain-related information in relation to high and low domain knowledge. *Journal of Verbal Learning and Berbal Behavior, 18,* 257–274.

Cochran, K. F. (1986, April). *Individual differences in working memory and text comprehension.* Paper presented at the meeting of the Rocky Mountain Psychological Association, Denver, CO.

Cohen, R. L. (1978). Cognitive deficits, learning disabilities, and WISC verbal-performance consistency. *Developmental Psychology, 14,* 624–634.

Cohen, R. L. (1981). Short-term memory deficits in reading disabled children, in the absence of opportunity for rehearsal strategies. *Intelligence, 5,* 69–76.

Cohen, R. L., Netley, C., & Clarke, M. A. (1984). On the generality of the short-term memory/reading ability relationship. *Journal of Learning Disabilities, 17,* 218–221.

Collins, A. M., & Loftus, E. F. (1975). A spreading activation theory of semantic processing. *Psychological Review, 82,* 407–428.

Collins, A. M., & Quillian, M. R. (1972). Experiments on semantic memory and language comprehension. In L. W. Gregg (Ed), *Cognition and learning.* New York: Wiley.

Connors, C. K., K. Kramer, & F. Guerra. (1969). Auditory synthesis and dichotic listening in children with learning disabilities. *Journal of Special Education, 3,* 163–170.

Copeland, A. P., Reiner, E. M. (1984). The selective attention of learning disabled children: Three studies. *Journal of Abnormal Child Psychology, 12,* 455–470.

Copeland, A. P., & Wisniewski, N. M. (1981). Learning disability and hyperactivity: Deficits in selective attention. *Journal of Experimental Child Psychology, 32,* 88–101.

Craik, F. I. M. (1977). Age differences in human memory. In J. E. Birren & K. W. Schaie (Eds.), *Handbook of the psychology of aging.* (pp. 95–129). New York: Van Nostrand.

Craik, F. I. M., & Simon, E. (1980). Age differences in memory: The role of attention and depth of processing. In L. W. Poon, J. L. Fozard, L. S. Cermak, D. Arenberg, & L. W. Thompson (Eds.), *New directions in memory and aging* (pp. 95–129). Hillsdale, NJ: Erlbaum.

Dallago, M. L. P., & Moely, B. E. (1980). Free recall in boys of normal and poor reading levels as a function of task manipulation. *Journal of Experimental Child Psychology, 30,* 62–78.

Daneman, M., & Carpenter, P. A. (1980). Individual differences in working memory and reading. *Journal of Verbal Learning and Verbal Behavior, 19,* 450–466.

Dempster, F. N. (1981). Memory span: Sources of individual and developmental differences. *Psychological Bulletin, 89,* 63–100.

Dempster, F. N. (1985). Short-term memory development in childhood and adolescence. In C. J. Brainerd (Ed.). *Basic processes in memory development* (pp. 209–248). New York: Springer-Verlag.

Dempster, F. N., & Cooney, J. B. (1982). Individual differences in digit span, susceptibility to proactive interference, and aptitude/achievement test scores. *Intelligence, 6,* 399–416.

Dawson, M. H., Hallahan, D. P., Reeve, R. E., & Ball, D. W. (1980). The effect of reinforcement and verbal rehearsal on selective attention in learning-disabled children. *Journal of Abnormal Child Psychology, 8,* 133–144.

Denckla, M. B., & Rudel, R. G. (1974). Rapid "automatized" naming of pictured objects, colors, letters, and numbers by normal children. *Cortex, 10,* 186–202.

Denckla, M., & Rudel, R. (1976). Rapid "automatized" naming (R.A.N.): Dyslexia differentiated from other learning disabilities. *Neuropsychologia, 14,* 471–479.

Deutsch-Smith, D., Deshler, D., Hallahan, D., Lovitt, S. R., Voress, J., & Ysseldyke, J. (1984). Minimum standards for the description of subjects in learning disabilities research reports. *Journal of Learning Disabilities, 7,* 221–225.

Dykman, R. A., Walls, R. C., Suzuki, T., Ackerman, P. T., & Peters, J. E. (1970). Children with learning disabilities: Conditioning, differentiation, and the effect of distraction. *American Journal of Orthopsychiatry, 40,* 766–782.

Elbert, J. C. (1984). Short-term memory encoding and memory search in the word recognition of learning-disabled children. *Journal of Learning Disabilities, 17,* 342–345.

Ericsson, K. A., & Simon, H. A. (1980). Verbal aspects as data. *Psychological Review, 87,* 215–251.

Farnham-Diggory, S. (1978). *Learning disabilities.* Cambridge, MA: Harvard University Press.

Flavell, J. (1976). Metacognitive aspect of problem solving. In L. Resnick (Ed.), *The nature of intelligence* (pp. 231–236). Hillsdale, NJ: Erlbaum.

Flavell, J. (1979). Metacognition and cognitive monitoring. *American Psychologist, 34,* 906–911.

Goldman, S. R., Hogaboam, T. W., Bell, L. C., & Perfetti, C. A. (1980). Short-term retention of discourse during reading. *Journal of Educational Psychology, 72,* 647–655.

Goyen, J. D., & Lyle, J. (1971). Effect of incentives upon retarded and normal readers on a visual-associate learning task. *Journal of Experimental Child Psychology, 11,* 274–280.

Goyen, J. D., & Lyle, J. (1973). Short-term memory and visual discrimination in retarded readers. *Perceptual and Motor Skills, 36,* 403–408.

Guthrie, J. T., & Goldberg, H. K. (1912). Visual sequential memory in reading disability. *Journal of Learning Disabilities, 5,* 41–46.

Guttentag, R. E. (1984). The mental effort requirement of cumulative rehearsal: A developmental study. *Journal of Experimental Child Psychology, 37,* 92–106.

Hagen, J. W., Jongeward, R. H., & Kail, R. V. (1975). Cognitive perspectives on the development of memory. In H. W. Reese (Ed.), *Advances in child development and behavior* (Vol. 10, pp. 57–97). Orlando, FL: Academic Press.

Haines, D., & Torgesen, J. K. (1979). The effects of incentives on short-term memory and rehearsal in reading disabled children. *Learning Disabilities Research Quarterly, 2,* 18–55.

Hallahan, D. P. (1975). Comparative research studies on the psychological characteristics of learning disabled children. In W. M. Cruickshank & D. P. Hallahan (Ed.), *Perceptual and learning disabilities in children* (Vol. 1, pp. 29–62). Syracuse, NY: Syracuse University Press.

Forrest-Pressley, DD. L., & Gillies, L. A. (1983). Children's flexible use of strategies during reading. In M. Pressley & J. R. Levin (Eds.), *Cognitive strategy research: Educational applications.* New York: Springer-Verlag.

Friedes, D. (1974). Human information processing and sensory modality: Cross-modal functions, information complexity, memory, and deficit. *Psychological Bulletin, 81,* 284–310.

Friedrich, D. (1974). Developmental analysis of memory capacity and information encoding strategies. *Developmental Psychology, 10,* 559–563.

Geiselman, R. E., Woodward, J. A., & Beatty, J. (1982). Individual differences in verbal memory performance: A test of alternative information-processing models. *Journal of Experimental Psychology: General, 111,* 109–134.

Gelzheiser, L. (1984). Generalization from categorical memory tasks to prose by learning disabled adolescents. *Journal of Educational Psychology, 76,* 1128–1138.

Gerber, M. M. (1983). Learning disabilities and cognitive strategies: A case for training or constraining problem solving. *Journal of Learning Disabilities, 16,* 255–260.

Geschwind, N. (1962). The anatomy of acquired disorders of reading. In J. Money (Ed.), *Reading disability: Progress and research needs in dyslexia* (pp. 115–129). Baltimore: Johns Hopkins Press.

Golden, A. J., McCutcheon, B. A., Delay, E. R., & Isaac, W. (1982). Perceptual speed and short term retention of visual stimuli in preschool children. *Journal of Applied Developmental Psychology, 3,* 329–335.

Hallahan, D. P. (1975). Distractibility in the learning disabled child. In N. M. Cruickshank & D. P. Hallahan (Eds.), *Perceptual and learning disabilities in children (Vol. 2): Research and theory.* (pp. 195–220). Syracuse, NY: Syracuse University Press.

Hallahan, D. P. Gajar, A. H., Cohen, S. B., & Tarver, S. G. (1978). Selective attention and focus of control in learning disabled and normal children. *Journal of Learning Disabilities, 11,* 231–236.

Hallahan, D. P., & Cruickshank, W. M. (1973). *Psychoeducational foundations of learning disabilities.* Englewood Cliffs, NJ: Prentice-Hall.

Hallahan, D. P., & Reeves, R. (1980). Selective attention and distractibility. In B. Keogh (Ed.), *Advances in special education* (Vol. 1, pp. 141–181). Greenwich, CT: JAI Press.

Harber, J. R. (1981). Learning disabilities research: How far have we progressed? *Learning Disability Quarterly, 4,* 372–381.

Hasher, L., & Zacks, R. T. (1979). Automatic and effortful processes in memory. *Journal of Experimental Psychology: General, 108,* 356–388.

Hinshelwood, J. (1917). *Congenital word blindness.* London: Lewis.

Hinton, G. E., & Anderson, J. A. (1981). *Parallel models of associative memory.* Hillsdale, NJ: Erlbaum.

Howe, M. L., Brainerd, C. J., & Kingma, J. (1985). Storage-retrieval processes of normal and learning disabled children: A stages-of-learning analysis of picture-word effects. *Child Development, 56,* 1120–1133.

Humphreys, M. S., Lynch, M. J., Revelle, W., & Hall, J. W. (1983). Individual differences in short-term memory. In R. Dillon & R. Schmeck (Eds.), *Individual differences in cognition* (pp. 35–63). Orlando, FL: Academic Press.

Hunt, E. B. (1985). Verbal ability. In R. J. Sternberg (Ed.), *Human abilities: An information processing approach.* (pp. 31–58). New York: W. H. Freeman.

Jackson, M. D., & McClelland, J. L. (1979). Processing determinants of reading speed. *Journal of Experimental Psychology: General, 108,* 151–181.

Jorm, A. J. (1979). The cognitive and neurological basis of developmental dyslexia: A theoretical framework and review. *Cognition, 7,* 19–33.

Jorm, A. F. (1983). Specific reading retardation and work memory: A review. *British Hournal of Psychology, 74,* 311–342.

Kail, R. V., & Bisanz, J. (1982). Cognitive strategies. In C. R. Puff (Ed.), *Handbook of research methods in human memory and cognition* (pp. 229–255). Orlando, FL: Academic Press.

Kavale, K. A., & Forness, S. R. (1985a). The historical foundation of learning disabilities: A quantitative synthesis assessing the valildity of Strauss and Werner's exogenous versus endogenous distinction of mental retardation. *Remedial and Special Education, 6,* 18–25.

Kavale, K. A., & Forness, S. R. (1985b). *The science of learning disabilities.* San Diego: College-Hill Press.

Kavale, K. A., & Nye, C. (1981). Research definitions of learning disabilities: A survey of the literature. *Learning Disability Quarterly, 4,* 383–388.

Keogh, B., Major-Kingsley, S., Omori-Gordon, H., & Reid, H. (1982). *A system of marker variables in the field of learning disabilities.* New York: Syracuse University Press.

Kintsch, W., & Dijk, T. A. (1978). Toward a model of text comprehension and production. *Psychological Review, 85,* 363–394.

Kneedler, R. D., & Hallahan, D. P. (1984). Self-monitoring as an attentional strategy for academic tasks with learning disabled children. In B. Gholson & T. Rosenthal (Eds.), *Applications of cognitive-developmental theory* (pp. 243–258). San Diego, CA: Academic Press.

Koorland, M. A., & Wolking, W. D. (1982). Effect of reinforcement on modality of stimulus control in learning. *Learning Disability Quarterly, 5,* 264–273.

Koppitz, E. M. (1971). *Children with learning disabilities: A five year follow-up study.* Orlando, FL: Grune & Stratton.

Kosslyn, S. M. (1984). Mental representation. In J. R. Anderson & S. M. Kosslyn (Eds.), *Tutorials in learning and memory: Essays in honor of Gordon Bower* (pp. 91–117). New York: W. H. Freeman.

Kuhn, T. S. (1979). *The structure of scientific revolutions.* Chicago: University of Chicago Press.

Kussmaul, A. (1877). Disturbances of speech. *Cyclopedia of Practical Medicine, 14,* 581–875.

Lehman, E. B., & Brady, K. M. (1982). Presentation modality and taxonomic category as encoding dimensions from good and poor readers. *Journal of I ˑarning Disabilities, 15,* 103–105.

Liberman, I. Y., Shankweiler, D., Orlando, C., Harris, K. S., & Berti, F. B. (1971). Letter confusion and reversals of sequence in the beginning reader: Implications for Orton's theory of developmental dyslexia. *Cortex, 7,* 127–142.

Loper, A. B., Hallahan, D. P., & Ianna, S. O. (1982). Meta-attention in learning disabled and normal students. *Learning Disabilities Quarterly, 5,* 29–36.

Lorsbach, T. C. (1982). Individual differences in semantic encoding processes. *Journal of Learning Disabilities, 15,* 476–480.

Lorsbach, T. C., & Gray, J. M. (1985). The development of encoding processes in learning disabled children. *Journal of Learning Disabilities, 18,* 222–227.

Lyon, R., & Watson, B. (1981). Empirically derived subgroups of learning disabled readers: Diagnostic characteristics. *Journal of Learning Disabilities, 14,* 256–261.

Maisto, A. A., & Sipe, S. (1980). An examination of encoding and retrieval processes in reading disabled children. *Journal of Experimental Child Psychology, 30,* 223–230.

Mandler, G. (1979). Organization and repetition: Organizational principles with special references to rote learning. In L. Nilsson (Ed.), *Perspectives on memory research* (pp. 293–315). Hillsdale, NJ: Erlbaum.

Manis, F. R. (1985). Acquisition of word identification skills in normal and disabled readers. *Journal of Educational Psychology, 77,* 78–90.

Mason, M. (1980). Reading ability and the encoding of item and location information. *Journal of Experimental Psychology: Human Perception and Performance, 6,* 89–98.

Mastropieri, M. A., Scruggs, T. E., Levin, J. R., Gaffney, J., & McLoone, B. (1985). Mnemonic vocabulary instruction for learning disabled students. *Learning Disability Quarterly, 8,* 57–63.

Mazer, S. R., McIntyre, C. W., Murray, M. E., Till, R. E., & Blackwell, S. L. (1983). Visual persistence and information pick-up in learning disabled children. *Journal of Learning Disabilities, 16,* 221–225.

McClelland, J. L., & Rumelhart, D. E. (1981). An interactive model of context effects in letter perception: I. An account of basic findings. *Psychological Review, 88,* 375–407.

McGrady, J. J., & Olson, D. A. (1970). Visual and auditory learning processes in normal children and children with specific learning disabilities. *Exceptional Children, 36,* 581–589.

McIntyre, C. W., Murray, M. E., Coronin, C. M., & Blackwell, S. L. (1978). Span of apprehension in learning disabled boys. *Journal of Learning Disabilities, 11,* 13–20.

Miller, P. H., & Bigi, L. (1979). The development of children's understanding of attention. *Merrill Palmer Quarterly, 25,* 235–250.

Mishra, S. P., Shitala, P., Ferguson, B. A., & King, P. V. (1985). Research with the Wechsler Digit Span Subtest: Implications for Assessment. *School Psychology Review, 14,* 37–47.

Monroe, M. (1932). *Children who cannot read.* Chicago: University of Chicago Press.

Morgan, W. P. (1896). *A case of congenital word blindness. British Medical Journal, 2,* 1378–1379.

Morrison, F. J., Giordani, B., & Nagy, J. (1977). Reading disability: An information processing analysis. *Science, 196,* 77–79.

Murdock, B. B. (1974). *Human memory: Theory and data.* New York: Wiley.

National Advisory Committee on Handicapped Children. (1968, January). *Special education for handicapped children. First annual report.* Washington, DC: U.S. Department of Health, Education, and Welfare.

Obrzut, J. E. Hynd, G. W., Obrzut, A., & Leitgeb, J. L. (1980). Time sharing and dichotic listening asymmetry in normal and learning disabled children. *Brain and Language, 11,* 181–194.

Obrzut, J. E., Hynd, G. W., Obrzut, A., & Pirozzola, F. J. (1981). Effect of directed attention on cerebral asymmetries in normal and learning disabled children. *Developmental Psychology, 17,* 118–125.

Ornstein, P., & Corsale, C. (1979). Organizational factors in children's memory. In C. R. Puff (Ed.), *Memory organization and structure* (pp. 219–258). Orlando, FL: Academic Press.

Ornstein, P. A., & Naus, M. J. (1978). Rehearsal processes in children's memory. In P. A. Ornstein (Ed.), *Memory development in children.* Hillsdale, NJ: Erlbaum.

Ornstein, P. A., & Naus, M. J. (1983). *Effects of the knowledge base on children's memory processing.* Unpublished manuscript.

Orton, S. T. (1925). "Word-blindness" in school children. *Archives of Neurology and Psychiatry, 14,* 581–615.

Orton, S. T. (1937). *Reading, writing, and speech problems in children.* New York: Norton.

Owen, F. W., Adams, P. A., Forrest, T., Stolz, L. M., & Fisher, S. (1971). Learning disorders in children: Sibling studies. *Monographs of the Society for Research in Child Development, 36,* (Serial No. 144). Chicago: University of Chicago Press.

Perfetti, C. A. (1985). Reading ability. In R. J. Sternberg (Ed.), *Human abilities: An information processing approach.* (pp. 59–82). New York: W. H. Freeman.

Perfetti, C. A., & Hogaboam, T. (1975). The relationship between single word decoding and reading comprehension skill. *Journal of Educational Psychology, 67,* 461–469.

Perfetti, C. A., & Lesgold, A. M. (1977). Discourse comprehension and sources of individual differences. In M. A. Just & P. A. Carpenter (Eds.), *Cognitive processes in comprehension* (pp. 141–183). Hillsdale, NJ: Erlbaum.

Perfetti, C. A., & McCutchen, D. (1984). Speech processes in reading. In N. Loss (Ed.), *Advances in speech and language (Vol. 7).* Orlando, FL: Academic Press.

Postman, L. (1976). Methodology of human learning. In W. K. Estes (Ed.), *Handbook of learning and cognitive processes* (Vol. 1, pp. 11–69). Hillsdale, NJ: Erlbaum.

Pressley, M., Borkowski, J. G., & Sullivan, J. T. (1984). Memory strategy instruction is made of this: Metamemory and durable strategy use. *Educational Psychologist, 10,* 94–107.

Pressley, M., Forrest-Pressley, D. L., Elliott-Faust, D., & Miller, G. (1985). Children's use of cognitive strategies, how to teach cognitive strategies, and what to do if they can't be taught. In M. Pressley & C. J. Brainerd (Eds.), *Cognitive approaches to memory development.* New York: Springer-Verlag.

Pressley, M., Heisel, B. E., McCormick, C. B., & Nakamura, G. V. (1982). Memory strategy Instruction. In C. J. Brainerd & M. Pressley (Eds.), *Progress in cognitive development research (Vol. 2): Verbal processes in children (pp. 125–159).* New York: Springer-Verlag.

Pressley, M., & Levin, J. R. (1986). Elaborative learning strategies for the inefficient learner. In S. J. Ceci (Ed.), *Handbook of cognitive, social and neuropsychological aspects of learning disabilities.* Hillsdale, NJ: Erlbaum.

Rabinowitz, J. C., Ackerman, B. P., Craik, F. I. M., & Hinchley, J. L. (1982). Aging and metamemory: The roles of relatedness and imagery. *Journal of Gerontology, 37,* 688–695.

Reid, D. K., & Hresko, W. P. (1981). *A cognitive approach to learning disabilities.* New York: McGraw Hill.

Rizzo, N. D. (1939). Studies in visual and auditory memory memory span with reference to reading disability. *Journal of Experimental Education, 8,* 208–244.

Samuels, J. (in press). Information processing and reading. *Journal of Learning Disabilities.*

Samuels, S. J., & Miller, N. L. (1985). Failure to find attention differences between learning disabled and normal children on classroom and laboratory tasks. *Exceptional Children, 51,* 358–375.

Satz, P., & Morris, R. (1981). Learning disability subtypes: A review. In M. Pirozzolo & M. Wittrock (Eds.), *Neuropsychological and cognitive processes in reading* (pp. 109–141). Orlando, FL: Academic Press.

Scruggs, T. F., Mastropieri, M. A., Levin, J. R., & Gaffney, J. S. (1985). Facilitating the acquisition of science facts in learning disabled students. *American Educational Research Journal, 22,* 575–586.

Senf, G. M., & Feshbach, S. (1970). Development of bisensory memory in culturally deprived, dyslexic and normal readers, *Journal of Educational Psychology, 61,* 461–470.

Shankweiler, D., Liberman, I. Y., Mark, S. L., Fowler, L. A., & Fischer, F. W. (1979). The speech code and learning to read. *Journal of Experimental Psychology: Human Learning and Memory, 5,* 531–545.

Shepard, L. A., & Smith, M. L. (1983). An evaluation of the identification of learning disabled students in Colorado. *Learning Disabilities Quarterly, 6,* 115–127.

Shepard, L. A., Smith, M. L., & Vojir, C. P. (1983). Characteristics of pupils identified as learning disabled. *American Educational Research Journal, 20,* 309–331.

Shiffrin, R. M., & Schneider, W. (1977). Controlled and automatic human information processing: II. Perceptual learning, automatic attending, and a general theory. *Psychological Review, 84,* 127–190.

Siegel, L., & Lindor, B. A. (1984). Short-term memory processing in children with reading and arithmetic learning disabilities. *Developmental Psychology, 20,* 200–207.

Small, S. (1980). *Word expert parsing: A theory of distributed word-based natural longuage understanding* (Tech. Rep. No. TR-954 NSG-7253). College Park, MD: University of Maryland, Department of Computer Science.

Spear, L. C., & Sternberg, R. J. (1986). An information-processing framework for understanding reading disability. In S. Ceci (Ed.), *Handbook of cognitive, social and neuropsychological aspects of learning disabilities.* Hillsdale, NJ: Erlbaum.

Speece, D. L., McKinney, J. D., & Applebaum, M. E. (1985). Classification and validation of behavioral subtyes of learning disabled children. *Journal of Educational Psychology, 77,* 66–77.

Spilich, G. J., Vesonder, G. T., Chiesi, H. L., & Voss, J. F. (1979). Text processing of domain-related information for individuals with high and low domain knowledge. *Journal of Verbal Learning and Verbal Behavior, 18,* 275–290.

Stanovich, K. E. (1982). Individual differences in the cognitive processes of reading: II. Text-level processes. *Journal of Learning Disabilities, 15,* 549–554.

Strauss, A. A., & Kephart, W. C. (1955). *Psychopathology and education of the brain-injured child* (Vol. 2): *Progress in theory and clinic.* Orlando, FL: Grune & Stratton.

Strauss, A. A., & Lehtinen, L. E. (1947). *Psychopathology and education of the brain-injured child.* Orlando, FL: Grune & Stratton.

Swanson, H. L. (1977a). Nonverbal visual short-term memory as a function of age and dimensionality in learning disabled children. *Child Development, 45,* 51–55.

Swanson, H. L. (1977b). Response strategies and dimensional salience with learning disabled and mentally retarded children on a short-term memory task. *Journal of Learning Disabilities, 10,* 635–642.

Swanson, L. (1978). Verbal encoding effects on the visual short-term memory of learning-disabled and normal readers. *Journal of Educational Psychology, 70,* 539–544.

Swanson, H. L. (1981). Vigilance deficit in learning disabled children: A signal detection analysis. *Journal of Child Psychology and Psychiatry, 4,* 393–399.

Swanson, H. L. (1983a). A developmental study of vigilance in learning disabled and non-disabled children. *Journal of Abnormal Child Psychology, 11,* 415–429.

Swanson, L. (1983b). Relations and among metamemory, rehearsal activity and word recall in learning disabled and nondisabled readers. *British Journal of Educational Psychology, 53,* 186–194.

Swanson, H. L. (1984a). Effects of cognitive effort and word distinctiveness on learning disabled and nondisabled readers' recall. *Journal of Educational Psychology, 76,* 894–908.

Swanson, H. L. (1984b). Semantic visual memory codes in learning disabled readers. *Journal of Experimental Child Psychology, 37,* 124–140.

Swanson, H. L. (1985). Assessing learning disabled children's intellectual performance: An information processing perspective. In K. D. Gadow (Ed.), *Advances in learning and behavior disabilities* (Vol. 4, pp. 225–272). Greenwich, CT: JAI Press.

Swanson, H. L. (in press). Do semantic memory deficiencies underlie learning disabled readers' hemispheric and encoding processes? *Journal of Experimental Child Psychology.*

Swanson, H. L., & Cooney, J. B. (1985). Strategy transformation in learning disabled and nondisabled students. *Learning Disabilities Quarterly, 8,* 221–230.

Swanson, H. L., & Obrzut, J. E. (1985). Learning disabled readers' recall as a function of distinctive encoding, hemisphere processing and selective attention. *Journal of Learning Disabilities, 18,* 409–418.

Sykes, D. H., Douglas, V. I., Weiss, G., & Minde, K. K. (1971). Attention in hyperactive children and the effect of methylphenidate (Ritalin). *Journal of Experimental Child Psychology, 12,* 375–385.

Tarver, S. G., Hallahan, D. P., Kauffman, J. M., & Ball, D. W. (1976). Verbal rehearsal and selective attention in children with learning disabilities: A developmental lag. *Journal of Experimental Child Psychology, 22,* 375–385.

Taylor, M. B., & Williams J. P. (1983). Comprehension of learning-disabled readers: Task and text variations. *Journal of Educational Psychology, 75,* 743–751.

Torgesen, J. K. (1975). Problems and prospects in the study of learning disabilities. In M. Heatherington (Ed.), *Review of child development research* (Vol. 5, pp. 385–440). Chicago: University of Chicago Press.

Torgeson, J. K. (1977). The role of nonspecific factors in the task performance of learning disabled children: A theoretical assessment. *Journal of Learning Disabilities, 10,* 27–34.

Torgesen, J. K. (1977). Memorization processes in reading-disabled children. *Journal of Educational Psychology, 69,* 571–578.

Torgesen, J. K. (1978a). Memorization process in reading-disabled children. *Journal of Educational Psychology, 69,* 571–578.

Torgesen, J. K. (1978b). Performance of reading disabled children in serial memory tasks: A review. *Reading Research Quarterly, 19,* 57–87.

Torgesen, J. K. (1981l). The relationship between memory and attention in learning disabilities. *Exceptional Education Quarterly, 2,* 51–59.

Torgesen, J. K. (1985). Memory processes in reading disabled children. *Journal of Learning Disabilities, 18,* 350–357.

Torgesen, J. K., Bowen, C., & Ivey, C. (1978). Task structure vs. modality of the Visual-Oral Digit Span test. *Journal of Educational Psychology, 70,* 451–456.

Torgesen, J. K., & Dice, C. (1980). Characteristics of research on learning disabilities. *Journal of Learning Disabilities, 13,* 531–535.

Torgesen, J. K., & Greenstein, J. J. (1982). Why do some learning disabled children have problems remembering? Does it make a difference? *Topics in Learning & Learning Disabilities, 2,* 54–61.

Torgesen, J. K., & Goldman, T. (1977). Rehearsal and short-term memory in second grade reading disabled children. *Child Development, 48,* 56–61.

Torgesen, J. K., & Houck, G. (1980). Processing deficiencies in learning disabled children who perform poorly on the digit span task. *Journal of Educational Psychology, 72,* 141–160.

Torgesen, J. K., Murphy, H. A., & Ivey, C. (1979). The effects of an orienting task on the memory performance of reading disabled children. *Journal of Learning Disabilities, 12,* 396–401.

U.S. Office of Education, (1976). Education of handicapped children: Assistance to states: Proposed Rulemaking. *Federal Register, 41,*

U.S. Office of Education, (1977). Education of handicapped children: Implementation of Part B of the Education of the Handicapped Act. *Federal Register 42*, PART II.

U.S. Office of Education. (1977). Education of handicapped children: Assistance to states: Procedures for evaluating specific learning disabilities. *Federal Register, 42*.

U.S. Office of Education. (1979). *Progress toward a free appropriate public education: A report to Congress on on the Implementation of PL 94-142: The Education for All Handicapped Children Act.* Washington, DC: U.S. Department of Health, Education, and Welfare.

Vellutino, F. R. (1977). Alternative conceptualizations of dyslexia: Evidence in support of a verbal-deficit hypothesis. *Harvard Educational Review, 47*, 334–345.

Vellutino, F. R. (1979). *Dyslexia: Theory and research.* Cambridge, MA: MIT Press.

Vellutino, F. R., Harding, C. J., Phillips, F., & Steger, J. A. (1975a). Differential transfer in poor and normal readers. *Journal of Genetic Psychology, 126*, 3–18.

Vellutino, F. R., & Scanlon, D. M. (1982). Verbal processing in poor and normal readers. In C. J. Brainerd & M. Pressly (Eds.), *Verbal processes in children* (pp. 189–264). New York: Springer-Verlag.

Vellutinio, F. R., & Scanlon, D. M. (1985). Free recall of concrete and abstract words in poor and normal readers. *Journal of Experimental Child Psychology, 39*, 363–380.

Vellutino, F. R., & Scanlon, D. M. (1985). Verbal memory in poor and normal readers: Developmental differences in the use of linguistic codes. In D. Gray & J. Kavanaugh (Eds.), *Biobehavioral measures of Dyslexia* (in press). Parkton, MD: York Press.

Vellutino, F. R. , Smith, H., Steger, J. A., & Kamin, M. (1975b). Reading disability: Age differences and the perceptual-deficit hypothesis. *Child Development, 46*, 487–493.

Vellutino, F. R., Steger, J. A., Harding, C. J., & Phillips, F. (1975c). Verbal vs. non-verbal paired-associates learning in poor and normal readers. *Neuropsychologia, 13*, 75–82.

Werner, H. (1948). *Comparative psychology of mental development.* New York: International Universities Press.

Wong, B. Y. L., Wong, R., & Foth, D. (1977). Recall and clustering of verbal materials among normal and poor readers. *Bulletin of the Psychonomic Society, 10*, 375–378.

Wong, B. Y . L. (1978). The effects of directive cues on the organization of memory and recall in good and poor readers. *Journal of Educational Research, 72*, 32–38.

Wong, B. Y. L. (1979). Increasing retention of main ideas through questioning strategies. *Learning Disability Quarterly, 2*, 42–47.

Wong, B. Y. L. (1982). Strategic behaviors in selecting retrieval cues in gifted, normal achieving and learning disabled children. *Journal of Learning Disabilities, 15*, 33–37.

Wong, B. Y. L. & Sawatsky, D. (1984). Sentence elaboration and retention of good, average and poor readers. *Learning and Disability Quarterly, 6*, 229–236.

Worden, P. E. (1983). Memory strategy instruction for the learning disabled. In M. Pressley & J. R. Levin (Eds.), *Cognitive strategy research: Psychological foundations* (Vol. 129–153). New York: Springer-Verlag.

Worden, P. E. (1986). Comprehension and memory for prose in the leaing disabled. In S. J. Ceci (Ed.), *Handbook of cognitive, social and neuropsychological aspects of learning disabilities* (Vol. 1, pp. 241–262). Hillsdale, NJ: Erlbaum.

Worden, P. E., Malmgren, & Gabourie, P. (1982). Memory for stories in learning disabled adults. *Journal of Learning Disabilities, 15*, 145–152.

Worden, P. E., & Nakamura, G. V. (1983). Story comprehension and recall in learning-disabled vs. normal college students. *Journal of Educational Psychology, 74*, 633–641.

CONTROL PROCESSES AS A WAY OF UNDERSTANDING, DIAGNOSING, AND REMEDIATING LEARNING DISABILITIES

Richard H. Bauer

ABSTRACT

The importance of the learning and memory processes that are under the learner's own control and the deficient use of control processes by learning-disabled (LD) and reading disabled (RD) children are discussed. Rehearsal, reorganization, underlining, taking notes, identifying important information, rate of presenting to-be-recalled information, and the use of source material and retrieval cues are deficient in disabled children. The rather remarkable success in improving learning and memory of disabled children by instruc-

Memory and Learning Disabilities
Advances in Learning and Behavioral Disabilities, Suppl. 2, pages 41–81.
ISBN: 0-89232-836-3

tions in the use of control processes is also considered. The deficient use of control processes by LD and RD children appears to be due to a lower level of skill in using control processes and to a lower level of awareness (metamemory) about control processes. Because skill and awareness of control processes are learned, it appears likely that the deficient use of control processes and lower awareness of control processes by disabled children are due to a slower rate of learning about control processes. Thus, disabled children have a basic deficit in learning how to learn.

In a classic book on learning, Clark Hull (1943) wrote "we must regard the processes of learning as wholly automatic" (p. 69). Hull's opinion on the automatic nature of learning was influenced to a great extent by associationist ideas of learning and by Pavlov's work on conditioned reflexes (1927). Associations were thought to be the prototype of all learning and were formed by contiguity of stimuli and frequency of pairing. Pavlov and others showed that stimuli which produce reflexive responses when paired with so called "neutral" stimuli resulted in conditioning. The nature of these conditioned stimuli are such that when presented to the organism a reflex occurs, and this reflex is to a large extent beyond the organisms control. Learning was not only thought to be automatic but given the proper conditioning, the learner could be taught virtually anything. The attitude that learning is not under the learner's control was epitomized by Watson's (1930) classical statement, "Give me a dozen healthy infants, well-formed, and my own specified world to bring them up in and I'll guarantee to take any one at random and train him to become any type of specialist I might select doctor, lawyer, artist, merchant-chief and, yes, even beggar-man and thief, regardless of his talents, penchants, tendencies, attitudes, vocations, and race of his ancestors" (p. 104).

Skinner (1938) pointed out that classical conditioning is a restricted and special case of learning and suggested that behavior is under more voluntary control. Although the organism had a certain degree of control, Skinner eschewed unobservables, such as learning and memory, and placed the control of behavior squarely on reinforcers provided by the environment. For Skinner learning, or at least behavior, was controlled by the proper application of reinforcers. Thus, the organism had control but only in so far as reinforced responses increased and nonreinforced responses were eliminated.

At the time S-R psychologists were espousing the automatic nature of learning, more cognitively orientated psychologists were proposing that both animals and humans exercise a considerable degree of control over their own learning. For example, Tolman (1951) suggested that rats tested various hypotheses to learn complex mazes, and Thorndike (1931) proposed that humans use subvocal repetition (rehearsal) to enhance learning. These early cognitive psychologists were the forerunners of currently very popular information processing models of human learning and memory.

The remainder of this chapter considers the learning and memory processes which are under the learner's control and the importance of control processes for learning disabilities. The intent is to examine the important aspects of learning disabilities, i.e., understanding deficits, diagnosing disabilities, and rehabiliting the disabled in terms of control processes. Furthermore, I attempt to convince the reader that viewing learning disabilities in terms of deficient control processes is the most heuristic and broadest way of considering learning disabilities and holds more promise for the future than other current theoretical formulations.

THE ROLE OF CONTROL PROCESSES IN LEARNING AND MEMORY

Control processes are an integral part of information processing models of human learning and memory. In general, information processing models propose that there are a number of stages with different underlying processes for each stage. On the one hand, there are certain fixed, structural characteristics that are built in and can not be directly modified by conscious control. On the other hand, a variety of learning and memory processes are under the learner's control. The learner has control over the information to-be-stored and the processes used to store and retrieve the information. Control processes may change from time to time in the same individual and differ from individual to individual.

Sensory Memory and Attention

As shown in Figure 1, sensory memory, short-term memory (STM), and long-term memory (LTM) are the major stages of information processing models. The first stage is thought to require attention to the relevant material, and attended to information is stored in modality specific sensory memory. The duration of sensory memory for visual (iconic) information is fairly well established at 0.5 sec. The duration information is stored in auditory (echoic) memory is more debatable and has been estimated at 0.5 to 2 sec. Approximately 10 items can be stored in iconic and echoic memory. Information in sensory memory is interfered with by presenting additional information in the same modality but is altered very little by stimuli in a different modality (for reviews see Atkinson & Shiffrin, 1971; Bower, 1977).

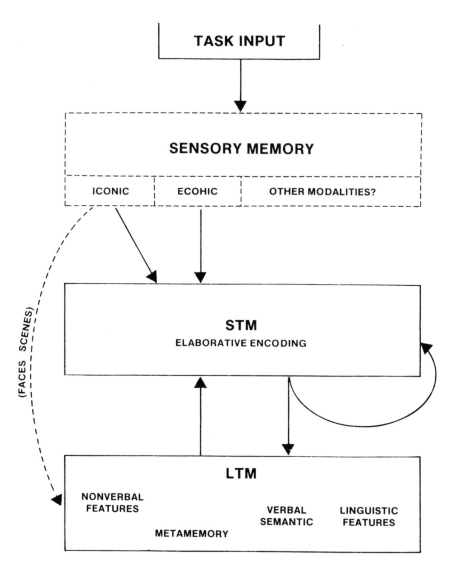

Figure 1. Schematic of a general memory model for verbal and nonverbal stimuli which depicts the flow of information in the system. Solid lines represent information over which the learner has considerable control, and dashed lines represent information over which the learner has very little or no control over.

As shown in Figure 1, the learner has control over information that enters sensory memory by altering attention. Processes of attention at the earliest stage are, in general, gross behavioral changes involving orientation so that the sensory organs are stimulated. Attention can be more complex in the sense of selecting among some stimuli and ignoring other stimuli that impinge on the receptors. Thus, attention can influence learning at the very outset by selecting information for entry into sensory memory. However, once information has entered sensory memory, there is no evidence suggesting that the learner can control the duration or amount of information stored in sensory memory.

STM

A portion of the information in sensory memory can be maintained for a longer time in STM by actively engaging in elaborative encoding processes, such as rehearsal, making sentences or other higher order groups, and identifying categories and associations. At this stage the learner selects the encoding processes to store the information and decides which information to store or ignore. However, ignored information is quickly lost from STM. The information that receives further processing is clearly under the learner's control, and the effective learner will be aware of which material is important to learn. Choosing which information to store is particularly important when the information presentation rate is not under the learner's control, such as in lectures and films, because elaborative encoding processes take time, and the presentation rate may be faster than the learner's rate of elaborative encoding. When the information presentation rate is under the learner's control, such as reading and studying textbooks and notes, the learner has the opportunity to exercise greater control by using a wider variety of control processes, e.g., underlining and taking notes, and by adjusting presentation rates to correspond to their elaborative encoding rates. In some instances STM processes may not be under the learner's control, as for example, when associated items are widely separated in time or by intervening information. However, teachers and textbook writers are usually aware that learning is easier when related information is presented together and present information accordingly.

Since information in STM is not yet permanently stored, attention is also an important consideration at this stage. Irrelevant stimuli which divert attention away from elaborative encoding will result in a rapid loss of information. The number of irrelevant stimuli in a particular environment is likely to be beyond the learner's control, but the learner has control over whether to continue using elaborative encoding or to divert attention to irrelevant stimuli.

LTM

Information for faces, scenes, and other complex visual stimuli that are not verbally labeled go directly from sensory memory to LTM (see Figure 1). Memory for complex, difficult to label visual stimuli is thought to be more rapid, automatic, and under less conscious control (e.g., Bower, 1977; Shiffrin & Schneider, 1977). Thus, memory for complex visual information is related to the fixed, structural characteristics of the memory system in that, other than directing the eyes to the appropriate stimuli and identifying distinctive characteristics, we typically have little direct control over storage of this type of information.

For permanent learning of verbal, semantic information the information must be maintained in STM for some period of time. Elaborative encoding processes not only maintain information in STM, but with enough elaborative encoding verbal information is transferred to LTM. To learn the names (phonological codes) for visual stimuli, the visual stimuli or an image of the stimuli must be connected with the appropriate phonological code in STM. When the phonological code and/or a representation of the visual stimuli have not yet been stored in LTM, the missing stimuli must be provided for entry into STM. Rehearsal and other elaborative encoding processes performed on the information in STM will result in more rapid transfer to LTM.

In most academic situations that students encounter the information must be retained after elaborative encoding has ceased and, for this reason, the effective learner will attempt to store information in LTM. More difficult material requires more elaborative encoding and, for this reason, in nonsubject paced tasks difficult material will have to be presented a number of times for more permanent storage. When the presentation rate is under the learner's control, the learner can decide whether the information has been stored well enough for later recognition or recall and, if the decision is affirmative, the learner is likely to stop elaborative encoding of this information and begin elaborative encoding on new information. More difficult material requires more elaborative encoding and the facile learner will present difficult material at a slower rate than easier material. Thus, when an adequate learner has control over the presentation rate, presentation rate will vary with task difficulty, prior knowledge, and the learner's ability.

Retrieval

Retrieval processes are to a large extent under the learner's control. Rehearsal is considered to be subvocal speech and when using rehearsal as a control process the learner needs only switch to overt speech for recall. Since rehearsal and recall are related, retrieval requirements of the task influence elaborative encoding. For example, when attempting to remember a telephone number, the facile learner will rehearse the digits in the same order in which they must be dialed, because rehearsing in one order facilitates dialing in the same order. When retrieval order is not critical and rehearsal is used as a control process, the learner is very likely to rehearse information in various orders which are designed to promote the maximum storage. If retrieval order is unimportant and to-be-recalled information is stored in both STM and LTM, retrieving less permanently stored information before permanently stored information is the more appropriate control process. Retrieving information in STM before information in LTM is more effective, because recalling information in STM interferes less with recall of information stored in LTM than the reverse recall order (Bauer, 1979a; Rundus, 1971).

Retrieval from LTM is an elusive phenomenon, in part because LTM retrieval is often quite rapid and requires little conscious effort or capacity, i.e., is more automatic. For example, recalling your father's name, your social security number, and reading are automatic in the sense that little conscious effort is required and the speed of retrieval is fast. Although retrieval of this highly over learned information is more automatic, the initial learning of the information required control processes, like rehearsal and reorganizing the material. It appears very likely that the names of all sorts of objects, like letters, digits, words, and lists of these items that are recalled rapidly and effortlessly by normal adults were intially learned by engaging in active control processes. Once the names and verbal labels have been transferred to LTM by control processes, the names and labels can be retrieved from LTM and manipulated in STM along with other information in STM. These manipulations are sometimes referred to as "working memory" (see Figure 1). Thus, in a complex task like reading there is a rapid flow of information between STM and LTM and the facile learner has transferred more of the task requirements to LTM (Atkinson & Shiffrin, 1971; Ericson, 1985; Logan, 1985; Shiffrin & Schneider, 1977).

There is a great deal of evidence that reaction times for highly over learned information are faster than for less well learned information. The longer reaction times for less familiar information is primarily due to the greater amount of time spent in retrieval processes (e.g., Shiffrin & Schneider, 1977). Retrieval failures from LTM have provided an opportunity to study LTM retrieval processes, because time consuming control proceses are required when LTM retrieval fails. The "tip of the tongue" phenomenon, which we have all experienced, involves knowing that one knows a name, fact, or other information, but we are unable to recall the information. To enhance retrieval, the person will often use various retrieval cues which are under their control to search for the information.

For example, in searching for a name, the learner might go through letters of the alphabet, try to reconstruct situations in which the name occurred, and imagine what the person looks like. These retrieval cues are associations stored in LTM, and the greater the number and recency of the appropriate associations, the more rapid and the greater the probability of retrieval. When the information is retrieved, there is an awareness that the answer is correct and the search terminates.

Metamemory

Because control processes will to a large extent determine the flow of information in the learning task and, ultimately, the level of performance, the learner's knowledge about control processes is critical. Knowledge of one's own learning and memory processes and abilities has been termed *metamemory* (Flavell & Wellman, 1977). Metamemory involves such characteristics as knowing what one knows and does not know, predicting the outcome of one's memory performance, efficiently apportioning control processes, and monitoring the outcomes of using various control processes. Episodic metamemory, repisodic metmemory, and control processes are the major components of metamemory. Episodic metamemory is awareness of one's memory abilities and characteristics in specific situations. Repisodic metamemory is knowledge about one's memory abilities and characteristics in general obtained from similar, reoccurring episodes. Metamemory is an important aspect of control processes, because the learner must be aware of various control processes, choose the best one from among their repertoire, monitor the efficiency of each control process, and be aware of when the information has been learned adequately enough for the recognition or recall requirements of the task.

Because repisodic metamemory is obtained from previous experiences, repisodic metamemory will play an important role in long term goals and asperations involving learning. For example, initial failure may result in a search for more adequate control processes which are designed to overcome failures. However, repeated failure by learning disabled (LD) children often occurs and results in avoidance of similar situations in the future (Licht, Kistner, Ozkaragoz, Shapiro, & Clausen, 1985). It should also be pointed out that the person's perceived abilities, as well as actual abilities, will influence long-term goal setting. A primary role of the academic counselor is to insure a reasonable degree of correspondence between actual and perceived learning and memory abilities and learning goals. Since learning and memory abilities may be difficult to change, the academic counselor is likely to accomplish this goal by enhancing the person's metaknowledge.

In specific tasks the mature learner is typically aware of the information they know and do not know, can recognise more difficult material, and use a variety of control processes, such as taking notes, underlining, asking questions, and going to other source materials (Brown & Smiley, 1978; Flavell & Wellman, 1977; Masur, McIntyre, & Flavell, 1973). To assist the learning process, some textbooks provide episodic metaknowledge to the learner. For example, important information is printed in boldface, goals of the lesson or chapter are clearly specified, and summaries and sample questions are provided.

Motivation

Because control processes require effort, motivation and reinforcement will have a major impact on control processes. At a molar level, choosing to enroll in a course, studying for a course, or engaging in some other unrelated activity are under the learner's control and are likely to be motivated by anticipated reward. Thus, one role of motivation is to influence goal setting. At a less molar level, motivation will influence attention and control processes; for example when one student continues to study in a noisy classroom and another becomes distracted by the same stimuli. When reinforcement is provided for recall of some information and not others, more control processes will be devoted to rewarded items and, consequently, rewarded information will be learned more rapidly (Harley, 1965). Thus, motivation and reward will increase control processes for some information and not others. Another role of reinforcement is to provide information concerning the correct response and the level of performance. When the learner is told that a response was incorrect, this provides information that more time should be spent processing information that is not yet learned.

Summary

In most situations the learner is clearly allowed to select the information to store, the control processes used to store and retrieve the information, and determine when the information has been adequately stored and retrieved. In addition, when the learner is allowed to present information at their own rate, the learner has still greater control and can alter presentation rates to correspond to other control processes being used to perform the task.

The discussion on control processes has centered around information processing models of learning and memory, primarily because these models are the most comprehensive and clearly specified models, and the present volume is concerned with learning and memory deficits. It should be pointed out that control processes involve regulation and evaluation in a wide variety of tasks. When a difficult task is first encountered, adequate task performance requires selecting the relevant aspects of the task and organizing control processes around the important aspects. The person must develop an ultimate goal and related subgoals and maintain various subgoals in relationship to each other until the final goal is attained. Control processes must be directed in an orderly manner, and when there are failures, other control processes must be adopted. When a subgoal is achieved, the person must move on to the next subgoal, which may require a shift in control processes. Continued application of control processes will result in transfer of information to LTM which results in more rapid responding and frees conscious effort for other control processes or other aspects of the environment. In consideration of control processes, at this point the reader may reflect about first learning to drive and compare this with current driving processes.

CONTROL PROCESSES OF DISABLED LEARNERS

In the remainder of this chapter the role deficient control processes play in learning and reading disabilities is considered, and it is pointed out that deficient control processes account for a broad range of behavioral differences between disabled children and nondisabled children. In general, discussion of control processes by LD and reading disabled (RD) children follows the same order as the previous section on the important role of control processes in learning and memory. The rather remarkable success in facilitating learning, memory, and comprehension by LD and RD children by instructions in control processes is also discussed. Finally, a general theory which accounts for the deficient use of control processes by LD and RD children is presented.

Sensory Memory and Attention

The older literature on learning disabilities stressed the importance of inattention as the basis for learning disabilities. For example, performance by LD children in simple and complex reaction time tasks is impaired to a greater degree by irrelevant and distracting stimuli (e.g., Atkinson & Seunath, 1973; Dykman, Walls, Suzuki, Ackerman, & Peters, 1970). In vigilance tasks requiring continuous, sustained attention in order to detect infrequent stimuli, LD children typically detect fewer signals and make more false alarms (e.g., Atkinson & Seunath, 1973; Dykman et al., 1970). In tasks that measure recall of central and incidental material, recall by LD children is lower than nonlearning disabled (NLD) children (e.g., Hallahan & Reeve, 1980). The lower recall by LD youngsters is alleged to be due to failure to filter out incidental material. Selective attention deficits were also used to account for the slower learning rate and lower memory task performance by LD children (Hallahan & Reeve, 1980).

More recent research using more sophisticated methods (signal detection analysis) indicates that what appears to be lower detection of auditory and visual stimuli by LD children is, in fact, due to a change in response criteria (Swanson, 1981). Pelham (1979) compared performance of LD and NLD children of three different ages in four different tasks that measure selective attention and concluded that LD children do not have a selective attention deficit. The interpretation that lower recall by the LD group in the central-incidental recall task is due to a selective attention deficit has been seriously criticized, because the amount of incidental recall does not differ in LD and NLD children; only recall of central (intentional) information, which requires elaborative encoding and other control processes, is lower in LD than NLD (e.g., Tarver, 1981).

Research using learning and memory tasks to examine attention and distraction have failed to support the contention that attention deficits are responsible for learning disabilities. For example, when random dot patterns or geometric patterns are presented for only 150 msec, recognition by LD and NLD subjects is no different when the test for recognition is 300 msec or less after presentation (Morrison, Giordani, & Nagy, 1977). Torgesen and Houck (1980) found that LD and NLD children perform equivalently on a digit span task as long as the rate of presentation was rapid (1 to 4 digits per sec), but the LD group recalled less than their NLD peers with slower presentation rates. Because rapid presentation is likely to tax attention more than slower presentation, these findings do not support the attention deficit hypothesis. Serial and free recall of short lists of colors, digits, and words with less than 4 sec between presentation and recall is comparable in LD and NLD children, indicating that the LD children attend to the information at the time of presentation (Bauer, 1977a, 1977b). These findings indicate that attention, sensory storage, and retrieval from sensory storage are not impaired in LD children.

A number of experiments have placed greater demands on attention by increasing the number of distracting and irrelevant stimuli in the test situation. Results of these studies show that increasing the number of irrelevant stimuli does not produce more detremental effects on performance of LD than NLD children. In a series of experiments line drawings or patterns were presented, and the children were occupied by a distracting task for several seconds. Another line drawing or pattern was presented immediately after the distracting task, and the children were required to say whether the drawings or patterns were the same or different. The distracting task increased the number of recognition errors by LD and NLD children to the same degree (Clifton-Everest, 1974; Ellis & Miles,

1978). Serial recall of nonsense syllables and free recall of words are reduced to a comparable degree in LD and NLD groups by performing an
irrelevant counting task between presentation and recall (Bauer, 1977a,
1977b). Nober and Nober (1975) demonstrated that detection of auditory
signals by LD and NLD students was reduced to a comparable degree in
noisy classrooms. Studies that have increased the number of irrelevant
stimuli fail to support the hypothesis that LD youngsters are more distractible.

The studies discussed above are but a few that fail to support the contention that LD children have an attention deficit. The reader is referred
to reviews by Douglas and Peters (1979) and Koppell (1979) for additional
evidence that attention deficits are not characteristic of this population.
Furthermore, these reviewers suggested that what appears to be an attention deficit is, in fact, an information processing deficit.

Elaborative Encoding

Elaborative encoding includes a variety of control processes, such as
rehearsal, reorganizing information, and identifying categories and associations. As compared to other learning and memory processes, elaborative encoding requires more conscious effort and takes a considerable
degree of time. As shown in Figure 1, elaborative encoding maintains
information in STM and with sufficient elaborative encoding the information is transferred to more permanent memory. The developmental increase in elaborative encoding and other control processes are well documented. For example, younger children are less likely to rehearse,
reorganize, underline, take notes, ask questions, and use a variety of other
task relevant control processes (e.g., Brown & Smiley, 1978; Flavell &
Wellman, 1977).

Time dependent processes.   Since elaborative encoding takes time and
elaborative encoding is used to maintain information for short periods of
time, a number of experiments have compared the time dependent memory
processes of LD and NLD children. When three letters or words are presented at a rate of one item per second and there is little or no delay
between presentation and recall, LD and NLD samples recall a comparable
amount (Bauer, 1977a; 1977b). However, the amount recalled by the LD
group decreases more rapidly as the delay between presentation and recall
increases (Bauer, 1977a; 1977b). Since elaborative encoding is used to
store information for brief periods of time, the faster decrease by LD
youngsters across time suggests that they are using less effective elaborative encoding processes. Torgesen and Houck (1980) presented digit
sequences at rates of from four per second to one per 2 sec and found

that recall by NLD children was more adversely influenced by presenting the information at a rapid rate. These findings suggest that the LD group was less likely than NLD peers to use the additional time to engage in elaborative encoding. In an immediate-free recall task with presentation rates of one word per 1-, 2-, and 4-sec recall of the first few list items (the primacy effect), which requires elaborative encoding, was lower in RD than NLD children (Bauer & Emhert, 1984). These findings suggest that less effective elaborative encoding is used by LD than NLD children. However, presenting the information at a slower rate increased the primacy effect of both RD and NLD subjects to the same degree. Since recall of primacy items requires elaborative encoding, it appears that both RD and NLD children use the additional time to engage in elaborative encoding.

Allowing subjects to present to-be-learned information at their own pace allows a broader range of control processes to operate, and in many situations, such as when studying textbooks and notes, the learner is allowed to present the information at their own pace. Because presentation rates and patterns in self-paced tasks are under the learner's control and time dependent control processes are impaired in LD children, presentation of to-be-recalled information would be expected to differ in LD and NLD samples. Bauer (1979a) found that in a multi-trial free recall task, the LD group presented the word list for a shorter time than NLD subjects, and LD children required more trials to criterion. Furthermore, mean study time per trial was positively correlated with measures of rehearsal and organization. These findings indicate that the greater study time by NLD children is due to more time spent engaging in elaborative encoding, and the greater time spent in elaborative encoding results in fewer trials to criterion. In accord with these findings, Dallago and Moely (1980) found that RD students spend less time than NLD peers studying line drawings before indicating a readiness to recall the information, and RD children recall less than NLD. Similarly, Wong and Wilson (1984) found that LD children spent less time studying prose and recalled less than NLD children.

Because presentation rates by LD children are inappropriate, we have begun a closer examination of presentation rates by LD and NLD students (Bauer & Newman, 1985). In this self-paced presentation task the information was presented visually, because in most self-paced learning tasks the information is presented visually. We were primarily interested in examining control processes, rather than reading processes, and for this reason digits rather the words or letters were presented. On each of 15 trials LD and NLD subjects, of 11 years of age ($n = 10$ per group) presented slides with one digit on each slide by pressing a remote control button of a slide projector. When the botton was pressed the nineth time a blank slide appeared, and this was the cue to recall the digits in the same order as they were presented. Unknown to the children, the time each slide was presented on the screen was recorded by a timer and printout counter. As shown in the upper panel of Figure 2, recall was lower by LD than NLD children, $p < .05$, and the percentage recalled decreased across serial positions, $p < .01$. The lower panel of Figure 2 presents the mean presentation time by LD and NLD groups as a function of serial positions. Analysis of variance showed that the main effect for groups was not significant. This nonsignificant main effect indicates that LD and NLD adolescents spent a comparable amount of time presenting the digits. The main effect for serial positions was significant, $p < .01$, indicating that the presentation time became slower as each additional digit of a sequence was presented. More importantly, the Groups x Serial Positions interaction was significant, $p < .05$. As can be seen in Figure 2, this interaction was due to the progressively slower presentation rate by NLD subjects as each additional digit of a sequence was presented and to the relatively constant rate by LD children as each additional digit was presented.

The differences in presentation rate and recall between the two groups have a number of implications. First, it appears reasonable that as the information load increases, (i.e., each additional digit of a sequence is presented), more time would be spent engaging in control processes, such as cumulative rehearsal and/or grouping the digits. The slower presentation rates by the NLD group indicate, then, that they spend more processing time as additional information is presented. However, LD children do not appear to spend more time engaging in elaborative encoding in response to the increasing demands of the task. These results are in accord with the finding that lower ability and average ability fifth graders spend as much time studing easier prose material but, unlike average ability students, lower ability students do not increase their study time for more difficult material (Owings, Peterson, Bransford, Morris, & Stein, 1980). Recall of the prose material was also lower in less abled than average students. The finding that time spent in presenting to-be-recalled information, reading, and studying prose is similar in RD, LD, and NLD children or even faster by LD and RD subjects than NLD peers but recall of RD and LD youngsters is lower than NLD age-mates (Bauer, 1979a; Paris & Myers, 1981; Wong & Wilson, 1984) indicate that the disabled groups do not compensate for their lower recall and reading ability by studying the material for a longer period of time. Thus, in a variety of tasks LD and RD students do not alter their presentation rates in response to task demands or their own abilities. Because many everyday, naturalistic learning situations are self-paced, these findings are likely to have important implications for teaching LD and RD children. At the very least, disabled children should be more informed about the importance of study-

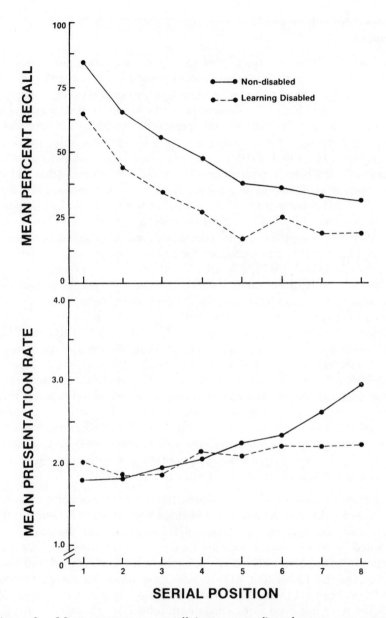

Figure 2. Mean percentage recall (upper panel) and mean presentation rate (lower panel) by nondisabled and learning-disabled children.

ing more difficult material and material they do not yet know for a longer period of time.

Free recall. The extensive knowledge of the information processing that normal children and adolescents use in immediate-free recall tasks increases the likelihood of understanding how information processing may differ in disabled learners. In immediate-free recall, normal adolescents and adults rehearse the most recently presented item along with previously presented items (cumulative rehearsal), up to about seven items (Atkinson & Shriffrin, 1971; Rundus, 1971). There is a high relationship between the amount of cumulative rehearsal devoted to the first several items and the probability of recalling these items (e.g., Atkinson & Shiffrin, 1971; Rundus, 1971) and forcing normal learners to rehearse only the last item presented reduces the primacy effect (Atkinson & Shiffrin, 1971). Young children rehearse only the last item presented, and this single item rehearsal is very likely to be responsible for the lower primacy effect of younger children (Douglass, 1981b; Flavell & Wellman, 1977). Younger children are also less likely to use a number of other elaborative encoding processes, such as subjectively reorganizing the material and making sentences (e.g., Brown & Smiley, 1978; Flavell & Wellman, 1977; Paris & Myers, 1981).

Results of studies examining immediate-free recall by LD, RD, and NLD children indicate that the primacy effect of the disabled group is lower than normally-achieving peers (Bauer, 1977a; 1979a; Bauer & Emhert, 1984; Peller-Porth & Bauer, 1984; Spring & Capps, 1974). Because recall of the first few items of each list requires cumulative rehearsal, these findings suggest that LD and RD children are less likely to use cumulative rehearsal and possibly other elaborative encoding processes. Recall of primacy items is also highly correlated with reading level, suggesting that the level of elaborative encoding is important for differences in reading ability (Bauer & Emhert, 1984; Spring & Capps, 1974).

Direct measures of rehearsal. Studies that have more directly measured rehearsal by disabled and non-disabled learners support findings in free recall tasks. Torgesen and Goldman (1977) and Haines and Torgesen (1979) recorded lip movements, which are indicative of rehearsal, of 7-year-old RD and NLD children during the delay between presentation and recall of pictures and found that RD subjects have fewer lip movements and recall less than NLD children. These findings suggest that younger RD students were not even using single item rehearsal to remember the pictures. Douglass (1981b) recorded overt rehearsals by LD and NLD children of two different ages (approximately 9 and 11 years) in a serial recall for pictures task and found that older NLD children used more cumulative rehearsal and recalled more than the other three groups. Similarly, Cermak (1983) recorded overt rehearsal and found that younger LD and NLD children and older LD children use single item rehearsal, whereas the older NLD group use more cumulative rehearsal. Use of cumulative rehearsal was also associated with higher recall.

Organization. Identifying organization in verbal material and imposing organization on verbal material are control processes which are known to facilitate recall. A number of reports indicate that NLD children recall randomly presented words consecutively from the same categories (i.e., words that are subsumed under the same subordinate) more frequently than LD and RD children, and recall by nondisabled peers is higher than disabled learners (Gelzheiser, 1984; Torgesen, 1977; Wong, 1978). The tendency to recall words consecutively from the same category is referred to as *category clustering.* Bauer (1979a) found that in a multi-trial free recall task, LD subjects cluster words less than NLD children, and clustering is highly correlated with the rate of acquisition in the same task. Dallago and Moely (1980) examined clustering of line drawings forming 10 categories and found that recall and clustering were higher in NLD than RD children. On the basis of these and other findings, Dallago and Moely concluded that LD children were not impaired in using semantic relationships to cluster but had difficulty generating effective study techniques. Similarly, on the basis of findings that reorganization of passages is higher in NLD subjects, Wong and Wilson (1984) concluded that LD children were less aware of how to effectively organize and study prose. The lower levels of reorganization and recall by LD children indicate that they are less likely to impose organization on verbal material. Since reorganization is under the learner's control, these findings support the hypothesis that control processes are impaired in children with learning disabilities.

Other Control Processes

Although control processes are required in a variety of complex, everyday tasks, very little research has been devoted to comparing control processes by disabled and non-disabled learners in more naturalistic situations. In one set of tasks, 8-year-old LD and NLD children were individually brought into a small room with four tables. Three tables contained the materials needed to solve the tasks along with many other items that were irrelevant for task solution, and the fourth table contained a board with pictures of items needed to solve each task. The children were tested in five task, requiring that they find objects needed to bake a cake, solve a math problem, and find shapes, letters, and words which matched pictures on the board. Although LD and NLD children solved the tasks, the NLD used more effective control processes. On the first trip to find the needed objects, more correct objects were brought back by the NLD group. More importantly, on additional trips NLD referred to the picture board to determine which items were still missing, whereas the LD children were less likely to use this control process. Referring to the picture board resulted in fewer trips per solution, less time to complete the tasks, and fewer hesitations by NLD children. Thus, what appears to be a simple control process of referring to the picture board is deficient in LD children (Kops & Belmont, 1985). These findings are important, because they indicate that control processes by LD children are deficient in nonverbal tasks, and they fail to use the control process even when using the control process reduces the amount of effort required to complete the tasks. In accord with these findings, Wong (1982) found that RD children were less likely to select adequate retrieval cues when learning prose passages and to check their retrieval cues than NLD students.

Various control processes used by RD and NLD children in the study of text material were examined by Paris and Myers (1981). Hesitations, repetitions, underlining, and self corrective behaviors for anomolous phrases in text were lower in the RD group, suggesting that processing of information that is not understood is lower in RD than non-disabled learners. In a follow-up study, RD and NLD students were required to read and study text material until they could recall the material. The use of notes, questions, and a dictionary to comprehend and recall the text were lower in the RD group. In addition, RD adolescents were lower in comprehension and recall of the text material, and use of these control processes was correlated with the amount recalled. Similarly, Brown and Smiley (1978) showed that older and higher level readers were more likely to rehearse, reorganize, underline, take notes, and ask questions than younger and less abled readers, and recall and comprehension were higher in older and more skilled readers. These findings indicate that differences in the use of a variety of control processes play an important role in the comprehension and recall differences of RD and nondisabled children.

In research designed to compare test taking strategies, LD and NLD students read passages from a standardized reading test and answered questions that could not be answered on the basis of information contained in the passages (Lifson & Scruggs, 1984). The answers by NLD group were approximately 60% correct, but LD children were significantly lower. In follow-up studies (Scruggs, Bennion, & Lifson, 1985), LD and NLD subjects read passages from a standardized test and answered questions about the passages. The children were then asked to indicate the basis for selecting their answers. The results showed that LD children performed at a lower level on questions that were based on reasoning processes. These findings indicate that LD children are deficient in using deductive reasoning processes.

Acquisition and LTM

Elaborative encoding not only maintains verbal, semantic information over short periods of time but results in the transfer of information to LTM (see Figure 1). Since elaborative encoding and other control processes of disabled learners are deficient, slower acquisition by these children is very likely to be due to deficient elaborative encoding. In support of this suggestion, recall of primacy items, which are maintained by cumulative rehearsal, and category clustering in immediate-free recall are highly correlated with acqustion rate of learning word lists and with trials to criterion in both experimenter-paced and subject-paced tasks (Bauer, 1979a). Immediate recall of digit and color sequences, which are likely to be maintained by elaborative encoding, are also highly correlated with acquisition of lists of digit and color sequences (Bauer, 1979b; 1982). In addition, when the length of to-be-learned word lists is varied according to the number of primacy items that can be recalled by each child in immediate-free recall, rate of acquisition by LD and NLD children is virtually identical (Bauer, 1979a). Thus, when the length of to-be-learned lists is varied according to the elaborative encoding ability of each child, acquisition differences between NLD and LD children are eliminated. These results provide strong evidence that the slower acquisition rates by LD students are due to deficient elaborative encoding processes.

There is also evidence that the names of visual stimuli are acquired at slower rates by disabled children, and they are less likely to rehearse verbal labels for visual stimuli. Jansky and de Hirsch (1972) found that the ability to name letters and pictures of objects at approximately 5 years of age were the best predictors of reading level 2 years later. A number of researchers have demonstrated that paired associate learning of nonsense figures with letters or words and nonsense syllables with geometric forms is lower by RD children (Done & Miles, 1978; Otto, 1961; Vellutino, 1979). Recall of unfamilar visual stimuli is higher by nondisabled than RD children, and nondisabled readers rehearse verbal labels to remember the unfamilar visual stimuli, whereas RD children do not use this control process. Furthermore, preventing rehearsal of the verbal labels by performing an irrelevant task reduced recall by NLD readers to the level of RD students (Hicks, 1981). These findings provide strong evidence that disabled readers learn the names of visual stimuli at a slower rate, because they do not use adequate control processes, such as rehearsal.

As shown in Figure 1, information for faces, scenes, and other visual stimuli that have not been labeled verbally are transferred directly from sensory memory to LTM. Furthermore, the learner has little direct control over memory for visual stimuli that have not been labeled verbally. Thus, memory for visual patterns relys more on the fixed, structural characteristics of the memory system, whereas verbal information requires more active control processes. Given the memory processes for nonverbally labeled and verbally labeled stimuli, if deficient control processes are primarily responsible for learning disabilities, memory for visual stimuli which have not been verbally labeled should be comparable in LD, RD, and NLD children, but memory for verbally labeled stimuli should be impaired in LD and RD students. Experiments comparing memory for verbal (letters, words, and digits) and nonverbal stimuli (nonsense figures) indicate that in the same LD, RD, and NLD children memory for nonsense figures is no different, but memory for verbal information is lower in disabled youngsters (Done & Miles, 1978; Hulme, 1981; Swanson, 1978, 1983). In addition, memory for faces is comparable in disabled and NLD children, but memory for verbal material is lower in the disabled group (Holmes & McKeever, 1979; Liberman, Mann, Shankweiler, & Werfelman, 1982). Swanson (1978) also demonstrated that providing verbal labels for nonsense designs increased recall by NLD children but had no effect on recall by RD subjects. These findings indicate that learning and memory per se are not impaired in disabled students; only learning and memory, which is based on control processes, are impaired in disabled learners. Therefore, comparison of learning and memory for information which requires control processes with learning and memory that does not require control processes provides clear support for the hypothesis that deficient control processes play a critical role in learning and reading disabilities.

Although transfer of verbal information to LTM is impaired in children with learning disabilities, once verbal information has been stored in LTM, rate of forgetting from LTM does not appear to be dysfunctional (Bauer, 1982; Otto, 1961; Vellutino, Steger, DeSetto, & Phillips, 1975).

Retrieval

When recall or recognition are low, one can infer that retrieval is impaired. Davis and Bray (1975) suggested that recall by LD children is lower because retrieval of some information interferes with retrieval of subsequent information. If this hypothesis is correct, recall of the first few items in serial recall should be comparable by LD and NLD children, but the differences between these groups should become progressively greater as each additional item is recalled. Contrary to this suggestion, serial recall of color sequences and digit sequences presented visually or aurally is lower in LD and ND subjects at all serial positions (Bauer, 1979b; see Figure 2). Thus, recalling some information does not impair recall of subsequent information more in LD children.

In spite of the fact that very little rehearsal is devoted to the last few items in immediate-free recall tasks, recall is also high for the last few items of each list (the recency effect). The last few items are thought to require attention, stimulus recognition, and memory for adequate recall, but recall of the last few items before recall of earlier items also contributes to the high recall of the last few list items (Bauer, 1979a; Rundus, 1971). Normal learners are apparently aware that (a) the last few items are less adequately stored than earlier items and (b) recall of the last few items interferes less with recall of earlier items than the reverse recall order. Examination of recall order in free recall by LD, RD, and NLD children shows that all three groups recall more of the last few items of each list before recalling earlier items (Bauer, 1979a; Bauer & Emhert, 1984). Therefore, in immediate-free recall, which allows the learner to recall the items in any order, LD and RD children use an adequate retrieval process.

A large number of studies have shown that reaction times to visual stimuli, typically naming and identifying the stimuli, are slower in disabled learners (for reviews see Biemiller, 1977–1978; Stanovich, 1982; Stanovich, in press). Because slower reaction times are indicative of slower retrieval from LTM, these findings would appear to indicate that disabled children are deficient in retrieving information from LTM. However, as discussed above, greater storage of information in LTM results in more rapid retrieval from LTM (e.g., Bower, 1977; Ericsson, 1985; Shiffrin & Schneider, 1977). Thus, on the basis of reaction times along, it is not clear whether slower naming speeds are due to deficient storage in LTM or to deficient retrieval from LTM. As is discussed in a later section of this chapter, additional data on learning and memory processes of disabled children suggests that slower reaction times are due to deficient storage of information in LTM.

Metamemory

Although research on the development of metamemory of children has increased dramatically in the last few years, comparison of metamemory of LD and NLD children has only recently begun. In a study on the effects of increased incentives on recall, Haines and Torgesen (1979) found that both LD and NLD subjects had a comparable increase in rehearsal and both groups reported being aware that incentives increased rehearsal. Thus, awareness of using rehearsal appears to be comparable in LD and NLD students, indicating that one aspect of episodic metamemory is similar in both groups. Scruggs, Bennion, and Lifson (1985) examined episodic metamemory of LD and NLD children in reading tasks. The children read passages from a standardized reading test and indicated which answers were correct and the confidence of their selections. The children were also asked to state how they selected the answer. On using strategies which involved referring to the passages, both groups had similar actual performance and were equally accurate in estimating their own performance. The number of questions that were answered correctly on the basis of reasoning processes that were not obtained from information contained in the passages was significantly higher in the NLD than LD sample, but the level of confidence for these answers was lower in the LD group. These findings suggest that when performance is adequate children with learning disabilities make accurate assessments of their own performance, but when performance is inadequate they over estimate their own performance.

Douglass (1981a) gave LD and NLD children a repisodic metamemory questionnaire and found that both groups had comparable awareness about the benefits of single item rehearsal, but the LD group had lower awareness of the benefits of cumulative rehearsal, categorizing, subjective organization, and forming associations. These findings suggest that LD children are less likely to use cumulative rehearsal, categorizing, and reorganization because they are less aware of the importance of these control processes for improving learning and memory. Both groups had similar awareness about the effects of study time, preparation for remembering, immediate and delayed recall, and memory abilities. Although LD students were aware that studying for a longer time is necessary for adequate recall, the finding that they do not spend as much time studying as their nondisabled peers (Bauer, 1979; Dallago & Moely, 1980; Wong & Wilson, 1984) and do not distribute their study time appropriately (Bauer & Newman, 1985) indicates that LD children do not apply their knowledge of studying longer to actually studying longer.

In a study which should serve as a model for the factors to investigate in metamemory studies, Paris and Myers (1981) examined repisodic metamemory, episodic metamemory, control processes, and recall. Ratings on the importance of underlining, taking notes, asking questions, looking up words in a dictionary, and writing down in their own words were taken from both RD and NLD children. Both groups were equally aware of the importance of these processes for comprehension of text, indicating that repisodic metamemory by RD and ND children is comparable. The same children were then required to read text material until they thought they knew the material. During reading and studying the text, the study processes were recorded. In spite of the fact that both groups had previously acknowledged the importance of several control processes, the RD subjects were less likely to actually use these control processes during the study of text, and they recalled less than their NLD peers. When asked to describe what they had been doing to learn the text material (episodic metamemory), both groups were equally aware of the processes they actually used during the study of text. These findings indicate that RD and NLD students were equally aware of important control processes, but the RD group were less likely to actually use these control processes when studying text. Furthermore, RD children were aware that they were not using adequate control processes.

Examination of the literature on metamemory and memory of disabled and nondisabled children indicates that in some instances both groups are aware of control processes that are necessary for adequate learning and memory. However, when tested in tasks where the contol processes are beneficial, children with learning disabilities are less likely to actually use the control processes and are aware that they are not using adequate control processes. These findings suggest that disabled learners are not using the control processes, because of lower skill and/or lower motivation to use control processes. In other instances (i.e., awareness of the beneficial effects of cumulative rehearsal, categorizing, organization, and forming associations) metamemory is lower in LD children, suggesting that they do not use these control processes because of lower awareness of their benefits to learning and memory.

Motivation

Because LD and RD children perform at a lower level on a variety of tasks which require control processes and the effective use of control processes requires adequate motivation, lower motivation may be the underlying basis for deficient use of control processes by disabled children. Although motivation plays an important role in performing many tasks, very little research has been devoted to comparing motivation of disabled and nondisabled learners. Increased reinforcement improves or has no effect on responding to relevant stimuli by LD students (Dawson, Hallahan, Reeve & Ball, 1980; Hallahan, Tarver, Kauffman, & Graybeal, 1978), but since nondisabled comparison groups were not included in these studies, there is no basis for making comparative statements about motivation. Reinforcement increased paired associate learning and serial recall by RD and NLD children to the same degree, suggesting that motivation is not lower in the RD group (Goyen & Lyle, 1972; Haines & Torgesen, 1979). Haines and Torgesen (1979) also found that providing greater incentives for recall increased lip movements and recall of both RD and NLD subjects to a comparable degree, suggesting that incentives increased recall by increasing rehearsal and, perhaps, other elaborative encoding processes. Torgesen and Houck (1980) found that increased incentives improved serial recall of digits by NLD and LD learners that had digit spans within the normal range, but incentives did not increase recall by LD children who had below normal digit spans. Failure of incentives to increase recall by LD children with below normal digit spans was attributed to a lack of control over processes required for performance of the digit span task.

We have recently examined immediate-free recall by LD and NLD children on trials without tangible reinforcement and when tokens worth five cents were given for recalling each additional word (Peller-Porth & Bauer, 1984). Because reinforcement increased recall of both groups to about the same degree, lower motivation does not appear to be responsible for the lower recall by LD children. In addition, tangible reward increased the primacy effect and recency effects of both LD and NLD subjects to a comparable degree, suggesting that increased motivation influenced processes that are responsible for recall of the first few items (cumulative rehearsal and other elaborative encoding processes) and the last few items (attention, stimulus recognition, and sensory memory).

If motivation is lower in LD children, one would expect them to present information at a faster rate in self-paced tasks. In a self-paced task requiring serial recall of digits, the overall presentation rates by LD and NLD groups were not significantly different (Bauer & Newman, 1985). Although in a self-paced multi-trial free recall task LD subjects presented the word list at a faster rate than their nondisabled peers, the faster presentation by the LD adolescents was apparently due to less time spent engaging in elaborative encoding and not due to lower motivation (Bauer, 1979a). Thus, the findings from self-paced tasks suggests that motivation is no different in LD and NLD children. Furthermore, comments in the literature and my own observations suggest that children with learning disabilities are motivated to perform learning and memory tasks.

FACILITATING LEARNING AND MEMORY BY IMPROVING CONTROL PROCESSES

Any model or theory of learning disabilities should provide successful suggestions for elevating the behavioral problems of disabled learners. Earlier theories suggested that LD children were deficient in intersensory integration or were deficient in basic visual processing. However, attempts to improve performance by LD children by training in intersensory integration and visual processing met with little or no success (For a review see Stanovich, 1981; Stanovich, in press). Since LD children do not use a variety of control processes, recent attempts to facilitate learning have centered around improving control processes.

There are four major issues that arise from research on attempting to enhance learning and memory by improving control processes. Three issues are related to the practical matter of whether (a) the manipulations improve performance in a task, (b) improvements are maintained across some period of time, and (c) there is generalization and transfer to other tasks. The effect of manipulations to enhance control processes on these three issues can be examined experimentally, and the interpretation of the results are relatively straight forward. The fourth issue is more theoretical and pertains to inferences that are made about the learning and memory processes of disabled learners. The fourth issue has led to erroneous conclusions about the learning and memory deficits of LD children. Because manipulations in the use of control processes only partially increase performance children with learning disabilities and do not result in equivalent performance by LD and NLD children, some researchers have concluded that deficient control processes are not responsible for performance differences of LD and NLD children (e.g., Hagen, Barclay, & Schwethelm, 1982; Torgesen & Houck, 1981). On the basis of the same findings, others have suggested that LD children have a structural deficit that may inhibit the spontaneous use of control processes or limit their effectiveness (Worden, 1983). Two interesting cases of increasing digit span (Ericsson, 1985) will serve as a nice example for why neither of these conclusions is warranted. During testing in a digit span task a college student (SF) discovered that longer digit strings could be maintained by grouping the digits in terms of running times. For example, "2942" would be a 29 min 42 sec run. Using this procedure SF recalled sequences of 80 digits. A second student (DD) was instructed in this technique, and after a slight improvement was able to recall sequences of over 100 digits. Now, suppose you are instructed in this technique and after the instructions your digit span is tested for about 1 hr. If you can not recall 80 or more digits, would you conclude that the difference in digit span between yourself and SF and DD is not due to grouping, or that you have a brain abnormality that prevents you from using the grouping technique? To the contrary, you are likely to conclude that the differences in digit span are due to differences in using the grouping technique and that you do not have a brain abnormality. Furthermore, the astute observer might conclude that given enough practice in using the grouping technique, their digit span would increase. In fact, 2 years of practice were required for SF and DD to obtain their high level of performance. The developmental literature also indicates that the efficient use of control processes like cumulative rehearsal and clustering develop over a few years (e.g., Brown & Smiley, 1978; Cermak, 1983; Douglass, 1981b; Flavell & Wellman, 1977; Masur et al., 1973). Because control processes are acquired over a few years time, even when control processes are deficient in LD and RD children, there is little or no reason to believe that instructions in control processes and a short testing session improve skill and ability to use control processes. Because instructions and training are very likely to have little impact on skill in using control processes, it appears very likely that instructions improve performance by increasing metaknowledge that a particular control process will be beneficial for performing the task.

Although the use of rehearsal by LD and RD students is low, surprisingly little attention has been paid to improving recall by promoting rehearsal. Recall of line drawings by 8-year-old RD and NLD children was increased by having the children point to and say aloud the name of the drawing, but the children were not specifically told to rehearse (Torgesen & Goldman, 1977). However, this procedure increased lip movements in both groups, suggesting that rehearsal was increased. In what appears to be the first study to investigate the effects of instruction in rehearsal on recall, Douglass (1981b) trained LD and NLD children of two different ages in the use of cumulative rehearsal and found that training eliminated the recall differences between the two groups. Rose, Cundick, and Higbee (1983) had one group of LD students read prose material with red dots positioned in the material. At the occurrence of a red dot, the children were instructed to rehearse the material between the dots. Another group of LD children were not provided with the cue or rehearsal instructions. Recall was significantly higher for children in the rehearsal condition than the unaided group. These results suggest that recall and reading comprehension could be enhanced by providing cues concerning which material should be rehearsed and instructions in using cumulative rehearsal.

Because reorganization processes are lower in disabled learners, manipulations designed to increase reorganization would be expected to increase recall. In one of the first studies to improve recall by improving control processes, RD and NLD children were shown how to sort pictures into categories and told to study and recall the pictures. Recall was improved in both groups, with a slightly greater increase in the RD subjects. Improved recall was accompanied by an increase in task relevant control processes, such as the number of pictures moved and rehearsed and a decrease in distracting behaviors, such as aimlessly looking around or investigating incidental aspects of the environment (Torgesen, 1977). Wong (1978) found that having RD and NLD children point to and name the category to which each word belonged increased recall and category clustering by RD students. Similarly, Dallago and Moely (1980) showed that presenting category cues and having RD and NLD children sort drawings of objects into their respective categories increased recall by both groups and decreased the number of distracting behaviors by the RD youngsters. Recall of prose was also increased by training LD children to reorganize sentences around a central theme (Wong & Wilson, 1984). Because recall by RD children is so readily enhanced by procedures that increase reorganization, it appears likely that instructions increase awareness that reorganization will be beneficial for performing the task. These findings also indicate that the lower use of control processes by these children results in more nontask oriented behaviors, which have been interpreted as inattention, and that increasing control processes by instructions reduces these inattentive behaviors.

Ceci, Lea, and Ringstrom (1980) separated LD subjects into groups with visual deficits, auditory deficits, and both visual and auditory deficits. The children in each group, along with NLD controls, were trained in semantic categorizing, nonsemantic categorizing (color or type of voice), or no instructions were given. Children were presented to-be-recalled information in the visual or auditory modality. Training in semantic categorizing enhanced recall by LD children with auditory deficits when the presentation modality was visual and enhanced recall by LD children with visual deficits when the presentation modality was auditory. Training in semantic categorizing had no influence on recall by LD children with both visual and auditory deficits. These findings indicate that training in semantic categorizing increased recall when the presentation modality was different than the modality in which LD children have their primary deficit. These findings have very important implications for facilitating learning and memory by disabled learners because they suggest that greater facilitation will result when the presentation modality is different than the modality that is associated with the primary deficit.

On numerous occasions Torgesen (e.g., Torgesen & Houck, 1980) has suggested that LD and RD children are inactive learners and are deficient in effortful processing. On the basis of this hypothesis manipulations designed to increase effort may facilitate recall by these children. Short and Ryan (1984) trained one group of less skilled readers to select and study important aspects of a story; another group was trained in the importance of spending effort to understand the story; and a third group was trained in both study processes and effort. Recall was not altered by training in effort alone. The improvement shown by groups trained in only study processes and both study processes and effort were equivalent, and both of these groups were improved to the point where they were similar to skilled readers. The finding that study time by the three groups of less skilled readers was similar suggests that the amount of effort devoted to the task was comparable. Thus, increasing effort had no effect by itself or when combined with training in better control processes. These findings suggest that effort per se is not impaired in less skilled readers; rather, the type of effort that is engaged in is the critical factor.

Although generalization and transfer of training in control processes to other situations and tasks are important issues, they have only recently been examined. Gelzheiser (1984) first examined recall and clustering of line drawings and prose passages by LD and NLD adolescents and then trained the former in the use of categories. Training included discriminating and finding categories and reorganizing material along various dimensions.

Prior to trainining, recall and clustering of line drawings by LD adolescents were lower than the NLD group, but after training recall and clustering, they were comparable in both groups. Training increased recall and organization of prose material, but the levels attained after training were still significantly below NLD youths.

The extent to which training in control processes is maintained after training was recently examined by Short and Ryan (1984). Less skilled readers trained to select and study important aspects of stories maintained their training effect after six sessions. However, LD children trained to increase comprehension of text in a special program did not maintain the training effect when transferred to a mainstream classroom (Jenkens, Barksdale, & Clinton, 1978).

Attempts to improve performance by disabled learners by instructions and training in control processes have been remarkably successful. Studies in which both disabled and NLD children were instructed and trained in control processes indicate that even with brief instructions and short testing session, disabled children are improved to the point where they are no longer significantly different from their NLD peers (Douglass, 1981b; Torgesen, 1977; Torgesen & Goldman, 1977). Even when both LD and NLD children are improved by instructions in control processes, the LD group was improved to the point where they are similar to NLD subjects prior to instructions (Ceci et al., 1980; Dallago & Moely, 1980). Studies which have tested both disabled and NLD children but only instructed the disabled group, show that on some measures both groups are similar, whereas on other measures LD children are still below NLD children (Short & Ryan, 1984). The effect of instructions in control processes also generalizes to other tasks (Gelzheiser, 1984) and extends past the training period (Short & Ryan, 1984).

Given the success in improving LD, RD, and NLD children by instructions and training in control processes, a movement focusing on improving control processes by students in the classroom is eminently warranted. Teachers should not only be trained to teach the subject matter but should also be trained to realize the importance of control processes and to recognize control processes that are beneficial for learning various subject matters. Furthermore, while learning various subjects, children should be (a) informed about the importance of using control processes, (b) intentionally instructed in the use of various control processes (i.e., metamemory should be increased), (c) given practice on how to use control processes (i.e., skill should be increased), and (d) reinforced for using adequate control processes (i.e., motivation should be increased). Because students are typically prevented from underlining and writing in textbooks, at the very least, publishers of textbooks should underline the most important information and provide short summary notes in the margin. Cues for when rehearsal, reorganization, visual imagery, and other control processes are likely to improve learning should also be provided in textbooks.

READING DISABILITIES

Below expected grade level in reading is a major characteristic of LD students. Therefore, any framework, model, or theory of disabled children must provide a reasonable account of reading disabilities. Furthermore, because control processes, metamemory, and learning and memory of RD children are impaired, any framework, model or theory of reading disabilities must provide a reasonable account of deficient control processes, metamemory, and learning and memory. At present there are two major data sets that provide the bases for two classes of theories on reading disabilities. One data set is the consistent finding that naming of visual stimuli is slower by RD than NLD children. This data set has resulted in a variety of suggestions that reading deficits can be accounted for by slower processing at lower levels, such as letter and word encoding and decoding. Another major data set is the finding that disabled readers are less likely to use effective control processes, which suggests that deficits in higher level processing are primarily responsible for reading disabilities. These two classes of theories are not mutually exclusive but are, in fact, closely interwoven. There are high correlations between naming speeds for linguistic material and elaborative encoding (Spring & Capps, 1974; Torgesen & Houck, 1980), naming speeds for linguistic material and reading ability (for a review see Stanovich, 1982; Stanovich, in press), and elaborative encoding and reading ability (Bauer & Emhert, 1984; Ericsson, 1985; Spring & Capps, 1974) indicating that reaction times, elaborative encoding, and reading are closely related.

Naming, Reading, and Elaborative Encoding

One major data base on RD children is the finding that reaction times for a variety of visual stimuli are slower in less skilled than skilled readers. For example, dyslexic children name random lists of objects, colors, numbers, and words at a slower rate than age-matched normal readers (Denckla & Rudel, 1976; Seymour & Porpodas, 1980; Spring & Capps, 1974). Children classified as RD but without dyslexia are slower than age-matched nondisabled readers in naming random lists of colors, pictures, digits, letters, pseudowords, and words (e.g., Beimiller, 1977-1978; LaBerge & Samuels, 1974; Manis, 1985; Perfetti & Hogaboam, 1975; Stanovich, 1982). Researchers examining the development of reading processes in NLD children have universally found that naming speeds for visual stimuli increase with age and, of course, reading increases with age. Naming speeds for lists of colors, drawings, digits, letters, pseudowords, words, and text increase from 7 to at least 12 years of age (Biemiller, 1977–1978; Ehri & Wilce, 1983; Gibson & Gibson, 1955; Perfetti & Hogaboam, 1975; Spring & Capps, 1974). Comparing naming speeds of disabled and NLD children of different ages indicates that across ages, naming speeds increase at a slower rate in dyslexic children and lower level readers than nondisabled readers (Biemiller, 1977–1978; Ehri & Wilce, 1983; Spring & Capps, 1974). These age related changes suggest that naming and reading speeds develop at a faster rate in nondisabled readers than below average and severely retarded readers.

Slower naming and reading speeds by younger and disabled readers have been interpreted in a variety of ways. Earlier theories proposed that basic visual processing deficits were responsible for slower naming and reading, but a large number of well done studies have failed to demonstrate that visual processing deficits are responsible for reading deficits (for reviews see Stanovich, 1982; Stanovich, in press; Swanson, 1978; Vellutino, 1979). Slower phonological recoding and slower transfer of information from visual to phonological codes have also been suggested as the basis for slower naming and reading (Manis, 1985; Perfetti, Finger, & Hogaboam, 1978; Spring & Capps, 1974; Stanovich, 1982). Because rapid responding is less effortful and more automatic, slower responding has been attributed to a deficit in automatic processing (LaBerge & Samuels, 1974; Sternberg & Wagner, 1982) and to a lower level of familiarity with the stimuli (Torgesen & Houck, 1980). As pointed out in the discussion on retrieval from LTM, slower reaction times are indicative of less adequate storage of information in LTM. Therefore, the slower naming and reading speeds by RD, LD, and younger children indicate that they have less adequate storage in LTM than nondisabled and older children. Although slower encoding, recoding, decoding, automaticity, and lower familiarity may account for the slower response speeds by younger and disabled readers, the basis for processing deficits at these lower levels has not been adequately explained. As discussed below, inadequate control processes are very likely to be responsible for the slower naming of visual stimuli by younger and disabled readers.

It has been proposed that slower processing of verbal information at lower levels reduces the time available for higher level processes involved in recall and comprehension of text (e.g., LaBerge & Samuels, 1974; Perfetti & Lesgold, 1977). More specifically, it has been suggested that RD students are not deficient in elaborative encoding processes per se, but that slower phonological encoding, stimulus encoding, and recognition reduce the time available for elaborative encoding processes (Chi, 1977; Shankweiler & Liberman, 1976; Spring & Capps, 1974), and deficient elaborative encoding reduces recall and comprehension (Stanovich, 1982). The preponderance of the evidence, however, does not support the suggestion that slower linguistic processing speeds reduce elaborative encoding. First, the differences in reaction times between RD and NLD children are quite small; the rate differences between these two groups for forms, digits, letters, and words are only about 160 msec per item. It appears unlikely that a difference of only 160 msec per item effectively reduces the time available for rehearsal and other elaborative encoding processes, especially when studies examining elaborative encoding typically present the information at the rate of one item per second and slower. Additional evidence that the factors responsible for slower reaction times for linguistic material by disabled readers are not responsible for elaborative encoding deficits comes from studies showing that recall of recency items by RD, LD, and NLD children is comparable, but recall of primacy items is lower by disabled children (Bauer, 1977a; 1979b; Bauer & Emhert, 1984; Peller-Porth & Bauer, 1984). If RD and LD children did not have enough time to encode the stimuli, they would have lower recall of recency items and primacy items. In addition, since recall of recency items requires stimulus encoding and recognition and recall of primacy items also requires elaborative encoding, on the basis of the hypothesis that slower stimulus encoding and recognition are responsible for elaborative encoding deficits, one would expect positive correlations between recall of primacy and recency items. However, correlations between recall of primacy and recency items are uniformly low and nonsignificant (Bauer, 1977a, 1979a; Bauer & Emhert, 1984). Furthermore, it is not clear how (a) instructions in rehearsal and other control processes could so rapidly improve recall and comprehension of disabled children by increasing the speed of naming and recognizing letters and words, and (b) slower naming and recognition can account for the poorer metamemory and control process of RD and LD children.

We (Bauer & Emhert, 1984) have recently examined the extent to which elaborative encoding per se by RD children is deficient in an immediate-free recall task when the task is structured so that visual to phonological coding is not required and there is adequate time for stimulus recognition and encoding. To eliminate visual encoding and visual to phonological recoding, the words were presented aurally. Because recall of recency items requires stimulus encoding and recognition, a lower recency effect by RD children would be consistent with the hypothesis that they did not have enough time to recognize and encode the words. Furthermore, because the word lists were presented at different rates (one word per 1-, 2-, or 4-sec), if RD subjects did not have enough time for stimulus encoding and recognition at the fastest rate, the recency effect would be expected to increase as the presentation rate decreased. The results showed that the recency effect of RD and NLD children was similar at all presentation rates, indicating that at all presentation rates both groups had enough time to encode and recognize the words. In spite of enough time to encode the words and the fact that visual to phonological encoding was not required, at all presentation rates the primacy effects of the RD group were lower than the NLD children. Because elaborative encoding is necessary for recall of the first few list items, the lower primacy effect by RD children indicates that they have an elaborative encoding deficit that can not be accounted for by slower stimulus encoding and recognition. Recall of primacy items was highly correlated with scores on a standardized reading test ($r = .70$), whereas recall of recency items was not significantly correlated with reading test scores. These findings provide further evidence that elaborative encoding processes are related to reading ability.

ACQUISITION OF NAMING, READING, AND CONTROL PROCESSES

While slower response speeds to linguistic material do not account for deficient elaborative encoding by younger and disabled readers, deficient elaborative encoding is likely to be responsible for the slower processing speeds for linguistic material. Considerable evidence indicates that when new and difficult tasks (such as learning to name objects, digits, letters, words, and reading) are first encountered, a great deal of time is spent using control processes to encode and retrieve the information. As the task continues to be performed, the need for time consuming control processes is reduced for some aspects of the task (such as naming and recognition of some items) because the use of control processes results in the transfer of information to LTM. More permanent storage reduces the need for control processes and leads to more rapid, less effortful, automatic encoding and retrieval. As the need for control processes is reduced for some aspects of the task, control processes can be directed toward higher level aspects of the task (e.g., semantic analysis and comprehension). Naming visual stimuli, reading, mathematics, other academic skills, and motor skills clearly require a great deal of control processes during acquisition, and performance of these tasks becomes more rapid, automatic, and less intentional and effortful as learning progresses (for excellent reviews of this area see Bower, 1977; Ericsson, 1985; Logan, 1985; Shiffrin & Schneider, 1977).

Prior to learning to read, visually presented letters, syllables, words, and numbers have very little meaning but by the time reading training begins the child has a fairly well developed verbal, phonological, articulatory, semantic language system stored in LTM. In order to name visually presented letters, syllables, words, and digits, the child must recode the visual stimuli into their appropriate phonological representation and, thereby, connect the visual representation with the phonological system stored in LTM. When first learning to name visual stimuli of all sorts, the object, letter, or digit is presented, and the appropriate phonological code is provided. Furthermore, at the very outset the parent or teacher is very likely to encourage the child to say the name (phonological code) while looking at the stimuli. Thus, while learning the names of visual stimuli, the child is not only being taught associations between visual stimuli and their phonological codes but is being taught to use single item rehearsal. Therefore, children that are developmentally delayed in using rehearsal would acquire the names of all sorts of visual stimuli at a slower rate (for evidence of slower acquisition of names by LD and RD children see Done & Miles, 1978; Hicks, 1980; Jansky & de Hirsch, 1972; Otto, 1961; Vellutino, 1979). For some time after the names have been learned, children that have a rehearsal deficit would be slower naming the visual stimuli, because less information has been transferred to LTM. In searching and detecting of letters and digits, college students used rehearsal for at least 600 trials and complete automatic responding required approximately 2,000 trials (Shiffrin & Schneider, 1977), indicating that even when rehearsal is used automatic responding develops very slowly. Thus, deficient rehearsal and possibly other elaborative encoding processes are very likely to be the basis for slower response speeds for linguistic material by younger and disabled readers. A developmental delay in using rehearsal would also account for the developmental delay in rapid naming by disabled readers (e.g., Biemiller, 1977–1978; Ehri & Wilce, 1983; Spring & Capps, 1974).

After children have some knowledge of the names of digits and letters, various sequences of this information begin to be taught, e.g., the alphabet, counting, spelling, and phonological recoding of letter sequences (syllables and words). While learning sequences, the instructor is very likely to present the material so that single item and cumulative rehearsal are demonstrated to the child, and the children are encouraged to use single item and cumulative rehearsal. Initial teaching of the concepts for simple addition and subtraction are typically taught by the instructor reorganizing and regrouping actual objects. Thus, before formal school begins and during the early school years children are not only being taught the names of objects and various subject matters, but they are indirectly or directly taught to use single item rehearsal, cumulative rehearsal, grouping, and reorganizing as control processes. Children that are deficient in learning rehearsal and other control processes would, therefore, have greater difficulty learning to spell and to read. For a review of the close relationship between spelling and reading deficits see Waters, Bruck, and Seidenberg (1985). Knowledge of grapheme to phoneme conversion would also be acquired at a slower rate in children with rehearsal deficits (for an excellent review of this deficiency by RD and younger children see Stanovich, in press). At later stages of academic training, children that are deficient in the use of control processes must still devote more control processing to lower levels of the task, such as encoding and retrieving words from LTM, and control processes devoted to lower levels reduces control processes for higher levels of the task, such as recall and comprehension. At later stages of development, when reading is used as a tool for learning history, the sciences, and other academic disciplines, the processing capacity of disabled learners is likely to be devoted to higher level reading processes, rather than organizing and integrating the material into a comprehensive schema for each discipline. Furthermore, even though reading may be mastered, LD and RD children would still have learning problems, if they have not learned how to recognize important material, takes notes, use source material like dictionaries, make inferences, and use other control processes. Thus, deficient use of control processes would be responsible for learning disabilities at virtually all ages.

The Basis for Deficient Control Processes

Since deficient control processes play a critical role in learning and reading disabilities, the basis for deficient control processes is considered here in greater detail. A structural or relatively permanent brain dysfunction which impairs the acquisition or use of control processes may be one basis for a deficiency. Although a brain abnormality may play a role in the deficient use of control processes, at the present time there are several reasons for rejecting this possibility. Perhaps the most important reason is that studies on facilitation of learning and memory by teaching LD and RD children about better control processes have demonstrated considerable improvement in relatively short periods of time. These training and instruction studies clearly do not support the possibility that the deficient control processes of disabled learners are fixed and unchangeable. Other reasons for rejecting the suggestion that a relatively permanent brain disorder is responsible for deficient use of control processes are that accepting this suggestion reduces the likelihood of searching for behavioral treatments that will benefit disabled children, and without clear and substantial evidence labeling children as "brain damaged" is unwarranted and unethical.

Other major hypotheses for the deficient use of control processes center around the level of awareness and the level of skill in using control processes. One possibility is that disabled learners are aware of adequate control processes and have the necessary skill to use these control processes but, for lack of motivation, do not use the control processes. While one may accuse disabled learners of lacking motivation, the findings discussed above indicate that motivation of disabled learners is no lower than motivation of nondisabled learners.

Another possibility is that disabled children are less aware of adequate control processes. Metamemory studies indicate that RD and LD are less aware of cumulative rehearsal, reorganization, categorizing, and forming associations (Douglass, 1981a). Instruction and training studies also suggest that disabled students may fail to recognize the benefits of using a control process in a particular task. A number of studies have shown that instructing LD, RD, and NLD children in control processes increases recall and comprehension of disabled learners to the level of NLD age-mates (Douglass, 1981b; Torgesen, 1977; Torgesen & Goldman, 1977). Because skillful use of control processes require a long period of time to acquire, it appears unlikely that instructions and the short testing session that are typically used would have much impact on skill or ability to use control processes. It appears more likely that in these studies performance was enhanced by increasing metaknowledge that particular control processes will be beneficial to performing the task.

A variety of findings indicate the disabled learners have lower skills in using control processes. Findings from metamemory studies indicate that RD and LD are aware of adequate control processes, but when tested in tasks where the control processes would be of benefit, they do not use the control processes (cf., Bauer, 1979a; Douglass, 1981b; Paris & Myers, 1981). Furthermore, disabled learners are aware that they are not using adequate control processes (Paris & Myers, 1981). When a learner does not use a beneficial control process of which they are aware, it appears likely that lower skill in using the control process is responsible. Instructions and brief training in control processes increase performance by LD and RD children, but performance by disabled learners is still below NLD children (Ceci et. al., 1980; Dallago & Moely, 1980). Because instructions in the use of control processes would provide metaknowledge concerning the benefits of the control processes, lower performance by disabled students even after instructions is probably due to a lower level of skill in using control processes.

There is a vast literature showing that control processes are acquired by NLD children from the earliest school years (e.g., Brown & Smiley, 1978; Flavell & Wellman, 1977), and both children and adults can be taught control processes which greatly enhance learning and memory (e.g., see the section on facilitating learning and memory). Therefore, lower awareness and skill in using control processes by LD and RD children may be due to a slower rate of learning about control processes. Studies comparing development of control processes by disabled learners support the suggestion that control processes are acquired at a slower rate by LD than

NLD children. In a task requiring serial recall for pictures, 9-year-old LD and NLD children and 11-year-old LD children used a similar amount of cumulative rehearsal and recall by these groups was similar. Older NLD children (approximately 11 years of age) used more cumulative rehearsal, and recall of the older NLD group was higher than the other three groups (Douglass, 1981b). Cermak (1983) examined rehearsal and recall of LD and NLD children of three different ages (approximately 9, 11.5, and 13.5 years of age) in a multi-trial free recall task for words. Younger NLD and LD subjects of all ages used single item rehearsal and recall of these groups was similar, whereas older NLD children used cumulative rehearsal and recall of this group was higher. Byrne and Arnold (1981) found that the primacy effect of 7-year-old RD and NLD learners was no different, but a number of studies have shown that the primacy effect of older disabled children in lower than the primacy effect of comparable aged NLD children (Bauer, 1977a; 1979a; Bauer & Emhert, 1984; Bauer & Newman, 1985; Peller-Porth & Bauer, 1984; Spring & Capps, 1974). Because elaborative encoding is necessary for recall of primacy items, it appears that the more rapid increase in the primacy effect in NLD children is due to a more rapid development of elaborative encoding. In general, these findings indicate that disabled learners acquire control processes at a slower rate than nondisabled age-mates. Thus, in a very real sense, disabled learners have not yet learned how to learn. The slower learning about control processes is very likely to be responsible for the inadequate use of control processes, lower awareness about control processes, slower learning, poorer memory and slower naming of visual stimuli by LD and RD children.

SUMMARY

Unlike earlier theories of human learning and memory, which were based on associations, modern information processing models stress the importance of the learner's own cognitive processes. Looking back at Watson's (1930) classical statement from a modern perspective suggests that Watson could have created a begger-man and thief, but creating a doctor, lawyer, artist, and merchant-chief would require that the child learn a number of control processes. From the very start of learning associations between visual stimuli and their phonolocial codes, children are being trained to use single item rehearsal as a control process. When the names of objects have been learned, children learn sequences of object names (e.g., the alphabet, counting, and spelling), and while learning sequences children are also being taught to use cumulative rehearsal. Using reorganization and grouping as control processes are likely to be learned, at least in part, during learning of simple mathematics. At older ages, control processes are not only learned by following the teachers example but, in some instances, the teacher intentionally teaches the use of control processes. Children that are deficient in learning control processes would not only be impaired in reading, spelling, mathematics and other subjects but would be less skillful in using control processes, generally less aware of control processes, and less aware of when a particular control process will be of benefit in a specific task. Deficient use of control processes would also result in less automatic naming of letters, words, and other visual stimuli, because less information has been transferred to LTM. The greater amount of control processing spent at lower levels, such as searching for phonological codes of written words, would detract from controlled processing necessary for higher levels of the task. Therefore, information processing models provide a comprehensive and parsimonious framework for considering learning and reading disabilities. Because control processes are learned and play such an important role in learning and memory at all ages, a concerted effort should be made to learn more about control processes and to intentionally teach control processes to both LD and ND children.

REFERENCES

Atkinson, B. R., & Seunath, O. H. M. (1973). The effects of stimulus change on attending behavior in normal children and children with learning disabilities. *Journal of Learning Disabilities, 6,* 569–573.

Atkinson, R. C., & Shiffrin, R. M. (1971). The control of short-term memory. *Scientific American, 225,* 82–90.

Bauer, R. H. (1977a). Memory processes in children with learning disabilities: Evidence for deficient rehearsal. *Journal of Experimental Child Psychology, 24,* 415–430.

Bauer, R. H. (1977b). Short-term memory in learning disabled and nondisabled children. *Bulletin of the Psychonomic Society, 10,* 128–130.

Bauer, R. H. (1979a). Memory, acquisition, and category clustering in learning-disabled children. *Journal of Experimental Child Psychology, 27,* 365–383.

Bauer, R. H. (1979b). Recall after a short delay and acquisition in learning disabled and nondisabled children. *Journal of Learning Disabilities, 12,* 596–608.

Bauer, R. H. (1982). Information processing as a way of understanding and diagnosing learning disabilities. *Topics in Learning and Learning Disabilities, 2,* 33–45.

Bauer, R. H., & Emhert, J. (1984). Information processing in reading-disabled and nondisabled children. *Journal of Experimental Child Psychology, 37,* 271–281.

Bauer, R. H., & Newman, D. (1985). *Self paced studying by learning disabled and nondisabled children.* Paper presented at the meeting of the American Psychological Association, Los Angeles.

Biemiller, A. (1977–1978). Relationship between oral reading rates for letters, words, and simple text in development of reading achievement. *Reading Research Quarterly, 13,* 221–253.

Bower, G. (Ed.) (1977). *Human memory: Basic processes.* Orlando, FL: Academic Press.

Brown, A. L., & Smiley, S. (1978). The development of strategies for studying texts. *Child Development, 49,* 1076–1088.

Byrne, B., & Arnold, L. (1981). Dissociation of the recency effect and immediate memory span: Evidence from beginning readers. *British Journal of Psychology, 72,* 371–376.

Ceci, S. J., Lea, S. E. G., & Ringstrom, M. D. (1980). Coding processes in normal and learning-disabled children: Evidence for modality-specific pathways to the cognitive system. *Journal of Experimental Psychology: Human Learning and Memory, 6,* 785–797.

Cermak, L. S. (1983). Information processing deficits in children with learning disabilities. *Journal of Learning Disabilities, 16,* 599–605.

Chi, M. (1977). Age differences in memory span. *Journal of Experimental Child Psychology, 23,* 266–281.

Clifton-Everest, J. M. (1974). The immediate recognition of tachistoscopically presented visual patterns by backward readers. *Genetic Psychology Monographs, 89,* 221–239.

Dallago, M. L. L., & Moely, B. E. (1980). Free recall in boys of normal and poor reading levels as a function of task manipulations. *Journal of Experimental Child Psychology, 30,* 62–78.

Davis, M. S., & Bray, N. W. (1975). Bisensory memory in normal and reading disability children. *Bulletin of the Psychonomic Society, 6,* 572–574.

Dawson, M. M., Hallahan, D. P., Reeve, R. E., & Ball, D. W. (1980). The effect of reinforcement and verbal rehearsal on selective attention in learning-disabled children. *Journal of Abnormal Child Psychology, 8,* 133–144.

Denckla, M. B., & Rudel, R. G. (1976). Rapid 'automatized' naming (R.A.N.): Dyslexia differentiated form other learning disabilities. *Neuropsychologia, 14,* 471–479.

Done, D. J., & Miles, T. R. (1978). Learning, memory and dyslexia. In M. M. Gruneberg, P. E. Morris, & R. N. Sykes (Eds.), *Practical aspects of memory* (pp. 551–577). Orlando, FL: Academic Press.

Douglas, V. I., & Peters, K. G. (1979). Toward a clearer definition of the attentional deficit of hyperactive children. In G. A. Hale & M. Lewis (Eds.), *Attention and the development of cognitive skills* (pp. 173–247). New York: Plenum.

Douglass, L. C. (1981a). *Metamemory in learning disabled children: A clue to memory deficiencies.* Paper presented at the meeting of the Society for Research in Child Development, Boston.

Douglass, L. C. (1981b). *A developmental study of rehearsal strategies in the serial recall of learning disabled and normal children.* Paper presented at the meeting of the Association for Children with Learning Disabilities, Atlanta.

Dykman, R. A., Walls, R. C., Suzuki, T., Ackerman, P. T., & Peters, J. E. (1970). Children with learning disabilities: Conditioning, differentiation, and the effect of distraction. *American Journal of Orthopsychiatry, 40,* 766–782.

Ehri, L. C., & Wilce, L. S. (1983). Development of word development of word identification speed in skilled and less skilled beginning readers. *Journal of Educational Psychology, 75,* 3–18.

Ellis, N. C., & Miles, T. R. (1978). Visual information processing in dyslexic children. In M. M. Gruneberg, P. E. Morris, & R. N. Sykes (Eds.), *Practical aspects of memory* (pp. 561–569). London: Academic Press.

Ericsson, K. A. (1985). Memory skill. *Canadian Journal of Psychology, 39,* 188–231.

Flavell, J. H., & Wellman, H. M. (1977). Metamemory. In R. V. Kail & J. W. Hagen (Eds.), *Perspectives on the development of memory and cognition* (pp. 3–33). Hillsdale, NJ: Erlbaum.

Foster, R., & Gavelek, J. (1983). Development of intentional forgetting in normal and reading-delayed children. *Journal of Educational Psychology, 75,* 431–440.

Gelzheiser, L. M. (1984). Generalization from categorical memory tasks to prose by learning disabled adolescents. *Journal of Educational Psychology, 76,* 1128–1138.

Gibson, J. J., & Gibson, E. J. (1955). Perceptual learning: Differentiation or enrichment? *Psychological Review, 62,* 32–41.

Goyen, J. D., & Lyle, J. G. (1972). Effect of incentives upon retarded and normal readers on visual-associate task. *Journal of Experimental Child Psychology, 11,* 274–280.

Hagen, J. W., Barclay, C. R., & Schwethelm, J. A. (1982). Cognitive development of the learning disabled child. In N. E. Ellis (Ed.), *International review of research in mental retardation* (Vol. 11, pp. 1–41). Orlando, FL: Academic Press.

Haines, D. J., & Torgesen, J. K. (1979). The effects of incentives on rehearsal and short-term memory in children with reading problems. *Learning Disabilities Quarterly, 2,* 48–55.

Hallahan, D. P., & Reeve, R. E. (1980). In B. K. Keogh (Ed.), Basis constructs and theoretical orientations *Advances in special education* (Vol. 1, pp. 141–181). Greenwich, CT: JAI Press.

Hallahan, D. P., Tarver, S. G., Kauffman, J. M., & Graybeal, N. L. (1978). Selective attention abilities of learning disabled children under reinforcement and response cost. *Journal of Learning Disabilities, 11,* 430–439.

Harley, W. F. (1965). The effect of monetary incentive in paired-associate learning using a differential method. *Psychonomic Science, 2,* 377–378.

Hicks, C. (1980). The ITPA Visual Sequential Memory task: An alternative interpretation and the implications for good and poor readers. *British Journal of Educational Psychology, 50,* 16–25.

Holmes, D., & McKeever, W. (1979). Material specific serial memory deficit in adolescent dyslexics. *Cortex, 15,* 51–62.

Hull, C. L. (1943). *Principles of behavior: An introduction to behavior theory.* New York: Appleton-Century-Crofts.

Hulme, C. (1981). The effects of manual training on memory in normal and retarded readers: Some implications for multisensory teaching. *Psychological Research, 43,* 179–191.

Jansky, J., & De Hirsch, K. (1972). *Preventing reading failure.* New York: Harper & Row.

Jenkins, J. R., Barksdale, A., & Clinton, L. (1978). Improving reading comprehension and oral reading: Generalization across behaviors, settings, and time. *Journal of Learning Disabilities, 11,* 5–15.

Koppell, S. (1979). Testing the attentional deficit notion. *Journal of Learning Disabilities, 12,* 52–57.

Kops, C., & Belmont, I. (1985). Planning and organizing skills of poor school achievers. *Journal of Learning Disabilities, 18,* 8–14.

LaBerge, D., & Samuels, S. J. (1974). Toward a theory of automatic information processing in reading. *Cognitive Psychology, 6,* 293–323.

Liberman, I. Y., Mann, V. A., Shankweiler, D., & Werfelman, M. (1982). Children's memory for recurring linguistic and nonlinguistic material in relation to reading ability. *Cortex, 18,* 367–375.

Licht, B. G., Kistner, J. A., Ozkaragoz, T., Shapiro, S., & Clausen, L. (1985). Causal attributions of learning disabled children: Individual differences and their implications for persistence. *Journal of Educational Psychology, 77,* 208–216.

Lifson, S., & Scruggs, T. E. (1984). Passage independence in reading comprehension items: A follow-up. *Perceptual and Motor Skills, 58,* 945–946.

Logan, G. D. (1985). Skill and automaticity: Relations, implications, and future directions. *Canadian Journal of Psychology, 39,* 367–386.

Manis, F. R. (1985). Acquisition of word identification skills in normal and disabled readers. *Journal of Educational Psychology, 77,* 78–90.

Masur, E. G., McIntyre, C. W., & Flavell, J. H. (1973). Developmental changes in appor-
   tionment of study time among items in a multitrial free recall task. *Journal of Experimental Child Psychology, 15,* 237–246.
Morrison, F. J., Giordani, B., & Nagy, J. (1977). Reading disability: An information processing
   analysis. *Science, 196,* 77–79.
Nober, L. W., & Nober, E. H. (1975). Auditory discriminations of learning disabled children
   in quiet and classroom noise. *Journal of Learning Disabilities, 10,* 57–60.
Otto, W. (1961). The acquisition and retention of paired associates by good, average and
   poor readers. *Journal of Educational Psychology, 52,* 241–248.
Owings, R., Petersen, G., Bransford, J. D., Morris, C. D., & Stein, B. S. (1980). Spontaneous
   monitoring and regulation of learning: A comparison of successful and less successful
   fifth-graders. *Journal of Educational Psychology, 72,* 250–256.
Paris, S., & Myers II, M. (1981). Comprehension monitoring, memory, and study strategies
   of good and poor readers. *Journal of Reading Behavior, 13,* 5–22.
Pavlov, I. P. (1972). *Conditioned reflexes* (G. V. Anrep, Trans.). London: Oxford University
   Press.
Pelham, W. E. (1979). Selective attention deficits in poor hearers? Dichotic listening, speeded
   classification and auditory and visual central and incidental learning tasks. *Child Development, 50,* 1050–1061.
Peller-Porth, V., & Bauer, R. H. (1984). *The effect of tangible reinforcement on information
   processing of learning disabled and nondisabled children.* Paper presented at the meeting
   of the Southwestern Psychological Association, New Orleans.
Perfetti, C., Finger, E., & Hogaboam, T. (1978). Sources of vocalization latency differences
   between skilled and less skilled young readers. *Journal of Educational Psychology, 70,*
   730–739.
Perfetti, C. A., & Hogaboam, T. (1975). Relationship between single word decoding and
   reading comprehension skill. *Journal of Educational Psychology, 67,* 461–469.
Perfetti, C. A., & Lesgold, A. M. (1977). Discourse comprehension and sources of individual
   differences. In M. M. Just & P. A. Carpenter (Eds.), *Cognitive processes in comprehension* (pp. 141–183). Hillsdale, NJ: Erlbaum.
Rose, M. C., Cundick, B. P., & Higbee, K. L. (1983). Verbal rehearsal and visual imagery:
   Mnemonic aids for learning-disabled children. *Journal of Learning Disabilities, 16,* 352–
   354.
Rundus, D. (1971). An analysis of rehearsal processes in free recall. *Journal of Experimental
   Psychology, 89,* 63–77.
Scruggs, T. E., Bennion, K., & Lifson, S. (1985). Learning disabled students' test-taking
   skills on reading achievement tests. *Learning Disability Quarterly, 8,* 205–210.
Seymour, P. H. K., & Porpodas, C. D. (1980). Lexical and non-lexical processing of spelling
   in dyslexia. In U. Firth (Ed.), *Cognitive processes in spelling* (pp. 443–473). London:
   Academic Press.
Shankweiler, D., & Liberman, I. Y. (1976). Exploring the relations between reading and
   speech. In R. M. Knights & D. J. Baker (Eds.), *Neuropsychology of learning disorders:
   Theoretical approaches* (pp. 297–313). Baltimore: University Park Press.
Shiffrin, R. M., & Schneider, W. (1977). Controlled and automatic human information pro-
   cessing: II. Perceptual learning, automatic attending and a general theory. *Psychological
   Review, 84,* 127–190.
Short, E. J., & Ryan, E. B. (1984). Metacognitive differences between skilled and less skilled
   readers: Remediating deficits through story grammar and attribution training. *Journal
   of Educational Psychology, 76,* 225–235.
Skinner, B. F. (1938). *The behavior of organisms.* New York: Appleton-Century-Crofts.
Spring, C., & Capps, C. (1974). Encoding speed, rehearsal, and probed recall of dyslexic
   boys. *Journal of Educational Psychology, 66,* 780–786.

Stanovich, K. E. (1982). Individual differences in the cognitive processes of reading: 1. Word decoding. *Journal of Learning Disabilities, 15*, 485–493.

Stanovich, K. E. (in press). Cognitive processes and the reading problems of learning disabled children: Evaluating the assumption of specificity. In J. Torgesen & B. Wong (Eds.), *Psychological and educational perspectives on learning disabilities*. Orlando, FL: Academic Press.

Sternberg, R. J., & Wagner, R. K. (1982). Automatization failure in learning disabilities. *Topics in Learning and Learning Disabilities, 2*, 1–11.

Swanson, L. (1978). Verbal encoding effects on the visual short-term memory of learning disabled and normal readers. *Journal of Educational Psychology, 70*, 539–544.

Swanson, L. (1981). Vigilance deficit in learning disabled children: A signal detection analysis. *Journal of Child Psychology and Psychiatry. 22*, 393–399.

Swanson, L. (1983). A study of nonstrategic linguistic coding on visual recall of learning disabled readers. *Journal of Learning Disabilities, 16*, 209–216.

Tarver, S. G. (1981). Underselective attention in learning-disabled children: Some reconceptualizations of old hypotheses. *Exceptional Education Quarterly, 2*, 25–35.

Thorndike, E. L. (1931). *Human learning.* New York: Appleton-Century-Crofts.

Tolman, E. C. (1951). *Collected papers in psychology.* Reprinted as *Behavior and psychological man.* Berkeley: University of California Press.

Torgesen, J. K. (1977). Memorization processes in reading-disabled children. *Journal of Educational Psychology, 69*, 571–578.

Torgesen, J. K., & Goldman, T. (1977). Verbal rehearsal and short-term memory in reading-disabled children. *Child Development, 48*, 56–60.

Torgesen, J. K., & Houck, D. G. (1980). Processing deficiencies in children who perform poorly on the digit span test. *Journal of Educational Psychology, 72*, 141–160.

Vellutino, F. R. (1979). *Dyslexia: Theory and research.* Cambridge, MA: MIT Press.

Vellutino, F. R., Steger, J. A., DeSoto, L., & Phillips, F. (1975). Immediate and delayed recognition of visual stimuli on poor and normal readers. *Journal of Experimental Child Psychology, 19*, 223–232.

Waters, G. S., Bruck, M., & Seidenberg, M. (1985). Do children use similar processes to read and spell words? *Journal of Experimental Child Psychology, 39*, 511–530.

Watson, J. B. (1930). *Behaviorism.* Chicago: University of Chicago Press.

Wong, B. (1978). The effects of directive cues on the organization of memory and recall in good and poor readers. *Journal of Educational Research, 72*, 32–38.

Wong, B. Y. L. (1982). Strategic behaviors in selecting retrieval cues in gifted, normal achieving and learning disabled children. *Journal of Learning Disabilities, 15*, 33–37.

Wong, B. Y. L., & Wilson, M. (1984). Investigating awareness of and teaching passage organization in learning disabled children. *Journal of Learning Disabilities, 17*, 477–482.

Worden, P. E. (1983). Memory strategy instruction with the learning disabled. In M. Pressley & J. R. Levin (Eds.), *Cognitive strategy research: Psychological foundations* (pp. 129–153). New York: Springer-Verlag.

SEMANTIC STRUCTURE AND PROCESSING:

IMPLICATIONS FOR THE LEARNING DISABLED CHILD

Jacquelyn G. Baker, Stephen J. Ceci and
Doug Herrmann

ABSTRACT

In this chapter we suggest that learning disabilities can best be understood
by examining homogeneous subgroups of disabled children who exhibit
similar cognitive profiles. One such group consists of children who experience
language/learning-disabilities (L/LD). This subgroup is the primary focus of
our presentation, and we argue that L/LD children experience difficulty in

Memory and Learning Disabilities
Advances in Learning and Behavioral Disabilities, Suppl. 2, pages 83–109.
Copyright © 1987 by JAI Press Inc.
All rights of reproduction in any form reserved.
ISBN: 0-89232-836-3

deriving meaning from verbally presented information, i.e., they are semantically deficient. The question of whether this semantic deficit occurs at the level of *structure* or at the level of *process* is addressed. While the former term refers to deficits in the manner in which knowledge residing in long-term memory is structured, the latter term refers to deficiencies in the deployment of basic cognitive operations such as encoding. Two experiments are described, and their findings are discussed in terms of this distinction. Although an understanding of the relationship between structure and process is still at a preliminary stage, results from the first experiment suggest that L/LD children are deficient at the specific level of semantic representation, while their general structural system is age-appropriate. In the second investigation, evidence is provided to suggest that they are deficient at some forms of semantic processing (i.e. automatic), while other forms of processing remain intact.

In comparison to other fields of inquiry, research aimed at understanding the cognitive underpinnings of learning disabilities is still in its infancy. Nonetheless, this is an important time in the short history of learning disabilities (LD) research. Nearly a generation of talent and resources has been devoted to researching and remediating learning disabilities. As this first generation comes to an end and a second generation approaches, it is only natural for researchers, clinicians, and educators to stop and query: "Are we moving any closer to understanding and remediating the academic problems of LD children?" From our perspective, the answer to this question must be mixed. In some respects little progress has been made. For the most part, we have been in search of global solutions to a global disability. That is, investigators have typically compared "learning disabled" with "nondisabled" children, often forgetting that learning disabilities were never intended to be researched (or remediated) as a unitary disorder. Initially, the label was created in an attempt to organize various academic problems under one diagnostic category (Doris, 1986; Gaddes, 1985; Torgeson, 1975). Only recently have researchers begun to recognize the tremendous variability with respect to LD children's cognitive capabilities. In those instances when investigators have incorporated this insight into their methodologies, progress has been made. In fact, progress seems most evident when the goal has been to describe and explain the cognitive processes underpinning the academic deficiencies of relatively homogeneous *subgroups* of LD children.

Many different approaches have been taken by investigators attempting to identify subgroups of LD children (for review see Fletcher & Morris, 1986). One camp identifies disabled subgroups on the basis of academic underachievement (Fletcher, 1985a; 1985b; Rourke, 1982; Siegel & Heaven, 1986). For example, Fletcher and his colleagues have identified four subtypes of disabled children (a) reading-spelling disabled, (b) spelling-arithmetic disabled, (c) reading-spelling-arithmetic disabled, and (d) arithmetic disabled. Others argue that subgroups are more appropriately distinguished on the basis s of behavioral and affective characteristics (Goldstein & Dundon, 1986). Finally, a third camp suggests that differentiation according to patterns of underlying cognitive and neuropsychological processes holds the key to LD subtyping (Johnson & Myklebust, 1967; Kirk, McCarthy, & Kirk, 1969). For example, Johnson and Myklebust have distinguished between children with perceptual vs. auditory disabilities.

One of the most prominent LD subgroups to have emerged from these investigations, and the group upon which we focus, consists of disabled children who are experiencing a language-related deficit (Ceci, Lea, & Ringstrom, 1980; Kail & Leonard, 1986). This verbal deficit is characterized by subtle, rather than all-encompassing, linguistic processing deficiencies (for reviews see Donahue, 1986; Vellutino & Scanlon, 1982). Although a common term has not yet been agreed upon, descriptive terminology for this subgroup has ranged from "language/learning disabled" (Ceci, 1984; Ceci & Baker, 1986; Suiter & Potter, 1978), to "language impaired" (Kail & Leonard, 1986), and "language deficient" (Fried-Oken, 1984). These children are of normal intelligence, but perform below expectancy in such language-related areas as reading comprehension, spelling, and vocabulary. Frequently, they are not impaired, however, in the areas of perceptual, neurological, social, or emotional functioning, at least not to the extent that difficulties in these areas become noticed by professionals.

For reasons that will soon become apparent, we suggest that language/learning disabled (L/LD) children experience a great deal of difficulty in deriving meaning from verbally presented information. Thus, the purpose of this chapter is to examine the existing literature on semantic memory and its relation to learning disabilities. Our focus is on the development of relational word meaning. Although space limitations prevent a review of sentential meaning, it is our belief that a discussion of semantic relations is the appropriate point of departure for our eventual understanding of the semantic system. Semantic memory is viewed here from two different but interrelated perspectives. From the first perspective, the structure of semantic memory is examined and discussed in terms of how it relates to memory, comprehension, and the development of the knowledge base for both L/LD and nondisabled (NLD) children. Second, the processes that allow for the elaboration and development of the semantic system are considered in terms of their implications for the atypical cognitive characteristics of the L/LD child.

This distinction between structure and process is a variant of the form vs. function duality. *Structure* refers to the organizational characteristics of semantic memory, e.g., how knowledge that resides in semantic memory is "dimensionalized" and differentiated. *Process,* in contrast, refers to operations carried out on information residing in semantic memory (Smith, 1977). It is important to make this distinction, we believe, because cognitive dysfunction can result from any one of three states: (a) adequate semantic structure but inadequate cognitive processes, (b) inadequate semantic structure but adequate cognitive processes, or (c) inadequate semantic structure and inadequate cognitive processes. In our attempt to understand the origins of semantic dysfunction, we are working under the assumption that deficits in either structure or process have a "spill-over" effect and impede the functioning of the other (e.g., inadequate encoding processes impede semantic acquisition and, hence, eventually impede semantic structure). Although at many points throughout this chapter structure and process are examined and discussed separately, clearly, the two are in symbiosis.

The reader should be forewarned at the outset that most of the studies we describe are comprised of samples of relatively heterogeneous groups of LD children, and, as we have already pointed out, L/LD children are but one subset of this population. In our effort to understand this specific subgroup, we rely on past studies of "generically" disabled children only as one step in the process of generating new hypotheses applicable to the subgroup of L/LD children. Finally, we test these new hypotheses, with the rest of our discussion focusing on two, as yet, unpublished empirical investigations recently conducted in our own laboratory.

LANGUAGE, COGNITION, AND THE SEMANTIC SYSTEM

Much of the seminal work in the area of language/learning disabilities has been conducted by Vellutino and his colleagues (Vellutino, 1979; Vellutino & Scanlon, 1982). They argue that not all cognitive processes share equal responsibility for producing a learning disability. Rather, many academic difficulties are caused by deficiencies restricted to the domain of language. To support this position, Vellutino and others have compared the performance of disabled and nondisabled children on a variety of verbal and nonverbal tasks. A brief review of L/LD children's most salient deficits suggests that they perform particularly poorly in such areas as verbal strategy use, word recognition, awareness of the sound-structure of speech, and semantic processing (Perfetti, 1985; Spear & Sternberg, 1986; Vellutino & Scanlon, 1982). It is unclear, at present, whether these language-based deficits are caused by some underlying process deficit (e.g., poor semantic coding), whether they are initially unrelated to cognitive processes but eventually constrain their operation (e.g., inadequate semantic knowledge will eventually hinder semantic coding because the latter relies on the former), or whether some third, and as yet unspecified possibility, exists. We do know, however, that most of these language disabilities are subtle rather than global. Evidence also suggests that, despite their subtle nature, these deficits are pervasive enough to cripple academic progress in such areas as reading, vocabulary, and spelling, as well as in other areas that involve the processing of oral or written language (e.g., social studies, math).

We have elected to focus on the semantic system for a number of reasons. For one, semantic relations must be processed in a wide variety of linguistic tasks, from analogical reasoning, to comprehension, and inference. Despite the diversity of these tasks, they all involve the common goal of "relation perception" (Herrmann & Chaffin, in press). Reasoning, comprehension, and induction are some of the hallmarks of verbal intelligence. Thus, a better understanding of LD children's semantic systems might, in turn, lead to the development of educational programs designed to boost L/LD children from current low levels of verbal "intelligence."

Our interest in the development of the semantic system is further motivated by a theoretical desire to understand its structural and operational underpinnings. The semantic system is a natural junction between language, memory, and the cognition. Thus, it is possible that an understanding of atypical characteristics of this system will also increase our understanding of the relationship that exists between comprehension and knowledge throughout the normal course of development.

Three major hypotheses have been set forth to explain semantic deficits in LD children (Vellutino & Scanlon, 1982): (a) poor vocabulary/lexical deficiency, (i.e., a structural deficit), (b) name retrieval dysfunction (i.e., a processing deficiency), and (c) generalized deficiency in apprehending meaning. (The latter deficit can result from either or both structural and processing deficits). Somewhat independently, investigators from the disciplines of linguistics and cognitive psychology have been at work attempting to address these hypotheses:

Linguistic Research

Linguistic research in the field of learning disabilities has, for the most part, focused on the *structure* of language and its relationship to LD children's knowledge and abilities. In general, they perform at age-appropriate levels on measures of single-word comprehension (Semel & Wiig, 1975). Similarly, on word association tasks, they appear to perform on par with NLD children (Bartel, Grill, & Bartel, 1973). That is, when LD youngsters are asked to provide a one-word response to a target word, they respond in a fashion identical to their NLD peers. One might interpret this evidence to suggest that the two groups categorize information in a similar manner. If this suggestion is correct, it would provide some measure of support for the idea that the *structure* of semantic memory is the same for both disabled and nondisabled learners. Yet, there is other evidence to suggest otherwise (Israel, 1984). To presage our later conclusion, we believe that a resolution to this apparent set of contradictory findings exists. Simply stated, we believe that structural differences do, in fact, exist between L/LD and NLD children, but these differences reflect subtle aspects of the semantic system, not global ones. Thus, on gross measures of structure, such as those tapped in many word association tasks, L/LD children may perform on par with NLD peers. It is only when one compares them on the fine-grained aspects of their semantic structure that one will observe differences.

Cognitive Research

Taking a different approach from that taken by linguists, cognitive psychologists have, for the most part, attempted to understand the processes underlying specific deficiencies in semantic memory (Rabinowitz & Chi, 1986). Such semantic processing abilities as lexical access and name retrieval have been examined and found deficient in LD children (Ceci, 1982; Denckla & Rudel, 1976).

In another line of research, disabled and nondisabled children have been compared in their abilities to rehearse and recall semantic information (Bauer, 1977; Torgeson & Goldman, 1977). Most of these investigations have concluded that LD children are inefficient at strategic processing. Such processing deficiencies have been further inferred from studies in which their recall improved as a result of training in the use of a particular type of strategy (Dallago & Moely, 1980; Torgeson, 1977).

One of the limitations of such studies is their tendency to emphasize process at the expense of structure. We argue that it is not enough to suggest that processing differences can explain L/LD deficiencies. As others have suggested, a theory of language processing assumes a theory of linguistic structure (Jackendoff, 1983; Marr, 1982). Thus, investigators who argue that either structure *or* process holds the key to the LD child's memory deficiencies are only partially correct, we believe.

Another problem with investigations that attempt to isolate processing deficiencies without accounting for structural influences is their inability to explain why processing difficulties exist in the first place. We maintain that semantic accessability and availability are a by-product of *both* semantic structure and process. Thus, the two are inextricable. One cannot explain or be explained without an understanding of the other. Hence, our purpose in the following pages is to take a small, first step towards the integration of these two areas of inquiry.

In addition to suggesting that the structure/process distinction is helpful in explaining L/LD children's language deficiencies, it is necessary to make use of another distinction. This distinction pertains to the kinds of processes that enable children to comprehend language. This distinction holds that some processes are implemented voluntarily, in a *purposive* fashion while other processes are *automatic*, occurring without a child's intention. This chapter goes further than earlier statements about comprehension by suggesting that purposive processes may operate (as they appear to do in many types of reasoning tasks) on information in semantic memory that is only loosely structured whereas automatic processes tend to operate on information that is well-developed in its structure. Thus, we argue that a proper analysis of L/LD children's deficiencies requires research that addresses both purposive and automatic processes. With this goal in mind, the first half of this chapter examines the nature of the L/LD child's deficiencies in purposive processing of semantic relations that may be only loosely structured, while the second part of the chapter examines the nature of their deficiencies in automatic processing in a verbal conditioning task that would seem to rely on activation of well-developed semantioc structures.

STRUCTURE OF SEMANTIC MEMORY

One explanation for the relatively poor language and memory performance of disabled learners is that group differences exist in the ease with which relations in semantic memory are activated (Ceci, 1984; Vellutino & Scanlon, 1982). An hypothesis invoked to explain such differences claims that both disabled readers and young, NLD students possess a less elaborated knowledge base, resulting in an inability to identify and organize category relations (Bjorklund, 1985; Bjorklund & Bernhottz, in press; Rabinowitz, 1984). In light of the evidence already presented, this hypothesis makes a good deal of sense. Linguistic abilities depend upon the degree to which semantic structure is elaborated. Thus, a deficient language structure will inevitably constrain one's ability to code, store, and retrieve semantic information. It is not terribly surprising then, that L/LD children are at a disadvantage when attempting to name, describe, and remember linguistic information, given deficits in their knowledge base.

In order to pinpoint L/LD student's linguistic disabilities, one direction to look for possible clues is the structure of the semantic memory system. A perusal of the literature on this topic is confusing, as seen by the finding that LD children do not differ from NLD peers in word associations (Bartel, Grill, & Bartel, 1973), but do differ in their probability of giving a paradigmatic response (Israel, 1984). Furthermore, some evidence suggests that when groups are matched on IQ, LD children do *not* organize information in long-term memory in a qualitatively different manner than NLD youngsters (Berger & Perfetti, 1977; Dallago & Moely, 1980; Torgeson, 1977). Conversely, others have reported the organizational structure of long-term memory to be quite different for LD and NLD children (Smiley, Oakley, Worthen, Campione, & Brown, 1977; Wong, 1979).

We have attempted to reconcile these discrepant findings by examining in greater detail the structure and organization of semantic memory. On both a theoretical and empirical level, we argue that these seemingly incompatible findings are not so surprising because in some subtle areas of semantic memory organization, L/LD children are deficient, while in more global areas they are performing similarly to NLD students. In order to support this argument, we first briefly examine theoretical models that aim to explain how semantic knowledge is structured within long-term memory, and then expand these models to account for both the typical and atypical semantic memory characteristics of L/LD children.

Network Theories of Semantic Memory

Investigators interested in how knowledge is represented have developed several models of the structure of semantic memory. The most elaborate of these models are referred to as semantic network theories. Over the years, a variety of these network theories have been invoked to explain the structure of knowledge as it is represented within long-term memory (Anderson, 1983; Collins & Loftus, 1975; Norman, Rumelhart, & the LNR Research Group, 1975). Underlying assumptions of network models suggest that concepts within long-term memory are represented as nodes connected by associative links. These links vary in strength, thus, the amount of activation that spreads is determined by the strength of the associative links between concepts (Rabinowitz & Chi, 1986). Activation spreads along network paths by a mechanism whereby nodes can cause their neighboring nodes to become active (Anderson, 1984). Thus, children and adults might determine semantic relatedness by judging if two words are connected by an associative link so that spreading activation from one encounters activation from the other.

For network models of semantic memory, the association is the finest level of analysis. Yet, one of the problems with using these theoretical models to explain the deficits experienced by the LD child is their inability to decompose the semantic unit into finer structural units. Using these existing models, we can point out that L/LD youngsters are quantitatively deficient on semantic memory tasks, but it is difficult to examine qualitative patterns of performance. Until we understand the finer details of semantic structure, including the relationships within *and* between concepts, remediation will remain a slow and painful process.

Relation Element Theory

Recent work from Eastern Europe (Klix, 1980; Klix & Meer, 1980) and from the United States and Britain (Chaffin & Herrmann, in press; Johnson-Laird, Herrmann, & Chaffin, 1984) has proposed an alternative to network models that explains comprehension in terms of the basic elements of linguistic concepts. The theories developed from this work appear to hold great promise for the cognitive and linguistic remediation of atypical populations. Unlike traditional semantic network theories which assert that the relationship between two concepts is determined by the strength of associative links, *relation element theory* maintains that semantic relations are comprehended by identifying the basic elements that comprise the relationship between two words.

Relation element theory is unique in that it attempts to explain the structural components of linguistic knowledge, as well as how structure can be incorporated within a semantic decision model in order to also account for the processes involved in the comprehension of semantic relations (Chaffin & Herrmann, 1984; Herrmann & Chaffin, in press). In brief, Herrmann and Chaffin (in press) have suggested that the processing of semantic relations involves a number of steps based on the evaluation of each basic element of which the relation is comprised after it has been retrieved from long-term memory. Comprehension of a particular relation involves an analysis of the meaning of two words to determine if these meanings are consistent with a relation element existing between the words. Within this theory, the same processes are not invoked uniformly across relations. Thus, the processing of various types of semantic relations is interwoven with structural requirements in important ways. Most importantly, each type of relation invokes a unique set of decision criteria (Herrmann, Chaffin, Conti, Peters, & Robbins, 1979).

Relation element theory further argues that semantic knowledge is structured on two levels, *general* and *specific* (Chaffin & Herrmann, in press). The *general* component includes definitional criteria distinguishing between families of relations. For example, the family of antonyms can be defined in terms of a pair in which the meaning of one word is in opposition to the meaning of its pair member (i.e. front/back). Opposition is further defined by the two critical features of, (a) bipolarity and (b) position, on a common dimension. This general level is most similar to traditional network explanations of semantic structure, as the association is the basic level of analysis.

In addition to the general level that is represented within semantic memory, relation element theory maintains that *specific* components also exist in semantic memory. *Specific* components distinguish characteristics within a family of relations (Chaffin & Herrmann, in press; Leech, 1974; Lyons, 1979). For example, in the particular case of antonyms, specific components might include opposition that is either represented on a continuum (e.g., hot/cold), is contradictory (e.g., life/death), or is directional (e.g., top/bottom). As we explain later, specific components also have been identified for the families of synonymy (e.g., dish/plate), class-inclusion (e.g., animal/dog), part-whole (e.g., pants/zipper), and case-relations (e.g., waiter/table).

To date, empirical work within relation element theory has involved only an examination of the way adults structure knowledge in long-term memory. Results suggest that adults possess different amounts of knowledge for general and specific semantic relations (Ross, 1985). Until now, relation element theory has not comprehensively examined the developmental course for both general and specific representations. Nonetheless, we have reason to hypothesize that children acquire knowledge of general and specific components at different rates, with the order of development proceeding from the general to the specific (Przybilski, Schmidt, & Sydow, 1980; Raschke & Sydow, 1985). This hypothesis is consistant with Eleanor Rosch's work in the acquisition of the concept of class-inclusion (Rosch, Mervis, Gray, Johnson, & Boyes-Braem, 1976). She has found that basic categories (e.g., desk, table) are acquired before their superordinate (e.g., furniture) or subordinate terms (e.g., roll-top desk, kitchen table). Similarly, Schwaneflugel, Bjorklund, Guth, Willenborg, and Boardman (1984) have found that children's ability to discriminate among features that are critical in defining a word increase with age. Keeping these findings in mind, our purpose now is to examine the theoretical and practical implications of relation element theory for the course of both typical and atypical memory development.

Types of Semantic Relations

Relation element theory comes out of a body of literature within the field of linguistics and psycholinguists that is unfamiliar to most cognitive psychologists attempting to understand the structure of LD children's semantic memory. This literature is comprised of a number of investigations that have attempted to map different types of semantic relations onto the semantic system (Chaffin & Herrmann, 1981; Klix & Meer, 1980; Kuczaj, 1982; Lyons, 1977). For the most part, this literature has identified five general types of relations: antonyms, synonyms, class-inclusion, part-whole and case relations. These five families can be distinguished on at least two levels. First, antonym relations are contrast relations and thus, they can be distinguished from the other four non-contrast relations. A second distinction can be made between logical and pragmatic relations. On the one hand, the logical relations, synonymy and class inclusion involve overlap in meaning between the two words comprising a relation. On the other hand, pragmatic relations (part-whole and case-relations) are related by a pragmatic association. And, as was already mentioned, relation element theorists maintain that subsumed within these general relations are specific relations, which can also be meaningfully distinguished from one another.

Before presenting the task utilized in the present investigation, we briefly review definitional criteria for the various types of general relations (as well as some specific relations) that psycholinguists have agreed upon:

Class-inclusion. The relation of class-inclusion exists when one class subsumes another, as in the relationship between a subordinate (e.g., apple) and a superordinate (e.g., fruit). Class-inclusion is important in understanding semantic development, as it imposes a hierarchical structure on the semantic system. This hierarchical system facilitates a child's acquisition of new words and relations (Kuczaj, 1982; Markman & Seibert, 1976). Examples of specific components include *collaterals* (e.g., fruit/potato), *coordinates* (e.g., leg/arm), and *superordinates* (e.g., flower/rose).

Part-whole relations. The part-whole relation can be described as the relationship between an object and its parts (Lyons, 1977). Like class-inclusion, a part-whole relationship involves the component of inclusion. The two relations differ in that class-inclusion subsumes a word's meaning and part-whole relations subsumes a physical feature. Examples of specific components include *membership* (e.g., team/player), *functional object* (e.g., wheel/bike), and *functional location* (e.g., toilet/bathroom).

Antonyms. Antonymy can roughly be characterized on the basis of opposition. As mentioned earlier, the conceptual characteristics of this general component include bipolarity that is represented along a common dimension. Specific components include (a) *contradictory* relations (e.g., dead/alive), comprised of two terms considered to be of a dichotomous or ungradeable nature (Lyons, 1977; Kuczaj, 1982), (b) *contrary* relations (e.g. hot/cold), which are made up of two continuous terms that are at opposite ends on a continuum. and (c) *directionals* (e.g., front/back), which represent opposition in time or space. (Unlike contradictory antonyms, contrary ones can be preceded by the adverb, "very").

Synonyms. Synonymy occurs when two words express the same or similar meanings (Kuczaj, 1982; Herrmann, 1978). Within this general component, specific components can be further differentiated according to the degree of overlap in word meaning. For example, *synonymity* (e.g., dish/plate) involves complete overlap of one word's meaning with another word's meaning, while *dimensional similarity* involves only partial overlap in meaning (e.g., jog/run). With both dimensional similarity and antonymy, the two words can be represented on a common dimension; however, dimensional similars are situated on the same side of the midpoint (Chaffin & Herrmann, 1986). A third type of specific relation involves *attribute similarity* (e.g., door/lid).

Case relations. Case relations differ from the four types of general relations already discussed in that an understanding of this relation does not rely solely on the meaning of the two terms of which it is comprised. Instead, an understanding of its nature results from experience with everyday events and objects (Chaffin & Herrmann, 1986). Specific relations include *agent-object* (e.g., king/crown), *instrument-object* (e.g., hammer/nail), and *agent-instrument* (e.g., singer/microphone).

Semantic Relations Task

In order to compare the structure of semantic knowledge between L/LD and non/LD children, we developed an analogical reasoning task comprised of 180 common relations recognizable by children. Table 1 provides examples of general and specific relations included on the *Semantic Relations Test* (SRT).

This task was developed in a format to complement an earlier version created specifically for adults (see Chaffin & Herrmann, 1986). For each of 45 questions, children were asked to identify one of three choices that was "most like" a target pair.

Three different types of questions were implemented to test childrens' knowledge of the general and specific relations mentioned earlier. In the first question type (heterogeneous-same), a target pair and correct response pair shared both general and specific components (see Table 2). Thus, the child could rely on knowledge of either general, specific, or both types of components to obtain a correct answer. In the second question type (heterogeneous-different), the target and correct response shared a general but not specific relationship. Finally, the third question type (homogeneous) contained a target pair and three response pairs of the same general relation. A correct response would depend on a match based only on knowledge of the specific relation.

Three groups of elementary and junior high school aged boys completed the SRT. The first group included 20 L/LD boys enrolled in self-contained classrooms for children with specific learning disabilities ($M = 12.8$ years old). They were classified as language-learning disabled on the basis of

Table 1. General and Specific Relations for the Childrens Semantic Relations Test

General	Specific	Example
Antonyms	1. Contrary	Whisper-Yell
	2. Contradictory	Life-Death
	3. Directional	Top-Bottom
Synonyms	1. Synonyms	Middle-Center
	2. Dimensionals	Town-City
	3. Attributes	Fork-Rake
Class Inclusion	1. Subordination	Animal-Dog
	2. Coordination	Ear-Nose
	3. Colaterals	Mammal-Bee
Case Relations	1. Agent/Object	Mailman-Letter
	2. Agent/Recipient	Whip-Lion
	3. Agent/Instrument	Writer-Pencil
Part Whole	1. Functional/Object	Shirt-Button
	2. Functional/Location	School-Class
	3. Membership	Team-Player

three criteria: (a) performance on language and reading achievement tests was *at least* 2 years below grade level; (b) possessed at least average IQs; and (c) a verbal/performance IQ discrepancy existed of at least 10 points, with the higher scale being the performance one (mean WISC-R scores:

Table 2. Hypothetical Examples of Semantic Relations Test Items (for Antonyms)

HOMOGENEOUS-Specific Knowledge			
top	front*	dead	cold
bottom	back	alive	hot
(direction)	(direction)	(contradictory)	(continuum)
HETEROGENEOUS-DIFFERENT-General Knowledge			
top	dead*	dish	vegetable
bottom	alive	plate	carrot
(direction)	(contradictory)	(synonym)	(class-inclusion)
HETEROGENEOUS-SAME-either general, specific or both			
top	front*	dish	vegetable
bottom	back	plate	carrot
(direction)	(directional)	(synonym)	(class-inclusion)

*denotes correct response

FS = 97, V = 87, P = 105). The second group was comprised of 21 NLD boys of junior high school (grades 7 and 8) age (M = 12.7 years). The third group, which consisted of 24, upper-level elementary (grades 5 and 6) school-age NLD boys (M = 10.6 years). was included in order to better address the question of whether L/LD students exhibit qualitatively distinct structural patterns of semantic knowledge, or if their semantic profiles are qualitatively similar to younger normal children (i.e., simply developmentally delayed).

The SRT was developed in a manner to allow examination of semantic structure and abilities at different levels of analysis. First, the test provides an overall score reflecting a child's generalized ability to comprehend semantic relations. The test also permits total scores for each of the five different semantic relations. And at the most detailed level of analysis, the test provides scores for comprehension of general and specific components for each relation.

We first examined the three groups' overall mean scores. This overall score was obtained by summing across homogeneous, heterogeneous-same, and heterogeneous-different question types for the five kinds of semantic relations. Statistically significant differences were found between the three groups, $F(2,62)$ = 4.65,p < .01. Pairwise comparisons revealed that L/LD children performed less accurately than their age-mates, while performing similarly to younger (fifth grade) NLD children. By themselves, these results are not surprising. On most cognitive tasks, LD children are found to perform below their peers.

We next compared the three groups' scores on the SRT for the five different relations, collapsing across scores for the three question types. Overall, there was no interaction between the group and type of relation.

Finally, we compared the three groups' scores for the five relations within each question type. Figure 1 presents mean group scores by relation for each question type: heterogeneous-different (general component), homogenous (specific component), and heterogeneous-same (general and/or specific components). An analysis of the data in the left panel of the figure indicated that L/LD children were less able to identify the correct answer to heterogeneous-same questions for the relations of antonymy, part-whole, and synonymity. Since this question can be answered on more than one basis, its interpretation is more complicated than either homogeneous or heterogeneous-different question types. Subjects may answer this kind of question on the basis of a general component alone or on the basis of a general component and a specific component, with the latter basis providing a confirmation that the pair chosen matches the stimulus pair's relation. Linguistic theory indicates that a specific component can be analyzed only after the presence of an appropriate general component has been confirmed. Thus, scores for the heterogeneous-same questions

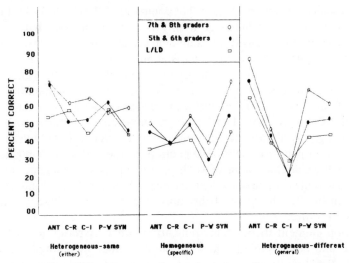

Figure 1. Mean percent correct as a function of group and type of semantic relation.

are expected to be comparable or better than scores for the heterogeneous-
different questions. Specifically, it is expected that scores for heterogeneous-same question types will be comparable if answers are based on a
general component only. Or, these scores will be higher if answers are
based on both general and specific components.

Comparison of the right and left panels of Figure 1 indicates that for
case relations, class-inclusion, and part-whole relations, L/LD students
and 5th graders scored higher on heterogenous-same than heterogeneous-
different questions. It appears that for these relations children based their
answers on both general and specific components. With regard to antonyms, L/LD youngster's scores actually decreased when they were provided the opportunity to base relational decisions on both general and
specific components, while correct responses to synonyms remained constant regardless of question type.

Additionally, all three groups scored lower on heterogeneous-different
(general) components for the relation of class inclusion. This pattern
changes when children are provided an opportunity to draw upon both
general and specific knowledge. That is, class inclusion scores are much
higher in the heterogeneous-same as opposed to the heterogenous-different
condition. Interestingly, prior developmental research has indicated that
the relation children have the most difficulty discriminating from others
is class inclusion (Landis, 1982), thus the low scores for this relation may
be another manifestation of this well-documented difficulty.

The results of this work suggest that comparing L/LD with NLD children on global measures of language ability is insufficient and that relevant information can be obtained by examining components of linguistic ability. It must be emphasized that our work is at an exploratory stage. Replication is needed as well as more in-depth examination of each of the general and specific components discussed. However, it can be concluded that like adults, children possess differential knowledge of general and specific types of semantic information. Furthermore, this ratio of general to specific seems to vary by ability and age. On a general level, L/LD children seem to perform on par with their NLD peers (i.e., they are as capable as age-mates in the understanding of such general linguistic concepts as case relations and class inclusion). Yet, by junior high there is a trend towards a delay in the development of the more intricate system underlying this general structure.

Relation element theory has implications for classroom instruction of disabled and non-disabled school children. Rather than simply teaching students the definitional characteristics of various types of semantic relations, it may be profitable to instruct children in the decision processes that interact with the structural characteristics of lexical knowledge. Clearly, relational element theory holds promise for our understanding of the L/LD child's difficulties in comprehending linguistic information. In an attempt to add another dimension to our understanding of the relationship between semantic structure and processing characteristics of these children, we next examine the automatic/purposive processing distinction mentioned earlier.

AUTOMATIC PROCESSING CHARACTERISTICS OF L/LD CHILDREN

Up to this point we have suggested that, at least for particular types of relationships, L/LD children structure semantic information in a qualitatively different manner from NLD age-mates. We suggest that structure constrains the optimization of those cognitive processes that depend on an elaborate semantic system. An implication of this assumption is that the structural differences between L/LD and NLD students may, in part, explain the memory deficiencies of the former. Although the precise causal relationship is as yet undetermined, we have suggested that one reason these structural differences may exist in the first place is that they may be related to the manner in which L/LD children *process* semantic information. To give just one example, if they routinely processed stimuli on a non-semantic level (phonetic, graphemic, spatial), this would be expected to result in an impoverished semantic memory. An impoverishment in semantic memory would be expected to have "ripple" effects on all forms of cognizing, including the effective use of encoding and retrieval processes. No matter how functional one's encoding and retrieval processes may be, children will be ineffective in deploying them if semantic memory does not contain the information to be encoded. Thus, processes are viewed as necessary but not sufficient to perform adequately.

The processing characteristics of disabled and non-disabled children have been examined from a number of different angles. One of the more profitable approaches has been to examine semantic processing deficits from the "levels of processing" perspective set forth by Craik and his colleagues (Craik & Lockhart, 1972). Craik's framework has provided a common frame of reference for investigators interested in understanding memory structure and process. It has also provided a base for examining and debating whether disabled learners experience "bottom-up" or "top-down" semantic processing deficiencies (Carr, 1981; Spear & Sternberg, 1986). On the one hand, a number of investigators have suggested that LD children experience bottom-up difficulties (for review see Spear & Sternberg, 1986), that is, they experience such a great deal of difficulty in word decoding (i.e. phonics) that very little attentional resources remain in order to derive meaning from what has been decoded. Conversely, others argue that LD youngsters experience top-down disabilities (Ceci, 1984). According to this position inadequate activation of higher-order meaning processes (such as inference) results in an inordinate amount of lower-level processing.

We prefer to distinguish the processing of semantic information as either automatic or purposive (Ceci, 1982, 1984). On the one hand, *automatic processing* is defined as a process that occurs mechanically, requiring no awareness or attention on the part of the subject. It does not benefit from practice and does not compete for resources of the limited-capacity attentional system (Hasher & Zacks, 1979; Posner & Snyder, 1976). Examples of this type of processing abound in both laboratory studies (e.g., shadowing one ear while a related word is presented to the non-attended ear) and everyday tasks (e.g., much of the meaning derived from this page of text is done so on an automatic level).

On the other hand, *purposive processing* entails the sort of controlled-strategies involved in encoding and retrieving semantic information (Schneider & Shiffrin, 1977). Purposive processing utilizes resources of the limited capacity memory system. Almost any task that requires conscious, highly focused attention falls into this category (e.g., deriving inferences).

Few experts agree on the contribution of each of these forms of processing to the deficits experienced by disabled learners. In fact, parallel with the top-down vs bottom-up controversy, two very different viewpoints exist: One group of researchers believe that disabled learners are deficient at purposive processing but are unimpaired at automatic processing (Bauer, 1982; Ceci, 1982, 1984; Simpson & Lorsbach, 1983; Stanovich & West, 1983). Their findings suggest that LD children are less apt to engage in conscious forms of semantic analysis, while automatic forms of processing remain, for the most part, unimpaired. Others argue, however, that LD children are inefficient at automatic processing, resulting in increased effort spent decoding words that for NLD peers are processed automatically, along with a decrease in the processing of word meaning (Laberge & Samuels, 1974; Sternberg & Wagner, 1982). While the former view suggests that LD children experience top-down processing difficulties, the latter position maintains that they lack bottom-up abilities.

One of the difficulties in resolving this debate has been the development of a methodology capable of separating automatic and purposive forms of semantic processing. Traditional paradigms have typically involved the use of either motor or vocal response times, which are themselves confounded with age-related changes. In our attempt to develop a methodology sensitive enough to disentangle the semantic processing characteristics of language deficient children, we were influenced by experimental work in the area of psychophysiology (Corteen & Dunn, 1974; Corteen & Wood, 1972; Dawson & Schell, 1982; Forster & Goirer, 1978; VonWright, Anderson, & Stenman, 1975).

Typically, these investigators have used a two-part experimental procedure involving classical conditioning in Phase 1 and dichotic shadowing in Phase 2. In Phase 1, subjects are presented with a list of words, some of which are designated as TARGET words by their association with a mild electric shock or a loud noise. A measure of conditioning to the TARGET word is subjects' skin conductance responses (SCRs) when the target word is presented in the absence of electric shock or loud noise (after several prior pairings). In most instances, SCRs are conditioned to the shock-associated target words after only a few presentations.

In Phase 2, a shadowing task is introduced. Subjects are presented the previous list of words dichotically and told to repeat only those words presented to one ear, while ignoring words presented to the opposite ear. Both Posner (1978) and Dawson and Schell (1982) have argued that attending to the shadowed ear involves the limited capacity (purposive) attentional system. Although subjects are usually unable to recall having heard words presented to their non-attended ear, they often have been found to produce physiological responses of the same magnitude as in the conditioning phase. These shock-associated target words, when presented to the non-attended ear, are thought to be receiving an automatic level of attention. Responses have also been found to generalize beyond the target word to synonyms and rhyme words of the targets (VonWright et. al., 1975).

In an attempt to examine automatic and purposive semantic processing in L/LD children, we adapted these methods to fit a format that we believed to be both motivating and appropriate for measuring subtle linguistic processing abilities of these children. So far, 24 boys (12 L/LD and 12 N/LD) have participated in this on-going investigation. All children were seated in front of a video game, wearing a stereo headset and a pair of finger electrodes to measure galvanic skin conductance responses throughout the experimental session. Children were told that their job was to manipulate a joystick to steer a spacecraft that appeared on the screen. The spacecraft was to be steered to various planets that were located randomly around the perimeter of the screen. They were informed that they would hear words through the stereo headset as they played the video game, but these words could be ignored until later when subjects would be asked to repeat (shadow) the words from one ear while ignoring those from the other. For the time-being, subjects were told that their goal was to visit as many of the planets on the screen (in a predetermined order) before being shot-down by one of the anti-aircraft rocket launchers that would be fired at the spacecraft from all corners of the screen. Unbeknown to the subjects, the game was programmed so that a rocket would destroy the spacecraft at pre-arranged times. Whenever, a rocket hit the spacecraft, the craft's destruction was accompanied by a visual display of its disintegration in addition to a burst of white noise producing the sensation of a loud crash.

Throughout this conditioning phase, 24 familiar words were auditorily presented via speech synthesizers in a randomized order. The word *Black* was designated as the target. Two-thirds of the time the target was presented, one of the rockets being fired from the four corners of the screen would hit the spacecraft and destroy it, with the simultaneous presentation of white noise and visual destruction of the spacecraft. On every third occurence of the presentation of the target word, the explosion and white noise were absent. Children were not told about the relationship between the target and the explosion, as the purpose of this phase was to classically condition a skin conductance response (SCR) to the target word. Conditioning was considered to be established when two consecutive no explosion occurrences of the target *each* resulted in an average SCR that exceeded 110% of the average SCR' of the word immediately preceding the target.

Once conditioned, children were told the video game was over. At this point they were asked to participate in the second phase of the experiment. They were instructed to listen and repeat aloud words presented to one of their ears while ignoring those words presented to the other ear. During this shadowing phase, SCRs were collected and averaged. In addition to the 24 words presented during the conditioning phase, 3 new words were added. Two of these words were semantically related to the target, BLACK: DARK and BROWN.[1]

Data of interest were the SCRs associated with the 27 words from the shadowing phase. Preliminary analyses reveal a statistically reliable interaction between group (L/LD vs. NLD) and channel (attended vs. non-attended). That is, L/LD children emitted significantly more SCRs to words presented to the attended (shadowed) channel, than they did to words presented to the non-attended ear, whereas NLD children emitted essentially the same number of SCRs to both attended and non-attended channels. This first bit of evidence lends some support to the hypothesis that L/LD children are deficient at automatic processing (Sternberg & Wagner, 1982).

In order to explore further these observed processing differences, we examined group responses to the target, phonetic, semantic, and unrelated words. As Figure 2 graphically reveals, nearly 90% of both groups of children emitted large SCRs to the target when it was presented to the attended ear. Similarly, the two groups emitted approximately the same number of SCRs to words semantically related to the target. It is important to note that semantically related words were more likely to produce a large

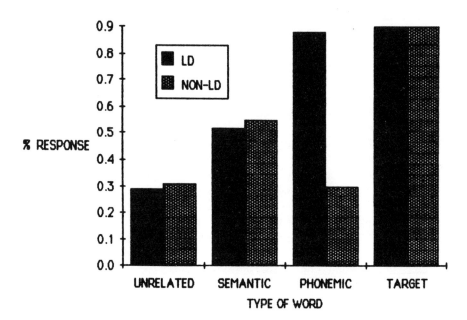

Figure 2.   Mean percent of words associated with large SCRs presented to the attended ear.

SCR than were unrelated words, even though they had not appeared during the previous conditioning phase.

As seen in Figure 3, the pattern was slightly different for the words presented to the non-attended ear. On average, N/LD children were more likely than the L/LD group to yield SCRs to the target and to words *semantically* related to it when these words were presented to the non-attended ear. Moreover, N/LD youngsters exhibited nearly the same number of SCRs to words presented to their non-attended ear as to those of their attended ear. They emitted SCRs to 80% of targets versus 66% for the L/LD group. On semantically related words, NLD subjects emitted SCRs to 55% of cases whereas the L/LD sample emitted SCRs to only 35% of semantically related words.

Although still preliminary in nature, these results lend support to the argument that L/LD children are deficient at automatic semantic processing (Wagner & Sternberg, 1982). L/LD children were not as likely as their NLD peers to manifest automatic semantic processing (as evidenced by the interaction between group and channel (attended/non-attended), and specifically by their diminished propensity to emit SCRs to semantically related words in the nonattended ear). Although these results were some-

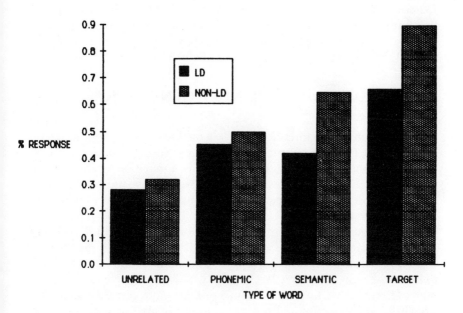

Figure 3. Mean percent of words associated with large SCRs presented to the nonattended ear.

what of a surprise to us, we are confident that the methodology employed in the present investigation is, to date, the most precise way of disentangling automatic from purposive forms of semantic processing.

What is one to make of these findings? Several alternative explanations exist. The most straightforward (and least parsimonious) explanation would be to report that L/LD children are deficient at automatic processing. The implication of this explanation is that they invest more purposive attention in the processing of words than do nondisabled students and consequently have little attentional "energy" left to process higher-order meaning. As it stands, this explanation is less than completely satisfactory because it ignores the fact that L/LD youngsters did automatically process rhyme words.[1] It would follow from this reasoning that nondisabled students were deficient at phonetic processing, however, this conclusion also may be unwarranted in that it relies on a "non-cross-over" interaction for its interpretation (the L/LD group's performance on the attended list surpassed the NLD sample's performance, whereas their performance on the non-attended list was similar). It could be argued, and there is some empirical data to support it, that LD children have more difficulty allocating their attention on dichotic tasks (Obrzut, Hynd, Obrzut, & Pirrozolo, 1981). If true, their inferior performance on the non-shadowed channel may merely underscore their rigid attentional style. Although this is post hoc conjecture, it does gain support both from studies documenting LD children's inferiority in switching attention on dichotic tasks and from studies using the priming paradigm, which have shown that the automatic semantic processing of LD children's equivalent to that of NLD peers.

SUMMARY: THE NEXT GENERATION

Our purpose in this chapter has been to examine the manner in which one subgroup of LD children structure and process semantic information. We believe that the approach outlined in here is a potentially profitable one for LD researchers, clinicians, and educators because it capitalizes upon a distinction that lies at the center of contemporary cognitive science, i.e. the structure versus process distinction. Although our own data are still preliminary, they appear to provide support for the view that L/LD children differ in fundamental ways from their nondisabled peers in the structure of their semantic memories and also possibly in the processes they deploy to instantiate this structure. We have provided some evidence to support both of these views, however, a number of questions remain unanswered. Primarily, are structure and process causally related or only correlates, mediated by a third and, as yet unknown, variable? Rather than develop two separate (and parallel) models to explain the structural and processing deficiencies of L/LD children, investigators should examine how structure and process interact to produce deficient performance.

In conclusion, it is important to point out that we have examined only semantic memory, and only in one subgroup of LD children. Nonetheless, our attempt to integrate structure and process has allowed us to move beyond the sterile single variable investigations that have characterized the first generation of cognitive research. As this first generation of LD research comes to an end, we are left with testable hypotheses with which to base future investigations. With a better understanding of basic cognitive theory, more integrative models, and the identification of more homogeneous subgroups of disabled children, the first generation's goal of understanding and remediating the cognitive underpinnings of specific learning disabilities may become the next generation's reality.

NOTE

1.   The third additional word rhymed with the target, *BACK*. Results of relevant analyses found that L/LD children emitted SCRs 88% of the time that rhymes were presented to the attended ear (versus only 30% for N/LD subjects) but only 44% of the time they were presented to the non-attended ear (versus 48% for N/LD group). Although these results are quite striking, a discussion of their significance is beyond the scope of the present paper.

REFERENCES

Anderson, J. R. (1983). *The architecture of cognition*. Cambridge, MA: Harvard University Press.

Anderson, J. R. (1984). Spreading activation. In J. Anderson & S. Kosslyn (Eds.), *Tutorials in learning and memory-Essays in honor of Gordon Bower* (pp. 61–90). San Francisco: W. H. Freeman.

Bartel, N., Grill, J., & Bartel, H. (1973). The syntactic-paradigmatic shift in learning disabled and normal children. *Journal of Learning Disabilities, 7,* 518–523.

Bauer, R. H. (1977). Memory processes in children with learning disabilities: Evidence for deficient rehearsal. *Journal of Experimental Child Psychology, 24,* 415–430.

Bauer, R. H. (1982). Information processing as a way of understanding and diagnosing learning disabilities. *Topics in Learning and Learning Disabilities, 2,* 33–45.

Berger, N., & Perfetti, C. (1977). Reading skill and memory for spoken and written discourse. *Journal of Reading Behavior, 9,* 7–16.

Bjorklund, D. F. (1985). The role of conceptual knowledge in the development of organization in children's memory. In C. J. Brainerd & M. Pressley (Eds.), *Basic processes in memory development: Progress in cognitive development research* (pp. 103–142). New York: Springer-Verlag.

Bjorklund, D. F., & Bernhottz, J. E. (in press). The role of knowledge base in the memory performance of good and poor readers, *Journal of Experimental Child Psychology*.

Carr, T. H. (1981). Building theories of reading ability: On the relation between individual differences in cognitive skills and reading comprehension. *Cognition, 9,* 73–114.

Ceci, S. J. (1982). The extraction of meaning from pictures and words: Automatic and purposive processing by L/LDs. *Topics in Learning and Learning Disabilities, 2,* 79–89.

Ceci, S. J. (1984). A developmental study of memory and learning disabilities. *Journal of Experimental Child Psychology, 38,* 352–371.

Ceci, S. J., & Baker, J. G. (1986). How shall we conceptualize the language-based difficulties of L/LDs? In S. J. Ceci (Ed.), *Handbook of cogntive, social, and neuropsychological aspects of learning disabilities* (Vol. 2, pp. 103–112). Hillsdale, NJ: Erlbaum.

Ceci, S. J., Lea, S. E. G., & Ringstrom, M. (1980). Coding characteristics of normal and learning disabled children: Evidence for modality-specific pathways to the cognitive system. *Journal of Experimental Psychology: Human Learning and Memory, 6,* 785–797.

Chaffin, R., & Herrmann, D. J. (1981). Semantic relationships and the generality of semantic-memory models. *Bulletin of the Psychonomic Society, 17,* 69–72.

Chaffin, R., & Herrmann, D. J. (1984). The similarity and diversity of semantic relations. *Memory and Cognition, 12,* 134–141.

Chaffin, R., & Herrmann, D. J. (in press). Relation Element Theory: A new account of the representations and processing of semantic relations. In D. Gorfein & R. Hoffman (Eds.), *Memory and learning: The Ebbinghaus Centennial Conference.* Hillsdale, NJ: Erlbaum.

Collins, A., & Loftus, E. F. (1975). A spreading activation theory of semantic processing. *Psychological Review, 82,* 407–428.

Corteen, R. S., & Dunn, D. (1974). Shock-associated words in a non-attended message: A test for awareness. *Journal of Experimental Psychology, 102,* 1143–1144.

Corteen, R. S., & Wood, B. (1972). Autonomic responses to shock associated words in an unattended channel. *Journal of Experimental Psychology, 97,* 308–313.

Craik, F. I., & Lockhart, R. G. (1972). Levels of processing: A framework for memory research. *Journal of Verbal Learning and Verbal Behavior, 11,* 671–684.

Dallago, M. L. P., & Moely, B. E. (1980). Free recall in boys of normal and poor reading levels as a function of task manipulations. *Journal of Experimental Child Psychology, 30,* 62–78.

Dawson, M. E., & Schell, A. M. (1982). Electrodermal responses to attended and nonattended significant stimuli during dichotic listening. *Journal of Experimental Psychology: Human Perception and Performance, 8,* 315–324.

Denckla, M. B., & Rudel, R. G. (1976). Naming of object drawings by dyslexic and other learning disabled children. *Brain and Language, 3,* 1–15.

Donahue, M. (1986). Linguistic and Communicative Development in Learning-disabled children. In S. J. Ceci (Ed.), *Handbook of cognitive, social, and neuropsychological aspects of learning disabilities* (Vol. 1, pp. 263–289). Hillsdale, NJ: Erlbaum.

Doris, J. (1986). Learning disabilities. In S. J. Ceci (Ed.), *Handbook of cognitive, social, and neuropsychological aspects of learning disabilities* (Vol. 1, pp. 3–53). Hillsdale, NJ: Erlbaum.

Fletcher, J. M. (1985a). Memory for verbal and nonverbal stimuli in learning disability subgroups: Analysis by selective reminding. *Journal of Experimental Child Psychology, 40,* 244–259.

Fletcher, J. M. (1985b). External validity of learning disability subtypes. In B. P. Rourke (Ed.), *Neuropsychology of learning disabilities: Essentials of subtype analysis* (pp. 187–211). New York: Guilford.

Fletcher, J. M., & Morris, R. (1986). Classification of disabled learners: Beyond exclusionary definitions. In S. J. Ceci (Ed.), *Handbook of cognitive, neuropsychological, and social aspects of learning disabilities* (Vol. 1, pp. 54–80). Hillsdale, NJ: Erlbaum.

Forster, P. M., & Govier, E. (1978). Discrimination without awareness. *Quarterly Journal of Experimental Psychology, 30,* 282–295.

Fried-Oken, M. (1984). *The development of naming skills in normal and language deficient children.* Unpublished doctoral dissertation, Boston University.

Gaddes, W. H. (1985). *Learning disabilities and brain function.* NY: Springer-Verlag.

Goldstein, D., & Dundon, W. D. (1986). Affect and cognition in learning disabilities. In S. J. Ceci (Ed.), *Handbook of cognitive, neuropsychological, and social aspects of learning disabilities* (Vol. 2, pp. 233–250). Hillsdale, NJ: Erlbaum.

Hasher, L., & Zacks, R. T. (1984). Automatic and effortful processes in memory. *Journal of Experimental Psychology: General, 108,* 356–388.

Herrmann, D. J. (1978). An old problem for the new psychosemantics: Synonymity. *Psychological Bulletin, 85,* 490–512.

Herrmann, D. J., & Chaffin, R. (in press). Comprehension of semantic relations as a function of the definitions of relations. In F. Klix (Ed.), *In memoriam Hermann Ebbinghaus.* Amsterdam: North-Holland.

Herrmann, D. J., Chaffin, R. J., Conti, G., Peters, D., & Robbins, P. H. (1979). Comprehension of antonymy and the generality of categorization models. *Journal of Experimental Psychology: Human Learning and Memory, 5,* 585–597.

Israel, L. (1984). Word knowledge and word retrieval: Phonological and semantic strategies. In G. Wallach & K. Butler (Eds.), *Language learning disabilities in school-age children* (pp. 230–250). Baltimore: Williams & Wilkins.

Jackendoff, R. (1983). *Semantics and cognition.* Cambridge, MA: MIT Press.

Johnson, D., & Myklebust, H. (1967). *Learning disabilities: Educational principles and practices.* Orlando, FL: Grune & Stratton.

Johnson-Laird, P. N., Herrmann, D. J., & Chaffin, R. (1984). Only connections: A review of semantic network models. *Psychological Bulletin, 96,* 292–315.

Kail, R., & Leonard, L. B. (1986). Sources of Word-finding Problems in Language-impaired Children. In S. J. Ceci (Ed.), *Handbook of cognintive, social, and neuropsychological aspects of learning disabilities* (Vol. 1, pp. 185–202). Hillsdale, NJ: Erlbaum.

Kirk, S. A., McCarthy, J., & Kirk, W. (1969). *The Illinois Test of Psycholinguistic Abilities* (rev. ed.). Urbana: Illinois University Press.

Klix, F. (1980). On structure and function of semantic memory. In F. Klix & J. Hoffmann (Eds.), *Cognition and memory* (pp. 11–26). Amsterdam: North-Holland.

Klix, F., & v.d. Meer, E. (1980). The method of analogy recognition for the determination of semantic relations in long-term memory. In F. Klix & J. Hoffman (Eds.), *Cognition and memory* (pp. 145–153). Amsterdam: North-Holland.

Kuczaj, S. A. (1982). Acquisition of word meaning in development of the semantic system. In C. J. Brainerd & M. Pressley (Eds.), *Verbal processes in children* (pp. 95–120). New York: Springer-Verlag.

Laberge, D., & Samuels, S. J. (1974). Toward a theory of automatic information processing in reading. *Cognitive Psychology, 6,* 293–323.

Leech, G. (1974). *Semantics.* Baltimore: Penguin Books.

Lyons, J. *Semantics* (Vol. 1). New York: Cambridge University Press.

Markman, E. M., & Seibert, J. (1976). Classes and collections: Internal organization and resulting holistic properties. *Cognitive Psychology, 8,* 561–577.

Marr, D. (1982). *Vision.* San Francisco: Freeman.

Norman, D. A., Rumelhart, D. E., & the LNR Research Group (1975). *Explorations in cognition.* San Francisco: Freeman.

Obrzut, J. E., Hynd, G. W., Obrzut, A., & Pirozzolo, F. J. (1981). Effect of directed attention on cerebral asymmetries in normal and learning disabled children. *Developmental Psychology, 17,* 118–125.

Perfetti, C. A. (1985). *Reading ability.* New York: Oxford University Press.

Posner, M. I. (1978). *Chronometric explorations of mind.* Hillsdale, NJ: Erlbaum.

Posner, M. I., & Snyder, C. R. R. (1976). Attention and cognitive control. In P. Rabbitt (Ed.), *Attention and performance VI*. Orlando, FL: Academic Press.

Przybilski, Schmidt, H-D., & Sydow, H. (1980). The development of semantic relations in childhood. In F. Klix & J. Hoffmann (Eds.), *Cognition and memory* (pp. 117–124). Amsterdam: North-Holland Press.

Rabinowitz, M. (1984). The use of categorical organization: Not an all-or-none situation. *Journal of Experimental Child Psychology, 38*, 338–351.

Rabinowitz, M., & Chi, M. T. H. (1986). An Interactive model of Strategic Processing. In S. J. Ceci (Ed.), *Handbook of cognitive, social, and neuropsychological aspects of learning disabilities (Vol. 2*, pp. 83–102). Hillsdale, NJ: Erlbaum.

Raschke, I., & Sydow, H. (1985, July). *Semantic relations: Their generality level in preschool age*. Paper presented at the symposium in memorium of Herman Ebbinghaus, East Berlin.

Rosch, E., Mervis, C., Gray, W., Johnson, D., & Boyes-Braem, P. (1976). Basic objects in natural categories. *Cognitive Psychology, 8*, 382–439.

Ross, J. L. (1985). Semantic relational comprehension: Components and correlates. *Conhecer A. Pessoa, 3*, 9–17.

Rourke, B. P. (1982). Central processing deficiencies in children: Toward a developmental neuropsychological model. *Journal of Clinical Neuropsychology, 4*, 1–18.

Schneider, W., & Shiffrin, R. M. (1977). Controlled and automatic human information processing: 1. Detection, search, and attention. *Psychological Review, 84*, 1–67.

Schwanenflugel, P. J., Bjorklund, D. F., Guth, M. E., Willenborg, M. F., & Boardman, J. L. (1984). *A developmental trend in the understanding of concept attribute importance*. Paper presented at the Meeting of the Southeastern Conference on Human Development, Athens, GA.

Semel, E., & Wiig, E. (1975). Comprehension of syntactic structures and critical verbal elements by children with learning disabilities. *Journal of Learning Disabilities, 8*, 53–58.

Siegel, L. S., & Heaven, R. K. (1986). Categorization of Learning Disabilities. In S. J. Ceci (Ed.), *Handbook of cognitive, social and neuropsychological aspects of learning disabilities* (Vol. 1, pp. 95–121). Hillsdale, NJ: Erlbaum.

Simpson, G., & Lorsbach, T. (1983). The development of automatic and conscious components of contextual facilitation. *Child Development, 54*, 760–772.

Smiley, S., Oakley, D., Worthen, D., Campione, J., & Brown, A. (1977). Recall of thematically relevant material by adolescent good and poor readers as a function of written versus oral presentation. *Journal of Educational Psychology, 69*, 381–389.

Spear, L. C., & Sternberg, R. J. (1986). An information-processing framework for understanding reading disability. In S. J. Ceci (Ed.), *Handbook of cognitive, social, and neuropsychological aspects of learning disabilities* (Vol. 2, pp. 3–32). Hillsdale, NJ: Erlbaum.

Stanovich, K. W., & West, R. F. (1983). On priming by a sentence context. *Journal of Experimental Psychology: General, 112*, 1–36.

Sternberg, R. S., & Wagner, R. K. (1982). Automatization failure in learning disabilities. *Topics in Learning and Learning Disabilities, 2*, 1–11.

Suiter, M. L., & Potter, R. E. (1978). The effects of paradigmatic organization on the language/learning disableds' (L/LDs') verbal recall. *Journal of Learning Disabilities, 11*, 247–250.

Torgesen, J. K. (1975). Problems and prospects in the study of learning disabilities. In E. M. Hetherinton (Ed.), *Review of child development research* (Vol. 5, pp. 128–147). Chicago: University of Chicago Press.

Torgesen, J. K. (1977). Memorization processes in reading-disabled children. *Journal of Educational Psychology, 72,* 141–160.

Torgesen, J. K., & Goldman, T. (1977). Verbal rehearsal and short--term memory in reading disabled children. *Child Development, 48,* 56–60.

Vellutino, F. R. (1979). *Dyslexia: Theory and research.* Cambridge, MA: MIT Press.

Vellutino, F. R., & Scanlon, D. (1982). Verbal processing in poor and normal readers. In C. J. Brainerd & M. Pressley (Eds.), *Verbal processes in children* (pp. 189–254). New York: Springer-Verlag.

VonWright, J., Anderson, K., & Stenman, V. (1975). Generalization of conditioned GSRs in dichotic listening. In P. M. A. Rabbitt (Ed.), *Attention and performance* (Vol. 5, pp. 87–101). London: Academic Press.

Wong, B. (1979). Strategic behaviors in selecting retrieval cues in gifted, normal achieving and learning disabled children. *Journal of Learning Disabilities, 15,* 33–37.

INFORMATION PROCESSING DEFICITS IN CHILDREN WITH LEARNING DISABILITIES

Laird S. Cermak and Patti Miliotis

ABSTRACT

This chapter explores the possibility that deficits in information processing influence the reading and memory abilities of learning disabled (LD) children. It proposes that these children do not analyze and encode verbal material on a normal level and that these deficits contribute to their linguistic difficulties, reading disorders, and problems with retention of verbal information. Studies will be reviewed which demonstrate that LD children are deficient in the speed with which they analyze the features of verbal material, in the level of sophistication they achieve during this initial analysis and in the strategies they develop to retain this material once it has been analyzed.

Memory and Learning Disabilities
Advances in Learning and Behavioral Disabilities, Suppl. 2, pages 111–122.
ISBN: 0-89232-836-3

Ever since Craik and Lockhart's (1972) paper on "Levels of Processing," it has generally been felt that information processing can be subdivided into several stages that contribute to the overall product called memory. The process is initiated by the level of analysis that an individual performs upon an incoming stimulus; however, memory is not totally determined by this analysis. Cermak (1976) has shown that some totally amnesic patients can perform highly sophisticated semantic feature analysis but still not retain anything of the information. The amnesic successfully analyzes the stimulus, but his/her analysis does not produce a lasting memory. Thus, normal retention must depend upon the ability to retain as well as to perform this analysis. This stage of processing has been defined as the "encoding" of material into memory. In this stage, the individual must cognitively manipulate the detected features of each item to compare and/or contrast these features with items already present in memory (i.e., categorizing) or previously analyzed in the current task (i.e., chunking). In addition to these two processing stages, Jacoby (1984) has also emphasized a third stage which he calls reconstruction. In this stage, which is essentially a retrieval stage, the desired item of information must often be reconstructed from the features that have been retained. Some individuals are more adept at this process than are others. Amnesics, for instance, have almost no capacity for this reconstructive process. While this stage has received almost no acknowledgement by investigators of learning disabilities, it is briefly discussed later in this chapter.

To summarize, encoding ability is defined as distinct from analytic ability. Some individuals with memory problems may fail to retain material as a consequence of their *analytic* deficiencies. Others may be unable to *encode* their analyses. LD children may be developmentally delayed in the rapid and proficient analysis of verbal information or they may be deficient in the encoding of that information. This chapter focuses on both these possibilities.

A description of LD children's ability to automatically process rudimentary features (visual, phonemic, nominal) of incoming information is presented first, which is followed by an analysis of their ability to abstract semantic features of verbal material. Next, the encoding difficulties experienced by LD children is discussed. Finally, a description of the difference between the processes involved in explicit memory (the conscious processing and retrieval of information) and implicit memory (which involves no conscious effort) is presented.

DEFICITS IN AUTOMATIC (PERCEPTUAL) ANALYSIS

The possibility that children with learning disabilities may demonstrate automatized processing disorders relative to their peers has recently received compelling support. Morrison, Giordani, and Nagy (1977) found that the processing deficit displayed by these children begins in the initial milliseconds following perception of a stimulus. Using Sperling's (1960) classic technique, Morrison et al. demonstrated that reading disabled children could "perceive" as much information from a stimulus display as could any normal reader of the same age. However, the reading disabled child began to lose information from this display faster than the normal child during a critical 500 to 2000 msec delay interval. This visual memory loss resulted in less information being available to the disabled child just one-half second after exposure.

Morrison et al. (1977) suggested that this rapid loss of information was the consequence of an inability to adequately analyze the incoming material. The LD child could perceive the material adequately but failed to automatically process the visual features of the information. Similar deficits were noted in the analysis of nonverbal geometric and abstract forms. This suggests that while learning disabilities are not solely the result of perceptual difficulties, the deficient processing that does occur during perception contributes to these children's decreased memory abilities.

In order to further explore these analytic deficits, Cermak (1983) used a modified version of Posner and Mitchell's (1967) chronometric analysis paradigm. This task was designed to assess the speed with which LD boys could process other rudimentary features of verbal information. In this task, two letters were exposed simultaneously to a child who was simply asked to indicate whether the two letters were the same or different. Under one condition, the children were asked to indicate whether the letters were physically the same (e.g., an *A* and an *A*) or different (e.g., an *A* and a *B* or an *A* and an *a*). In a second condition, the children were asked to indicate whether the letters were nominally the same (e.g., an *A* and an *A* or an *A* and an *a*) or different (e.g., an *A* and a *B*). Speed of response was determined as the time between presentation of the letters and the child's depression of an appropriate response key. Results indicated that although the LD children performed normally under the physical identity instructions, they were significantly worse than their contemporaries under the nominal identity instructions. This impairment on the nominal instructions was most evident when the children had to say "different" on the basis of the nominal (AB) features of the stimuli.

Similar results were found using two other categories of stimuli (i.e., letters vs. numbers and four-sided vs. three-sided figures). Under the letter-number condition "nominally alike" meant that both stimuli were numbers as opposed to letters while "physically identical" meant that the letter or number was exactly the same. In the figure condition "nominally alike" meant triangular as opposed to rectangular shapes whereas, "physically the same" meant the same shape exactly. The LD children performed the physical identity task normally, but they were significantly impaired on the nominal identity task for both letters vs numbers and the figures.

This outcome demonstrated that LD children can perform normally on a simple perception task but that they have difficulties analyzing the features in the stimulus array. LD children may eventually engage in the same processing as normals, but they do so less automatically. This places them at a severe disadvantage under conditions where rate of processing is important. Even when rate is not emphasized, their tendency toward a less sophisticated analyses of the material might result in a less firm basis for retention. As a consequence, there would be a more rapid decay of to-be-retained material and a lower probability of the child's being able to reconstruct the desired material even under the appropriate cueing instructions.

DEFICITS IN COGNITIVE (PHONEMIC, SEMANTIC) ANALYSIS

The analysis of incoming information involves not only the ability to "automatically" detect visual and nominal features of verbal stimuli but also the ability to abstract those features of verbal information that allow the material to be differentiated from other incoming material. These features include the phonemic and the semantic dimensions of the material. The ability to differentiate these features constitutes one's cognitive (nonautomatic) analysis of the verbal material.

One of the first demonstrations that LD children have impairments in these analytic abilities was by Shankweiler, Liberman, Fowler, and Fisher (1979). Their experiment involved the recall of five consonants drawn from sets of rhyming (B C D G P T V Z) or nonrhyming consonants (H K L Q R S W Y). Unlike normal children, the LD children were not affected by acoustic overlap between the rhyming consonants. They consistently made more errors on recall of the five letters than did the normal control child, but they made no more errors on the rhyming set than on the nonrhyming set. The normal control children made nearly twice as many errors on the rhyming set than on the nonrhyming set. This implied that the normal control children were attempting to retain the material on the basis of a phonemic form while the disabled children were not since there was more phonemic confusion for good learners than for poor. This finding is consistent with the hypothesis that LD children have an extremely rudimentary deficit in analysis of even the phonemic features of verbal information. A similar outcome and interpretation has been reported by Goodglass, Denes, and Calderon (1974) for adults with language disorders. Broca's aphasics demonstrated the same invulnerability to phonemic interference. It may be that language disorders impair the ability to analyze the phonemic features of verbal stimuli. Consequently, one is forced to rely on lower level orthographic features to retain the material.

Further support comes from a study by Cermak (1983) in which lists of words were presented to each child at a rate of one word per second. In one condition, the children were instructed to listen to each word and to raise their hand whenever they heard a word repeated. These repeated words were separated by either 0, 2, 4, 6, or 8 intervening words. In a second condition, the children were instructed to raise their hand whenever they heard a word that rhymed with another word in the list. In a third condition, the children were instructed to raise their hand whenever they heard a word belonging to the same category as a preceding word in the list. Fifteen lists were presented in each of the conditions—three lists at each retention interval as determined by the number of intervening words.

Both phonemic and semantic analytic impairments were demonstrated for all LD children in their early school years (8 to 10) and for all but the most verbal of these children in their later years. Whether the older, highly verbal children suffered from any residual effects of this problem could not be determined by this task because it was too easy for them. The results were consistent with the idea that the LD child's verbal memory difficulties are related to a deficit in cognitive analysis since their performance was normal on the repetition task and impaired on the phonemic and semantic conditions.

On the basis of this study, Cermak (1983) concluded that the ability to perform phonemic and semantic analyses was developmentally delayed for LD children. In order to evaluate the extent to which this disability might be improved through instructions, Cermak (1983) utilized a paradigm (Craik & Tulving, 1975) in which instructions to attend to specific semantic features of a word were given in order to improve the probability of retrieval of that word. Instructions to attend to the physical features of a word (induced by questions such as, "Is this word written in capital letters?") were not expected to increase the recall of the words. However, instructions to analyze the phonemic features of a word (induced by a question such as, "Does this word rhyme with 'bring'?") were expected to increase the probability of retrieval. Semantic instructions (created by questions such as, "Does this word fit in the sentence, 'The man picked up the ———'?") were expected to result in superior recall. Cermak and Reale (1978) had reported that such phonemic and semantic instructions did not help adults with organic forms of amnesia, however, it was hoped that LD children could benefit from such instructions.

The children were shown 60 words presented one at a time. They were asked either an orthographic, phonemic or semantic question about each word as described above. "Yes/No" responses were indicated by pressing an appropriate response key, attached to a timer. Following list presentation, the children were asked to recognize the 60 words from among a list of 180 words. All the LD children, regardless of age or IQ scatter, recognized as many orthographically and phonemically-analyzed words as did the normal children. Furthermore, they recognized only slightly fewer semantically analyzed words. Thus, the LD children benefited from instructions to analyze each word on a semantic level. Interestingly, though, it took them considerably more time than the normal readers to answer the questions about each word. Apparently, it took the LD children more time to analyze the specific features of the words, but the "pattern" of analytic time was the same as that of the normal children. Semantic analysis took longer than phonemic which, in turn, took longer than orthographic.

The finding that LD children were capable of analyzing the appropriate features of verbal information under optimal conditions (i.e., with appropriate instructions and sufficient time) makes therapeutic intervention seem possible. However, the task reported above was a simple one and another investigation (Swanson, 1984) was not so optimistic. Swanson found that LD children were less able to perform analytic tasks as the level of cognitive effort needed to perform that task increased. In this study, children were asked to solve anagrams and later to recall the words they had generated from those anagrams. The amount of effort needed to solve the anagrams, determined either by the difficulty of solution or the amount of time allowed for solution, correlated with the probability of retrieval for normal children. In contrast, increased task difficulty was not associated with enhanced recall for the LD children. Thus, the well documented normal relationship between effort and degree of memory (see also Perfetti & Lesgold, 1978), did not seem to exist for the LD children. This result diminishes the potential value of therapeutic intervention because it demonstrates that effortful analysis does not improve recall for the LD child.

ENCODING (CHUNKING, CATEGORIZING) DEFICITS

A major source of difficulty that LD children experience during their attempts to memorize material has been highlighted by Gelzheiser, Solar, Shepard, and Wozniak (1983). These authors recorded a brief statement made by a LD student following an attempt to retain a passage containing four paragraphs about diamonds. The student reported that she could identify major themes of the story, but could not categorize the various pieces of information under these major topics. She was able to abstract the essence of the story, but was unable to use this as a framework to organize the retention of the specific passage.

This suggests that LD children may be capable of abstracting categories of words from serially presented lists of words, but they may not be able to chunk (i.e., categorize together) these words for use at later retrieval. Cermak (1983) has presented evidence to support this thesis in a study in which children with and without learning disabilities were asked to learn a list of 20 common nouns in 5 trials. The children were told to rehearse the words aloud during each trial. Then, at the conclusion of each trial, they were asked to recall as many of the words as they could. Three types of word lists were used: a random list of unrelated words; a list containing five words from each of four categories randomly distributed within the list; and a list containing five words from each of four categories with the words presented in category blocks. The LD children recalled fewer words than their normal counterparts following all types of presentation. A developmental trend was observed among the normal readers, with recall probability increasing with age. This trend was consistent across all three conditions. However, a developmental trend was not consistently found for the LD children. The older LD children recalled no more words than did the younger LD children following the unrelated word presentation. However, once order was imposed (i.e., both related words conditions), probability of recall increased with age. Apparently the older LD children were not as adept as the older normal readers at imposing order where none existed, but they could detect and utilize semantic categorization to some extent (albeit not as well as normals) when it did exist within the list presentation.

When the rehearsal protocols were examined it became clear that the LD children had utilized a less sophisticated rehearsal strategy than had the normal children. The LD children between the ages of 8 and 14 years rehearsed in a manner typical of normal learners in the 8-to-10-year old range. They rehearsed only the word presently before them. In contrast, the older normal readers rehearsed several words concurrently, the one before them plus several others presented prior to the current word. The single-word strategy resulted in significantly more overt repetitions of each word but also in less organization of the total list. It was interesting to find that the older LD children had retained this rather immature rehearsal strategy long after their contemporaries had discarded it. This must have placed them at a distinct disadvantage when it came time to remember the words, since they could draw only from a disjointed series of episodes rather than a well-organized network of responses in which one word recall might possibly evoke others. This rehearsal strategy was utilized even for the categorized (blocked or unblocked) word lists on which the older LD children's recall performance had improved. Thus, they must have realized the existence of the categories but could not use this realization to aid their rehearsal.

Swanson (1983) arrived at a similar conclusion when he found that LD children rarely reported the use of an organizational strategy when they were required to rehearse several items. He reasoned that, since these children were capable of multi-item rehearsal, the problem was not a production deficiency in rehearsal but, instead, was a failure to perform elaborative processing of each word. Elaborative rehearsal was defined as the processing that goes beyond the initial level of analysis to include more sophisticated features of the words and ultimately the comparison of these features with others in the list. In other words, to include encoding as it has been defined here. Swanson pointed out that elaborative rehearsal provides a plan of retrieval for normal individuals, but it is not utilized by the LD children who appear to rely on rote, single item, rehearsing.

If it is true that LD children rehearse each item of information independently and on a level below their contemporaries, then it also follows that each of these items ought to be highly sensitive to loss when rehearsal is disrupted. To test this hypothesis, Cermak et al. (1981) asked a group of 12 to 16 year olds to retain three words across retention intervals ranging from 0 to 24 seconds. These words were unrelated and, therefore, not easily amenable to chunking. During the retention interval the children were engaged in a secondary (distractor) task that involved either semantic processing (i.e., looking for words from a particular category), phonemic processing (i.e., looking for rhymes), or visual processing (i.e., looking for a specific pattern). It was felt that the purely visual task would not distract the LD children from rehearsing the material but that the phonemic and semantic distractor tasks would disrupt their rehearsal. The normal children, on the other hand, could perform a more sophisticated cognitive analysis of the material which would allow greater encoding differentiation between the to-be-retained material and the disrupting task. The results substantiated this hypothesis because the LD children proved to be normal in retention when nonverbal distraction occurred and below normal (even after only six seconds) with either phonemic or semantic distraction.

Swanson (1978) has suggested that the LD child's rehearsal and retention of nonverbal materials might not be quite so easily disrupted as their verbal retention. He asked children to view randomly generated shapes one at a time and then gave them a probe stimulus. They were then asked to point to the stimulus (now face down on the table), which matched the probe. Swanson found that LD children could perform this task as well as normals. However, he also found that when the normal control children were taught a name for each stimulus they improved dramatically, but the LD children did not. The LD children did not show a visual memory deficit but they did exhibit a dysfunction as soon as a visual-verbal integration had to be performed. The child seemed able to attach verbal lables to visual stimuli but this did not improve his memory performance because he lost the label as soon as others had to be retained.

DEFICITS IN RETRIEVAL

It has been mentioned that the final stage in the process of retaining and retrieving verbal information is the ability to retrieve material known to be in memory. As also noted, very little attention has been paid to this ability, or disability, in LD children. One way to assess this ability is to measure the response time needed to retrieve material from a highly overlearned and limited set of stimuli. Elbert (1984) found that LD children took more time than normals just to determine that a probe word was a member of a small set of memorized words (Sternberg's technique, 1969). This indicated that they could not scan their memory as easily as normals and this, in turn, is strong evidence for the notion that children with learning disabilities may have processing deficits in retrieval as well as in their analysis and encoding. However, this area of deficiency needs to be investigated in a much more detailed and precise manner similar to that undertaken for analysis and encoding.

IMPLICIT MEMORY

All the preceding sections of this chapter have focused upon the explicit aspects of memory. *Explicit memory* is defined as the recall, or recognition, of an episode (Graf & Schacter, 1985). The subject is aware that he is recalling a specific event. In addition, he is conscious that he has personally experienced that event. *Implicit memory* is a form of memory in which the individual is not aware that he has experienced the specific event nor that he is retaining that event. Such memory is demonstrated whenever a learning experience has an effect upon subsequent behavior even though the individual cannot consciously remember that the learning occurred. For instance, an item in a store may seem desirable for reasons the buyer may not consciously remember; anxiety may be induced by a stimulus the person does not recall having seen before; and a word may be given as a response to a category cue even though the subject fails to recognize that it had been previously presented.

Jacoby (1984) has proposed that these two forms of retention (explicit and implicit) are independently represented in memory. Memory with awareness (explicit memory) requires that the individual exert a conscious effort to retain the material. Thus, level of processing, type of rehearsal, and organizational strategy can affect the probability of retaining this episode. Memory without awareness (implicit memory) does not require conscious effort on the part of the individual. Consequently, it is not sensitive to such factors as level of processing, analytic instructions, or method of presentation. It seems likely that LD children would be less deficient in implicit memory since little to no effort is involved and conscious cognitive effort seems to be lacking in these children's explicit memory (Swanson, 1984).

Jacoby and Dallas (1981) have introduced a procedure that allows the investigation of explicit and implicit memory within the same paradigm and over a very short retention interval. In this procedure, the influence of a prior exposure of a word on a subject's ability to *identify* that word when present at extremely short durations is contrasted with the ability to *recognize* that word among a series of other alternatives. Recently, we adapted this task for use with children and, in a preliminary investigation, assessed LD children's ability to perform these tasks. A short list of 10 words was presented to the children who were then asked to recognize 5 of these items within a list of 10 words. After this was completed, the children were asked to identify words presented at very short intervals (beginning at 15 msecs). Five of these words had been presented in the original list but had not appeared on the recognition list. Five were new words that had not previously appeared. When a word could not be identified it was presented again and again at successively longer intervals (5 msec increments) until identification was possible.

The LD children were impaired on the identification task relative to normal controls for both primed (previously presented) and unprimed (new) words. Surprisingly, however, they could recognize as many of the words as could the control children. Two features of the LD children's performance on this task should be highlighted. First, they *did* show a priming effect even though their identification of the primed words was slower than the normal children's identification of unprimed words. The LD children took 57 msecs to identify new (unprimed) words and 34 msecs for primed words while the controls took 25 msecs for new and 17 msecs for primed words. Thus, both groups showed approximately the same amount of savings (60%) for primed over unprimed words. Secondly, the recognition for both groups was nearly perfect (95% for the LD and 97% for the normal group). This outcome of nearly perfect recognition may have produced the comparable priming percentages. Whether decreased levels of recognition would have similar effects remains to be determined.

What can be concluded is that when explicit memory is exceptionally good for LD children, then implicit memory is normal (even though performance based on this memory is slow). If explicit memory could be diminished (through increased word lists or more difficult words, etc.), then the question of normal implicit memory in LD children could be assessed with more precision. If the two memory systems are independent, then even as recognition becomes more impaired, identification may remain normal. If it does not remain normal, then future research efforts must be made to determine whether this means that both implicit and explicit retention are impaired or whether both are based on the same impaired trace or whether they are mutually dependent upon one another. The paradigm holds a good deal of promise for future investigations and it could be used in therapeutic intervention. If implicit retention is normal, then much could be accomplished by improving a LD child's performance whether he is aware of prior exposures or not. Less emphasis on explicit recall and recogntion could then be placed on the child during therapy.

CONCLUSIONS

It appears that an entire spectrum of information processing abilities may be developmentally delayed in children with learning disabilities. This is due, in part, to the fact that one aspect of processing builds upon another. However, it also seems to be related to problems exhibited by these children within each stage of processing. LD children exhibit difficulties in the initial analysis of the features of verbal information as manifested by their slow rate of automatic processing. Their level of cognitive processing is also impaired as demonstrated by their inability to differentiate material on a phonemic or semantic level. Furthermore, problems exist in the encoding of these features, even when the children are given proper instructions and sufficient processing time. Maintenance of verbal material over short time intervals in the face of distraction is easily disrupted for these children. Finally, these children appear to have difficulties reconstructing the desired material from the features they have stored. Unfortunately, it is likely that these deficits are not limited to the verbal sphere, since evidence exists at each level implicating a nonverbal processing deficit as well. Clearly, in-depth research on all these processing abilities in very young children should proceed so that early detection of this disability can be documented.

ACKNOWLEDGMENTS

The authors wish to thank Margaret O'Connor and Sharon Cermak for their helpful suggestions during the preparation of this chapter. Some of the research reported in this chapter was supported by grant HD-09508 from the National Institute of Child Health and Human Development and by the Medical Research Service of the Veterans Administration.

REFERENCES

Cermak, L. S. (1976). The encoding capacity of a patient with amnesia due to encephalitis. *Neuropsychologia, 14*, 311–326.

Cermak, L. S. (1983). Information processing deficits in children with learning disabilities. *Journal of Learning Disabilities, 16,* 599–605.

Cermak, L. S., & Reale, L. (1978). Depth of processing and retention of words by alcoholic Korsakoff patients. *Journal of Experimental Psychology: Human Learning and Memory, 4,* 165–174.

Cermak, L. S., Goldberg-Warter, J., DeLuca, D., Cermak, S., & Drake, C. (1981). The role of interference in the verbal retention ability of learning disabled children. *Journal of Learning Disabilities, 14,* 291–295.

Craik, F. I. M., & Lockhart, R. S. (1972). Levels of processing: A framework for memory research. *Journal of Verbal Learning and Verbal Behavior, 11,* 671–684.

Craik, F. I. M., & Tulving, E. (1975). Depth of processing and retention of words in episodic memory. *Journal of Experimental Psychology, General, 104,* 268–294.

Elbert, J. C. (1984). Short-term memory encoding and memory search in the word recognition of learning-disabled children. *Journal of Learning Disabilities, 17,* 342–345.

Gelzheiser, L. M., Solar, R. A., Shepard, M. J., & Wozniak, R. H. (1983). Teaching learning disabled children to memorize: A rationale for plans and practice. *Journal of Learning Disabilities, 16,* 421–425.

Goodglass, H., Denes, G., & Calderon, M. (1974). The absence of covert verbal mediation in aphasia. *Cortex, 10,* 264–269.

Graf, P., & Schacter, D. L. (1985). Implicit and explicit memory for new associations in normal and amnesic subjects. *Journal of Experimental Psychology: Learning, Memory and Cognition, 11,* 501–518.

Jacoby, L. L. (1984). Incidental vs. intentional retrieval: Remembering and awareness as separate issues. In L. R. Squire & N. Butters, (Eds.), *The neuropsychology of memory.* New York: Guilford.

Jacoby, L. L., & Dallas, M. (1981). On the relationship between autobiographical memory and perceptual learning. *Journal of Experimental Psychology: General, 3,* 306–340.

Morrison, F. J., Giordani, B., & Nagy, J. (1977). Reading disability: An information-processing analysis. *Science, 196,* 77–79.

Perfetti, C., & Lesgold, A. (1978). Discourse comprehension and source of individual differences. In M. Just & P. Carpenter (Eds.), *Cognitive processes in comprehension.* Hillsdale, NJ: Erlbaum.

Posner, M. I., & Mitchell, R. F. (1967). Chronometric analysis of classification. *Psychological Review, 74,* 392–409.

Shankweiler, D., Liberman, I. Y., Marks, L. S., Fowler, C. A., & Fischer, F. W. (1979). The speech code and learning to read. *Journal of Experimental Psychology: Human Learning and Memory, 5,* 531–545.

Sperling, G. (1960). The information available in brief visual presentations. *Psychological Monographs, 74,* (Whole No. 498).

Sternberg, S. (1969). Memory scanning: Mental processes revealed by reaction time experiments. *American Scientist, 57,* 421–457.

Swanson, L. (1978). Verbal encoding effects on the visual short-term memory of learning disabled and normal readers. *Journal of Educational Psychology, 70,* 539–544.

Swanson, H. L. (1983). Relations among metamemory, rehearsal activity and word recall of learning disabled and nondisabled readers. *British Journal of Educational Psychology, 53,* 186–194.

Swanson, H. L. (1984). Effect of cognitive effort on learning disabled and nondisabled reader's recall. *Journal of Learning Disabilities, 17,* 67–74.

A DIMENSIONAL APPROACH TO COGNITIVE DEFICIENCIES

John W. Hagen, David A. Saarnio and
Eric D. Laywell

ABSTRACT

The chapter is organized into three sections. In the first, the cognitive-developmental view of learning disabilities is reviewed. The distinction between structural and control processes is made, major sources of variance hypothesized to account for memory development are discussed, and a model is offered that incorporates these factors into a taxonomy of person and task characteristics enabling assessment and prediction in research on cognitive deficiencies. In the second section, research from the authors' laboratory on the cognitive abilities of children with chronic illness is presented using such research as an example of the importance of a noncategorical

Memory and Learning Disabilities
Advances in Learning and Behavioral Disabilities, Suppl. 2, pages 123–145.
Copyright © 1987 by JAI Press Inc.
All rights of reproduction in any form reserved.
ISBN: 0-89232-836-3

approach to research on developmental disabilities. In the final section, the cognitive-developmental model and the work on chronically ill children are combined into a dimensional model for research on cognitive deficiencies. This approach involves the consideration of patterns of performance in the cognitive, academic, and behavioral areas exhibited by children who have been labeled into existing diagnostic categories. Three dimensions, diagnostic category, descriptors that cut across categories, and developmental level are presented as providing a framework within which current data can be organized and new predictions can be generated.

In a recent survey of professionals involved with learning disabilities, one of the overriding concerns of respondents was that of arriving at a consensus of what constitutes a learning disability (Adelman & Taylor, 1985). The basis for such a concern is obvious in any perusal of the literature on learning-disabled (LD) children or adults. There exists substantial disagreement regarding the nature of learning disabilities (e.g., Tucker, Stevens, & Ysseldyke, 1983). They are viewed by many to be the result of neurophysiological problems, whereas others view them as primarily behavioral problems in cognitive functioning. Some believe learning disabilities as specific to very limited domains, whereas others see them as more general problems. There are many ways of viewing learning disabilities, with at least some proponents for each. One point of agreement is that there exist some groups of children (and adults) who exhibit problems in certain academic domains (e.g., reading and/or mathematics), such that they lag behind their peers and that their achievement does not match their potential as assessed on aptitude tests (e.g., IQ tests) (Smith, 1983; but see McLoughlin & Netick, 1983, for a discrepant view).

The paradoxical nature of aptitude-achievement discrepancies and the observation that learning disabilities occur in more than one domain have led many researchers to believe that children with learning disabilities may have some general cognitive problems rather than problems in specific skills (e.g., Torgesen, 1977a). Those problems are thought to affect certain domains more than others, resulting in the argument for domain-specificity of learning disabilities. This view is part of the reason that so much attention has been devoted to the study of memory in children with learning disabilities. Memory is a general cognitive process that pervades most cognitive and academic tasks. It has been studied the most thoroughly of any aspect of cognitive processing in recent years, because of the central role played by memory in contemporary models of information processing. The fact that children diagnosed as learning disabled have been found to perform poorly on a variety of memory tasks, relative to their nondisabled peers, suggests that memory processes are a useful, if not necessary, focus of research on learning disabilities. Within this context, the focus of this chapter is on memory and related cognitive processes. However, our purpose is to offer arguments supporting the position that current approaches to the study of memory and cognitive processes in children with learning disabilities, as well as other children with cognitive problems, are inadequate for understanding the nature of their problems. A different approach to the study of cognitive deficiencies is needed that takes into account the diversity of problems exhibited by LD children, as well as their cognitive strengths.

The modal approach to research on memory and learning disabilities at this point in time is to take a sample of children identified by schools as learning disabled and to contrast their performance to that of nondisabled children, generally attempting to equate for aptitude between the two samples. Such an approach is problematic in at least two ways. First, it ignores the diversity of criteria used to identify children as learning disabled. Keogh (1983) argues that "system identified samples probably represent only one subset of the condition as a whole . . . [and that] system-selected samples tell us something about a particular system and the children selected into it . . . [but do] not necessarily convey information about other aspects of the condition" (p. 25). Second, it ignores the tremendous diversity in the skills and deficiencies of LD children within and across school systems, with both the skills and deficiencies overlapping to varying degrees with those of other populations of children. It is important to note that such overlap extends to both those children who show low levels of achievement *and* those who do not (Ysseldyke & Algozzine, 1983). In essence, given the diversity of criteria used to identify learning disabilities and the variations in skills and deficits, one cannot expect to find that specific memory deficits will be similar across different samples of children. In fact, it has been demonstrated that memory performance in LD children varies at least as a function of type of learning problem (e.g., reading, arithmetic) and the nature of the stimuli (e.g., Fletcher, 1985).

In this chapter, we argue for a dimensional approach to research and theory on cognitive deficiencies, purposely implying that such an approach extends beyond learning disabilities per se. Our view is that diagnostic labels are limited in their usefulness in terms of explaining cognitive limitations and abilities. Rather, the analysis of patterns of performance across dimensions should be used to characterize children with academic and cognitive problems. This approach has a number of advantages over other existing approaches, including that (a) it is functional, focusing on the deficiencies and proficiencies of children so that areas or domains in need of remediation can be identified and the extant skills of the children can be used as bases for remediation; (b) it is developmental in nature, taking into account the variation in skills or lack thereof that occurs across childhood; and (c) it deemphasizes the stigma and ambiguity associated with any given label.

This chapter is organized in the following manner. Section I presents a brief overview of the cognitive-developmental view of learning disabilities. In Section II we discuss research on cognitive abilities in children with chronic illnesses. This work is presented as a way of exemplifying both the extent of possible bases for cognitive deficiencies and the need for a dimensional approach. In the last section, the dimensional model is presented that serves as an heuristic guide for research and theory on cognitive deficiencies.

THE COGNITIVE DEVELOPMENTAL APPROACH

In this section our view of learning disabilities is introduced by contrasting two of the prevailing approaches to research on learning disabilities. The purpose of this discussion is to make clear both the basis for our views and the assumptions we make in our theoretical approach to cognitive deficiencies.

Evidence for the Importance of Control Processes

There is a continuing controversy in the literature on learning disabilities concerning the relative importance of structural features versus control processes. *Structural features* are relatively permanent and not easily influenced by short-term treatment (Campione & Brown, 1977). These structural features include long-term memory, capacity for short-term memory, and other invariant, nonoptional aspects of an individual's cognitive system. *Control processes* are skills and information acquired individually through experience. The distinction between structural features and control processes is analogous to the distinction between hardware and software in a computer. The questions are, to what extent do structural features and control processes contribute to learning disabilities, and should control processes be considered as anything other than a neurophysiological phenomenon?

Cruickshank (1983), a major proponent of the structural view, asserts that "First, all learning is neurological. It can be nothing else" (p. 28). Because learning involves synapses, fibers, and other structures, any problem in learning must boil down to structural problems. Even though many researchers (e.g., Torgesen 1982) argue that research in the area of learning disabilities has thus far determined that LD children do not engage in organized, goal-directed behaviors that facilitate performance on academic tasks, such deficits are viewed by the structuralists as failures in structural featues. Cruickshank's argument for the prime importance of structural features may be valid. However, presently our technologies are insufficient to provide purely neurophysiological answers to all questions concerning learning disability. Hall (1980) suggests that "the functional and structural properties implied by the definition as necessary for the processing of information are, at present, largely unknown" (p. 80). Certain structures (amygdala, hippocampus, etc.) are known to be critical for humans to demonstrate their long-term memory, but where and how these long-term memories are actually stored is not known.

Our approach to cognitive deficiencies is a cognitive-developmental one. This approach focuses on the control processes rather than the structural features of an information-processing system (e.g., see Atkinson & Schiffrin, 1968). It is not the case that researchers using this approach discount possible structural differences between children who do and do not have varying cognitive problems. Most severe intellectual deficits do have biological components (Zigler, 1982). However, because the nature of structural differences is not yet understood for most problems, because brain-behavior relationships are not yet understood, and because the structural differences are probably subtle if they exist (see Kavanaugh & Yemi-Komshian, 1985; Wong, 1979), taking a cognitive-developmental approach allows researchers to concentrate on observed, potentially correctable problems in adaptive cognitive processing in various settings and tasks. They can consider proximate solutions and ignore for the time being the distal causes. As Cruickshank (1983) acknowledges, "a definition is relatively worthless unless it results in action" (p. 28). In this chapter we are concerned with those deficits that are not obviously a result of organic brain dysfunction.

From our viewpoint, individual differences in cognitive performance can appropriately be viewed as extensions of developmental differences. It has been recognized for some time that, in memory, development progresses from a stage of mediation deficiency, to production deficiency, and then to efficient processing of information to be remembered (e.g., Hagen, 1971). Children with learning disabilities exhibit this same developmental pattern but at considerably older chronological ages (CA) (Newman & Hagen, 1982). A major concern, then, is why children exhibiting cognitive deficiencies do not learn to regulate effectively the flow of information within their cognitive systems as do children without such deficiencies. Problems are especially apparent in tasks requiring planful, strategic, adaptive behavior. What is known about "normal" cognitive development can be used as a basis for evaluating deficient performance, developing hypotheses regarding the causes of atypical performance, and developing remediational techniques to bring children with cognitive problems closer to their normally performing peers.

The general consensus among cognitive-developmental researchers is that at least three factors are involved in performance on any cognitive task: strategies, metacognition, and domain-specific knowledge.

In normal development, much of the variability in cognitive performance across the ages from the preschool years into adolescence can be attributed to differential use of strategies (see Kail & Hagen, 1977; Ornstein, 1978). For example, compared with young children (e.g., early elementary and below), older children are much better at selectively attending to relevant information and ignoring incidental or irrelevant information (Hagen & Hale, 1973; Miller, 1985), at rehearsing (Ornstein & Naus, 1978) and organizing (Moely, 1977) information for memory, and at retrieving information from memory (Ackerman, 1985; Kobasigawa, 1977). Strategies provide the means of increasing the functional capacity of our limited-capacity cognitive system.

Metacognition is used here to refer to both awareness and executive control of cognitive processing (see Brown, Bransford, Ferrara, & Campione, 1983; Wellman, 1983, for distinctions and elaborations). For efficient task performance and/or strategy use, one must be aware of one's own cognitive strengths and limitations, of what the requirements are for the task at hand, and what strategies might be useful in various situations or tasks. In other words, successful cognitive performance is dependent on knowing when, why, and how to apply strategies (Flavell & Wellman, 1977; Paris & Cross, 1985). Further, one must be able to coordinate strategies, allocate limited cognitive resources, monitior one's learning and performance, modify plans and strategies as the need arises, and perform other "executive" decisions throughout most cognitive activities. In essence, for nonautomatic cognitive processing (Shiffrin & Schneider, 1977; Shiffrin, Dumais, & Schneider, 1981), awareness and regulation are essential aspects of efficient performance. (See Torgesen et al. of the present volume for further discussion of metacognition.)

The third requisite factor for efficient memory or cognitive performance is domain-specific knowledge (Pressley, Borkowski, & Schneider, in press). Often refered to as "knowledge base" (Bjorklund, 1985; Chi & Rees, 1983; Glaser, 1984; Naus & Ornstein, 1983), this factor corresponds to one's store of information within (and cumulatively, between) domains that provides a basis for comprehending, organizing, and integrating the relevant information for the task at hand. Knowledge base is a key element in the use of strategies and metacognitive knowledge; for example, strategy use, resource allocation, and cognitive monitoring should all be varied as a function of familiarity with pertinent information. Alternatively, sufficient domain-specific knowledge may obviate the need for strategies in given tasks (Chi, 1978), whereas insufficient knowledge may hinder strategy use (Lindberg, 1980).

It is clear that strategies, metacognition, and knowledge base all can impact on developmental changes in cognition (e.g., see Brown et al., 1983; Pressley et al., in press), and it is likely that all three factors impact on individual differences as well (Butterfield & Ferretti, 1985; Torgesen & Kail, 1980). For example, LD children, relative to nondisabled children, tend to use strategies inefficiently or not at all in various tasks, as do children with other cognitive deficiencies (Bauer, 1982; Brown, 1974; Cermak, 1983; Campione & Brown, 1977; Hagen, Barclay, Schwethelm 1982; Torgesen, 1977a). In tasks that require active, strategic information processing, children who are LD or mentally retarded (MR) will do poorly, although given instruction, their performance may improve (Brown & Barclay, 1977; Newman & Hagen, 1981; Tarver, Hallahan, Kaufman, & Ball, 1977; Torgesen, 1977b). Given the complexity of learning and remembering as proposed by this model, it is not surprising that there are so many potential pitfalls in the process and that many children do not attain mastery in all tasks.

The Hagen and Barclay Model

Hagen and Barclay (1982; Hagen et al., 1982) have proposed a model that incorporates these factors into a frame of reference for research on cognitive deficiencies. It is insufficient to describe LD children or other children with cognitive problems as lacking in strategies, awareness, or knowledge. In any given evaluative or academic situation, there are certain task characteristics and requirements that must be met for successful task performance. At the same time, the person may or may not have the abilities necessary to meet those requirements. Hagen et al. proposed that in looking at the relationship between task and person dimensions, a taxonomy can be formed by the varying combinations of knowledge and strategies, with metacognition overlapping both factors. Thus, a task can be viewed as requiring strategies or not, and requiring knowledge or not. Similarly, an individual may have the requisite strategies and/or knowledge or not. Some predictions based on this taxonomy are illustrated in Table 1 for the person dimension.

A crucial aspect of this model is that children that are now characterized in a similar manner (e.g., as lacking strategies) but are from different populations (e.g., LD and MR children) can be differentiated by this model. For example, if one compares the research on memory in MR and LD children, one will find that most of the research characterizes both groups of children in a similar manner, as nonstrategic, inactive learners. However, if in fact these children do belong to different groups, such a characterization is insufficient to predict what instructional procedures would be best suited for each of them. The model proposed by Hagen et al.

Table 1.   A strategy and knowledge taxonomy indicating expected performance levels given different deficiencies

		Strategy Deficiency?	
		YES	NO
Knowledge Deficiency?	YES	Poor overall performance	Good performance on training problems but no unprompted maintenance or generalization
	NO	Variable performance depending on type of problem presented	Good overall performance

Note: From *Coming of Age, Vol. 3, The Best of ACLD.* W. Cruickshank and J. Lerner 1982, Syracuse Publications. Copyright 1982. Reprinted with permission.

(1982) predicts different patterns to be exhibited by these two groups, primarily in that LD children would be expected to perform substantially better on some tasks than MR children, and similarly on other tasks. The point is that such a taxonomy based on person and task characteristics enables assessment and predicitons based on patterns of performance across the varying combinations of strategies and knowledge. In addition, if children from different populations exhibit similar performance patterns, such children could be treated similarly for instructional purposes.

Although the aforementioned taxonomy represents an improved method for assessment and prediction, the model proposed by Hagen et al. (1982) does have a number of limitations. Three of the major ones are (a) the model assumes that *having* knowledge or strategies will lead to the *use* of knowledge or strategies, which is not necessarily the case; (b) the model lacks an explicit developmental dimension; and (c) the model ignores other characteristics of children that may impact on cognitive performance.

While children with learning disabilities and mild mental retardation have been considered thus far, it is evident that other groups of children also exhibit cognitive deficiencies and related problems in academic performance. Included are the economically disadvantaged, emotionally impaired, and chronically ill. During the past decades, there has been considerable interest among researchers in both psychology and pediatrics on the effects of health and illness on children's functioning. It is becoming increasingly clear that illness affects cognitive functioning, and some children with chronic illness are "at risk" for learning disability or other cognitive problems. We shall now consider recent research on children with chronic illnesses before returning to the cognitive model being proposed in this chapter.

COGNITIVE AND ACADEMIC ABILITIES IN CHILDREN WITH CHRONIC ILLNESSES

Research from the psychological and biobehavioral perspectives on children with various biological conditions and illnesses has increased greatly during the past decade. Recognition of the problem of chronic illnesses in children has led to many important chapters and volumes (e.g., Haggerty, 1983; Gortmaker & Sappenfield, 1984; Hobbs & Perrin, in press) as well as national conferences. Between 5 and 10 % of children in the United States are affected by chronic illness sometime during their childhood or adolescence (Perrin, 1986). Chronic illness has a major impact on the child and family and must be considered from the context of three systems that affect development: the family, the school, and the health care delivery system.

> Since chronic illnesses are of long duration, typically require specialized treatments and daily regimens, and often involve certain restrictions or modifications in activities and diet, parents and teachers must be educated in terms of the specifics of medical management . . . as well as about the more general impact of chronic illnesses on developmental processes. (Hagen, Anderson, & Barclay, p.2, in press)

While there has been considerable research on psychological aspects of chronic illnesses, the majority of the work until recently focused on personality and adjustment. However, the recognition that these conditions often have profound effects on cognitive development and academic performance has led to research focused specifically on these areas (e.g., Hagen et al., 1985; Ryan, Vega, & Drash, 1985). The same issues that are raised concerning the hypothesized causes of learning disabilities are applicable here. Does the illness itself include physical, neurological, or biochemical factors that affect learning, motivation, or performance? Are there consequences of the illness that affect the child's ability to perform to capacity such as medications, physical restrictions, diet, or absence from school? Are these children especially susceptible to motivational problems such as learned helplessness, lack of intentionality or inactivity to approaching various problems? No doubt biological factors that affect development are involved in many if not most physical illnesses. However, the same arguments that were made earlier in this chapter concerning the possible reasons for failure to perform in memory and other cognitive tasks for children with learning disabilities must be considered here. The study of children with specific physical illnesses should, indeed, provide insights into our understanding of cognitive deficits and learning/academic problems more generally. Unlike most learning disabilities, the defining criteria here are clear-cut; and further, for most chronic diseases considerable information is available concerning the biological and medical aspects of the disorder and their impact on the afflicted child's development. Further, comparing children with an illness that affects directly the central nervous system (e.g., seizure disorders) to children with an illness of similar severity but with little impairment of the CNS (insulin-dependent diabetes) could provide insights into the issues of structural deficits and control processes.

Cognitive Aspects of Insulin-Dependent Diabetes Mellitus

During the past several years our research has focused on two groups of children and adolescents with serious illnesses: insulin-dependent diabetes mellitus and seizure disorders, specifically, three types of epilepsy.

There are two types of diabetes: insulin-dependent diabetes mellitus (IDDM) and noninsulin-dependent diabetes mellitus (NIDDM). When the onset of the disease is in childhood, adolescence or even early adulthood, it is almost always IDDM. Individuals with IDDM must take injections of insulin daily for the rest of their lives. Blood glucose must also be monitored several times per day, and perhaps the most demanding part of the regimen involves the coordination of insulin, diet, and physical activity. The younger the diabetic child, the more involved the parents are in the management and control of the disease. Even when the strictest management is employed, some children are not able to achieve good medical control. Given the difficulties imposed by this disease, it is not surprising that research has revealed that children and families have problems coping in several areas. While some of these children are vulnerable in their psychological adjustment, controlled studies have demonstrated that the majority score within the normal range on standardized test of personality and adjustment.

Studies of children with diabetes have found that they are typically within the average range in intellectual and cognitive abilities (Ack, Miller, & Weil 1961; Appelboom-Fondu, Verstraeten, & Van Loo Reynaers, 1977; Koski, 1969; Steinhausen, Bonner, & Koepp, 1977). However, their performance on tasks measuring specific aspects of attention, learning, and memory may be impaired (Ryan, Vega, & Drash, 1985). Those children with an early-onset of the disease, before age 5, may be especially vulnerable. In our research (Hagen et al., 1985), two groups of diabetic children, 8 to 16 years at the time of testing, were studied: those diagnosed before 5 years of age, and those with disease onset at 5 years or older. A control, or comparison sample of children matched for sex and chronological age with the diabetics was included.

In performance on subtests of the WISC-R, children with diabetes scored significantly lower than did control children. Among the children with diabetes, those with an onset of the disease at 4 years or earlier scored lower than those with later onset on the following: vocabulary, digit span, and block design. On the central-incidental memory task (Hagen, 1967) there were no differences among the three groups on recall of central information, but the early onset group scored significantly higher than either the late onset or the control group on incidental memory. High incidental performance is indicative of lack of use of appropriate task strategies. Further, the pause-time memory task (Belmont & Butterfield, 1969) was administered to all children. Latency of time between response items is measured as well as accuracy. It was found that the early-onset group responded more quickly and scored significantly less accurately than did either of the other two groups. Analyses of performance by serial position (see Figure 1) demonstrated that strategies to facilitate recall of early items in the serial recall task were invoked by the comparison subjects most frequently, by the late-onset group next, and by the early-onset group least frequently. The control subjects showed an optimal active-passive rehearsal strategy for encoding information that resulted in a high level of overall recall.

The differences found in performance between the two groups of diabetic children cannot be explained by evidence in existing literature. However, some revealing differences among the groups in this study were found in the parent's reports of medical and school history. As shown in Table 2, the children in the early onset group were found to be much more likely to have experienced loss of consciousness, convulsions, or seizures than the children in the late onset or control groups. Insulin reactions of a severe nature were also much more common. Children with early disease onset repeated a grade and/or had remedial services more often than children in the other groups. Thus, even though IDDM is not typically associated with learning disabilities, major cognitive deficiencies, or problems in school performance, the findings of this study indicate that there are some possible areas of difficulty for children with diabetes, and that children who are diagnosed before 5 years of age appear to be at risk in some areas of both cognitive and academic performance.

In a project currently underway in our laboratory, children with seizure disorders are being evaluated on the same measures used in the study with diabetic youngsters. Since seizure disorders involve disturbances in certain aspects of brain functions as well as some problems in encoding of information, it is expected that the types and severity of problems in these children will be greater than those found in children with diabetes. Results will be forthcoming in the next year.

The performance of children with physical illness illustrates that many of the same dependent variables which have been found to typify areas

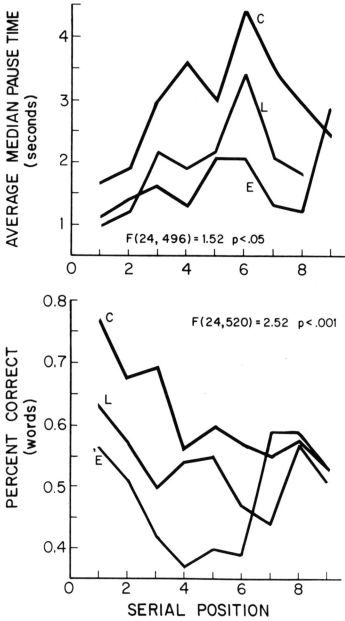

Figure 1. Pause-Time Memory Task: Latency (seconds) and percent correct (words remembered) as a function of serial position recall.

Table 2. Parent Report of Medical and School History in Early Onset, Late Onset, and Control Groups

	GROUPS (% sample)				
	EARLY ONSET	*LATE ONSET*	*CONTROLS*	*E vs. L*	*E vs. C*
MEDICAL HISTORY					
Loss of consciousness	60	13	17	**	**
Convulsion/Seizure	33	7	10		*
Serious head injury	20	0	7		
Insulin reaction with loss of consciousness and/or hospitilization	53	13	—	*	
Reactions while asleep	47	0	—	*	
SCHOOL HISTORY					
Repeated grade	20	7	0		**
Remedial educational services this year	40	13	7		**
Remedial educational services any year	53	27	17		**

** p .01
* p .05

135

of learning disability also pertain to chronically ill children. In order to account for cognitive deficiencies in any group of children it is necessary to consider factors or dimensions that are associated with and distinguish the various disorders.

Generic Approach to Chronic Illness

While most of the research on chronic illness in children has been disease-specific, during the past 10 years there has been considerable attention devoted to the noncategorical, or generic approach to childhood illness (Stein, & Jessop, 1984). While the categorical approach assumes that clinical diagnoses provide substantial information about the sequelae of chronic diseases, the generic approach assumes that specific child and family variables as well as the clinical diagnosis contribute to the sequelae of chronic diseases. For example, Stein and Jessop (1984) have developed rating scales to measure the *burden* the illness places on the child and family. Two children with the same illness but at different chronological age (CA) levels, with different levels of performance in school, and with different family circumstances might have *burden indexes* that are very different; however, two children with different illnesses but both early adolescents with similar problems in school might score very similarly. This research had identified those dimensions that cut across categories of illness and point to the common issues faced by children and their families.

This approach is especially well suited to the research and applied work of developmental and educational psychologists. Explicit recognition is given to the dimensions with which we are accustomed to studying and working with children, i.e., development, coping mechanisms, motivation and emotional considerations, influences of family, teachers and peers, and cognition. In a seminal paper, Pless and Pinkerton (1975) argued that knowledge of the medical diagnosis per se does not tell us how to treat the psychological and social needs of the child. It is the task of researchers to take seriously the importance of descriptive information available and to develop approaches that identify relevant dimensions that cut across diagnostic categories. This argument should be equally applicable to the categories that have evolved for labeling children with problems specifically in the cognitive domain, such as learning disability and mental retardation. We have already considered the model offered by Hagen and Barclay (1982). We shall now extend the rationale underlying the generic approach and combine it with features of Hagen and Barclay's model to offer the dimensional approach.

THE DIMENSIONAL APPROACH

Cognitive deficiencies occur in children of varying developmental levels and with varying conditions. We have already shown that children with learning disabilities are not unique with respect to the type of problems they exhibit or their susceptibility to remediation. For example, many children with learning disabilities and diabetes show similar cognitive problems. The cognitive-developmental approach, with its emphasis on the key roles of attention and memory, provides a framework for conceptualizing the cognitive development of children across many different diagnostic categories, from the mildly retarded, to the learning disabled, to those with illnesses that affect cognitive abilities and learning performance.

The mere fact of labeling children as, say, learning disabled or mentally retarded, does little to describe their particular problem areas or to suggest remediational practices that will yield enhanced performance or abilities. The labels provide some information, but the diversity of abilities and deficiencies within labelled populations suggests that treating all children with LD or MR alike is not practical. Within and between populations, children differ on many factors. For example, data collected by Speece, McKinney, and Appelbaum (1985), in the form or teacher ratings, yielded seven distinct subtypes of children in their school-identified sample of LD children, with the various subgroups differing substantially in their behavior patterns. The point is that special populations of children are multifaceted, just as are groups of normal children. The dimensional approach offered here provides a way to take into account the similarities that cut across categories as well as the differences within categories of diagnoses.

Three sets of dimensions must be included. As indicated in Figure 2, the first dimension includes the diagnostic categories under consideration, here mental retardation, learning disability, emotional impairment, and specific chronic illnesses. The second dimension is made up of these factors that cut across diagnostic categories, such as etiology, intellective and cognitive factors, academic performance, motivation, behavior, socioeconomic status, and culture. For example, it has been argued by many (e.g., Haggerty, 1983) that one of the most profound factors influencing a child's ability to cope with a condition, regardless of category of diagnosis, is the family's economic status. Each of these dimensions must be considered in trying to understand the child's adaptation and functioning, regardless of his/her diagnosed condition.

The third dimension is the developmental level of the child. Too often investigators do not take into account the impact of the condition at dif-

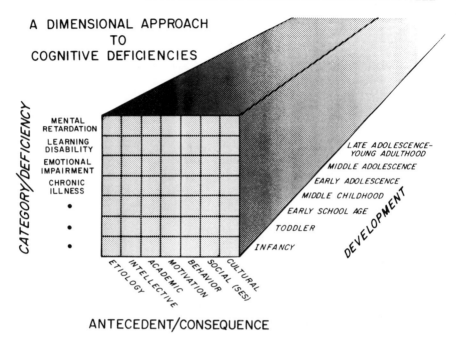

Figure 2. A Dimensional Approach to Cognitive Deficiencies: Diagnostic
     categories x Antecedent/consequence conditions x Developmental
     level.
Note: From *Topics in Early Childhood Special Education* 5:4. Gary Garwood, PRO-ED Publications.
Copyright 1986 (Winter). Reprinted with permission.

ferent developmental stages (for further discussion of this argument see
Anderson, 1984). This failing is understandable because research in special
populations is often hampered by problems in subject procurement because
of the limited numbers of children available with clear diagnoses and at
particular CA levels. However, since both biological and psychological
processes change with age, the impact of these changes cannot be ignored
when studying the responses of the child with a handicapping condition.

In order to make the arguments concerning the dimensional approach
as applicable as possible to the purposes of this volume, we shall now
examine in some detail a selected aspect of Figure 2, namely the cognitive
and academic performance of children who have been diagnosed into the
categories that we have considered thus far. Table 3 presents the diagnostic
categories on the rows and cognitive and academic dimensions on the
columns. In each cell, we have provided a brief summary of information
that is currently available concerning the status of functioning or performance.

Characteristics of children that cross category boundaries become apparent when applying the dimensional model. For example, problems in attention and/or memory have been found to occur in children in all categories. This fact supports the argument that memory is critical in understanding cognitive deficiencies, and it also supports the argument that a focus of research on the development of memory should include the study of differences across diagnostic categories. The cognitive developmental model specifies areas in which differences might occur (e.g., strategies vs. knowledge). The inclusion of developmental level in research allows for testing of predictions concerning the nature and extent of deficiencies and potential for remediation.

The importance of the consideration of distinct subgroups within categories is also illustrated in Table 3. There seem to be three subgroups within those children diagnosed as having seizure disorders. General intellectual level and school performance vary among these subgroups, and it should be expected that memory and other aspects of cognition would vary as well. From a functional standpoint, children in the upper subgroup in terms of intelligence may be more similar both cognitively and academically to children in other diagnostic categories than they are to children with seizures in the other two subgroups.

It should be recalled that differences in cognition and academic performance for children with diabetes Type I were found to be a function of age of onset. These findings illustrate the importance of the inclusion of developmental level as it affects the onset and course of the disorder. This factor has not yet received enough attention in the research on disorders, yet in most of the disorders being considered here diagnosis is not made at birth or during infancy. Thus, the label was acquired at some time when the child is at a particular developmental level. Mental retardation and learning disability are often not assigned to the child until he/she enters school. Yet, one should expect that performance in certain cognitive tasks should be affected before this age level.

Children diagnosed as learning disabled exhibit a wide range of difficulties, a point stressed in this chapter as well as in many others in this volume. According to our model, the researcher and the diagnostician should focus on the cognitive processes of these children rather than the content areas where problems may be occuring. However, their problems in other areas should not be ignored. From Table 3, the overlap between the LD and EI categories is apparent in several areas. Problems in attention and in social behavior obviously covary, but can it be demonstrated that the cause-effect relationships are different for these two groups?

The cognitive developmental approach has provided a conceptual framework and generated empirical evidence indicating that not only are control processes/strategies important, but that knowledge and metacognition must be considered as well (Hagen & Barclay, 1982). The dimen-

Table 3. Intellective and School Performance

	Intellective		School	
	General Intelligence	Specific Deficits	Academic	Behavioral-Social
Mentally Retarded	Low IQ	Memory Attention Problem Solving	Low achievement overall Special Education	Sometimes behavioral and social problems
Learning Disability	Average/low normal IQ	Memory Attention Reading • dyslexia	Two or more grade levels below in achievement. • reading • math • other Special Education	Acting out Distractibility Hyperactivity
Emotionally Impaired	Normal distribution IQ (displaced to low normal) Sometimes low verbal intelligence	Attention Thought disorders	Majority are low achievers Special Education	Acting out Distractibility Hyperactivity Depression
Seizure Disorders	Ave./above IQ Low normal IQ Mental retardation	Memory Attention Medication effects	Majority are low achievers Special Education	Hyperactivity Passivity Absences Seizures
Type I Diabetes	Normal distribution IQ	Memory Attention (especially in early onset)	Majority are average or better achievers Early onset: more academic problems	Insulin reaction or hypoglycemia Absences

140

sional approach offered here extends the cognitive developmental approach to the consideration of (a) those factors which are hypothesized to be antecedents/consequences of deficiencies, and (b) the developmental level of children.

CONCLUSIONS

In this chapter, we have proposed a three-dimensional, multi-level model for research on learning disabilities and other cognitive deficiencies. The core of this model is the functional, developmental characterization of cognitive deficiencies according to patterns of performance across cognitive, behavioral, and social factors. Although others have argued for a cross-categorical approach by proposing a focus on specific learning deficits and the abolition of traditional diagnostic categories (e.g., Hallahan & Kauffman, 1977), there is at present too little evidence to argue for this position now (e.g., see Epstein & Cullinan, 1983). The model proposed here provides a framework for investigating the utility of such an approach. If the dimensional model is pursued and enough evidence becomes available, the logical outcome might be the self destruction of the categories as listed in the left-hand margin. New groupings of children would emerge, with prescriptions for intervention readily apparent.

The cognitive-developmental model has proven to be very useful in our understanding of cognitive development in LD children and other cognitively-related deficiencies. The research on memory has provided insight into the critical role of control processes, knowledge and strategies. However, there is still much more that we need to understand in order to deal effectively with these children. It is now time to build upon the knowledge we have and expand the focus of research to include other factors that are inextricably intertwined with memory and cognitive processes.

REFERENCES

Ack, M., Miller, M., & Weil, M. (1961). Intelligence of children with diabetes mellitus. *Pediatrics, 28*, 764–770.

Ackerman, B. P. (1985). Children's retrieval deficit. In C. J. Brainerd & M. Pressley (Eds.), *Basic Processes in Memory Development* (pp. 1–46). New York: Springer-Verlag.

Adelman, H. S., & Taylor, L. (1985). The future of the LD field: a survey of fundamental concerns. *Journal of Learning Disabilities, 18*, 423–427.

Anderson, B. J. (1984). The impact of diabetes on the developmental tasks of childhood and adolescence: A research perspective. In M. Natrass & J. Santiago (Eds.), *Recent advances in diabetes* (pp. 165–171). London: Churchill Livingstone.

142   J. W. HAGEN, D. A. SAARNIO and E. D. LAYWELL

Appelboom-Fondu, J., Verstraeten, F., & Van Loo-Reynaers, J. (1977). Comparative study of psychological aspects between diabetic and hemophilic children. *Pediatric and Adolescent Endocrinology, 3*, 29–35.

Atkinson, R. C., & Schiffrin, R. M. (1968). Human memory: A proposed system and its control processes. In K. W. Spence & J. T. Spence (Eds.), *The psychology of learning and motivation (Vol. 2*, pp.89–195). Orlando, FL: Academic Press.

Bauer, R. H. (1982). Information processing as a way of understanding and diagnosing learning disabilities. *Topics in Learning and Learning Disabilities, 2*, 33–45.

Belmont, J. M., & Butterfield, E. C. (1969). The relations of short-term memory to development and intelligence. In L. P. Lipsitt & H. W. Reese (Eds.), *Advances in child development and behavior* (Vol. 4 pp. 29–82). Orlando, FL: Academic Press.

Bjorklund, D. F. (1985). The role of conceptual knowledge in the development of organization in children's memory. In C. J. Brainerd & M. Pressley (Eds.), *Basic processes in memory development* (pp. 103–142). New York: Springer-Verlag.

Brown, A. L. (1974). The role of strategic behavior in retardate memory. In N. R. Ellis (Ed.), *International review of research in mental retardation* (Vol. 7, pp. 77–166). Orlando, FL: Academic Press.

Brown, A. L., & Barclay, C. R. (1977). The effects of training specific mnemonics on the metamnemonic efficiency of retarded children. *Child Development, 47*, 70–80.

Brown, A. L., Bransford, J. D., Ferrara, R. A., & Campione, J. C. (1983). Learning, remembering, and understanding. In J. H. Flavell & E. M. Markman (Eds.), *Handbook of child psychology* (Vol. 3, pp. 77–166). *Cognitive development*. New York: Wiley.

Butterfield, E. C., & Ferretti, R. P. (1985). Towards a theoretical integration of cognitive hypotheses about intellectual differences among children. In J. G. Borkowski & J. D. Day (Eds.), *Memory and cognition in special children*. Norwood, NJ: Ablex.

Campione, J. C., & Brown, A. L. (1977). Memory and metamemory development in educable retarded children. In R. V. Kail & J. W. Hagen (Eds.), *Perspectives on the development of memory and cognition* (pp. 367–403). Hillsdale, NJ: Erlbaum.

Cermak, L. S. (1983). Information processing deficits in children with learning disabilities. *Journal of Learning Disabilities, 16*, 599–605.

Chi, M. T. H. (1978). Knowledge structures and memory development. In R. S. Siegler (Ed.), *Children's thinking: What develops?* (pp. 73–96). Hillsdale, NJ: Erlbaum.

Chi, M. T. H., & Rees, F. T. (1983). A learning framework for development. In M. T. H. Chi (Ed.), *Contributions to human development: Trends in memory development research* (Vol. 9, pp. 73–107). Basel: Karger.

Cruickshank, W. (1983). Learning disabilities: A neurophysiological dysfunction. *Journal of Learning Disabilities, 16*, 27–29.

Epstein, M. H., & Cullinan, D. (1983). Academic performance of behaviorally disordered and learning-disabled pupils. *Journal of Special Education, 17*, 303–307.

Flavell, J. H., & Wellman, H. M. (1977). Metamemory. In R. V. Kail & J. W. Hagen (Eds.), *Perspectives on the development of memory and cognition* (pp. 3–33). Hillsdale, NJ: Erlbaum.

Fletcher, J. M. (1985). Memory for verbal and nonverbal stimuli in learning disability subgroups: Analysis by selective reminding. *Journal of Experimental Child Psychology, 40*, 244–259.

Glaser, R. (1984). Education and thinking: The role of knowledge. *American Psychologist, 39*, 93–104.

Gortmaker, S. L., & Sappenfield, W. (1984). Chronic childhood disorders: Prevalence and impact. *Pediatric Clinics of North America, 31*, 3–18.

Hagen, J. W. (1967). The effect of distraction on selective attention. *Child Development, 38,* 685–694.

Hagen, J. W. (1971). Some thoughts on how children learn to remember. *Human Development, 14,* 262–271.

Hagen, J. W., Anderson, B., Barclay, C. R., Goldstein, G., Kandt, R., Genther, C., Feeman, D., Segal, S., & Bacon, G. (1985). *Cognitive and school performance in diabetic children.* Presented at the Biennial Meetings of the Society for Research in Child Development, Toronto.

Hagen, J. W., & Barclay, C. R. (1982). The development of memory skills in children: portraying learning disabilities in terms of strategy and knowledge deficiencies. In W. Cruickshank (Ed.), *Coming of age: The best of ACLD* (Vol. 3, pp. 127–141). New York: Syracuse University Press.

Hagen, J. W., Barclay, C. R., & Schwethelm, B. (1982). Cognitive development of the learning-disabled child. In N. Ellis (Ed.), *International review of research in mental retardation* (Vol. 11, pp. 1–41). Orlando, FL: Academic Press.

Hagen, J. W., & Hale, G. A. (1973). The development of attention in children. In A Pick (Ed.), *Minnesota symposia on child psychology* (Vol. 7, pp. 117–140). Minneapolis: University of Minnesota Press.

Haggerty, R. J. (1983). Epidemiology of childhood disease. In D. Mechanic (Ed.), *Handbook of health, health care and health professions* (pp. 101–119). New York: Free Press.

Hall, R. J. (1980). An information-processing approach to the study of exceptional children. *Advances in Special Education* (Vol. 2, pp. 79–110). Greenwich, CT: JAI Press.

Hallahan, D. P., & Kauffman, J. M. (1977). Labels, categories, behaviors: ED, LD, and EMR reconsidered. *Journal of Special Education, 11,* 139–149.

Hobbs, N., & Perrin, J. M. (in press). *Chronically ill children and their families: Problems, prospects and proposals from the Vanderbilt Study.* San Francisco: Jossey-Bass.

Kail, R. V., & Hagen, J. W. (Eds.). (1977). *Perspectives on the development of memory and cognition.* Hillsdale, NJ: Erlbaum.

Kavanaugh, J. F., & Yemi-Komshian, G. (1985). *Developmental dyslexia & related reading disorders* (NIH Publication No. 80–92). Bethesda, MD: National Institutes of Health.

Keogh, B. K. (1983). Classification, compliance, and confusion. *Journal of Learning Disabilities, 16,* 25.

Kobasigawa, A. (1977). Retrieval strategies in the development of memory. In R. V. Kail & J. W. Hagen (Eds.), *Perspectives on the development of memory and cognition* (Vol. , pp. 177–201). Hillsdale, NJ: Erlbaum.

Koski, M. (1969). The coping process in childhood diabetes. *ACTA Paediatrica Scandinavica* (Suppl. 198). 1–56.

Lindberg, M. A. (1980). Is knowledge base development a necessary and sufficient condition for memory development? *Journal of Experimental Child Psychology, 30,* 401–410.

McLoughlin, J. A., & Netick, A. (1983). Defining learning disabilities: A new and cooperative direction. *Jounal of Learning Disabilities, 16,* 21–23.

Miller, P. H. (1985). Metacognition and attention. In D. L. Forrest-Pressley, G. E. MacKinnon, & T. G. Waller (Eds.), *Metacognition, cognition, and human performance* (Vol. 2, pp. 181–221). Orlando, FL: Academic Press.

Moely, B. F. (1977). Organizational factors in the development of memory. In R. V. Kail & J. W. Hagen (Eds.), *Perspectives on the development of memory and cognition* (pp. 203–236). Hillsdale, NJ: Erlbaum.

Naus, M. J., & Ornstein, P. A. (1983). Development of memory strategies: analysis, questions, and issues. In M. T. H. Chi (Ed.), *Contributions to human development: Trends in memory development research* (Vol. 9, pp. 1–30). Basel: Karger.

Newman, R. S., & Hagen, J. W. (1981). Memory strategies in children with learning disabilities. *Journal of Applied Developmental Psychology, 1,* 297–312.

Ornstein, P. A. (Ed.). (1978). *Memory development in children.* Hillsdale, NJ: Erlbaum.

Ornstein, P. A., & Naus, M. J. (1978). Rehearsal processes in children's memory. In P. A. Ornstein (Ed.), *Memory development in children* (pp. 69–99). Hillsdale, NJ: Erlbaum.

Paris, S. G., & Cross, D. R., (1985). Ordinary learning: pragmatic connections among children's beliefs, motives, and actions. In J. Bisanz, G. L. Bisanz, R. V. Kail (Eds.), *Learning in children* (pp. 137–169). New York: Springer-Verlag.

Perrin, J. M. (1986). Chronically ill children: An overview. In S. G. Garwood (Ed.), *Topics in Early Childhood Special Education* (Vol. 5, pp. 1–11). *Chronically Ill Children.* Austin, TX: Pro-Ed.

Pless, I., & Pinkerton, P. (1975). *Chronic childhood disorder: Promoting patterns of adjustment.* London: Henry Kimpton.

Pressley, M., Borkowski, J. G., & Schneider, W. (in press). Good strategy users coordinate metacognition, strategy use, and knowledge. In R. Vastas, & G. Whithurst (Eds.), *Annals of child development* (Vol. 4). Greenwich, CT: JAI Press.

Ryan, C., Vega, A., & Drash, A. (1985). Cognitive deficits in adolescents who develop diabetes early in life. *Journal of Pediatrics, 75,* 921–927.

Shiffrin, R. M., & Schneider, W. (1977). Controlled and automatic human information processing: II. Perceptual learning, automatic attending, and a general theory. *Psychological Review, 84,* 27–90.

Shiffrin, R. M., Dumais, S. T., & Schneider, W. (1981). Characteristics of automatism. In J. R. Long, & A. P. Baddeley (Eds.), *Attention and performance IX* (pp. 223–238). Hillsdale, NJ: Erlbaum.

Smith, C. P. (1983). *Learning disabilities.* Boston: Little, Brown.

Speece, D. L., McKinney, J. D., & Appelbaum, M. I. (1985). Classification and validation of behavioral sybtypes of learning disabled children. *Journal of Educational Psychology, 77,* 67–77.

Stein, R. E. K., & Jessop, D. J. (1984). General issues in the care of children with chronic physical conditions. *Pediatric Clinics of North America, 31,* 189–198.

Steinhausen, H., Borner, S., & Koepp, P. (1977). The personality of juvenile diabetics. *Pediatric and Adolescent Endocrinology, 3,* 1–7.

Tarver, S. G., Hallahan, D. P., Kaufman, J. M., & Ball, D. W. (1976). Verbal rehearsal and selective attention in children with learning disabilities: a developmental lag. *Journal of Experimental Child Psychology, 22,* 375–385.

Torgesen, J. K. (1977a). The role of nonspecific factors in the task performance of learning disabled children: a theoretical assessment. *Journal of Learning Disabilities, 10,* 33–40.

Torgesen, J. K. (1977b). Memorization processes in reading-disabled children. *Journal of Educational Psychology, 69,* 571–578.

Torgesen, J. K. (1982). The learning disabled child as an inactive learner: educational implications. *Topics in Learning and Learning Disabilities, 2,* 45–52.

Torgesen, J., & Kail, R. V. (1980). Memory processes in exceptional children. In B. K. Keogh (Ed.), *Advances in special education* (Vol. 1, pp. 55–99). Greenwich, CT: JAI Press.

Tucker, J., Stevens, L. J., & Ysseldyke, J. F. (1983). Learning disabilities: The experts speak out. *Journal of Learning Disabilities, 16,* 6–14.

Wellman, H. M. (1983). Metamemory revisited. In M. T. H. Chi (Ed.), *Contributions to human development (Vol. 9): Trends in memory development research* (pp. 31–51). Basel: Karger.

Wong, B. (1979). The role of theory in learning disabilities research. Part I, an analysis of problems. *Journal of Learning Disabilities, 12,* 19–29.

Ysseldyke, J. F., & Algozzine, B. (1983). LD or not LD: That's not the question. *Journal of Learning Disabilities, 16,* 29–31.

Zigler, E. (1982). Developmental versus difference theories of mental retardation and the problem of motivation. In E. Zigler & D. Balla (Eds.), *Mental retardation: The developmental-difference controversy* (pp. 163–186). Hillsdale, NJ: Erlbaum.

PROBLEMS IN THE SEARCH FOR MEMORY DEFICITS UNDERLYING LEARNING DISABILITIES AND READING DEFICIENCY

James W. Hall, Margaret B. Tinzmann and
Michael S. Humphreys

ABSTRACT

A number of logical and methodological problems in research concerning the role of memory in learning disabilities and reading deficiency are considered, and relevant research published within the past 5 years is examined in the light of those problems. We conclude that research of this sort aimed toward discovering generalizations regarding learning disabilities as a cat-

Memory and Learning Disabilities
Advances in Learning and Behavioral Disabilities, Suppl. 2, pages 147–174.
ISBN: 0-89232-836-3

egory has been and will be of little value either practically or theoretically and should be abandoned, largely because of problems of sample definition and identification that are inherent in such work. Research directed toward understanding factors contributing to reading difficulties is more promising, but much of that work also has been problematic in various ways and has not yet yielded much of practical value. Problems here include generalizing to the ill-defined categories of dyslexic and reading disabled children, the misuse of IQ matching, the use of preselected samples or sample pools, inconsistencies in sample definitions, and the failure to differentiate between children with problems specific to reading and those with more general achievement deficiencies. Recent research appears to be increasingly sophisticated both theoretically and methodologically, but the identification of specific processing deficits associated with specific performance deficiencies (e.g., in reading) remains an elusive goal. There is no convincing evidence of a causal link between any specific cognitive deficit and deficiencies specific to reading. Indeed, there is no convincing evidence that any such deficit plays an important role in reading deficiency for most children; it remains plausible that most such problems are mainly the result of specific experiential deficits rather than of any basic deficit in memory or cognition. We close with several recommendations concerning research and teaching.

It is widely believed that there are substantial numbers of children who exhibit performance deficiencies in some restricted skill domain, but acquire intellectual skills and knowledge outside that domain with normal ease (i.e., there is no deficiency in general intelligence). A further assumption is that such deficiencies are, at least in many cases, the result of a functional deficit in some quite specific cognitive mechanism or process, and memory processes have been among the most common nominees for such deficits. The term *learning disabilities* is commonly applied to individuals thought to be characterized by various specific deficiencies of this sort. Terms such as *reading disabled* and *dyslexic* often are applied to those individuals whose performance deficiency is specific to reading.

Several years ago Ceci, Ringstrom, and Lea (1981) concluded that "the literature relating LD [learning disabilities] to memory deficits is in a state of utter confusion" (p. 159). There is little reason to reach any other conclusion now; research concerning memory and learning disabilities has made no important contribution either to theory or to practice except to disconfirm enduring misconceptions. The research on memory and reading deficiency is promising from a theoretical perspective, but as yet has not established causal links between specific processing deficits in memory and cognition and specific reading deficiencies. Indeed, at this point there is no good evidence that any such deficits underlie the performance difficulties of a substantial proportion of children identified as learning disabled or reading disabled (also see Hall & Humphreys, 1982, and Morrison & Manis, 1982).

In part, this state of affairs is due to a number of conceptual and methodological problems in much of the relevant research. Some of these issues were considered in an earlier paper by Hall and Humphreys (1982). The various points raised at that time had arisen from an inspection of a considerable body of research published up through 1980 as well as from research experience of our own. In preparation for the present chapter we reviewed a substantial body of research published more recently. Although some shifts were noticeable, we were struck by the extent to which a number of problems remain prevalent, particularly with respect to sample selection and generalizations from samples to populations. Our focus here is mainly on those problems and our recommendations for alternative practices. Other issues, especially concerning methodology for identifying processing deficits and causality with respect to such deficits, are considered much more briefly. We close the chapter with summary comments on the likely role of memory deficits in learning disabilities and reading deficiency, and by outlining research and instructional approaches that we believe are most reasonable in these areas.

When the terms *learning disability* and *reading disability* are used, it is not always clear whether "disability" refers to the behavioral or performance (e.g., achievement) deficiency displayed by the individual or whether it refers to the deficit underlying the performance deficiency. For the sake of clear communication on that point, in this chapter we use learning disability, reading disability, and *performance deficiency* to refer to the behavioral level, and underlying *deficit* to refer to factors (cognitive and otherwise) that might account for that deficiency.

In our review of the research we inspected the issues from 1981 through 1985 of the following seven journals in which relevant research often is published: *Exceptional Children, Journal of Educational Psychology, Journal of Experimental Child Psychology, Journal of Learning Disabilities, Journal of Reading Behavior, Learning Disabilities Quarterly,* and *Topics in Learning and Learning Disabilities.* From these we identified articles reporting research that (a) focused on learning disabilities or more specifically defined deficiencies, and (b) included memory-related terms or concepts (using a quite loose criterion) in discussions of the purpose or results of the study. In all, 40 articles were selected in this way, and those articles reported a total of 55 separate empirical studies. Those reports then were examined in some detail, with particular emphasis on methodology.

LD CATEGORY STUDIES

These are studies in which the investigator compared a sample of learning disabled (LD) children or adults with some non-learning disabled (NLD) sample for the purpose of generalizing about possible cognitive deficits in the broader LD population, i.e., deficits characterizing individuals who form the category labeled learning disabled. Thirteen (nearly 25%) of the 55 studies were of this type, which seems to us to be a marked decline from earlier years, although we have no documentation for that conclusion. In 8 of those 13 the sample was undifferentiated. By undifferentiated we mean that the sample has not been broken down by specific performance deficiencies or patterns of such deficiencies. In the remaining five LD category studies, the samples were differentiated by pattern of achievement deficiency or pattern of performance on tests presumably thought to tap important aspects of cognitive processing.

Two sampling issues are discussed. First, there is the problem of generalizing from a sample to a population when sample identification procedures cannot be specified operationally. This, we maintain, is the case for all LD category research. The second problem concerns the use of undifferentiated LD samples, i.e., samples representing the full range of variability typical of school-identified LD children. The use of such samples does not lend itself to the identification of a link between an observed cognitive deficit and some *specific pattern* of performance deficiencies, which is the crucial requirement for such research if it is to be maximally useful from either a practical or a theoretical perspective. Finally, approaches to differentiation within LD samples are considered quite briefly. For further discussion and documentation regarding the points made in this section (and others as well), the reader is referred to publications by Capobianco (1964), Cruickshank (1972), Hall and Humphreys (1982), Harber (1979), Keogh, Major, Reid, Gandara, and Omori (1978), and Torgesen (1979), and especially the impressive work by Ysseldyke and his colleagues (Algozzine & Ysseldyke, 1983; Epps, Ysseldyke, & McGue, 1984; Ysseldyke, Algozzine, & Epps,1983; Ysseldyke, Algozzine, & Thurlow, 1983; Ysseldyke, Thurlow, Graden, Wesson, Algozzine, & Deno, 1983).

The Impossibility of Operationally Defining LD Samples

A central and inherent problem in this type of study is that it is not possible to describe the sample in the way that would be necessary to know what population it represents. The problem here is the diversity and subjectivity involved in the LD identification process, beginning with the selection of children who undergo testing in the first place. Most commonly the first step in the procedure is a referral by a teacher. There is considerable evidence that nonintellective factors play a major role in such referrals (e.g., Christenson, Ysseldyke, & Algozzine, 1982; Ysseldyke, Algozzine, Regan, & McGue, 1981). Thus, of all children who display particular performance deficiencies, some will be referred and identified as learning disabled and others will not, depending in part on the nonintellective behaviors to which teachers and others respond. The result is that the particular patterns of test scores of LD children are no different than for many children not so identified; the difference is in other aspects of behavior that are never quantified or reported, or in the idiosyncracies of teachers. That is, an individual who will be referred for further testing by one teacher may not be referred by another, even at the same grade level and in the same school.

The second point in which there is enormous subjectivity and variability is in the final stage, following referral and "diagnostic" testing, where some final placement decision is made, often heavily influenced by the clinical judgment of a school psychologist or other specialist. Ysseldyke, Algozzine, and Thurlow (1983) nicely illustrate this problem in their description of two school psychologists whose rates of identification of children as learning disabled were "radically different," despite working in the same school district. (See Epps, Ysseldyke, and McGue [1984] for impressive evidence on the subjectivity and resulting unreliability of LD placement judgments.)

What are the implications of this state of affairs for the selection of an LD research sample? It seems clear that selecting a sample consisting of children already identified as learning disabled, which is the approach taken by all of the LD category studies we reviewed, is problematic. The investigator cannot report the operational procedures and criteria for sample selection because neither the investigator nor anyone else knows at an operational level just what those were. Furthermore, it is known that there is great variability in this respect, even within a particular school district. Therefore, when samples are preselected (by school or clinic personnel, generally), it is impossible to meet the requirements necessary for the generalization of the results to the LD category.

The obvious alternative is for an investigator to assume complete control of the LD identification procedure, but that proves to be unsatisfactory as well, if the goal is to uncover generalizations about LD children. If an investigator takes control of sample selection, there are two choices as to how to proceed. One is to attempt to follow procedures that are judged to be typically used in LD identification. This would involve getting teachers to suggest candidates for the sample, administering a battery of tests, then making some final judgement taking into account all available information. Both the nominations by teachers and the final judgment would involve the sort of subjectivity that created the problem with pre-selected samples in the first place, so there would be little gain from this approach. Alternatively, the investigator could eliminate the subjectivity by using objective criteria alone. For example, tests could be administered to all the children in certain grades in one or more schools, with some set of discrepancy criteria (e.g., achievement markedly lower in reading than other areas) set in advance for the research sample. This would meet the requirement of operational specification of sampling and sample charac-teristics, but one could no longer hope to generalize results to the category of LD children as they now exist. Obviously, this does not constitute a gain if one's objective is to uncover generalizations about the LD category.

The Problem with Undifferentiated LD Samples

We can imagine two potential gains from research that attempts to iden-tify cognitive deficits contributing to learning disabilities. First, consider the practical advantages of knowing that a particular type of performance deficiency is likely to be due to a deficit in a particular aspect of processing. Training then can be directed toward that aspect of processing with the hope of remediating the deficit, leading to improved performance in what-ever tasks are dependent on that aspect of processing. Or, if the process in question is resistent to training, it might be possible to compensate for the deficit by working out alternative approaches to tasks for which the process ordinarily is important. Theoretically, it also would be a gain to discover causal relations between basic cognitive processes and perfor-mance on particular classes of socially important tasks, such as reading.

Note that these gains are not achieved unless it is possible to link a specific class of performance deficiencies (e.g., word decoding in reading) with a specific process or aspect of processing (e.g., speed of short-term memory search). Thus, one might expect investigators to take pains to select LD samples that are differentiated with respect to the types of per-formance deficiencies represented. This might take the form of using only a single LD subtype in a study or using a more diverse sample in which the various subtypes are identified. In fact, the use of differentiated sam-ples appears to have increased markedly over the past several years, per-haps due to the numerous criticisms levied against the use of undiffer-entiated LD samples (e.g., Hall & Humphreys, 1982). Nevertheless, stud-ies using undifferentiated LD samples continue to be published, as evi-denced by the five studies of this type among those we reviewed. We shall consider the problems associated with this approach and certain cir-cumstances in which studies using undifferentiated samples may be useful.

In the reports of LD studies it is easy to see from the means and standard deviations of the groups that there is a very large degree of overlap between the LD and NLD children with respect to the dependent measures (e.g., cognitive processing tasks). That is, there are a number of LD children who are higher than the mean of the NLD group and a number of NLD children who are lower than the mean of the LD group. To our knowledge there are no exceptions to this state of overlapping distributions, i.e., there are no cases in which all or nearly all of a sizeable LD sample performed below all or nearly all of the NLD sample on whatever cognitive tasks were used. Indeed, a significant difference between means can, and often does, result even in cases wherein a majority of the LD sample scores within the range of scores obtained by the NLD sample. Clearly, the best that can be said is that *some* LD children are deficient in Process X, and the "some" may be a relatively small proportion; characterizing the LD population in this fashion would be misleading, although it has not been uncommon.

If research is (correctly) characterized as a continuing and cumulative enterprise, then one might argue that finding that some LD children are characterized by a particular cognitive deficit is not a bad start toward establishing links between processing deficiencies and performance problems. At this point, the investigator might look more closely within the data to identify and further study those particular LD children who displayed unusually poor performance on experimental tasks. That is, a study of this sort might be valuable if it were the beginning of a planned set of studies designed to define with increasing specificity the nature of the cognitive deficit and the particular pattern of performance deficiencies to which it contributes. However, in none of the LD category studies we reviewed was there a report of post hoc analyses that might lead to a specification of the particular achievement deficiencies that were associated with the deficit in processing. Nor were any indications given that there would be follow-up studies focusing on those unusually poor processors. Thus, these studies are uninformative regarding associations between cognitive processing deficits and learning disabilities, a serious limitation from both a theoretical and a practical perspective. Theoretically, it is of questionable value to know that some unknown portion of children with diverse performance deficiencies are deficient in a particular process. Practically, if there are treatment (e.g., instructional) implications of such a deficit, to whom do they apply?

There is a circumstance in which results using an undifferentiated LD sample may be informative. This is the case in which the results are negative with respect to a particular cognitive deficit, the LD sample is a reasonably large one that may be assumed to include the full range of children typically identified as learning disabled, and the measurement procedures are adequate (sufficiently sensitive to the existence of a cognitive deficit). Under such circumstances the failure to observe any processing difference between an LD and NLD sample indicates that the process in question is not a major factor for any substantial subset of the LD population sampled. This is one of the few instances in which negative results may be more informative, or at least more useful, than positive ones. An example here are studies in which such LD samples did not differ from NLD samples in rates of forgetting over 24 hours (Hall, Humphreys, & Wilson, 1983). Note, though, that it may be quite difficult to provide an entirely convincing argument with respect to the crucial assumption that the sample used was sufficiently representative of LD samples more broadly. The use of multiple LD samples would be helpful in that respect.

The "True" LD Child

According to some definitions of learning disabilities the LD individual is characterized by a deficit in some "basic" aspect of cognitive processing. Other definitions go so far as to specify that there is brain pathology involved. The important distinction here is between an hypothesis and a definition. If one hypothesizes that such deficits are peculiar to children identified as learning disabled, then those hypotheses may be regarded as disconfirmed. However, if one includes the presence of such deficits as part of one's definition of learning disability, then one must conclude that most children identified as learning disabled are not learning disabled. This position is not uncommon. In describing our results to LD teachers and others we quite often have been met with the rejoinder that whereas our results and conclusions may be correct for many or most LD children, they are not correct for children who are *really* learning disabled. The problem, we are told, is that many children who are not really learning disabled nevertheless are so classified, either by error or because they need the special help that is provided by such placement. If we studied only the true LD child, the argument goes, we indeed would find various basic cognitive processing deficits.

Although this argument may seem unproductive, it deserves serious consideration, in our judgment. Historically, it was believed that there were children who were true outliers with respect to particular perceptual or cognitive processes, but at the same time were perfectly normal with respect to other aspects of intellectual functioning. (These are the children to whom such labels as dyslexic originally were intended, we suspect.) In fact, there seems little reason to doubt this belief; we assume that such children do exist. It is easy to understand that they would be the focus of special concern, so as to avoid their being misclassified (e.g., as mentally retarded) and so they could receive appropriate instruction. The desire for research to more fully understand the nature and consequences of the deficit also seems reasonable, both from a practical and from a theoretical perspective.

It seems clear now that over the years these children have been "lost in the shuffle," so to speak. These are not the children who typically are "diagnosed" as being learning disabled nor do they make up any substantial proportion of LD research samples. There probably are many reasons for this "watering down" of the concept of learning disabilities. Certainly one problem has been the limitations of instruments and procedures by which deficits can be detected. Perhaps also such children are more rare than once was believed; our own estimate is that they make up less than 5% of those individuals identified as learning disabled. Certainly the temptation to help children who need help, whatever factors might underlie their difficulties, must have been another factor. In any case, contemporary LD research offers little possibility of understanding this category of individuals or even any rough idea of how many such individuals there are. It would be worthwhile, we believe, to make efforts to track down children of this sort, even a small sample, and study them intensively using experimental techniques that have been developed over the past two decades for the study of cognitive processes. From a theoretical perspective that would seem more promising than the current approach of experimentation with the hodge-podge of children who make up the bulk of LD individuals.

Summary Comments on LD Category Research

The specific criteria for LD identification cannot be documented because of the subjectivity and variability involved at various points in the decision processes. This severely restricts generalizations from samples to the broader LD population. The failure to differentiate among different patterns of performance deficiencies compounds that already serious problem. Differences found between LD and NLD samples apply only to a segment of children identified as learning disabled, and it is not possible to determine just what segment that is. This seriously limits the practical value of results, and may lead to inappropriate applications of them and inaccuracies in conceptions regarding LD children. Thus, in some instances these studies may result in a step backward, and seldom have they made a positive contribution, so far as we can see. Fortunately, there appears to have been a decline in the frequency of this type of study.

RESEARCH ON READING DEFICIENCY

At a general level, most of the studies in this category seem to be directed toward the discovery of factors that account for reading difficulties in individuals not characterized by general mental deficiency. There appears to be the assumption that specific cognitive deficits of one sort or another are involved in such cases, and the research is aimed at the identification of those deficits. Because the population of interest is (presumably) more homogeneous with respect to performance deficiencies in these than in LD studies, one might expect that the limitations associated with undifferentiated samples are avoided. We might also expect less ambiguity with respect to the population to which generalizations may be made. That is, one might imagine that samples of poor readers could be selected with a minimum of subjectivity and variability. However, the points made with respect to research with undifferentiated LD samples are pertinent to many of the studies in this category as well, as is demonstrated here. A number of other conceptual and methodological difficulties also characterize many of the studies, and several of these are discussed in detail. There are important differences among the studies, and certain of the specific approaches taken offer considerably more promise than others. For discussions of many of the issues that we raise here see Hall and Humphreys (1982), Morrison and Manis (1982), and Valtin (1980).

Definitional Ambiguities, Subjectivity, and Generalization Problems

In a number of the reading deficiency experiments generalizations about populations labeled *reading disabled* or *dyslexic* or *learning disabled readers* were made. The research involved comparing presumed samples of those populations with individuals who display no reading deficiency in their performance, using cognitive tasks of various sorts. The sampling issues are, in the main, similar to those encountered with respect to LD category research.

The problem inherent in generalizing about RD or dyslexic children and adults is that there is no generally accepted definition for these categories, either at the operational or the conceptual level. The Encyclopedia Brittanica (1978) classifies dyslexia as a type of agnosia, which in turn is classified as an aphasia resulting from brain pathology of some sort. This idea of dyslexia being a particular subcategory of reading difficulty that is especially severe and involves underlying deficits in perceptual processing seems to be a quite common one. None of the authors of the studies we reviewed was explicit regarding such assumptions; most seemed to use the term interchangeably with reading disability. Some explicitly classified reading disability as a subset of learning disability, whereas others use the term in a more operational sense. The striking differences in conceptualizations about reading disabilities and especially about dyslexia seem bound to result in a good bit of confusion on the part of the research consumer, if not the researcher.

As might be imagined, sample identification procedures vary widely as well. In at least three of these studies the investigator reported in some detail the criteria used for sample membership, but the pool of children from whom the sample was selected already had been identified by schools or other agencies as learning disabled. (In some cases it was not possible to tell whether or not preselected sample pools had been used.) In several other studies samples were selected from children already identified as reading disabled; the subjectivity and variability in such identification procedures have been documented by Vinsonhaler, Weinshank, Wagner, and Polin (1985). In these cases the investigator only reported in detail the steps taken to reduce a preselected group of LD or RD children to the subset of that group included in the final research sample. Thus, the same kind of ambiguity about population characteristics exists here as with the preselected LD samples, although it may not be so apparent to the reader.

In some cases the sole criterion appeared to be reading level in relation to grade level, whereas in others a disparity between reading achievement and IQ was used. In some studies the basis for calculated expected achievement was not described. There was considerable variability in the magnitude of the discrepancies that were used as criteria; to take one extreme, in three experiments (Brady, Shankweiler, & Mann, 1984) the "poor readers" *averaged* only 0.5 years below expected achievement levels, so that apparently a fair proportion of those poor readers were reading very near to expected levels. In only three studies was there an attempt to ensure that the achievement deficiencies of the subjects were specific to reading rather than more pervasive across intellectual skills (e.g., arithmetic). Most researchers took pains to match (or try to match) the poor and good readers on IQ or some other measure of general intelligence but several did not. When IQ matching was attempted there was considerable variability in the tests used, some involving heavy verbal components and others explicitly avoiding verbal intelligence tests. Just as striking as the variability in these respects was the almost complete absence of discussions of that variability in interpretations of results and attempts to integrate the results with those from other studies.

Efforts to Control for General Intelligence

Although labels and sampling procedures varied, it is clear that the population of interest in most of the studies under discussion were individuals whose reading skill is lower than would be expected on the basis of their general intellectual performance. The assumption, seldom made explicit, seemed to be that if reading difficulties occur in children who are otherwise quite bright (i.e., normally intelligent), then whatever cognitive processing deficit is involved must be one that is independent of general intelligence (IQ). That is, there presumably are two sets of cognitive processes that influence the acquisition of reading skills, one summarized by the concept of general intelligence as reflected by IQ and the other independent of general intelligence. If one is to identify the latter it is necessary to control for the former. This reasoning apparently accounts for the fact that in most of the studies of reading deficiency as well as in most LD category studies some effort was made to equate poor and normal reading groups on IQ or in performance on some IQ subtest. There are a number of problems with this approach, leading some critics to conclude that attempts to match good and poor readers on IQ is undesirable (Crowder, 1982; Hall & Humphreys, 1982; also see Torgesen, 1985 for a discussion of certain difficulties with IQ matching).

The execution of IQ matching often is inadequate, particularly when studies are considered together. Wolford and Fowler (1984) found that in 21 of 22 studies reviewed in which IQ matching was attempted, the normal reading group was higher than the reading-deficient group (also see Torgesen, 1985). In many cases the difference was quite small, but in others it was substantial. The studies reviewed here fit that pattern well. In the 14 studies in which an IQ match was attempted, and IQ data were reported, mean IQ was higher for the normal readers in 10 cases. A second problem with the execution of matching that we saw with some frequency was the use of different tests for the two groups in the IQ matching procedure, making comparisons virtually meaningless. This problem has been noted and discussed by others (e.g., Harber, 1981).

Hall and Humphreys (1982) raised a third issue concerning the execution of IQ matching, namely, that statistical regression effects may result in an overestimate of the goodness of match in some cases (also see Kahneman, 1965, as well as our later discussion of measurement error and regression effects). To illustrate this point, suppose that an investigator begins selecting poor readers by identifying those children who are 2 years or more behind in reading, a fairly common approach, and selects a sample of good readers who are reading at or above grade level. Now, to ensure (presumably) that the samples do not differ in general intelligence, the researcher matches them on IQ. Because so many of the poor readers are below average in IQ, matching requires that the researcher select to a disproportionate degree those poor readers with the highest IQs. When the extreme scores in a distribution are selected, one can be certain that those scores are farther from the mean of the distribution than are the true scores. That is, repeated IQ testing of those subjects would show some regression toward the mean of the distribution. This means that the true IQs of a sample selected in this way will be overestimated, resulting in an overestimate of the goodness of match. This effect may be quite small in most studies, but taken together with IQ means of the poor readers that are somewhat below those of the good readers anyway, it may contribute significantly to a failure in matching.

The fourth difficulty with IQ matching applies specifically to studies aimed at generalizations about the populations labeled reading disabled or dyslexic (see Valtin, 1978–1979). It is generally acknowledged that RD or dyslexic children are well below average in IQ and include a substantial proportion of individuals below the normal range. Indeed, if that were not true researchers would not have to make special efforts to achieve a match on IQ. The problem created by excluding lower IQ children from samples to achieve an IQ match with normal readers is that the representativeness of the sample is undermined. That is, only generalizations to the subpopulation of RD or dyslexic individuals with similar IQ distributions rather than to the general population are warranted. The limitations on generalizability that are inherent in IQ matching are not restricted to the RD and dyslexic categories. The correlation in the population in the elementary school grades between IQ and reading is positive and quite high (generally about .6 in our studies with children in Grades 2 and 3). Thus, poor readers, as a group, are well below average in IQ, and not at all well represented by samples from which low-IQ children have been systematically excluded. Of course, in these studies the whole idea is to find the cause(s) of reading difficulty in otherwise able individuals, and we do not mean to criticize that goal. But it should be kept clearly in mind that if certain cognitive deficits were to be identified for that subset of poor readers, that same cognitive deficit might or might not be involved in reading difficulties more generally.

The final issue concerning IQ matching is more subtle than the others. The assumption seems to be that by equating the groups with respect to IQ, general intelligence may be ruled out as a possible cause of whatever differences might be found in performance on experimental tasks. In our judgment this reasoning reflects a confusion about what is meant by "general intelligence" and what is measured by IQ tests. There is no need to rule out general intelligence as a cause of reading difficulties in these samples because general intelligence is not a *cause* of anything. General intelligence is a rather loose psychometrically based concept that most often is operationalized in terms of performance on IQ or similar tests. What we call general intelligence (IQ test performance) is a product of a variety of specific cognitive processes and mechanisms. Matching groups (or individuals) on IQ (or on any particular test subscale) does not mean that they are the same in the effectiveness of *each* of the processes that contribute to that score, but only that they are similar in the outcome of these various processes; the particular patterns of processing effectiveness may differ even though the product of them is similar. Therefore, matching on

IQ may not be taken to mean anything at all at the level of specific cognitive processes. Put most simply, at the level of processes that might affect reading (or any other area of performance) we do not know what is and what is not matched when we match on IQ test performance. Nor are we substantially better informed when the match occurs on the basis of tests or subtests with more specific labels, because performance on those tests also reflects the operation of a number of different cognitive processes. Even when groups are matched on IQ, it remains a possibility that group differences in performance on some experimental task are nevertheless due to differences in the efficiency of processes that affect IQ, i.e., to components of general intelligence at a process level.

It is not clear why children who are relatively low both in reading and in general intelligence would be excluded from samples by many researchers interested in the relationship between specific processing characteristics and reading competence. It is as though our knowledge of a high correlation between IQ and reading competence amounts to an explanation of poor reading by such children, i.e., that these children are poor readers *because* they are low in intelligence. In fact, though, this constitutes an explanation only at the most superficial level, and certainly not in terms of the particular cognitive processing differences that are crucial in accounting for individual differences in reading. That is, it remains to determine just what aspects of memory and cognition are responsible for reading difficulty in low IQ children and precisely how those mechanisms operate. The approach taken by Briggs and Underwood (1982), and Chabot, Petros, and McCord (1983), in which no exclusions from the samples on the basis of IQ, offer the possibility of achieving that goal.

Pseudo-Specificity of Reading Deficiencies

The greater specificity of the performance deficiencies in the research on reading deficiency is more apparent than real in most such studies. To us it would seem that when a sample is described as reading disabled or dyslexic, or when authors attribute certain processing deficits to RD or dyslexic children, there is an implication of specificity. That is, we would expect that the central performance problem of the sample members is in reading, so that the search is for a processing deficit especially associated with poor reading. Consistent with this perspective, Reitsma (1983) referred to dyslexics as "children with persistent reading problems but normal in all other respects," and carefully distinguished such individuals from his sample of poor readers for whom such specificity had not been established. Some investigators describe the sample as *specific* reading disabled, apparently confirming the notion of specificity of deficiencies. Others use more neutral terms such as "poor readers" or "unskilled readers." However, even in those cases most of the researchers made an effort to restrict their sample to individuals who do not differ from normal readers in terms of general intelligence (a point that we will discuss shortly), suggesting that interest is in performance deficiencies limited to, or centered in, reading.

Given this emphasis, one might expect that some care would be taken to ensure that these samples indeed were characterized by deficiencies specific to or at least centered in reading. In fact though, in 36 of the 40 studies there is no reason to believe that these samples were especially deficient in reading, because no achievement data other than for reading were used in sample identification or were reported in the articles; the four exceptions were two experiments by Lund, Hall, Wilson, and Humphreys (1983) and two by Paris and Myers (1981) in which the poor readers were similar to the normal readers in math achievement.

Given the substantial intercorrelations among achievement measures for different intellectual skills, we may be quite certain that the bulk of the subjects selected on the basis of low reading achievement only are also low in other areas, e.g., in mathematics achievement. In short, with the four exceptions cited above, the samples under discussion were not so differentiated from LD samples (where low general achievement is a common characteristic) as the terminology used to describe them would imply. Indeed, if an investigator selected children low in mathematics instead of reading, many of the same subjects would turn up in that sample because of the strong relationship between the two. In either case the sample really would consist largely of children for whom the term "underachiever" was common in the years preceding the increased popularity of terms such as *learning disabled* and *reading disabled*. Nevertheless, the authors of these studies consistently discussed their results in terms of factors relating to deficiencies in *reading,* and in not a single case was there any discussion or even acknowledgement of the nonspecificity of the deficiency.

The above considerations led us to use a somewhat different approach in our work concerning reading deficiency. Instead of matching good and poor readers on IQ (or some other measure of general intelligence), we defined our sample primarily in terms of a discrepancy between math and reading achievement. That is, the poor readers in our samples were children whose math scores were in line with expectations based on IQ, but whose reading scores were markedly lower (see Hall, Wilson, Humphreys, Tinzmann, & Bowyer, 1983). This ensured that we really were studying children whose performance problems were centered in reading rather than underachievement more generally. What we ended up with were samples of poor readers whose math and IQ scores were roughly the same as for our normal readers.

A number of studies with such samples were done involving a wide variety of tasks, including free recall, serial recall, paired-associate learning, recognition memory, rates of long-term forgetting in a free recall task, phonetic confusions in serial recall of letters, and memory for event frequency. With one exception, the poor and good readers were indistinguishable on these tasks (see Hall, Humphreys, & Wilson, 1983; Hall, Wilson, Humphreys, Tinzmann, & Bowyer, 1983; Lund, Hall, & Wilson, 1983). The exception occurred with tasks that required memory for order information (Wilson, 1983), where poor readers consistently performed worse. This difference, although consistent across tasks and statistically significant for each such task, was not large. In short, what was most striking to us was the degree of similarity, rather than differences, in cognitive processing between the groups. In contrast, most of the reading deficiency studies that we have reviewed have reported group differences, and the range of tasks involved is remarkably wide. Perhaps the contrast in specificity of reading deficiencies between these and the studies that we conducted account for the differences in results.

Overestimation of Deficiencies and Discrepancies in RD Samples

The problem of concern here is that when individuals are identified on the basis of extreme scores relative to the population mean, the extremity of their *true* scores will be overestimated, as has been pointed out earlier. That is, if these same individuals were retested, their performance, as a group, would be less extreme. Such statistical regression occurs whenever the measure used is less than perfectly reliable. The lower the reliability, and the greater the original deviation from the mean, the greater the regression.

There are various ways that such statistical regression can mislead the investigator (and the reader) beyond the problem in IQ matching discussed earlier. First, if subjects are selected on the basis of low performance in a particular area (e.g., reading), the degree of the performance deficiency of the sample will appear to be considerably greater than it is. Suppose, for example, the criterion is that the child be one SD or more lower in reading than in IQ, and 20 children meet that criterion following initial reading and IQ testing. One may be quite certain that several of those 20 children are misclassified (i.e., that repeated testing would show that their true discrepancy is less than one SD) and that the true mean score in reading is higher than that reported. The same result occurs when the subjects are selected on the basis of low reading relative to math performance (or the reverse). The overestimate of specificity also occurs when subjects are selected on the basis of low performance relative to expected performance in a given area, e.g., a discrepancy between obtained and expected reading scores expressed as grade-equivalent scores. Scores in other skill areas (e.g., math) will be found to be higher than the reading scores, but the degree of that difference will be due in part to measurement error. In all these cases measurement error magnifies the true discrepancy between sample means, so that what may look like a sample characterized by a performance deficiency centered mainly in a particular area (e.g., reading) might in fact be a sample of low achievers. The degree of that effect depends on test reliabilities, the magnitude of the correlation between the measures, and the magnitude of the discrepancy (see Hall & Humphreys, 1982, for further details).

The problem of measurement error and statistical regression in sample selection and description is almost universally ignored in research on learning disabilities and reading deficiency. As a result, in most studies the magnitude of deficiencies and discrepancies is overestimated by the scores that are reported. The consequences of this outcome are varied, depending in part on the logic of the particular study, the sensitivity of the experimental tasks used, and other specific characteristics of the methodology. Studies in which discrepancy (difference) scores are involved and in which sensitivity of measurement is likely to be quite low are especially susceptible to these measurement error effects. For example, Fletcher (1985) reported data concerned with possible differential deficits between groups that differed in their achievement pattern in reading, spelling, and arithmetic. To do this, children were grouped as low in arithmetic only, low in reading and spelling only, low in spelling and arithmetic only, and low in all three areas. An inspection of the reading, spelling, and arithmetic means and SDs that were reported for these groups showed sharp distinctions among them that were in line with the logic just described. However, one may be certain that the groups were not nearly so distinctive in their achievement patterns as it appeared, because measurement error effects were likely to be quite large and no steps to assess or avoid these effects were taken. That combined with small numbers of subjects in certain of the groups (10 and 13 in two of them) means that the experiment probably was considerably less sensitive to certain effects of interest than was intended. A second illustration is a study by Waters, Bruck, and Seidenberg (1985) in which subjects were grouped in terms of patterns of performance in reading and spelling, with only 12 subjects per group and no steps to avoid measurement errors in forming those groups. Other studies in which measurement errors in sample selection seem likely to have played an especially problematic role include those in which samples were separated into small groups of "dysphonetics" and "dyseidetics" (Bayliss & Livesey, 1985; Godfrey, Syrdal-Lasky, Millay, & Knox, 1981), and one involving small groups with different WISC profiles (Cermak, Goldberg-Warter, DeLuca, Cermak, & Drake, 1981).

There is a simple approach by which classification errors due to statistical regression may be minimized (though not entirely eliminated), and that is to retest the subjects who originally met the sample criterion, then to eliminate those who no longer meet that criterion (see Lund et al., 1983, for an example of this approach). There also are techniques by which it is possible to estimate the magnitude of such regression effects (Kahneman, 1965), but they depend on test reliability data that may not always be available for the particular class of subjects involved.

ISOLATING DEFICITS: AMBIGUITIES REGARDING PROCESSES AND CAUSALITY

Limitations in Experimental Tasks

The goal of most researchers has been to devise research designs and experimental tasks that permit one to interpret group differences in highly analytical ways. Thus, with respect to memory, one would not be satisfied in saying that the groups differed in free recall of words, for example, but would wish to pinpoint the particular factor(s) that accounted for the recall difference. This is an extremely difficult goal to attain. In discussing the complexities involved, Torgesen (1985) described three categories of factors that might underlie performance on memory tasks. First, there are basic mechanisms of the memory systems. These control, for example, the speed with which memory search occurs and the capacity of working memory. Using a computer analogy, these may be thought of as the hardware of the memory system. They are the kinds of factors that apparently are referred to in neurological hypotheses about learning disabilities and dyslexia. Second, there are differences in the amount and organization of information in memory, sometimes referred to as semantic memory differences or knowledge differences. Such differences may arise in part from differences in experience (e.g., differences in verbal experience may result in differences in vocabulary) but also from differences in the efficiency of basic mechanisms that are involved in the storage of information. Third, performance on many memory tasks is influenced by the nature and extent of controlled processing, i.e., the particular strategies or study activities deliberately initiated by the learner. Individual differences in strategy use may reflect differences in semantic memory (which, in turn, may reflect either experiential or basic mechanism differences) or motivational differences. Thus, it is minimally instructive at a theoretical level to find that LD children often use less effective study strategies than do NLD children.

Developments in the general field of memory and cognition over the past two decades has made possible a marked increase in the sophistication of approaches to understanding sources of individual differences on various memory and cognitive tasks (see Humphreys et al., 1983). However, our knowledge about memory processes and our ability reliably to measure specific processes remains limited, and these limitations restrict progress in research on individual differences, including that relating to reading deficiency. Largely because of those limitations, and perhaps also because of the difficulty in keeping up with the cutting edge of theory and methodology in memory and cognition, even the more sophisticated of the studies we reviewed are not free of ambiguities with respect to the interpretation of results. We illustrate some of these difficulties next.

In a study by Bauer and Emhert (1984) it was inferred that RD children were deficient in "elaborative encoding" on the basis of lower recall of items in the primacy position but not of items in other list positions. The crucial assumption that differences in the primacy effect reflect differences in the amount or quality of elaborative rehearsal is open to serious question. A plausible alternative is that such differences are due to differences in the extent to which subjects retrieve earlier items as they go through a list. If such study-phase review was more characteristic of the normal readers, that difference might produce higher recall of the primacy items whether or not the rehearsal was more elaborative, as that term is ordinarily used. As a second example, consider a recent observation that false recognitions of semantically related distractors in a recognition test were more frequent for normal than for LD children in Grade 6 (Lorsbach & Gray, 1985). The difference here was attributed to differences in strategic rather than in semantic encoding, whereas the design of the experiment in no way rules out the possibility that nonstrategic differences were involved.

The increased sophistication of the research has been accompanied by the increased importance of quite technical considerations that, although quite subtle in some cases, may be important with respect to interpretation of findings. For example, it is common now for researchers to use two or more tasks, varying in the extent to which they tap various processes, then to look at interactions between groups and tasks as a way of pinpointing a particular processing problem (see Hall & Humphreys, 1982, for a discussion of this approach). This is a powerful approach provided that one may be certain about the processes that are being tapped by the various tasks and that scaling characteristics permit straightforward interpretation of interactions. Problems regarding scaling sometimes are subtle and researchers in the area seem not to be sufficiently sensitive to them. The result is that interactions that may be spurious may nevertheless be interpreted in a substantive way by experimenters. For a discussion of such problems in general, the reader is referred to publications by Baron and Treiman (1980), and Loftus (1978), and to see how they may apply in research on reading deficiency, see the analysis by Hall, Wilson, Humphreys, Tinzmann, and Bowyer (1983) of experimental results reported by Shankweiler, Liberman, Mark, Fowler, and Fischer (1979). Additional relevant discussions are found in Hall and Humphreys (1982) and Humphreys et al. (1983).

These examples were not selected to illustrate weak research. Our intention was to illustrate limitations and problems that are apt to be found in the more impressive research programs wherein researchers are attempting to become highly analytical regarding processes under investigation. Given the state of the art in cognitive psychology generally (as yet immature but rapidly developing) and the complexity of memory and cognition, it perhaps should not be surprising that research based heavily on that area would not easily yield up definitive answers to such difficult questions. In addition, the use for individual differences research of tasks developed in the memory and cognition laboratory is complicated by problems concerned with reliability of measurement and, in the present context, feasibility of use with school-age children. No single experiment or evidence from performance from a single paradigm will suffice to achieve the desired level of specificity with respect to processing. What is needed is an approach over a series of studies in which a number of different tasks and conditions are used to eliminate alternative accounts and narrow down the possibilities as to the precise nature of the deficit. This convergence strategy with respect to research on reading deficiency has been discussed in greater detail by Hall and Humphreys (1982) and by Humphreys et al. (1983).

The studies that we reviewed vary considerably in the extent to which they reflect this cumulative convergent strategy. Studies by Bauer and Emhert (1984), Brady et al., (1983), Ceci et al., (1981), Hanson, Liberman, and Shankweiler (1984), Lund et al., (1983), Perfetti and Lesgold (1979), Torgesen and Houck (1980), and Vellutino and Scanlon (1985) represent portions of quite extensive and influential research programs that are in line with that strategy, some of which have been going on for more than a decade. To evaluate such studies one must consider them in the context of these research programs. Other studies appeared to be more-or-less "one-shot" studies. The value of the latter depends largely on how well they may be integrated with the work of others, which in turn depends largely on similarities across investigators in the nature of the methods (including subject selection) used. Unfortunately, the degree of variability often is so great that when results appear to be in conflict one is hard put to identify likely sources of the inconsistency.

Even in the more systematic and long-standing research programs concerning reading deficiency, it has proven difficult to isolate specific processing deficits and to understand their relationship to reading competence. Perhaps the greatest impact on current thinking has been from the work of the Haskins Institute group and others concerning the problems of poor readers in encoding the phonological features of words. That work has been highly programmatic, and converging evidence from a number of different studies (e.g., Hanson et al., 1984) has pointed toward such an association (but see Hall, Wilson, Humphreys, Tinzmann, & Bowyer, 1983). However, there remain questions regarding the prevalence of phonological coding problems among poor readers, the precise nature of the problem, the origin of the deficit, the relationship between the process(es) involved and general intelligence, and whether the relationship with reading is causal. A recent paper by Torgesen (1985) provides a much more complete discussion of this evidence and of the questions that remain.

The Magnitude of Observed Differences

A quite striking characteristic of all the studies of reading deficiency that we have reviewed is that, as with LD category studies, the differences found between good and poor readers on experimental tasks are not impressively large, statistical significance aside. Indeed, those differences are so small that they could be accounted for in most cases by unusually low performance of a rather small fraction of the deficient readers. Weener (1981) has documented this observation in considerable detail, and discussed a number of implications. The fact that a particular deficit might be characteristic of only 15 or 20% of a sample does not necessarily mean that the finding is uninteresting, particularly from a theoretical perspective. But it does mean that generalizations to RD or poor readers as a group are unwarranted, and if taken seriously by practitioners could lead to unfortunate placement or instructional decisions. Also, given the relatively small difference required for statistical significance between group means, and the particular issues involved, it would be desirable to report data concerning the distribution of the scores in the groups, as Weener has suggested. If it is the case that only some subset of poor readers are markedly deficient in a process tapped by a given experimental task, then one might expect a bimodal distribution of scores by the poor readers. That is, the subset of poor readers with normal processing would look just like the good readers, and the subset of process-deficient poor readers would form a distribution of its own below that. We have never seen such a distribution of scores in a sample of poor readers, and that is one reason that we remain skeptical of the idea that poor readers are, to any marked degree, characterized by anomalous cognitive processing.

Establishing and Understanding Causality

Finding a processing difference between LD and NLD children does not, by itself, establish a causal link; poor performance on classroom tasks and on laboratory memory tasks might both result from some third factor. Indeed, the performance deficiency might lead to poorer performance on certain laboratory memory tasks. Morrison and Manis (1982) discussed problems in establishing causal links between processing deficits and reading deficiencies a few years ago. They also reviewed the relevant literature and came to the conclusion that such links had not yet been established in the case of any of the processing deficiencies that had been proposed. Their conclusion is equally applicable today, in our judgment (also see Torgesen, 1985).

Establishing causality in this context is an extraordinarily difficult task, and again a converging-evidence approach is required to become confident in this respect. Two general strategies for this purpose were suggested by Hall and Humphreys (1982). One of these involves longitudinal studies beginning well in advance of formal instruction in reading. The idea is to administer a set of tasks by which individual differences in various aspects of cognitive processing may be assessed, then following the subjects to the point that individual differences in various reading subskills may be measured. This approach is not foolproof, however, because it is logically possible that some unmeasured factor might produce a low level of performance on some cognitive task during the preschool years and reading difficulty later. Thus, some additional evidence might be required to become confident regarding causality. Two other limitations are the time involved and the difficulty of obtaining reliable measures of specific aspects of processing in preschool children.

A second, and much less difficult, approach involves the use of control conditions consisting of younger children whose reading progress is normal but whose actual reading performance is similar to the (older) poor readers under study, as in a recent experiment by Young-Loveridge (1985). The logic, put briefly, is as follows. Suppose that a difference in performance on Task X is found between good and poor readers in Grade 3, suggesting that a deficit in the cognitive processes tapped by Task X may be responsible for the reading difficulty. To reach such a conclusion it is necessary to rule out the possibility that such a deficit merely accompanies the lower reading level characteristic of the Grade 3 poor readers, but is not the cause of that difficulty. The possibility that the latter is the case may be checked by including younger children whose normal reading level is the same as that of the older poor readers. If the deficit performance is found with those younger normal readers, then one is led to reject the notion that the deficit is a cause of the reading difficulty. If that deficit is not characteristic of the younger children, then the causal relationship is not proved, but it may be judged to be more probable. Although this seems to be a promising approach toward establishing causality, it remains one that is seldom used. Indeed, researchers seem particularly unimaginative with respect to using additional control subjects and tasks to eliminate alternative interpretations of observed differences between good and poor readers on the tasks of interest.

SUMMARY COMMENTS ON THE ROLE OF MEMORY IN LEARNING DISABILITY AND READING DEFICIENCY

Memory Deficits?

It seems certain that the average performance of the population of children identified as learning disabled is well below the average of NLD children in performance on a wide variety of tasks involving memory. This might be expected, given that the LD population is well below average in measures of general intelligence, suggesting that the processes that underlie performance on IQ tests and various tasks involving memory are less efficient in the LD population. Many LD children appear to differ little if at all with respect to basic cognitive mechanisms from NLD children of similar intelligence (see Hall et al., 1983). The fact that some such children are lower achievers than would be expected on the basis of IQ data probably is a result of a variety of non-cognitive factors, just as in the case of NLD underachievers. In any case, the diversity within the school-identified population places severe restrictions on meaningful generalizations regarding cognitive processing characteristics of that population as a whole.

Because of the strong relationship between IQ and reading competence, we may be reasonably certain that the bulk of the variation in reading within the general population at any given age/grade level is a result of individual differences in processes underlying general intelligence. Furthermore, even when poor readers are matched with normal readers in some summary measure of general intelligence (e.g., IQ), differences in one or more of the specific processes that underlie IQ are not ruled out. There is no convincing evidence that the performance deficiencies involved are a result of any *additional* types of cognitive deficit, i.e., deficits in some aspects of cognitive processing that are not related to general intelligence (also see Torgesen, 1985). Nor is there any reason to suspect that whatever deficits exist are a result of brain pathology, except perhaps in a small proportion of cases. In fact, as with LD children, it seems likely to us that most children who are reading below expected levels do so because of the cumulative effects of noncognitive factors, including especially differences in the amount of verbal experience and appropriate instruction.

Recommendations Concerning Research

A number of problems in the way samples are selected and sample data are reported were discussed in some detail. Specifically, we suggest that LD category research concerning cognitive deficits be abandoned, that the use of preselected samples or sample pools be avoided, that IQ matching is seldom appropriate, that double-testing be done to avoid problems arising from measurement errors, and that achievement in areas other than reading be determined and reported. If the population of interest consists of children with deficiencies specific to reading, then these additional achievement data should be used to ensure that the sample does not include underachievers more generally. Journal editors seem to be in a key position to facilitate these changes.

Elsewhere it has been suggested that researchers concerned with relationships between basic cognitive processes and performance in various areas such as reading make greater use of more classic approaches to individual difference research (see Humphreys et al., 1983, for a more extended discussion of such possibilities). Reliable measures of individual differences in various aspects of cognitive processing and performance (e.g., in reading) would be administered to a large unselected sample of the population of interest (e.g., elementary school children). Then the researcher would use more traditional individual-difference methodologies (quite sophisticated techniques are available) to examine relationships between these sets of measures. The result would be a set of empirically-derived hypotheses regarding relationships between particular processes and particular aspects of performance.

To bring this off, considerable effort would be needed first to develop sufficiently reliable and specific processing and performance measures, building on some of the procedures already used in research concerning reading competence and on those developed for use in memory and cognition experiments. An investment of this sort will be necessary sooner or later, it seems to us, no matter what research strategy is used. A second requirement would be the use of much larger samples than are typical in LD and reading research, in part because of the requirements of the statistical techniques involved, but also to be certain that there is adequate representation at the extremes (especially the low extremes) of the distributions. This would make it possible to detect truly anomolous characteristics that some have attributed to children with severe reading problems, if such characteristics indeed exist. This requirement is expensive in the short run, but we suspect would be more efficient and economical in the long run. It also would require a larger research team, with broader expertise than ordinarily is involved in any given research program. It would seem reasonable to work out ways to draw upon the diverse talents of a number of leading reading researchers along with specialists in individual difference research technology and specialists in areas other than reading (e.g., mathematics).

To verify the hypotheses generated in this way, the approach we suggest would be the direct opposite of that generally taken, where extreme groups in performance are selected, then compared on measures of processing. Instead, one could select groups on the basis of the processing measure(s), then compare them in performance on, say, specific reading subskills. This would produce a symmetry between conceptions of causality and research operations. Processing deficits are suspected of causing performance deficits, so in contrast to usual procedures, one would first define levels of the independent variable (processing characteristics), then look for differences in the dependent variable (performance in reading). This approach to testing hypotheses about cognitive deficits and performance deficiencies is, in our judgment, more convincing than the usual reverse practice. We suspect that the reasons that it is less often used are in part matters of convenience, i.e., ready availability of preselected subjects or subject pools. This tendency to sacrifice quality for convenience is apparent in much of the LD and RD research that we have examined. For example, why else would one use preselected samples or report IQ scores from different tests for the different groups under comparison rather than administering a common test to all subjects?

Implications for LD Practitioners

So far as we can see, the research concerning cognitive deficits in LD and RD children has been of little or no value to those who plan and implement instruction except to suggest that assumptions about such deficits or their neurological bases are probably incorrect for most children and irrelevant to most instructional decisions in any case. We suggest that practitioners take a position that is atheoretical with respect to cognitive processing and that focuses, instead, on the difficulties exhibited by the child (see Lewis, 1983, and Ysseldyke et al., 1983, for more extended discussions along these lines). The idea is that important skills, such as reading, consist of the integration of various subskills and knowledge components built up through experience (including formal instruction) over long periods of time, and that poor skill performance must, therefore, be due to a breakdown of one or more components or their integration. The challenge is to identify the various components (generally through task analysis procedures) and, for given individuals, to find out just where that breakdown is occurring so that instruction can be directed specifically to its repair.

REFERENCES

Algozzine, B., & Ysseldyke, J. (1983). Learning disabilities as a subset of school failure: The over-sophistication of a concept. *Exceptional Children, 50,* 242–246.

Baron, J., & Treiman, R. (1980). Some problems in the study of differences in cognitive processes. *Memory and Cognition, 8,* 313–321.

Bauer, R. H., & Emhert, J. (1984). Information processing in reading-disabled and nondisabled children. *Journal of Experimental Child Psychology, 37,* 271–281.

Bayliss, J., & Livesey, P. J. (1985). Cognitive strategies of children with reading disability and normal readers in visual sequential memory. *Journal of Learning Disabilities, 18,* 326–332.

Brady, S., Shankweiler, D., & Mann, V. (1983). Speech perception and memory coding in relation to reading ability. *Journal of Experimental Child Psychology, 35,* 345–367.

Briggs, P., & Underwood, G. (1982). Phonological coding in good and poor readers. *Journal of Experimental Child Psychology, 34,* 93–112.

Capobianco, R. F. (1964). Diagnostic methods used with learning disability cases. *Exceptional Children, 31,* 187–193.

Ceci, S. J., Ringstrom, M., & Lea, S. E. G. (1981). Do language-learning disabled children (L/LDs) have impaired memories? In search of underlying processes. *Journal of Learning Disabilities, 14,* 159–173.

Cermak, L. S., Goldberg-Warter, J., DeLuca, D., Cermak, S., & Drake, C. (1981). The role of interference in the verbal retention ability of learning disabled readers. *Journal of Learning Disabilities, 14,* 291–295.

Chabot, F. J., Petros, T. V., & McCord, G. (1983). Developmental and reading ability differences in accessing information from semantic memory. *Journal of Experimental Child Psychology, 35,* 128–142.

Christenson, S., Ysseldyke, J., & Algozzine, B. (1982). Institutional constraints and external pressures influencing referral decisions. *Psychology in the Schools, 19,* 341–345.

Crowder, R. J. (1982). The demise of short-term memory. *Acta Psychologica, 50,* 291–323.

Cruickshank, W. M. (1972). Some issues facing the field of learning disabilities. *Journal of Learning Disabilities, 5,* 5–13.

Epps, S., Ysseldyke, J. E., & McGue, M. (1984). I know one when I see one—differentiating LD and non-LD students. *Learning Disability Quarterly 7,* 89–100.

Fletcher, J. M. (1985). Memory for verbal and nonverbal stimuli in learning disability subgroups: Analysis by selective reminding. *Journal of Experimental Child Psychology, 40,* 244–259.

Godfrey, J. J., Syrdal-Lasky, A. K., Millay, K. K., & Knox, C. M. (1981). Performance of dyslexic children on speech perception tests. *Journal of Experimental Child Psychology, 32,* 401–424.

Hall, J. W., & Humphreys, M. S. (1982). Research on specific learning disabilities: deficits and remediation. *Topics in Learning and Learning Disabilities,* 68–78.

Hall, J. W., Humphreys, M. S., & Wilson, K. P. (1983). Differences in long-term retention in relation to early school achievement. *American Journal of Psychology, 96,* 267–287.

Hall, J. W., Wilson, K. P., Humphreys, M. S., Tinzmann, M. B., & Bowyer, P. M. (1983).

Phonetic-similarity effects in good and poor readers. *Memory & Cognition, 11*, 520–527.

Hanson, V. L., Liberman, I. Y., & Shankweiler, D. (1984). Linguistic coding by deaf children in relation to beginning reading success. *Journal of Experimental Child Psychology, 37*, 378–393.

Harber, J. R. (1981). Critical evaluation of published research: Some guidelines. *Learning Disability Quarterly, 4*, 260–270.

Humphreys, M. S., Lynch, J. J., Revelle, W., & Hall, J. W. (1983). Individual differences in short-term memory. In R. F. Dillon & R. R. Schmeck (Eds.), *Individual differences in cognition* (Vol. 1, pp. 35–64). Orlando, FL: Academic Press.

Kahneman, D. (1965). Control of spurious association and the reliability of the controlled variable. *Psychological Bulletin, 64*, 326–329.

Keogh, B. K., Major, S. M., Reid, H. P., Gandara, P., & Omori, H. (1978). Marker variables: A search for comparability and generalizability in the field of learning disabilities. *Learning Disability Quarterly, 1*, 5–11.

Lewis, R. B. (1983). Learning disabilities and reading: Instructional recommendations from current research. *Exceptional Children, 50*, 230–241.

Loftus, G. R. On interpretation of interactions. (1978). *Memory and Cognition, 6*, 312–319.

Lorsbach, T. C., & Gray, J. W. (1985). The development of encoding processes in learning disabled children. *Journal of Learning Disabilities*, 222–227.

Lund, A. M., Hall, J. W., & Humphreys, M. S. (1983). Frequency judgment accuracy as a function of age and school achievement (learning disabled vs nonlearning-disabled) patterns. *Journal of Experimental Child Psychology, 35*, 236–247.

Morrison, F. J., & Manis, F. R. (1982). Cognitive processes and reading disability: A critique and proposal. In C. J. Brainerd & M. Preessley (Eds.), *Advances in cognitive development (Vol. 2): Verbal processes in development.* New York: Springer-Verlag.

Paris, S. G., & Myers, M. (1981). Comprehension monitoring, memory, and study strategies of good and poor readers. *Journal of Reading Behavior, 13*, 5–22.

Perfetti, C. A., & Lesgold, A. M. (1979). Coding and comprehension in skilled readers and implications for reading instruction. In L. B. Resnick & P. Weaver (Eds.), *Theory and practice of early reading,* (Vol. 1, pp. 57–84). Hillsdale, NJ: Erlbaum.

Reitsma, P. (1983). Printed word learning in beginning readers. *Journal of Experimental Child Psychology, 36*, 321–339.

Shankweiler, D., Liberman, I. Y., Mann, S. L., Fowler, L. A., & Fischer, F. W. (1979). The speech code and learning to read. *Journal of Experimental Psychology: Human Learning and Memory, 5*, 531–545.

Torgesen, J. K. (1985). Memory processes in reading disabled children. *Journal of Learning Disabilities, 18*, 350–357.

Torgesen, J. K. (1979). What shall we do with psychological processes? *Journal of Learning Disabilities, 12*, 514–521.

Torgesen, J. K., & Houck, G. (1980). Processing deficiencies in learning disabled children who perform poorly on the digit span task. *Journal of Educational Psychology, 72*, 141–160.

Valtin, R. (1980). Deficiencies in research on reading deficiencies. In J. F. Kavanaugh & R. L. Venezky (Eds.), *Orthography, reading, and dyslexia.* Baltimore, Md.: University Park Press.

Valtin, R. (1978–1979). Dyslexia: Deficit in reading or deficit in research? *Reading Research Quarterly, 14*, 210–221.

Vellutino, F. R., & Scanlon, D. M. (1985). Free recall of concrete and abstract words in poor and normal readers. *Journal of Experimental Child Psychology, 39*, 363–380.

Vinsonhaler, J. R., Weinshank, A. B., Wagner, C. C., & Polin, R. M. (1983). Diagnosing children with educational problems: Characteristics of reading and learning disabilities specialists, and classroom teachers. *Reading Research Quarterly, 18,* 134–164.

Waters, G. S., Bruck, M., & Seidenberg, M. (1985). Do children use similar processes to read and spell words? *Journal of Experimental Child Psychology, 39,* 511–530.

Weener, P. (1981). On comparing learning disabled and regular classroom children. *Journal of Learning Disabilities, 14,* 227–232.

Wilson, K. P. (1983). *Performance of good and poor readers across a variety of memory tasks.* Unpublished doctoral dissertation, Northwestern University.

Wolford, G., & Fowler, C. A. (1984). Differential use of partial information by good and poor readers. *Developmental Review, 4,* 16–35.

Young-Loveridge, J. M. (1985). Use of orthographic structure and reading ability: What relationship? *Journal of Experimental Child Psychology, 40,* 439–449.

Ysseldyke, J., Algozzine, B., & Epps, S. (1983). A logical and empirical analysis of current practice in classifying students as handicapped. *Exceptional Children, 50,* 160–166.

Ysseldyke, J. E., Algozzine, B., Shinn, M. R., & McGue, M. (1982). *Journal of Special Education, 16,* 73–85.

Ysseldyke, J., Algozzine, B., & Thurlow, M. (1983). On interpreting institute research: A response to McKinney. *Exceptional Education Quarterly, 4,* 145–147.

Ysseldyke, J. E., Thurlow, M., Graden, J., Wesson, C., Algozzine, B., & Deno, S. (1983). Generalizations from five years of research on assessment and decision making: The University of Minnesota Institute. *Exceptional Education Quarterly, 4,* 75–93.

NEUROPSYCHOLOGICAL BASIS OF ATTENTION AND MEMORY IN LEARNING DISABILITIES

George W. Hynd, John E. Obrzut and
Sara M. Bowen

ABSTRACT

The term *learning disabilities* has come to be associated with disorders in auditory discrimination, visual perception, sequential processing, cross-modal integration, semantic memory, and so on. In short, deficits have been identified in nearly every conceivable perceptual and cognitive process among these children. It is argued in this chapter that learning disabled (LD) children suffer neurodevelopmental anomalies that manifest in lateralized processing mechanisms. This neurophysiologically based perspective argues

Memory and Learning Disabilities
Advances in Learning and Behavioral Disabilities, Suppl. 2, pages 175–201.
ISBN: 0-89232-836-3

that many if not most deficits across modalities and various cognitive processes including memory reflect basic deficiencies in the allocation of attentional resources that persist throughout development. It is believed that this perspective is consistent with the historical evolution of the syndrome of learning disabilities and is reflective of the neuropathological and neuropsychological literature in this area.

While a great many investigators have examined the educational and psychological parameters that distinguish the learning disabled (LD) from the normal child, it has only been recently that progress has been made in articulating the neuropsychological basis of attention and memory in LD children. This is indeed important because it not only addresses the often neglected etiological factors associated with learning disabilities but also focuses in on those basic neurological processes that contribute to, and are reflected in, the well documented disorders of higher cognitive processing found in these children.

While it has long been presumed that learning disabilities have a neurological etiology (e.g., Bastian, 1898; Hinshelwood, 1895, 1900, 1902; Kirk, 1962; Orton, 1928), the precise nature of the neurodevelopmental deficit remained unknown. This lack of any clear understanding of the precise neuropathology of learning disabilities led to ambiguity in definitional efforts.

For example, Orton (1937) was one of the first to suggest that individuals with learning problems suffered from incomplete or delayed functional lateralization. Orton suggested that the dysfunction was neurophysiological in origin and would be amenable to remediation and/or maturation. Orton's theory, however, was unclear and, according to Knights and Bakker (1976), proposed little more than a label to describe unobservable events within individuals who have learning problems. Nonetheless, the theory of maturational lag received further support through the work of Lenneberg (1967), Critchley (1970), and especially by Satz and his colleagues (e.g., Satz, Rardin & Ross, 1971; Satz & Sparrow, 1970).

Only recently has this neurodevelopmental delay model been challenged by those who argue that children do not grow out of their learning disabilities and that the associated attentional and memory problems persist into adulthood (Hynd, Cohen, & Obrzut, 1983). According to this deficit perspective, malfunction is due to disruption of the developing brain, "be it at the cellular or the molecular level, or is due to a failure of its genetic control" (Kinsbourne, 1983, p. 1). These deficits can include but are not restricted to malfunction of the language-dominant hemisphere, failure of cerebral lateralization to be completed, and callosal insufficiency (Kinsbourne, 1983). Gaddes (1980) described the LD individual as one "with no positive evidence of neurological dysfunction [but] may be hypothesized to have disorder'' (p. 18). He further stated that there is little question that neurological deficits are involved in producing cognitive and perceptual impairments (Gaddes, 1980). Recent research by the present authors indicated that differences between normal and LD children are not due to delayed cerebral dominance but rather to attentional deficiencies associated with lateralized language function. In this same vein, Kinsbourne (1970) had earlier proposed that each hemisphere selectively directs attention to the opposite side of space. Thus, additional deficits in LD children and adolescents may be due to their inability to shift attention appropriately in processing information. These issues are addressed in detail in this chapter.

However, in the light of the lack of specificity of the early notions regarding the presumed nature of the neurodevelopmental delay associated with learning disabilities, the difficulties encountered in formulating a coherent definition of learning disabilities becomes easier to understand. Kirk (1962) first defined learning disability as:

> a retardation, disorder, or delayed development in one or more of the processes of speech, language, reading, spelling, writing, or arithmetic resulting from a possible cerebral dysfunction and/or emotional or behavioral disturbances and not from mental retardation, sensory deprivation, or cultural or instructional factors. (p. 253)

Kirk (1962) later warned against the excessive use of technical names such as dysphasia and strephosymbolia in describing deficits seen in LD children. He found descriptions of actual behavioral or learning deficits more useful in discussing children's problems. Kirk's initial move away from medical-technical jargon in defining learning disabilities led to more educationally oriented descriptions.

In 1968, the National Advisory Committee on Handicapped Children presented a new definition to Congress. This definition served as the basis of the 1968 Learning Disabilities Act (Kirk & Kirk, 1983) and was included in Public Law 94–142. This definition was as follows:

> The term 'specific learning disability' means a disorder in one or more of the basic psychological processes involved in understanding or in using language, spoken or written, which may manifest itself in an imperfect ability to listen, think, speak, read, write, spell, or to do mathematical calculations. The term includes such conditions as perceptual handicaps, brain injury, minimal brain dysfunction, dyslexia, and developmental aphasia. The term does not include children who have learning problems which are primarily the result of visual, hearing, or motor handicaps, or mental retardation, of emotional disturbance, or of environmental, cultural, or economic disadvantage. (*Federal Register*, Dec. 29, 1977, p. 65083)

This broad definition, while still officially used, had several weaknesses: the phrase "basic psychological processes" is vague and does not specifically delineate what deficits that child may have. Smith (1983) attributed this vagueness to the fact that professionals cannot, as yet, clearly define the psychological processes underlying learning disabilities, nor can they be sure that these processes are amenable to remediation. Another problem with the definition was the implication that children who have other handicapping conditions, such as visual or hearing impairment or emotional disturbance, cannot be diagnosed learning disabled as well.

Perhaps most importantly from the present author's perspective is the fact that Kirk (1962) carefully avoided any articulate mention as to the nature of the neurological dysfunction associated with learning disabilities. Thus, the definition which finally appeared in 1977 suggested that the term *learning disabilities "includes* such conditions as" but was apparently not limited to only those disorders where the psychological or educational deficits could be correlated to neurologically-based deficits. By and large, this omission of any formal tie to a neurological etiology led to a situation where a child could be diagnosed as learning disabled simply on the basis of (a) deficit academic performance, (b) a discrepancy (usually statistically-based) between IQ and achievement, and (c) no evidence of compromising factors (e.g., lack of opportunity, cultural differences). The absence of any statement as to the neurological etiology and substantiating correlated evidence probably led to significantly more children diagnosed as learning disabled than the neurological evidence would support.

In this decade, the National Joint Committee for Learning Disabilities (NJCLD) formed from representatives of six professional associations, introduced a revised definition for learning disabilities. The group agreed on the following definition:

> Learning disabilities is a generic term that refers to a heterogeneous group of disorders manifested by significant difficulties in the acquisition and use of listening, speaking, reading, writing, reasoning, or mathematical abilities. These disorders are intrinsic to the individual and *presumed to be due to central nervous system dysfunction*. Even though a learning disability may occur concomitantly with other handicapping conditions (e.g., sensory impairment, mental retardation, social and emotional disturbances) or environmental influences (e.g., cultural differences, insufficient/inappropriate instruction, psychogenic factors), it is not the direct result of those conditions or influences. (Hammill, Leigh, McNutt, & Larsen, 1981, p. 336, emphasis added)

This new definition served to clarify some of the problems with the definition included in the *Federal Register*. It stated explicitly that disorders were due to presumed central nervous system dysfunction. This statement attempted to clarify the ambiguity inherent in the phrase "basic psychological processes" (Smith, 1983).

Also, the NJCLD definition, by excluding the word children, made an effort to recognize that problems may be encountered by adolescents and adults as well as by young children (McLoughlin & Netick, 1983). The definition also avoided explicit reference to any discrepancy between actual and expected achievement, thus forcing professionals to redesign assessment and diagnostic procedures away from "formulas" that quantify discrepancies. The move away from detecting "significant difficulty in acquisition" has gained popularity of late (McLoughlin & Netick, 1983; McLeod, 1983). McLeod (1983) further contended that there is no specific level at which one *ought* to be achieving, it is the responsibility of educators to decide which students are achieving so far below the norm that they will need aid.

An additional important change in the NJCLD definition was the recognition that learning disabilities may occur concomitantly with other handicapping conditions. According to the Federal definition, there could be no visually or hearing impaired LD individuals, however, these sensory impaired individuals may qualify for services and have an even greater need than some other LD groups (Sabatino, 1983). The point must be clear that learning disabilities are not the direct result of other handicaps or of environmental factors but it is conceivable that multiple problems can be present in an individual. Therefore, in contrast to the exclusionary clause in the Federal definition, an individual could be hearing impaired and learning disabled or even mentally retarded and learning disabled as well. Although the primary diagnostic category may be multi-handicapped due to more than one concomitant handicapping condition, learning disabled may well be one of those conditions. This lent support to the contention that the LD population is indeed a heterogeneous group that is comprised of persons with a myriad of different problems.

From a neurological perspective this is completely consistent. Clinically, children who have neurological problems frequently have learning disabilities. For example, children who survive acute lymphocytic leukemia often suffer learning disabilities possibly as a result of receiving intrathecal methotrexate and/or intracranial radiation (Elbert, Culbertson, Gerrity, Guthrie, & Bayles, 1985). Deficits in memory, cognition, verbal-motor integration, and verbal fluency have been documented in these children (Goff, 1982; Massari, 1982). Also, evidence continues to accumulate that suggests infants of very low birth weight, of whom about 80% between 1,000 to 1,500 grams survive (Horwood, Boyle, Torrance, & Sinclair, 1982), nearly 64% end up in special education classes by the age 10 years (Nickel, Bennett, & Lamson, 1982).

Thus, it does seem that there exists a growing population of children who may have documented neurological problems whose deficits correlate with learning disabilities. However, what about those children who do not have any known history of neurological trauma or disease who seem to possess cognitive deficits typical of the LD child? Is there any evidence as to the neuropsychological or neurophysiological basis for these deficits that substantiate the notion that learning disabilities have a neurological etiology that may manifest in attention or memory deficits?

This chapter attempts to address these two questions. To adequately address these issues the literature in several areas must be discussed. In this manner it is hoped that a clear conceptualization will emerge as to how the neurophysiological etiology relates to the deficient attention and memory processes found in LD children. An overview of the literature associated with cerebral lateralization is first presented with a focus on our work with dichotic listening asymmetries in normal and LD children. Then, a brief review of attentional theories and the cytoarchitetonic or neuropathological studies of reading disabled children's brains is presented. Finally, a brief but integrated conceptualization of brain-behavior relationships in LD children is discussed such that the research in other chapters of this volume may be placed in a neurophysiological context.

FUNCTIONAL CEREBRAL LATERALIZATION IN LEARNING DISABILITIES

The notion that language was lateralized to the left cerebral hemisphere was expressed before the time of Broca. It was Broca (1861), however, who formally provided evidence for such lateralization of linguistic processes. Orton (1937) was one of the first to postulate that incomplete or delayed lateralization of language resulted in cognitive deficits in LD children. Although researchers such as Lenneberg (1967) and Satz et al. (1971) suggested that language lateralization proceeded in infancy from bilateral to unilateral specialization and that lateralization progresses developmentally, evidence of this developmental process was inconclusive. More recent research suggests that language lateralization is predetermined and can be demonstrated early in the neonatal period (Caplan & Kinsbourne, 1976; Kinsbourne & Hiscock, 1977, 1978). Historically, lateralization has been assessed through measures of lateral preference (e.g., handedness), however, there appears to be limited evidence that handedness is related to the degree of cerebral dominance in children (Obrzut & Hynd, 1981).

More current techniques to measure functional lateralization include the measurement of perceptual asymmetries through dichotic listening and visual half-field presentation. Dichotic listening techniques have been used extensively as a non-invasive procedure to assess language lateralization in normals (Kimura, 1961) and more recently with LD children (Ayres, 1977; Hynd, Obrzut, Weed, & Hynd, 1979; Hynd et al., 1983; Obrzut, Hynd, Obrzut, & Leitgeb, 1980). The research indicates that dichotic listening tasks access central auditory processes and lateralized language ability. Additionally, in studies of patients in whom cerebral dominance had been established by the sodium amytal test (Wada & Rasmussen, 1960), the dichotic listening task has appeared to be a reliable and stable measure of cerebral dominance for auditory and language functions (Gaddes, 1980). Those with known left hemisphere representation of language function displayed an ear effect that would be expected during a dichotic listening task using verbal material. This experimental dichotic listening technique was originally developed by Broadbent (1958) in conjunction with his mechanical model of memory.

The Dichotic Listening Paradigm

In the dichotic listening task, paired verbal stimuli (e.g., consonant vowel syllables, digits, words) are presented simultaneously, one to each ear. The stimuli reported by the subject will usually be evidence of an "ear effect" where the subject will report more correctly the stimuli in a favored ear (see Figure 1). Through this dichotic listening task, Kimura (1967) reported that subjects perceived information received in the right ear more accurately than information received in the left ear. Since contralateral auditory pathways transmit information more quickly (Kimura, 1967), the ear opposite the language dominant hemisphere will perceive correctly a greater number of the dichotically presented stimuli. Kimura's contention that contralateral pathways are more effective than ipsilateral pathways in auditory perception suggests that this right ear advantage (REA) was due to language functioning being controlled in the left hemisphere. This contention that an REA is thought to reflect left hemisphere representation for language has been generally accepted (Kinsbourne & Hiscock, 1981).

Linguistic Asymmetries in Normal and LD Children

Research using dichotic listening techniques with LD children has been designed to determine if they are less lateralized than their normal counterparts in language functioning (as originally suggested by Orton, 1937) and to determine if there is any evidence of a developmental increase in functional lateralization with increasing age. Several studies (e.g., Satz et al., 1971) using dichotic listening to determine cerebral dominance in LD children revealed an REA for this population. The results of these studies tend to contradict the hypothesis that these children are not as well lateralized for language functioning as their normal counterparts.

The fact that normal children exhibit a left hemisphere dominance for language functions and, therefore, a right ear advantage in dichotic listening, has been well established by Kimura (1961, 1963) and has been supported in subsequent studies (Bever, 1971; Satz et al.; 1971, Sommers & Taylor, 1971). Satz et al. (1971) did suggest that children with learning

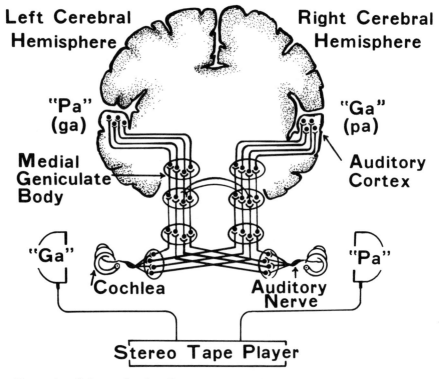

Figure 1. Schematic of auditory pathways involved in dichotic listening. Because crossed auditory pathways are more numerous/prepotent, a dichotic stimuli presented to the right ear ("Pa") is perceived in the left auditory cortex. The dichotic ear effect occurs because the right perceptual field (right ear) is favored in linguistic stimuli recognition by the left auditory cortex. The crossed auditory pathways are more numerous and seem prepotent in auditory stimulus recognition, because pathways cross at both the level of the pons at the trapezoid body and at the level of the midbrain at the inferior colliculus.

Note: From *Dyslexia: Neuropsychological Theory, Research and Clinical Differentiation* by G.W. Hynd and M. Cohen, 1983, Orlando, FL: Grune & Stratton. Copyright 1983 by Grune & Stratton, Inc. Reprinted by permission.

disabilities show a delay in left hemisphere language development. Their study concluded that deficits in performance may be associated with younger children, but that these deficits tend to attenuate with age in LD children. Conversely, additional studies (Ullman, 1977; Schulman-Galambos, 1977) indicated no developmental trend in the establishment of cerebral dominance and that the left hemisphere was predisposed for the processing of language at birth.

Recently, a series of studies using groups of LD children and normal counterparts have been carried out by Obrzut and Hynd and their associates (Hynd et al., 1979; Hynd & Obrzut, 1981; Obrzut, Hynd, Obrzut, & Pirozzolo, 1981) in an attempt to investigate the developmental hypothesis. The LD subjects in these studies were classified on the basis of an extensive evaluation including an IQ score $\geq$ 80; evidence of a processing deficit and a two year achievement deficit in reading and math. In the study by Hynd et al. (1979), the REA in 48 normal and 48 LD children was assessed. Both groups were matched according to age, gender, and handedness and were divided into two age groups in order to examine possible developmental differences. Results of this study showed that both the LD and normal subjects demonstrated a significant REA, although normals reported right ear stimuli more accurately. Also, no developmental trend was evidenced between the groups indicating that "while there may be differences between the performance of learning disabled and normal children on a dichotic task, both are lateralized for speech representation and do not evidence developmental characteristics" (Hynd et al., 1979, p. 450). Table 1 summarizes these results.

The finding that a distinct difference was observed in the overall performance of the LD and normal children, despite no apparent differences in cerebral lateralization, has led to a hypothesis with regard to how the former process and attend to information. Hynd et al. (1979) contended that the differences between the groups of children were attributed to deficits in the ability to selectively attend. In the LD subjects this deficit resulted from a higher rate of guessing during the task. This variability in performance due to differing abilities to attend selectively had been suggested previously by Bryden and Allard (1978) in their review of dichotic

Table 1. Mean Number of Correctly Reported CV Syllables for Each Ear by the Normal and Learning-Disabled Children

	Developmental Level (age range)	Left Ear			Right Ear	
		N	$\bar{X}$	SD	$\bar{X}$	SD
Learning disabled	Younger (7–0 to 9–6)	24	10.21	2.67	11.83	3.31
	Older (9–7 to 11–11)	24	8.38	3.56	12.67	5.32
Normal	Younger (7–0 to 9–6)	24	11.67	3.56	14.17	4.59
	Older (9–7 to 11–11)	24	10.58	2.60	14.79	2.61

Note: From "Development of Cerebral Dominance: Dichotic Listening Asymmetry in Normal and Learning Disabled Children" by G. W. Hynd, J. E. Obrzut, W. Weed, and C. R. Hynd, 1979, *Journal of Experimental Child Psychology, 28.* Copyright 1979 by Academic Press. Reprinted by permission.

listening studies. Bryden and Allard (1978) suggested that children may have difficulties in disentangling simultaneously occurring sounds and, therefore, resort to random guessing in their responses.

Attentional Mechanisms in Linguistic Asymmetries

Kinsbourne (1970) first proposed an attentional model for functional asymmetry. He proposed that each hemisphere is dominant for interpretation of different stimuli. Expectation of incoming stimuli will activate the appropriate hemisphere and causes a shift in attention toward the opposite side of space. At the same time, the perception of stimuli in the other hemisphere is suppressed. Thus, awareness and expectancy of verbal stimuli activates the left hemisphere and shifts or biases attention toward the right side of space. However, if LD children have attentional deficits, as suggested by Hynd et al. (1979), they may not have the ability to suppress the non-dominant hemisphere in verbally related tasks and are, therefore, unable to focus attention appropriately for linguistic tasks. Attention deficits, per se, do not cause learning disabilities. However, this inability to focus attention is often manifested in LD children and probably is a direct consequence of neuropathological deficits.

In an effort to examine these attentional factors Obrzut et al. (1981) conducted a study with normal and LD youngsters using both free recall and directed attention conditions in the dichotic task. Directed attention conditions included instructing the children to report what they heard only in the right ear for one set of trials and only what they heard in the left ear for another set of trials. These preliminary cuing conditions were used in an attempt to control for the effects of variability in selective attention.

Results in support of Hynd et al. (1979) indicated again that both groups clearly demonstrated a significant REA and that no developmental trend was evidenced. However, it was interesting to note that when asked to direct attention to the left ear only, the LD group was able to reverse the ear effect and showed a dramatic LEA, while the normal group continued to show a REA. Also, when attention was directed toward the right ear, both groups showed a significant REA, but the LD subjects could increase the magnitude of the between-ear difference significantly over the normals (Obrzut et al., 1981). It was concluded that the tendency for LD children to show LEA in the directed left condition reflected a greater susceptibility to attentional biases.

These results suggested that LD children have not developed the ability to suppress the non-dominant hemisphere during verbal tasks (Kinsbourne, 1974) and that these children may not have developed the ability to verbally

Table 2. Mean Number of Correctly Reported Dichotic Consonant-Vowel Syllables by Group, Age Level, and Condition

	Listening Condition					
	Free Recall		Directed			
			Left		Right	
Subject Group/Age Level	Left	Right	Left	Right	Left	Right
Normal						
Younger						
M	10.56	13.31	11.38	13.69	10.94	14.19
SD	1.86	2.39	3.16	3.00	2.41	1.91
Older						
M	11.06	13.81	10.88	13.19	11.06	13.88
SD	1.48	2.51	1.36	1.94	2.08	2.42
Learning Disabled						
Younger						
M	9.56	13.63	12.44	9.13	6.56	19.81
SD	1.75	1.46	3.54	2.96	1.67	2.54
Older						
M	8.88	13.44	11.94	9.69	6.56	18.50
SD	2.73	3.76	3.19	3.32	3.20	5.06

Note: Age range for younger group = 7.42-10.41 years, for older group = 10.42-13.17 years. *Note:* From "Effects of Directed Attention on Cerebral Asymmetries in Normal and Learning-Disabled Children" by J. E. Obrzut, G. W. Hynd, A. Obrzut, and F. J. Pirozzolo, 1981, *Developmental Psychology, 17*, p. . Copyright 1981 by the American Psychological Association. Reprinted by permission.

mediate appropriate perceptual events. Therefore, these children perform as if the two cerebral hemispheres interact minimally in processing. This leads to interference from the nondominant hemisphere and difficulty in focusing attention as well as normal children. Hynd et al. (1979) have postulated that this occurs because of deficits in transcollosal functioning. Table 2 summarizes these results.

Within this framework, an additional issue warrants further consideration. The examination of attentional deficits within different subtypes of LD children may also be important. For example, Boder (1970) defined three distinct types of learning/reading disabled children. These groups, which she labeled dysphonetic, dyseidetic, and dysphonetic-dyseidetic (alexic), differ in their approach to reading and spelling tasks. The *dysphonetics* appear to have deficits in phonetic skills while *dyseidetics* can decipher words phonetically but have problems perceiving whole words and remembering nonphonetic sight words. The *alexic* reader is one who can neither remember sight words nor can he use phonetic skills in word analysis. Obrzut (1979) examined these independent groups on a dichotic listening task to see if they differed. His results indicated that dysphonetics (those with auditory-linguistic deficits) *and* visuo-spatial deficits) showed poorer auditory lateralization and greater deficits in attention than did dyseidetics (those with only visuo-spatial deficits). This suggests that while LD children as a group show overall attentional deficits, there may be significant differences within the population itself. This issue is very much overlooked in the literature.

Thus, the research examining perceptual linguistic asymmetries in LD children has yielded data indicating that this group is as well lateralized as their normal counterparts, but appear not to use appropriate attentional strategies in processing information. Also, in contrast to the theory of developing laterality (Orton, 1937, Lenneberg, 1967), no developmental trend in cerebral dominance for normal or LD children has been conclusively proven. Research has yielded very little evidence that there are any systematic changes in cerebral lateralization with age. There even exists evidence that these linguistic asymmetries can be documented in newborn infants (Molfese & Molfese, 1979). As shown in previous studies, the REA remains relatively consistent across age groups. The hypothesis that LD populations have deficits in their ability to attend selectively, as stated by Hynd and his colleagues (1979, 1983), appears to be a valid explanation for performance decrement in LD children.

To fully understand how deficient attentional mechanisms (which obviously play such a vital role in memory) reflect a neuropathological/neurodevelopmental etiology, one must first have some basic understanding as to how attention is conceptualized at a physiological level.

NEUROPHYSIOLOGICAL MECHANISMS OF ATTENTION AND ITS RELATION TO LINGUISTIC ASYMMETRIES

The study of attention has been both lauded and maligned in the course of the development of modern psychology. Early experimental psychologists, such as Wundt and Titchner extolled the virtues of the study of attention as a "major achievement" in experimental psychology (Parasuraman & Davies, 1984). James (1890) was a forerunner in introducing the concept of attention into psychology in his book *Principles of Psychology*. In it, he speaks of attention as a deliberate and active process and as having some limited capacity in dealing with incoming stimuli (James, 1890). Later, Titchner (1908) viewed attention as it affected consciousness, in that attention both determined consciousness and influenced consciousness.

Despite the extensive research on attention carried out by experimentalists such as Wundt and Titchner, the study of attention fell into disrepute as behavioral psychology became dominant during the first part of this century. Considering the strong emphasis placed on observable behavior and empirical measures, the idea of attention was seen as too vague, too mentalistic, and too dependent upon introspection to suit the stimulus response bound behavioral psychologists (Horton & Turnage, 1976). Behaviorists did not want to speculate on any processes intervening between stimulus and response, and attention was considered one of the "intervening variables" (Eysenck, 1982).

Attention was, therefore, all but ignored for close to three decades. Advances in neuroanatomy and neuropsychology coupled with the development of cognitive psychology laid a solid foundation for the re-emergence and recognized importance of the study of attention in psychology. In this regard, studies of selectivity and limited capacity will be briefly discussed.

Attempts to describe what attention is and how it is measured have traditionally served to confound the reader and even weaken the term in some respects. Although attention was an important feature in introspection, even introspective psychologists could not agree with one another on the basic theoretical knowledge pertaining to attention (Broadbent, 1958). It is of interest to note also that even Hebb, whose writings on attention equalled Broadbent in helping to resurrect attention theory, once defined attention as, "various properties of mind, undefinable and impossible to understand" (Hebb, 1949, p. 125).

Defining Attention—Its Physiological Basis

Definitions of attention vary in relation to one's perspective. Attention can be defined in terms of its physiological components (French, 1957; Hebb, 1949; Heilman & Valenstein, 1979; Luria, 1980; Moruzzi & Magoun, 1949), in terms of perception (James, 1890; Tichener, 1908), and in terms of selective filtering of incoming stimuli (Broadbent, 1958; Cherry, 1959; Deutsch & Deutsch, 1963; Kimura, 1967; Kinsbourne, 1970; Treisman, 1969). Understanding attention can be as diverse as the many schools of thought that have attempted to study and explain it. For instance, attention can be measured through altered neural firings (Hernandez-Peon & Haybarth, 1955; Hernandez-Peon, 1969) in a strictly neurophysiological sense. Attention can be measured psychologically as well, by examining how an organism orients themself for incoming stimuli (Pavlov, 1927), how they filter out relevant stimuli (Broadbent, 1957, 1958; Kimura, 1967; Treisman, 1969), and how they respond to stimuli they have processed (Deutsch & Deutsch, 1963).

According to James (1890, p. 381), attention was "the taking possession by the mind, in clear and vivid form, of one out of what seem several simultaneously possible objects or trains of thought." Attention can be defined as the selective aspect of perception and response (Treisman, 1969). It is the perceiving in relation to a task or goal, internally or externally motivated (Hale & Lewis, 1979). It is the conscious or unconscious focusing of one or more sense organs on some incoming stimuli, be it visual, auditory, tactile, olfaction, taste, or a combination thereof. Attention can also be described in terms of vigilance, which Mackworth (1957, p. 390) described as "a state of readiness to detect and respond to certain small changes occurring at random time intervals in the environment." In simple terms, attention can be measured as the level of awareness that an organism has toward his environment, the extent to which they know what is going on around them.

Attention, in its simplest terms, was described by Pavlov (1927) as merely a reflex action by an organism, in response to even the slightest change in the environment, such that the organism could "orient" itself appropriately toward that change. Still later work by biologists and physiologists helped to uncover the neurological basis of attention and arousal. The earliest of these pioneers, Moruzzi and Magoun (1949) discovered that stimulating the cortex of the brain was not sufficient to arouse the brain. In experiments using a cat, they found that stimulation to the reticular formation in the brain would wake the sleeping cat, where stimulation to the cortex area would not. Moruzzi and Magoun (1949) named this arousal unit the reticular activating system. Accordingly, the reticular activating system (RAS) serves as a general alarm to simply arouse the brain, not relay any specific messages (French, 1957). The RAS arouses the cortex so that incoming sensory stimuli can be perceived in the appropriate cortical region. French suggests that the RAS continues, "functioning to keep the individual in a conscious state . . . in the waking state the RAS plays a part, in combination with the cortex, in focusing attention and probably in many other mental processes" (pp. 56–59). The reticular activating system, in addition to its role in arousal, is responsible for filtering sensory input, for accepting what we need to perceive and rejecting what is irrelevant (French, 1957), and for monitoring and integrating neural signals.

The importance of the RAS is evident by examining its extensive neural connections. It extends from the pons and medulla through the thalamus and hypothalamus through the limbic system (Heilman & Valenstein, 1979) particularly the hippocampus (Mostofsky, 1970), and then diffuses many neural projections into portions of the frontal cortex (Luria, 1980). Through this network of neural projection fibers, the RAS, as stated before, serves to arouse the cortex and direct incoming stimuli toward the appropriate cortical area.

Research by Heilman and Valenstein (1979), working from an earlier model, examined the role of the corticolimbic-reticular loop in attention and arousal. This structure functions as a linking system in which the cortex analyzes incoming stimuli to determine its novelty and significance and the reticular formation then mediates the general level of arousal accordingly (Heilman & Valenstein, 1979). This research has served to provide evidence of a physiological mechanism for controlling attention.

Development of psychological theories for attention began primarily with the work of Broadbent (1958) in his postulation of the filter theory. With regard to attentional theories arising from Broadbent, the remaining discussion focuses on theories specific to selective attention. As defined by Horton and Turnage (1976), selective attention is the process of making a distinction between information that is attended to and that which is ignored at any moment.

Theories of Selective Attention

Broadbent's (1957, 1958) filter theory of attention stemmed from the work of Cherry (1959). Broadbent used a dichotic listening technique to examine the idea that some messages are received and processed while others are rejected. The mechanism that Broadbent (1958) describes in his theory is called a "filter," hence the name "filter theory." Broadbent postulated that when several messages are presented simultaneously, they are processed through the sensory channels and directed into a "selective filter" where certain messages are then channeled on to a higher processing area, while other messages are stored in a sensory "preperceptual" system. Messages held in the sensory buffer and not passed on are forgotten quickly before actually being processed. This theory fits well with the findings of Cherry (1959). The messages held in sensory buffer are analogous to the rejected messages and are dissipated before they are processed cognitively. The selective filter in Broadbent's (1958) theory serves as a perceptual "bottleneck" to prevent information overload in the perceptual system. Otherwise, we would be constantly bombarded with environmental stimuli and have no way to sort out what is relevant and what is not.

Broadbent's (1957, 1958) filter theory presumes an all-or-none operation in the filter. His theory assumes that one message is attended to and one message is rejected, so that no content of the rejected message would be noticed. Moray (1959) found that while the rejected message is usually ignored, if pertinent information, such as the subject's name, is presented within that message, then the message can be noticed. Additional evidence that the rejected message is not completely ignored was presented by Treisman (1964). She proposed that the information in the rejected message was not completely ignored and forgotten, but attenuated. She postulated that the selective filter is not always at a preperceptual level but can fluctuate depending on the message.

Treisman's (1964) theory proposes that recognition of sensory inputs is accomplished through a hierarchy of analyses based on physical cues, syllabic patterns, words, and word meanings. Threshold levels for deciding if a message will be attended to are set according to the significance of the message. Important messages such as one's name or "help!" may have a lower threshold and will be attended to, no matter if they are contained in a rejected message. Treisman (1964) suggested that all incoming information is processed to a certain degree but is passed on through the filter with regard to its particular significance at the time.

Deutsch and Deutsch (1963) approached the selection problem from a different viewpoint. They examined the bottleneck as it occurs when selecting a response. Deutsch and Deutsch believed that all incoming stimuli receive perceptual analysis and that a "message will reach the same perceptual and discriminatory mechanisms whether attention is paid to it or not" (p. 83). They asserted that incoming signals were processed according to importance, and that only the most important signals coming in will be acted on. Further, Deutsch, and Deutsch (1963) proposed that the importance of incoming stimuli set fluctuating "levels" and that these levels correlate with states of arousal. This proposal is relevant to the findings in which particularly salient stimuli are attended to in otherwise ignored messages. The problem with this theory, however, is that it does not address the presenting problem of some kind of pre-screening of incoming stimuli.

As can be seen with regard to selective attention, information can be filtered and then the rejected message is forgotten or the rejected message can be only weakened and stored for later processing. Or, all information can be processed and then responses selected. Regarding the notion of "rejected" and "attended" messages within the auditory context, it is helpful to examine some theories of how input travels through the sensory channels and arrives in the processing area.

Selective Auditory Attention and Linguistic Asymmetries

As noted previously, Kimura (1967) proposed an anatomical explanation for perceptual asymmetries in the auditory modality. Since language was presumed to be controlled in the left hemisphere (Wada & Rasmussen, 1960), the left hemisphere exerted functional dominance in verbal materials. Through dichotic listening tasks, Kimura was able to report that subjects reported information received in the right ear more accurately than information received in the left ear. Kimura (1967) contended that although each ear has connections with the auditory receiving area in each hemisphere, the pathways "connecting the ears to their opposite hemispheres are apparently more effective than the ipsilateral pathways" (p. 164). In selective attention, it may be these stronger correlational stimuli that become the attended messages. The contralateral pathways are capable of "occluding impulses arriving along the ipsilateral pathways" (Kimura, 1967), therefore, weakening the message before they reach the filter area.

Kinsbourne (1970) applied an attentional model to support and explain Kimura's (1967) contentions. He proposed that each hemisphere is dominant for interpretation of different stimuli but that presentation of stimuli activates the appropriate hemisphere and thus biases attention toward the contralateral side of space. If attention is biased to one side, there is a "greater readiness of the perceptual mechanism to respond to material in the attended location" while stimuli presented in the non-dominant hemisphere is suppressed. This theory uses Kimura's anatomical model in an exploration of selective attention. Kinsbourne's contention serves as a foundation for interpreting dichotic listening studies in which the majority of children have shown a significant right-ear superiority (Kimura, 1963; Hynd et al., 1983).

Levels of Processing and Selective Linguistic Asymmetries

In the context of a neurophysiologically-based but psychologically mediated mechanism for selective attention, the notion of levels of processing becomes important. If in fact LD children are similar to their normal counterparts in cerebral linguistic asymmetrical organization as suggested by Hynd et al. (1983), then it makes some conceptual sense that if the deficit represents the mediation or filtering of linguistic processing, that progressively poorer performance according to processing level will be manifested by LD children. As Belmore (1980) suggested:

> A comparison of ear asymmetries for verbal material processed at different levels of linguistic analysis would provide valuable information about the nature of functional asymmetries for human language. If the left hemispheric superiority is limited to the level of speech perception, any phonetically encoded signal which is understood as speech should produce an REA, and this REA should be relatively insensitive to variations in the meaningfulness of initial processing. If, however, the left hemisphere is also specialized for more complex aspects of language use, then variations in the type of linguistic processing might be expected to produce systematic differences in the nature or the magnitude of the REA. (p. 658)

Results of previous studies (Cermak, 1983; Obrzut, Obrzut, Bryden, & Bartels, 1985) indicated that LD children's information-processing ability was impaired relative to that of their normal counterparts. Obrzut et al. (1985) suggested that children with learning disabilities may have "deficiencies of processor capacity" within the language areas of the left hemisphere. This suggests that while they may be impaired due to attentional deficits, they may have inadequate processing abilities as well. Swanson and Obrzut (1985) found that lateral asymmetries only existed at low levels of linguistic encoding between LD and normal children. More recently, however, Bowen, Hynd, and Wisenbaker (in press) documented that not only do the deficiencies discussed here with LD youngsters fail to disappear in adulthood, but that the greater the discriminate load on the linguistic processor, the greater the deficit in performance evidenced by them as compared to the normal group. This result was especially noted in the directed attentional paradigms as discussed earlier.

The notion that linguistic asymmetries reflect regulated attentional mechanisms in normal children is important to those who contend that learning disabilities reflect deficient, not delayed, lateralized linguistic processing modes (e.g., Hynd et al., 1983). If in fact children with learning disabilities have poorly regulated but highly selective attentional mechanisms, then the superior ability of these children to shift ear effects can be explained (Obrzut et al., 1981). They may possess selective attention strategies but have difficulty in applying them appropriately especially when more difficult levels of processing are required. In large part, these children behave neuropsychologically as if they were suffering a disconnection syndrome where normally organized functional systems existed but were operating inefficiently due to neurodevelopmental deficits. If the neuropathological basis of these deficiencies could be demonstrated then support would be generated for the neurological basis of the poorly regulated attentional mechanisms discussed here and support provided for the idea that LD children will not outgrow their deficiencies. They may well improve with time and maturation in terms of their attentional and memory capabilities due to compensation, but if neuroanatomical deficits can be documented, then changes due to "neurological maturation" or some "catch-up" phenomena seems unlikely at best.

NEUROPATHOLOGICAL BASIS OF LEARNING DISABILITIES

With specific regard to severe reading disorders or dyslexia, Critchley (1964) suggested that should autopsies be conducted on LD children's brains, no abnormality would be found. Despite evidence to the contrary (e.g., Drake, 1968; Galaburda & Eidelberg, 1982; Galaburda & Kemper, 1979), there are those who continue to argue strongly that learning disabilities have nothing to do with neurological pathology (e.g., Ross, 1976; Smith, 1982).

Autopsy Findings in Children with Learning Disabilities

Originally conceived of as having a neuropathological etiology (e.g., Bastian, 1898), the first autopsy of a LD child's brain yielded positive findings. Consistent with Bastian's (1898) and Hinshelwood's (1900; 1902) theories as well as that of Luria (1980) in which the region of the angular gyrus was implicated, Drake (1968) found an abnormal convolutional pattern in the parietal lobes bilaterally involving the region of the angular gyrus. Also, the associated area of the corpus callosum was thinned. These deficits, which are consistent with the disruption of a widespread functional neurolinguistically-based system for reading (see Figure 2) (Hynd & Hynd, 1984, 1985), are due not to brain damage but rather to deviant neuroanatomical development.

Considering that the results of over 600 autopsies on the brains of mentally retarded persons exist in the literature (e.g., Crome, 1960; Freytag & Lindenberg, 1967), it is remarkable that after Drake's report in 1968 that 11 years passed before a second more detailed study appeared. Reflecting Crome's (1960) prediction that, "it seems likely that future refinements in techniques will raise to the surface other, still submerged anomalies" (p. 903), Galaburda and Kemper (1979) reported on the cytoarchitectonic abnormalities in a dyslexic adult. They found focal dysplasias including ectopic cortex, disordered cortical layering and polymicrogyria scattered throughout the left cerebral hemisphere; involving also the thalamus (Galaburda & Eidelberg, 1982). The continued work of Gal-

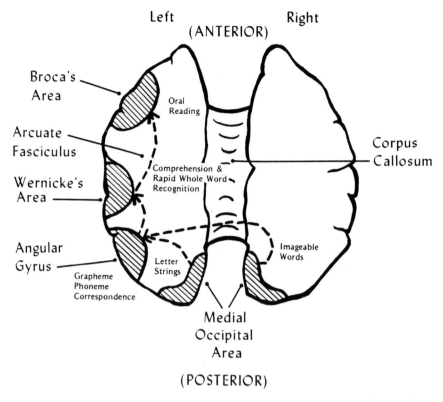

Figure 2. The brain as viewed in horizontal section. The major pathways
and cortical regions thought to be involved in reading are depicted.
Neurolinguistic processes important in reading are also noted.

Note: From "Dyslexia: Neuroanatomical/Neurolinguistic Perspectives" by G. W. Hynd and C. R. Hynd,
1984, *Reading Research Quarterly, 19.* Copyright 1984 by the International Reading Association,
Inc. Reprinted by permission.

aburda and his colleagues (e.g., Galaburda & Mesulam, 1983; Galaburda,
Sherman, Rosen, Aboitiz, & Geschwind, 1985) is extremely important in
continuing to articulate the neuropathology of learning disabilities (see
Figure 3). While a variety of prenatal factors may be implicated in the
occurrence of neurodevelopmental abnormalities in the brains of these
children and adults (see Hynd & Willis, in press for a review), it should
be clear that the evidence as to the neuropathological basis of learning
disabilities once hypothesized to not exist by Critchley (1964), does in
fact exist.

Relationship to Attention and Memory Deficits

The central question to be addressed in this context is how do these
neurodevelopmental abnormalities produce or correlate to attentional

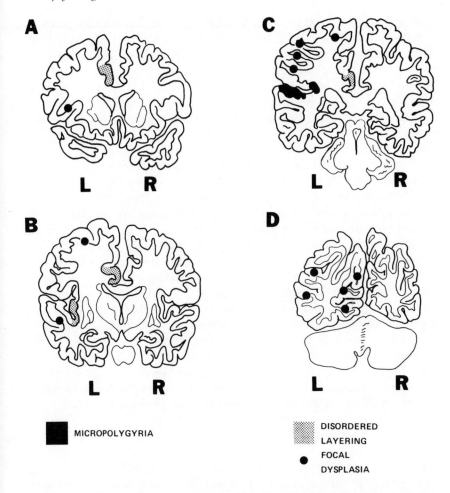

Figure 3. The brain at several coronal levels. Cross-hatching represents
areas of mild cortical dysplasia in the left cingulate gyrus, rostral in-
sula, and focally throughout the left hemisphere. Note the increased
frequency of focal lesions posteriorly. Area in black represents the
polymicrogyria.

Note: From "Cytoarchitectonic Abnormalities in Developmental Dyslexia: A Case Study" by A. M.
Galaburda and T. L. Kemper, 1979, *Annals of Neurology, 6.* Copyright 1979 by Little, Brown
and Company. Reprinted by permission.

processes so vital to memory? The data from the previously reviewed
studies on linguistic asymmetries may help answer this question.

First of all, by referring back to Figure 2 it can be seen that the hypothesized functional system involved in reading, as an example, involves
both cerebral hemispheres, but primarily the left cerebral hemisphere.
Data from the dichotic studies indicates that for the LD child, language

is lateralized to the left cerebral hemisphere as it is in the vast majority of normals (Hynd et al., 1983). The autopsy studies by Galaburda et al. (1985) indicate that the neurodevelopmental abnormalities found typically involve the left cerebral hemisphere, where language is presumably localized. Since the hypothesized functional system involved in reading (Hynd & Hynd, 1985) is so widespread, involving primarily the left cerebral hemisphere, it can be understood how nearly any neurodevelopmental anomaly localized to the left hemisphere could disrupt the optimal functioning of the cortex necessary for attention on linguistic tasks such as in fluent reading. This conceptualization would not only account for the considerable variability in strengths and weakness among these children on psychological tests but would, according to Kinsbourne's (1970) hypothesis regarding hemispheric attentional mechanisms, account for the disconnection syndrome earlier proposed by Hynd et al. (1979, 1983) where the attentional abilities or "filters" (Broadbent, 1958) of the two hemispheres operate relatively independently. Important in this context is the presumption that the subtle neurodevelopmental anomalies disrupt the normal patterns of cerebral hemispheric functioning but are not sufficient to induce patterns of cerebral reorganization. Also, important is the notion that the impaired linguistic system in LD children never matures sufficiently to allow for the more fixed pattern of left hemispheric dominance over the right on perceptual tasks as suggested for normals by Kinsbourne (1974). Thus, for LD children the hemispheric mechanisms of attention important in directing arousal contralaterally in space never develop normally where they are regulated and used appropriately in an integrated fashion. Thus, they may perform on attentional and memory tasks variably depending on whether or not stimuli-appropriate attentional mechanisms or "filters" are brought into focus.

The preceding two paragraphs are speculation at this point and these ideas need to be further examined, especially as they relate to attentional shifting interactions with levels of information processing. It may well be that the most important research along these lines will focus on the interactions that may occur between experimenter manipulated intra-individual biases in attention, levels of linguistic processing, and categorically variable recall conditions among subtypes of LD children.

CONCLUSIONS

The concept of learning disabilities has evolved through many permutations variously referred to as dyscalculia, congenital word blindness, amnesia, visualis verbalis, dyslexia (Pirozzolo, 1979) and most recently a much broader and all inclusive term of *learning disabilities*. From the earliest of accounts there has been a presumption that learning disabilities have a neurological etiology. Based on rapidly accumulating evidence, the efforts of those who criticize the conceptualization of the neurological basis of learning disabilities should turn to articulating even further a standardized neuropsychologically-based nosology of subtypes. This is one of the most urgent of needs.

Important as a foundation for such an effort would be the recognition that there exists a potentially tremendous diversity of neurodevelopmental anomalities that could produce learning disabilities (Hynd & Willis, in press) and that the neuropsychological profiles of the various subtypes will be equally as diverse. Consequently, researchers and clinicians should take heart at the rich variability in the abilities and disabilities of LD children as documented in the other chapters of this volume. Such diversity should argue strongly that not fewer conceptualizations as to brain-behavior relations are needed but many more interactive ones which at their core focus on expanding our notions of the attentional and memory mechanisms so important to all of our behavior.

REFERENCES

Ayres, A. J. (1977). Dichotic listening performance in learning-disabled children. *American Journal of Occupational Therapy, 31,* 441–446.

Bastian, H. C. (1898). *Aphasia and other speech defects.* London: H. K. Lewis.

Belmore, S. M. (1980). Depth of processing and ear differences in memory for sentences. *Neuropsychologia, 18,* 657–663.

Bever, T. G. (1971). The nature of cerebral dominance in speech behavior of the child and adult. In R. Huxley & E. Ingram (Eds.), *Language acquisition: Models and methods* (pp. 231–261). Orlando, FL: Academic Press.

Boder, E. (1970). Developmental dyslexia: A new diagnostic approach based on the identification of three subtypes. *Journal of School Health, 40,* 289–290.

Bowen, S., Hynd, G. W., & Wisenbaker, J. (1986). *Cerebral lateralization, dichotic listening, and selective attention in adults with learning disabilities.* Manuscript submitted for publication.

Broadbent, D. E. (1957). A mechanical model for human attention and immediate memory. *Psychological Review, 64,* 205–215.

Broadbent, D. E. (1958). *Perception and communication.* New York: Pergamon.

Broca, P. (1861). Nouvelle observation d'aphemie produite par unelesion de la muite postorieure des deuxieme et troisieme circonvolutions frontales. *Bulletin de la Society Anatomique de Paris, 36,* 398–407.

Bryden, M. P., & Allard, F. (1978). Dichotic listening and the development of linguistic processes. In M. Kinsbourne (Ed.), *Asymmetrical function of the brain* (pp. 285–312). New York: Cambridge University Press.

Caplan, P. J., & Kinsbourne, M. (1976). Baby drops the rattle: Asymmetry of duration of grasp by infants. *Child Development, 47,* 532–534.

Cermak, L. L. (1983). Information processing deficits in children with learning disabilities. *Journal of Learning Disabilities, 16,* 599–605.

Cherry, E. C. (1959). Some experiments on the cognition of speech with one and with two ears. *Journal of the Acoustical Society of America, 25,* 975–979.

Critchley, M. (1964). *Developmental dyslexia.* London: Heinemann.

Critchley, M. (1970). *The dyslexic child.* London: Heinemann.

Crome, L. (1960). The brain in mental retardation. *British Medical Journal, 1,* 897–904.

Deutsch, J. A., & Deutsch, D. (1963). Attention: Some theoretical considerations. *Psychological Review, 70,* 80–90.

Drake, W. E. (1968). Clinical and pathological findings in a child with a developmental learning disability. *Journal of Learning Disabilities, 1,* 486–502.

Elbert, J. C., Culbertson, J. L., Gerrity, K. M., Guthrie, L. J., & Bayles, R. (1985). *Neuropsychological and electrophysiological follow-up of children surviving acute lymphocytic leukemia.* Paper presented at the annual meeting of the International Neuropsychological Society, San Diego.

Eysenck, M. W. (1982). *Attention and arousal: Cognition and performance.* New York: Springer-Verlag.

Federal Register (Thursday, 29 December 1977). Washington, DC. (65082–65085). In C. R. Smith (1983), *Learning disabilities: The interaction of learner, task and setting.* Boston: Little, Brown.

French, J. D. (1957). The reticular formation. *Scientific American, 196,* 54–60.

Freytag, E., & Lindenberg, R. (1967). Neuropathologic findings in patients of a hospital for the mentally deficient. A study of 359 cases. *Johns Hopkins Medical Journal, 121,* 379–392.

Gaddes, W. H. (1980). *Learning disabilities and brain function.* New York: Springer-Verlag.

Galaburda, A. M., & Eidelberg, D. (1982). Symmetry and asymmetry in the human posterior thalamus: II. Thalamic lesions in a case of developmental dyslexia. *Archives of Neurology, 39,* 333–336.

Galaburda, A. M., & Kemper, T. L. (1979). Cytoarchitectonic abnormalities in developmental dyslexia: A case study. *Annals of Neurology, 6,* 94–100.

Galaburda, A. M., & Mesulam, M. M. (1983). Neuroanatomical aspects of cerebral localization. In A. Kertesz (Ed.), *Localization in neuropsychology* (pp. 21–58). Orlando, FL: Academic Press.

Galaburda, A. M., Sherman, G. F., Rosen, G. D., Aboitiz, F., & Geschwind, N. (1985). Developmental dyslexia: Four consecutive patients with cortical anomalies. *Annals of Neurology, 18,* 222–233.

Goff, J. R. (1982). *Memory deficits and distractability in survivors of childhood leukemia.* Paper presented at the annual meeting of the American Psychological Association.

Hammill, D. D., Leigh, J. E., McNutt, G., & Larsen, S. C. (1981). A new definition of learning disabilities. *Learning Disabilities Quarterly, 4,* 336–342.

Hebb, D. O. (1949). *The organization of behavior.* New York: Wiley.

Heilman, K. M., & Valenstein, E. (1979). *Clinical neuropsychology.* New York: Oxford University Press.

Hernandez-Peon, R. (1964). Attention, sleep, motivation, and behavior. In R. C. Heath (Ed.), *The role of pleasure in behavior* (pp. 195–217). New York: Harper and Row.

Hernandez-Peon, R., & Hagbarth, K. E. (1955). Interaction between afferent and cortically induced reticular responses. *Journal of Neurophysiology, 18,* 44–45.

Hinshelwood, J. (1895). Word-blindness and visual memory. *Lancet, 2,* 1564–1570.

Hinshelwood, J. (1900). Congenital word-blindness. *Lancet, 1,* 1506–1508.

Hinshelwood, J. (1902). Congenital word-blindness, with reports of two cases. *Ophthalmic Review, 21,* 91–99.

Horton, D. L., & Turnage, T. W. (1976). *Human learning*. Englewood Cliffs, NJ: Prentice-Hall.

Horwood, S. P., Boyle, M. H., Torrance, G. W., & Sinclair, J. C. (1982). Mortality and morbidity of 500-to 1,499-gram birth weight infants liveborn to residents of a defined geographic region before and after neonatal intensive care. *Pediatrics, 69*, 613–620.

Hynd, G. W. (1978). *An investigation of the developmental relationship between memory attribute preference and cerebral dominance*. Unpublished doctoral dissertation, University of Northern Colorado.

Hynd, G. W., & Cohen, M. (1983). *Dyslexia: Neuropsychological theory, research and clinical differentiation*. Orlando, FL: Grune & Stratton.

Hynd, G. W., Cohen, M., Obrzut, J. E. (1983). Dichotic consonant-vowel (CV) testing in the diagnosis of learning disabilities in children. *Ear and Hearing, 4*, 283–286.

Hynd, G. W., & Hynd, C. R. (1984). Dyslexia: Neuroanatomical/neurolinguistic perspectives. *Reading Research Quarterly, 19*, 482–498.

Hynd, C. R., & Hynd, G. W. (1985). *Regional cerebral blood flow in developmental dyslexia*. Paper presented at the annual meeting of the International Reading Association, New Orleans.

Hynd, G. W., & Obrzut, J. E. (Eds.) (1981). *Neuropsychological assessment and the school-age child: Issues and procedures*. Orlando, FL: Grune & Stratton.

Hynd, G. W., Obrzut, J. E., Weed, W., & Hynd, C. R. (1979). Development of cerebral dominance: Dichotic listening asymmetry in normal and learning disabled children. *Journal of Experimental Child Psychology, 28*, 445–454.

Hynd, G. W., & Willis, W. G. (in press). *Pediatric neuropsychology*. Orlando, FL: Grune & Stratton.

James, W. (1890). *The principles of psychology* (2 vols.). New York: Holt.

Kimura, D. (1961). Cerebral dominance and the perception of verbal stimuli. *Canadian Journal of Psychology, 15*, 166–171.

Kimura, D. (1963). Speech lateralization in young children as determined by an auditory test. *Journal of Comparative Physiological Psychology, 56*, 899–902.

Kimura, D. (1967). Functional asymmetry of the brain in dichotic listening. *Cortex, 3*, 163–178.

Kinsbourne, M. (1970). The cerebral basis of lateral asymmetries in attention. *Acta Psychologica, 33*, 193–201.

Kinsbourne, M. (1974). Mechanisms of hemispheric interaction in man. In E. M. Kinsbourne & W. L. Smith (Eds.), *Hemispheric disconnection and cerebral function*. Springfield, IL: Charles C Thomas.

Kinsbourne, M. (1983). Models of learning disability. *Topics in Learning and Learning Disabilities, 3*, 1–13.

Kinsbourne, M., & Caplan, D. (1979). *Children's learning and attention problems*. Boston: Little, Brown.

Kinsbourne, M., & Hiscock, M. (1977). Does cerebral dominance develop? In S. J. Segalowitz & L. A. Gruber (Eds.), *Language development and neurological theory*. Orlando, FL: Academic Press.

Kinsbourne, M., & Hiscock, M. (1978). Cerebral lateralization and cognitive development. In M. Grady & E. Luecke (Eds.), *Education and the brain* (Vol. 108, pp. 10–12). Chicago: University of Chicago Press.

Kirk, S. A. (1962). *Educating exceptional children*. Boston: Houghton Mifflin.

Kirk, S. A., & Kirk, W. D. (1983). On defining learning disabilities. *Journal of Learning Disabilities, 16*, 20–21.

Knights, R. M., & Bakker, D. J. (Eds.) (1976). *The neuropsychology of learning disorders*. Baltimore: University Park Press.

Lenneberg, E. H. (1967). *Biological foundations of language.* New York: Wiley.

Luria, A. R. (1980). *Higher cortical functions in man* (2nd ed.). New York: Basic Books.

Mackworth, N. H. (1957). Some factors affecting vigilance. *Advancements in Science, 53,* 389–393.

Massari, D. (1982). *Late neuropsychological effects in children with ALL.* Paper presented at the annual meeting of the American Psychological Association.

McLeod, J. (1983). Learning disability is for educators. *Journal of Learning Disabilities, 16,* 23–24.

McLoughlin, J. A., & Netick, A. (1983). Defining learning disabilities: A new and cooperative direction. *Journal of Learning Disabilities, 16,* 21–23.

Molfese, D. C., & Molfese, V. J. (1979). Hemisphere and stimulus differences as reflected in the cortical responses of newborn infants to speech stimulus. *Developmental Psychology, 15,* 505–511.

Moray, N. (1959). Attention in dichotic listening: Affective cues and the influence of instructions. *Quarterly Journal of Experimental Psychology, 11,* 56–60.

Moruzzi, G., & Magoun, H. W. (1949). Brain stem reticular formation and activation of the EEG. *Electroencephalography and Clinical Neuropsychology, 1,* 455–473.

Mostofsky, D. I. (1970). *Attention: Contemporary theory and analysis.* New York: Appleton-Century-Crofts.

Nickel, R. E., Bennett, F. C., & Lamson, F. N. (1982). School performance of children with birthweights of 1,000 g or less. *American Journal of Diseases of Children, 136,* 105–110.

Obrzut, J. E. (1979). Dichotic listening and bisensory memory skills in qualitatively diverse dyslexic readers. *Journal of Learning Disabilities, 12,* 24–33.

Obrzut, J. E., & Hynd, G. W. (1981). Cognitive development and cerebral lateralization in children with learning disabilities. *International Journal of Neuroscience, 14,* 139–145.

Obrzut, J., Hynd, G. W., Obrzut, A., & Leitgeb, J. L. (1980). Time sharing and dichotic listening asymmetry in normal and learning-disabled children. *Brain and Language, 11,* 181–194.

Obrzut, J. E., Hynd, G. W., Obrzut, A., & Pirozzolo, F. J. (1981). Effects of directed attention on cerebral asymmetries in normal and learning-disabled children. *Developmental Psychology, 17,* 118–125.

Obrzut, J. E., Obrzut, A., Bryden, M. P., & Bartels, S. G. (1985). Information processing and speech lateralization in learning-disabled children. *Brain and Language, 25,* 87–101.

Orton, S. T. (1928). Specific reading disability—strephosymbolia. *Journal of the American Medical Association, 90,* 1095–1099.

Orton, S. T. (1937). *Reading, writing, and speech problems in children.* New York: Norton.

Parasuraman, R., & Davies, D. R. (1984). *Varieties of attention.* Orlando, FL: Academic Press.

Pavlov, I. P. (1927). *Conditioned reflexes.* Oxford: Clarendon Press.

Pirozzolo, F. J. (1979). *The neuropsychology of developmental reading disorders.* New York: Praeger Press.

Ross, A. O. (1976). *Psychological aspects of learning disabilities and reading disorders.* New York: McGraw-Hill.

Sabatino, D. A. (1983). The house that Jack built. *Journal of Learning Disabilities, 16,* 26–27.

Satz, P., Rardin, D., & Ross, J. (1971). An evaluation of a theory of specific developmental dyslexia. *Child Development, 42,* 2009–2021.

Satz, P., & Sparrow, S. (1970). Specific developmental dyslexia: A theoretical formulation. In D. J. Bakker & P. Satz (Eds.), *Specific reading disability: Advances in theory and method* (pp. 17–39). Rotterdam: Rotterdam University Press.

Schulman-Galambos, C. (1977). Dichotic listening performance in elementary and college students. *Neuropsychologia, 15,* 577–584.

Smith, C. R. (1983). *Learning disabilities: The interaction of learner, task, and setting.* Boston: Little, Brown.

Smith, F. (1982). *Understanding reading* (3rd ed.). New York: Rinehart & Winston.

Sommers, R. K., & Taylor, M. L. (1972). Cerebral speech dominance in language-disordered and normal children. *Cortex, 8,* 224–232.

Swanson, H. L., & Obrzut, J. E. (1985). Learning disabled reader's recall as a function of distinctive encoding, hemispheric, processing and mode of processing. *Journal of Learning Disabilities, 18,* 409–418.

Titchener, E. B. (1908). *Lectures on the elementary psychology of feeling and attention.* New York: Macmillan.

Treisman, A. M. (1964). Monitoring and storage of irrelevant messages in selective attention. *Journal of Verbal Learning and Verbal Behavior, 3,* 449–459.

Treisman, A. M. (1969). The effect of irrelevant material on the efficiency of selective listening. *American Journal of Psychology, 77,* 533–545.

Ullman, D. G. (1977). Children's lateral preference patterns: Frequency and relationships with achievement and intelligence. *Journal of School Psychology, 15,* 36–43.

Wada, J. A., & Rasmussen, N. J. (1960). Intracarotid injection of sodium amytal for the lateralization of cerebral speech dominance. *Journal of Neurosurgery, 17,* 266–282.

PHONOLOGY AND THE PROBLEMS OF LEARNING TO READ AND WRITE

Isabelle Y. Liberman and Donald Shankweiler

ABSTRACT

Learning to read and write depends on abilities that are language-related but that go beyond the ordinary abilities required for speaking and listening. Research has shown that the success of learners, whether they are children or adults, is related to the degree to which they are aware of the underlying phonological structure of words. Poor readers are often unable to segment words into their phonological constituents and may have other phonological deficiencies as well. Their difficulties in naming objects and in comprehending sentences, for example, may also stem from a basic problem in the phonological domain.

Memory and Learning Disabilities
Advances in Learning and Behavioral Disabilities, Suppl. 2, pages 203–224.
Copyright © 1987 by JAI Press Inc.
All rights of reproduction in any form reserved.
ISBN: 0-89232-836-3

At the start of formal instruction in reading, the child or adult can speak and understand many words and uncountably many more sentences. Experience tells us, however, that while such command of the language may be necessary for reading, it is not sufficient. But why not? Surely, we must answer that question if we are to understand, and take appropriate action about, the difficulties that so often attend the development of literacy.

Broadly speaking, there are two sets of hypotheses about where the difficulties might lie. One set may be categorized generally as nonlanguage related. Many hypotheses of that kind have been advanced, but perhaps the most widely held (by many clinicans and the lay public, at least) proposes that children who fail have visual perceptual derangements in which they see letters or words wholly or partially backwards. Since the printed word is conveyed to the reader visually, the possibility of some visual defect in the handicapped individual must, of course, be considered. However, we know from the extensive research efforts of many investigators over the years (see Stanovich, 1982, and Vellutino, 1979, for reviews of the evidence) that difficulties in reading are not commonly attributable to perceptual derangements.

Our own research and that of others in the field have persuaded us that learning to read and write depends in large part on special language-related skills that go beyond the primary abilities required in producing and understanding speech. But where in language do those skills lie? Early in our research we guessed that many, perhaps most, are in the phonological domain (Liberman, 1971, 1973), and so we put our attention there. For several reasons, that seemed a plausible guess and, therefore, the right place to start: first, because an alphabetic orthography—the kind we must, as a practical matter, be concerned with—represents the phonology, however approximately; second, because the smooth running of the "higher" processes of syntax and semantics presumably depends, at the very least, on the existence of a proper representation in the "lower" domain of phonology (see Liberman, 1983; Liberman, Shankweiler, Liberman, Fowler, & Fischer, 1977, for a discussion of these points). The results of research have, we think, justified our assumptions, providing evidence that characteristics of phonological processing do, indeed, underlie some of the difficulties that poor readers and spellers have. Our aim in this paper is to describe those difficulties and present some of the evidence.

PHONOLOGY AND READING THE WORD

To see what phonology has to do with reading, we must first remind ourselves of what it has to do with language. Perhaps the best way to do that is to imagine what language would be like if there were no phonology. In that case, each word in the language would have to be represented by a signal (for example, a sound) that differed holistically from the signals for all other words. The obvious consequence would be that the number of words could be no larger than the number of holistically different signals a person can efficiently produce and perceive. Of course, we do not know precisely what that number is, but surely it must be small (especially in the case of speech) by comparison with the tens or even hundreds of thousands of words that a language commonly comprises. What a phonology does for us, then, is to provide a basis for constructing a large and expandable set of words (all the words that ever were, are, and will be) out of two or three dozen signal elements. These signal elements, often called phonemes, are themselves represented (though only after complex transformations) by the sounds of speech.

All this is to say that phonology is real and not invented by linguists, and, more important, that, whatever else they may be, words are always phonological structures. No matter that the meaning of a word, or its grammatical status, is ambiguous, unknown, or subject to dispute; it is always a string of abstract phonological elements, and, within quite narrow limits, all speakers of the language are in close, if only tacit, agreement about the form of that string. It follows, then, that to have perceived or produced a word, however that may be done, is to have engaged a phonological structure. To misperceive or misproduce a word is to have engaged the wrong phonological structure. We take all of that as given by the very nature of language, as distinguished from such other forms of communication like, for example, pictures.

But why, then, should reading words be difficult in an alphabetic orthography, given that such a transcription represents, if only approximately, the phonological structure that the reader must grasp; and what, as a practical matter, can the teacher do about it? We and our colleagues have offered details in earlier papers (Liberman, 1971, 1973, 1983; Liberman, Liberman, Mattingly, & Shankweiler, 1980a; Liberman, Shankweiler, Camp, Blachman, & Werfelman, 1980). Here, it is only appropriate to summarize the argument.

To understand the problem one faces when required to read a word, we must first consider, if only briefly, how the word is perceived when spoken. As we said, the word is formed by a phonological structure, so when the word is perceived, it is this structure that is accessed. But the speaker of the word did not produce the phonological units one at a time, each in its turn, that is, did not spell the word out aloud. Rather, the speaker "coarticulated" the phonological units (i.e., assigned the consonant we know as 'b,' for example, to the lips, and the vowel we know as 'a,' for example, to a shaping of the tongue, and then produced the two at pretty much the same time). The advantageous result of such coarticulation is that speech proceeds at a satisfactory pace (have you ever tried to understand speech when it was spelled to you, letter by painful letter?), but a further result, and a less advantageous one for the would-be reader, is that there is now, inevitably, no direct correspondence in segmentation between the underlying phonological structure and the sound. Thus, though the word "drag" has four phonological units and, correspondingly, four letters, it has only one pulse of sound, the four elements of the underlying phonological structure having been thoroughly overlapped and merged. How, then, do listeners recover the discrete units of the phonological structure from the seamless sound, thereby making contact with the word as it must be stored in their lexicons?

The long and comprehensive answer has been provided in other papers from our laboratory (see in particular A. M. Liberman, Cooper, Shankweiler, & Studdert-Kennedy, 1967; A. M. Liberman & Mattingly, 1985; A. M. Liberman & Studdert-Kennedy, 1978). The short and, for our purposes, sufficient answer is that the phonological segments are recovered from the sound by processes that are deeply built into the aspect of our biology that makes us capable of language. This is to say that in listening to speech, the processes by which we perceive the phonological structure conveyed by speech go on automatically, below the level of conscious awareness. In listening to speech, we are no more consciously aware of the processes by which we arrive at the word than we are consciously aware in vision of the way we use binocular disparity to perceive the relative distance of objects in our field of view.

But reading is different in that it is, in some significant measure, a secondary, less natural, use of language—part discovery, part invention. It follows, then, that even though its processes must at some point make contact with those of the natural and primary system, special skills are required if the proper contact is to be made. We take the point of that contact to be the word, which is, of course, represented in the print by a transcription of the phonological structure. But this transcription will make sense to the child only if he or she understands that it has the same number of units as the word. Only then will the relation between the print and the word be apparent.

Thus, readers can understand, and properly take advantage of the fact, that the printed word *drag* has four letters, only if they are aware that the spoken word "drag," with which they are presumably already quite familiar, is divisible into four segments. They will probably not know that spontaneously, because, as we have said, the relevant processes of speech perception, which they already command, are automatic and unconscious. And it may be somewhat difficult to teach them what they need to know because, given the overlap of phonological information that characterizes the spoken word, there is no way to produce the consonant segments in isolation. The teacher can try, of course, to "sound out" the word, but in so doing will necessarily produce a nonsense word comprising four syllables, "duhruhahguh." Such instruction may be better than none at all, but it may not help the child understand why it makes sense to represent the meaningful monosyllable "drag" with four letters. In the next sections, we offer some of the evidence which shows that novice readers do indeed find it hard to see why, and, further, that their difficulty in this regard is associated with poor reading ability.

Awareness of Basic Phonological Structure

We know that the child's awareness of phonological structure does not happen all at once, but develops gradually over a period of years. Some 12 years ago, we began to examine developmental trends in phonological awareness by testing the ability of young children to segment words into their constituent elements (Liberman, Shankweiler, Fischer, & Carter, 1974). We found that normal preschool children performed rather poorly. We learned, however, as we had suspected, that of the two types of sublexical phonological units, syllables and phonemes, the phonemes presented the greater difficulty. None of the 4 year olds whom we tested could accurately count the number of phonemes in familiar monosyllabic words, though about half managed an accurate count of syllables in multisyllabic words. At the age of 5 years, a similar pattern emerged: Over half succeeded in the syllable task but less than a fifth could achieve phoneme counting. Only 10% failed the syllable counting task at the end of the first school year, whereas 30% were still failing phoneme counting.

It was clear from these results that awareness of phoneme segments is harder to achieve than awareness of syllable segments, and develops later, if at all. More relevant to our present purposes, it was also apparent that a large number of children may not have attained either level of understanding of linguistic structure (phoneme or syllable) even at the end of a full year in school. We turn now to the evidence that awareness of linguistic structure, which so many children lack, may be important for the acquisition of reading and spelling.

Awareness of Phonological Structure and Literacy

Much evidence is now available to suggest that awareness of the phonological constituents of words (or as it is sometimes called, metalinguistic awareness) is most germane to the acquisition of literacy. This evidence comes from studies, including some that have been carried out in languages other than English, which have shown that this awareness is predictive of reading success in young children (Alegria, Pignot, & Morais, 1982; Bradley & Bryant, 1983; Liberman, 1973; Lundberg, Olofsson, & Wall,

1980; Mann & Liberman, 1984; deManrique & Gramigna, 1984; Treiman & Baron, 1981). One study worthy of special mention as one of the most extensive was carried out in Sweden (Lundberg, Olofsson, & Wall, 1980). Among the many abilities, both related and unrelated to language, considered in that study, the ability to segment words into phonemes was the single most powerful predictor of future reading and spelling skills in a group of children tested at the end of their kindergarten year.

A more modest but similar study from our laboratory (Mann & Liberman, 1984) was a longitudinal comparison of a group of children as kindergarteners and first graders. It had the aim of discovering the best kindergarten predictors of reading success. The ability to segment words by counting their constituent syllables was selected instead of phoneme counting as the measure of awareness. We knew, given the results of our earlier study, that syllable segmentation ability (unlike phoneme segmentation) was already in place in over half of the children before the first grade; therefore, we considered syllable awareness would be less open to criticism as possibly confounded by reading instruction. Of the 26 children later classified as good readers in the first grade, 85% had ''passed'' the syllable counting test when they were kindergarteners. In contrast, only 56% of the average readers and 17% of the poor readers had been successful.

In a recent study by our research group (Liberman, Rubin, Duques, & Carlisle, 1985) metalinguistic awareness in the phonological domain has been found to be also highly predictive of spelling success. This study relating the invented spellings (Read, 1971) of kindergarteners to their performance on other language-related tasks suggests that their proficiency in spelling is more closely tied to phonological awareness than to other aspects of language development. Of the eight language-based tasks administered to this group, three made a difference statistically and accounted for 93% of the variance in invented spelling proficiency. These three unquestionably tapped phonological skills. Listed in descending order of importance, they included a phoneme analysis test patterned after Lundberg et al. (1980); a test of the ability to supply the correct grapheme when phonemes are dictated; and a test of the ability to delete phonemes from spoken words, adapted from the Test of Auditory Analysis Skills (Rosner, 1975). A fourth, a picture naming test, contributed 1% to the variance but did not quite attain significance. It is less obviously phonological in nature, but, as we shall note in a later section, it may be viewed as a subtle indicator of phonological difficulties. The four remaining language-based tasks did not make a difference in the kindergarteners' performance on the invented spelling test. It is notable that though these four tasks all reflect certain aspects of language development, they do not require the degree of awareness of internal phonological word structure that is tapped by the others. Three of these tasks (receptive vocabulary, letter naming/ writing, and word repetition) do not include the analytic phonological component at all; the fourth (syllable deletion) taps it at a less abstract level closer to the basic unit of articulation.

These results and the many others that could be cited (Blachman, 1983; Fox & Routh, 1980; Goldstein, 1976; Helfgott, 1976; Zifcak, 1981) certainly suggest that readiness for reading and spelling is related to metalinguistic awareness of the internal structure of words. There is now some evidence that this relationship also implies that phonological awareness may help the child learn to read. This evidence comes from a pair of experiments (Bradley & Bryant, 1983), the first of which looked at the performance of a large number of 4- and 5-year-olds, none of whom could read, on a metalinguistic task requiring categorization of the "sounds" (phonemic constituents) in words. As in previous studies, high correlations were found between phonological awareness (in this case measured by the sound categorization scores) and the children's reading and spelling scores 3 years later. The relationship remained strong even when the influence of intellectual level at the time of the initial tests was removed.

However, as the authors themselves correctly point out, simply to show that children's skills in metalinguistic awareness are predictive of their success or failure in reading later on does not by itself prove that the relationship is necessarily a causal one. It is possible, in principle at least, that the measured relationship occurred because both abilities are highly correlated with a third ability and that this unidentified third ability is the controlling factor. In order to get around this problem, the authors carried out a second experiment. This was a training study using subsamples of the original group, carefully matched for age and IQ, but with initially low scores on phonological judgments. For one subgroup, the training sessions directed the child's attention to shared initial, medial, and final phonemes in consonant-vowel-consonant words. A second group was also taught this information, but in addition was shown how phonemes in the test words could be represented by letters of the alphabet. A third group received instruction in semantic classification of the same set of words, but no attention was given to the phonological relationships or the spelling. As a control, a fourth group received no special training at all. It was found at the end of the project that the children receiving training in phonological categorization were superior to the semantically trained group on standardized tests of reading and spelling, and those trained with alphabetic letters in addition to the phonological training were even more successful (particularly in spelling).

Together, this pair of experiments, which combines longitudinal and training procedures, offers the strongest evidence to date of a possible causal link between phonological awareness and reading and writing abilities. At the very least, they support other studies showing that there are methods for training phonological awareness that can be used successfully with young children (Content, Morais, Alegria, & Bertelson, 1982; Olofsson & Lundberg, 1983). Beyond that, they also indicate that this training can have beneficial effects on children's progress in learning to read and spell (see Vellutino, in press, for another phonological training procedure with salutary effects on literacy).

There remains some question, however, concerning the extent to which phonological awareness, which we have seen to be important for reading and spelling success, arises spontaneously, as it were, as part of general cognitive development, or whether, alternatively, it develops only after specific training or as a spinoff effect of reading instruction.

The question as to whether word-related metalinguistic abilities develop spontaneously or must be taught is a crucial one, with obvious implications not only for preschool instruction, but also for the design of literacy teaching programs geared to adults. It was explored in an unusual investigation by a group of Belgian researchers who examined the phonological awareness of illiterate adults in a rural area of Portugal (Morais, Cary, Alegria, & Bertelson, 1979). They found that the illiterate adults could neither delete nor add phonemes at the beginning of nonsense words, whereas others from the same community who had received reading instruction in an adult literacy class succeeded in performing those tasks. The authors concluded that awareness of phoneme segmentation does not develop spontaneously even by adulthood, but arises as a concomitant of reading instruction and experience. A closer look at the results reveals that within the literate group, those who had obtained certificates for passing the course performed significantly better on the measures of phoneme segmentation skill than those who had taken the course but had not attained the level of proficiency required for a certificate. This kind of variation should not, of course, be ignored. It is entirely plausible that those adults who took the course and did not do well may resemble younger poor readers in other studies: Their failure to develop awareness of phonological structure may have hindered them in learning to read.

Another relevant study is one recently carried out in mainland China with subjects grouped according to whether they had or had not ever been exposed to alphabetic instruction (Read, Ahang, Nie, & Ding, 1984). The results of this study again suggest that reading instruction may be a critical factor in developing phonological awareness. The critical finding is that given a phoneme addition-deletion task (similar to that used with the Portuguese subjects), individuals who at some time in their educational experience had been exposed to *pinyin*, the official alphabetic spelling system, performed that task very well. In contrast, those whose only literacy training had been in the Chinese logographic characters and who had had no experience with the alphabet did not. Thus, it appears that people who are literate but who have not developed alphabetic literacy may not develop a metalinguistic strategy at the phoneme level.

In view of these findings, we believed that it should prove of value to explore further the cognitive characteristics of adult poor readers. In previous work, we had concentrated on children who were having difficulties learning to read. Now, we proposed to examine the characteristics of adults who despite years of exposure to alphabetic reading instruction as children had not achieved full literacy. We were interested in particular to learn whether their performances would be similar to those of younger learners who were having difficulty. We consider a recent study of a community literacy class that was conducted by members of our research group (Liberman, Rubin, Duques, & Carlisle, 1985) as only a first step toward that goal, but one that nonetheless provides promising leads.

In a comparison of the reading and spelling of our adult subjects, we found, as would be expected in any comparison of recognition and production measures, that their reading of single real words was better than their spelling of such words. But on nonsense words, for which some explicit reference to the phonological structure is obligatory rather than optional (as it may be in dealing with real words), the advantage of recognition over production was eliminated. The performance of the adults on both reading and spelling of nonsense words was quite poor and virtually identical in quality, bespeaking what seemed to be a serious deficiency in the ability to deal analytically with phonological structure.

The performance of the adult poor readers in another task, one directly measuring language analysis at the phonemic level, lends credence to the hypothesis that they may indeed have such a deficiency. On a very simple phoneme analysis task requiring only that subjects identify the initial, medial, or final sound in words (an exercise commonly encountered in first-grade classrooms), they managed to produce correct responses on only 58% of the items. Moreover, they clearly found the task particularly frustrating and unpleasant. This inability of adults with literacy problems to perform well on tasks requiring explicit understanding of phonological structure has also been found by other investigators (Byrne & Ledez, 1983; Marcel, 1980; Morais et al., 1979; Read & Ruyter, 1985).

A recent study of adult prisoners of low literacy (Read & Ruyter, 1985) provides strong confirmation of these pilot findings of ours. In their report of this new investigation, the authors note that their subjects remain poor readers despite cognitive maturity, environmental experience with the written language, and adequate general intelligence. The greatest difficulty displayed by these adults is in decoding unfamiliar words and in the segmentation skills that underlie decoding—particularly in tasks that demand awareness of the location of phonemes within a syllable. The subjects are much better at recognizing familiar words and also in tasks that do not require internal phonemic analysis, such as identifying the initial consonant and judging overall similarities in words. The authors remark that whatever the causes of the difficulty (poor educational opportunity and/or motivation), a prominent characteristic now is a disability in decoding new and unfamiliar words and in phonemic segmentation. Moreover, the deficits clearly cannot be attributed to a general maturational lag, for they do not disappear in these adults of adequate intelligence.

Despite much evidence of the kind we have been considering here, there remains a question as to whether the deficiency may be in fact not necessarily phonological, or even linguistic, but rather attributable to a deficiency in general analytic ability (Wolford & Fowler, 1983). This question is addressed directly, and, in our view, very convincingly, in a recent study by the Brussels group of experimenters. They have recently shown (Morais, Cluytens, & Alegria, 1984) that poor readers (children aged 6 to 9 years with severe reading disability) were poorer than normal readers in segmenting words into their constituent parts, but performed as well as normal readers in a similar task that required them to deal not with words but with musical tone sequences. Thus, evidently the deficiency that the poor readers were exhibiting was not due to a general analytic disability, but was rather specifically language-related and, more than that, specifically phonological in nature.

The possible presence in poor readers of a general analytic deficiency rather than a deficiency specifically in the phonological realm was a question also addressed in yet another recent study (Pratt, 1985). There two complementary experiments were carried out—one with good and poor readers in adult education classes and the other with good and poor readers in the third grade. Both reader groups in each case were given linguistic awareness tasks and a nonspeech control task identical in format to one of the linguistic tasks. Significant differences between the good and poor readers at both levels were found on all three linguistic awareness measures but not on the nonspeech control task.

Thus, it appears again that the deficiency the poor readers were exhibiting was not due to some general analytic disability, but was, instead, specifically language-related and, more than that, specifically phonological in nature.

As we have seen, there is now a wealth of evidence pointing to metalinguistic deficiencies in the phonological domain in individuals of various ages, languages, and cultural backgrounds, who have difficulty in attaining literacy. We suggest that perhaps it would be reasonable now to consider seriously the possibility that the deficiency in these individuals who are resistant to ordinary methods of literacy instruction may not be limited to metalinguistic awareness, but may reflect a more general deficiency in the phonological domain. Some of the evidence for this conjecture is discussed in the next two sections.

PHONOLOGY AND NAMING

We now turn to consider the significance of the well-known fact that children who are poor readers often have some degree of difficulty in producing the names of things. At first blush, this would appear to be a problem completely separate from their difficulties in reading. But, in our view, the failures in calling up the appropriate name of an object and the failures in identifying words in print may both relate in some degree to the poor readers' difficulties with language at the level of the phonology.

Several investigators have found that errors in naming are characteristic of children with reading disability (Denckla & Rudel, 1976; Jansky & de Hirsch, 1973; Katz, 1986; Mattis, French & Rapin, 1975; Wolf, 1981). The existence of a naming problem can be demonstrated by a picture naming test of the sort that is commonly used in testing aphasic patients. The data we discuss here were obtained using an adaptation of the Boston Naming Test (Kaplan, Goodglass, & Weintraub, 1976), in which the subject is presented with pictured objects one at a time and is required to name each item as it appears.

The fact that poor readers tend to misname things could lead one to infer that the problem is semantic. But, as we shall see, this may be a wrong inference. The first step toward a correct analysis of the poor reader's naming difficulties is to recognize that there are several different aspects to the naming task. First, the perceiver has to apprehend the object in perception. The object must be recognized for what it is. Then a search of the internal lexicon must be carried out to find the word that best names the object. Finally, the word must be articulated in overt speech. An error can arise at any stage from perceptual apprehension to phonetic output. Thus, an error in naming does not automatically reveal its source, which can only be discovered by further analysis.

The experiments needed to pinpoint the source of mistakes in naming have rarely been carried out. Katz's (1986) study is noteworthy in this regard. Words selected for the study were pictured items from the Boston Naming Test that were considered appropriate for children aged 8 to 10 years. High-frequency and low-frequency words were equally represented in this revised version of the test.

In tabulating the results, Katz noted the relationship between each naming error and the target word (i.e., the word judged to be the best name for the object depicted). He showed that although the poor readers produced more incorrect names than the good readers, their responses were not arbitrary. Indeed, they often resembled closely the phonological structure of the correct word. For example, when the picture presented was of a globe, one child's response was to produce the nonword, "gloave" which, though incorrect, is identical to the target word except in the last phonological segment. Such an error is consistent with the hypothesis that the child has identified the object in question, but has difficulty producing the word.

In other cases, the child produced a real word in response to the test picture. Again, the response often bore a close phonological resemblance to the target word phonologically. Thus, a frequent response to the picture of a volcano was the word, "tornado"—quite different in meaning but with the same number of syllables, an identical stress pattern, and similar vowel constituents. Without further tests, however, the interpretation of such a response would be ambiguous. Katz resolved these ambiguities by questioning the child. When, in this instance, the subject was subsequently quizzed about the characteristics of the pictured object, he correctly described a volcano and not a tornado. Thus, it was clear that the child was quite aware of the meaning of the object. Many other cases in which an ambiguous response was produced were resolved similarly: It often turned out that the child's problem had to do not with meaning, but with the phonological structure of the target word. Thus, whether the poor readers' responses were nonwords (as in the first example) or incorrect real words (as in the second example), the source of the error was often phonological.

Further indications that phonology and not semantics may have been at the basis of these poor readers' naming errors are provided by the results of a test of identification of pictured objects in which the previous procedure was reversed. In this reversed procedure, the examiner produced the name and the child had to select the one picture from a set of eight that best depicted the meaning of the word. Each item that had previously been misnamed on the naming test was subsequently tested for recognition in this manner. In most cases, correct retrieval was demonstrated. Thus, it was apparent that the poor readers had acquired internal lexical representations of most of the objects whose names they could not produce accurately. As Katz (1986) points out, distorted production of the word for an item that has been correctly identified could stem either from an incomplete specification of the phonological word in the lexicon, or from deficient retrieval and processing of the stored phonological information. Which of these possibilities is correct is not relevant to the question at issue here. What is relevant is that, in either case, the source of the poor readers' difficulty had to do with the phonologic aspect of words and not with their meanings.

PHONOLOGY AND SENTENCE COMPREHENSION

Having seen that deficiencies in the phonological domain may be responsible for difficulties in reading words, and also for some of the well-known problems of naming, we turn to the role of phonological abilities in sentence comprehension. Recent investigations have noted that poor readers frequently have difficulties understanding complex sentences, not only in reading but also in speech (Byrne, 1981; Vogel, 1975). Our principal task in this section is to say why one would suppose that the deficit that underlies poor readers' difficulties in sentence understanding is phonologic, and how we have gone about testing this idea.

We begin by making three points: First, understanding sentences requires short-term memory. Second, short-term memory depends on the ability to exploit phonologic structure. Third, young children who are poor readers are known to have special limitations in short-term memory and deficiencies in the use of phonological structure. We take up each of these points in turn and attempt to show the connections between them. First, we discuss how short-term memory is relevant for comprehension; then we suggest how the short-term memory system depends on phonological structures; and finally we introduce evidence that the comprehension problems of poor readers may stem not from lack of syntactic abilities but from weaknesses in the phonologic system.

It has been suggested that short-term storage must play a central role in the operation of the syntactic and semantic processors because ascriptions of syntactic structure and propositional content must be based on briefly holding sequences of words in memory (Liberman, Mattingly, & Turvey, 1972). Thus, verbal short-term memory is needed for processing connected discourse, whether it is apprehended through the medium of the printed page or by speech. Although use of short-term memory is not unique to reading, we argue that reading may place special demands on this system.

The hypothesis regarding need for short-term memory might seem to be weakened by recent data from several sources indicating that the processes supporting sentence comprehension are to a considerable extent performed "on line" (e.g., Frazier & Fodor, 1978; Frazier & Rayner, 1982). Partly in response to such findings, most recent current conceptions of sentence parsing mechanisms have the parser operating on small chunks of the text (groups of two or three words). In our view, these developments actually strengthen the argument that short-term memory is essential to ongoing language processing. It is precisely because this memory system has such a limited capacity for retention of the verbatim record that fast-acting processing routines must have evolved (Crain & Shankweiler, in press). There is much evidence that the temporary memory system, on which the processing of connected language depends, briefly preserves the phonology and its phonetic derivatives; short-term memory is thus said to depend on an internal phonetic code (Conrad, 1964, 1972; Crowder, 1978).

In relating this information about memory to the performance of beginning readers, it is significant, first, that the memory deficits of young children who are poor readers appear to be limited, by and large, to the linguistic domain. For example, we have found that they have no more difficulty than good readers with memory for faces, nonsense designs, and other stimuli not amenable to verbal labeling (Katz, Shankweiler, & Liberman, 1981; Liberman, Mann, Shankweiler, & Werfelman, 1982). In addition, there is reason to believe that poor young readers are specifically deficient in use of the short-term memory code. Thus, it has been found that poor readers in the early elementary grades who perform poorly also on tests of immediate recall do not code the phonetic properties of words as fully as good readers (Brady, Shankweiler, & Mann, 1983; Liberman et al., 1977; Olson, Davidson, Kliegl, & Davies, 1984; Shankweiler, Liberman, Mark, Fowler, & Fischer, 1979).

Considerable evidence already exists pointing to a connection between poor readers' difficulties in remembering sequences of spoken words (and other materials that can be coded as words) and their failure to exploit phonological structure as a vehicle for short-term retention (Mann, Liberman, & Shankweiler, 1980). The suggestion has also been made (Byrne, 1981; Mann et al., 1980; Shankweiler et al., 1979; Vellutino, 1979) that short-term memory limitations might account as well for the problems poor readers sometimes display clinically in oral sentence comprehension. This possibility was strengthened by the finding that poor readers are worse than good readers not only in recall of arbitrary strings of words, but also in recall of both meaningful and meaningless (but syntactically accurate) sentences (Mann et al., 1980).

Until a recent study by Mann, Shankweiler, and Smith (1984), however, no experiment had expressly addressed the question of whether the sentence comprehension problems of poor readers might not be to some degree phonologic in nature, rather than syntactic. The test of syntactic competence selected to make this determination tapped the subject's understanding of relative clauses. The relative clause, which allows the embedding of sentences within one another, was chosen because it is a device of central importance to grammatical function. Syntactically complex, it is apt to be misinterpreted by young children (Tavakolian, 1981) and also by older persons with language disorders (Caramazza & Zurif, 1976).

Good and poor readers in the third grade were tested for comprehension of four different orally presented relative clause structures. In constructing the test sentences, account was taken of the grammatical fact that a relative clause may attach either to a subject noun phrase or to a direct-object noun phrase, and, further, that the relative pronoun that substitutes for the missing noun phrase (in the relative clause) can take either the subject role or the direct-object role.

Comprehension of the tape-recorded sentences was tested by the children's manipulation of toy animals. Rote recall for the sentences was also tested, but on a later day; the children listened to the recordings again and were asked to repeat each sentence as accurately as possible. The pattern of errors for good and poor readers in comprehension and recall for each type of relative-clause sentence was then examined. One way an error of sentence interpretation can arise is from simplification of the structure of a sentence containing a relative clause. For example, the sentence might be interpreted as having two main clauses joined by *and* rather than having a relative clause modifying a noun phrase. Such an erroneous parsing of a sentence containing an object-relative clause, as in the example, "The dog stood on the turtle that chased the sheep," would result in a response by the child in which the dog stands on the turtle and chases the sheep. If it were found that poor readers made chiefly this kind of error, it could be taken to imply that their grammar is less differentiated than that of normal adults and more mature children of their own age. Such a finding would constitute evidence of a primary deficiency in syntactic competence. But, in the event, that is not what happened.

Turning to the results of the test of comprehension, we consider first the errors for each of the four sentence types, separately for good and poor readers. It was found that the poor readers made consistently more errors than the good readers. It was expected, on the basis of past research on language acquisition (Tavakolian, 1981), that there would also be differences in difficulty among the sentence types, and, in fact, such differences were found even in children as old as these (8 to 10 years). But when the four sentence types were ranked in order of difficulty for good and poor readers separately, the ordering was found to be the same for both groups. The poor readers were generally worse than the good readers in comprehension of relative clause sentences, but within this broad class, they were affected by syntactic variations in the same way as the good readers. The results give no evidence, then, that the poor readers were deficient on any facet of the grammar pertaining to the interpretation of these relative clause sentences. The competence they displayed in this regard was essentially like that of the good readers. A similar result was obtained in a second experiment on interpretation of reflexive pronouns that employed the same subjects (Shankweiler, Smith, & Mann, 1984).

We must account, however, for the other major finding of the study: The poor readers' performance, though similar in pattern, was not equivalent in proficiency to that of good readers in comprehension of any of the four relative clause structures. The best clue we have as to why the poor readers were less accurate is given by comparing their performance on the test of rote recall, where it was found that the poor readers also made significantly more errors. Again, the differences between the groups did not favor one type of sentence more than another. When the recall scores and the comprehension scores on individual subjects are compared statistically, a significant degree of correlation is found. These results are also in complete agreement with recall findings obtained earlier (Mann et al., 1980) with comparable groups of good and poor readers. They fit well with much earlier work that indicates, as we have seen, that poor readers perform consistently more poorly than good readers on a variety of tests of verbal short-term memory. Thus, the failure of the poor readers to do as well as the good readers on the test of sentence comprehension is probably a reflection, at least in part, of verbal short-term memory deficiencies in the poor reader group.

Although these studies do not totally resolve the question of whether the poor readers have a deficit in syntactic competence as such, there is nothing in the findings that would specifically indicate such a deficit. Instead, the findings suggest that our disabled readers have acquired the grammar they need for understanding these complex sentences, though they do not always interpret them correctly. When they deviate from good readers, it would appear to be because they cannot remember the words and their order of occurrence as well. Thus, the findings we have to date support the claim that the poor readers' difficulties in comprehension may ultimately stem from failure to exploit the phonological structure in short-term memory. Therefore, we would suppose that the difficulties in understanding sentences, like the difficulties in reading words and naming objects, are at root phonological.

The phonological deficiencies we have uncovered in poor readers' performance on tasks involving spoken language have definite consequences for reading, and it is to reading comprehension itself that we now turn. It is important to appreciate that the problems that poor readers characteristically have in comprehension of text stem in large part from their slow and inaccurate word decoding skills. Because short-term memory is, for everyone, both fleeting and limited in capacity, the rate at which material is read into short-term memory is critical. Perfetti and his colleagues (Perfetti & Hogaboam, 1975) have suggested that poor readers cannot use their short-term memory efficiently because of the "bottleneck" created by slow word recognition. Thus reading sentences with comprehension would be hampered, even if all the component words were identified correctly, but too slowly to be processed efficiently. The problem is even more serious, however, than we have indicated so far. Poor readers, as we have seen, have not just the normal limitations of short-term memory; their short-term memory spans are abnormally curtailed. Therefore, poor readers' problems in reading complex sentences may be especially acute.

The point that we would add to this account of the bottleneck hypothesis is that, in view of the findings of Mann et al. (1984), we do not have to invoke a syntactic deficit in order to account for problems in reading sentences. We see that a low-level deficit in use of the orthography to gain access to word representations may have major repercussions on the higher-level syntactic and semantic processes required for text comprehension, especially when compounded by a short-term memory problem. Our research leads us to believe that reading comprehension difficulties may reflect processing limitations originating in the phonology, and not necessarily absence or malformation of the higher level structures of the sentence grammar.

SUMMARY AND CONCLUSIONS

In our research we have sought to identify the language-related sources of difficulty in learning to read and write. To this end, we have explored the difficulties of poor readers in reading words, in naming, and in sentence comprehension. First, we discussed evidence suggesting that it is difficult for the beginning reader to grasp that words have parts: phonemes, syllables, and morphemes. A language user does not need to be aware of what the parts are in order to speak and understand speech because the built-in speech apparatus processes them automatically. But to learn to use an alphabet, to read and to spell, the learner needs to become aware of the parts to make the connection between speech and writing. Awareness of sublexical structure draws upon a set of phonological (or, more accurately, morphophonological abilities [Liberman et al., 1980a]). Possession of these abilities distinguish people who are good readers and spellers from those who are less skilled. Though native abilities may account to a considerable degree for the differences, experience in reading and writing also plays a significant role.

Poor readers not only have problems in identifying printed words, they also frequently have problems finding the most appropriate words for things in speaking. By quizzing poor readers about the objects they misname, it has been learned that the source of the naming error is not always a semantic confusion. Frequently, the source of the problem is not having ready access to the mental structures that store information about the phonological properties of particular words in the vocabulary (Katz, 1986).

In the last section of the paper we showed that difficulties in the phonologic domain are sufficient to cause problems in sentence understanding. In order to process complex sentences accurately, one needs to have the ability to retain the words of the sentence and their order, briefly, while the information is processed through the several levels from sound to meaning. Poor readers do not remember ordered series of linguistic items (words and objects that can readily be coded as words) as well as good readers. Their special-purpose phonetic working-memory system is deficient. This is probably not a general cognitive deficit, since nonlinguistic memory tests do not distinguish poor readers from good readers. The processing limitation, which is apparently specific to systems that support language use, can affect comprehension when the sentence structure is complex even though the basic grammar is, to the best of our knowledge, intact. It can also lead to severe difficulties in the comprehension of printed text because short-term memory function is hobbled by slow and inaccurate word recognition.

We have identified three problems of the poor reader: (a) difficulty in becoming aware of sublexical structure for the purpose of developing word-recognition strategies, (b) unreliable access to the phonological representations in the internal lexicon for naming objects and for performing metalinguistic tasks involving phonological properties of words, and (c) the deficient use of phonetic properties as a basis for the short-term working memory operations that underlie the processing of connected language in any form. We cannot fail to notice that all of these are deficits in lower level abilities. It is an important task for future research to determine how these abilities, each of which involves the phonological component of the language apparatus, are related in development and pathology.

There is now much evidence that metalinguistic abilities in the phonological domain can be taught at all ages with significant success. Moreover, there is increasing evidence that such phonological instruction has beneficial effects on proficiency in reading words. We know relatively little about the role of instruction in developing and maintaining or expanding the phonetic short-term memory system required for sentence comprehension. But whether or not phonetic memory function can be improved by instruction, we know that pressure on short-term memory is reduced as reading strategies become more efficient. Thus, fostering phonological development in the beginning reader may serve to improve not only the reading of words, but also the comprehension of sentences. Various ways to promote phonological development have been outlined elsewhere (Bradley & Bryant, 1983; Liberman et al., 1980b; Olofsson & Lundberg, 1983). However, the creative teacher who understands the basic problems the child faces in learning to read and write will have no trouble devising other, equally appropriate, techniques.

ACKNOWLEDGMENT

This research was supported, in part, by grant HD-01994 to Haskins Laboratories from the National Institute of Child Health and Human Development. We are grateful to Alvin M. Liberman for his criticisms of earlier drafts of this paper. We also thank Stephen Crain for his comments on the manuscript. This paper is adapted from "Phonology and the Problems of Learning to Read and Write" by I. Y. Liberman & D. Shankweiler, 1985, *Remedial and Special Education, 6,* 8–17.

REFERENCES

Alegria, J., Pignot, E., & Morais, J. (1982). Phonetic analysis of speech and memory codes in beginning readers. *Memory & Cognition, 10,* 451–456.

Blachman, B. (1983). Are we assessing the linguistic factors critical in early reading? *Annals of Dyslexia, 33,* 91–109.

Bradley, L., & Bryant, P. E. (1983). Categorizing sounds and learning to read—a causal connection. *Nature, 301,* 419–421.

Brady, S., Shankweiler, D., & Mann, V. (1983). Speech perception and memory coding in relation to reading ability. *Journal of Experimental Child Psychology, 35,* 345–367.

Byrne, B. (1981). Deficient syntactic control in poor readers: Is a weak phonetic memory code responsible? *Applied Psycholinguistics, 2,* 201–212.

Byrne, B., & Ledez, J. (1983). Phonological awareness in reading-disabled adults. *Australian Journal of Psychology, 35,* 185–197.

Caramazza, A., & Zurif, E. B. (1976). Dissociation of algorithmic and heuristic processes in language comprehension: Evidence from aphasia. *Brain and Language, 3,* 572–582.

Conrad, R. (1964). Acoustic confusions in immediate memory. *British Journal of Psychology, 55,* 75–84.

Conrad, R. (1972). Speech and reading. In J. Kavanagh & I. Mattingly (Eds.), *Language by ear and by eye: The relationships between speech and reading* (pp. 205–240). Cambridge, MA: MIT Press.

Content, A., Morais, J., Alegria, J., & Bertelson, P. (1982). Accelerating the development of phonetic segmentation skills in kindergarteners. *Cahiers de Psychologie Cognitive, 2,* 259–269.

Crain, S., & Shankweiler, D. (in press). Syntactic complexity and reading acquisition. In A. Davison, G. Green, & G. Herman (Eds.), *Critical approaches to readability: Theoretical bases of linguistic complexity.* Hillsdale, NJ: Erlbaum.

Crowder, R. G. (1978). Language and memory. In J. F. Kavanagh & W. Strange (Eds.), *Speech in the laboratory, school, and clinic* (pp. 331–375). Cambridge, MA: MIT Press.

Denckla, M. B., & Rudel, R. G. (1976). Naming of object-drawings by dyslexic and other learning disabled children. *Brain and Language, 3,* 1–15.

Fox, B., & Routh, D. K. (1980). Phonetic analysis and severe reading disability in children. *Journal of Psycholinguistic Research, 9,* 115–119.

Frazier, L., & Fodor, J. D. (1978). The sausage machine: A new two-stage parsing model. *Cognition, 6,* 291–325.

Frazier, L., & Rayner, K. (1982). Making and correcting errors during sentence comprehension: Eye movements in the analysis of structurally ambiguous sentences. *Cognitive Psychology, 14,* 178–210.

Goldstein, D. M. (1976). Cognitive-linguistic functioning and learning to read in preschoolers. *Journal of Educational Psychology, 68*, 680–688.

Helfgott, J. (1976). Phoneme segmentation and blending skills of kindergarten children: Implications for beginning reading acquisition. *Contemporary Educational Psychology, 1*, 157–169.

Jansky, J., & deHirsch, K. (1973). *Preventing reading failure*. New York: Harper and Row.

Kaplan, E., Goodglass, H., & Weintraub, S. (1976). *Boston naming test*. Boston: Boston University School of Medicine.

Katz, R. B. (1986). Phonological deficiencies in children with reading disability: Evidence from an object-naming task. *Cognition, 22*, 225–257.

Katz, R. B., Shankweiler, D., & Liberman, I. Y. (1981). Memory for item order and phonetic recoding in the beginning reader. *Journal of Experimental Child Psychology, 32*, 474–484.

Liberman, A. M., Cooper, F. S., Shankweiler, D. P., & Studdert-Kennedy, M. (1967). Perception of the speech code. *Psychological Review, 74*, 431–461.

Liberman, A. M., & Mattingly, I. G. (1985). The motor theory of speech perception reconsidered. *Cognition, 21*, 1–37.

Liberman, A. M., Mattingly, I. G., & Turvey, M. (1972). Language codes and memory codes. In A. W. Melton & E. Martin (Eds.), *Coding processes and human memory* (pp. 307–334). Washington, DC: Winston and Sons.

Liberman, A. M., & Studdert-Kennedy, M. (1978). Phonetic perception. In R. Held, H. W. Leibowitz, & H.-L. Teuber (Eds.), *Handbook of sensory physiology, Vol. VIII: Perception* (pp. 143–178). New York: Springer-Verlag.

Liberman, I. Y. (1971). Basic research in speech and lateralization of language: Some implications for reading disability. *Bulletin of the Orton Society, 21*, 71–87.

Liberman, I. Y. (1973). Segmentation of the spoken word and reading acquisition. *Bulletin of the Orton Society, 23*, 65–77.

Liberman, I. Y. (1983). A language-oriented view of reading and its disabilities. In H. Myklebust (Ed.), *Progress in learning disabilities* (Vol. 5, pp. 81–101). New York: Grune & Stratton.

Liberman, I. Y., Liberman, A. M., Mattingly, I. G., & Shankweiler, D. (1980a). Orthography and the beginning reader. In J. F. Kavanagh & R. L. Venezky (Eds.), *Orthography, reading, and dyslexia* (pp. 137–153). Austin, TX: Pro-Ed.

Liberman, I. Y., Mann, V. A., Shankweiler, D., & Werfelman, M. (1982). Children's memory for recurring linguistic and non-linguistic material in relation to reading ability. *Cortex, 18*, 367–375.

Liberman, I. Y., Rubin, H., Duques, S. L., & Carlisle, J. (1985). Linguistic skills and spelling proficiency in kindergarteners and adult poor spellers. In D. B. Gray & J. F. Kavanagh (Eds.), *Biobehavioral Measures of Dyslexia*, Parkton, MD: York Press.

Liberman, I. Y., & Shankweiler, D. (1979). Speech, the alphabet and teaching to read. In L. B. Resnik & P. A. Weaver (Eds.), *Theory and practice of early reading* (Vol. 2, pp. 109–134). Hillsdale, NJ: Erlbaum.

Liberman, I. Y., Shankweiler, D., Camp, L., Blachman, B., & Werfelman, M. (1980b). Steps toward literacy. In P. Levinson & C. Sloan (Eds.), *Auditory processing and language: Clinical and research perspectives* (pp. 189–215). Orlando, FL: Grune & Stratton.

Liberman, I. Y., Shankweiler, D., Fischer, F. W., & Carter, B. (1974). Explicit syllable and phoneme segmentation in the young child. *Journal of Experimental Child Psychology, 18*, 201–212.

Liberman, I. Y., Shankweiler, D., Liberman, A. M., Fowler, C., & Fischer, F. W. (1977). Phonetic segmentation and recoding in the beginning reader. In A. S. Reber & D. L. Scarborough (Eds.), *Toward a psychology of reading: The proceedings of the CUNY Conferences* (pp. 207–225). Hillsdale, NJ: Erlbaum.

Lundberg, I., Olofsson, A., & Wall, S. (1980). Reading and spelling skills in the first school years, predicted from phonemic awareness skills in kindergarten. *Scandinavian Journal of Psychology, 21,* 159–173.

Mann, V. A., & Liberman, I. Y. (1984). Phonological awareness and verbal short-term memory: Can they presage early reading problems? *Journal of Learning Disabilities, 17,* 592–599.

Mann, V. A., Liberman, I. Y., & Shankweiler, D. (1980). Children's memory for sentences and word strings in relation to reading ability. *Memory & Cognition, 8,* 329–335.

Mann, V. A., Shankweiler, D., & Smith, S. (1984). The association between comprehension of spoken sentences and early reading ability: The role of phonetic representation. *Journal of Child Language, 11,* 627–643.

deManrique, A. M. B., & Gramigna, S. (1984). La segmentacion fonologica y silabica en ninos de preescolar y primer grado. *Lectura y Vida, 5,* 4–13.

Marcel, A. (1980). Phonological awareness and phonological representation: Investigation of a specific spelling problem. In U. Frith (Ed.), *Cognitive processes in spelling* (pp. 373–403). London: Academic Press.

Mattis, S., French, J. H., & Rapin, I. (1975). Dyslexia in children and young adults: Three independent neuropsychological syndromes. *Developmental Medicine and Child Neurology, 17,* 150–163.

Morais, J., Cary, L., Alegria, J., & Bertelson, P. (1979). Does awareness of speech as a sequence of phonemes arise spontaneously? *Cognition, 7,* 323–331.

Morais, J., Cluytens, M., & Alegria, J. (1984). Segmentation abilities of dyslexics and normal readers. *Perceptual and Motor Skills, 58,* 221–222.

Olofsson, A., & Lundberg, I. (1983). Can phonemic awareness be trained in kindergarten? *Scandinavian Journal of Psychology, 24,* 35–44.

Olson, R. K., Davidson, B. J., Kliegl, R., & Davies, S. E. (1984). Development of phonetic memory in disabled and normal readers. *Journal of Experimental Psychology, 37,* 187–206.

Perfetti, C. A., & Hogaboam, T. (1975). The relationship between single word decoding and reading comprehension skill. *Journal of Educational Psychology, 67,* 461–469.

Pratt, A. (1985). *The relationship of linguistic awareness to reading skill in children and adults.* Unpublished doctoral dissertation, University of Rhode Island.

Read, C. (1971). Pre-school children's knowledge of English phonology. *Harvard Educational Review, 41,* 1–34.

Read, C., Ahang, Y., Nie, H., & Ding, B. (1984). *The ability to manipulate speech sounds depends on knowing alphabetic spelling.* Paper presented at the International Congress of Psychology, Acapulco, Mexico.

Read, C., & Ruyter, L. (1985). Reading and spelling skills in adults of low literacy. *Remedial and Special Education, 6,* 43–52.

Rosner, J. (1975). *Helping children overcome learning difficulties.* New York: Walker.

Shankweiler, D., Liberman, I. Y., Mark, L. S., Fowler, C. A., & Fischer, F. W. (1979). The speech code and learning to read. *Journal of Experimental Psychology: Human Learning and Memory, 5,* 531–545.

Shankweiler, D., Smith, S. T., & Mann, V. A. (1984). Repetition and comprehension of spoken sentences by reading-disabled children. *Brain and Language, 23,* 241–257.

Stanovich, K. E. (1982). Individual differences in the cognitive processes of reading: 1. Word decoding. *Journal of Learning Disabilities, 15,* 449–512.

Tavakolian, S. L. (1981). The conjoined-clause analysis of relative clauses. In S. Tavakolian (Ed.), *Language acquisition and linguistic theory* (pp. 167–187). Cambridge, MA: MIT Press.

Treiman, R., & Baron, J. (1981). Segmental analysis ability: Development and relation to reading ability. In G. E. MacKinnon & T. G. Waller (Eds.), *Reading research: Advances in theory and practice* (Vol. 3, pp. 159–197). Orlando, FL: Academic Press.

Vellutino, F. R. (1979). *Dyslexia: Theory and research.* Cambridge, MA: MIT Press.

Vellutino, F. R. (1985). Phonological coding: Phoneme segmentation and code acquisition in poor and normal readers. In D. B. Gray & J. F. Kavanagh (Eds.), *Biobehavioral Measures of Dyslexia.* Parkton, MD: York Press.

Vogel, S. A. (1975). *Syntactic abilities in normal and dyslexic children.* Baltimore, MD: University Park Press.

Wolf, M. (1981). The word-retrieval process and reading in children and aphasics. In K. Nelson (Ed.), *Children's language* (Vol. 3). New York: Gardner.

Wolford, G., & Fowler, C. A. (1983). Perception and use of information by good and poor readers. In T. Tighe & B. Shepp (Eds.), *Perception, cognition, and development: Interactional analyses* (pp. 267–292). Hillsdale, NJ: Erlbaum.

Zifcak, M. (1981). Phonological awareness and reading acquisition. *Contemporary Educational Psychology, 6,* 117–126.

IMPLICATIONS OF MNEMONIC-STRATEGY RESEARCH FOR THEORIES OF LEARNING DISABILITIES

Thomas E. Scruggs, Margo A. Mastropieri and
Joel R. Levin

ABSTRACT

In recent years, a sizeable number of studies investigating the use of mnemonic strategies by learning disabled (LD) students has been reported in the literature. Research investigating the use of the "keyword method" and related mnemonic techniques has consistently demonstrated the power and versatility of such instructional strategies with LD populations. To date, research has been conducted on native and foreign vocabulary learning, learning of single and multiple attributes in geology and natural history,

Memory and Learning Disabilities
Advances in Learning and Behavioral Disabilities, Suppl. 2, pages 225–244.
ISBN: 0-89232-836-3

prose learning, and the effects of extended mnemonic instructions. None of the research reported in this chapter was designed to test specific theories of learning disabilities. However, the consistently positive results of mnemonic research are not supportive of several theories that may have predicted the failure of such techniques with LD populations, including perceptual deficit, visual-auditory integration, and distractibility theories. In contrast, results of mnemonic strategy research support strategy deficit and information-processing deficit theories, which suggest learning disabilities are potentially remediable by means of task-specific learning strategy instruction.

On several occasions throughout the last 20 years, researchers who have probed into the specific skills and deficits of handicapped learners have advocated tapping the untapped potential of mnemonic strategies (e.g., Jensen & Rohwer, 1963; Lebrato & Ellis, 1974; Martin, 1978; Taylor & Turnure, 1979). More recently, Worden (1983, pp. 147–148) has called for research investigating the effects of mnemonic strategies on learning-disabled (LD) students' performance of real-world tasks. What we regard here as mnemonic strategies are systematic techniques for improving one's memory, or mnemonic devices (Bellezza, 1983; Levin, 1981). In contrast to frequently assessed memory strategies in LD populations (e.g., spontaneous rehearsal and semantic organization—see, for example, Worden, 1983, and the various chapters in this volume), mnemonic strategies have been relatively understudied.

Rather, mnemonic strategies had been relatively understudied until just a few years ago. Since that time, however, a sizeable number of studies investigating the use of mnemonic strategies by LD students has appeared in the literature. Consistent with mnemonic-strategy outcomes in non-handicapped populations (e.g., Levin, 1985; Pressley, Levin, & Delaney, 1982), the resulting effect sizes have been the largest ever to appear in the LD literature. In this chapter we summarize these impressive mnemonic-strategy effects. We then attempt to reconcile these effects with various theoretical explanations that have been offered to account for the etiology of learning disabilities.

First, we present an overview of LD students' memory deficits, and the corresponding remedial strategies that have been empirically investigated. We then provide a detailed description of a versatile mnemonic strategy, followed by a discussion of several mnemonic-strategy applications with students classified as learning disabled. Finally, a contribution to theoretical accounts of learning disabilities is offered. Although none of the mnemonic research conducted to date has evaluated these accounts directly, it will become clear that the results of such research lend support to certain theoretical positions while casting doubt on others.

MEMORY DEFICITS IN LEARNING-DISABLED
STUDENTS

There is no paucity of empirical research documenting the memory deficiencies of LD students. These deficits have been noted in their short- and long-term memory, rate of memory search, and spontaneous use of such memory strategies as rehearsal, clustering, and elaboration (e.g., Pressley, Heisel, McCormick, & Nakamura, 1982; Pressley & Levin, in press; Torgesen & Kail, 1980; Worden, 1983). Among other things, LD students perform more poorly than their nondisabled peers: (a) when processing items that are presented at a slower rate (Torgesen & Houck, 1980); (b) when remembering primacy items (Bauer, 1977, 1979; Tarver, Hallahan, Kauffman, & Ball, 1976); and (c) when identifying semantically similar information (Cermak, Goldberg-Water, Deluca, Cermak, & Drake, 1981; Dallago & Moely, 1980). Worden (1983) and Torgesen (1980) speculated that LD students perform poorly because they do not spontaneously apply "elaboration" strategies (Rohwer, 1973); that is, they do not generate potentially useful semantic relationships and inferences when processing information (see also Bransford, Stein, Vye, Franks, Auble, Mezynski, & Perfetto, 1982; and Pressley & Levin, in press).

In response to these observed deficits, researchers have implemented task and instructional variations in order to improve LD students' performance. For example, when Bauer (1979) adjusted the list length to be within LD students' short-term memory span, he found that both acquisition and retention percentage rates were similar for LD and nondisabled students. Dallago and Moely (1980) required LD students to sort list items into five semantic categories prior to recall, and concluded that the sorting task significantly improved the students' recall. Likewise, Wong (1978, Wong, Wong, & Foth, 1977) improved LD students' recall of categorizable words by presenting items by category, telling students to learn conceptually-related items together, and providing category-based retrieval cues. Torgesen and Goldman (1977) found that the provision of rehearsal instructions improved LD children's ability to remember picture sequences to the point where their average performance equalled that of nondisabled children.

The preceding studies have documented memory deficits in LD students, as well as improved performance resulting from instruction in both lower-level strategies (e.g., rote rehearsal) and higher-level strategies (e.g., category clustering and semantic organization). Investigations of this kind provide strong empirical support for strategy-deficit theories of learning disabilities. Yet, two important questions emerge from this research: First, can LD students benefit from alternative, more complex, mnemonic strategies that have proven to be extremely effective in nondisabled populations (Pressley, Levin, & Delaney, 1982)? Second, can LD students successfully apply mnemonic strategies to educationally valid tasks and content? In the following section, we describe a specific strategy from which most of the mnemonic-research applications with handicapped learners has evolved.

THE MNEMONIC KEYWORD METHOD

This mnemonic strategy was formally introduced and explicated by Richard Atkinson in 1975 (although it should be noted that the essence of the keyword method had been both advocated by memory experts and investigated by memory researchers for many years prior to that). Atkinson (1975, Atkinson & Raugh, 1975) originally used the keyword method to improve college students' acquisition of foreign-language vocabulary. Basically, the keyword method is a systematic strategy for the efficient storage and retrieval of factual information, incorporating what Levin (1983) has referred to as the "three R" components of associative mnemonic strategies: Recoding, Relating, and Retrieving.

We now illustrate use of the keyword method in the context of foreign-vocabulary learning. In order to remember that the Italian vocabulary word *testa* means *head,* the learner could first Recode *testa* into a word that is acoustically similar, familiar, and easily pictured, such as *test.* Then, the recoded "keyword" *(test)* would be Related to the target meaning *(head)* via an interactive image, phrase, sentence, or illustration. For this example, a good interaction might be a person tapping his/her *head* in obvious thought while taking a *test.* Finally, to Retrieve the meaning of *testa,* the re-presented word *testa* leads directly to the keyword proxy *test,* which in turn leads directly to the interaction between a test taker and a puzzled head, yielding the desired response *head.* As was mentioned earlier, adaptations of the keyword method have been profitably applied by nonhandicapped learners in a variety of content domains (see, for example, Levin, 1985; and Pressley, Levin, & Delaney, 1982).

As Levin (1981) has pointed out, the effectiveness of the keyword method has its roots in theories of learning and memory. For example, proficient associative learning and memory depend upon well-established connections between stimuli and responses (e.g., Anderson & Bower, 1973). Establishing such connections involves the two associative-learning stages referred to by Underwood and Schulz (1960) as the response-learning stage and the associative stage. The *response-learning* stage involves increasing one's familiarity with the items to be learned, whereas the *associative* stage refers to building stimulus-response linkages. The keyword method is a mnemonic strategy that facilitates mastery of each of these stages. Specifically, for the *testa* example, the recoding component of the keyword method transforms the unfamiliar item *testa* into the more familiar, concrete, word *test*. This component would be expected to benefit the response-learning stage because of empirical evidence documenting that meaningful stimuli are more reliably processed than unfamiliar stimuli (e.g., Paivio, 1971; Underwood & Schulz, 1960). Also, because semantic elaborations substantially improve learning and memory in both handicapped and nonhandicapped learners (e.g., Pressley & Levin, in press; Rohwer, 1973; Taylor & Turnure, 1975), the relating component would be expected to benefit the associative stage. In the case of *testa*, the semantic elaboration or interaction consists of the test taker's head puzzling over a test item. Finally, the direct retrieval path leading from the stimulus (here, *testa*) to the keyword *(test)*, and then from the keyword to the elaborated response *(head)*, should provide the learner with ready access to the recoded and related components, respectively (see Desrochers & Begg, in press, for additional theoretical discussion).

MNEMONIC-STRATEGY INSTRUCTION WITH LEARNING-DISABLED STUDENTS

In this section we present the results of recent applications of mnemonic strategies by LD students. We begin with mnemonic-strategy studies focussing on LD students' learning of single- and multiple-item attributes. We then consider research on LD students' mnemonic vocabulary learning, including such students' ability to maintain a previously instructed strategy on a subsequent vocabulary-learning task. We conclude by discussing some direct educational implications of mnemonic instruction, both through a recent classroom mnemonic intervention and through studies in which LD students have effectively applied mnemonic strategies to the recall of information from factual prose passages.

Before reviewing this research, we wish to offer the following prefatory comment. Because there are several competing theoretical accounts of learning disabilities, it was not at all a foregone conclusion that LD students would benefit from mnemonic-strategy instruction. Indeed, certain theories would lead one to expect that with LD students as the target population, mnemonic facilitation is not possible. For example, those who hold that learning disabilities result primarily from deficits in visual perception (e.g., Frostig & Maslow, 1973), as well as those who hold that learning disabilities involve primarily a "lack of ability to integrate visual and auditory modalities" (e.g., Lerner, 1976), would not likely expect mnemonic instruction to be successful with clinically diagnosed LD students. In addition, those who hold that pictures can potentially inhibit the learning of distractible LD students (Harber, 1980) might expect pictorial-based mnemonic strategies to be detrimental for such students. Thus, the implications of mnemonic-strategy successes in LD populations for these and other theories about learning disabilities are considered at the end of the chapter.

Attribute Learning

Single attributes.   Mastropieri (1983) combined the keyword method with the mnemonic "pegword method" to teach LD adolescents single attributes of North American minerals (see Mastropieri, Scruggs, & Levin, 1985, for a complete description). The attribute of interest was the hardness level (ranging from 1 to 10) of each of several minerals. With her combined strategy, Mastropieri first taught students rhyming "pegwords" to represent hardness levels 1–10, where 1 is *bun*, 2 is *shoe*, 3 is *tree*, etc. Keywords were then provided for the mineral names, along with an illustration that depicted an interaction between the pegworded hardness levels and the keyworded mineral names. For example, for *topaz* which has a hardness level of *8*, the illustration consisted of a *top* (keyword for *topaz*) spinning on a *gate* (pegword for *8*). Students were also instructed to follow three steps when asked for each mineral's hardness level: First, they should think of the keyword for the mineral name (e.g., *top* for *topaz*). Second, they should try to remember what was happening in the picture with the keyword in it (e.g., a *top* was spinning on a *gate*). Finally, they should respond with the appropriate number for the associated pegword (e.g., *8* for *gate*).

In this experiment, ninth-grade LD students were divided into two reading achievement levels (relatively higher and relatively lower), and were then randomly assigned either to the just-described mnemonic condition or to one of two other conditions: free study or direct questioning (directed-rehearsal), with the latter condition providing task structure, experimenter-student interaction, and student responding. It was found that at both levels of reading achievement, LD students who were mnemonically instructed substantially outperformed students in either of the two comparison conditions, with mean recall percentages of 75% (mnemonic), 36% (free study), and 28% (direct questioning). A similar mnemonic advantage was exhibited on a 24-hour delayed-recall test.

In a followup study employing identical procedures and conditions with nonhandicapped learners 2 years younger (seventh graders), Mastropieri, Scruggs, and Levin (1985) replicated the superiority of mnemonic instruction. In addition, the nonsignificant advantage of free study over direct questioning observed in the ninth-grade LD sample was statistically significant in the seventh-grade nondisabled sample, with mean recall percentages of 83% (mnemonic), 50% (free study), and 27% (direct questioning).

A similar investigation assessed the effects of mnemonic instruction when delivered to LD high-school students in their regular classroom groups (Mastropieri, Scruggs, & Levin, in press), rather than individually (as in the Mastropieri, 1983, study). In this experiment, mnemonic instruction was compared with an adaptation of a rehearsal condition recommended by Becker, Engelmann, Carnine, and Maggs (1982). This rehearsal condition (commonly referred to as "direct instruction") included the following prescribed components: experimenter-directed questions, rapid pacing, choral responding on cue, immediate feedback, and cumulative review. As in the previous experiments, students who were given mnemonic instruction by far outperformed students in the comparison direct-instruction condition, with mean recall percentages of 80% and 50%, respectively.

Multiple attributes. Several experiments expanded the just-described research on mineral hardness levels to encompass the additional mineral attributes of *color* and *common use*. Scruggs, Mastropieri, Levin, and Gaffney (1985) taught specific hardness levels, colors, and uses to LD middle-school students who were randomly assigned to mnemonic, free-study, or one of two direct-instruction conditions. The second direct-instruction condition ("reduced list" direct instruction) required that subjects study only half as many minerals (4) as did subjects in the three other conditions (8). In the mnemonic condition, all three mineral attributes were incorporated into a thematically linked illustration. For example, for *wolframite* (No. 4 on the hardness scale, black in color, and used in making light bulbs), students were shown an illustration of a *black* (color) *wolf* (keyword for *wolframite*) standing on a stage *floor* (pegword for *4*) that was lit up by *light bulbs* (use). To control for the potentially motivating effect of illustrations per se, nonmnemonic illustrations (line drawings of the actual minerals) accompanied the materials provided for subjects in the two direct-instruction conditions. The findings replicated those of the previously discussed experiments, in that the performance of mnemonically instructed students (an average of 69% correct) was considerably higher than that of students in both the free-study and full-list direct-instruction conditions (averages of 30% and 24% correct, respectively). Of additional interest, students in the reduced-list direct-instruction condition not only learned fewer total attributes than did mnemonically instructed students, but they also learned a descriptively lower percentage of their 12 possible attributes ($M = 49\%$) than did mnemonic subjects learn of their 24 possible attributes ($M = 69\%$). The mean percentages for the full-list and reduced-list direct-instruction conditions represent virtually the same total number of correctly remembered attributes in both cases (about 5.8 attributes). The latter results are in striking contrast to previously discussed short-term memory data, where improvements in LD students' learning have been detected when either list lengths or inter-item intervals have been reduced (e.g., Bauer, 1979; Worden, 1983).

In a related study, we (Mastropieri, Scruggs, McLoone, & Levin, 1985) sought to determine whether multiple-attribute information could be remembered when initially presented in the form of attribute dichotomies (i.e., soft vs. hard minerals, pale vs. dark in color, and home vs. industry use). The primary rationale for this study was to investigate the possibility that LD students might become confused by the fact that several minerals shared the same attribute classification (i.e., four different minerals were hard, four were soft, etc.). Mnemonic subjects were taught the attribute dichotomies via illustrations that symbolized and integrated the relevant information. For example, for *wolframite* (described as a soft mineral, dark in color, and used in the home) students were shown an interactive illustration that depicted a *blackened-in* (symbolizing *dark* color) *wolf* (keyword for *wolframite*) scaring a *baby* (symbolizing *soft* mineral) in a *living room* setting (symbolizing *home* use). Subjects in one comparison condition were taught according to the basic principles of direct instruction, and those in a free-study condition were instructed to study on their own a typed list of the minerals and their associated attributes. The mean attribute recall of mnemonic subjects (95%) surpassed that of subjects in the two other conditions, with free-study students (77%) remembering somewhat more attributes than did students in the direct-instruction condition (64%).

In a further extension of attribute learning via mnemonic instruction, the mnemonic approach was compared with an alternative representation of the same information (Scruggs, Mastropieri, Levin, McLoone, Gaffney, & Prater, 1985). As was indicated earlier, Dallago and Moely (1980) have provided evidence that semantic organization positively affects LD students' free recall. Even more to the point, Engelmann and Carnine (1981) have suggested that visual-spatial representations of "fact systems" also enhance handicapped students' learning. A visual-spatial organizational format that incorporated the present mineral-attributes information was fashioned after an example presented by Engelmann and Carnine, and compared with the previously described mnemonic strategy applied to the same information. In Experiment 1, specific mineral attributes were taught to middle-school LD students; and in Experiment 2, dichotomized attributes were taught to fifth- and sixth-grade LD students. In both experiments, mnemonically instructed students remembered many more mineral attributes in comparison to subjects in either the visual-spatial or a free-study condition. The respective condition means for specific-attribute recall (Experiment 1) were 58%, 28%, and 26%; and for dichotomous-attribute recall (Experiment 2) they were 87%, 65%, and 60%.

It should be noted that although the visual-spatial organization did not facilitate LD students' performance on the mineral-attributes task, there may be other contexts in which the use of these and other semantic-based pictorial strategies are beneficial. For example, Mastropieri and Peters (in press) demonstrated that LD students' recall of prose-embedded information could be improved through the provision of spatially organized "maps." Similarly, there is now a good deal of evidence to suggest that the prose learning of handicapped learners can be facilitated through either the provision or generation of text-relevant pictures (see, for example, Levin, Anglin, & Carney, in press; and Pressley & Levin, in press). It is likely that pictorial organizations and representations are helpful only when the material to be learned is already (partially) meaningful or familiar to the students, unlike the "strange" mineral names and their attributes that were presented to students in the Scruggs et al. (1985) study. A similar argument has been advanced concerning the empirically documented impotency of nonmnemonic pictures and figural organizations in the context of students learning the meanings of unfamiliar vocabulary items (e.g., Levin, 1981; Levin & Pressley, 1985). Application of mnemonic strategies to LD students' vocabulary learning is the topic to which we now turn.

Vocabulary Learning

In two experiments, Mastropieri, Scruggs, Levin, Gaffney, and Mc-Loone (1985) taught LD middle-school students the definitions of 14 low-frequency English vocabulary words according to either mnemonic- or direct-instruction procedures. In Experiment 1, mnemonically instructed students were shown illustrations in which the keywords were related to the associated definitions. For example, for *peavey* (meaning *hook*), the illustration consisted of a *pea* (keyword for *peavey*) being used as bait on a fish *hook*. Direction-instruction students were taught the vocabulary words and their definitions following the previously mentioned principles of direction instruction. Following instruction, mnemonic students correctly remembered an average of about 80% of the definitions of the vocabulary items, in contrast to only about 31% by direct-instruction subjects.

In Experiment 2 of the same investigation, the direct-instruction condition of the first experiment was compared with a "partially self-generated" mnemonic variation in which students were required to generate their own internal interactive images—rather than viewing experimenter-provided illustrations. (We include the term "partially" because the students did *not* have to generate their own keywords.) Although the size of the mnemonic advantage was reduced relative to that of Experiment 1, once again the average performance of mnemonic-instruction students (69% correct) was statistically higher than that of direct-instruction students (47% correct). The comparatively smaller effect associated with student-generated mnemonic imagery than with experimenter-provided mnemonic illustrations is consistent with previous theory and data in the associative-learning literature. In particular, it has been documented that students' skill in constructing their own facilitative elaborative images improves with age, ability, and experience—in contrast to the uniformly large benefits resulting from experimenter-provided elaborative illustrations (see, for example, Levin, 1976; Pressley, 1977; and Pressley & Levin, 1978).

In sum, the results of the foregoing experiments suggest that relative to direct instruction, mnemonic instruction constitutes a much more potent vocabulary-remembering strategy for LD students, and that this is true whether the mnemonic interactions are provided as illustrations (Exp. 1) or generated as internal images (Exp. 2). Additional support for the benefits of mnemonic vocabulary instruction in LD populations may be found in the studies of Taylor (1981) and Berry (1983).

McLoone, Scruggs, Mastropieri, and Zucker (in press) extended the experimenter-provided/subject-generated findings just cited by determining whether middle-school LD students who were given explicit mnemonic-strategy instruction on one vocabulary-learning list could independently apply the same strategy on a second list. Mnemonic-instruction students were provided with an initial strategy-training session that included a vocabulary list with mnemonic illustrations and subsequent feedback related to the use and efficacy of the mnemonic strategy. These students were then given a list of vocabulary items for which they were required to apply the "three R" mnemonic-strategy components independently, namely generating both their own keywords and interactive images, and following the previously instructed retrieval steps. Subsequent interviews with mnemonic subjects indicated that they effectively applied the mnemonic strategy on the second list; as performance evidence, in comparison to directed-rehearsal subjects, mnemonic subjects exhibited a considerable vocabulary-recall advantage (means of 41% and 74%, respectively).

The results of the vocabulary-learning investigations provide empirical support for the argument that LD students' learning can be dramatically increased in an important area of school functioning. In addition, information has been gained to suggest that LD students can *independently* generate effective mnemonic components when required to do so. Along with recent efforts to enhance LD students' metacognitive skills and strategies (e.g., Brown & Palincsar, 1982; Graves, 1986; Wong, this volume), the mnemonic research reviewed thus far indicates that LD students definitely *can* be taught a potent repertoire of cognitive strategies. Post-learning interview data collected in conjunction with some of this research further reveal that LD students are well aware of the efficacy of mnemonic strategies (see, for example, Scruggs, Mastropieri, McLoone, Levin, & Morrison, in press).

Other Mnemonic Applications

In the mnemonic research summarized in the preceding section, we have seen that students instructed to learn a lesson mnemonically have remembered substantially more information from that lesson than have students in various comparison conditions. But how would mnemonically instructed students fare if they had to apply different mnemonic strategies to several related lessons delivered across several days of instruction? A preliminary answer to this question was recently provided by Tolfa-Veit, Scruggs, and Mastropieri (1986). In that investigation, LD middle-school students were taught information about dinosaurs over a 3-day period, with individual recall tests administered each day and a cumulative recall test administered on the fourth day. In one of the three lessons, mnemonic students were taught vocabulary information about several dinosaurs in a manner similar to that of Mastropieri, Scruggs, Levin, Gaffney, and McLoone (1985, Exp. 1). In a second lesson, mnemonic students were taught three categorized attributes of the dinosaurs in a manner similar to that of Mastropieri, Scruggs, McLoone, and Levin (1985). Finally, in a third lesson, the pegword method was used to teach mnemonic students eight possible reasons for dinosaurs' extinction (in order of their plausibility), in a manner similar to that of Mastropieri, Scruggs, and Levin (1985). On each day, students in the control condition were taught the same information, but in the context of directed-rehearsal and semantic-organizational strategies.

Results indicated that mnemonically instructed subjects outperformed control subjects by a wide margin on both the individual and cumulative recall tests. In contrast to what some learning-disabilities theorists' might have predicted (e.g., Hallahan & Reeve, 1980), it was found that within-lesson intrusions were much more prevalent among *control* subjects, and among-lesson intrusions were nonexistent. Analysis of treatment effects also revealed that the advantage exhibited by mnemonic subjects remained relatively constant over the 3 days. Such results suggest that LD students can benefit from multiple mnemonic interventions over several days of instruction. Although research documenting the effectiveness of mnemonic strategies over weeks or months of instruction remains to be conducted, the Tolfa-Veit et al. (1986) findings speak to the potential utility of mnemonic instruction in actual classrooms (as opposed to laboratory settings).

In another mnemonic-research application, Scruggs et al. (in press) assessed the potential benefits of embedding mnemonic illustrations in expository prose passages. Although such mnemonic prose learning had previously proven effective in nonhandicapped populations (see, for example, Levin, 1982), some might argue that LD students would be distracted by the presence of pictures in prose (e.g., Harber, 1980). In the Scruggs et al. (in press) study, high-school LD students read passages about either dichotomized mineral attributes (Exp. 1) or specific mineral attributes (Exp. 1), which consisted of elaborated prose versions of the mineral materials described earlier. In both experiments, students who read mnemonically illustrated passages remembered more mineral attributes than did students who read the same passages accompanied by figural taxonomic representations (i.e., diagrammed hierarchies) of the minerals and their attributes. Moreover, in Experiment 2, the mnemonic advantage was manifested both on a 1-week delayed-recall measure and on one that required subjects to infer attribute categories that were not explicitly mentioned in the text.

Thus, not only did LD students who were given mnemonic illustrations not suffer in the Scruggs et al. (in press) study; they derived substantial benefits from such illustrations. The results of a few additional investigations corroborate the conclusion that the application of mnemonic strategies can produce prose-learning benefits among students with poor reading-comprehension skills (Peters & Levin, in press), including students diagnosed as reading disabled (Goin, Peters, & Levin, 1986). Mnemonic instruction therefore appears to constitute a powerful, but as yet untapped, prose-learning resource well worth exploring in special education.

IMPLICATIONS FOR THEORIES OF LEARNING DISABILITIES

The mnemonic-research studies described in this chapter were all designed to assess the educational potential of mnemonic instruction, rather than to test fundamental assumptions underlying various current theories of learning disabilities. Nonetheless, we believe that the findings derived from applied mnemonic-strategy research do have implications for these theories, which we summarize in the remainder in the chapter. Such derived implications of course need to be formally tested in subsequent controlled experiments that directly address the assumptions in question, but as a preliminary guide to the direction of such research we mention several theoretical positions that either *are* or *are not* supported by recent mnemonic-strategy findings.

Perceptual Deficit Theory

Mnemonic-research findings do not support the perceptual deficit theory. This is the oldest and most persistent theory of learning disabilities, dating back to observations of ophthamologists (e.g., Hinshelwood, 1900) of deficits in visual perception, and which was maintained (Orton, 1937) and extended into more recent times (e.g., Cruickshank, 1972)—see Kavale and Forness (1985) for a review. The perceptual-deficit hypothesis suggests that problems in visual perception are at the heart of reading and other academic deficiencies. Although organic perceptual deficiencies surely comprise a proximate cause for some disabled learners, recent research suggests that as a group (i.e., on the average) disabled readers do not differ from nondisabled readers on certain visual-perceptual tasks, such as immediate visual recall (Morrison & Manis, 1982; Vellutino, 1979).

In specific regard to mnemonic-research findings, it seems highly unlikely that students who are deficient in their ability to integrate visual information would benefit from pictorially-based mnemonic strategies. Although such strategies are often accompanied by a predominant verbal component, sometimes they are not. Thus, it must be assumed either that the visual-perceptual skills of the LD students included in these studies have been adequate or that the pictorial-mnemonic materials employed have been so perceptually rich that they have compensated for the students' presumed deficiencies.

Visual-Auditory Integration Theory

Some researchers (e.g., Kirk & Kirk, 1971; Lerner, 1976) have suggested that LD students cannot adequately integrate visually and auditorially presented information. This assumption led to the development of such diagnostic measures as the Illinois Test of Psycholinguistic Abilities (Kirk, McCarthy, & Kirk, 1968). It also stimulated efforts to (a) identify students as either "visual learners" or "auditory learners" and (b) develop remedial materials and procedures that either capitalized on or compensated for individuals' learning-modality aptitudes (see, for example, Cronbach & Snow, 1977). Such efforts are still widely advocated in the field of special education today (e.g., Barbe & Swassing, 1979: D'Zamko & Raiser, 1986). Some have argued that research relevant to this theory of learning disabilities has suffered from the use of unreliable and invalid assessment devices (Arter & Jenkins, 1979). More critically, for reasons related to inadequate measurement, incorrect theory, or both, individually tailored methods and materials have generally not increased the academic performance of LD students (Kavale & Forness, 1985, in press).

Concerning mnemonic research, it is hard to imagine that students who are deficient in their ability to integrate visual and acoustic information would benefit as much as they do from mnemonic instruction. For mnemonic instruction to succeed, the recoding, relating, and retrieving components must all be functioning in the prescribed manner (e.g., Bower, 1970; Levin, McCormick, Miller, Berry, & Pressley, 1982; McCarty, 1980), and these involve several successful inter-modality (verbal to pictorial and vice versa) stimulus transformations (see also Bower, 1972; Levin, 1972; Paivio, 1971). It is unlikely that students with visual-auditory integration deficiencies could manage these necessary transformations and integrations.

Distractibility Theory

Some psychologists and educators have suggested that LD students have difficulty sustaining attention, and that such attentional deficits contribute to cognitive failures in reading and other academic areas. In fact, differences on certain sustained attention tasks have been observed (see Hallahan & Reeve, 1980, for a review). Morrison and Manis (1982), however, argue that with memory factors controlled, little difference in attention is found between disabled and nondisabled learners; in fact, attentional problems may be posited to be the effect rather than the cause of reading problems.

As was noted earlier, some have suggested that text-embedded illustrations function to distract LD students, which is presumably why such students do not exhibit pictorial prose-learning benefits (Harber, 1980). Apart from Harber's basic assertion being empirically false with respect to nonmnemonic illustrations (Levin et al., in press), the mnemonic prose-learning research conducted to date also serves to weaken a distractibility argument. As long as the pictures that are distracting the student are relevant to the desired instructional outcome (as when text-relevant illustrations or appropriately constructed mnemonic illustrations are used in a prose-memory situation [Levin, 1983]), then pictorial facilitation is almost invariably produced (Levin et al., in press). In contrast, when prose-learning pictures are not appropriate to the task on hand, or when other critical "ground rules" (Levin & Lesgold, 1978) are violated when probing for pictorial prose-learning facilitation (such as when written prose passages are presented to students with inadequate decoding skills [e.g., Harber, 1983]), then pictorial facilitation would certainly *not* be anticipated.

Strategy Deficit and Information-Processing Deficit Theories

As was noted at the outset, a number of researchers believe that the observed deficits in LD students' learning are attributable in part to such students' lack of spontaneous application of effective cognitive and metacognitive strategies, ranging from simple rehearsal and monitoring to more complex semantic-elaborative strategies (e.g., Pressley & Levin, in press; Torgesen, 1980; Worden, 1983). Mnemonic-strategy research has similarly documented that LD adolescents in free-study conditions do not spontaneously employ the kind of effective mediational strategies that have been observed in cognitively advanced students (Scruggs & Mastropieri, 1985).

The repeated finding that rehearsal-based direct instruction does not improve LD adolescents' acquisition of factual information might suggest that simple rehearsal is a component of LD students' spontaneous information-processing repertoire. Alternatively, it supports the claim that in contrast to *serial learning,* where a cumulative-rehearsal strategy has been found to be beneficial for LD students (e.g., Torgesen & Goldman, 1977), the same kind of rote rehearsal does not constitute an effective *associative-learning* strategy (see, for example, Pressley & Levin, in press; and Rohwer, 1973). When mnemonic strategies are employed, however, the associative learning of LD students has improved dramatically. Both the assumptions and supporting data associated with the strategy deficit position are consistent with the now classical "production deficiency" notion (e.g., Flavell, 1970); that is, although inefficient learners do not spontaneously employ effective learning strategies, when they are instructed or induced to do so their performance benefits greatly. In this view, the causes of learning difficulties are clearly remediable.

Lack of strategy use per se cannot be the whole story, however. When the performances of LD and nondisabled students are compared following mnemonic-strategy instruction, the latter still exhibit an advantage (ranging from slight to moderate). Thus, even though mnemonic-strategy instruction reduces some of the pre-existing performance differences between LD and nonLD students, it does not eradicate them completely. Differences between such students in prior knowledge and experiences, as well as in linguistic proficiency and other information-processing skills (e.g., Swanson, in press; Vellutino, 1979) are certainly not inconsistent with a strategy-deficit hypothesis and, in fact, may go a long way toward supplementing it (see, for example, Pressley, Borkowski, & Schneider, [in press]).

CONCLUDING COMMENTS

We conclude this chapter by calling for all who are concerned with the causes and consequences of learning disabilities to re-examine their respective theoretical orientations in light of the numerous strategy-training efforts (including the mnemonic applications reported here) that have proven effective in enhancing the cognitive performance of students who are presumed to be "handicapped" learners. With specific regard to mnemonic strategies, we have seen that LD students can be instructed to apply such strategies successfully in both laboratory and more educationally valid learning situations. The most optimistic findings of that research go well beyond simple demonstrations of mnemonic-strategy efficacy, arguing in addition that many learning handicaps are in fact quite malleable and remediable under high-quality, properly sequenced, instruction. Further applied research involving LD students can do much to specify the precise nature of those optimal instructional procedures.

We do not regard mnemonic strategies as a monolithic educational panacea that should be used in the service of *all* instructional objectives. Mnemonic strategies are optimally suited for remembering factual information. For those who shun factual-memory objectives in the name of more highly valued objectives such as thinking, reasoning, and problem solving, bear in mind that one must first remember relevant factual information before one can think, reason, or solve problems with it. Remembering is exactly what mnemonic strategies enable one to do, better than any other learning strategy yet investigated, in both nondisabled and LD populations.

REFERENCES

Anderson, J. R., & Bower, G. H. (1973). *Human associative memory*. Washington, DC: V. H. Winston.

Arter, J. A., & Jenkins, J. R. (1979). Differential diagnosis-prescriptive teaching: A critical appraisal. *Review of Educational Research, 4*, 517–555.

Atkinson, R. C. (1975). Mnemotechnics in second-language learning. *American Psychologist, 30*, 821–828.

Atkinson, R. C., & Raugh, M. R. (1975). An application of the mnemonic keyword method to the acquisition of a Russian vocabulary. *Journal of Experimental Psychology: Human Learning and Memory, 104*, 126–133.

Barbe, W. B., & Swassing, R. H. (1979). *Teaching through modality strengths: Concepts and practices*. Columbus, OH: Zaner-Bloser.

Bauer, R. H. (1977). Memory processes in children with learning disabilities. *Journal of Experimental Child Psychology, 24*, 415–430.

Bauer, R. H. (1979). Memory, acquisition, and category clustering in learning-disabled children. *Journal of Experimental Child Psychology, 27*, 365–383.

Becker, W. C., Engelmann, S., Carnine, D. W., & Maggs, A. (1982). Direct instruction technology: Making learning happen. In P. Karoly & J. J. Steffen (Eds.), *Improving children's competence: Advances in child behavioral analysis and therapy* (Vol. 1, pp. 151–204). Lexington, MA: Heath.

Bellezza, F. S. (1983). Mnemonic-device instruction with adults. In M. Pressley & J. R. Levin (Eds.), *Cognitive strategy research: Psychological foundations* (Vol. , pp. 51–73). New York: Springer-Verlag.

Berry, J. K. (1983). Unpublished data. University of Wisconsin, Madison.

Bower, G. H. (1970). Imagery as a relational organizer in associative learning. *Journal of Verbal Learning and Verbal Behavior, 9,* 529–533.

Bower, G. H. (1972). Mental imagery and associative learning. In L. Gregg (Ed.), *Cognition in learning and memory.* New York: Wiley.

Bransford, J. D., Stein, B. S., Vye, N. J., Franks, J. J., Auble, P. M., Mezynski, K. J., & Perfetto, G. A. (1982). Differences in approaches to learning: An overview. *Journal of Experimental Psychology: General, III,* 390–398.

Brown, A. L., & Palincsar, A. S. (1982). Inducing strategic learning from texts by means of informed, self-control training. *Topics in Learning and Learning Disabilities, 2,* 1–17.

Cermak, L. S., Goldberg-Water, J., DeLuca, D., Cermak, S., & Drake, C. (1981). The role of interference in the verbal retention ability of learning disabled children. *Journal of Learning Disabilities, 14,* 291–295.

Cronbach, L. J., & Snow, R. E. (1977). *Aptitudes and instructional methods.* New York: Irvington.

Cruickshank, W. M. (1972). Some issues facing a field of learning disabilities. *Journal of Learning Disabilities, 5,* 380–383.

Dallago, M. L. L., & Moely, B. E. (1980). Free recall in boys of normal and poor reading levels as a function of task manipulations. *Journal of Experimental Child Psychology, 30,* 62–78.

D'Zamko, M. E., & Raiser, L. (1986). A strategy for individualizing directed group instruction. *Teaching Exceptional Children, 18,* 190–195.

Desrochers, A., & Begg, I. (in press). A theoretical account of encoding and retrieval processes in the use of imagery-based mnemonic techniques: The special case of the keyword method. In M. Pressley & M. A. McDaniel (Eds.), *The mnemonic and imaginal bases of learning.* New York: Springer-Verlag.

Englemann, S. & Carnine, D. (1982). *Theory of instruction: Principles and applications.* New York: Irvington.

Flavell, J. H. (1970). Developmental studies of mediated memory. In L. Lipsitt & H. Reese (Eds.), *Advances in child development and behavior* (Vol. 5, pp. 181–211). Orlando, FL: Academic Press.

Frostig, M., & Maslow, P. (1973). *Learning problems in the classroom.* Orlando, FL: Grune & Stratton.

Goin, M. T., Peters, E. E., & Levin, J. R. (1986, April). *Effects of pictorial mnemonic strategies on the reading performance of students classified as learning disabled.* Paper presented at the annual meeting of the Council for Exceptional Children, New Orleans.

Graves, A. W. (1986). A study of the efficacy of direct instruction and metacomprehension training on finding main ideas by learning disabled children. *Learning Disabilities Research, 1* (1), 90–100.

Hallahan, D. P., & Reeve, R. E. (1980). Selective attention and distractibility. In B. K. Keogh (Ed.), *Advances in special education* (Vol. 1, pp. 141–181). Greenwich, CT: JAI Press.

Harber, J. R. (1980). Effects of illustrations on reading performance: Implications for further LD research. *Learning Disability Quarterly, 3,* 60–70.

Harber, J. R. (1983). The effects of illustrations on the reading performance of learning disabled and normal children. *Learning Disability Quarterly, 6,* 55–60.

Hinshelwood, J. (1900). Congenital word-blindness. *Lancet, 1,* 1506–1508.

Jensen, A. R., & Rohwer, W. D., Jr. (1963). The effect of verbal mediation on the learning and retention of paired-associates by retarded adults. *American Journal of Mental Deficiency, 68,* 80–84.

Kavale, K. A., & Forness, S. R. (1985). *The science of learning disabilities*. San Diego: College-Hill.

Kavale, K. A., & Forness, S. R. (in press). A matter of substance over style: A quantitative synthesis assessing the efficacy of modality testing and teaching. *Exceptional Children*.

Kirk, S. A., & Kirk, W. D. (1971). *Psycholinguistic learning disabilities: Diagnosis and remediation*. Chicago: University of Illinois Press.

Kirk, S. A., McCarthy, J. J., & Kirk, W. D. (1968). *The Illinois test of psycholinguistic abilities* (rev. ed.). Urbana: University of Illinois Press.

Lebrato, M. T., & Ellis, N. R. (1974). Imagery mediation in paired-associate learning by retarded and nonretarded subjects. *American Journal of Mental Deficiency, 78,* 704–713.

Lerner, J. W. (1976). *Children with learning disabilities* (2nd ed.). Boston: Houghton-Mifflin.

Levin, J. R. (1972). When is a picture worth a thousand words? In *Issues in imagery and learning: Four papers* (Theoretical Paper No. 36). Madison: Wisconsin Research and Development Center for Cognitive Learning.

Levin, J. R. (1976). What have we learned about maximizing what children learn? In J. R. Levin and V. L. Allen (Eds.), *Cognitive learning in children: Theories and strategies*. (Vol. , pp. 105–134). Orlando, FL: Academic Press.

Levin, J. R. (1981). The mnemonic '80s: Keywords in the classroom. *Educational Psychologist, 16,* 65–82.

Levin, J. R. (1982). Pictures as prose-learning devices. In A. Flammer & W. Kintsch (Eds.), *Discourse processing* (Vol. 1, pp. 412–444). Amsterdam: North-Holland.

Levin, J. R. (1983). Pictorial strategies for school learning: Practical illustrations. In M. Pressley & J. R. Levin (Eds.), *Cognitive strategy research: Educational applications* (Vol. , pp. 213–237). New York: Springer-Verlag.

Levin, J. R. (1985). Educational applications of mnemonic pictures: Possibilities beyond your wildest imagination. In A. A. Sheikh & K. S. Sheikh (Eds.). *Imagery in education: Imagery in the educational process* (Vol. 2, pp. 63–87). Farmingdale, NY: Baywood.

Levin, J. R., Anglin, G. J., & Carney, R. N. (in press). On empirically validating functions of pictures in prose. In D. M. Willows & H. A. Houghton (Eds.), *Illustrations, graphs and diagrams: Psychological theory and educational practice*. New York: Springer-Verlag.

Levin, J. R., & Lesgold, A. M. (1978). On pictures in prose. *Educational Communication and Technology Journal, 26,* 233–243.

Levin, J. R., McCormick, C. B., Miller, G. E., Berry, J. K., & Pressley, M. (1982). Mnemonic versus nonmemonic vocabulary learning strategies for children. *American Educational Research Journal, 19,* 121–136.

Levin, J. R., & Pressley, M. (1985). Mnemonic vocabulary instruction: What's fact what's fiction. In R. F. Dillon (Ed.), *Individual differences in cognition* (Vol. 2, pp. 145–172). Orlando, FL: Academic Press.

Martin, C. J. (1978). Mediational processes in the retarded: Implications for teaching reading. In N. R. Ellis (Ed.), *International review of research in mental retardation* (Vol. 9, pp. 61–84). Orlando, FL: Academic Press.

Mastropieri, M. A. (1983). *Mnemonic strategies with learning disabled students*. Unpublished doctoral dissertation, Arizona State University, Tempe.

Mastropieri, M. A., & Peters, E. E. (in press). Maps as schema for prose recall. *Journal of Educational Research*.

Mastropieri, M. A., Scruggs, T. E., & Levin, J. R. (1985). Memory strategy instruction with learning disabled adolescents. *Journal of Learning Disabilities, 18,* 94–100.

Mastropieri, M. A., Scruggs, T. E., & Levin, J. R. (in press). Direct instruction vs. mnemonic instruction: Relative benefits for exceptional learners. *Journal of Special Education*.

Mastropieri, M. A., Scruggs, T. E., Levin, J. R., Gaffney, J., & McLoone, B. (1985). Mnemonic vocabulary instruction for learning disabled students. *Learning Disability Quarterly, 8*, 57–63.

Mastropieri, M. A., Scruggs, T. E., McLoone, B., & Levin, J. R. (1985). Facilitating the acquisition of science classifications in LD students. *Learning Disability Quarterly, 8*, 299–309.

McCarty, D. L. (1980). Investigation of a visual imagery mnemonic device for acquiring face-name associations. *Journal of Experimental Psychology: Human Learning and Memory, 6*, 145–155.

McLoone, B. B., Scruggs, T. E., Mastropieri, M. A., & Zucker, S. (in press). Mnemonic instruction and training with LD adolescents. *Learning Disabilities Research.*

Morrison, F. J., & Manis, F. R. (1982). Cognitive processes and reading disability: A critique and proposal. In C. J. Brainerd & M. Pressley (Eds.), *Verbal processes in children: Progress in cognitive development research* (Vol. 1, pp. 59–93). New York: Springer-Verlag.

Orton, S. T. (1937). *Reading, writing, and speech problems in children.* London: Chapman and Hall.

Paivio, A. (1971). *Imagery and verbal processes.* New York: Holt.

Peters, E. E., & Levin, J. R. (in press). Effects of a mnemonic imagery strategy on good and poor readers' prose recall. *Reading Research Quarterly.*

Pressley, M. (1977). Imagery and children's learning: Putting the picture in developmental perspective. *Review of Educational Research, 47*, 585–622.

Pressley, M., Borkowski, J. G., & Schneider, W. (in press). Cognitive strategies: Good strategy users coordinate metacognition and knowledge. In R. Vasta & G. Whitehurst (Eds.), *Annals of child development.* Greenwich, CT: JAI Press.

Pressley, M., Heisel, B. E., McCormick, C. B., & Nakamura, G. V. (1982). Memory strategy instruction with children. In C. J. Brainerd & M. Pressley (Eds.), *Progress in cognitive development research: Verbal processes in children* (Vol. 2, pp. 125–159). New York: Springer-Verlag.

Pressley, M., & Levin, J. R. (1978). Developmental constraints associated with children's use of the keyword method of foreign language vocabulary learning. *Journal of Experimental Child Psychology, 26*, 359–372.

Pressley, M., & Levin, J. R. (in press). Elaborative learning strategies for the inefficient learner. In S. J. Ceci (Ed.), *Handbook of cognitive, social, and neuropsychological aspects of learning disabilities.* Hillsdale, NJ: Erlbaum.

Pressley, M., Levin, J. R., & Delaney, H. D. (1982). The mnemonic keyword method. *Review of Educational Research, 52*, 61–91.

Rohwer, W. D., Jr. (1973). Elaboration and learning in childhood and adolescence. In H. W. Reese (Ed.), *Advances in child development and behavior* (Vol. 8, pp. 1–57). Orlando, FL: Academic Press.

Scruggs, T. E., & Mastropieri, M. A. (1985). Spontaneous verbal elaboration in gifted and non-gifted youths. *Journal for the Education of the Gifted, 9*, 1–10.

Scruggs, T. E., Mastropieri, M. A., Levin, J. R., & Gaffney, J. S. (1985). Facilitating the acquisition of science facts in learning disabled students. *American Educational Research Journal, 22*, 575–586.

Scruggs, T. E., Mastropieri, M. A., Levin, J. R., McLoone, B. B., Gaffney, J. S., & Prater, M. (1985). Increasing content area learning: A comparison of mnemonic and visual-spatial direct instruction. *Learning Disabilities Research, 1*, 18–31.

Scruggs, T. E., Mastropieri, M. A., McLoone, B., Levin, J. R., & Morrison, C. R. (in press). Mnemonic facilitation of learning-disabled students' memory for expository prose. *Journal of Educational Psychology.*

Swanson, H. L. (in press). Learning disabled readers verbal coding difficulties: A problem of storage or retrieval. *Learning Disabilities Research.*

Tarver, S. C., Hallahan, D. P., Kauffman, J. M., & Ball, D. W. (1976). Verbal rehearsal and selective attention in children with learning disabilities: A developmental lag. *Journal of Experimental Child Psychology, 22,* 375–385.

Taylor, A. M., & Turnure, J. E. (1979). Imagery and verbal elaboration with retarded children: Effects on learning and memory. In N. R. Ellis (Ed.), *Handbook of mental deficiency, psychological theory, and research* (Vol. 1, pp. 659–697). Hillsdale, NJ: Erlbaum.

Taylor, S. C. (1981). *The keyword mnemonic method for teaching vocabulary: Its use by learning disabled children with memory difficulties.* Unpublished doctoral dissertation, Oklahoma State University.

Tolfa-Veit, D., Scruggs, T. E., & Mastropieri, M. A. (1986). Extended mnemonic instruction with learning disabled students. *Journal of Educational Psychology, 78,* 300–308.

Torgesen, J. K. (1980). Conceptual and educational implications of use efficient task strategies by learning disabled children. *Journal of Learning Disabilities, 13,* 364–371.

Torgesen, J. K., & Goldman, T. (1977). Verbal rehearsal and short-term memory in reading-disabled children. *Child Development, 72,* 141–160.

Torgesen, J. K., & Houck, D. O. (1980). Processing deficiencies of learning-disabled children who perform poorly on the digit span test. *Journal of Educational Psychology, 72,* 141–160.

Torgesen, J., & Kail, R. J., Jr. (1980). Memory processes in exceptional children. In B. K. Keogh (Ed.), *Advances in special education: Basic constructs and theoretical orientations* (Vol. 1, pp. 55–99). Greenwich, CT: JAI Press.

Underwood, B. J., & Schulz, R. W. (1960). *Meaningfulness and human learning.* Philadelphia: Lippincott.

Vellutino, F. R. (1979). *Dyslexia: Theory and research.* Cambridge, MA: MIT Press.

Wong, B. Y. L. (1978). The effects of directive uses on the organization of memory and recall in good and poor readers. *Journal of Educational Research, 72,* 32–38.

Wong, B. Y. L., Wong, R., & Foth, D. (1977). Recall and clustering of verbal materials among normal and poor readers. *Bulletin of the Psychonomic Society, 10,* 375–378.

Worden, P. E. (1983). Memory strategy instruction with the learning disabled. In M. Pressley & J. R. Levin (Eds.), *Cognitive strategy research: Psychological foundations* (Vol. 1, pp. 129–153). New York: Springer-Verlag.

STRATEGIES AND MNEMONICS GO TO SCHOOL

Margaret Jo Shepherd and Lynn M. Gelzheiser

ABSTRACT

In this chapter, we discuss the research base for recommendations that learning disabled students be taught memorization strategies and mnemonics in school. We suggest that existing evidence of strategy use among these students does not support the characterization of learning disabled students as strategy deficient, or provide a sufficient rationale for strategy instruction. We conclude that little is known about the type of instruction that would enable them to use memorization strategies effectively in school. Similarly, we suggest that the educational benefit of mnemonic instruction with learning disabled students is yet to be demonstrated. We characterize the evidence needed to support recommendations for instruction in the use of memorization strategies and mnemonics.

Memory and Learning Disabilities
Advances in Learning and Behavioral Disabilities, Suppl. 2, pages 245–261.
Copyright © 1987 by JAI Press Inc.
All rights of reproduction in any form reserved.
ISBN: 0-89232-836-3

Special educators, ourselves among them, were intrigued by Torgesen's (1977) finding that intervention would increase poor readers' use of memorization techniques and enhance recall. While Torgesen did not use school tasks, his results suggested that instruction to use memorization techniques might increase the amount of information which learning disabled students could acquire in school.

Learning disabled or poor reader groups recall less than their normally achieving peers on a range of memorization tasks (for a discussion, see Moore, Kagan, Sahl, & Grant, 1982). For example, without instruction as to how to study, they recalled less than normally achieving groups on serial recall tasks (Bauer, 1977; 1979; Bauer & Emhert, 1984; Ford, Pelham, & Ross, 1984; Kastner & Rikards, 1974; Spring & Capps, 1974; Swanson, 1983; Tarver, Hallahan, Kauffman, & Ball, 1976; Torgesen, 1977; Torgesen & Goldman, 1977). Learning disabled groups also recalled less on free recall tasks (Bauer, 1979; Dallago & Moely, 1980; Gelzheiser, 1984; Shepherd, Gelzheiser, & Solar, 1985; Torgesen, 1977; Torgesen, Murphy, & Ivey, 1979; Wong, Wong, & Foth, 1977), and on a paired associate task (Shepherd et al., 1985).

On each of the memorization tasks reviewed above, recall is enhanced by the use of appropriate strategies: rehearsal, category organization, and elaboration. Evidence obtained on these tasks is used to support the suggestion that learning disabled groups' relatively poor recall is due to a failure to use appropriate strategies. Deficiency in strategy use among learning disabled students has been interpreted using Flavell's (1970) concept of a production deficiency, meaning that the learning disabled student has the capability to carry out a strategy but does not produce the strategy. The characterization of learning disabled youngsters as production deficient is further supported by evidence that the recall of learning disabled groups increases when they are told to use the appropriate strategy (for a review, see Worden, 1983).

It has also been suggested that for learning disabled students, production deficiencies may explain more than poor performance on recall tasks. Some hypothesize that a production deficiency is general and characterizes their approach to many learning tasks. In fact, a general production deficiency hypothesis has been proposed as an explanation for learning disabilities (Barclay & Hagen, 1982). Torgesen (1980) proposed a similar hypothesis describing learning disabled students as inactive learners.

Proponents of a production deficiency/inactive learner hypothesis suggest that it has implications for instruction that go beyond recommendations to teach learning disabled students how to memorize (Torgesen, 1980). Advocates for the hypothesis recommend teaching a range of learning strategies to them. It has also been suggested that if learning disabled students learned to use mnemonics, they would acquire more information in school (Mastropieri, Scruggs, & Levin, 1985a). Several texts used in programs preparing special education teachers present these same arguments. Authors of these texts have characterized students with learning disabilities as production deficient or as inactive learners and have recommended that, in schools, they be taught to use learning strategies and mnemonics (Hallahan & Kauffman, 1986; Kirk & Chalfant, 1984; Lerner, 1985; Reid & Hresko, 1981; Smith, 1983).

The purpose of this chapter is to discuss the extent to which existing research on strategies and mnemonics should inform decisions about instruction. Since research on learning disabled students' use of strategies for memorizing was designed to answer theoretical questions, it is unlikely to have clear implications for practice. Research on mnemonics was designed to inform practice; we discuss the extent to which it answers questions that are pertinent to good practice.

TERMINOLOGY

In this chapter, we discuss instances of deliberate or intentional learning, which we refer to as *memorization*. When memorizing, people work to acquire information, expecting that they will eventually use it. A variety of memorization techniques are available.

Some memorization techniques, including rehearsal, category organization, and elaboration, seem to be acquired by students without direct instruction (Brown, Bransford, Ferrara, & Campione, 1983). Students use these techniques independently, as *strategies,* to attain the goal of memorizing information (Paris & Cross, 1983). Other memorization techniques, including keyword, pegword, yodai, and pictorial *mnemonics,* are not used without direct instruction. These more complex techniques involve the use of representations which structure how students store and retrieve information. For example, to represent letter/sound associations, Ehri, Deffner, and Wilce (1984) used pictorial mnemonics such as a flower with a stem shaped to form the letter *f*. In most studies using mnemonics, students are not expected to create the representation, but rather are expected to use representations created by the examiner.

Instruction can encourage students to use rehearsal, category organization, and elaboration. While *strategy instruction* is useful shorthand, it is important to realize that strategy instruction does not work directly (Resnick, 1984). Instruction shows students how to carry out a rehearsal, category organization, or elaboration *routine.* They are also told that these activities can be used to attain the goal of improved recall. At first, students may not fully understand this relationship, so that rehearsal, category organization, and elaboration are not strategies for memorizing. Instead, they may be used by the student to attain the goal of complying with the instructor's request (Paris & Cross, 1983). When rehearsal, category organization, and elaboration are used independently to attain the goal of increased recall, they become memorization strategies.

We stress these distinctions because different mental activity is required to implement a routine, strategy, or mnemonic (Paris & Cross, 1983). Further, students carrying out routines, strategies, and mnemonics allocate processing capacity differently. When implementing a strategy, capacity must be allocated to planning and carrying out the strategy. In contrast, when the examiner imposes the mnemonic or prompts students to use a routine, the student does not need to allocate capacity to planning. This capacity is free to be allocated to other activities. If processing capacity is finite (Kahneman, 1973), performance may be better under conditions of examiner support than under conditions of strategy use.

PRODUCTION DEFICIENCY AS A RATIONALE FOR INSTRUCTION

As we have already pointed out, authors of special education texts state that learning disabled students are production deficient, and suggest that they be encouraged to use strategies for memorizing, other learning strategies, and mnemonics. Such statements suggest that evidence is sufficient to accept a production deficiency/inactive learner hypothesis. In this section, we consider the support for the hypothesis. Data on use of rehearsal, category organization, and elaboration are reviewed, since production deficiency views of learning disabilities are supported with such evidence. We then review data pertinent to the hypothesis that learning disabled students are generally production deficient or inactive learners. Finally, we discuss whether evidence is sufficient to treat production deficiencies as fact, and to warrant general recommendations for strategy instruction and mnemonic instruction.

A number of studies have investigated learning disabled students' uninstructed use of a rehearsal strategy, using measures such as lip movements that indicate word repetition, or serial position curves that reveal a primacy effect. In some investigations, students with learning disabilities given serial recall tasks were less likely than normally achieving students to use rehearsal (Bauer, 1977; 1979; Bauer & Emhert, 1984; Spring & Capps, 1974; Tarver et al., 1976; Torgesen, 1977; Torgesen & Goldman, 1977). Ford et al. (1984) found group differences in rehearsal using examiner ratings of study behavior, but these differences were not confirmed when serial position curves were examined. Kastner and Rikards (1974) obtained group differences in use of rehearsal when students were asked to memorize novel stimuli, but groups did not differ in rehearsal of familiar stimuli. In two other investigations, learning disabled and normally achieving groups did not differ in use of rehearsal (Griswold, Gelzheiser, & Shepherd, in press; Swanson, 1983).

With free recall tasks, group differences in use of category organization strategies were also not consistent across studies. In some investigations, groups differed in use of a categorical grouping strategy during study, as indicated by moving or sorting items (Gelzheiser, 1984; Torgesen, 1977; Torgesen et al., 1979). Groups did not differ in study period organization in other investigations (Shepherd et al., 1985; Wong et al., 1977). In these same investigations, differences between groups in the use of a categorical clustering strategy during recall were found in some instances but not in others. Differences between groups were found in some studies using a variety of measures of clustering; Bauer (1979) found differences using a Modified Ratio of Repetition (MRR); Shepherd et al. (1985) found differences using an Adjusted Ratio of Clustering (ARC); Torgesen et al. (1979) found differences using a Ratio of Repetition (RR); and Wong et al. (1977) found differences using an Item Clustering Index (ICI). Groups did not differ in clustering in other studies using ARC (Gelzheiser, 1984), RR (Dallago & Moely, 1980), and ICI (Torgesen, 1977) measures.

An elaboration strategy can be defined as generating an interactive picture or sentence which associates items to be learned. While limited evidence is available about learning disabled students' uninstructed use of elaboration (Worden, 1983), in one study, they were less likely than normally achieving subjects to report use of an elaboration strategy on a paired associate task (Shepherd et al., 1985).

Evidence thus indicates that learning disabled groups are not consistently strategy deficient. Further, in instances where strategy deficits were found, the deficit was merely relative. That is, learning disabled groups were strategy deficient *relative* to normally achieving groups. We know of no instance when all members of a learning disabled sample failed to employ the appropriate strategy.

We raise this issue because a group's relative deficiency in a skill provides limited information about how individual group members should be taught. A learning disabled group's deficiency (relative to normally achieving students) simply indicates that they may be more likely to benefit from strategy instruction than normally achieving students. Unfortunately, when authors of texts for special education teachers recommend that learning disabled youngsters be given strategy instruction, they often fail to acknowledge that strategy deficiency is only relative. Instead, they make global recommendations to teach strategies to learning disabled students, as if none of them use appropriate strategies, and all normally achieving peers do.

In fact, when percentages of students using appropriate strategies are reported, strategy use in samples of learning disabled students is more common than one might expect. In one investigation, 95% of the learning disabled subjects were observed to use rehearsal (Griswold et al., in press). In another study, 50% of younger learning disabled and 83% of older learning disabled subjects reported that they had used rehearsal (Swanson, 1983). In a third study, 38% of poor readers used rehearsal (Ford et al., 1984). In two studies, 31% (Torgesen et al., 1979) and 23% (Shepherd et al., 1985) of learning disabled subjects used a category organization strategy appropriately during study. Further, 35% of the learning disabled group reported use of elaboration on a paired associate task (Shepherd et al., 1985).

Proficiency in strategy use among normally achieving students is also relative. When reported, many normally achieving age-mates did not use appropriate strategies. For example, in one investigation, 38% of the normally achieving subjects were not observed to use rehearsal where appropriate (Ford et al., 1984). In two studies, 69% (Shepherd et al., 1985) and 32% (Torgesen et al., 1979) of normally achieving subjects failed to use appropriate strategies on a free recall task and 42% reported that they did not use elaboration on a paired associate task (Shepherd et al., 1985). One might conclude from these data that it is inappropriate to restrict recommendations for strategy instruction to learning disabled children and adolescents.

The hypothesis that learning disabled students are generally production deficient or inactive learners is typically supported with accumulated evidence from studies using single tasks (Hagen & Barclay, 1982; Torgesen, 1980). The hypothesis can be tested directly by giving one group of learning disabled students a variety of tasks and measuring use of strategies across tasks. When tested directly, the hypothesis of a general production deficiency was not supported. Individual subjects used appropriate strategies on some tasks and failed to use appropriate strategies on others (Johnson, 1985; Warner & Bull, 1984).

This finding is not surprising, given what is known about strategy acquisition among normally achieving students. Measures of rehearsal and category organization were not highly correlated among a group of students of mixed ability levels (rs ranged from $-.02$ to $.28$, Kirby & Ashman, 1984). Kail (1979) inferred strategy use from primacy recall and free recall scores and found only a limited relationship between use of rehearsal and a categorical retrieval strategy ($r = .02$ for younger and $r = .28$ for older normally achieving students). Of course, these demonstrations that strategy use is not a general trait are consistent with a developmental view of strategy acquisition. Typically, strategies appropriate to different tasks emerge at different ages (Flavell, 1985).

Evidence obtained on memorization tasks and pertinent to questions of strategy deficiency among learning disabled students can be summarized as follows. They are less likely than normally achieving peers to use elaboration when memorizing. Group differences in rehearsal, categorical organization during study, and categorical organization during recall are obtained in some instances and are not obtained in others. Differences in strategy use are relative; some learning disabled students use rehearsal, category organization, and elaboration, and many normally achieving age-mates fail to use appropriate strategies. For an individual, strategy use is likely to vary from task to task, rather than being uniform across tasks.

The evidence summarized above leads us to two conclusions. Because strategy use varies among individuals within groups and varies across tasks, it is illogical to make general recommendations to provide strategy instruction for students with learning disabilities. Further, data are not sufficient to warrant acceptance of a production deficiency/inactive learner hypothesis as an explanation for learning disabilities, or as a rationale for instruction.

PERMISSIBLE INFERENCES ABOUT STRATEGY INSTRUCTION

Authors of special education texts suggest that learning disabled children and adolescents be taught to use strategies for memorizing, but are silent about the type of instruction required. Barclay and Hagen (1982) suggest that only a minimum of instruction may be needed to teach learning disabled students to use strategies. In this section, we discuss what can be inferred about strategy instruction from existing research.

Most of the studies in which learning disabled students have been taught rehearsal, category organization, and elaboration used minimal instruction, no more than one lesson. Typically, a routine was described and modelled, and one or two practice trials were provided with simple stimuli. These studies can be organized along a continuum, according to how independently the student memorized.

Learning disabled students memorized least independently in two studies where they were told how to study prior to each study period (Dallago & Moely, 1980; Torgesen, 1977). If subjects did not employ the instructed routine during the study period, the examiner prompted and assisted them. Torgesen also cued use of a categorical retrieval routine during recall on a free recall task. Under these conditions, the recall of the learning disabled group improved on tasks that required rehearsal (Torgesen, 1977) and on free recall tasks (Dallago & Moely, 1980; Torgesen, 1977). In both studies, after instruction learning disabled groups recalled as well as normally achieving groups.

In another set of studies, students were told how to study immediately prior to their only study period. They were not prompted or assisted during study. Under such conditions, recall improved, but differences in performance between learning disabled and normally achieving groups were not eliminated. Wong et al. (1977) cued the use of categorical study and retrieval routines. Cued learning disabled groups recalled more than those not told how to study, but did not recall as well as cued normally achieving age-mates. When told to use elaboration, the recall of the learning disabled sample improved on a paired associate task, although not to the level of an instructed normally achieving group (Solar, 1984).

In a third group of studies, students were told how to study before a first test trial, but then received other test trials without prompts. In these test conditions, minimal strategy instruction was often not helpful for learning disabled students. Ford et al. (1984) found that direction to use rehearsal improved performance, but did not eliminate group differences in recall. In fact, training increased group differences for recall of later items. Moore et al. (1982) found that a learning disabled group showed improved recall of digits after instruction to use rehearsal. However, this improvement was not maintained; 8 to 10 months later subjects had to be re-instructed to use rehearsal. Compared to an uninstructed group, a learning disabled group taught to use rehearsal had higher central recall on the Hagen Central-Incidental task (Dawson, Hallahan, Reeve, & Ball, 1980). However, in another study using the same task, learning disabled students taught to use rehearsal did not differ significantly from an uninstructed group in central recall (Tarver et al., 1976). After instruction to use rehearsal, Swanson (1983) found that the recall of a learning disabled group did not improve from baseline level. They recalled less than normally achieving peers, although the groups were comparable in strategy use. Using a free recall task, Newman and Hagen (1981) obtained similarly disappointing results. On an unprompted test trial that occurred immediately after a prompted test trial, an instructed learning disabled group did not recall more than an uninstructed group.

Taken together, these studies suggest that learning disabled students' recall after minimal instruction is positively related to the degree of examiner direction provided during study. They are most likely to use instructed routines and to recall well when minimal instruction is accompanied by explicit directions from the examiner during study. Under these conditions, instructed learning disabled groups recall more than uninstructed groups, and recall differences between learning disabled and normally achieving groups may be eliminated. Often, when learning disabled students are expected to work more independently, group differences in recall are not eliminated. In fact, in a number of these studies, minimal instruction did not improve the recall of learning disabled groups.

On the basis of this trend, one would predict that minimal strategy instruction would not enhance recall under conditions where the learning disabled student was expected to study independently. Gelzheiser, Cort, and Shepherd (1985) tested this prediction. They pretested subjects and selected groups of learning disabled and normally achieving students who were matched on the basis of recall. The two groups were taught to use a category organization routine. In one lesson, they were told to study by sorting items into categories and rehearsing. Subjects completed four practice trials, during which use of the routine was prompted as needed. Two days after instruction, strategy use was tested (i.e., subjects were given a test trial in which they were not reminded how to study). While instructed groups showed increased evidence of strategy use on the posttest, their recall did not improve from pretest levels. Additionally, although the learning disabled and normally achieving samples had been matched at pretest, at posttest the former recalled less than the latter.

This study confirmed the prediction that minimal instruction is not sufficient for learning disabled students to learn to use a category organization strategy effectively. It suggests that if most studies had tested strategy use, minimal instruction would not have been shown to be effective with learning disabled students. In fact, under conditions of self-directed study, minimal instruction may create, rather than reduce, recall differences between learning disabled and normally achieving groups.

In school, teachers seldom prompt individual students as they study; rather, students memorize independently. If instruction to use a memorization routine is to have educational benefit, it must result in strategy use. Because minimal instruction does not result in effective strategy use by learning disabled students, research on minimal strategy instruction has little to say about good practice.

Gelzheiser (1984) reports the effects of more extensive strategy instruction with learning disabled students. Two groups of learning disabled adolescents were taught to use a category organization strategy in five lessons, which totalled 3 hours of instruction. Subjects were taught to identify the class of tasks where a category organization routine would be helpful. One group was taught this concept in a more explicit fashion than the other group. In all other respects, the instruction provided to the two groups was comparable. All instructed subjects practiced using the routine by memorizing a variety of materials of increasing difficulty. Prompts were faded across practice trials. Subjects received both feedback about their performance and a monetary reward contingent upon recall and were reminded that use of the instructed routine would result in increased recall.

Several days after instruction, the youths were tested to determine whether they would use the strategy to memorize materials like the training materials, and on a prose recall transfer task. They were not prompted how to study on either test. The learning disabled groups' strategy use and recall improved on the test using familiar materials. A majority of the instructed adolescents also transferred the strategy. The learning disabled group that had received the most explicit instruction recalled more on the transfer test than the uninstructed subjects.

Most learning disabled students can learn to use and transfer a strategy in such a way that recall improves. Three hours of instruction is sufficient to teach them to use and transfer a strategy. The amount of instruction required to attain the goal of independent strategy use among learning disabled students is, as yet, unknown.

MEMORIZATION IN SCHOOL

It has been suggested that memorization research would have direct application to practice if school tasks were used (Torgesen, 1980). This may be an oversimplification. It is true that the information typically memorized in strategy research (lists of common objects and digits) differs from content memorized in school, and for that reason, the research is not directly helpful to teachers or learning disabled students. Research and practice differ more fundamentally, however, in the way that memorization and strategies are conceptualized. For research to be informative to practice, it must use school tasks *and* it must be designed in accordance with the views of memorization and strategies held by teachers.

In research designed to investigate the effects of strategies for memorizing, memorization has been studied for its own sake. Information was memorized but not used, except to be recalled for a test. In schools, memorization is not valued for its own sake. Certain information is memorized to be used; other facts are acquired as a foundation for concepts. While some information may be learned just for a test, most teachers would argue that this is not the goal of learning in school.

A further limitation of existing research is that it was designed to answer questions about strategies. Strategies were emphasized, and the content to be learned was incidental. The emphasis placed on strategies in memorization research does not have a counterpart in schools. In schools, strategies for memorizing are simply means to acquire content that teachers believe is important and useful.

The limitations of memorization research that simply uses school content can be illustrated with studies in which learning disabled students were taught to use mnemonics. We argue that the practical value of these studies is restricted because memorization is apparently valued for its own sake and mnemonics are emphasized at the expense of content.

A series of studies has assessed the effectiveness of teaching learning disabled students to use keyword and pegword mnemonics (for a review, see Mastropieri et al., 1985a). Students were presented with an interactive picture and keyword or pegword which were prepared by the examiner. Students were taught how to use these mnemonics with "school tasks": synonyms for vocabulary words and attributes of minerals. Students readily acquired the information.

Yet, memorization in these studies does not seem to occur for the reasons that students might memorize in school. When keyword mnemonics were used to teach vocabulary words (Mastropieri, Scruggs, Levin, Gaffney, & McLoone, 1985), learning disabled students memorized synonyms for a test. Although presumably the purpose of learning vocabulary is to enhance communication, it was not demonstrated that they could use the vocabulary when speaking and writing, or that comprehension improved when reading text that included the vocabulary. We suspect that students would not use these words effectively, since the meanings that students are taught appear to be imprecise.

In other studies of mnemonics, students have been asked to memorize content that is unlikely to be memorized in school. In the mineral attribute studies (Mastropieri, Scruggs, & Levin, 1985b; Scruggs, Mastropieri, Levin, & Gaffney, 1985), students were asked to memorize information from a reference table in a science text (Bishop, Lewis, & Sutherland, 1976). While this information was included in a text, the authors of the text did not indicate that students should memorize the information. The objectives identified in the teacher's manual and study questions for students at the end of the chapter do not require that the mineral attributes be memorized. Instead, the objective of the section is that students identify minerals following procedures used by geologists. Students perform a series of tests to determine seven attributes of an unidentified mineral specimen. When the tests are completed, all of the attributes of the unknown mineral are compared to the attributes of minerals listed in the reference table. The mineral is identified when a mineral is found in the reference table whose attributes are the same as those of the tested mineral specimen.

One might ask if memorizing mineral attributes from the table would facilitate mineral identification. In the mnemonic instruction studies, minerals could not be identified using the information that students memorized. Students memorized only one or two of the seven attributes needed to identify minerals. While the lesson objective could be accomplished if all seven attributes of all the minerals were memorized, it is difficult to justify memorizing this much information.

RESEARCH GOES TO SCHOOL

We have argued that existing research on memory strategies and mnemonics does not answer questions pertinent to practice, and suggest that those questions need to be tested directly. Direct tests of the effectiveness of memorization techniques must meet several criteria. The conditions of instruction should be comparable to the conditions of instruction in classrooms. Students should memorize information that they memorize in school and use information in ways comparable to expectations for learning in school. Both recall and use of the information should be assessed.

To determine the effectiveness of memorization techniques in school, information must be identified that teachers expect learning disabled students to memorize. From these sources, information that can be memorized using mnemonics and rehearsal, category organization, and elaboration strategies could be selected as content for memorization studies.

It is unlikely that there will be consensus about what information learning disabled students should memorize. While teachers may not agree about the specific information that students should memorize, they probably use comparable criteria to determine what facts should be memorized. Research that would be informative to teachers would have students memorize content selected using these criteria. Teachers select content to be learned because it is of value, especially for learning disabled students. Further, they judge memorization to be an appropriate way to learn the content.

The value of information to be memorized is determined by its presence in the curriculum and the frequency with which the information is likely to be used. For example, information that seems valuable to memorize includes letter/sound associations, addition and subtraction facts, the names of senators and congressmen who represent you, and conversions such as 12 eggs equals a dozen, 36 inches equals a yard, and 365 days equals a year. Other content in the curriculum can be memorized but is not because students do not need to know this material. This includes information that has limited or highly specialized utility and the kind of extensive information usually contained in reference books.

The judgment that memorizing is an appropriate way to learn particular information is a second criterion used to select content. This judgment involves distinguishing between learning, memorizing, and comprehending. Memorizing seems most appropriate when the information to be learned cannot be understood per se. Some parts of the curriculum, such as letter/sound associations, fall into this category. However, in other parts of the curriculum the distinction cannot be made so clearly and both memorization and comprehension may be required. For example, the multiplication tables may be learned most efficiently through instruction that emphasizes both memorization and comprehension. A student may then acquire some multiplication facts using the principle of repeated addition and others through rote memorization.

Memorization is usually judged not to be an appropriate way to learn information that can be conceptually organized. Typically, it is more important for students to understand the organization of such information than to memorize the particular facts. For example, the structure of veins and arteries is appropriately learned by applying the principle that form follows function in anatomy (for a discussion, see Brown et al., 1983). Although the particular facts about veins and arteries could be memorized in a rote fashion, students who learn the facts using a mnemonic may fail to learn the principle.

Once information has been identified that teachers expect students to memorize, the decision can be made whether to teach students to memorize the information using a strategy or mnemonic. Almost any information can be rehearsed, and students often rehearse when they prepare for tests. Rehearsal is the way that most junior high school learning disabled and normally achieving students learned vocabulary words and their meanings (Griswold, et al., in press). However, rehearsal is not always a powerful strategy, and when much information must be memorized, it may not be particularly helpful.

In instances when much information must be learned, category organization and elaboration are more powerful strategies because they require the student to transform the information to be learned (Neimark, 1976). However, it is difficult to identify occasions when a category organization strategy would be useful in school. Students are rarely asked to memorize information that is randomly ordered but which could be categorized. Instead, information is organized when it is presented to students. On those occasions when a teacher does not organize the information, it is unlikely that students would have sufficient knowledge of the topic to organize the information for themselves.

There would appear to be a number of occasions in school when arbitrary associations must be memorized. Elaboration techniques can be used to make these associations meaningful and easier to learn. Techniques such as pictorial (Ehri et al., 1984), Yodai (Higbee & Kunihira, 1985), keyword, and pegword mnemonics have been used to teach letter/sound associations, mathematics operations, and vocabulary in a second language, among other things.

The usefulness of elaboration is limited, however. Use of pictured elaborations is restricted to information that can be represented in concrete form. The information to be memorized must be distilled to a single idea, or more than one mnemonic must be generated. When students are asked to learn a number of related facts, elaboration techniques may not allow them to learn fine distinctions between the facts. For example, in one chapter of a science text (Bishop et al., 1976) students are expected to learn definitions of several terms referring to collections of heavenly bodies: *solar system, galaxy, constellation,* and *universe.* It would be difficult to generate elaborations that capture distinctions between these terms.

Once content has been identified that would be memorized in school and could be memorized using a mnemonic or strategy, the way that students will use this content should be considered. Research that would inform practice would show that learning disabled students can apply information that they have memorized using strategies and mnemonics. This would add a second phase to research. In this second phase, learning disabled students would be taught to use the information and then the extent to which students could apply the memorized information would be assessed.

CONCLUSIONS

Research that includes instruction does not necessarily inform decisions about teaching in the classroom. Research on memorization that would be of value to teachers and learning disabled students must do more than ask students to memorize "school" materials. The research must also confront the age-old debate as to the appropriate roles of learning, memorizing, and comprehending in education. In sum, unless the conditions of instruction in research are similar to those found in the classroom and memorization is conceptualized in the way that it is viewed in schools, research does not have direct application to practice.

Too often, particular types of instruction have been recommended for students with learning disabilities without evidence that such instruction would be effective. We have described limits to our understanding of the effectiveness of strategy and mnemonic instruction and limits to the way that existing research can be used to inform decisions about instruction in the use of memorization techniques with learning disabled students. In the presence of these limits, we believe that strategy instruction and mnemonic instruction must be treated as experimental classroom methods. That is, when teachers identify individual learning disabled students as candidates for instruction in the use of particular memorization techniques, they can justify such instruction by documenting its effectiveness with the particular student. In this way, teachers can show that strategies and mnemonics enable students to learn what they need to learn in school.

Recommendations for strategy and mnemonic instruction for learning disabled students cannot be justified on the basis of the appeal of a production deficiency/inactive learner hypothesis. Those familiar with the history of learning disabilities are well aware of the danger of recommending instruction on the basis of an hypothesis about psychological processing deficits among learning disabled students.

ACKNOWLEDGEMENT

We thank Eric Larsen, Bob Pruzek, Lee Swanson, and Jim Turnure for their comments on earlier versions of this chapter.

REFERENCES

Barclay, C. R., & Hagen, J. W. (1982). The development of mediated behavior in children: An alternative view of learning disabilities. In J. P. Das, R. F. Mulcahy, & A. E. Wall (Eds.), *Theory and research in learning disabilities* (pp. 61–84). New York: Plenum.

Bauer, R. H. (1977). Memory processes in children with learning disabilities: Evidence for deficient rehearsal. *Journal of Experimental Child Psychology, 24,* 415–430.

Bauer, R. H. (1979). Memory, acquisition and category clustering in learning-disabled children. *Journal of Experimental Child Psychology, 27,* 365–383.

Bauer, R. H., & Emhert, J. (1984). Information processing in reading-disabled and nondisabled children. *Journal of Experimental Child Psychology, 37,* 271–281.

Bishop, M. S., Lewis, P. G., & Sutherland, B. (1976). *Focus on earth science.* Columbus, OH: Charles Merrill.

Brown, A. L., Bransford, J. D., Ferrara, R., & Campione, J. (1983). Learning, understanding, and remembering. In J. H. Flavell & E. Markman (Eds.), *Handbook of child psychology: Vol. 3, Cognitive development* (4th ed.) (pp. 77–166). New York: Wiley.

Dallago, M. L. L., & Moely, B. E. (1980). Free recall in boys of normal and poor reading levels as a function of task manipulations. *Journal of Experimental Child Psychology, 30,* 62–78.

Dawson, M. M., Hallahan, D. P., Reeve, R. E., & Ball, D. W. (1980). The effect of reinforcement and verbal rehearsal on selective attention in learning-disabled children. *Journal of Abnormal Child Psychology, 8,* 133–144.

Ehri, L. C., Deffner, N. D., & Wilce, L. S. (1984). Pictorial mnemonics for phonics. *Journal of Educational Psychology, 76,* 880–893.

Flavell, J. H. (1970). Developmental studies of mediated memory. In H. W. Reese & L. P. Lipsitt (Eds.), *Advances in child development and behavior* (Vol. 5, pp. 182–211). Orlando, FL: Academic Press.

Flavell, J. H. (1985). *Cognitive development* (2nd ed.). Englewood Cliffs, NJ: Prentice-Hall.

Ford, C. E., Pelham, W. E., & Ross, A. O. (1984). Selective attention and rehearsal in the auditory short-term memory task performance of poor and normal readers. *Journal of Abnormal Child Psychology, 12,* 127–142.

Gelzheiser, L. M. (1984). Generalization from categorical memory tasks to prose by learning disabled adolescents. *Journal of Educational Psychology, 76,* 1128–1138.

Gelzheiser, L. M., Cort, R., & Shepherd, M. J. (1985). *Testing the production deficiency hypothesis: Is minimal strategy instruction sufficient for learning disabled children?* Manuscript submitted for publication.

Griswold, P. C., Gelzheiser, L. M., & Shepherd, M. J. (in press). Does a production deficiency hypothesis account for the vocabulary learning of learning disabled and normally achieving adolescents? *Journal of Learning Disabilities.*

Hallahan, D. P., & Kauffman, J. M. (1986). *Exceptional children: Introduction to special education* (3rd ed.). Englewood Cliffs, NJ: Prentice-Hall.

Higbee, K. L., & Kunihira, S. (1985). Cross-cultural applications of Yodai mnemonics in education. *Educational Psychologist, 20,* 57–64.

Johnson, S. (1985). [Learning disabled, underachieving, and normally achieving adolescents' use of memory strategies on three recall tasks.] Unpublished raw data.

Kahneman, D. (1973). *Attention and effort.* Englewood Cliffs, NJ: Prentice-Hall.

Kail, R. (1979). Use of strategies and individual differences in children's memory. *Developmental Psychology, 15,* 251–255.

Kastner, S. B., & Rickards, C. (1974). Mediated memory with novel and familiar stimuli in good and poor readers. *Journal of Genetic Psychology, 124,* 105–113.

Kirby, J. R., & Ashman, A. F. (1984). Planning skills and mathematics achievement: Implications regarding learning disability. *Journal of Psychoeducational Assessment, 2,* 9–22.

Kirk, S. A., & Chalfant, J. C. (1984). *Academic and developmental learning disabilities.* Denver, CO: Love Publishing.

Lerner, J. (1985). *Learning disabilities: Theories, diagnosis, and teaching strategies* (4th ed.). Boston: Houghton Mifflin.

Mastropieri, M. A., Scruggs, T. E., & Levin, J. R. (1985a). Maximizing what exceptional students can learn: A review of research on the keyword method and related mnemonic techniques. *Remedial and Special Education, 6,* 39–45.

Mastropieri, M. A., Scruggs, T. E., & Levin, J. R. (1985b). Mnemonic strategy instruction with learning disabled adolescents. *Journal of Learning Disabilities, 18,* 94–100.

Mastropieri, M. A., Scruggs, T. E., Levin, J. R., Gaffney, J., & McLoone, B. (1985). Mnemonic vocabulary instruction for learning disabled students. *Learning Disability Quarterly, 8,* 57–63.

Moore, M. J., Kagan, J., Sahl, M., & Grant, S. (1982). Cognitive profiles in reading disability. *Genetic Psychology Monographs, 105,* 41–93.

Neimark, E. D. (1976). The natural history of spontaneous mnemonic activities under conditions of minimal experimental constraint. In A. D. Pick (Ed.), *Minnesota symposia on child psychology* (Vol. 10, pp. 84–118). Minneapolis: University of Minnesota Press.

Newman, R. S., & Hagen, J. W. (1981). Memory strategies in children with learning disabilities. *Journal of Applied Developmental Psychology, 1,* 297–312.

Paris, S. G., & Cross, D. R. (1983). Ordinary learning: Pragmatic connections among children's beliefs, motives, and actions. In J. Bisanz, G. L. Bisanz, & R. Kail (Eds.), *Learning in children* (pp. 137–169). New York: Springer-Verlag.

Reid, D. K., & Hresko, W. P. (1981). *A cognitive approach to learning disabilities.* New York: McGraw-Hill.

Resnick, L. B. (1984). Comprehending and learning: Implications for a cognitive theory of instruction. In H. Mandl, N. L. Stein, & T. Trabasso (Eds.), *Learning and comprehension of text* (pp. 431–443). Hillsdale, NJ: Erlbaum.

Scruggs, T. E., Mastropieri, M. A., Levin, J. R., & Gaffney, J. S. (1985). Facilitating the acquisition of science facts in learning disabled students. *American Educational Research Journal, 22,* 575–586.

Shepherd, M. J., Gelzheiser, L. M., & Solar, R. A. (1985). How good is the evidence for a production deficiency among learning disabled students? *Journal of Educational Psychology, 77,* 553–561.

Smith, C. R. (1983). *Learning disabilities: The interaction of learner, task, and setting.* Boston: Little, Brown.

Solar, R. A. (1984). The effect of minimal instruction on the paired associate task performance of learning disabled adolescents (Doctoral dissertation, Teachers College, Columbia University, 1983). *Dissertation Abstracts International, 42,* 07A.

Spring, C., & Capps, C. (1974). Encoding speed, rehearsal, and probed recall of dyslexic boys. *Journal of Educational Psychology, 66,* 780–786.

Swanson, H. L. (1983). Relations among metamemory, rehearsal activity and word recall of learning disabled and nondisabled readers. *British Journal of Educational Psychology, 53,* 186–194.

Tarver, S. G., Hallahan, D. P., Kauffman, J. K., & Ball, D. W. (1976). Verbal rehearsal and selective attention in children with learning disabilities: A developmental lag. *Journal of Experimental Child Psychology, 22,* 375–385.

Torgesen, J. K. (1977). Memorization processes in reading-disabled children. *Journal of Educational Psychology, 69,* 571–578.

Torgesen, J. K. (1980). Conceptual and educational implications of the use of efficient task strategies by learning disabled children. *Journal of Learning Disabilities, 13,* 364–371.

Torgesen, J. K., & Goldman, T. (1977). Verbal rehearsal and short-term memory in reading disabled children. *Child Development, 48,* 56–60.

Torgesen, J. K., Murphy, H. A., & Ivey, C. (1979). The influence of an orienting task on the memory performance of children with reading problems. *Journal of Learning Disabilities, 12,* 396–401.

Warner, M. M., & Bull, K. S. (1984). *Putting metacognitive training for the LD adolescent in perspective: The issues of control and meaning.* Unpublished manuscript.

Wong, B., Wong, R., & Foth, D. (1977). Recall and clustering of verbal materials among normal and poor readers. *Bulletin of the Psychonomic Society, 10,* 375–378.

Worden, P. E. (1983). Memory strategy instruction for the learning disabled. In M. Pressley & J. R. Levin (Eds.), *Cognitive strategy research: Psychological foundations* (pp. 129–153). New York: Springer-Verlag.

VERBAL CODING DEFICIT IN LEARNING DISABLED READERS:
REMEMBERING PICTURES AND WORDS

H. Lee Swanson

ABSTRACT

This chapter views learning disabled (LD) readers as having functionally *independent* visual and verbal coding systems. It is assumed that such readers fail to effectively establish visual and verbal coding interconnections, which impairs their episodic memory of visual information. One way this faulty interconnection is manifested is by verbal codes failing to adequately provide disabled readers with an "additive" component to enhance the recall of visual information. In contrast, skilled readers were viewed as having an *interdependent* coding system in which words (verbal code) applied to a visual form activate a network of both verbal and nonverbal association and

Memory and Learning Disabilities
Advances in Learning and Behavioral Disabilities, Suppl. 2, pages 263–304.
Copyright © 1987 by JAI Press Inc.
All rights of reproduction in any form reserved.
ISBN: 0-89232-836-3

hereby produces an efficient semantic processing input. Semantic processing is assumed to facilitate storage because, with multiple input, even if some of the input traces have dissipated or become fragmented, skilled readers are able to recover information from remaining stimulus properties. The present chapter reviews some data supporting this hypothesis as well as extending the hypothesis by suggesting that a deficient lexical system may contribute to disabled readers' independent coding operations on a picture-naming task. This hypothesis assumes that there are at least three distinct information processing stages that play an important role in the processing of pictorial information. These stages (modality-specific, semantic, and lexical processing) are reviewed and some recent data testing the model are presented.

The present chapter was directed at the question of how information is integrated in the minds of skilled and disabled readers as a function of diverse coding schemes—particularly for pictures and words. An important aim of this chapter is to bring the phenomena of verbal coding under a flexible theoretical framework; the favored view is that information from verbal and visual sources is predominantly represented in a semantic (conceptual) form for skilled readers and a modality-specific visual form for disabled readers. A three stage model is presented that provides some insight into the question of what circumstances favor individual differences in modality-specific performance, and the circumstances that encourage performance that carries no detectable residues of stimulus-specific information. Hopefully, this chapter will bring us closer to a more adequate understanding of skilled and disabled readers conceptual functioning.

A number of investigators have suggested that verbal coding underlies the episodic memory difficulties of learning disabled (LD) readers (e.g., Ceci, 1984; Ceci, Lea, & Ringstrom, 1980; Mann, Liberman & Shankweiler, 1980; Perfetti, 1985; Perfetti & Lesgold, 1979; Swanson, 1984; Shankweiler, Liberman, Mark, Fowler & Fisher, 1979; Torgesen & Houck, 1980; Vellutino & Scanlon, 1982, 1985). For example, verbal coding deficiencies have been found to be critically related to poor readers' ability to access a name (e.g., Denkla & Rudel, 1976; Perfetti, 1985), detect the recursive and invariant characteristics of words and sentences (e.g., Guthrie, 1973; Vogel, 1983), verbally rehearse names (Bauer, 1977; Torgesen & Goldman, 1977), and to translate visual information into a phonetic form (e.g., Shankweiler et al., 1979). In addition, many other studies have widely varied the type of visual ability required on tasks and have failed to find a relationship between visual coding (i.e., visual information processing ability) and reading skill, thereby implicating the verbal coding process as a possible explanation of learning disabilities (see Stanovich, 1982a, 1982b; Vellutino & Scanlon, 1982, for an extensive review).

Recently, a multiple coding hypothesis has been proposed as a possible framework for interpreting such children's faulty verbal coding on picture-naming tasks (Swanson, 1984b, in press). The hypothesis views LD readers as having functionally *independent* visual and verbal coding systems. Such readers fail to effectively establish verbal and visual coding interconnections, which impairs their episodic memory of visual information. More directly, verbal codes fail to adequately provide disabled readers with an "additive" component to enhance the recall of visual information. In contrast, the existence of an *interdependent* coding system in skilled readers assumes that a word (verbal code) applied to a visual form activates a network of both verbal and nonverbal associations and hence produces an efficient semantic processing input. Such semantic processing might be expected to facilitate storage because, with multiple input, even if some of the input traces have dissipated or become fragmented, skilled readers may be able to recover information from remaining stimulus properties. The present chapter reviews some data supporting this hypothesis as well as extending the hypothesis by suggesting that a deficient lexical system may contribute to disabled readers' independent coding operations on a picture-naming task (also see Perfetti, 1985, for a review of lexical access theory). This hypothesis assumes that there are at least three distinct information processing stages that play an important role in the processing of pictorial information. These stages (modality-specific, semantic, and lexical processing) are each reviewed and the data from several of my studies on picture-naming (as well as related tasks) are presented. After the three stages model is reviewed, some recent data are presented testing the model.

MODALITY-SPECIFIC PROCESSING

In the first stage of a picture naming task, we assume that a visual processing system generates a visual representation based on abstract information from the picture stimulus (e.g., Marschark & Paivio, 1977; Paivio, 1978; Paivio & Desrochers, 1980). This visual representation, through a recognition process, is matched with various representations in long-term memory (e.g., Ceci, 1980; Jolicoeur, Gluck, & Kosslyn, 1984; Kail & Siegel, 1977). Based on the picture-word literature, we assume that this first stage of processing represents the way information is initially acquired (e.g., Paivio, 1971, 1978; however see Anderson & Bower, 1973; Nelson & Castano, 1984; Pylshyn, 1973). Hence, different underlying representations (i.e., verbal and visual codes) or modality-specific meanings will be accessed. Regardless of what these visual representations might entail, this stage of processing appears to be comparable between LD and nondisabled readers in the processing of nonverbal stimuli (see Vellutino & Scanlon, 1982, 1985, for a review). We briefly review data in support of this assumption.

To test the assumption that a modality-specific coding system is efficiently utilized in both ability groups, a focus was placed on the nonverbal development of skilled and disabled readers. Our underlying assumption was that if both ability groups cannot access a verbal/semantic system, a separate independent store (e.g., visual coding system) must be used to retrieve information. Access to a semantic system can be controlled by using items for recall that are rated low in verbal codability. Thus, if disabled readers' recall of nonverbal information is comparable to skilled readers, it is likely than that similar underlying mental representations may account for recall performance. In the present studies, items to-be-recalled consisted of 8-point random shapes normed as nonverbal for adults (see Vanderplas & Garvin, 1959; for the verbal association and content values). Shapes are illustrated in recent articles by Swanson (1978, 1984b, in press). As a measure of nonverbal coding, association and content values for skilled and LD readers are given for each item in Table 1. The association value (A) was the percentage of children stating "yes" when asked if shapes reminded them of anything familiar. The content value (C) was the total percentage of labels associated with shapes when children were asked if they could provide a label for stimulus items. Association and content responses in Table 1 were comparable to Vanderplas and Garvin's (1959) nonverbal item classification for adults, < 1.50.

To assess the retrieval of visual information (i.e., random shapes), we utilized a probe-type serial recall task adapted from Atkinson, Hansen, and Bernbach (1964). The basic paradigm consists of a sequential spati-

Table 1. Mean Percentage of Item Association (A) and Content Responses (C) for Dimensionally and Reading Groups

| | Random Shape Number Sequence | | | | | | | | | | |
| | Percent I | | Percent II | | Percent III | | Percent IV | | Percent V | | Percent VI | |
Group	A	C	A	C	A	C	A	C	A	C	A	C
3-D (objects)												
Group I	20	13	20	07	20	00	13	07	13	07	20	07
Group II	20	13	27	27	27	27	20	07	20	20	13	13
2-D (pictures)												
Group I	20	13	20	07	13	20	13	07	13	13	13	07
Group II	13	13	27	27	20	10	20	13	20	20	20	13

[a]Random number assigned to each similar item pair of the two- and three-dimensional stimuli.

otemporal presentation of pictures. A reverse probe response mode was used, where the probe itself was displayed and the child attempts to select the picture in the array that matches it. Results obtained from this task exhibit the typical serial position curve, with prominent primacy and recency effects. Strong primacy performances with children are assumed to reflect a cumulative rehearsal strategy, while a strong recency performance represents attention mechanisms (Bauer, 1977). However, an alternative appraisal of serial position effects may suggest that primacy performance may reflect spatial memory rather than cumulative rehearsal (see Berch, 1979, for a review). Regardless, it is important to realize that this recall task requires that attention be paid to all shapes, whether labeld or not, and therefore the relative contribution of verbal and/or visual coding can be critically assessed. Correct recall would require that all shapes be intensively searched for attributes (i.e., spatial or size dimensions) that support recall performance. Subjects in all of the studies to be reviewed were impaired in their ability to use overt cumulative rehearsal (i.e., children were stopped from verbalizing names of previous serial positions) because it has been suggested that control processes (e.g., rehearsal) favorably bias the effects of verbal coding (e.g., Nelson & Brooks, 1973; Paivio's, 1975). The dependent measure across serial positions was d'. This measure provides an unbiased index of memory trace strength (see Berch, 1975, 1979; Hochhaus, 1972; Murdock, 1982, for a discussion).

In the first experiment (Swanson, 1978a), 15 skilled and 15 LD readers (M CA 9.1), matched on IQ and sex, were presented with two and three dimensional representations of nonverbal 8-point shapes. The results produced no statistical difference between ability groups in nonverbal serial recall short-term memory performance (this includes primacy and recency performance). In order to obtain additional evidence related to recall between ability groups, a measure of response bias (C_j index) based on the false alarm rate was determined. As shown in Table 2, the greatest re-

Table 2. Mean Response Bias Values (C_j)

Group	Serial Positions					
	1	*2*	*3*	*4*	*5*	*6*
3-D (objects)						
Group I	1.80	1.19	.88	1.08	1.49	1.68
Group II	1.92	1.44	.97	1.36	1.58	1.70
2-D (pictures)						
Group I	1.33	1.54	.96	1.26	1.37	1.53
Group II	1.79	1.18	1.16	1.02	1.85	1.85

[a]Group I—learning disabled children.
[b]Group II—normal reading children.

sponse bias (i.e., lowest scores) for both groups (normal vs. learning-disabled) and dimensionality (two- vs. three-dimensional) was in serial positions 3 and 4. Both ability groups and dimensionality conditions reflected a bias for choosing the middle serial positions, a finding similar to other studies using disabled and nondisabled samples (e.g., Calfee, 1970; Swanson, 1977). In short, this study yielded similar serial recall strategies (e.g., middle serial position response bias, primacy and recency effects) between ability groups. These findings led support to the notion that the two ability groups were comparable in nonverbal coding efficiency.

A disappointing finding in the above study was that the nature of the stimulus, whether two or three dimensional, did not have a significant effect on recall performance in either group. This outcome was contrary to our expectations since certain developmental theories (e.g., Piaget & Inhelder, 1956; as well as Flavell, 1970; Gibson, 1971) would have led us to predict that stimulus redundancy or salience (e.g., extra cue of depth) enhances item retrievability. At the very least, remedial programs have suggested perceptual salience (three dimensional) improves disabled children's visual memory performance (Roach & Kephart, 1966; Symmes, 1972). Another puzzling finding in the present study, as well as a related study in which nonverbal development was considered (Swanson, 1977), was the absence of a primacy effect (as defined by the first serial position when compared to middle positions) in the two but not three dimensional treatment. As shown in Figure 1, nonverbal recall patterns of LD children follows normal development (Calfee, 1970; Corsini, Pick, & Flavell, 1968; Ryan, Hegion, & Flavell, 1970; i.e., age-related primacy-recency effects, poor recall of medial positions), yet no primacy effect occurred on the two-dimensional condition. This finding also occurs for skilled readers (1977; Swanson, 1978a). Since instructional procedures thwarted verbal rehearsal, (as indicated by the lack of primacy effect), it was assumed ability group performance was due to an inability to attach a visual code or to visually rehearse (see Morrison, Holmes, & Haith, 1974, for a related hypothesis) the first serial position. In sum, the two experiments reviewed support the assumption that LD reader's nonverbal recall on a probe recall task is similar to nonverbal short-term memory responses of normal reading children. Implied in these findings is the notion that the two groups of children were equally efficient in modality-specific coding (i.e., coding of nonverbal information).

The issue of concern in the next two experiments reviewed was the extent to which skilled and disabled readers memory of visual information was dependent upon a verbal process. There is a long history of data in the experimental literature suggesting that prior label pretraining facilitates the later recall of nonsense shapes (e.g., Daniels & Ellis, 1972; Nagae, 1977; Warren & Horn, 1982). However, efforts to fully understand memory

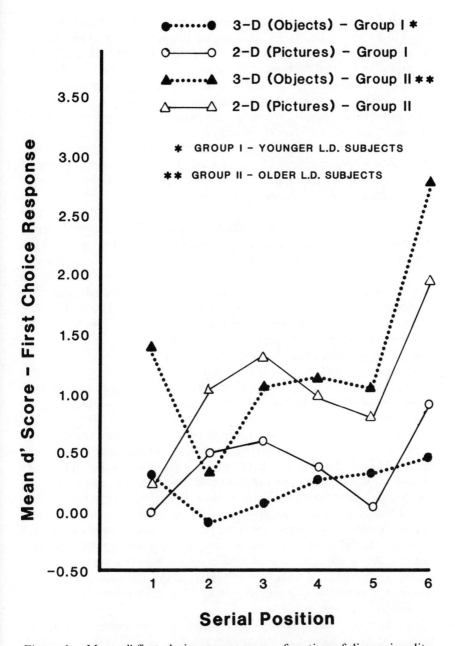

Figure 1. Mean *d'* first choice response as a function of dimensionality, age, and serial position. From "Nonverbal visual short-term memory as a function of age and dimensionality in learning disabled children" by H. L. Swanson, (1977). *Child Development, 48,* 51–55. Adapted by permission.

of visual materials and how such materials are coded have been somewhat retarded by the difficulty in generalizing findings across ability groups (Swanson, 1978b). An experimental model that may provide a tentative account of individual differences in memory representation is dual coding theory (e.g., Paivio, 1971). A dual or modality-specific hypothesis assumes that their exists an appropriate associative connection between two separate memory stores (i.e., pictures are named, the referents of words are imagined, and readers translate a concept from one code to another). However, can one assume that there exists in both ability groups appropriate associative connections between the two separate memory stores? Thus, an important question to be answered is whether the reading ability groups differ in their multiple coding process.

To answer the above question some criteria must be established that allows one to infer whether disabled readers utilize a distinctively different or similar memory representation than skilled readers during multiple input (visual and verbal) operations. In order to establish such criteria, let us first consider the dependent measure. The d' measure is taken to be an unbiased index of memory strength that reflects mediational stages that intervene between a stimulus and response (Berch, 1977; Murdock, 1982). The use of such an unbiased index of memory strength has several advantages in testing the assumptions of common versus dual (modality-specific) coding. For example, differences in memory responses (d' scores) between verbal and nonverbal conditions can be used to infer whether the coding processes are identical or not. If verbal and nonverbal conditions are contacting distinct modality-specific representations, as a dual coding theory hypothesizes (e.g., Paivo & Desroaches, 1980), then the coding conditions should show unequal effects in memory strength (d'). Further, this criterion, nonequality in memory strength, can only be considered valid in determining whether ability groups code multiple inputs in qualitatively different fashion if (a) both ability groups can associate a verbal code to visual information (i.e., both groups have comparable access to a verbal system); (b) both group are comparable in encoding (i.e., pretraining conditions in learning the name-shape assignment are comparable); (c) retrieval of visual information produces comparable recall patterns between ability groups using nonverbal coding conditions; and (d) a nonequality in retrieval exists between ability groups when recall conditions require the mixing of two memory codes. These four criteria were used to interpret our next experiment.

This next experiment (Swanson, 1978b) tested the above issues by utilizing a probe-memory task. Sixty matched (IQ, sex, CA) skilled and LD readers in 4 groups of 15 served as subjects (IQ: $M = 101.5$; CA $M = 9.1$; gender: 10 males and 5 females). Stimuli were the same nonverbal random shapes used in the earlier studies. A pilot study found no significant differences between ability groups in verbal content and association responses (criterion a). Children in both learning groups were randomly assigned for participation in named and unnamed stimulus conditions. During pretraining conditions children from both the LD and the normal-reading group were assigned to the named or an unnamed condition in which they had equal practice in discriminating both top and bottom contours of the shapes in a matching-to-sample task, but were not given names. Children in the named condition gave the name of the test shape when it was shown, with correction after 3 seconds. Labels were assigned to each of the shapes such that the label was a meaningful "representation" of the shapes to some extent. No differences were found between ability groups in trials to criterion on name-shape learning (criterion b). Further, a posttest after recall trials indicated that children retained labels for each shape (criterion a).

After each pretraining condition, children were administered a probe recall task. Procedures were similar to the previous studies reviewed. Main differences in the present investigation were that a pretraining period was given to meet the labeling criterion and children were instructed to use the pretrained label each time stimuli were presented. Using the Flavell et al. (1966) procedures, instances where stimulus names were actually spoken or could be lip-read were recorded on the delay portion of each trial. In terms of results, nonsignificant ratios for the number of children using labels for each of the six stimuli were found comparing LD and normal readers on named conditions using the Flavell et al. (1966) procedure. LD children used overt labeling to the same extent as skilled readers (criteria a). Overall, the correct recall of probed serial positions was more difficult for the LD than for the skilled readers. The effects of name training were significant, but group effects, as shown in Figure 2, were obscured by significant interaction of Group X Task (named vs. unnamed) Training (criteria d).

Tests of simple main effects indicated that name training influenced performance on the recall task for skilled readers, while unnamed recall performance for the LD reader was better compared with named conditions, although not significantly so, $p < .05$. As shown in Figure 2, a significant effect for reading ability group was found for the named condition, while no significant difference in recall performance was found between reading groups for the unnamed condition (criterion c). The main effect of serial position was also significant, while the interactions of ability group and name versus unnamed condition by serial position did not reach significance. Again, no significant primacy effect occurred for either reader on the unnamed conditions. An analysis of response biases, using the C_j index, produced a typical recall pattern for the middle serial positions. Thus, it is apparent from these three studies, no general response pattern

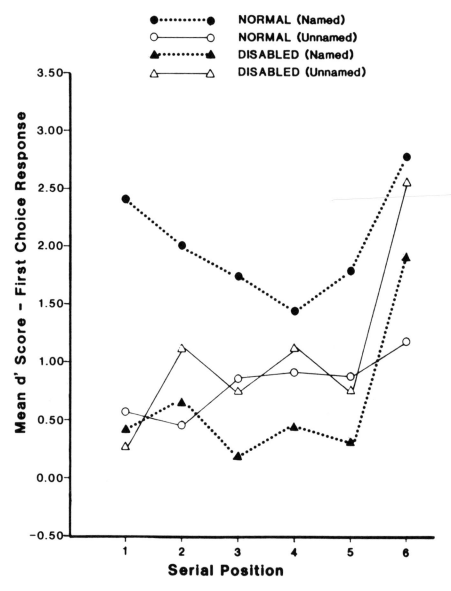

Figure 2. Mean *d'* first choice response as a function as group, labeled and nonlabeled stimulus and serial position. From "Verbal coding effects on the visual short-term memory of learning disabled and non-disabled readers" by H. L. Swanson (1978). *Journal of Educational Psychology, 70,* 539–544. Copyright 1978 by the American Psychological Association. Adapted by permission.

accounting for recall differences unique to LD or skilled readers is evidenced (criterion c).

In a developmental study (Swanson, 1983, Experiment 3), the same methods, materials, and learning and testing procedures from the previous study were used. Subjects in this experiment consisted of 24 normal and 24 LD children separated into two age groups of 12, with each subject matched on IQ and sex. Nine males and three females were in each cell. Computed mean IQ scores from the Otis-Lennon intelligence test and mean chronological ages for the older children were 109.1 (SD = 7.03) and 12.6 (SD = .56) for skilled readers, respectively, and 107.2 (SD = 9.03), and 12.5 (SD = 1.03) for disabled readers, respectively. Young children's mean IQ scores and chronological ages were 107.5 (SD = 4.21) and 7.5 (SD = 1.36) for normals, respectively, and 100.6 (SD = 4.32) and 7.0 (SD = 1.03) for disabled readers, respectively. Classification of LD children again was further determined by the Reading subtest on the Metropolitan Achievement Test. Mean percentile scores were 20.1 (SD = 8.12) for older and 20.3 (SD = 5.11) for younger disabled readers. Percentile scores were 75.2 (SD = 4.41) for older and 79.0 (SD = 6.20) for normal readers.

The d' score constituted the overall memory measure. To simplify the figure, adjacent serial positions were paired (1-2, 3-4, and 5-6). As shown in Figure 3, recall of probed serial positions was significantly more difficult for younger than older children and skilled readers significantly out recalled disabled readers. The main effect for name training was not reliable, but was again obscured (as shown in Figure 3) by an interaction of Name Training X Group. Tests of simple main effects indicated that name training significantly influenced recall performance for skilled, but not disabled readers. As shown in Figure 3, a simple main effect on reading ability group was found for the named condition, while no significant difference in recall was found between groups for the unnamed condition. Thus, a reading disability can not be attributed to developmental deficiencies in visual coding.

What can be concluded from these four studies in relation to modality-specific processing? First, it is clear that mixing visual and verbal codes has a deleterious consequence on LD readers' performance. When labels are used to encode nonverbal forms, there is a decrease in disabled readers' performance when compared with the unnamed (nonverbal) conditions. Because encoding was comparable between ability groups (i.e., paired associative learning), we assume that a *functional* independence exists between the two store systems in disabled readers. It appears that the mixing of two inputs together, when the coding of one input is known to be weak (i.e., verbal code; Shankweiler et al., 1979; Vellutino et al., 1975a, 1975b), produces decrements to the LD subject in terms of recall. In con-

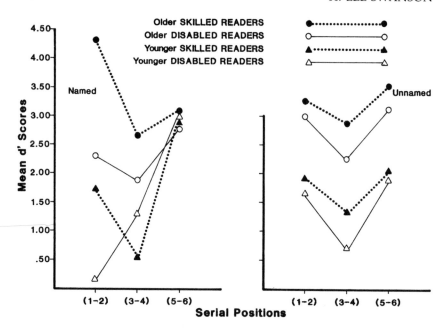

Figure 3.   Mean *d'* first choice response as a function of group, label and
nonlabeled stimulus and serial position. From "A study of nonstrategic linguistic coding on visual recall of learning disabled readers"
by H. L. Swanson (1983). *Journal of Learning Disabilities, 16,* 209–
216. Copyright 1983, by Professional Press, adapted by permission.

trast, skilled readers are able to establish interconnections between the
two stores and thus yield an additive effect in recall. Second, both ability
groups are comparable in their processing of visual information, via a
modality-specific code. For example, no developmental lags were apparent
on the disabled readers part in their processing of nonverbal information.

Finally, the data suggest that qualitatively different memory representations may underlie disabled and skilled readers' modality-specific processing. Because the training instructions did not encourage the semantic
linking of the verbal and visual systems (i.e., the common properties of
both visual and verbal input were *not* emphasized in the training instructions), we assume that both ability groups processed visual information
in a modality-specific manner. Based on the results, it appears that two
different or distinctive underlying representations may have been used by
skilled readers in an additive fashion, while disabled readers failed to make
an appropriate connection between the two separate stores (one linking
pictures with names). More specifically, skilled readers memory performance in one condition surpassed the second, suggesting then the former
must have required more complex processing of multiple codes (thus cri-

terion d was met). However, does such processing by skilled readers merely reflect the additive effect of two distinct multiple codes? The next series of studies sheds some light on this issue.

SEMANTIC PROCESSING

In the second stage of picture-word processing, visual codes are associated with one or more corresponding verbal codes. This *linking* of visual and verbal information is done through a process of determining properties common to both verbal and visual input. This linking occurs because a semantic network is activated (e.g., Kintsch, 1974; te Linde, 1982; Paivio, 1978; Snodgrass, 1984). When compared with visual coding alone, the semantic network provides a means of further mediating and referencing the various attributes of the visual stimulus. This further referencing is done by effectively organizing or indexing (e.g., class affiliation, subordinate and subordinate properties) the two (visual, verbal) memory inputs (e.g., Jolicoeur et al., 1984; te Linde, 1982). In relation to reading ability, several studies (e.g., Ceci et al., 1980; Perfetti, Hogaboam & Bell—reported in Perfetti & Lesgold, 1979; Swanson, 1984b; Vellutino, Steger, DeSetto, & Phillips, 1975a, 1975b) suggest that LD readers have difficulty linking visual and verbal information into semantic network. We briefly review studies from our laboratory that support this second stage, and draw our conclusions from two different memory tasks.

Picture-Naming Task

The studies to be reviewed use the same probe-recall procedures discussed earlier and manipulated the name training conditions in order to better understand the locus of disabled readers recall interference and facilitation. In the first study (Swanson, 1984b, Experiment 1) reviewed, skilled and LD readers, matched on CA ($M = 12.9$) and IQ ($M = 106.3$), viewed nonsense pictures with or without labels. In the former condition, labels were either semantically relevant (the experimenter directed the subject to the particular visual properties clearly associated with the name) or irrelevant (no connection was indicated between the common properties of a name and shape) with respect to the distinctive characteristics of the pictures. Based on these experimental conditions, predictions related to how ability group represent memory information can be derived from the two memory coding models: common code versus dual codes. Both memory coding models hypothesize that verbal labeling increases retrieval of visual presented information (see Klatzky & Rafnel, 1976; Warren & Horn, 1982). For example, the common code model assumes that labeling a picture at input insures that semantic processing of the picture occurs and thereby increases the likelihood that semantic information becomes part of the resulting memory code (Bartlett, Till, & Levy, 1980; Nelson, 1979; Nelson & Castano, 1984; Nelson, Reed, & McEvoy, 1977). Likewise, the dual coding model suggests that code redundancy has an additive (i.e., positive) effect on performance (Paivio, 1978). Of course, both models have different explanations under which naming a picture at input influences subsequent recall. A name that has a meaningful representation with respect to the corresponding picture will be recalled better than other conditions, and meaningless labels will provide no better recall than unnamed pictures (see Klatzky & Rafnel, 1976, for a rationale). That is, a meaningless name (with respect to the contour of the shapes) would access the same conceptual representation as the picture. According to the dual coding model, a verbal code is independent of the visual code and therefore retrieval will be no better recalled with meaningful than nonmeaningful labels, but both conditions will be better recalled than the no label condition.

While these arguments are rather traditional, we suggest an alternative conceptualization (see Snodgrass, 1984, for a review). We assume that readers are flexible in the way they process pictorial information and that, within the limits of their semantic system, they are capable of varying their coding strategies so as to process visual information within a modality-specific knowledge system or a conceptual/semantic system. We assume that, based on reading ability, subjects will adopt whichever strategy will maximize recall effects. More specifically, its hypothesized that skilled readers use modality-specific representations and amodality-independent semantic system when it is to their advantage to do so. In contrast, disabled readers, because of their difficulty in indexing the common properties of visual and verbal input, (i.e., mixing two codes together), favor processing information through the visual modality system (Stage 1). Further, procedures that induce disabled readers to mix the two codes together (as in a picture-naming task) produces costs to the LD reader in terms of recall.

Except for a manipulation of name-shape instruction, methods, materials, and procedures in the present study were comparable to the earlier studies (Swanson, 1978a, 1978b; 1983) reviewed. As shown in Figure 4, recall was higher for skilled (CA = 13.3, MIQ = 107.6) than disabled readers (CA = 12.8, IQ M = 106.1). Name training conditions interacted with ability group performance. Tests of simple main effects indicated that skilled readers recalled more name-associated and name nonassociated items than disabled readers, while no ability group differences were found for the unnamed condition. For skilled readers, recall of name associated and name nonassociated items were not significantly different, while both

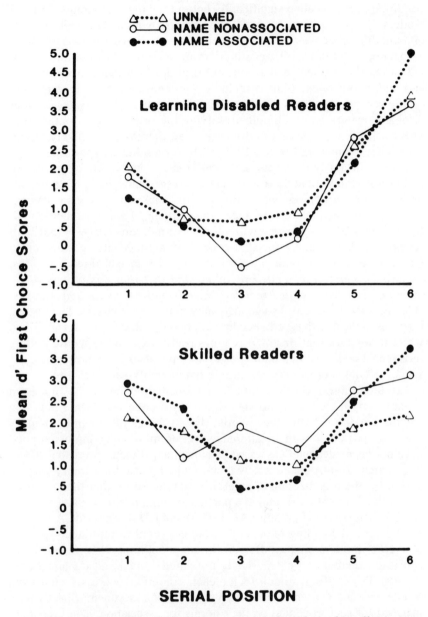

Figure 4. Mean *d'* first choice response as a function of reading group, treatment, and serial position. From "Semantic and visual memory codes in learning disabled readers" by H. L. Swanson (1984). *Journal of Experimental Child Psychology, 37,* 124–140. Copyright 1984 by Academic Press. Adapted by permission.

conditions were recalled significantly better than unnamed items. For LD readers, unnamed items were recalled better than named, while no significant difference was found between name associated versus name nonassociated conditions. There was a Group X Serial Position interaction indicating that skilled readers out perform disabled readers on primacy and middle positions, while disabled readers out perform skilled readers on the recency positions. This finding was interpreted as suggesting that disabled readers have difficulty resolving the order of information in a linear array (i.e., indexing information) and therefore selectively attend to recency items (see Mason, 1978; 1980; for a related hypothesis).

The important finding was that while the facilitative effects of verbal coding for skilled readers was unrelated to the name shape assignment, verbal coding conditions were superior to visual coding (unnamed) conditions. This unequal performance between named and unnamed conditions and equal performance within named conditions suggests that both semantic coding (name-associated condition) and modality specific coding (name nonassociated condition) are likely to occur in skilled readers. *Thus, criterion d must be extended to reflect the fact that coding variability within and between skilled readers depends on task instruction.* For disabled readers, there was also an inequality in treatment effects. The results, however, indicated that verbal coding interfered with effective recall. Thus, while it appears that disabled readers prefer modality-specific coding (nonverbal coding), such coding does not appear to have appropriate associative connections between the verbal modality-specific store.

The limitation of these results is that a semantic system has not been directly implicated (i.e., no significant difference was found between naming conditions). In other words, the attributes of semantic memory (i.e., the indexing or organizational aspect of interconnecting two inputs) have not been adequately assessed. The next experiment (Swanson, 1984b; Experiment 2) introduced a new task in which episodic memory was assessed for the organization of an entire stimulus set, rather than focusing on recall of individual stimuli at a particular serial position. Skilled (MCA = 12.7, MIQ = 108.0, reading M = 77.3) and LD readers (MCA = 12.2, MIQ = 102.7, Reading M = 21.4) were expected to reproduce (sketch) nonverbal random shapes after pretraining conditions that included categorically related and categorically unrelated named and unnamed conditions. Twenty-four stimuli (8 for each condition) were selected from Vanderplas and Garvin's (1959) nonverbal shape assortment. Shapes were matched for each condition on their norms for association values, content, and shape complexity. The verbal pretraining included stimulus words of two types: categorically related (animal, dog, cat, bird) and unrelated words (e.g., baby, hammer, square). A pretraining condition also included the tracing of unfamiliar shapes for both the named and unnamed con-

Table 3. Mean Percentage of Correct and Correct Ratio of Repetition
Score (CRR) as a Function of Naming Condition

	Categorically related	*Unrelated*	*Unnamed*
Learning Disabled			
Percent correct	24.40	30.03	37.16
Clustering-subordinate	30.70	29.95	29.25
Clustering-superordinate	20.70	27.41	31.69
Skilled Readers			
Percent correct	45.62	46.74	40.53
Clustering-subordinate	32.35	23.80	31.69
Clustering-superordinate	42.75	33.55	29.25

From Swanson, H., 1984, *Journal of Experimental Child Psychology,* reprinted with the permission of
Academic Press.

ditions. After tracing was completed, children were shown a single composite without labels. Children studied the composite and after a short distractor task were asked to reproduce all the forms. Mean percent of correct reproduction and retrieval organization (based on the pretraining condition in which a composite of all shapes was provided in tree like fashion) by name training condition are shown in Table 3. Skilled readers correctly reproduce more shapes than disabled readers on the named but not the unnamed conditions. Within conditions, skilled readers superior performance occurred on named, while disabled readers superior performance occur on unnamed conditions. As shown in Table 3, ability group differences in terms of the interference and facilitative recall patterns related verbal conditions replicated the previous studies.

Retrieval organization was next analyzed for superordinate and subordinate levels of clustering within and between the two input (visual and verbal) systems. For example, retrieval may follow a vertical or top to bottom organization (superordinate) or an organization directed by subordinate relationships (organization by levels). When clustering scores were analyzed by subordinate levels, no significant difference occurred between ability groups within labeling conditions. These results suggest that ability groups did not differ in their use of interitem associations. Although superordinate organization scores on the unnamed condition did not differ between ability groups, organization scores were higher for skilled compared to disabled readers on the categorically related word condition. Thus, a general semantic code (one representing superordinate relations) was more likely to be used by skilled than disabled readers. Interestingly, superordinate organization scores were higher for disabled readers than skilled readers on the categorically unrelated word condition. Coupled with the recall performance, these latter results suggest that disabled readers focus on interitem associations *within* a specific coding systems more so than skilled readers. The results also suggest that when words are conceptually unrelated, skilled readers restructured the visual composite to form their own hierarchical scheme. Support for this interpretation comes from the finding that skilled readers' percentage of correct reproduction for the unrelated word condition was comparable to the categorically related condition. Thus, skilled readers attempt to connect and define a visual representation in terms of its semantic properties. A post-hoc analysis within groups supports this finding in that organization differences between treatments were categorical > unrelated > unnamed; for skilled and unnamed > unrelated > categorical for disabled readers, respectively. These results provide evidence for the notion that skilled readers prefer amodal representations but can rely on modality-specific (as evidenced by their recall on the unrelated word condition) when it is to their advantage to do so. In contrast, while disabled readers engage in modality-specific representations, they have difficulty mixing multiple inputs codes at a semantic level when required to do so.

Neuropsychological Tasks

There is evidence to suggest that verbal and visual coding may underlie hemispheric processing preferences or biases in recall (e.g., Paivio, 1971; Sidtis, Volpe, Holtzman, Wilson, & Gazzaniga, 1981). For example, the left-hemispheric processing tends to specialize in the processing of verbal coded material, while right hemispheric tends to specialize in the processing of visually coded material. While assumptions related localized processing are questionable (e.g., Friedman & Polson, 1981; Obrzut, Hynd, Obrzut, & Pirozzolo, 1981), it is possible that the two independent hemisphere may interconnect or share resources at a semantic level (see Sidtis et al., 1981; Swanson & Mullen, 1983). Thus, additional support for the hypothesis that disabled readers verbal and visual coding processes are functionally independent is reflected by their inability to utilize superordinate word classifications shared between the two hemispheres. Further, consistent with the findings on the picture-naming tasks, one would expect that recall differences would occur between ability group in terms of the verbal processing demands placed on the two cerebral hemispheres. One means to test these assumptions is to look at ability group recall performance as a function of ear presentations and the level-of-word processing. In our study (Swanson & Mullen, 1983), two age groups of LD (MCA = 12.2, MCA = 8.8) and skilled readers (MCA = 11.6, MCA = 8.6) were compared on diotic (identical word information presented to *both* ears simultaneously) and dichotic listening recall task for semantically organized (e.g., red, green, blue), phonemically organized (e.g., set, pit), and categorically unrelated word lists. Free recall scores are presented in Table 4 as a function of age and ability group and type of word processing. The most important result was that the Group X Task (dichotic, diotic) X Type of word processing interaction was significant. Skilled readers' recalled more semantically and phonemically organized words in the right ear (left hemisphere) and more phonemically organized words on the diotic (both) task then disabled readers. Within groups, disabled readers recall more words on diotic and left ear (right hemisphere) presentations than right ear presentations. In contrast, skilled readers recalled more words from the right ear than other presentations.

Overall, the results suggest that disabled readers are comparable to skilled readers in processing linguistic information in the right hemisphere (left ear presentation) and transcallosally (diotic presentation). While its tempting to conclude that LD readers' verbal coding deficits are related to the processing of linguistic information in the left hemisphere, a subsequent analysis of retrieval patterns would caution such an interpretation. As in the previous experiment (Swanson, 1984b, Experiment 2), an analysis of *hierarchial* clustering for the semantically and phonemically organized word lists provided only one significant effect, skilled readers recalled more superordinate categories than LD readers. The nonsignificant main effect and interactions related to ear presentation suggests that skilled readers link the resources in the two independent hemispheres (see Freidman & Polson, 1981; Friedman, Polson, Dafoe, & Gaskill, 1982, for a discussion of this notion) by taking advantage of the superordinate properties of words. That is, support is found for the notion that skilled readers appear to link two independent hemispheric resources through a semantic system.

Additional evidence for this interpretation was found in our recent study (Swanson & Obzrut, 1985) in which LD and nondisabled readers were compared on dichotic listening recall tasks that included semantic, phonemic, and structural orienting instructions. As expected, performance was a function of group, orienting instructions, and ear presentation on measures of ear lateralization, free recall, retrieval clustering, and selective attention. Most importantly, the results demonstrated that group recall differences interact with orienting instructions. The effects of orienting instructions were pronounced for nondisabled readers but not for LD readers, suggesting that the two ability groups differ in the accessing information from semantic memory. Further, interactions related to orienting instructions suggested that memory traces were composed of various resources from each hemisphere (as inferred from ear laterality scores), which further determined the quality of recall. Specifically, the results

Table 4. Mean Percentage Correct Recall as a Function of Age, Group, Mode of Presentation, and Level of Word Processing

	Both Ears			Right Ear			Left Ear		
	Semantic	Phonemic	Unrelated	Semantic	Phonemic	Unrelated	Semantic	Phonemic	Unrelated
Older									
Disabled	.44	.28	.29	.36	.36	.26	.44	.33	.26
	(.11)	(.09)	(.11)	(.16)	(.14)	(.11)	(.16)	(.11)	(.06)
Nondisabled	.45	.38	.35	.44	.42	.35	.43	.33	.30
	(.18)	(.12)	(.08)	(.13)	(.13)	(.13)	(.13)	(.11)	(.07)
Younger									
Disabled	.37	.28	.23	.29	.24	.26	.38	.28	.26
	(.12)	(.11)	(.12)	(.11)	(.13)	(.09)	(.12)	(.08)	(.06)
Nondisabled	.33	.30	.20	.42	.29	.22	.37	.31	.29
	(.12)	(.10)	(.04)	(.16)	(.09)	(.05)	(.11)	(.11)	(.09)

Note: Standard deviation in parentheses.
From "Hemispheric specialization in learning disabled readers' recall as a function of age and level of processing" by Swanson, H.L. & Mullen, R. (1983). Journal of Experimental Child Psychology, 35, 457–477. Copyright by Academic Press. Adapted by permission.

suggested that LD readers' semantic memory appeared to be deficient in (a) the amount of information it contained and (b) the internal organization and coherence of that information.

In summary, the previous studies suggest that inadequate superordinate structures from a semantic system underlie LD readers' ineffective verbal coding. Collectively, the studies suggest that label training increases memory for visual forms in skilled readers, but labeling seems to uniformly reduce recall of LD readers. Our results, consistent with others (e.g., Vellutino & Scanlon, 1982), suggest that visual coding is not impaired in LD readers, since their performance was like that of skilled readers under the no-labeling condition. We realize it is impossible to make a final decision between dual (modality-specific) coding versus common coding (amodal) memory theory as an unequivocal framework for capturing ability group differences in how visual information is mentally represented. The available evidence on disabled readers' recall performance tends to favor the former position. For disabled readers, the two codes appear to aggregate negatively or (at least) the potency between the two codes differs (unequal performance). As consequence of this type of aggregation, multiple input does not increase recall of pictorial information. In contrast, the results suggest that skilled readers are flexible, depending on task, in activating a referential or superordinate level of representation, which influences how memory traces are combined in an additive manner. This finding renders the modality-specific representations as important, but also suggests that skilled readers may, depending on the task, use a semantic code (amodal code) to unify the distinct features of two modality systems. Thus, our results supported the notion that each and every processing task will not yield consistent evidence for or against a common versus dual code hypothesis (e.g., Snodgrass, 1984).

LEXICAL PROCESSING

In the final stage, a lexical system is activated in order to provide internal input to the semantic network (see Kintsch, 1974; Lachman & Lachman, 1980; Norman & Rumelhart, 1975; for a discussion related to the distinction between semantic and lexical networks). The lexical system provides an attachment of *word meaning* to the organization or indexing of memory codes. For example, word meaning has been known to influence semantic processing by increasing an item's relatedness (Scarborough, Gerard, & Cortese, 1984) perceptual recognition (e.g., Jacoby, 1983) as well as integrating representations of bilingual language systems (e.g., see Scarborough et al., 1984, for a review). Of course, it may be argued that the semantic network encompasses the entire vocabulary of an individual and therefore "word meaning" is not an independent system (Kuczaj, 1982; Mervis, 1983). Therefore, no claims are made about the organization of the lexical system relative to its semantic properties. However, as indicated from clinical studies on patients with amnesia and aphasia (e.g., Gardner, 1974; Squire & Cohen, 1982), it is assumed that the lexical system represents a repository or vocabulary of acquired names for conceptual categories in the semantic system. In relating the lexical and semantic stages to reading ability, here is evidence suggesting that disabled readers suffer from lexical deficiencies that may encumber them on semantic coding tasks (e.g., Denkla & Rudel, 1976a, 1976b; Fleisher, Jenkins, & Pany, 1979; Guthrie, 1973).

Except for a study to be discussed later in the chapter, our work in this stage of processing has been meager. Indirect evidence is available suggesting that effective semantic processing is linked to the *effort* of accessing information from a lexical system (Swanson, 1984b). Processing effort (or cognitive effort) was determined in this study when manipulations were made on primary tasks of differing difficulty that required the accessing of information from a lexical system (e.g., identifying a word), and subsequent recall performance on a secondary task. In the study of concern (Swanson, 1984a, Experiment 3), primary tasks included correctly solving anagrams of varying difficulty and secondary tasks included word recall of correctly solved anagrams. It is generally accepted that anagram solution relies on the accessing of a lexical system (e.g., Fink & Weisberg, 1981; Rubenstein, Lewis, & Rubenstein, 1971). In the present study we explored the notion that differences in word recall between ability groups were related to effort of accessing information for a lexical system. One purpose of this study was to examine whether distinctive word features activated during recall differed between reading ability groups. An understanding of the word features activated in each group is assumed to be couched in the interaction between stimulus structure (word list organization) and memory processes (orienting instructions). In the present study, subjects consisted of 24 skilled (MCA = 8.6, MIQ = 105.0) and 24 (MCA = 8.8, MIQ = 99.4) LD readers matched as closely as possible on CA and IQ. Prior to recalling each anagram solution, children answered questions about the targeted word. The conditions related to each of the orienting questions are shown in Figure 5.

The purpose of the *nonrelational* orienting condition was to direct children's attention to the distinctive features "between" words. This condition directed children to answer "yes" or "no" to a question about whether a previously presented target word and a newly presented target word had the same meaning. All appropriate responses for the semantically organized and uncategorized word lists required a "no" response. Admittedly, a bias exists in these conditions in that all correct responses

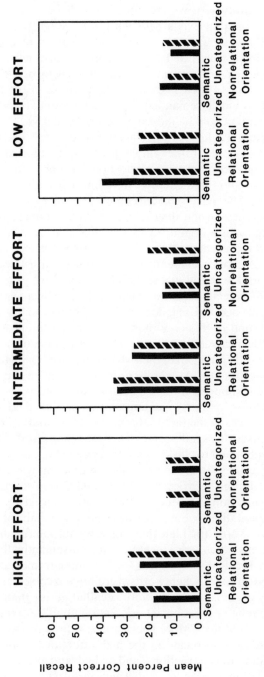

Figure 5. Mean total percentage of correct word recall of words as a function of group, semantic orientation instructions (relational vs. nonrelational), processing effort, and word organization. From "Effects of cognitive effort and word distinctiveness on learning disabled and nondisabled readers' recall" by H. L. Swanson (1984). *Journal of Educational Psychology, 76,* 894–908. Adapted with permission.

285

were "no." However, it was reasoned that distinctive encoding occurs when minimal overlap exists between the targeted items (e.g., Hunt & Mitchell, 1982). A negative response was assumed to minimize the semantic overlap of words and thereby enhance distinctive encoding. To insure that children were attending to the differences between words, they were asked to justify their response. The purpose of the *relational* condition was to provide a semantic context (superordinate category) against which information could be judged as being distinctive. For the relational orienting condition, children were again asked "yes" or "no" questions about individual words. For example, for the uncategorized list they were asked if the word was of the same category as the previous one. All correct responses were "no" and children were intermittently required to justify their response. The purpose of this condition was to assess the effects of item distinctiveness when instructions include a superordinate context. For the categorically organized lists, children were asked whether the targeted word represented one of the four categories (e.g., animal, eating, utensil). All categories embedded within the word list were included in the task orientation question and therefore required "yes" response. The purpose of this condition was to minimize item distinctiveness (i.e., "yes" responses) while accentuating context (superordinate category). It assumed that the confound in this condition would lessen the probability of high recall, i.e., "distinctiveness" occurs when processing includes a "minimal overlap" of words rather than their shared features (see Hunt & Mitchell, 1982; for a discussion). All children correctly solved the anagram tasks and correctly responded to task orienting questions.

Processing time for each anagram solution produced no statistically significant differences in the factorial aspects of this study. Thus, processing time was an insensitive index of lexical processing effort. Significant main effects were obtained for task orientation and list organization on the percent correct recall scores. An important interaction was found for Group × Task Orientation × Processing Effort and Group × Processing Effort × List Organization. In general, the results suggest that (a) relational (semantic) orientations were superior to nonrelational; (b) skilled readers recalled more words for high than for low and intermediate processing effort conditions when words were organized semantically, whereas disabled readers recalled more words for low and intermediate than for high processing effort tasks when words were organized semantically; and (c) semantically organized words were recalled better than uncategorized words in the relational (context) orientation condition, though not in the nonrelational condition. More specifically, skilled readers were superior to disabled readers in recall on the high effort task under the relational semantic orientation instructions, and on high and intermediate effort task under nonrelational orientation instructions. LD readers recalled more semantically organized words than skilled readers during the relational orientation for the low effort condition. Within the skilled reading group, the effect of lexical processing effort on recall was related to list organization. Recall scores for skilled readers by processing effort (collapsed across task orientation conditions) were: intermediate > high = low, for uncategorized lists, and high > intermediate > low, for semantically organized lists, respectively. The LD readers recall ordering by stimulus organization was: low > intermediate > high, for semantically organized lists, and intermediate > high = low, for uncategorized word lists, respectively.

In summary, the results show that individual variations occur in how lexical processing effort facilitates later recall. As suggested by the ability Group × Effort × List Organization interaction, when the process demands are high, disabled readers change the level of their initial processing so as to recall an optimal number of word features. This resolution occurs when processing intensity places more strain on the lexical system than can be effectively accommodated. We review some recent information that more directly tests the aforementioned three stage model.

RECENT LABORATORY STUDIES

The aforementioned systems (i.e., visual, semantic, lexical) discussed in this chapter provide a tentative framework for capturing ability group differences in memory coding. The model is not dependent upon a resolution of the common code or multiple code controversy (see Snodgrass, 1984) because it suggests that both amodal and modality specific effects may capture ability group differences. These ability group differences can be accounted for in two ways. First, ability group differences may be accented when experimental procedures require a transition for modality-specific representations (Stage 1) to modality independent representations (Stage 2). Second, because several studies (e.g., Vellutino & Scanlon, 1985) suggest that reading ability group differences in recall occur at the semantic stage of processing, it is possible to assess the manner in which semantic processing is influenced by a lexical system. That is, to what extent is the activation of semantic network (i.e., the references of visual and verbal knowledge) influenced by ability group differences in a lexical system? Within this context, the present studies address the question, Is the LD reader's semantic network during the processing of pictorial information influenced by a "high" or "low" repository of lexical information?

In addition to the preceding question, the present series of studies addressed two related questions. First, are ability group differences in picture-word recall related to the verbal codability of pictorial information; and if so, what coding mechanisms influence such ability group performance? An answer to this two part question is important because it determines whether ability group differences are independent or dependent upon the verbal qualities of pictorial information. Several studies (e.g., Swanson, 1978a, 1978b; Vellutino & Scanlon, 1982) provide evidence that disabled readers retrieve visual information on a level comparable to skilled readers when items are of low verbal codability. It is assumed that low codable items eliminate the advantage accrued to skilled readers by virtue of their ability to utilize verbal codes in short-term memory. However, several inconsistent results in ability group performance have occurred when a manipulation has been made of high and low item codability (e.g., Cummings & Faw, 1976; DiLollo, Hanson, & McIntyre, 1983; Gascon & Goodglass, 1970; Morrison, Giordinia, & Nagy, 1977, Wolford & Fowler, manuscript). For example, a number of studies have demonstrated performance differences between skilled and disabled readers with both verbal and nonverbal stimuli and on nonverbal tasks (Morrison et al., 1977; also see Morrison & Manis, 1982, for a review). Based on our earlier studies, it is possible that the conflict in findings may reflect the coordination of resources from the semantic system. This coordination of information is reflected in the information transmitted between long-term and short-term memory.

The second question focuses on the relationship between visual form and meaning in language. More specifically, Is meaning independent or dependent of pictorial surface form? In relation to reading ability, several authors (e.g., Byrne & Shea, 1979; Goodman & Burke, 1972; Haber, & Haber, 1981) indirectly have suggested that disabled readers separate the surface form of pictures from the meaning features of language. That is, disabled readers tend to divorce the verbal code from pictorial information in order to analyze the distinctive visual features of information. However, it is uncertain about what kind of information processing costs occur because of disabled readers utilization of separate and distinct codes. One possibility is that these "costs" may be represented in terms of down grading verbal codes in favor of processing visual representations. One hypothesis to be tested in this study is that during label training for low codable shapes, both ability groups attempt to relegate (down grade) verbal codes to a secondary process in their mental representation of visual information. However, in contrast to disabled readers, skilled readers efficiently map visual information onto preexisting semantic information in long-term memory. Thus, skill readers processing of meaning and surface form is an independent process.

Study 1

The first study determined whether disabled readers activate a semantic system independent of the verbal codability of visual information and effectively coordinate semantic information between two memory structures (i.e., long-term and short-term memory). To this end, a comparison was made between named and unnamed training conditions on the serial recall of pictured shapes that were of either high or low verbal codability. Names were either semantically relevant or irrelevant with respect to the contour (form) of the pictured shape. The inclusion of relevant and irrelevant name conditions is based upon the assumption that a relevant name (with respect to the shape contour) has a more meaningful (i.e., semantic) representation of pictorial information than nonassociated name, thus better facilitating access to an "amodal" representation of pictorial information (see Klatzky & Rafnel, 1976). Support for the notion that skilled readers prefer processing word-picture information in an amodal fashion would be found if the name-associated conditions produce higher recall than name-nonassociated condition. However, a more flexible hypothesis, as discussed earlier suggests that in contrast to disabled readers, skilled readers are able to make strategic transitions between amodal and multiple coding representation and, therefore, recall differences are not expected to occur between name training conditions.

This first experiment does not assess the independent effects of LD readers' semantic and lexical systems on the coding of multiple input. Based on our previous study, (e.g., Swanson, 1984b, Experiment 1), however, it was assumed that names would provide skilled readers with a means of indexing visual information independent of the contour of the shape. This independence between the shape and name assignment during retrieval performance suggests that a highly developed semantic system is in operation (see Klatzky & Rafel, 1976, for a discussion). Except for the use of verbally codable shapes in the high codable condition, procedure, stimuli, and test procedures were similar to the previously reviewed picture-name tasks.

As shown in Figure 6, the main effect of ability group and name-training was not significant but was obscured by an interaction of ability Group × Name Training. Tests of simple main effects indicated that skilled readers, when compared to LD readers, recalled more name associated and name nonassociated shapes. For skilled readers, name conditions resulted in higher recall than unnamed conditions, while no difference in recall was found between the named conditions. LD readers recalled more unnamed shapes than name associated and name nonassociated shapes, while name nonassociated shapes were recalled more often than name associated shapes.

In order to better interpret ability group and item codability effects, a separate analysis of d' scores was done. Assuming that serial position performance involves two independent stores, then the overall probability of an item being recalled according to Watkins (1974) is $Rj = Pm + Sm - (Pm - Sm/R)$, where R is the overall recall probability, Pm is primary memory or short-term memory storage, Sm is secondary memory or long-

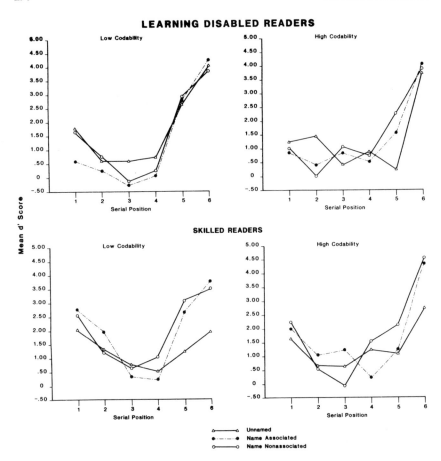

Figure 6. Mean *d'* performance as a function of reading group, stimulus codability, name training and serial position.

term memory storage (which is calculated as the mean of the two middle serial positions), and R is the recall of the last item (this is used as an estimate of the probability that items are entering short-term storage). On the assumption that disabled readers differ from skilled readers in short-term storage, the following formula was used (see Glanzer, 1982; Watkins, 1974, for a review) to compute performance on the primacy and recency positions: Pm = Rj (Rj − Sm)/(Rj − Sm). Rj, in this case was equal to the performance of mean *d'* scores of serial position 1 and 2 (primary position) and serial position 5 (recency position). An analysis of variance on primary and recency storage scores, utilizing the factors discussed earlier was performed.

Table 5. Short-term Memory Storage by Item Codability, Name Training, and Ability Group (Item Codability)

	High Codability			Low Codability		
	Primacy	*Recency*	*Row M*	*Primacy*	*Recency*	*Row M*
Learning Disabled						
Unnamed	− .16	−1.00	− .58	.08	2.34	1.21
Name Associated	− .60	.58	− .02	.14	2.56	1.35
Name Nonassociated	−1.00	1.38	.19	1.43	2.72	2.07
Column *M*	− .59	.31		.55	2.54	
Skilled readers						
Unnamed	.17	.77	.47	.96	.27	.62
Name Associated	.27	− .69	− .21	2.10	2.71	2.41
Name Nonassociated	.05	1.37	.71	.83	2.88	1.86
Column *M*	.17	.48		1.31	1.93	

As shown in Table 5, low scores reflect the accessing of resources from long-term memory, while high scores reflect the accessing of resources from short-term memory. We interpret the minus d' scores as reflecting an unduly restrictive transference of information from long-term memory to a memory stage (e.g., short-term memory) where it would facilitate retrieval. Main effects for item codability, serial position, and ability group were found. These results suggest that short-term memory resources are more readily used for low codable than high codable items and that recency rather than primacy positions demand more of these resources.

The interpretation of the main effect for ability group must be qualified since a four-way interaction occurred. In general, this interaction suggests that disabled readers' short-term memory resources are superior to skilled readers on the recency but inferior on the primacy positions. Thus, skilled readers' recall performance appears to represent a "balance" between resources activated from long-term and short-term memory. In contrast, disabled readers appear to have difficulty coordinating semantic resources from the two independent memory systems. The inadequate coordination of long-term memory resources (i.e., semantic information) in disabled readers is most apparent on the high codable primacy position, especially under name-training conditions. No other theoretically important findings occurred.

The present study supports the notion that verbal codes influence skilled readers' episodic memory of visual information because they activate a semantic system. Regardless of an item's verbal codability, labels appear to favorably influence the skilled reader's coding operations and thus produce an additive effect in recall. In contrast, the disabled reader's poor episodic memory reflects the fact that verbal codes fail to provide an additive effect in recall. The initial coding of items influenced recall in the sense that highly codable items disrupted the disabled reader's efficient short-term memory storage operations while low codable items "free-up" short-term memory resources. It appears that disabled readers have difficulty coordinating resources from a semantic system between two memory structures (long-term and short-term memory). This inference is supported from the finding that disabled readers recall of visual information is disrupted when visual codes are semantically processed (i.e., when name training instructions directly link, via the name associated condition, the common properties of verbal and visual information). Thus, the results suggest that the disabled reader's representation of visual information is qualitatively different from that of the skilled reader. Specifically, disabled readers processing reflects a type of restrictive modality-specific representation while skilled readers appear to benefit from conditions that emphasize both amodal (name-associated condition) and modality-specific (name-nonassociated condition) representations.

Study 2

The next study indirectly assesses the extent to which skilled and disabled readers' (N = 18 in each group) semantic processing of visual information is influenced by a lexical system. To this end, the effects of training when both *shapes* and *names* were of *low* verbal codability were assessed. Words were selected from Paivio, Yuille, and Madigan's (1968) norms judge to be low in concreteness, imagery, and meaningfullness. It was assumed that if names were of low verbal association value, as well as nonrepresentative of shape contour, then a meager repository of information could be accessed from the lexical store. That is, based on the proposed three stage model, it was assumed that the semantic network would not be effectively activated during multiple coding operations because very little internal input would be provided from the lexical system. Thus, skilled readers would fail to establish interdependent verbal and visual interconnections, and such a failure would produce episodic memory performance comparable to disabled readers.

As shown in Figure 7, skilled readers performed slightly better than the disabled but the results were not significant. The findings were then compared with the previous experiment. When a statistical comparison was made between d' scores (these may interpreted as standard scores) for skilled readers in Study 1's low codable condition on the unnamed items to skilled readers' recall in the present study, performance was comparable. In contrast, disabled readers in the unnamed condition in Study 1 performed better when compared with this study's disabled readers on the named condition (M = 1.69 vs. M = .59). These results suggest that a semantic network must be activated before an additive recall effect occurs in the processing of multiple input for skilled readers. In contrast, disabled readers fail to effectively interconnect multiple codes together.

Study 3

This next study again compared name-training conditions, except LD readers were subdivided into high (LD-HV) and low (LD-LV) lexical ability. The issue under consideration was whether disabled readers, who have average lexical skills, can invoke a semantic representation of visual information comparable to skilled readers. The theoretical assumption was that the activation of a semantic network during multiple input operations is influenced by a lexical system. Thus, the additive effects of multiple inputs on recall performance would be most pronounced in the skilled reading and high lexical LD group. This study sought to identify LD subjects who were comparable in reading comprehension (i.e., decoding of visual printed text), but varied in terms of lexical knowledge (vocabulary).

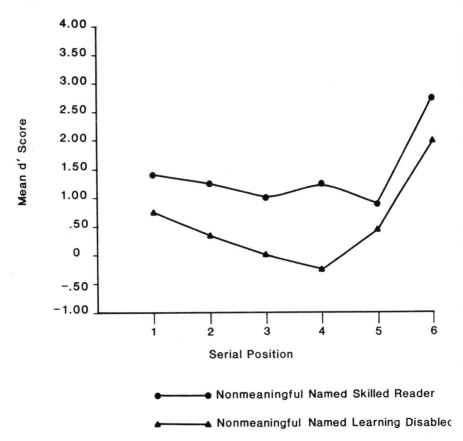

Figure 7.   Mean *d'* performance as a function of reading group and serial
         position.

To begin with, a pool of 84 LD children from a large eastern urban school
district was selected. All children were administered the reading comprehension and vocabulary subtests of the SRA Reading Achievement
Series (Thorpe, Lefever, & Naslund, 1969) as well as the Edinburgh
Handedness Inventory (Oldfield, 1970). The first measure was selected
because the vocabulary skills are assessed within a visual context (e.g.,
written passage). Further, the vocabulary subtest uses words from written
passages identical to these of the reading comprehension section administered immediately before. Therefore, we reasoned that any performance
discrepancies existing between vocabulary and reading comprehension
subtests would reflect lexical skills. The KR–20 reliability on the vocabulary subtest ranges from .76 to .92. The latter measure was administered

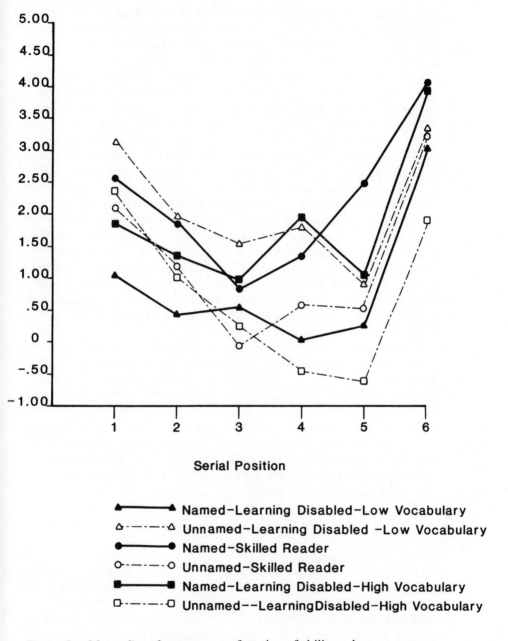

Serial Position

▲——————▲ Named–Learning Disabled–Low Vocabulary
△–·——·–△ Unnamed–Learning Disabled –Low Vocabulary
●——————● Named–Skilled Reader
○–·——·–○ Unnamed–Skilled Reader
■——————■ Named–Learning Disabled–High Vocabulary
□–·——·–□ Unnamed––LearningDisabled–High Vocabulary

Figure 8.   Mean *d'* performance as a function of ability subgroups, name-
   training, and serial position.

in order to provide some control over subject hemispheric processing preferences. This is because it has been recently argued that the left hemisphere is specialized for lexical access and is responsible for the verbal coding of visually-presented items (see Barry, 1981).

All skilled and LD readers, within a split plot design, participated in two treatment conditions. The two treatment conditions included named and unnamed pretraining. Materials, training instructions, and test procedures were identical to Study 1, except that the name-associated condition and high codable shapes were eliminated. As shown in Figure 8, a significant interaction was found for ability Group × Label Training. For the named conditions, tests of simple main effects indicated that skilled readers recalled more items than the LD-LV readers and LD-HV readers outrecalled LD-LV readers. No significant difference in recall was found between LD-HV and skilled readers. Thus, the results suggest that disabled readers who are high in vocabulary skills can effectively utilize multiple input. For the unnamed conditions, the LD-LV readers recalled more items than skilled and LD-HV readers. Skilled readers recalled more unnamed items than LD-HV readers, but the results were not significant. Within the name-training conditions, skilled and LD-HV readers recalled more items on the named than unnamed conditions. In contrast, LD-LV readers recalled more unnamed than named items.

In general, the results suggest that high vocabulary-learning disabled readers benefit from multiple input operations while low vocabulary learning disabled subjects do not. Thus, support is found for the notion that a lexical store influences coding operations. The results further suggest that LD readers who are deficient in lexical skills favor processing information through the visual coding system and, in some cases, are superior in this network when compared with children with higher vocabulary skills. The three studies taken together support the notion that the aforementioned stages may adequately capture some of the word and picture naming effects that occur between ability groups.

GENERAL CONCLUSIONS

Our studies to date suggest that children of normal intelligence who have problems in reading fail to use multiple input in an additive fashion. The experiments show that name-training seems to uniformly impede the recall of disabled readers. An exception to this finding was noted when disabled readers were subgrouped into high and low vocabulary skills. Collectively, the results of the name-training conditions reflect disabled readers' inability to activate a retrieval route that adequately relies on a semantic network. In addition, the results are consistent with others (e.g., Swanson, 1978a,

1978b; Vellutino, & Scanlon, 1982, 1985, for review), suggesting that visual coding is not impaired in LD readers, since their performance was like that of skilled readers under the unnamed condition. Two theoretical questions raised prior to the reviewing our recent studies and the theoretical framework for the results are now summarized.

In response to the first question related to the verbal codability of visual items, it is assumed from the LD literature that recall differences between ability groups is dependent upon the initial verbal codability of visual information. The relative effects of ability group recall become more pronounced with increasing opportunities for making verbal association to visual information. Unfortunately, this assumption was not clearly supported (no significant ability Group × Item Codability interaction occurred). When compared to other studies this lack of significant interaction in Study 1 may be due to the fact that stimulus complexity (e.g., number of points on a shape) and rehearsal were controlled. When an analysis was made of memory storage operations, however, the results clearly suggested that individual variations do exist in the semantic resources that can be effectively activated from long-term memory. For high codable items, it appears that disabled readers are inefficient in activating long-term memory resources, while skilled readers can effectively coordinate the semantic information accessed from long-term and short-term memory. Thus, support is found for the notion that ability group recall differences are not so much a matter of high versus low codable items as they are a function of the activation of semantic memory resources coordinated between the two independent memory stores.

In response to the second question on whether meaning is independent of visual form and verbal meaning, the results of the first study suggest that for skilled readers different instructions may reveal, on the one hand, evidence for independence or amodality and the other, dependence or modality-specific differences. In contrast, disabled readers' representation of information is dependent upon visual form and verbal meaning (i.e., a modality-specific system). The name-training effects for disabled readers during Study 1 suggest that semantic processing (name-associated condition) produced some processing costs or interference effects in recall. What appears to take place is disabled readers use a retrieval route unrelated to the verbal coding system and that instructions that emphasize the name mediating or indexing the various attributes of a single shape either "fragment" the visual code or block a preferred retrieval route. One can only speculate, but the results may indicate that remedial reading approaches that emphasize visual form and meaning are misdirected (e.g., see the Peabody Rebus Reading Program, Woodcock & Clark, 1969), while mnemonic procedures that capitalize on an intact retrieval route, i.e., imagery (see Scruggs et al., this volume; Levin, 1983; Paivio, 1983, for a discussion of the key-word method), holds promise in remediating reading difficulties. Regardless of this speculation, it appears that the verbal code that occupies a unique place in the skilled reader's memory does not carry its usual potency in disabled readers.

How can these three studies be placed within current information processing theory? A model for picture and word processing effects that predicts both amodal and modality-specific effects, depending on the task and reading ability, can be proposed. The model incorporates the notion that a semantic system mediates between two (verbal and visual) distinct memory codes, and subjects (based upon reading ability) will either maximize or minimize the input. Based on this model, three applications to LD and skilled readers' performances can be made. First, visual coding for both ability groups can be partially independent of verbal coding. Effective retrieval of visual information during the unnamed condition occurs for both ability groups under conditions in which verbal coding is unlikely. This implies that for both ability groups, visual processing (e.g., storage and retrieval) can occur in an independent visual memory system.

Secondly, the presentation of visual information activates a process that determines what the child "verbally" knows about the stimulus object. However, as shown in our final study and the anagram study (Swanson, 1984a), when lexical stores are meager, disabled readers fail to effectively access a semantic system and thereby benefit from multiple inputs. The results also suggest that multiple coding deficiencies are not characteristic of all LD readers. For example, high vocabulary LD readers had normal retrieval of visual information and did not appear to have difficulty utilizing labels to enhance recall. This finding suggests that other sources of variance in reading disabilities need to be explored. The fact that the high vocabulary LD group produced the poorest performance (although not significant) on the nonlabel-condition does suggest, however, than an important dimension of reading ability may be related to balancing cognitive resources associated with verbal and visual codes.

In summary, this chapter proposes a three stage model as a framework for interpreting LD readers' coding operations. It is proposed that a deficient lexical system contributes to disabled readers' rigid modality-specific coding operations by failing to provide input to the semantic system. In contrast, skilled readers' coding operations reflect a flexible transition between amodal and modality-specific knowledge systems. Because of inefficiencies in accessing semantic information, disabled readers have difficulty coordinating resources between two independent memory stores (long-term and short-term store) as well as processing information independent of the surface.

REFERENCES

Anderson, J. R., & Bower, G. H. (1973). *Human associative memory*. Washington, DC: Winston.

Atkinson, R., Hansen, D., & Bernbach, N. (1964). Short-term memory with children. *Psychonomic Science, 255–256.*

Barry, C. (1981). Hemispheric asymmetry in lexical access and phonological encoding. *Neuropsychologia, 19,* 473–478.

Bartlett, J. C., Till, R. E., & Levy, J. (1980). Retrieval characteristics of complex pictures: Effects of verbal coding. *Journal of Verbal Learning and Verbal Behavior, 19,* 430–449.

Battig, W., & Montague, W. (1969). Category norms for verbal items in categories: A replication and extension of the Connecticut category norms. *Journal of Experimental Psychology Monograph, 80,* 3, pt. 2.

Bauer, R. H. (1977). Memory processes in children with learning disabilities: Evidence for deficient rehearsal. *Journal of Experimental Child Psychology, 24,* 415–430.

Berch, D. (1975). Measures of sensitivity and response bias for the probe-type serial memory task. *Experimental Child Psychology, 20,* 154–158.

Berch, D. (1977). Absolute judgment of recency: A reexamination of children's short-term memory data. *Psychological Bulletin, 84,* 1261–1266.

Berch, D. (1979). Coding of spatial and temporal information in eposidic memory. In H. Reese (Ed.), *Advances in child development and behavior.* Orlando, FL: Academic Press.

Byrne, B., & Shea, P. (1979). Semantic and phonetic memory codes in beginning readers. *Memory & Cognition, 7,* 333–338.

Calfee, R. C. (1970). Short-term recognition memory in children. *Child Development, 41,* 145–161.

Ceci, S. J. (1980). A developmental study of multiple encoding and its relationship to age-related changes in free recall. *Child Development, 51,* 892–895.

Ceci, S. J. (1984). A development study of learning disabilities and memory. *Journal of Experimental Child Psychology, 38,* 352–371.

Ceci, S., Lea, S., & Ringstrom, M. (1980). Coding process in normal and learning disabled children. *Journal of Experimental Psychology: Human Learning and Memory, 6,* 785–795.

Cermak, L. (1983). Information processing deficits in children with learning disabilities. *Journal of Learning Disabilities, 16,* 599–605.

Chi, M. T. H. (1978). Knowledge structures and memory development. In R. S. Siegler (Ed.), *Children thinking: What develops?* (pp. 73–96). Hillsdale, NJ: Erlbaum.

Chi, M. T. H. (1983). A learning framework for development. In M. T. H. Chi (Ed.). *Trends in memory development* (Vol. , pp. 71–107). New York: S. Karger.

Corsini, D. A., Pick, A. D., & Flavell, J. H. (1968). Production deficiency of nonverbal mediators in young children. *Child Development, 39,* 53–58.

Craik, F. I., & Simon, E. (1980). Age differences in memory: The roles of attention and depth of processing. In L. Poon et al. (Eds.) *New directions in memory and aging* (pp. 95–112). Hillsdale, NJ: Erlbaum.

Cummings, E. M., & Faw, T. T. (1976). Short-term memory and equivalence judgments in normal and retarded readers. *Child Development, 47,* 286–289.

Daniels, T. C., & Ellis, H. C. (1972). Stimulus codability and long-term recognition memory for visual form. *Journal of Experimental Psychology, 96,* 83–89.

Denckla, M., & Rudel, R. (1976). Rapid 'automatized' naming (R.A.N.) Dyslexia differentiated for other learning disabilities. *Neuropsychologia, 14*, 471–479.

Denckla, M., & Rudel, R. (1976b). Naming of pictured objects by dyslecic and other learning disabled children. *Brain and Language, 3*, 1–15.

DiLollo, V., Hanson, D., & McIntyre, J. S. (1983). Initial stage of visual information process in dyslexia. *Journal of experimental psychology: Human perception and performance, 9*, 923–935.

Fink, T. E., & Weisenberg, R. W. (1981). The use of phonetic information to solve anagrams. *Memory & Cognition, 9*, 402–410.

Flavell, J. (1970). Developmental studies of mediated memory. In H. W. Reese & L. Lipsett (Eds.) *Advances in child development and behavior* (Vol. 5). Orlando, FL: Academic Press.

Flavell, J., Beach, D., & Chinsky, J. (1966). Spontaneous verbal rehearsal in memory tasks as a function of age. *Child Development, 37*, 283–299.

Fleisher, L. S., Jenkins, J. R., & Pany, D. (1979). Effects on poor readers' comprehension of training in rapid decoding. *Reading Research Quarterly, 15*, 30–48.

Friedman, A., & Polson, M. (1981). Hemispheres as independent resource systems: Limited-capacity processing and cerebral specialization. *Journal of Experimental Psychology: Human Perception and Performance, 7*, 1031–1058.

Friedman, A., Polson, M. C., Dafoe, C., & Gaskill, S. (1982). Dividing attention within and between hemispheres: Testing a multiple resources approach to limited-capacity information processing. *Journal of Experimental Psychology: Human Perception and Performance, 8*, 625–650.

Gardner, H. (1974). The naming of objects and symbols by children and aphasic patients. *Journal of Psycholinguistic Research, 3*, 133–149.

Gascon, G., & Goodglass, H. (1970). Reading retardation and the information content of stimuli in paired associate learning. *Cortex, 6*, 417–429.

Geiselman, R. E., Woodward, J. A., & Beatty, J. (1982). Individual differences in verbal memory performance: A text of alternative information processing models. *Journal of Experimental Psychology: General, 111*, 109–134.

Gibson, E. J. (1971). Perceptual learning and the theory of word perception. *Cognitive Psychology, 2*, 351–368.

Glanzer, M. (1982). Short-term memory. In C. R. Puff (Ed.), *Handbook of research methods in human memory and cognition* (pp. 63–93). Orlando, FL: Academic Press.

Goodman, Y., & Burke, C. L. (1972). *Reading Miscue Inventory: Procedure for diagnosis and evaluation*. New York: MacMillan.

Guthrie, J. T. (1973). Reading comprehension and syntatic responses in good and poor readers. *Journal of Educational Psychology, 65*, 294–299.

Haber, R., & Haber, L. (1981). The shape of a word can specify its meaning. *Reading Research Quarterly, 16*, 334–345.

Hagen, J., Meacham, J., & Masibov, B. (1970). Verbal learning, rehearsal and short-term memory. *Cognitive Psychology, 1*, 47–58.

Hagen, J., Jongeward, R., & Kail, R. (1975). Cognitive perspectives on the development of memory. In H. Reese (Ed.), *Advances in child development and behavior* (Vol. 10). Orlando, FL: Academic Press.

Hasher, L., & Zacks, R. T. (1979). Automatic and effortful processes in memory. *Journal of Experimental Psychology: General, 108*, 356–388.

Hochhaus, I. (1972). A table for the calculation of d' and B. *Psychological Bulletin, 77*, 326–375.

Hunt, R. R., & Mitchell, D. (1982). Implement effects of semantic and nonsemantic distinctiveness. *Journal of Experimental Psychology: Learning, Memory and Cognition, 8*, 81–87.

Jacoby, L. L. (1983). Perceptual enhancement: Persistent effects of experience. *Journal of Experimental Psychology: Learning, Memory, and Cognition, 9,* 21–38.

Jolicoeur, P., Gluck, M., & Kosslyn, S. (1984). Picture and names: Making the connection. *Cognitive Psychology, 16,* 243–275.

Kail, R. V., & Siegel, A. W. (1977). The development of mnemonic encoding in children: From perception to abstraction. In R. V. Kail & J. W. Hagen (Eds.), *Perspectives on the development of memory and cognition.* Hillsdale, NJ: Erlbaum.

Kintsch, W. (1974). *The representation of meaning in memory.* Hillsdale, NJ: Erlbaum.

Klatzky, R., & Rafnel, K. (1976). Labeling effects on memory for nonsense pictures. *Memory and Cognition, 4,* 717–720.

Kolers, P., & Gonzales, E. (1980). Memory for words, synonyms, and translation. *Journal of Experimental Psychology: Human Learning and Memory, 6,* 53–65.

Kosslyn, S. M., & Pomerantz, J. R. (1977). Imagery propositions and the form of internal representation. *Cognitive Psychology, 9,* 52–76.

Kuczaj, S. A. (1982). Acquisition of word meaning in development of the semantic system. In C. J. Brainerd & M. Presley (Eds.), *Verbal processes in children* (pp. 95–123). New York: Springer-Verlag.

Lackman, R., & Lackman, J. L. (1980). Picture naming: Retrieval and activation of long-term memory. In L. W. Poon et al. (Eds.), *New directions in memory and aging* (pp. 313–343). Hillsdale, NJ: Erlbaum.

Levin, J. R. (1983). Pictorial strategies for school learning: Practical illustrations. In M. Pressley & J. R. Levin (Eds.), *Cognitive strategy research: Educational applications* (pp. 213–237). New York: Springer-Verlag.

Lupker, S., & Katz, A. (1981). Input, decision, and response factors in picture-word interference. *Journal of Experimental Psychology: Human Learning and Memory, 7,* 269–283.

Mann, V. A., Liberman, I. Y., & Shankweiler, D. (1980). Children's memory for sentences and word strings in relation to reading ability. *Memory and Cognition, 5,* 623–629.

Marschark, M., & Paivio, A. (1977). Integrative processing of concrete and abstract sentences. *Journal of Verbal Learning and Verbal Behavior, 16,* 217–231.

Mason, M. (1978). From print to sound in mature readers as a function of reading ability and two forms of orthographic regularity. *Memory and Cognition, 6,* 568–581.

Mason, M. (1980). Reading ability and the encoding of item and location information. *Journal of Experimental Psychology: Human Perception and Performance, 6,* 89–98.

Mervis, C. B. (1983). Acquisition of a lexicon. *Contemporary Educational Psychology, 8,* 210–236.

Morrison, F. J. (1978). Reading disabilities: Methodological problem in information processing analysis: A reply. *Science, 200,* 802.

Morrison, F. J., Giordinia, B., & Nagy, I. (1977). Reading disability: An information processing analysis. *Science, 196,* 77–79.

Morrison, F. J., Holmes, D. L., & Haith, M. M. (1974). A developmental study of the effect of familiarity on short-term visual memory. *Journal of Experimental Child Psychology, 18,* 412–425.

Morrison, F. J., & Manis, F. R. (1982). Cognitive processes and reading disability: A critique and proposal. In C. J. Brainerd & M. Pressley (Eds.), *Verbal processes in children* (Vol.   , pp. 59–93). New York: Springer-Verlag.

Murdock, B. B. (1982). Recognition memory. In C. R. Puff (Ed.), *Handbook of research methods in human memory and cognition* (pp. 30–96). Orlando, FL: Academic Press.

Nagae, S. (1977). Recognition of random shapes as a function of complexity, relevancy and verbal labels and encoding strategy. *Japanese Psychological Research, 19,* 136–142.

Nelson, D. L. (1979). Remembering pictures and words: Appearance, significance and name. In L. S. Cermack & F. I. Craik (Eds.), *Level of processing in human memory* (pp. 45–76). Hillsdale, NJ: Erlbaum.

Nelson, D. L., & Brooks, D. H. (1973). Functional independence of pictures and verbal memory codes. *Journal of Experimental Psychology, 98,* 44–48.

Nelson, D. L., & Castano, D. (1984). Mental representations for pictures and words: Same or different. *American Journal of Psychology, 97,* 1–15.

Nelson, D. L., Reed, V. S., & McEvoy, C. L. (1977). Learning to order pictures and words: A model of sensory and semantic coding. *Journal of Experimental Psychology: Human Learning and Memory, 3,* 485–497.

Norman, D. A., & Rumelhart, D. E. (1975). *Explorations in cognition.* San Francisco: Freeman.

Obrzut, J., Hynd, G., Obrzut, A., & Pirozzolo, F. (1981). Effect of directed attention on cerebral asymmetries in normal and learning disabled children. *Developmental Psychology, 17,* 118–125.

Oldfield, R. (1971). The assessment and analysis of handedness: The Edinburgh inventory. *Neuropsychologigia, 9,* 97–113.

Paivio, A. (1971). *Imagery and verbal processes.* New York: Holt, Rinehart & Winston.

Paivio, A. (1975). Perceptual comparisons through the mind's eye. *Memory and Cognition, 3,* 635–647.

Paivio, A. (1978). Mental comparisons involving abstract attributes. *Memory and Cognition, 6,* 199–208.

Paivio, A. (1983). Strategies in language learning. In M. Pressley & J. Levin (Eds.), *Cognitive strategy research: Educational applications* (pp. 189–210). New York: Springer-Verlag.

Paivio, A., & Desrochers, A. (1980). A dual-coding approach to bilingual memory. *Canadian Journal of Psychology, 34,* 388–399.

Paivio, A., Yuille, J., & Madigan, S. (1968). Concreteness, imagery and meaningfulness values for 925 nouns. *Journal of Experimental Psychology.* Monograph Supplement, *76,* #1, part 2.

Perfetti, C. A. (1985). Reading ability. In R. J. Sternberg (Ed.), *Human abilities: An information processing approach* (pp. 59–102). New York: Freeman.

Perfetti, C. A., & Hogaboam, T. W. (1975). The relationship between single word decoding and reading comprehension skill. *Journal of Educational Psychology, 67,* 461–469.

Perfetti, C. A., & Lesgold, A. (1979). Coding and comprehension in skilled reading and implications for instruction. In L. B. Resnick & P. A. Weaver (Eds.), *Theory and practice of early reading.* Hillsdale, NJ: Erlbaum.

Piaget, J., & Inhelder, B. (1956). *The child's perception of space.* New York: Humanities Press.

Proctor, R., & Ambler, B. (1975). Effects of rehearsal strategy on memory for spacing and frequency. *Journal of Experimental Child Psychology: Human Learning and Memory, 1,* 640–647.

Pylyshn, Z. (1973). What the Mind's Eye Tells the Mind's Brain: A Critique of Mental Imagery. *Psychological Bulletin, 80,* 1–24.

Roach, E., & Kephart, N. (1966). *The Purdue perceptual motor survey.* Columbus, OH: Merrill.

Ross, B., & Youniss, J. (1969). Ordering of nonverbal items in children's recognition memory. *Journal of Experimental Child Psychology, 8,* 20–32.

Ryan, S., Hegian, A., & Flavell, J. (1970). Nonverbal mnemonic mediation in pre-school children. *Child Development, 40,* 539–550.

Rubenstein, H., Lewis, S. S., & Rubenstein, M. A. (1971). Evidence for phonemic recoding in visual word recognition. *Journal of Verbal Learning and Verbal Behavior, 10,* 645–657.

Scarborough, D. L., Gerard, L., & Cortese, C. (1984). Independence of lexical access in bilingual word recognition. *Journal of Verbal Learning and Verbal Behavior, 23,* 84–89.

Shankweiler, D., Liberman, I., Mark, I., Fowler, C., & Fisher, F. (1979). The speech code and learning to read. *Journal of Experimental Psychology: Human Learning and Memory, 5,* 531–545.

Sidtis, J., Volpe, B., Holtzman, J., Wilson, D., & Gazzaniga, M. (1981). Cognitive interaction after corpus callosal section: Evidence for transfer of semantic activation. *Science, 212,* 344–346.

Snodgrass, J. G. (1984). Concepts and their surface structure. *Journal of Verbal Learning and Verbal Behavior, 23,* 3–22.

Squire, L. R., & Cohen, N. J. (1982). Remote memory, detrograde amenesia, and the neuropsychology of memory. In L. S. Cermak (Ed.), *Human memory and amnesia* (pp. 275–304). Hillsdale, NJ: Erlbaum.

Stanovich, K. E. (1982a). Individual differences in the cognitive processes of reading I: Word decoding. *Journal of Learning Disabilities, 15,* 485–493.

Stanovich, K. E. (1982b). Individual differences in the cognitive processes of reading II: Text-level processes. *Journal of Learning Disabilities, 15,* 549–554.

Swanson, H. L. (1977). Nonverbal visual short-term memory as a function of age and dimensionality in learning disabled children. *Child Development, 48,* 51–55.

Swanson, H. L. (1978a). Comparison of normal and learning disabled children on a nonverbal short-term memory serial position task. *Journal of Genetic Psychology, 133,* 119–127.

Swanson, H. L. (1978b). Verbal encoding effects on the visual short-term memory of learning disabled and normal readers. *Journal of Educational Psychology, 70,* 639–544.

Swanson, H. L. (1983). A study of nonstrategic linguistic coding on visual recall of learning disabled readers. *Journal of Learning Disabilities, 16,* 209–216.

Swanson, H. L. (1984a). Effects of cognitive effort and word distinctiveness on learning disabled and nondisabled readers' recall. *Journal of Educational Psychology, 76,* 894–908.

Swanson, H. L. (1984b). Semantic and visual memory codes in learning disabled readers. *Journal of Experimental Child Psychology, 37,* 124–140.

Swanson, H. L. (1986). Multiple coding processes rin learning disabled and skilled readers. In S. J. Ceci (Ed.), *Handbook of cognitive, social and neuropsychological aspects of learning disabilities* (pp. 203–228). Hillsdale, NJ: Erlbaum.

Swanson, H. L., & Mullen, R. C. (1983). Hemispheric specialization in learning disabled readers' recall as a function of age and level of processing. *Journal of Experiment of Child Psychology, 35,* 457–477.

Swanson, H. L., & Obrzut, J. E. (1985). Learning disabled readers' recall as a function of distinctive encoding, hemispheric processing and selective attention. *Journal of Learning Disabilities, 18,* 409–418.

Symmes, J. (1972). Unexpected reading failure. *American Journal of Orthopsychiatry, 33,* 395–414.

te Linde, J. (1982). Picture-word differences in decision latency. A test of common-coding assumptions. *Journal of Experimental Psychology: Learning, Memory, and Cognition, 8,* 584–598.

Thorndyke, E. L., & Lorge, I. (1944). *The teacher's workbook of 30,000 words.* New York: Columbia University Teachers College.

Thorpe, R. P., Lefever, D. W., & Naslund, R. (1969). SRA Reading Achievement Series. New York: Science Research Associates.

Torgesen, J., & Goldman, I. (1977). Verbal rehearsal and short-term memory in reading disabled children. *Child Development, 48*, 56–60.

Torgesen, J. K., & Houck, D. G. (1980). Processing deficiencies of learning-disabled children who perform poorly on the Digit Span Test. *Journal of Educational Psychology, 72*, 141–160.

Torgesen, J. K., Rashotte, C. A., Houck, D. G., Portes, P., & Greenstein, J. (In press). Studies of rationally defined subgroups: Learning disabled children with short-term memory problems. *Alexander R. Luria Research Monograph Series* New York: Syracuse University Press.

Vanderplas, J., & Garvin, I. (1959). The associative values of random shapes. *Journal of Experimental Psychology, 57*, 147–154.

Vellutino, F. (1977). Alternative conceptualization of dyslexia. Evidence in support of a verbal-deficit hypothesis. *Harvard Educational Review, 47*, 334–345.

Vellutino, F. R., Harding, C. J., Phillips, R., & Steger, J. (1975). Differential transfer in poor and normal readers. *Journal of Genetic Psychology, 126*, 3–18.

Vellutino, F. R., Pruzek, R. M., Steger, J. A., & Meshoulam, U. (1973). Immediate visual recall in poor readers as a function of orthographic-linguistic familiarity. *Cortex, 9*, 368–384.

Vellutino, F. R., & Scanlon, D. M. (1982). Verbal processing in poor and normal readers. In C. J. Brainerd & M. Presley (Eds.), *Verbal processes in children* (pp. 189–264). New York: Springer-Verlag.

Vellutino, F. R., & Scanlon, D. M. (1986). Verbal memory in poor and normal readers: Developmental differences in the use of linguistic codes. In D. Gray & J. Kavanagh (Eds.), *Biobehavioral measures of dyslexia*. Parkton, MD: York Press.

Vellutino, F. R., Steger, J. A., DeSetto, L., & Phillips, F. (1975a). Immediate and delayed recognition of visual stimuli in poor and normal readers. *Journal of Experimental Child Psychology, 19*, 223–232.

Vellutino, F. R., Steger, J. A., Karman, M., & DeSetto, L. (1975b). Visual form perception in deficient and normal readers as a function of age and orthographic linguistic familiarity. *Cortex, 11*, 22–30.

Vogel, S. A. (1983). A qualitative analysis of morphological ability in learning disabled and achieving children. *Journal of Learning Disabilities, 16*, 416–420.

Warren, L. R., & Horn, J. W. (1982). What does naming a picture do? Effects of prior picture naming on recognition of identical and same-name alternatives. *Memory and Cognition, 10*, 167–175.

Watkins, J. J. (1974). The concept and measurement of primary memory. *Psychological Bulletin, 81*, 695–711.

Wolford, G., & Fowler, C. (manuscript). Processing of verbal and nonverbal information in normal and disabled readers.

Woodcock, R., & Clark, C. (1969). *Peabody Rebus Reading Program*. Circle Pines, MN: American Guidance Services.

ACADEMIC DIFFICULTIES OF LEARNING DISABLED CHILDREN WHO PERFORM POORLY ON MEMORY SPAN TASKS

Joseph K. Torgesen, Carol A. Rashotte,

Jonathan Greenstein, Griffith Houck

and Pedro Portes

ABSTRACT

This paper presents the results of an extended series of studies that were focused on 9- and 10-year-old learning disabled (LD) children of normal general intelligence who performed very poorly on memory span tasks. The goals of the research were (a) to identify the basic information processing difficulties that interfered with performance on span tasks and (b) to investigate the ways that these processing problems might also interfere with performance on academic tasks. Evidence is reviewed suggesting that this subgroup of LD children has particular difficulties processing the phono-

Memory and Learning Disabilities
Advances in Learning and Behavioral Disabilities, Suppl. 2, pages 305–333.
Copyright © 1987 by JAI Press Inc.
All rights of reproduction in any form reserved.
ISBN: 0-89232-836-3

logical features of verbal stimuli. Two studies are presented which illustrate the particular reading difficulties that may be associated with this processing deficiency. Implications for remediation are discussed.

The purpose of this chapter is to explain findings from a series of experiments that have focused on learning disabled (LD) children who have extreme difficulties on tasks requiring the short-term retention of verbal information. These children, although of normal general intelligence, are severely impaired in their immediate verbatim recall of verbal information when it is presented on a single trial. Although we used a number of different kinds of tasks in our research, the one studied most frequently, and the one used to select children for study in the first place, was the memory span, or digit span task. This task requires children to repeat random sequences of digits or other items that are presented either aurally or visually.

We focused our research on children with extreme memory span difficulties for three reasons. First, a large volume of research (Heulsman, 1970; Torgesen, 1978) has indicated that, on the whole, children with learning disabilities perform more poorly on memory span tasks than do children who learn normally in the classroom. However, at the time we began our research, the reasons for LD children's performance problems on span tasks were not well understood.

A second reason for studying LD children with severe memory problems was to see if these problems could be accounted for in terms of difficulties in using appropriate control processes or memory strategies. Earlier work we had conducted with heterogeneous groups of LD children had suggested that they frequently performed poorly because they did not use efficient cognitive strategies like verbal rehearsal or categorization (Torgesen, 1977; Torgesen & Goldman, 1978; Torgesen, Murphy, & Ivey, 1979). However, the subjects in these studies did not have extreme memory problems, and, because of the way our tasks were structured, the studies may have been particularly sensitive to individual differences in the use of mnemonic strategies. In contrast, the present series of studies was conducted on a carefully selected subgroup of LD children with the most extreme memory problems. Furthermore, the task used to select them was more tightly structured, in that it did not allow as much room for subject directed mnemonic activities during presentation of the stimuli to be remembered as tasks we had used previously.

Finally, we focused study on children with span difficulties because both theory and data suggest that short-term, or working, memory plays an important role in supporting performance on many complex tasks such as reading (for recent reviews see Baddeley, 1982; Crowder, 1982; Torgesen, Kistner, & Morgan, 1986). Although it is true that the memory span task may not be the best measure of the total working memory system (Daneman, 1984), it is clear that span tasks do tap some of the important processes that determine the functional capacity of working memory (Baddeley, 1985; Baddeley & Hitch, 1974).

Given these reasons for studying children with severe short-term memory (STM) problems, our research program had two major goals. First, we wanted to understand more about the specific processing difficulties that interfere with some LD children's performance on memory span tasks. Second, we wanted to establish empirical and theoretical links between poor performance on memory span tasks and failure on important academic tasks. We pursued this latter goal by two methods. First, we hoped to identify a basic processing operation that could be theoretically linked to difficulties on both the span task and specific academic tasks. No one believes, for example, that children cannot read because they cannot recall sequences of digits. Rather, our hope was to identify an information processing skill that might be important to performance on both tasks so that it could provide a theoretical link between them. Our second method was to compare the performance, on various academic tasks, of LD children with severe span problems against that of both LD children without span problems and with normal children. In doing this, we hoped to identify unique patterns of performance on academic tasks that might be closely associated with severe span difficulties.

In this chapter, we focus primarily on the academic difficulties of LD children with severe performance problems on memory span tasks. In the first part of the paper, we briefly review the common methodological features of our studies and summarize our investigations of the basic processes that account for severe performance problems on span tasks. Following this brief review, we present data from two experiments that examine the reading and math skills of children in our target experimental group.

COMMON METHODOLOGICAL FEATURES

As the research considered in this chapter was conducted over a period of several years, it is based on results from several different cohorts of experimental and control children. In all of our studies, we employed at least two control groups in addition to the target group of children with severe performance problems on span tasks. One of these control groups consisted of LD children who were matched with target group children on age and IQ, but who did not have memory span difficulties. The second control group was composed of children equivalent to the LD control group except that they were achieving at a normal rate in school.

In defining our subgroup of LD children with serious problems in the short-term retention of verbal information, we employed five exclusionary criteria. First, since level of intelligence is one of the most important background variables in studies of learning disabilities, and since span performance correlates moderately with IQ, we required that all subjects have full scale IQs (measured either by the WISC-R or Stanford Binet) of 85 or above. Second, the children had to be between the ages of 9 and 11 years at the time they were selected. We restricted the age range to children in the upper elementary grades not only because there is considerable age-related variance in performance on short-term memory (STM) tasks, but also because we wanted to increase the probability that our subjects had severe and chronic academic learning problems.

Our third criterion was that all children be at least 1.5 grade levels behind in either math or reading achievement. We did not require an academic deficit in a specific area because we wanted to study the ways severe STM problems are related to academic failure. We had no a priori expectations as to which type of academic tasks would be most affected. The fourth criterion, absence of gross behavioral problems, was assessed from the psychological evaluations made on each child by school psychologists. Additional information was obtained from conversations with each subject's learning disabilities resource room teacher. Children who were regarded as having major behavioral problems by either the psychologist or teacher were excluded from further consideration in the study.

Our final criterion involved measurement of the central defining feature of the subgroup: their deficiencies in the short-term retention of information. We used a two level screening procedure to select LD children with the most serious problems in this area. First, we formed a pool of all subjects in five LD resource rooms who met the other criteria and who had been identified by school psychologists (on the basis of performance on standardized psychometric measures of STM) as having specific problems with short-term retention. We then tested each child by having them repeat sequences of digits (varying in length between 2 and 7) presented aurally at the rate of one digit/sec. In the selection of subjects for our initial series of experiments (Torgesen & Houck, 1980), we simply eliminated any subjects whose poor and variable performance on this task appeared to reflect problems in cooperation or concentration on the task. In selecting groups in subsequent years, we employed a similar screening procedure, and simply eliminated from consideration any children who could recall correctly any sequences of more than four digits on three separate trials of the span task. Thus, the subjects selected for all of our experiments were cooperative and showed consistently low performance in recalling sequences of digits. We did not explicitly control for socio-economic background (although the requirement for IQ above 85 almost certainly restricted our range on this variable), race, or sex of subject in our initial experiments because we wanted to see if children who varied on these dimensions would have different explanations for their STM problems.

In selecting our LD control group, we identified children who met the same criteria as the LD target group, but whose performance on tests of STM fell in the normal range. Specifically, these subjects had to have scaled scores on the Digit Span subtest of the WISC-R between 9 and 11, or on the Auditory Sequential Memory Subtest of the ITPA (Kirk, McCarthy, & Kirk, 1968) between 32 and 40. All LD control children were taken from the same resource rooms as children in the target group. These children had been diagnosed as having a variety of other processing disorders involving perceptual-motor functions, language skills, or attention. The second control group was composed of children making normal academic progress (overall academic achievement scores between the 35th and 65th percentiles). These children also performed in the average range on the Digit Span subtest. For ease in describing the results of our research, we will henceforth refer to the LD children with short-term memory problems as the LD-S group, the LD children with normal short-term memory functions as the LD-N group, and the normal achievers as the N group.

INVESTIGATIONS OF PROCESSING DEFICIENCIES

Initial Studies

The goal of our initial studies of the LD-S group was to refine working hypotheses about the basic processing deficits of children in the subgroup. For example, although we defined membership in the LD-S group by level of performance on a simple task like digit span, we initially had no firm hypothesis about the reasons for poor performance on this task. Other research suggested a variety of possible causes for individual differences on span tasks (Dempster, 1981). For LD children, among the more likely causes of poor performance on tests of short-term memory were (a) inefficiency in the use of mnemonic strategies (Bauer, 1979; Torgesen, 1977), (b) problems in recognizing and coding verbal information (Shankweiler, Liberman, Mark, Fowler & Fisher, 1979), (c) short "attention span" (Sattler, 1974), (d) disruptive levels of anxiety (Hodges & Spielberger, 1969), (e) poor motivation (Hallahan, Tarver, Kauffman & Graybeal, 1978), or

(f) specific problems with the perception of temporal order (Bakker, 1972). Initially, our goal was to eliminate as many of these competing hypotheses as possible in order to establish an explanation for the difficulties of our subgroup in the short-term retention of information.

Thus far, we have completed 12 experiments that focus on identifying the processing deficit responsible for poor performance of our subgroup on memory span tasks. Eight of these experiments were reported in an earlier paper (Torgesen & Houck, 1980), and four others have yet to be published (Torgesen, Greenstein, & Portes, 1985). All of these studies used eight subjects in each of the three groups mentioned earlier. One of the most basic findings from the first group of studies was that the performance deficit of children in the LD-S group was both severe and stable over the short and long term. The average age of subjects was 10 years, but the children in the LD-S group performed on the digit span task like 5 and 6 year olds. In addition, their performance on span tasks showed no measurable improvement during the course of an entire year of experimentation. Children in the LD-S group were also less variable in performance on span tasks among themselves and within subjects across repeated trials than were children in either the LD-N or N groups.

The introduction of material incentives for good performance had no effect on the recall of children in the target group, although the performance of children in both control groups was raised slightly. Problems with short "attention span" did not appear to explain the memory performance deficits of children in the LD-S group, because these children were as able as children in the control group to attend to strings of digits they did not have to recall. Both the relatively good performance of LD-S children on the attention tasks and their failure to improve in performance on span tasks as they became more familiar and comfortable with the tasks and experimental situation led us to conclude that their poor performance on span tasks could not be explained by debilitating levels of anxiety. Finally, the results of three separate experiments combined to indicate that only a small proportion of the performance deficits of LD-S children could be accounted for in terms of inefficient use of simple mnemonic strategies like verbal rehearsal. One of these experiments, for example, presented stimuli at different rates and found that even at a very fast rate of presentation (4 digits/sec), recall differences among groups remained the same.

Although most of the experiments in the first series ruled out a variety of potential explanations for the performance deficits of LD-S children, one experiment did support an hypothesis that could account for the pattern of performance we observed. In this experiment, the subjects were asked to perform span tasks involving the recall of digits, simple words, and nonsense syllables. Differences in recall were greatest for digits, next greatest for words, and were nonsignificant for nonsense syllables. Since these stimuli differed from one another only in familiarity to the children, we concluded that "children in the LD-N and N groups had developed a much more efficient coding system for highly familiar stimuli than had children in the LD-S group" (Torgesen & Houck, 1980, p. 158). Although it appeared that LD-S children might have special difficulties coding familiar stimuli for storage in short-term memory, the precise nature of these coding difficulties was not clear.

The LD-S subgroup did appear to be quite homogeneous with regard to the basic processing deficiencies underlying poor performance on span tasks. In the original series of experiments, only one subject was substantially different from the others in the group. This subject performed more like the subjects who had been eliminated during the subject selection phase than the other children in the subgroup. The low and variable performance on span tasks of this subject appeared to be more related to attentional or motivational problems than the kinds of processing deficits shared by the rest of the children in the subgroup. These children were consistently similar to one another in their response to the experimental manipulations, with individual performance patterns closely resembling that of the group as a whole.

Subsequent Experiments on Processing Deficits

In our second set of four studies (Torgesen, Greenstein, & Portes, 1985), we again studied groups of eight children in each of the three groups (LD-S, LD-N, and N) described earlier. Because these studies involved different children than those in the first series, our first experiment tested the replicability of two important findings from the first set of studies. We again obtained a "familiarity effect" in that type of stimulus (digits vs. letters) had a greater effect on the performance of children in the control groups than it did on the LD-S children. The control groups showed a larger recall advantage on the more familiar stimuli (digits) than they did for the less familiar items (letters). Second, changes in rate of presentation of digits (from 1 to 4 digits/sec) affected all groups similarly. As with the initial series of experiments, children in the LD-S group responded homogeneously to the manipulations in this experiment.

Our second experiment in this series attempted to test the generality of the memory deficit shown by children in the LD-S group. Children in all three groups were tested on nine different memory tasks. Two of these tasks involved recognition memory; one involved immediate recall of sequences of abstract visual forms; another required recall of picture names after sorting the pictures into conceptual categories; one involved recall of sequences of digits in reverse order; and four involved some type of verbatim recall of ordered verbal material (memory for sequences of nameable pictures, memory for sequences of digits presented visually, memory for meaningful sentences, and memory for digit sequences presented aurally). There were the usual large differences between the LD-S and control groups on the latter four tasks, but the pattern of performance was different for the other five. All three groups were different from one another on the recall of digit sequences in reversed order, and differences among groups were not significant for the other four tasks.

The pattern of performance of the LD-S children on the recognition memory tasks (both involving auditory presentation of items) indicated once again that these children can attend effectively to stimuli as they are being presented. In contrast to their performance on recall tasks, LD-S children can meet the memory requirements of recognition tasks because recognition memory does not require as complete a representation of the word in memory as is required for recall. In addition, neither of the recognition memory tasks required the children to remember the order of the items, only the items themselves.

The good performance of LD-S children on the sorting task in this experiment is important because it suggests that, if they are able to code items in terms of their semantic features (as opposed to the type of coding they use on STM tasks), they can recall them as well as children in the two control groups. This result helps us to understand how children in the LD-S group can appear to be normally intelligent in spite of their severe difficulties in retaining certain types of information.

The last two experiments in this series answered specific questions about the memory coding problems of children in the LD-S group. In one experiment, we determined that the requirement to recall items in order on span tasks was not differentially difficult for children in the LD-S and control groups. That is, there were still large differences in recall among groups when the children were not required to recall items in order, or when recall score did not depend on correct recall of order. In comparison to children in the control groups, the LD-S children had difficulty recalling both the order of items as well as the items themselves. A fourth experiment was similar to a series reported by Shankweiler, Liberman, Mark, Fowler, and Fischer (1979) using much younger children with reading problems. In these experiments, the utility of phonetic codes for remembering sequences of familiar verbal material is varied by requiring children to recall either rhyming or nonrhyming letters. When the sequences to be recalled were varied in this manner, it affected the performance of children in the control groups the most, presumably because they can take most complete advantage of phonetic distinctiveness among the nonrhyming items. Thus, the "familiarity effect" observed in our earlier experiments is probably due to the fact that items that are most familiar are also most easily processed by control group children in terms of well integrated and easily accessed phonetic codes.

The Nature of the Processing Difficulty

Some investigators have argued that LD children with STM difficulties may have specific difficulties perceiving or coding temporal order (Bakker, 1972; Cohen, 1982). Although we cannot completely rule out this hypothesis as at least a partial explanation for the recall difficulties of LD-S children on span tasks, the concept does not seem necessary to explain our results. For example, both our own experiments and those of Bakker (1972) and Katz, Shankweiler, and Liberman (1981) have found that ordering difficulties of LD children occur only on items that can be represented by a verbal-phonetic code. When this finding is considered in light of other data suggesting that one function of phonetic codes is to preserve item order in STM (Drewnowski & Murdock, 1980; Salame & Baddeley, 1982), then the deficits in ordered recall shown by LD-S children when using highly familiar verbal material seem completely explicable in terms of an underlying difficulty in using phonetic codes to store material in STM. The principle of parsimony suggests that we need not invoke the concept of specific deficits in temporal order perception or retention in the absence of evidence that requires it.

Given that the performance problems of LD-S children are primarily explicable in terms of difficulties processing items that must be stored briefly on the basis of a verbal-phonetic code, there are still a number of possible ways to conceptualize this difficulty. For example, it is possible to view their processing problems as resulting from either the lack of availability of normal phonetic codes, or as a difficulty in accessing phonetic codes that are in other respects quite normal.

Although there is evidence in support of both of these interpretations (Torgesen, Kistner, & Morgan, in press), we currently favor a perhaps more general explanation in terms of the operational efficiency of processing phonetic codes. This explanation is more general than either of the two hypotheses just mentioned because operational inefficiency might result from slow access to codes, degraded codes, or a combination of both of these factors. The concept of operational efficiency was used by Case, Kurland, and Goldberg (1982) to explain age-related changes in memory span performance. These authors demonstrated that memory span was directly proportional to the speed with which the names of verbal items could be repeated. They also showed that, if operational efficiency (in terms of naming rates) for items was equated between adults and children, developmental differences in span were eliminated.

An explanation of the performance problems of LD-S children in terms of operational efficiency of processes involved in generating phonetic codes is consistent with some relatively weak data from our first series of experiments (Torgesen & Houck, 1980) that showed differences in naming rate for verbal items between LD-S and control children. It is also consistent with some stronger, but still not entirely satisfactory data that we report later in this chapter.

One final, and quite different explanation of the performance problems of LD-S children arises from the work of Baddeley (1981, 1985) and his associates on the working memory system. These investigators have proposed that working memory for verbal material has two components; a working space that can be devoted to a variety of conscious processing operations, and an "articulatory rehearsal loop" that is a slave system devoted entirely to storing sequences of phonetically coded items. If LD-S children had an inadequate or poorly developed rehearsal loop, they would show some of the same difficulties storing phonetically codeable items that we have documented in our experiments. Although the "articulatory rehearsal loop" hypothesis can explain some of our data, it cannot explain all of it. For example, in both our earlier (Torgesen & Houck, 1980) and later (Torgesen, Greenstein, & Portes, 1985) series of experiments, we showed that span differences were not reduced at all under extremely fast rates of presentation and were only slightly reduced in a condition that interfered with rehearsal processes. It appears that rehearsal loop differences can account for some of the differences among our groups, but they cannot for all of them.

Although some interesting theoretical questions about the coding difficulties of children in the LD-S group still remain, we have acquired a much stronger conceptualization of their memory difficulties than we had at the beginning of our research. In fact, over the past half decade, a broad range of research has converged on the fact that many young children who have difficulties mastering beginning school tasks in spite of normal intelligence may have difficulties processing or coding the phonological features of language (Torgesen, 1985). Our research shows that these difficulties can persist into middle childhood, at least for a subgroup of LD children. The processing disability documented in our research should affect performance on any task that places stress on phonetic coding skills.

EFFECTS OF PHONOLOGICAL CODING PROBLEMS ON ACADEMIC TASKS

Thus far, we have completed six experiments that have investigated patterns of performance of children in the LD-S group on several complex tasks. We briefly review results from four of these studies and then present two more experiments in greater detail.

Spelling and Language Comprehension Tasks

One of our earlier studies showed that LD-S children had special difficulties learning new spelling words when compared to other LD children (Foster & Torgesen, 1983). Furthermore, these difficulties were not easily remediable by alterations in the way LD-S children studied in preparation for a spelling test. Whereas the performance of other LD children improved with more efficient study techniques, the performance of children in the LD-S groups remained poor even when they were required to study more systematically. Three other experiments (Torgesen, Rashotte, & Greenstein, 1985) showed that the phonological coding problems of LD-S children did not affect their ability to comprehend normal prose when it was presented aurally. Although they had difficulty remembering the specific words used to convey the meaning of passages, they were equally adept with the children in the two control groups in recalling the gist of passages that varied from paragraph to story length. This research is consistent with other experiments (Baddeley & Lewis, 1981; Mann, Shankweiler, & Smith, 1984) in showing that only a certain type of complex prose places heavy demands on the functional capacity of working memory while it is being processed for meaning. With ordinary sentence structure and passage complexity, children in the LD-S group have no disadvantage in language comprehension when compared to other LD and normal children.

General Reading and Math Skills

As a preliminary to more specific study of LD-S children's academic skills, we first compared their performance against other LD children on standardized tests of reading and math. Since we had standardized test data available for three separate groups of LD-S children and appropriate control groups (selected over a period of 5 years, with eight subjects in each group), we were able to examine reading and math performance for 24 LD-S and 24 LD control children. Table 1 presents total reading grade equivalent scores from the Comprehensive Test of Basic Skills for children identified as part of three different subject cohorts. These data were analysed in a 2(LD-S vs. LD-N) × 3(cohort group) × 2(math vs. reading) repeated measures ANOVA. This analysis found main effects for the contrast between LD-N and LD-S children, $F(1,42) = 4.37, p < .05$, and for the difference between subject areas, $F(1,42) = 28.2, p < .01$. In addition, there was a significant interaction between type of subject and academic area, $F(1,42) = 6.2, p < .05$. Tests of simple main effects indicated that the LD-S group performed significantly poorer than the LD-N group only on the reading section of the test. Furthermore, although both groups

Table 1.   Reading and Mathematics Scores for Children in the LD-S
and LD-N Groups

Academic Subject	Cohort Group					
	1		*2*		*3*	
	LD-S	LD-N	LD-S	LD-N	LD-S	LD-N
Reading	2.7	3.1	2.3	3.4	2.7	3.4
	(.7)	(1.0)	(.4)	(1.0)	(.8)	(.7)
Math	3.4	3.3	3.1	3.5	3.5	3.9
	(1.0)	(.7)	(.7)	(.9)	(.5)	(.4)

Note:
LD-S = learning disabled children with sort-term memory problems; LD-N = learning disabled children
who perform normally on STM tasks.

performed better in math than in reading, the difference between content
areas was reliable only for the LD-S group.

These data provide some initial indication that children in the LD-S
group may have particular difficulties in reading when compared to other
LD children who have different kinds of processing difficulties. The scores
used in this analysis, however, were very broad measures of reading and
math skills. The reading measure, for example, combined scores from
both reading vocabulary (ability to decode and interpret individual words)
and reading comprehension (ability to understand the meaning of passages).

We decided to concentrate further study on the word reading, or word
decoding, skills of LD-S children for two reasons. First, our previous
experiments had already shown that children in the LD-S group do not
have a generalized language comprehension deficit. Thus, if these children
did show problems in reading comprehension, their difficulties would likely
be due to the unique requirements of decoding written to spoken language,
rather than to a comprehension problem per se. Second, previous work
(Stanovich, 1982) has shown that children who lag significantly behind in
the attainment of general reading skills are particularly impaired in their
abilities to decode individual words from written to spoken form.

Accuracy of Word Reading and Sound Blending

Description of subjects.   The subjects for our first study of word reading
skills were selected in a manner similar to that described in the first part
of this paper. Table 2 presents the information on characteristics of children
in the LD-S, LD-N, and N groups. The groups were equivalent in average
age, and the two LD groups did not differ in intelligence from one another.

Table 2. Comparison of Subject Groups on Selection Criteria

	Subject Group				
Criteria	LD-S		LD-N		N
Age (in months)	123.5		124.5		122.9
	(9.9)		(8.5)		(8.9)
School Achievement					
Reading	2.7		3.4		5.2
	(.8)		(.7)		(.3)
Math	3.5		3.9		4.9
	(.5)		(.4)		(.4)
Intelligence	100.2		96.5		—*
	(9.1)		(7.0)		—
Sex of Subject	7M	1F	7M	1F	7M	1F
Race (White & Black)	4B	4W	5W	3B	5W	3B

Note:
LD-S = learning disabled children with short-term memory problems; LD-N = learning disabled children who perform normally on STM tasks; N = children learning in average range in classroom.
* Intelligence tests were not given to children in the N group, but their mean standard score on the Digit Span Subtest of the WISC-R was 10.3 (S.D = .5).

The achievement levels of all children in the normal group fell between the 35th and 65th percentile for their age group, and their mean percentile was 47.

Experimental procedures. This experiment was conducted in one session lasting approximately 45 minutes. The testing was accomplished in a quiet room in a mobile research trailer. Three tasks were given in randomized order to all subjects. On all three tasks, subjects' verbal responses were recorded on a cassette tape recorder. One task was the reading and mathematics portion of the Wide Range Achievement Test (Jastak & Jastak, 1978), which was administered according to instructions contained in the test manual. The second task involved pronounciation of the sounds represented by single letters, consonant blends and digraphs, and single and multi-syllable words. These stimuli were typed and presented in lists on a single sheet of paper. In all, the children were asked to pronounce 18 single letters and blends, 15 single-syllable, 15 two-syllable, and 10 three-syllable nonsense words. The nonsense words were constructed according to standard English spelling rules. Examples of words from the list include: "heb, gleat, frachet, frildinub." The children were encouraged to "sound out" each nonsense word or letter combination. There were no time limits, although if no progress was made within 20 secs, the children were asked to try another word.

The final task administered in this study was the sound blending subtest from the Illinois Test of Psycholinguistic Abilities (Kirk, McCarthy, & Kirk, 1968). On this task, both real and nonsense words are divided into smaller sound segments that are presented at the rate of 2 segments per second with a distinct break between the sounds. For example, the word "big" is divided into the segments "b-i-g" and "babies" is presented as "b-a-b-ie-s." The subject's task is to verbalize the word after it was presented in segments. All words were presented via tape recorder. Although instructions for standard administration of this task include provisions for stopping before all items are administered, all items of the task were administered to subjects in this study.

Dependent measures. These instruments produced a number of different scores for each subject. The Wide Range Achievement test was scored according to standard procedures and a grade level score in reading and math was computed for each subject. For the pronounciation task, a variety of scores were produced. The accuracy of pronounciation of each type of letter group (1 and 2 letter groups, 1, 2, and 3 syllable words) was scored independently. The one and two letter groups were simply scored as correct or incorrect. The single and multi-syllable words were assigned 2 points if the pronounciation was perfect, 1 if there was a single minor error in pronounciation, and 0 if there was more than a single minor error. A final scoring category on the pronounciation task assessed the number of words for which the sound of the first letter was pronounced correctly.

All responses were scored from tape recordings. In all cases, the coder listened to the entire set of responses for each subject before beginning scoring, and an attempt was made to allow for consistent individual differences in the way sounds were articulated. The reliability of the coding system was assessed by comparing the scoring of two judges who independently scored 8 protocols. The percent agreement for all categories ranged from .85 to .98, with a mean of .94.

The sound blending task contained 32 items. Responses were scored as correct if the subject was able to blend the sound segments together so that the correct word could be rapidly pronounced with no noticeable breaks between sound segments.

Results and discussion. The pattern of performance on the Wide Range Achievement Test was similar that reported earlier for the Comprehensive Test of Basic Skills. The means for grade level scores in reading (SDs in parentheses) of the LD-S, LD-N, and N groups were 3.0 (.9), 3.8 (.7), and 5.6 (.9), respectively. Both LD groups are obviously impaired in reading, and the LD-S group was poorer than the LD-N group in their word reading skills, $t(14) = 2.3, p < .05$. The grade equivalent scores in math for the same three groups were 3.5 (.5), 3.9 (.5), and 4.5 (.3). Although the difference between the LD groups in math skills was not significant, it was in the same direction as the overall mean difference in the earlier comparison involving three sample groups. Given the small sample size in the present analysis, it is probable that differences in math skills between groups are real, but they are clearly not as large as the differences in reading.

In order to make performance levels comparable across different scoring categories for the letter and nonsense word pronounciation task, raw scores were converted into percentages. Table 3 reports the percent of the total score obtained by each group for each category. Because variances across scoring categories were unequal, and also because we were primarily interested in differences among groups on individual scoring categories, the data were analyzed in a series of one-way ANOVAs. The $F(2,21)$ values for these individual analyses were as follows: (a) one and two letter groups, 2.01, (b) one syllable words, 8.85, (c) two-syllable words, 14.5, (d) three-syllable words, 9.9, and (e) number of words beginning with correct letter sound, 1.6. Since, with these degrees of freedom, an F value of 3.46 is required for statistical significance, only the categories that measured accuracy in pronounciation of syllables produced significant differences among groups.

When the significant ANOVAs were followed up with Neuman-Keuls individual contrasts, an interesting pattern of differences emerged. For single syllable words, the LD-S group was different from both control groups, who did not differ significantly from one another. However, on all categories that involved pronounciation of multi-syllable words, both

Table 3. Percent Correct on Letter and Word Pronounciation Tasks

	Subject Group		
Scoring Category	*LD-S*	*LD-N*	*N*
One and two letter groups	61.1	79.9	77.0
	(28.9)	(11.4)	(15.0)
One syllable words	38.1	61.6	80.0
	(23.1)	(22.5)	(10.7)
Two syllable words	21.2	35.0	72.1
	(19.7)	(23.2)	(14.6)
Three syllable words	1.2	6.9	26.9
	(2.3)	(12.5)	(16.7)
Words beginning w/correct sound	94.7	98.5	100.0
	(9.8)	(2.3)	(0.0)

Note:
LD-S = learning disabled children with short-term memory problems; LD-N = learning disabled children who perform normally on STM tasks; N = children learning in average range in classroom.

LD groups were similar, and both were different from the normal readers. Thus, in comparison to normal readers, both LD groups showed significant difficulties in the pronounciation of nonsense words, but the LD-S group experienced difficulties even on one-syllable words, while children in the LD-N group performed better in this category. The differences between the LD-S and the LD-N groups, or those between the LD-N and normal groups do not appear to be due to lack of knowledge of individual letter-sound correspondences. On both the pronounciation of individual letter groups and correct pronounciation of the first letter in each word, there were no reliable differences between groups.

The results from this task suggest that children in the LD-S group have particular difficulties using their knowledge of letter sound correspondences to construct the complete sounds represented by nonsense words. Although the task used in this experiment was quite complex, so that performance problems could occur for a variety of reasons, Baddeley (1982) has suggested that some children might have difficulty with such tasks because of functional limitations on the ability to store phonetically coded items while they are being processed. If this were the case for children in the LD-S group, they should show performance problems on any task that required them to retain discrete sound elements while blending them into whole words.

In fact, the LD-S children in this experiment did manifest striking difficulties in performance on the sound blending task. The means and SDs for LD-S, LD-N, and N groups on this task were: 8.1 (2.3), 14.7 (2.7), and 13.9 (2.5), respectively. These differences are statistically reliable F (2.21) = 15.9, $p < .01$, and follow-up analysis showed that the LD-S group was different from both control groups.

To summarize, this experiment presents some preliminary information about a possible source of difficulty in reading for LD-S children that can be linked to their functional limitation in performance on STM tasks. While it is true that both LD groups experienced difficulty in constructing the sounds represented by nonsense words, the performance of LD-S children broke down at a simpler level than did that of children in the LD-N group. Children in the target group experienced severe difficulty even on single-syllable words, while the performance of children in the LD-N groups was not seriously impaired (in comparison to normal readers) until multi-syllable words were encountered. In addition, the children in the target group also showed limited ability to blend sounds together even when the requirement to decode the sounds from written to auditory representation was not present. Thus, limited functional capacity to store phonetically codeable stimuli may play a more primary role in the reading difficulties of LD-S than LD-N children.

Differences in Word Reading Rate

In addition to accuracy, another important dimension of word reading skill is speed. There is very good evidence that poor readers, in general, recognize even accurately read word more slowly than children with normal reading skills (Stanovich, 1986). Thus, the next study we report here examined the rate at which children in the LD-S group could recognize words that they could read with a high degree of accuracy. We were particularly interested to see if they were substantially slower in rate than other LD children. The second purpose of this study was to test for changes in word reading rate with practice. We were interested both in the absolute amount of improvement shown by children in each of our groups as well as possible differences among them in the rate at which reading speed increased.

Experimental procedures. The subjects and the setting in this experiment were the same as those in the previous one. The main item of equipment used in the experiment was a TEI microcomputer. The computer was used to present stimuli and time responses to the nearest millisecond. A response board that contained two buttons spaced approximately 12 cm apart was linked to the computer. All stimuli for the learning trials were presented on a cathode ray tube with diagonal measurement of 26 cm. The letter stimuli were approximately 75 mm square. The child sat at a small table with the screen of the CRT approximately 250 cm from his eyes. The experiment took place in three sessions on successive days. All children in all groups followed the same format and order of activities in each session. In order to insure maximum performance on this task and throughout the experiment, children received contingent rewards for good performance. Subjects could earn points on the various testing ar.d practice activities that were traded in for toys or candy at the conclusion of the experiment. Following is a listing of first session activities in the order they took place:

1. *Naming rate for digits, words, and nonsense syllables.* This task required children to name as rapidly as possible lists of digits, words, and nonsense syllables. The digits used were 1 through 9 (excluding 7), and they were included in the naming task in order to estimate improvements in naming speed that might occur simply as a result of familiarization with the naming task. Since digits were already highly familiar to all subjects and involved very simple, or unitized (Ehrie & Wilce, 1983), grapheme-phoneme relationships, improvements in naming rate for these items should primarily reflect adaptation to the task. The words on the word naming task were "cat, mom, see, red, big, him, dog." The nonsense syllables

were simple CVC trigrams and included, "bim, fos, dac, ret, seg, nad, tav." Thirty-six of each type of stimuli were arranged randomly in three rows of 12 stimuli on separate sheets of typing paper. The stimuli were typed using IBM Orator typeface and the rows were double spaced with red lines drawn between rows. The child's task was to rapidly name the stimuli proceeding from left to right in each row and from the top to bottom row. Two trials with each type of stimulus were given in the first session. For the first trial, the subjects named digits, then words, then nonsense syllables. For the second trial, they named words, then nonsense syllables, then digits. The first and second trials for each type of stimulus employed different random sequences of stimuli. Timing was done with a stopwatch and performance was recorded on a cassette recorder. The clock was started when the children named the first stimulus of a series and was stopped when the last stimulus was named.

2. *Practice with the nonsense words.* The object of this activity was to give subjects some initial practice in remembering which items were in the set of nonsense syllables they were to learn. Since the practice programs on the computer required children to correctly identify the particular nonsense syllables they were learning in this experiment (in contrast to other nonsense syllables of the same type), they had to learn which items belonged to the "target" set. The experimenter had the child read each syllable in the target set aloud five times. Then the child was asked to recall as many of the items from the set as possible in any order. Following recall, the child read the words once again, and attempted to recall all the items in the set. This study-recall cycle was conducted a total of five times.

3. *Visual cancellation task.* Items from the target set of nonsense syllables were interspersed randomly with distractor syllables and typed in four columns on a piece of typing paper. There were 28 nonsense syllables in each column, with a double vertical space between syllables. Each of the seven items from the target set appeared 8 times among the total array of 112 syllables. The child's task was to rapidly scan down each column and place a mark on target items while saying their name out loud. Children were told to work as fast as they could without making mistakes. This was a practice activity and did not contribute data to the experiment.

4. *Choice reaction time—control task.* The first reaction time task was used to obtain an estimate of speed of performance when the materials to be recognized were already highly familiar. If the stimulus appearing in the middle of the CRT was "XXX," the subject pushed the left button on the response panel. If the stimulus was "OOO," then the right button was to be pushed. The children were encouraged to go as fast as they could, but were also told to avoid mistakes. When the child indicated readiness to begin, the experimenter started a set of trials. Each set con-

tained 10 trials composed of equal numbers of "XXX" and "OOO" stimuli randomly distributed across the set. The stimuli were displayed on the screen until the child made a response, and inter-trial interval was 1 sec. Five sets of trials were given.

5. *Choice reaction time—experimental task.* This task was structured identically to the control task, except that children saw either nonsense words from the target set or syllables not in the set. Subjects had to press the left button if the syllable was a member of the target set, or they pushed the right button if it was not a member of the set. Again, the children were encouraged to go as fast as they could without making mistakes. Prior to the beginning of this task, subjects read through a list of target syllables five times in order to refresh their memory of the words in the set. Five sets of trials were given.

6. *Practice tasks.* These tasks were included following the control and experimental task in order to give subjects additional practice identifying and naming syllables from the target set. In the first task, a target syllable and nontarget syllable were displayed on the screen at the same time. The words were adjacent to one another, separated by about 5 cm. The child pressed whichever button corresponded to the side on which the target word appeared. Each set was composed of 10 trials, and four sets of trials were administered. On this task, children had to say the name of the target word aloud as they pushed the button. If an error was made, the words did not disappear from the screen. The subject had to respond correctly before moving on the next trial.

A second practice task was called the "Great Race Game." It was much the same as the experimental task, except that the first stimulus of a set appeared on the far left side of the screen. As the child responded correctly, each subsequent word appeared further to the right on the screen. The object was to reach a finish line in under the time limit for the set. When an error was made, an error signal flashed, and the subject had to wait one second before correcting the mistake. On this task, trials followed one another immediately after a correct response was made. Subjects were once again required to say the names of the target syllables out loud as they responded to them. Four sets of trials were given.

In the second session of this experiment, the following tasks were administered in the order given:

1. *Naming rate for digits, words, and nonsense syllables.* The naming rate task was administered in the same manner as in session one. Different arrangements of stimuli were used for each naming trial.

2. *Choice reaction time-control task.* Five sets of trials were administered in the same manner as session one.

3. *Choice reaction time-experimental task.* Five sets of trials were given.

4. *Practice tasks.* Six sets of trials were administered for each task.

In the third session of the experiment, the only task administered was the digit, word, and nonsense syllable reading task.

Dependent measures. The major dependent measures in this experiment were reading rate for digits, words, and nonsense syllables, and response time for the control and experimental choice reaction time tasks. Also of interest were the error rates for all groups on each task. Speed and accuracy data will first be presented for the digit, word, and nonsense syllable naming task.

Results and discussion. Errors for the reading tasks were coded from the taped records of performance. Error rates for the digit naming task were very low in all three sessions for all three groups (less than .05%). On the word naming task, children in the LD-S group made slightly more errors (2.4%) than children in the LD-N (1.1%) or N (.04%) group in the first session. However, there were only very slight differences among groups in the last two sessions, with the LD-S group making an average of 0.7% errors and the other two groups averaging 0.05% and 0.02% errors, respectively. For the nonsense syllables, the LD-S group again made more errors (11% on the initial trial) than the other groups (6% and 1.4%, respectively) with the difference between groups declining dramatically for the last two sessions (LD-S = 1.1%, LD-N = 0.4%, N = 0.2%).

The response times in secs./stimulus for the three types of stimuli are presented in Figure 1. Each data point represents an average for both trials in a session. As can be seen, the LD-S children in each case had the longest response times. Since the group with the slowest response times also had the largest error rate, the direction of differences in Figure 1 cannot be due to speed-accuracy trade-offs among groups. Because variances in response times were unequal across stimuli, results for each type of stimulus were analyzed in separate 3 (groups) × 3 (sessions) repeated measures ANOVAs. For digits, both the main effects for groups, $F(2,21) = 22.9, p < .01$, and sessions, $F(2,42) = 3.3, p < .05$, were reliable, as was the interaction between them, $F(4,42) = 4.8, p < .05$. Analysis of simple main effects showed that the effect of sessions was reliable only for the N group ($p < .01$). In addition, group differences were reliable for all three sessions ($p < .05$). Newman-Keuls contrasts among groups for each session indicated that all three groups were different from one another in the second and third sessions, but the differences were not large enough in the first session to make individual differences significant.

A slightly different pattern of results was obtained for reading rates on

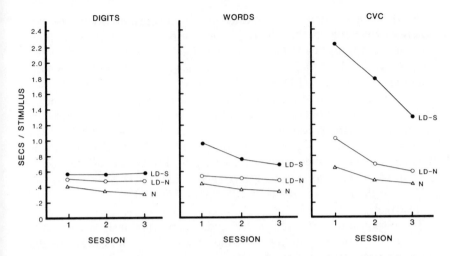

Figure 1. Naming rates across three sessions for digits, words, and nonsense syllables.

Note: LD-S = learning disabled children with short-term memory problems; LD-N = learning disabled children who perform normally on STM tasks; N = children learning in average range in classroom.

the simple words. Again, both group, $F(2,21) = 9.6, p < .05$, and session effects, $F(2,42) = 21.7, p < .01$, were reliable, as was the interaction, $F(4,42) = 3.2, p < .05$. However, in this case, analysis of simple effects showed a significant decrease in reaction time for all three groups, with the largest decrease occuring for the LD-S group. In addition, there were reliable group differences in all three sessions, and individual contrasts indicated that the LD-N and N groups performed similarly, with both being different than the LD-S group ($p < .05$).

The results for the nonsense syllables were similar to those for the words, although the differences among groups were more extreme. In fact, all the effects for nonsense syllables were substantial, with the F values for the group, session, and interaction effects being 17.0, 98.3, and 18.2, respectively. Analysis of simple effects and individual contrasts again showed that all groups increased their reading rates across sessions (with the LD-S group improving most), and the only reliable group differences occurred between the LD-S and the other two groups.

In terms of absolute amount of reading rate decrease, it is clear that the LD-S children improved most on both syllable and word reading tasks. For example, between the first and third sessions, the difference in rate between the LD-S and LD-N children was reduced by 41% for nonsense syllables, and by 47% for words. However, the reduction in reading rate difference between the LD-S and other groups across sessions does not mean that these latter groups did not improve substantially in rate with practice. The actual percent increase for all three groups was quite similar for nonsense syllables (LD-S = 41%, LD-N = 41%, N = 30%). For simple words, the LD-S group did show a greater percentage increase than the other groups (LD-S = 29%, LD-N = 10%, N = 13%).

The choice reaction time task also provided a measure of reading rate for nonsense syllables, but on this task, the subjects did not have to pronounce the syllables. Rather, they had to recognize which syllables were members of the target group they were to learn. Overall error rates for the choice reaction time tasks were very low. For 10 sets of trials on the control task, the error rates were: LD-S = 2.0%, LD-N = 2.2%, N = 1.5%. For the experimental task, the values were 4.4%, 3.2%, and 3.0%, respectively.

The response times for the control and experimental tasks are presented in Figure 2. In order to obtain three data points for each task, the median response times (for correct answers) from the first two, middle two, and last two sets of trials were averaged together. These data were analyzed in a 3 (groups) $\times$ 3(trials sets) $\times$ 2(task) repeated measures ANOVA. There was a significant effect of groups, $F (2,21) = 3.7$, $p < .05$, trial sets, $F (2,42) = 29.4$, $p < .01$, and task, $F (1,21) = 217.9$, $p < .01$. In addition, the interaction between groups and type of task was significant, $F (2,21) = 7.81$, $p < .01$. No other interactions were reliable. The interaction between groups and type of task was followed up with separate two-way analyses for each task. Only on the experimental task were differences among groups significant, $F (2,21) = 6.3$, $p < .05$. Individual contrasts indicated that children in the LD-S group were different from those in both of the other groups, who performed equivalently.

In contrast to the naming rate task, the LD-S group did not show either a greater absolute or proportionate amount of improvement on the experimental task than the other two groups. Between the first and last trials, the LD-S group's response time decreased 16%, while the decrease for the LD-N and N groups were 21% and 28%, respectively.

The data from this last experiment add to our understanding of children in the LD-S group in several important ways. First of all, there were clear differences in speed of processing for simple words and nonsense syllables that could be read with a high degree of accuracy. For the nonsense syllables, these differences occurred both when the syllables had to be pronounced verbally, as well as when they had to be simply recognized as members of a target group.

It is a bit puzzling that the differential improvement in rate shown on the syllable naming task did not also occur on the choice reaction time task. Since the format of these two tasks differed in at least two important ways (verbalization vs. no verbalization; continuous performance vs. dis-

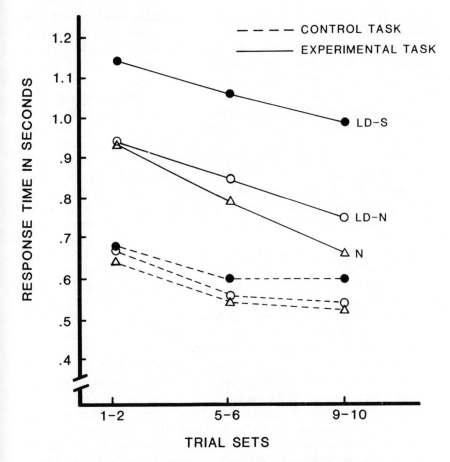

Figure 2. Response times for control and experimental tasks.
Note: LD-S = learning disabled children with short-term memory problems; LD-N = learning disabled children who perform normally on STM tasks; N = children learning in average range in classroom.

crete trials), it is difficult to identify a particular cause of the different pattern of performance on the tasks. In addition, the subjects did not actually begin the choice reaction time task until they had received many practice trials reading the nonsense syllables. Thus, some of the initial disadvantage the LD-S children showed in naming the nonsense syllables in the first session was ameliorated by the time the choice reaction time task was administered.

It does seem unlikely that the difference in pattern of performance on these tasks was the result of differences between tasks in the requirement to generate phonetic codes for the nonsense syllables. Although the choice reaction time task did not require subjects to say the names of syllables outloud, they did have to match the syllables against their memory of which items were in the target set. Since this distinction could not be reliably made by looking at only parts of the syllables, it seems likely that the entire sound pattern represented by a syllable had to be generated in order to make an accurate response. This interpretation is supported by data and theory from the experimental study of memory (Klatsky, 1975) that suggests non-meaningful materials such as nonsense syllables are stored primarily in terms of their acoustic or phonetic features. Thus, the stable difference among groups on the choice reaction time task probably represents differences in the time it took children in the different groups to generate the phonetic code in memory. The absence of differences among groups on the control task suggests that these differences were not the result of simple differences in decision time or reaction speed among groups.

The absolute differences in naming rate for digits in our last study are consistent with the pattern reported in our earlier research (Torgesen & Houck, 1980). Although stronger than the earlier data, the present results are still not entirely satisfactory, in that naming rate differences are not isomorphic to span differences. That is, if both rate and span differences are due to differences in operational efficiency of processes required to identify and extract phonemic codes from long-term memory, then the LD-S group should be different from both the LD-N and N groups, who should be similar to one another. As it is, all three groups of children appear to name digits at different rates.

While a similar pattern of differences for naming rate and span would constitute strong evidence for an "operational efficiency" hypothesis, the absence of such an isomorphism is not critical evidence against the hypothesis. For example, the difference between LD-N and N groups in naming rate for digits could be due to other, more general, characteristics of LD children that both LD-N and LD-S children share, but which are not the same as those required to identify phonemic codes for verbal stimuli. If the rate decrement caused by these other processes were absent, then LD-N and N children would be much more similar to one another, and both would be different from LD-S children. It is possible to view the pattern of differences in word and nonsense syllable naming as consistent with this latter possibility.

If, for example, there were a real difference between LD-S and both control groups in operational efficiency of processes involved in the manipulation of phonemic codes, tasks that require children to extract multiple codes as well as perform integrative operations on them should magnify differences between groups. Both word and nonsense syllable naming undoubtedly require more processing operations on phonemic codes per item named than does digit naming. These tasks not only produced the most striking differences between the LD-S and the two control groups, but also these differences were isomorphic to differences among groups on the span task. Thus, LD-S children might have extreme difficulties on span tasks and complex naming tasks for the same reason: both kinds of tasks require them to efficiently extract and operate on multiple phonemic codes over brief periods of time.

IMPLICATIONS FOR REMEDIATION AND PROGNOSIS

We have not yet conducted any research on remediation techniques for the LD-S subgroup. We are also aware that the knowledge we possess about our subgroup may still be inadequate to suggest effective remedial procedures or valid prognostic statements. For example, we know nothing about the developmental course of the processing disability we have identified. How does the problem characteristic of LD-S children influence performance in preschool or early elementary aged children? Some of the research reported by the group at Haskins Laboratories (Mann, 1986) suggests that the kind of processing problems shown by LD-S children may be more wide spread among children in the early elementary grades. That is, these investigators have demonstrated phonetic coding difficulties in relatively heterogeneous groups of poor readers in the first and second grades. It might be that our target group would be indistinguishable from other poor readers at the beginning of their schooling and are only unique in that they retain the processing disability while other poor readers do not. We also do not know about the developmental course of the disability we have identified beyond the age of 9 or 10 years. In order to make useful prognostic statements about the children in our target group, we need longitudinal data on their progress, both on the criterion task and on academic tasks like individual word reading.

Although there are still important gaps in our knowledge, we do have some initial expectations about the direction a search for effective remedial techniques should take. It is clear, for example, that we will not focus on methods to increase memory span performance, per se. Since the poor STM performance of LD-S children is seen as only one symptom of a problem involving processing verbal information that must be coded in terms of its phonetic features, there is no reason to expect that training in memory span would effectively ameliorate the basic problem. Intensive training on span tasks might lead to improvement in performance through the development of more sophisticated mnemonic strategies, but this would not alter the most important problem LD-S children experience on span tasks. At most, intensive practice on digit span tasks might lead to improved processing of digits, but this would not affect the mass of other verbal information that must be processed in school.

At present, there are two possible approaches to remediation that seem most clearly applicable to the children in our subgroup. One of these approaches has already been used with some success with heterogeneous groups of young poor readers, while the other remains largely in the experimental phase. The first approach is based on the finding that poor readers in the early grades are characterized by general difficulties in the phonemic analysis of speech (Lewkowicz, 1980; Mann, 1986). That is, poor readers have more difficulty than good readers in recognizing the phonemic structure of words. A number of studies (Bradley & Bryant, 1985; Fox & Routh, 1976; Williams, 1980) have shown that early training in phonemic analysis leads to improved acquisition of reading skills.

A study reported by Bradley and Bryant (1978) suggested that a group of poor readers as old as 10 years of age still remained deficient in the ability to analyze the phonemic structure of words. Thus, it is possible that our target group, with demonstrated difficulties in processing phonetically coded information, might be extreme examples of the type of poor reader studied by Bradley and Bryant. Unfortunately, we have not yet collected information on the phonemic analysis skills of children in our subgroup. However, if they should prove particularly deficient in this area, intensive training in phonemic analysis of speech could be one approach to remediation for them.

The other approach to instruction for children in the LD-S group is derived from the results of our last experiment. This experiment showed that the reading rate disparity between LD-S children and those in the control groups was reduced by intensive, speed-oriented practice. It may be that LD-S children are particularly in need of practice that focuses on the attainment of rapid, or overlearned, responses at each stage in the acquisition of reading skill. One way to conceptualize the results of our practice experiment is to propose that the improvement of children in the LD-S group resulted from the formation of more unitized (Ehrie & Wilce, 1983) codes for the stimuli they were required to read. When first reading a nonsense syllable, for example, they had to access and integrate three different phonetic segments (the phonetic codes for three separate letters). However, intensive practice may serve to reduce the number of separate codes that must be accessed for each syllable, allowing it to be processed as more of a unit. In this conceptualization, the LD-N and N groups were initially much faster at reading nonsense syllables because they could access and integrate separate phonetic codes more efficiently. However, as codes for children in all groups became more unitized with practice (or as the processing requirements for nonsense syllables became more like those for digits), the differences in speed of response among groups declined. Thus, children in the LD-S group may be much more in need of practice that emphasizes speed of response than other LD children, for speed of response is the most effective measure of the formation of unitized codes for words.

Since many reading programs allow progress on the basis of accuracy rather than speed of reading (Lesgold & Resnick, 1982), LD-S children may not get the practice they need to form efficiently accessible codes for individual words. Another reason to suspect that LD-S children are not getting enough speed oriented practice comes from research (Berliner & Rosenshine, 1977; Thurlow, Graden, Greever, & Ysseldyke, 1982) indicating that the actual amount of time children spend practicing reading in the early grades is highly variable and overall is very low. It is very difficult for teachers to provide large amounts of closely monitored, speed oriented practice by traditional methods.

One approach we are experimenting with at present is the use of microcomputers to deliver the enormous amounts of practice that LD-S children may need in order to be able to read effectively (Torgesen, 1986). Programs we are working with focus on both the acquisition of rapid, context free word recognition skills (sight word vocabulary) as well as the rapid utilization of word analysis and phonemic blending skills. These programs require that children respond at a given level of speed, as well as accuracy, before moving on to the next lesson or set of materials.

REFERENCES

Baddeley, A. (1981). The concept of working memory: A view of its current state and probable future development. *Cognition, 10*, 17–23.

Baddeley, A. (1982). Reading and working memory. *Bulletin of the British Psychological Society, 35*, 414–417.

Baddeley, A. (1985). *Developmental applications of Working memory*. Unpublished manuscript, MRC Applied Psychology Unit, Cambridge, England.

Baddeley, A. D., & Hitch, G. (1974). Working memory. In G. A. Bower (Ed.), *The psychology of learning and motivation*. (Vol. 8, pp. 47–89). Orlando, FL: Academic Press.

Baddeley, A., & Lewis, V. (1981). Inner active processes in reading: The inner voice, the inner ear, and the inner eye. Lesgald & Perfetti (Eds.), *Interactive processes in reading* (pp. 86–121). Allsdale NJ: Erlbaum.

Bakker, D. J. (1972). *Temporal order in disturbed reading*. Rotterdam, The Netherlands: Rotterdam University.

Bauer, R. A. (1979). Memory, acquisition, category clustering in learning-disabled children. *Journal of Experimental Child Psychology, 27*, 365–383.

Berliner, D. C., & Rosenshine, B. (1977). The acquisition of knowledge in the classroom. In R. C. Anderson, R. J. Spiro, & W. E. Montague, (Eds.), *Schooling and the acquisition of knowledge* (pp. 63–91). Hillsdale, NJ: Erlbaum.

Bradley, L., & Bryant, P. E. (1978). Difficulties in auditory organization as a possible cause of reading backwardness. *Nature, 221*, 746–747.

Bradley, L., & Bryant, P. (1985). *Rhyme and reason in reading and spelling*. Ann Arbor: University of Michigan Press.

Case, R., Kurland, D. M., & Goldberg, J. (1982). Operational efficiency and the growth of short-term memory span. *Journal of Experimental Child Psychology, 33*, 386–404.

Cohen, L. (1982). Individual differences in short-term memory. *International Review of Research in Mental Retardation, 11*, 43–77.

Crowder, R. C. (1982). *The psychology of reading*. New York: Cambridge University Press.

Daneman, M. (1984). Why some people are better readers than others: A process and storage account. In R. J. Sternberg, (Ed.), *Advances in the psychology of human intelligence* (Vol. 2, pp. 367–385). Allsdale, NJ: Erlbaum.

Dempster, F. N. (1981). Memory Span sources of individual and Developmental differences. *Psychological Bulletin, 89*, 63–100.

Drewnowski, A., & Murdock, B. (1980). The role of Auditory Features in memory span for words. *Journal of Experimental Psychology: Human Learning and Memory, 6*, 319–332.

Ehri, L., & Wilce, L. (1983). Development of word identification speed in skilled and less skilled beginning readers. *Journal of Educational Psychology, 75*, 3–18.

Foster, K., & Torgesen, J. K. (1983). The effects of directed study on the spelling performance of two subgroups of learning disabled children. *Learning Disabilities Quarterly, 6*, 252–257.

Fox, B., & Routh, D. K. (1976). Phonemic analysis and synthesis as word-attack skills. *Journal of Educational Psychology, 68*, 70–74.

Hallahan, D. P., Tarver, S. G., Kauffman, J. M., & Graybeal, N. L. (1978). Selective children under reinforcement and response cost. *Journal of Learning Disabilities, 11*, 42–51.

Hodges, W., & Spielberger, C. (1969). Digit span: An indicatant of trait or state anxiety? *Journal of Consulting and Clinical Psychology, 33*, 430–434.

Huelsman, C. B. (1970). "The WISG subtest syndrome for disabled readers". *Perceptual and motor skills, 30*, 535–550.

Jastak, J. F., & Jastak, S. (1978). *The Wide Range Achievement Test* (rev. ed.). Wilmington, DE: Jastak Associates.

Katz, R. B., Shankweiler, D., & Liberman, I. Y. (1981). Memory for item order and phonetic recoding in the beginning reader. *Journal of Experimental Child Psychology, 32*, 474–484.

Kirk, S. A., McCarthy, J. J., & Kirk, W. D. (1968). *Illinois test of psycholinguistic abilities, revised edition*. Urbana: University of Illinois Press.

Klatzky, R. L. (1975). *Human memory: Structures and processes*. San Francisco: W. H. Freeman.

Lesgold, A. M., & Resnick, L. B. (1982). How reading difficulties develop: Perspectives from a longitudinal study. In J. P. Das, R. F. Mulcahy, & A. E. Wall (Eds.), *Theory and research in learning disabilities* (pp. 155–188). New York: Plenum.

Lewkowicz, H. K. (1980). Phonemic awareness training: What to teach and how to teach it. *Journal of Educational Psychology, 72*, 686–700.

Mann, V. A. (1986). Why some children encounter reading problems: The contribution of difficulties with language processing and phonological sophistication to early reading disability. In J. K. Torgesen & B. Y. L. Wong (Eds.), *Psychological and educational perspectives on learning disabilities* (pp. 133–160). Orlando, FL: Academic Press.

Mann, J. A., Shankweiler, D., & Smith, S. T. (1984). The association between comprehension of spoken sentences and early reading ability: The role of phonetic representation. *Journal of Child Language, 11*, 627–643.

Salame, P., & Baddeley, A. (1982). L   ;ption of short-term memory by unattended speech: Implications for the structure of working memory. *Journal of verbal learning and verbal behavior, 21,* 150–164.

Sattler, J. M. (1974). *Assessment of children's intelligence.* Philadelphia, PA: Saunders.

Shankweiler, D., Liberman, I. Y., Mann, S. L., Fowler, L. A., & Fisher, F. W. (1979). The speech code and learning to read. *Journal of Experimental Psychology. Human Learning and Memory, 5,* 531–545.

Stanovich, K. E. (1982). Individual differences in the cognitive processes of Reading I: Word decoding. *Journal of Learning Disabilities, 15,* 485–493.

Stanovich, K. E. (1985). Cognitive processes and the reading problems of learning disabled children: Evaluating the assumption of specificity. In J. K. Torgesen, & B. Y. L. Wong (Eds.), *Psychological and educational perspectives on learning disabilities* (pp. 87–132). Orlando, FL: Academic Press.

Thurlow, M. L., Graden, T., Greever, T. W., & Ysseldyke, J. E. (1982). *Academic responding time for learning disabled and non learning disabled students* (Technical Report #72). Institute for Research on Learning Disabilities, Minneapolis, Minnesota.

Torgesen, J. K. (1977). Memorization processes in reading disabled children. *Journal of Educational Psychology, 69,* 571–578.

Torgesen, J. K. (1978). Performance of reading disabled children on serial memory tasks: A review. *Reading Research Quarterly, 19,* 57–87.

Torgesen, J. K. (1985). Memory processes in reading disabled children. *Journal of Learning Disabilities, 18,* 350–357.

Torgesen, J. K. (1986). Using computers to help learning disabled children practice reading: A research based perspective. *Learning Disabilities Focus, 1,* 72–81.

Torgesen, J. K., Greenstein, J., & Portes, P. (1985). *Further studies of learning disabled children with performance problems on memory span tasks.* Unpublished manuscript, Florida State University.

Torgesen, J. K., & Goldman, T. (1977). Rehearsal and short-term memory in second grade reading disabled children. *Child Development, 48,* 56–61.

Torgesen, J. K., & Houck, G. (1980). Processing deficiencies in learning disabled children who perform poorly on the digit span task. *Journal of Educational Psychology, 72,* 141–160.

Torgesen, J. K., Kistner, J., & Morgan, S. (in press). Component processes in working memory. In J. Borkowski & J. Day (Eds.), *Memory and cognition in special children: Perspectives on retardation, learning disabilities, and giftedness.* Norwood, NJ: Ablex.

Torgesen, J. K., Murphy, H., & Ivey, C. (1979). The effects of an orienting task on the memory performance of reading disabled children. *Journal of Learning Disabilities, 12,* 396–401.

Torgesen, J. K., Rashotte, C. A., & Greenstein, L. (1985). *Language comprehension in learning disabled children who perform poorly on memory span tests.* Unpublished manuscript. Florida State University.

Williams, J. P. (1980). Teaching decoding with an emphasis on phoneme analysis and phoneme blending. *Journal of Educational Psychology, 72,* 1–15.

DIRECTIONS IN FUTURE RESEARCH ON METACOGNITION IN LEARNING DISABILITIES

Bernice Y. L. Wong

ABSTRACT

This paper focuses on potential research areas in metacognition with learning disabled (LD) individuals. Specifically, five areas are considered. They include (a) research on normally-achieving and LD children's acquisition of metacognitive skills in reading, (b) research on classroom teachers' direct instruction of metacognitive skills in reading, (c) a more comprehensive and unified front in metacognitive research in reading, writing and spelling, (d) metacognition and motivation, and (e) metacognition and coping with failure. Respective rationales for conducting research in these five areas accompany discussions of each of them.

Memory and Learning Disabilities
Advances in Learning and Behavioral Disabilities, Suppl. 2, pages 335–356.
Copyright © 1987 by JAI Press Inc.
All rights of reproduction in any form reserved.
ISBN: 0-89232-836-3

The theoretical construct of *metacognition* originated with Flavell (1976), and it refers to a person's awareness of his/her cognitive processes and self-regulation. Metacognitive deficiencies, or more specifically, deficiencies in metamemory were used to explain children's failure to use inculcated mnemonic strategies in aid of recall (Flavell, 1976). *Metamemory* is a subset of metacognitive processes and refers to awareness of memory processes. Initially, research generated by the metacognition construct focused on metamemorial processes in children, but it soon spread beyond metamemory to other areas such as metalinguistic awareness, meta-attention, and reading. The importance of metacognition in reading was cogently argued by Brown (1980), and research in support of the role of metacognition in reading has been summarized in excellent reviews by Baker and Brown (1984a; 1984b).

Since the seminal paper by Ann Brown (1980) in which she related metacognition to reading, there has been interest in applying the theoretical construct of metacognition to generate research in learning disabilities (Bos & Filip, 1982; Loper, Hallahan, & Ianna, 1982; Torgesen, 1979; Wong & Jones, 1982). The studies by Loper et al. and Torgesen examined meta-attention and metamemory in LD and normally achieving children, respectively. The studies by Bos and Filips (1982) and Wong and Jones (1982) were intervention studies involving training comprehension-monitoring in LD and normally achieving students.

Both the relevance and limitations of metacognition to learning disabilities have been weighed (Wong, 1982; 1985; 1986). In the present paper, the author focuses on what she sees as potential areas for future research on metacognition in learning disabilities. Specifically, five areas are considered. These comprise (a) research on normally achieving and LD children's acquisition of metacognitive skills in reading, (b) research on classroom teachers' direct instruction of metacognitive skills in reading, (c) a more comprehensive and unified front in metacognitive research in reading, writing and spelling, (d) metacognition and motivation, and (e) metacognition and coping with failure.

ACQUISITION OF METACOGNITIVE SKILLS IN READING

Metacognitive Skills in Reading

As just mentioned, research on metacognitive skills in reading have been summarized and comprehensively reviewed by Baker and Brown (1984a). Chief among these skills are awareness of the goal or purpose in reading, comprehension monitoring (which comprises of two components:

awareness of one's comprehension breakdowns and using suitable strategies to amend the breakdowns), matching reading goal with an appropriate reading strategy (e.g., skimming, scanning for particular information in a newspaper or book), and allocation of attention (e.g., focusing attention on important parts of what is read). All these areas have been well researched (Baker & Brown, 1984a; 1984b).

The existent metacognitive research can be categorized into two groups of studies: the first investigated differences in metacognitive skills between older and younger or good and poor readers. This research yielded valuable information. Consistently, younger and poorer readers were found to show deficient metacognitive skills. For example, they thought the purpose of reading was decoding rather than comprehension (Cannery & Winograd, 1979; Garner & Kraus, 1982; Paris & Myers, 1981). They did not vary reading rate with nature of the reading purpose (Forrest & Waller, 1980). Moreover, they showed little debugging strategies in reading (Garner & Reis, 1981). The second group of studies involves metacognitive skills training (Hare & Borchardt, 1982; Palincsar, 1982; Winograd, 1984; Wong & Jones, 1982). These intervention studies had been successful in inducing appropriate comprehension-monitoring and summarization skills.

These metacognitive research findings have been most instructive. Perhaps we should now take time to reflect on a question concerning the acquisition of metacognitive skills in reading. Specifically, how do good readers or successful learners acquire those metacognitive skills in reading? What are the instructional conditions within the classroom that promote such acquisition?

One may ask: Why should we consider such an acquisitional question? Does it not suffice to continue with well-designed intervention studies? After all, our intervention studies to date have a reasonable batting average of success! The justification and importance of developing an acquisitional frame to analyze intervention research is that it provides a much broader and sounder conceptual basis for intervention. One does not decry the usefulness of the intervention studies on metacognition. However, they have been generated on either a hypothesized metacognitive deficiency among poor or LD readers (Palincsar, 1982; Wong & Jones, 1982), or on empirically observed metacognitive deficiencies (Bos & Filips, 1982; Winograd, 1984). In short, the reported metacognitive intervention studies had used a conceptually shallow, shot-gun approach. Effective but devoid of a developmental or acquisitional frame, the variables manipulated in these intervention studies may in retrospect be fragmentary and isolated. Hence, we need to rethink intervention in light of the previously posed acquisitional question. Additionally, knowing the instructional conditions within the classroom that promote children's acquisition of metacognitive skills in reading should provide us with clear guidelines to future instructional studies involving LD children.

Classroom Instructional Variables

Children spend many hours at school learning diverse academic skills from teachers. It is, therefore, reasonable to assume that through observation, at least for successful learners, they may well learn metacognitive skills in reading from effective classroom teachers who explicitly model such skills. But do effective classroom teachers explicitly model metacognitive skills in reading? A study by Schallert and Kleiman (1979) suggests that they do.

Schallert and Kleiman (1979) observed classroom teachers teach a lesson on sequoia trees. They noted that effective teachers demonstrated four specific kinds of behaviours that facilitated children's learning. These were "tailoring the message" to suit the level of prior knowledge among the children, "activating prior knowledge, focusing attention, and monitoring comprehension." Of these, attention-focusing and comprehension-monitoring are relevant to the subtheme of our paper here, and we confine our discussion to them.

In focusing the children's attention, effective classroom teachers posed direct questions, reinforced correct answers, and encouraged appropriate guessing and comments. They also monitored the children's attention and strove to keep it targetted on the lesson. More importantly, effective teachers directed children to attend selectively to important parts of the lesson. They brought about such selective attention focusing through repeatedly and explicitly saying to the class, "This is important."

These teachers also carefully monitored children's understanding and retention of the information in the new lesson. They did this through frequent questioning at various points in the teaching of the lesson, as well as at the end of the lesson.

Like comprehension-monitoring, attention-focusing is a metacognitive skill. This is because focusing attention on important parts of the text implies awareness of what constitutes important parts of the text. The description of what effective teachers did in the Schallert and Kleiman (1979) study indicates clearly that those teachers explicitly modelled metacognitive skills in reading. To become good readers, children must internalize those metacognitive skills that their teachers consciously model for them (Schallert & Kleiman, 1979).

It appears then that classroom instructional variables or what the teacher does pedagogically bears importantly on the acquisitional question of how do children acquire metacognitive skills in reading. Hence, we may profitably research the question of what kinds of metacognitive skills in reading when effectively and explicitly modelled by classroom teachers would induce those skills in children. Equally profitable would be research on children's internalization processes that mediate their acquisition of metacognitive skills in reading.

Why should we be involved in researching children's internalization processes here? The reason lies in the instructional implications. Wertsch and Stone (1985) showed the interesting evolvement in a very young child's internalization of the self-regulatory aspect of language. Initially, this 2.5-year-old girl learned the interpersonal, communicative aspect of language use. Later, through social interactions with her mother in a play-setting of assembling a puzzle in the presence of a model puzzle, she discovered the additional, equally important self-regulatory aspect of language use. Wertsch and Stone (1985) showed how this very young child went through a stage where her inner speech was still geared towards social communication rather than self-regulation. Finally, they documented her generating speech that indicated understanding of the regulatory aspect of language. Wertsch and Stone's (1985) analysis of the young child's internalization of the self-regulatory aspect of language derives from Vygotsky's theoretical analysis of young children's egocentric speech.

Wertsch and Stone's (1985) research is instructive for us in our search for understanding how children develop or acquire metacognitive skills in reading. Analogous to the very young child's process of attaining self-regulation in speech (Wertsch & Stone, 1985), school children may need much exposure and interaction with a model (the classroom teachers) of metacognitive skills, and gradually internalize those skills. If we can document in sufficient details this internalization process (or processes), and the variations in it (them) among good, average, and LD readers, we would gain much valuable insight and information for use in our teaching of metacognitive skills in reading.

The focus in this section has been the question of acquisition of metacognitive skills in reading. The conclusion here is that teachers play an important role in children's acquisition of those metacognitive skills. It implies teachers should explicitly model metacognitive skills in reading with sufficient frequency so that children can internalize them. To push this instructional implication further, can we have classroom teachers teach metacognitive skills in reading directly? We turn now to consider classroom research that supports the feasibility of implementing such an idea.

DIRECT INSTRUCTION OF METACOGNITIVE SKILLS

To date, we do not have reports on classroom teachers' direct instruction of metacognitive skills in reading. But we do have reports on classroom teachers' successful implementation of vocabulary teaching program and comprehension skills program (Beck, Perfetti, & McKeown, 1982; Palincsar, 1982). Recently, however, there is one study on classroom teachers' direct instruction of a metacognitive strategy in young children (Orsetti,

1984). Specifically, young children were taught to self-monitor errors in spelling.

Using two intact classrooms of grade one children, Orsetti (1984) randomly assigned one class to receive an error-monitoring self-questioning training strategy. To control for experimenter effect, Orsetti and the second grade one teacher alternated weekly in teaching spelling to the experimental and control classes. Additionally, to control for the effects of concurrent phonetic training in class, the spelling words were chosen from a source different than that used in the reading program. A total of 60 spelling words were used (20 phonetically regular, 20 phonetically irregular, and 20 two-syllable words). They were all from Thomas and Brawn's (1979) spelling program, which is used in schools within British Columbia, Canada.

The children from the two intact classrooms were pretested on the Peabody Picture Vocabulary Test and a screening test in spelling to insure no differences in verbal intelligence and knowledge of the spelling words to-be-taught. The pretest data indicated no between-group differences (Peabody means for experimental and control classes were 104.3 (SD = 12.8) and 101.4 (SD = 12.6), respectively; mean scores on spelling screening test were 3.57 (SD = 0.95) and 3.87 (SD = 0.97), respectively.

The children were given six new spelling words per week, across 10 weeks of instruction. Four times a week, the children were given a spelling lesson. Each lesson lasted about 20 minutes and was given to both classes at the same time on the same day in the separate classes. The teaching format was adhered to rigorously. The instructional steps for both experimental and control groups are given in Table 1. After the children had learned to spell all 60 words, they were given systematic reviews on it. Altogether the children's spelling acquisition of the 60 words were reviewed twice. An immediate posttest followed the conclusion of the second review. A maintenance test followed after 3 weeks. The results are given in Table 2. The results indicated that children trained in error-monitoring surpassed significantly their untrained peers in spelling performance both at the immediate and the delayed posttests. Clearly, instructing young children in error-monitoring through self-questioning increased their spelling proficiency. However, it is pertinent to point out that had they not received concurrent phonetic training in their reading program, they might not have achieved such substantial gains in spelling accuracy (cf. Gerber, 1982).

Orsetti's (1984) study indicates that classroom teachers can successfully implement direct instruction of metacognitive skills. However, we emphasize the pertinent prerequisites to her successful study, namely, the unswerving cooperation, coordination, and tremendous organization between the teachers in team-teaching. Nevertheless, successful teaching

Table 1. Instructions in Orsetti's (1984) Study

Control Group	Treatment Group
Teacher presents word visually.	Same
Teacher says word, students repeat.	Same
Teacher defines word if necessary.	Same
Teacher uses word in sentence.	Same
Children copy word in book.	Same
Teacher checks to verify accuracy.	Same
Children asked to cover word and spell word again. Check with first word to see if correct. If incorrect, children asked to correct.	* ● Cover word in book ● Repeat word to self and listen for the sounds. ● Print word. ● Direct children to ask themselves "Do I have the sounds I hear?" ● Does it look right? ● Underline any part not sure of. ● Uncover word and check. ● Correct word if necessary.
Repeat for second and third spelling of each word.	Repeat * above for second and third spelling of each word.
Children advised to learn and remember words for later use.	Same
Children reinforced their effort by saying, "I have worked hard to be good speller."	Same

of grade one children in a metacognitive strategy for monitoring spelling errors does provide some optimism and encouragement to classroom instruction of metacognitive skills in reading. Because metacognitive skills are crucial in efficient reading (Baker & Brown, 1984a), teachers should consciously and conscientiously promote their students' acquisition of those skills. Research on teachers' direct instruction of metacognitive skills in academic subjects is obviously needed.

Apart from the above areas, we discern three more potential areas for metacognitive research. These include (a) the need for a more comprehensive and unified front in metacognitive research in reading, writing and spelling, (b) metacognition and motivation, and (c) metacognition and coping with failure.

Table 2. Means, Standard Deviations, and Ranges in Children's
Spelling Performance on the Immediate and Delayed Posttests

	Immediate Posttest			*Delayed Posttest (3 weeks delay)*		
	M	*SD*	*Range*	*M*	*SD*	*Range*
Treatment Class	53.96	5.54	42-60	54.52	5.43	38-60
Control Class	45.48	7.28	32-58	47.00	7.58	32-60

from Orsetti, 1984

NEED FOR A MORE UNIFIED FRONT IN METACOGNITIVE RESEARCH

To date, with the exception of a few studies in spelling (Gerber, 1982), learning disabilities professionals engaged in metacognitive training research have concentrated exclusively on reading comprehension and studying skills (Bos & Filips, 1982; Ellis, 1983; Palincsar, 1982; Schmidt, 1983; Schumaker, Deshler, Alley, Warner, & Denton, 1982; Wong & Jones, 1982; Wong, Wong, Perry, & Sawatsky, 1986). This exclusive focus inadvertently and unnecessarily restricts the range of metacognitive research in learning disabilities, and precludes a more thorough understanding of the role of metacognition in students' successful academic functioning. Metacognition is conceptualized to play a central role in students' successful learning in any learning situation (Brown, 1980). In order to assess fully its role in students' academic successes and failures, we must extend our research endeavours beyond the domain of reading to include other areas of academic learning. Two such areas that appear to promote an understanding of the role of metacognition are writing and spelling. The following is an exposition of how metacognition is intricately involved in competent writing (composition), and hence the rationale for instructional research here with LD students. Elsewhere we have written on the role of metacognition in spelling (Wong, 1986).

Writing is a complex intellectual skill in which the component skills interact recursively (Flower & Hayes, 1980; Hayes & Flower, 1980). To illustrate these component skills and how they interact recursively, we shall use the theoretical model proposed by Hayes and Flower (1980). This heuristic model is chosen because it was derived from the authors' analyses of think-aloud protocals of college adult good and poor writers in a 2-year period. Although it is placed in a broader context that includes the writer's task environment and the writer's long-term memory, the model proposed by Hayes and Flower focuses on the writing process. Specifically, they propose three processes in writing: Planning, Translating, and Reviewing. The *Planning* process takes information from the writer's task environment (e.g., writing assignment) and from the writer's long-term memory (e.g., knowledge of topic in assignment) and uses such information to establish goals and a writing plan to shape the writer's composition to meet those goals. The *Translating* process is responsible for producing the text. The *Review* process serves to improve the quality of the produced text. Both the Planning process and the Review process contain subprocesses to enable their respective functions. The Planning process has three subprocesses: Generating, Organizing, and Goal-setting. The *Generating* process serves to retrieve information relevant to the writing task from long-term memory. The activation of relevant prior knowledge from long-term memory is assumed to be prompted by information about the topic of the writing task, and the audience in the task environment. The *Organizing* process selects the most useful materials retrieved by the Generating process and organizes them into a writing plan. The *Review* process has two subprocesses: Reading and Editing. The *Editing* process serves to identify and correct violations in writing conventions and semantic inaccuracies and to evaluate materials in accordance to the writing goals. Overriding the principal writing processes of Planning, Translating, and Reviewing is the *Monitor,* which basically serves the function of an executive monitoring system (Hayes & Flower, 1980, pp. 10–20).

One's writing does not proceed in a linear fashion. Typically, the writer jumps back and forth between the various principal processes and subprocesses in writing. This recursive nature in the interactions among these component processes and subprocesses is best understood by considering what a writer does during writing. For example, during writing (Translation process), the writer may suddenly realize the need to generate a new goal or subgoal to organize the material that s/he is producing. Thus, s/he switches from the Translating process to the Planning process. A second example of recursive interactions of the writing components and subcomponents would be when the writer realizes that s/he has strayed from the prior established goal in their writing, or s/he found the written argument for the thesis weak, and decides on an appropriate course of remedy. In this example, the writer is mobilizing the Editing subprocess within the principal process of Review (Hayes & Flower, 1980). Thus, the writer had jumped from a principal writing process, Translating, to a subprocess in writing, Editing. When the problem is fixed, s/he returns to Translating (Hayes & Flower, 1980).

The Role of Metacognition in Writing

The role of metacognition in writing is readily seen in competent writers. Competent or good writers are very aware of the goals of their writing, and the audience they have targetted in their respective pieces of writing. Their writing goals and targetted audience shape their writing by providing a frame of reference to which they constantly return in monitoring the relevance and clarity of their writing. Within the process of writing, there is much conscious, deliberate self-regulation. On the basis of subjects' protocol analyses, Flower and Hayes (1980) claimed that much of writing skill revolves around one's ability to "monitor and direct one's own writing process." After ideas are generated, competent writers spend much time planning: They select among the ideas generated; they organize the sifted ideas into a related hierarchy; and they plan on how to communicate these ideas to the intended audience. During such planning, writers may realize new ideas or connections between ideas hitherto not foreseen; or the necessity of introducing new subgoals. Plans themselves may undergo changes as a result of the writers' continual crystallization of the "problem" they have focussed on in their writing (Flower & Hayes, 1981). In short, much recursive thinking activities occur during writers' planning of their papers. The important point is that the writer's planful behavior shows clear, deliberate, goal-directed coordination (i.e., metacognition).

When competent writers have written a portion of their writing or the first draft, they engage in self-evaluation of their written products (Beach, 1976; Nold, 1981). Typically, as they review their writing, they seek to analyze if they have met their writing goals, whether or not they have used the appropriate language with their intended audience, whether or not they have written what they mean to write (precision in communicating their intent and meaning), and whether or not their writing conforms to expected writing conventions (Flower, 1979). Such self-evaluation indicates self-monitoring and self-regulation in accordance with clear evaluative criteria. As the competent writers pore through their writing, they revise and modify their writing to meet such internal evaluative criteria satisfactorily. Clearly, metacognitive skills are involved in such critical self-evaluation and subsequent revisions of one's writing.

Another aspect of competent writers that demonstrates metacognition pertains to their juggling of several constraints in writing (Flower & Hayes, 1980). As described above, writers need to attend to their writing goals, the production of "reader-based prose" and writing conventions (structure, semantics, and spelling). These constraints exert simultaneous demands on the writer's attention. Given the limitations in human information-processing capacity, the writer must decide on priorities in allocating his/her attention and cognitive efforts. S/he may temporarily hold at bay the concerns that s/he cannot attend to. For example, competent writers may focus on expressing clearly and precisely what they think and leave for later revision, spelling problems or uncertainties. Another example of how competent writers juggle these constraints in writing is their preferred way of revision. Nold (1981) reported that competent writers first revised globally and then locally. They added and deleted big chunks of writing first before examining sentences and words. Such conscious, deliberate allocation of one's cognitive/attentional resources implicates metacognition.

While it has been argued that competent writers demonstrate metacognition in their writing, it remains to be considered how less competent writers lack it, and whether teaching the latter metacognitive skills in writing promotes the quality of their writing. Less competent writers, be they children, adolescents, or adults, are found to follow the "think it, say it" mode of writing (Flower, 1979). Specifically, they show no planning in writing; their writing goals are not clearly articulated; and they have no awareness of the audience to which their writing addresses. They simply write as free associated ideas and thoughts enter their heads. Flower (1979) dubbed such writing as "writer-based prose", while she dubbed the opposite way of writing exemplified by competent writers, "reader-based prose." Along similar lines, but focusing on children, Bereiter and Scardamalia (1982) use "knowledge-telling strategy" to describe children's writing. Children tend to "tell what they know about a topic" in writing.

Stallard (1974) pinpointed some differences between good grade 12 writers and their peers who were average writers. He found the good adolescent writers spent more time at contemplating or reflecting on what they had written. They also spent more time and effort at writing and revising. In revising, they changed words, indicating attention to communication problems, and conscious attempts at achieving precision in communication. Moreover, they spent longer time in the pre-writing period choosing or limiting a topic and considering the purpose of their papers. Although this kind of pre-writing behavior indicates planfulness, it is limited to the topic and purpose of the paper and not extended to the writing of the entire paper, or even to the writing of individual paragraphs. Nevertheless, the good grade 12 writers in Stallard's study showed unmistakeable elements of production of "reader-based prose." They were aware of the need to communicate clearly to the audience; they actively reflected on what they have written; and they showed some planfulness. In short, they possessed certain metacognitive skills in writing.

Stallard's (1974) findings hinted at the importance of reflective processes in students' writing. Of import to instructional researchers and teachers is the efficacy of teaching children reflective processes in writing. Scardamalia, Bereiter, and Steinbach (1984) reported an interesting study in which they succeeded in teaching 6th graders independent reflective processes in writing. These researchers conducted their training by first teaching the children to select and use appropriate cue cards that elicited self-questioning during composition. Examples of these cue cards are: "An even better idea is . . . "; "I'm not very clear about what I just said so . . . "; and "A goal I think I could write to . . . ." The children were taught to incorporate phrases such as those into think-aloud-while-planning episodes. Specifically, each child stood in front of the class while thinking aloud, choosing particular cue cards when necessary. To facilitate children's selection, the cue cards were grouped according to function (e.g., under "Planning cues used for opinion essays," "New Idea," "Elaborate," "Improve"). While one child carried on with his/her think-aloud planning, the whole class helped to monitor and analyze that child's thinking. The second training step involved thought modelling. The teacher modelled planning for the children, and the children modelled for one another with and without cue cards. Moreover, there were follow-up discussions of the thinking strategies that were shown. The third training step was direct instruction of the notion of dialectic. This notion was explained to the 6th graders as rising above opposing arguments by producing a reconciliating idea that takes into account the validity of both sides.

The results were very good. Sixth graders given the training produced substantially more reflective statements both in planning and in writing. By reflective statements is meant that the children wrote "what you'd expect to find in a magazine/collection of essays." This study by Scardamalia et al. (1984) obviously has important implications for teaching writing processes in class. More important, it suggests that the development of important elements in competent writing can be attained by elementary school children through well-planned instruction. For the purpose of this section of the paper, the findings are important in demonstrating that teaching some metacognitive skills in writing resulted in qualitatively better writing. Reflective processes in this study involves the capacity of the child to decenter, to be aware of the need to be balanced in producing the reconciliation statement, and to monitor and evaluate one's written product against explicit criteria. Such processes clearly involve metacognition.

METACOGNITION AND MOTIVATION

Metacognition was posited to mediate strategy transfer (Borkowski, Johnson, & Reid, in press). As mentioned at the start of this paper, the original context of this theoretical construct arose from research on memory processes in which young children trained in mnemonic strategies were found to fail to generalize the learned strategy. It was thought that young children lack awareness or knowledge of memory processes, and ways of facilitating remembering. They lack metamemory (Flavell, 1976). Teaching them when, where, how and why they should deploy a learned strategy in aid of remembering (i.e., increasing their metamemory) should remedy the lack of strategy generalization (Brown, 1978).

Subsequent research investigating this proposed link between meta-memory and strategy transfer indicated inconsistent support for it. There was no one-to-one correspondence between metamemory and strategy transfer (Cavanaugh & Perlmutter, 1979). In order to explain the insuf-ficiency of metacognition in enabling trainees' strategy transfer, some re-searchers involved in metacognitive research have proposed the necessary inclusion of motivational variables in strategy interventions (Borkowski et al., 1985; Palmer & Goetz, in preparation; Wong, 1986). Borkowski et al. (1985) have advanced the most articulate notions on this topic. In their model on factors that influence strategy transfer, they place motivation within a metacognitive framework with a clear reciprocal relationship be-tween motivation and metacognition. Space does not permit an elaboration of their model here. Essentially, Borkowski et al. (1985) argue that in effective strategy training, metacognitive (executive) training must be paired with motivation training (reattribution training) to effect strategy generalization.

In the conceptualization of Borkowski et al. (1985), motivation refers to the process involved in attributions, self-efficacy, and learned help-lessness. Basically, they think that many LD children do not understand the relationship between effortful, strategic behavior and successful per-formance. Consequently, they fail on generalization tasks. Why do LD children lack understanding of the importance of effortful, strategic be-haviors? Consideration of their motivational problems would enlighten us here. One has to recall the histories of academic failures of LD children and realize how the kinds of repeated failures across a broad array of academic tasks promote a particular belief system and attributional pat-terns. These LD children have developed the belief that they lack abilities, that they are "dumb." Moreover, when they succeed in an academic task, they tend to attribute it to "luck," something that is beyond their control; when they fail, they tend to attribute it to their lack of abilities (Licht, 1983). Such belief system and attributional patterns result in (a) LD chil-dren depriving themselves opportunities in developing the understanding that with effort and appropriate strategy, they may well increase their success in academic tasks; (b) their lack of persistence in face of failure or giving up readily with a difficult task; and (c) a low expectancy of achievement that extends beyond academics (Licht, 1983). It is obvious how these resultant problems lead to LD children's further academic failures since they are unlikely to expend effort at learning. Thus, there is a vicious circle starting with the LD children's academic failures in the initial grades, which produce maladaptive attributions and belief system, and which in turn generate behaviors ill-suited to academic achievements. Subsequent academic failures reinforce those maladaptive attributions and belief system (Licht, 1983; Borkowski et al., (1985).

A plethora of empirical data attests to the maladaptive belief system and attributional patterns in LD children and children with learned helplessness (Licht & Kistner, 1986). Dweck (1975) found that mastery-oriented children persisted in face of failure and generated alternate strategies. Failure-oriented (learned-helpless) children, however, lacked both persistence and the propensity towards generating alternate strategies. Similar maladaptive attributions in LD children have been described by Pearl, Bryan, and Donahue (1980). Moreover, Pearl, Bryan, and Herzog (1983) found such attributional problems in a bowling game. That they found such attributional problems outside of academics suggests the LD children's maladaptive belief system and attributions are well entrenched and extensive. Corroborative findings on this point are found by Butkowsky and Willows (1980).

To what extent can LD children's maladaptive attribution patterns and belief system be changed? There is some convincing evidence that reattribution training can redress LD children's problems in their belief system and attributions. In such training, the LD children are taught how effort can help them succeed, and since they are generating the effort, they are responsible for the success. Thus, they learn to be more internal in locus-of-control, and to attribute the performance outcome to effort expenditure (Dweck & Repucci, 1973; Licht & Kistner, 1986). In recent analyses of reattribution training, attention has been drawn to the necessity of including appropriate strategy as well as effort to underlie successful performance outcomes (Licht, 1983).

Most recently, Borkowski et al. (in press) conducted a study that presents a cogent case for linking metacognition training and reattribution training. There were three treatment conditions: (a) the executive training condition, (b) the executive plus attribution training condition, and (c) the control. The executive training condition focused on general self-control (i.e., metacognition) and specific strategy training. The executive plus attribution training added reattribution training to what was given in the executive training condition. The control condition provided specific strategy training as in the other two conditions, but without the executive or attribution training components found in the other two conditions. Of instructional import is that Borkowski et al. increased the children's antecedent as well as program-generated (program specific) attributions. Specifically, concerning antecedent attributions, Borkowski et al. discussed with the trainees beliefs about causes of failure and provided them an opportunity in which to perform successfully an item that was failed previously by using the self-control procedure taught. They also trained the children to contemplate on beliefs about the causes of success. More specific program-generated attributions were trained by giving feedback to the children about their experimental task performances. The experimental tasks included pair-associate and sort-recall-readiness tasks. The experimenters selected two items, one which the child succeeded in recalling by using the strategy, and one which s/he failed to recall because of not using the strategy. The experimenters used these two items to teach the child relationships between strategy use and good recall, and between the absence of strategy use and poor recall.

The subjects were children from second, third, and fourth grade. They were labelled hyperactive by their teachers on the basis of ratings on the Conners' Teacher Rating Scales (Conners, 1973). However, about 60% of them were also diagnosed as learning disabled. The treatment condition of most interest was clearly the second one, executive plus reattribution training. Measurements were made at intervals of 3 weeks after training and at a 10-month follow-up. The dependent measures included: strategy transfer on lab tasks, impulsivity as measured on the Matching Familiar Figures Test, strategy use in the classroom as gauged by grades and impulsive behavior, and changes in attributions and increases in strategic knowledge as measured on a metamemory test. The results indicated the children in the executive plus attribution training condition surpassed significantly and consistently children in the other two treatment conditions on both follow-up posttest occasions. Without attribution training, children in the Executive training condition (metacognition training) produced attribution changes comparable to those in the control condition. Clearly, these findings from Borkowski et al. (in press) speak unequivocally for the necessity in according motivational variables an equal place to metacognitive training in strategic interventions.

METACOGNITION AND COPING WITH FAILURE

The Importance of Coping with Failure

In the early grades, through teacher evaluative feedback and social comparison, children develop perceptions of themselves as successful or unsuccessful learners. They learn what academic tasks they excel in, and others in which they do not, or even fail at. Children's reactions to academic failure depend on how they interpret it; what they think cause it; and whether or not they can cope with the failure (Cullen, 1982). Because children around the age of 7 years become increasingly aware of the role of ability in performance (Nicholls, 1978), those who encounter more frequently academic failures may run the risk of attributing their failures to deficient ability. The literature on learning disabilities indicates that such is the case. This attributional pattern erodes the LD children's motivation to learn and explains their passive learning style (Licht & Kistner, 1986). In contrast, successful learners have developed effective strategies in dealing with task failure. Clearly, it is important for children who are unsuccessful learners in school to acquire effective coping skills so that their motivation to learn is not stifled by fear and expectancy of failure.

What does coping with failure mean? From a theoretical point of view, coping with failure means effectively analyzing the conditions or factors associated with the failure experience and using a strategy, problem-solving approach to reverse the failure into success. In short, one focuses on the constructive aspects of failure and realizes that "the real culprits threatening learning are not so much failure and error-making as they are inappropriate goal-setting, ineffective goal awareness, undesirable performance conditions, ineffective task assessment and evaluation, and unproductive attributions for failure" (Clifford, 1984, p. 118). A *positive* analysis of failure in terms of its contributing factors, coupled with a strategy explanation for it, would turn the failure experience into a problem-solving situation. Consequently, the failed individual could focus on searching for a more effective problem-solving strategy with renewed effort and confidence that subsequent failure would not necessarily imply poor ability (Clifford, 1984).

To learn how children cope with failure, Cullen (1982) investigated children's responses to failure through individual interviews. A total of 90 children were involved in her study. They were evenly divided into 45 boys and 45 girls, and came from socioeconomic strata that ranged from working class to upper middle class. The children were attending the first term of their standard two year in Australia, which is roughly equivalent to our second grade. In the individual interviews, Cullen asked them about their responses to failure in 10 situations, which included individual academic tasks such as reading, spelling and math, group activities as in social studies and science, a class discussion, an individual craft project, games in class and the playground, and a homework assignment. An example of the interview question is: "You are working on a math problem and you get stuck. What would you do then?"

Cullen (1982) developed and used the following response categories to analyze the data from the children's responses to the interview items: Coping responses included social resource (asking someone for help), general effort (tries again), specific effort (describes renewed effort by referring to a specific strategy, e.g., self-checking or monitoring), learned skill (describes a task-specific skill, e.g., breaking a word into syllables), study skill (refers to use of dictionary, maths equipment, instructions, etc.), and cognitive (thinks about task requirements). Negative coping responses included anxiety (refers to anxiety, embarrassment, or guilt), anger (refers to anger, aggression, or frustration), justification (gives an excuse for the failure), denial (does not accept responsibility for the failure), social comparison (shows concern for what others think), and withdraws (gives up). On the bases of the responses, Cullen was able to categorize the children into 4 groups: strategy-oriented children, action-oriented children, anxiety-oriented children, and anger-oriented children. Strategy-oriented children scored high on the questions. They used primarily high-level coping responses or strategies such as the use of study skills or specific effort-renewal. The responses of a typical strategy-oriented child are shown below (Cullen, 1982, p. 3):

> (specific effort): "I'd look and see if I'd done something wrong and if I'd done something wrong I could fix it. I might have missed one of the pieces out and I'd have to do that part again" (individual craft activity).
>
> (learned skill). "I'd put it in syllables and if that didn't work I'd go on reading and then go back to it" (reading task).
>
> (study skill). "I'd check the instructions to see where I'd gone wrong" (spare-time maths game).
>
> (cognitive). "Well I gave a wrong answer. I'd think about it, think of a better answer and put my hand up" (class discussion).

This strategy-oriented child was further observed to use language to direct and co-ordinate her actions. Such language use highlights the important role of strategy-oriented thinking in her problem-solving.

Action-oriented children also had high coping scores. However, their coping was of low quality in that their coping responses involved general effort renewal and asking for external help. The responses of a typical action-oriented child are illustrated as follows: The child repeatedly said s/he would "try again" or "start again" and therefore exhibited the desired behaviour of persistence. However, such effort renewal was not tied to specific task strategies. Their use of language throughout the given puzzles seemed to provide a motivational function that maintained task persistence and interest. However, to maximize on such motivation, the child needed to learn specific ways of coping with task failure (i.e., generating task specific strategies).

The anxiety-oriented children scored low on the coping measure, using primarily negative affective responses that indicated anxiety, embarrassment, or guilt about failure. Such children appeared to be very concerned with being evaluated poorly in class discussions or group activities. The illustrative case of such a child showed that he said he would feel embarrassed if his answer to a question was wrong. The same child seemed very conscious and concerned if others notice he was doing something wrong in a math game. He sought reassurance frequently from the experimenter that his performance was adequate. Thus, this child and others like him appeared to show an excessive concern with others' evaluation and social comparison.

The anger-oriented children scored low and used primarily negative responses that consisted of either withdrawing from the task or statements indicating anger, aggression, or frustration about failure. Typical of responses from such children is the following boy's (Cullen, 1982, p. 4).

"Bust it, throw it away" (individual craft activity)

"I'd do nothing 'cause I'd be mad" (a maths problem)

"Get mad. I'm no good at work" (a reading activity)

"I get lots of crosses and sometimes I push people's desks around instead of doing the work" (incorrect homework)

"Go away" (maths game with another boy).

This boy, however, did indicate an appropriate response when he said he would ask his mother to help him with spelling a word.

The coping behaviours of Cullen's (1982) strategy-oriented children are reminiscent of the behaviours of mastery-oriented children in Diener and Dweck's (1978) study. Following failure, mastery-oriented children spontaneously generated self-monitoring statements that reflected attention to the degree of effort or concentration they were exerting. Such self-monitoring seemed to provide them with a check on their task-related behaviour. Diener and Dweck (1978) found 84% of the mastery-oriented children engaged in active self-monitoring. In contrast, the learned-helpless children generated no self-instructions nor showed any self-monitoring. Of import is the nature of the mastery-oriented children's self-instructions. These self-instructions clearly focused on improving performance. Some examples of such self-instructions were: "I should slow down and try to figure this out" and "The harder it gets, the harder I need to try."

Thus, strategy-oriented children (Cullen, 1982) and mastery-oriented children (Diener & Dweck, 1978) showed striking commonalities in actively bringing under control a difficult task, banishing negative affective thoughts or distractions, focusing attention on solving the task through trying out alternate strategies, and closely monitoring and checking their problem-solving and attention to the task. These children were aware of how to deal with initial task failure or a difficult, challenging task. They were "aware of learning as a self-directed process which requires active involvement of the learner" (Cullen, 1982, p. 4). Of importance to the topic of metacognition and coping with failure is that these children coordinated their awareness of the active nature of learning with the appropriate course of strategic actions. Such awareness and coordinated strategic action, with concomitant self-monitoring, indicates metacognition among strategy-oriented (Cullen, 1982) and mastery-oriented (Diener & Dweck, 1978) children.

The importance of coping with failure among school children is readily understandable since ample research data attest to the debilitating effects on children's self-concept, motivation to learn, and academic achievements when they do not tackle failure constructively (Clifford, 1984; Licht, 1983). Metacognitive skills appear to play a role in children's coping with failure successfully in that children possessing them can generate alternate task-specific problem-solving strategies and stay on task through self-monitoring (Cullen, 1985). Hence, future research appears warranted on teaching children to cope with failure through metacognitive skills training.

CONCLUSION

The purpose of this paper is to consider potential areas for future metacognitive research in learning disabilities. Because of the interest in metacognitive research in learning disabilities, I thought it would be useful to share some thoughts on what may provide potentially interesting and useful avenues for future metacognitive research. Since these thoughts emanate from one person's perspective, the suggested areas are obviously by no means exhaustive. Of comfort is my belief, however, that repercussions from continual metacognitive research in cognitive psychology and reading would generate other exciting ideas for research on metacognition by learning disabilities professionals.

REFERENCES

Baker, L., & Brown, A. L. (1984a). Metacognition skills of reading. In D. P. Pearson (Ed.), *Handbook on research in reading* (pp. 353–394). New York: Longman.

Baker, L., & Brown, A. L. (1984b). Cognitive monitoring in reading. In J. Flood (Ed.), *Understanding reading comprehension* (pp. 21–44). Newark, DE: International Reading Association.

Beach, R. (1976). Self-evaluation strategies of extensive revisers and nonrevisers. *College Composition and Communication, 27,* 160–64.

Beck, J. L., Perfetti, C. A., & McKeown, M. G. (1982). The effects of long-term vocabulary instruction on lexical access and reading comprehension. *Journal of Educational Psychology, 74,* 506–521.

Bereiter, C., & Scardamalia, M. (1982). From conversation to composition: The role of instruction in a developmental process. In R. Glaser (Ed.), *Advances in instructional psychology* (Vol. 2, pp. 1–64). Hillsdale, NJ: Erlbaum.

Borkowski, J. G., Johnston, M. B., & Reid, M. K. (in press). Metacognition, motivation, and the transfer of control processes. In S. J. Ceci (Ed.), *Handbook of cognition, social, and neuropsychological aspects of learning disabilities.* Hillsdale, NJ: Erlbaum.

Bos, C., & Filip, D. (1982). Comprehension monitoring skills in learning disabled and average students. *Topics in Learning and Learning Disabilities, 2,* 79–85.

Brown, A. (1978). Knowing when, where, and how to remember: A problem of metacognition. In R. Glaser (Ed.), *Advances in instructional psychology* (pp. 77–165). Hillsdale, NJ: Erlbaum.

Brown, A. L. (1980). Metacognitive development and reading. In R. J. Spiro, B. B. Bruce, & W. F. Brewer (Eds.), *Theoretical issues in reading comprehension* (pp. 453–481). NJ: Erlbaum.

Butkowsky, J. S., & Willows, D. M. (1980). Cognitive-motivational characteristics of children varying in reading ability: Evidence for learned helplessness in poor readers. *Journal of Educational Psychology, 72,* 408–422.

Cannery, G., & Winograd, P. (1979). *Schemata for reading and reading comprehension performance* (Tech. Rep. No. 120). Urbana: University of Illinois, Center for the Study of Reading.

Cavanaugh, J. C., & Perlmutter, M. (1982). Metamemory: A critical examination. *Child Development, 53,* 11–28.

Clifford, M. M. (1984). Thoughts on a theory of constructive failure. *Educational Psychologist, 19,* 108–120.

Cullen, J. L. (1985). Children's ability to cope with failure: Implications of a metacognitive approach for the classroom. In D. L. Forrest-Pressley, G. E. MacKinnon & T. G. Waller (Eds.), *Metacognition, cognition, and human performance* (Vol. 2, pp. 267–300). Orlando, FL: Academic Press.

Cullen, J. (1982). Learning to cope with failure in the early school years. *Set* (research information for teachers), *1,* Item 6.

Diener, C. J., & Dweck, C. S. (1978). An analysis of learned helplessness: Continuous changes in performance, strategy, and achievement cognitions following failure. *Journal of Personality and Social Psychology, 36,* 451–462.

Dweck, C. S. (1975). Achievement. In M. E. Lamb (Ed.), *Social and personality development* (pp. 114–130). New York: Holt, Rinehart & Winston.

Dweck, C. S., & Repucci, N. D. (1973). Learned helplessness and reinforcement responsibility in children. *Journal of Personality and Social Psychology, 25,* 109–116.

Ellis, E. (1983). *The effects of teaching learning-disabled adolescents metacognitive strategies for self-generating task-specific learning strategies.* Unpublished doctoral thesis, University of Kansas.

Flavell, J. H. (1976). Metacognitive aspects of problem solving. In L. B. Resnick (Ed.), *The nature of intelligence* (pp. 231–235). Hillsdale, NJ: Erlbaum.

Flower, L. S. (1979). Writer-based prose: A cognitive basis for problems in writing. *College English, 41,* 13–18.

Flower, L. S., & Hayes, J. (1981). Plans that guide the composing process. In C. H. Frederiksen & J. F. Dominic (Eds.), *Writing: The nature, development, and teaching of written communication* (Vol. 2, pp. 39–57). Hillsdale, NJ: Erlbaum.

Flower, L. S., & Hayes, J. R. (1980). The dynamics of composing: Making plans and juggling constraints. In L. W. Gregg & E. R. Steinberg (Eds.), *Cognitive processes in writing* (pp. 31–50). Hillsdale, NJ: Erlbaum.

Forrest, D. L., & Waller, T. G. (1980). *What do children know about their reading and study skills?* Paper presented at the annual meeting of the American Educational Research Association, Boston.

Garner, R., & Kraus, C. (1982). Good and poor comprehender differences in knowing and regulating reading behaviors. *Educational Research Quarterly, 6,* 5–12.

Garner, R., & Reis, R. (1981). Monitoring and resolving comprehension obstacles: An investigation of spontaneous text lookbacks among upper-grade good and poor comprehenders. *Reading Research Quarterly, 16,* 569–582.

Gerber, M. M. (1982). *Effects of self-monitoring training on spelling performance of learning-disabled and normally-achieving students.* Paper presented at AERA meeting, New York City.

Hare, V. C., & Borchardt, K. M. (1982). *Direct instruction of summarization skills.* Unpublished manuscript, University of Illinois at Chicago.

Hayes, J. R., & Flower, L. S. (1980). Identifying the organization of writing processes. In L. W. Gregg & E. R. Steinberg (Eds.), *Cognitive processes in writing* (Vol. , pp. 3–30). Hillsdale, NJ: Erlbaum.

Licht, B. G. (1983). Cognitive-motivational factors that contribute to the achievement of learning-disabled children. *Journal of Learning Disabilities, 16,* 483–490.

Licht, B. G., & Kistner, J. A. (1986). Motivational problems of learning-disabled children: Individual differences and their implications for treatment. In J. K. Torgesen & B. Y. L. Wong (Eds.), *Psychological and educational perspectives on learning disabilities* (pp. 225–265). Orlando, FL: Academic Press.

Loper, A. B., Hallahan, D. P., Ianna, S. O. (1982). Meta-attention in learning-disabled and normal students. *Learning Disability Quarterly, 5,* 29–36.

Nicholls, J. G. (1978). The development of the concepts of effort and ability, perception of academic attainment and the understanding that difficult tasks require more ability. *Child Development, 49,* 800–814.

Nold, E. W. (1981). Revising. In C. H. Frederiksen & J. F. Dominic (Eds.), *Writing: The nature, development, and teaching of written communication* (Vol. 2, pp. 67–79). Hillsdale, NJ: Erlbaum.

Orsetti, M. E. (1984). *An error-monitoring strategy for teaching spelling.* Unpublished master's thesis, Simon Fraser University.

Palincsar, A. S. (1982). *Improving the reading comprehension of junior high students through reciprocal teaching of comprehension-monitoring strategies.* Unpublished doctoral dissertation, University of Illinois.

Palmer, D. J., & Goetz, E. T. (1985). *Selection and use of study strategies: The role of the studier's beliefs about self and strategies.* Unpublished manuscript, Texas A & M University.

Paris, S. G., & Myers II, Meyer. (1981). Comprehension monitoring, memory, and study strategies. *Journal of Reading Behavior, 13,* 5–22.

Pearl, R. A., Bryan, T., & Donahue, M. (1980). Learning-disabled children's attributions for success and failure. *Learning Disability Quarterly, 3,* 3–9.

Pearl, R. A., Bryan, T., & Herzog, A. (1983). Learning-disabled and nondisabled children's strategy analyses under high and low success conditions. *Learning Disability Quarterly, 6,* 67–74.

Scardamelia, M., Bereiter, C., & Steinbach, R. (1984). Teachability of reflective processes in written composition. *Cognitive Science, 8,* 173–190.

Schallert, D. L., & Kleiman, G. M. (1979, June). *Some reasons why teachers are easier to understand than textbooks* (Reading Educ. Rep. No. 9). Urbana: University of Illinois, Center for the Study of Reading.

Schmidt, J. L. (1983). *The effects of four generalization conditions on learning-disabled adolescents written language performance in the regular classroom.* Unpublished doctoral thesis, University of Kansas.

Schumaker, J. B., Deshler, D. D., Alley, G. R., Warner, M. M., & Denton, P. H. (1982). Multipass: A learning strategy for improving reading comprehension. *Learning Disability Quarterly, 5,* 295–304.

Stallard, C. K. (1974). An analysis of the writing behavior of good student writers. *Research in the Teaching of English, 8,* 206–218.

Thomas, V., & Brawn, C. (1979). *The Canadian spelling program.* Toronto: Gage.

Torgesen, J. K. (1979). Factors related to poor performance on rote memory tasks in reading-disabled children. *Learning Disabilities Quarterly, 2,* 17–23.

Wertsch, J. V., & Stone, A. (1985). The concept of internalization in Vygotsky's account of the genesis of higher mental functions. In J. V. Wertsch (Ed.), *Culture, communication, and cognition: Vygotskian perspectives* (pp. 162–179). Cambridge: Cambridge University Press.

Winograd, P. (1984). Strategic difficulties in summarizing texts. *Reading Research Quarterly, 19,* 404–425.

Wong, B. Y. L. A cognitive approach to teaching spelling. *Exceptional Children,* 1986, *53,* 169–173.

Wong, B. Y. L. (1985). Metacognition and learning disabilities. In T. G. Waller, D. Forrest-Pressley, & E. MacKinnon (Eds.), *Metacognition, cognition and human performance* (Vol. 2, pp. 137–180). Orlando, FL: Academic Press.

Wong, B. Y. L. (1986). Metacognition and special education: A review of a view. *Journal of Special Education.*

Wong, B. Y. L. (Ed.). (1982). Metacognition and learning disabilities. *Topics in Learning and Learning Disabilities, 2.*

Wong, B. Y. L., & Jones, W. (1982). Increasing metacomprehension in learning-disabled and normally-achieving students through self-questioning training. *Learning Disability Quarterly, 5,* 228–240.

Wong, B. Y. L., Wong, R., & Perry, N. (1986). The efficacy of a self-questioning summarization strategy for use by underachievers and learning-disabled adolescents in social studies. *Learning Disabilities Focus, 2,* 20–35.

SUBJECT INDEX